TO MY BEST GIRL

COURAGE, HONOR, AND LOVE IN THE CIVIL WAR:

The Inspiring Life Stories of
Rufus Dawes and Mary Beman Gates

STEVE MAGNUSEN

First published by Dog Ear Publishing
4011 Vincennes Road
Indianapolis, IN 46268
www.dogearpublishing.net

ISBN: 978-1-4575-6276-1

Cover: Photos and letters courtesy of the Dawes Arboretum Archives.
Flag reproduction with permission from the Wisconsin Veterans
Museum. Iron Brigade medal from author's collection as obtained from
Civil War Recreations. Author photo by Judy Piersall.
Design by Dog Ear Publishing.

This book is printed on acid free paper.
Printed in the United States of America

This book is dedicated

To My Best Family

and in respectful memory of

Rufus R. Dawes and Mary Gates Dawes

Acknowledgements

Rufus Dawes and Mary Beman Gates Dawes merit first mention. I hope this presentation of their youthful lives together, which by their eloquent writings resonates through the years, does them justice.

Their family members told their own stories and provide us with so much amazing history and documentation. Most prolific are Julia Cutler, William P. Cutler, Ephraim C. Dawes, Lucy Dawes, Betsey Shipman Gates, Beman Gates, and Mary Frances Dawes Beach.

Peggy Dempsey's book *The Dawes House: The Place Where You Are Always Welcome* inspired me to investigate the archives. And her presentation of Aunt Julia Cutler's daily Civil War journal, through http://JuliaCutlerJournal.blogspot.com, has been a marvelous resource. Thank you, Peggy, plus husband and family descendant Rich, for your support, assistance, and inspiration. I am forever grateful.

At the end of a productive yet tiring day of research, and while having dinner in Marietta, Ohio, at Austyn's Restaurant on historic Front Street, I made a chance acquaintance with two ladies who arrived next to me and who inquired as to my note-taking. To my amazement, Barb Moberg introduced herself as a great-great-granddaughter! It was discovered we share a common link to Libertyville, Illinois. I am still flabbergasted! Barb serves the Dawes family as president of the DWDWRA (The Descendants of William Dawes Who Rode Association). Judy Piersall is a direct descendant of early Marietta settlers and is a board member for the Betsey Mills Club, once the home of Mary Gates and family. She arranged a tour graciously conducted by Franci Bolden. To Barb Moberg, husband Jack, and to Judy Piersall, thank you so much for your friendship and assistance ever since that amazing dinner meeting.

Historian Leslie Wagner and archivist Sarah Aisenbrey, both with the Dawes Arboretum near Newark, Ohio, have been exceedingly helpful and encouraging. Thank you for your wonderful assistance and for the important work you perform in preserving so much Dawes family history.

Linda Showalter, special collections librarian at Marietta College, has provided superior stewardship of the many historical documents in her care and keeping. Her friendly and timely assistance is most appreciated.

Scott Britton, executive director of the Castle in Marietta (mariettacastle.org) shares my passion for the Dawes story. Scott was first described to me as "everything Rufus Dawes." He is also a first-rate historian and storyteller. Scott, thank you for your incomparable insight, knowledge, and support, and for the tour and history of the First Congregational Church.

Many thanks to Jean and Bruce Sech. Bruce volunteered to drive and accompany me on a week-long Iron Brigade battlefields tour in July 2016. And to Jim and Joan Schnieders. Jim joined me in a research visit to Mauston, Wisconsin. Bill Paradise, David Schnieders, and Rick Cromie, all fine writers, have provided great insight and comments. Dr. Bruce Hopen provided medical history insight. Thank you all.

Hal Jespersen (cwmaps.com) has expertly supplied the map cartography that displays the complex battlefield actions, terrain features, and unit positions much more clearly than any text could. Hal, I am, your obedient servant.

The staff at Dog Ear Publishing have patiently and professionally guided me through to completion. Thank you, Angela, Amber, Matt, Megan, Stephanie and all who have made this narrative come to life.

Finally, thanks to my wife, Margie, and family members Greg, Jessica, Mitch, Heather, Marcy, Elaine, Bud, Jim, Tom, Bridget, Beth, Paul, and their families for tolerating my nineteenth-century mindset these past few years. And to the memory of Mom, Dad and brother, Tom who we lost too young.

Contents

Introduction

This book attempts to relate and recreate the experiences of two young individuals who became embroiled in the cauldron of our nation's Civil War, a conflict that would overwhelm the nation for four destructive years and consume hundreds of thousands of lives. This is a war story. It is a love story.

The narrative is presented as part biography, part history, and part historical fiction. Biography because the characters have a noteworthy background and their remarkable life stories are worth telling. History because the various events described within are accurate and did happen, and the people involved, with very few exceptions, were real-life individuals. Historical fiction because many of the conversations and some situations have been created, but are, I believe, reasonable depictions based on my research of the people and events.

The main character is probably unknown to most Americans, though Civil War historians and armchair enthusiasts are certainly familiar with him. His name is Rufus R. Dawes of Marietta, Ohio, and Juneau County, Wisconsin. His life experiences were extraordinary even before the outbreak of the war, which exploded upon the nation when he was twenty-two.

A young lady, Mary Beman Gates, of Marietta, Ohio, is the other leading character. She was not yet nineteen when open warfare broke upon the nation. She found love unexpectedly and became fully engulfed in the conflict while serving on "the home front," for better and for worse. Her life changed forever.

I became a Civil War enthusiast at age nine when my parents packed four kids into our bare-bones Pontiac for a hot summer family trip to Washington, D.C., and Gettysburg. At Gettysburg, I was mesmerized listening to the battlefield tour guide describe the scene along a stone wall, site of the famous "Angle" and the "Copse of Trees," the target of Pickett's Charge.

Since then I have read and collected numerous books on the war, and I developed a special interest in the Iron Brigade upon reading the excellent chronicle of that famous unit authored by Indianapolis native Alan Nolan. I began to collect other books about the Iron Brigade, including those authored by Lance Herdegen, William Beaudot, Craig Dunn, William Venner, and others. The most vivid account is arguably *Service with the Sixth Wisconsin Volunteers*. This book is evidence that Rufus Dawes played a key role in the exemplary history of this famous "western" volunteer fighting force. I read the recorded history and thought I understood his heroic contribution to America.

A new book emerged—*The Dawes House: The Place Where You Are Always Welcome*, written by Peggy Dempsey, herself part of the Dawes family tree. Peggy also created an online blog, recreating years of insightful war-journal entries recorded during the war by an amazing woman, Julia Cutler, Rufus's aunt living near Marietta, Ohio. I urge the reader to investigate both. Peggy's wonderful book and the terrific blog she created opened my eyes to a much more involved story. Many family letters, diaries, and journals have been preserved through the years, and I was prompted to investigate.

That investigation involved research trips to the Dawes Arboretum near Newark, Ohio; to the beautiful and historic city of Marietta, Ohio, and its library, museums, historical society, cemetery grounds, and the Marietta College Special Collections Library; to historical society archives in Madison and Juneau County, Wisconsin; to the Newberry Library in Chicago; and to state libraries in Indianapolis and Columbus. I toured specific Iron Brigade action sites on nine battlefields, all well-managed by the National Park Service. The letters and journals and manuscripts revealed a treasure trove of detail not previously published. As I delved into them, my admiration and respect for Rufus and Mary and their families became forever enriched.

What began as nothing more than a trip to satisfy a curiosity soon became an inspiration to do more. The fascinating story of Rufus and Mary begged to be told, obviously from a historical perspective, but more so as an example of strength of character, courage, and love amidst chaos and tragedy. My sincere goal is to portray the story of Rufus and Mary accurately and respectfully. My hope is that they become alive again in the mind of the reader. If so, I believe you will understand and appreciate the sacrifices they made for our country and the exceptional example their actions provide to all generations of Americans.

In a broader sense, their struggles reflect experiences endured by thousands of other couples and families during the Civil War and in all conflicts before and after. Untold numbers of young Americans have faced similar trials in answer to the call for service throughout our history. This book is meant to also honor their sacrifices—past, present, and future.

Along the way, I have walked in the footsteps of heroes and patriots, and I have met incredible people who realize the significance of ordinary people like Rufus and Mary—those who sacrificed so much to help secure for our nation what is too often forgotten or dismissed. I have been inspired by the great fortune of meeting and corresponding with family descendants. I am truly thankful for the wonderful support and assistance rendered by Barb and Jack Moberg and by Peggy and Rich Dempsey. The patience and encouragement received from my family and friends have sustained me throughout.

Steven R. Magnusen

Indianapolis, Indiana

Chapter One

A Bright Beginning: Clouds on the Horizon

October 1, 1838, Malta, Ohio

She begins her letter with the words "My dear Parents." Twenty-nine-year-old Sarah Cutler Dawes, living now in the small Ohio town of Malta on the Muskingum River, is informing her mother and father that they are grandparents once again. The baby, "whom we call Rufus," had been born on the Fourth of July 1838. The name Rufus seemed to fit the occasion. His namesakes are a Boston cousin who has made a name for himself as a poet, being a contemporary of Edgar Allen Poe, and the second, Revolutionary War General Rufus Putnam.

Putnam was the leader of forty-eight daring pioneers who, in the summer of 1788, established the first United States settlement in the land north of the Ohio River. Almost all of the settlers were Revolutionary War veterans and their families. The settlement was located where the Muskingum joined the Ohio, and they named the town Marietta, in honor of the French queen, Marie Antoinette, recognizing the critical support given by France during the American Revolution. Sarah called Marietta her hometown, though she had grown up on a large farm in the nearby hilly countryside adjacent to the Ohio River.

Amid the Independence Day fireworks and celebratory gunfire, Sarah's husband, Henry Dawes, proudly announces that little Rufus has arrived with a bang! *Yes, easy for him to say*, thinks Sarah. This little dark-haired boy is her fifth child since their marriage nine years past. The siblings, one boy and three girls, had arrived in regular intervals. They are more than a handful, but she thanks God they have all survived infancy, at least so far. The local cemetery is filled with many headstones etched with the names of small children and with the graves of several young mothers, lost in childbirth or by disease.

In fact, she had suffered through a terribly painful delivery with Rufus, and now that it is over and she has recovered, she recounts some detail to her parents:

> My suffering was very great and I was near <u>very</u> near unto death and even Mr. D who is not easily frightened concluded that a few more great spasms or turns of cramps "would carry me off," indeed my breath was sometimes gone some minutes …

But now she shares a mother's joy:

> My dear little babe is a fine healthy child, very quiet, his eyes very black, he is already a great comfort to me, O how I wish you could see him.[1]

The family lives on the second floor of her husband's wood-frame mercantile store. Sarah is exhausted much of the time. Crying babies, soiled underclothes, sibling quarrels, cooking, sewing, washing, and cleaning. It never ends. Women who share her educated background are few in Malta, and she is not able to cultivate many friends, even if she had the time. Still, she is a doting mother, educating her children and reading to them in the evenings by candlelight, huddled close to the fire with them during dark and cold winter months. Kate, Sarah's oldest at age eight, is now able to help some, but Sarah's family is too distant to assist. They are 40 miles south, along the north bank of the wide Ohio River, at her childhood home, the Old Stone House. She smiles when recalling the memories there.

Sarah's father, Ephraim Cutler, age seventy-one now but active as ever, had migrated from Massachusetts to settle in what became southeast Ohio. It was the summer of 1795, and the area was still a wilderness then, part of the Northwest Territory—all the land north of the Ohio and east of the Mississippi Rivers. For centuries, the land had been home to numerous native tribes who naturally opposed the intrusions. Resulting bloody conflicts arose through the years. By 1795, American forces led by General "Mad" Anthony Wayne had defeated the Ohio tribes. The resulting Treaty of Greenville opened the southern two-thirds of what would become Ohio to unhindered American settlement.

Twenty-seven-year-old Ephraim thought the new start in open land would benefit his wife's health. But it had been a grueling trip for his family—a thirty-one-day river voyage via flatboat from Pennsylvania.

Low Ohio River water levels and dysentery had plagued them from the start. Ephraim and his wife, Leah, sadly buried two of their four young children "in the wilderness" along the Ohio River before reaching Marietta. They were two stepsiblings, Polly and Hezekiah, who Sarah Cutler Dawes never had a chance to know, gone before she was born, as was Leah, who died in 1807 at the age of forty-two. Sarah is the first-born of her father's second wife, Sally Parker, ten years younger than Ephraim. Sarah and four younger siblings grew up in the large, happy home her father had built in 1806–09 using stone from the quarry he owned near the Ohio, some 6 miles or so downstream from Marietta.

Sarah knows her father to be one of the most prominent men in Ohio. As a young man in Connecticut, he became a property agent for the Ohio Company of Associates, comprised largely of former Revolutionary War officers turned land speculators. They used warrants granted to them by Congress as payment for their war service to help purchase massive unoccupied acreages north of the Ohio River. The young federal government needed revenue, and thus the fledgling Continental Congress approved the Northwest Ordinance of 1787, opening the huge territory for sale to pioneer settlers. Ephraim's father, Rev. Manasseh, famous in his own right, had helped draft the Ordinance, had authored provisions ensuring the settlement to be slave-free, and, as one of the Ohio Company founders, had aggressively lobbied congressmen to secure its passage. Manasseh traveled to Marietta in 1788 and spent a year there working with close associate Rufus Putnam to coordinate and document the various land sales.

For Ephraim, the new land meant there were many opportunities and much to be accomplished. He managed his large farm; developed a salt spring, quarry, and grindstone business; became a militia commander; and was appointed justice of the peace and judge. He helped establish one of the first library associations and served as a territorial representative. He represented his district at the Ohio Constitutional Convention, casting the deciding vote to veto a proposal that would have opened the new state to slavery. He was active in promoting education, becoming a trustee of the newly formed university in Athens. He supported the abolitionist movement, in fact assisted in the Underground Railroad that secretly conducted escaped slaves to safety in the north. He was a leader in his church. To Sarah, Ephraim is larger than life, absent many days at the state capitol or on business, but a loving father when he is home.

Sarah misses everything about her family, even after nine years of marriage. More to the truth of the matter, she misses them *because* of nine years of marriage. She and Henry had been introduced through their fathers, each being judges in the same Muskingum Valley circuit court. It was to be a marriage more of practicality than of love.

Henry had been given a small business in Malta by his father. He needed a wife to start a family and take care of the household. Sarah was blessed with a loving family, she was a pious Christian, and she was well-educated considering the times and her gender. She was not an attractive woman, however. Suitors were not knocking on the door. She was eligible and available, Henry's family was respected, and he had a bright future. To all concerned, the marital arrangement seemed like a good and practical match. The small ceremony occurred at her family home on a cold afternoon in January 1829, and the couple left immediately for Henry's two-story Malta store and warehouse. Sarah was not yet twenty; Henry, five years older. Lucretia Catherine, nick-named Kate, was born fourteen months later.

Henry Dawes was ambitious and could boast of an impressive family history. His family, like Sarah's, had its roots in Boston. His grandfather William was an early Revolutionary War patriot, one of the Sons of Liberty, and close neighbor to fellow patriots Dr. Joseph Warren and Paul Revere. One night, acting on covert intelligence, Warren gave a secret assignment to the thirty-year-old William "Billy" Dawes and Revere: Ride from Boston to warn Samuel Adams and John Hancock that British soldiers are being sent to Lexington, intent on capturing the patriot leaders and seizing nearby weapon stores. Dawes had cultivated friendships with the British soldiers guarding the narrow Boston Neck. This influence served him well, as the gate guards allowed him to pass through on the only land route to Lexington, closing it off to everyone else. Revere took the water route, a night crossing of Boston Harbor by small boat to a waiting horse.

The land route assigned to Dawes was four miles longer than Revere's path. After warning residents along the way and through Cambridge, Dawes rendezvoused with Revere in the dark night near Lexington. While riding together toward Concord and being joined by a young doctor named Samuel Prescott, a British mounted patrol unexpectedly halted the trio. Revere was captured, but Dawes and Prescott bolted away on horseback in different directions, both being pursued. With presence of mind as he approached some farm buildings, Dawes shouted out, "Halloo, boys! There's two of them behind me!" loud enough for the Brits to hear. The ruse worked. Fearing an ambush, the pursuers broke off, allowing Dawes to escape.

This was the famous "midnight ride" made on April 18, 1775. Area minutemen were alerted along the way, and the next morning's violent encounter between American militia and British soldiers precipitated the Revolutionary War. William Dawes was therefore a key participant in the initial actions leading to America's independence from English rule. He fought at Bunker (Breed's) Hill, where his patriot friend Dr. Warren was killed in action, and then served throughout the war as a militia commander.

Years later, one of William's sons, William Mears Dawes, was appointed by President Jefferson as surveyor and inspector for the port of Thomaston, Maine. Sarah's husband, Henry, was born there in 1804, but at age thirteen moved with his family to farmland in Morgan County, Ohio, near Malta. Henry's father became well-known, serving in the state legislature and as an associate judge. In those capacities, he came to know Ephraim Cutler. He continued the family military tradition by commanding a militia cavalry unit.[2]

But that was history. Whatever Henry's grandfather and father had done for the American Revolution and for Ohio had no real influence on the behavior of Henry as a husband and father. For Henry is a vain man with a mean streak and domineering attitude. He is a strict disciplinarian and a rough lover. In his mind, a wife and children are to obey and submit, and Sarah, brought up to believe in the sanctity of marriage, does so.

She feels increasingly trapped in a relationship that has slowly turned into her private misery. But women do not talk about their problems. Sarah is sure other wives have it more difficult. Her children are her reason for living. And Henry does provide for them, the basics at least, for he is not one to waste money on frivolous things. His total focus is his business and local politics. Family fun is impractical. Worse yet, much worse, there is abuse, both verbal and physical, and the children are not exempt. Still, she will try to carry on.

By the fall of 1839, life with Henry has worsened and become unbearable. In one fit of rage, Henry threatened her life over a bizarrely fabricated charge of infidelity. Her young children need love and stability. Rufus is only fourteen months old and sickly, and Sarah is now pregnant with her sixth child. She must find a way out, and at last decides to somehow seek her father's help. Ending a marriage is a legally complicated matter under existing state law. Indeed, to discourage acts of divorce or separation, such cases require review and disposition by the Supreme Court of Ohio. The fear of public embarrassment keeps many from choosing this course, but for Sarah, and for the sake of the children, the abuse needs to end. Her opportunity comes on October 13, 1839, when Henry leaves Sarah and the children at her parent's home at the Old Stone House while he travels upriver to Pittsburg on business.

Henry is away for two weeks, giving Sarah ample time to tearfully express to her parents the awful situation she and her family are facing. Judge Ephraim Cutler is an influential politician; he knows the law, and he loves his daughter. Ephraim meets Henry at the door as he returns from his trip to retrieve his cringing family. Escorting him into the parlor, Ephraim informs his son-in-law that Sarah and the children will not be returning with him due to the abuse they have suffered. Henry is furious, both with Sarah and her father. If he has been severe, he says, it is with the desire to be master of his house. His pride hurt, he demands that any separation be a final one. Ephraim prefers no litigation, just leave his daughter and grandchildren alone. That lasts until spring 1840, when Henry arrives and takes away the oldest son, eight-year-old Henry Manasseh. Sarah relents in an attempt at appeasement, with assurance that young Henry M. ("Hen" to the family) will be allowed summer visits to the Old Stone House.

In late May of 1840, Sarah gives birth to her sixth child, another son. She names him Ephraim Cutler Dawes in honor of her father. Nothing much more is heard from Henry until March 1841. For motives unknown, he then petitions the Ohio Supreme Court to serve Ephraim and Sarah with a writ of habeas corpus for all his children being held by them, except for infant Ephraim. Henry has not gone away. Judge Ephraim retains a lawyer who counters with a plea for alimony. As the legal battle involving the supreme court begins, local newspapers keep the populace informed along the way. Much of the legal testimony derives from a series of he said/she said depositions and is inconclusive. But the statement of a former hired girl stands out, and the judges are ultimately influenced by her recollections. She recalled an incident when six-year-old Kate was "whipt with a cow hide" so severely her clothes could not be fastened for several days.

The court's decision is rendered on November 11, 1841. Sarah and the children will remain apart from Henry, who must provide $400 per year as alimony. Henry is allowed part of the summers with the children. There is a shock, however. When the two sons, Rufus and Ephraim, turn ten years of age, they become the "possessions" of Henry, joining their older brother, Henry Manasseh, already living in Malta.[3]

Henry's anger toward his father-in-law, Ephraim Cutler, is deep and lasting. Having a son named after the man he holds responsible for his family breakup is too much to accept. He will never refer to his last child as Ephraim. On boyhood visits and when in "possession" at age ten, Henry addresses the boy by a different name. He chooses Daniel Webster Dawes—certainly not "Ephraim."

Dawes-Gates Ancestral Lines (DGAL), Dawes Arboretum Archives (DAA)

Ephraim Cutler

Pioneer, farmer, businessman, judge, legislator, abolitionist, "filled many places of usefulness and honor and labored to promote education, religion and true freedom."

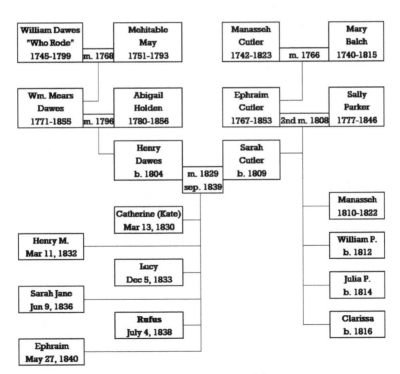

DAWES–CUTLER GENEALOGY

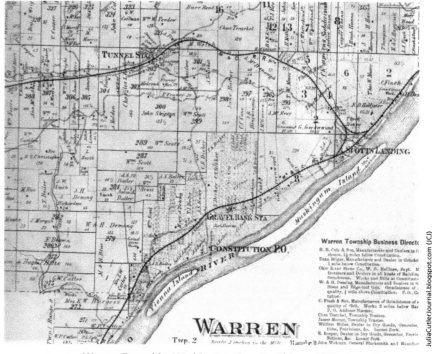

Warren Township, Washington County, Ohio, c. 1870

Key map features: Gravel Bank RR Station, Scott's Landing, Constitution Post Office, Cutler farm properties, stone and grindstone works, church, school, and Burgess home. Marietta is several miles upriver, to the northeast.

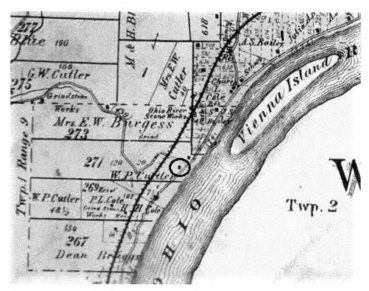

Blowup from large map above, showing the Old Stone House location circled in the center of the map at the River Road–Veto Road intersection. House no longer exists.

1840–1848, Constitution, Warren County, Ohio

Young Rufus Dawes lives an idyllic rural family life along the bank of the Ohio River, growing up in his maternal grandparent's spacious stone home. It is a full house: grandparents Ephraim and Sally; uncle William and aunts Julia and Clarissa; mother Sarah; and siblings Catherine (Kate), Lucy, Sarah Jane, and Ephraim. The home sees constant activity and lively dinner conversation. The Cutler family owns sizeable farm-land nearby and employs several hired hands. The Dawes children are assigned responsible chores at an early age and help with a variety of farm animals—from chickens to hogs to sheep to cattle and horses.

Rufus loves horses and watches as farmhands break in the young ponies. As a nine-year-old, he takes an overnight trip on horseback with his uncle William and a farmhand, riding a colt named Bonnie that he had broken himself. It is a feat that his aunt Julia mentions in her journal, surprised that the youngster could master a frisky colt. She makes note the next day that Rufus and William "returned safely this evening," obviously relieved young Rufus had met no harm trave-ling the rough terrain.

The Old Stone House is frequented regularly by travelers along the river road connecting Marietta and Belpre, where an Ohio River ferry connects to Parkersburg, Virginia. Ephraim established a post office near his home, and local farm families often linger to discuss topics of the day. Rufus and his siblings therefore become acquainted with neighboring children, developing friendships and generally running around, having fun.

Rufus meets many influential people who come to see his grand-father and uncle, and he listens in on their conversations—at least until he is shooed away by his mother to complete a chore. Uncle William, Sarah's unmarried brother, seems ancient, but he is only in his mid-thirties and already a leading Ohio politician by the time Rufus is old enough to understand such things. He remembers the family pride and large celebration hosted at the Old Stone House when William was elected speaker of the Ohio House of Representatives. Rufus had little interest in the politics, but he was happy for Uncle William and happier still for all the treats on the celebratory buffet table.

Uncle William has many meetings at the Old Stone House about politics and with men wanting to build a railroad to Cincinnati. That is a fascination to young Rufus—what boy would not be excited about a steam locomotive traveling 30 miles an hour! They are even talking about building a railroad station almost across the road, with the station signs to read "Constitution," named for the mythical town his grandfather had created for his home and farm. Rufus could just imagine boarding a steam-powered train for places now unknown. One evening he overhears talk about something that seems rather silly—an *underground* railroad that operates at night. He wonders how that could work.

Rufus often watches and waves at the magical paddlewheel steamboats going up and down the Ohio River. These boats even steam up the Muskingum to points inside Ohio, including his father's town of Malta. Marietta is a wonderful place for a young boy. His trips on the wagon or buggy into town are always an adventure. The summer visits allowed to Henry M. are cherished—an older brother to look up to. And fishing for catfish on the banks of the Muskingum is the best time of all. When they accompany one of the adults having business in town, the boys are often free to fish where the rivers join. On hot days they jump in and swim, ever mindful of the currents and eddies that can carry them away.

Marietta has shops, and wharves teeming with interesting people of all classes, and churches seemingly on every street, and a college! Uncle William is something called a "trustee" of the college, and Rufus gets to know the campus and meets the dean and students. He hopes that someday he will be a student there also.

These times along the Ohio and Muskingum Rivers do have their sobering moments. Steamboat accidents and boiler explosions happen periodically, with loss of limb or life not unusual. And in late June 1846, his grandmother Sally passes away at age sixty-nine. She was a loving person, and the family will miss her greatly. Grandfather is devastated at the loss of his second wife, but his resiliency perseveres, and he continues to manage the business and farm affairs unabated. Everyone knows and understands that death from disease or accident is always lurking at the door. Eight-year-old Rufus learns to understand it as well, but the pain of losing someone close still hurts badly. Life moves on, and the Old Stone House celebrates a marriage in September 1846 as Aunt Clarissa weds a local minister named Walton, the couple moving west to Illinois a short time later.

Virginia and large plantations and slavery are a short distance away, south of the Ohio River. Rufus has often heard the adults in the family discussing their opposition to slavery, but as a boy on the farm, it is not an issue that affects him. That all changes one warm summer day—the day that long rowboat drifts by him and his brothers.

It is a cloudy morning, and the boys are fishing along the Muskingum near the remains of the old Campus Martius stockade when they see the boat approach. It is heading downstream toward the Ohio's south bank, to Virginia. Its passengers are three rough-looking fellows armed with shotguns. But they are not the ones who catch Rufus's attention. A family of four Negroes—the man with a bloodied face, the woman openly weeping, and the two children trembling in fear—pass them not thirty feet away.

They are runaways, captured in Ohio by hired slave catchers, and are now on their way back to their owner, some rich Virginia plantation baron. Rufus knows from dinner conversations that it is legal to capture runaway slaves inside of free states. He knows that it is unlawful for anyone in a free state to assist runaway slaves. And he remembers the passion displayed by his grandfather Ephraim and uncle William against these laws. Their instruction to him is to obey the law but to heed good conscience—to step forward in opposition to any law that unfairly harms another, even the slave race. His duty is to do what is right.

Rufus can do nothing now except watch in open-mouth astonishment at what he is witnessing. In bed that night, he cannot forget the faces of that poor, miserable slave family. The children were about his age. Their owner was sure to make an example of the father—a lashing for sure, perhaps sell him to split the family. Slavery is an evil cancer, and it lives in persons not far away.[4]

Some weeks later, in the middle of the night, wagon noises outside his open bedroom window wake him from slumber. Rufus shares the room with his brother Ephraim and his mother, and she is awake, as well. A hoot-like owl call echoes nearby, the sound made by a man, not an owl. It is answered with a similar call from the south side of the river. In the dim light of a partial moon, Rufus and his mother can discern a rowboat hurriedly approaching the Ohio shore from across the wide and shimmering river, loaded with several dark figures. He knows what it means. His grandfather and uncle are at work, conducting that Underground Railroad business, in opposition to an unfair federal law. He is proud of them, but he is instantly caught up in the suspense and worried that they might be caught. He has seen the hired men in boats along the river, watching out for runaways. His mother also knows the consequences of discovery.

It is dangerous activity, subject to legal action and even violent retribution from slave owners in Virginia and their friends on the north side of the Ohio River. But over the years, many families of conscience had come together to assist runaways, developing a series of safe houses, often in hidden rooms within their own homes. A secret conveyance system to points north is coordinated by code. Uncle William's good friend, David Putnam Jr., a descendant of Marietta founding father Rufus Putnam's family, is often at the Old Stone House, coordinating "railroad" activities. He is a huge man, over six foot three, who had been forced to use his physical strength several times to fight off confrontations with pro-slavery toughs. His large home is in Harmar, just across the Muskingum River from Marietta. Rufus remembers family discussion of a news account last winter, reported by Mr. Beman Gates, editor of the *Marietta Intelligencer,* about a mob that intended to recapture two slaves and burn down Putnam's home:

> The alarm was given through Harmar that a mob had assembled at [David Jr.] Putnam's house and had threatened to destroy it; that a large number of men were there from Wood County [then Virginia] and more were coming. ... [The mob was] vexed to learn that the negroes were dressed up in cloaks, marched unnoticed through the crowd, furnished with horses, and started post haste for Queen Victoria's dominions [Canada].[5]

Grandfather Ephraim and Uncle William had chuckled at the cleverness. But the issue did not end there. A lawsuit against Putnam was filed by Virginia plantation owner George Henderson, owner of the Briars plantation. Being a known "conductor," Putnam and his family would be subject many times to threats and even home invasions from slave hunters.[6]

This has not yet happened to the Cutlers, but it is a threat. Sarah kneels to pray for the safety of all those concerned, both slaves and those

(Mother's Letters (ML), DAA)

The Old Stone House, Painting by Sala Bosworth

1875 Depiction of Constitution, Ohio
The Old Stone House is centered at extreme left, with the Burgess home to the right (north).

taking risks to free the slaves, members of her family. She tells Rufus to pray also. He does not want to turn away from the window, but does as he is told, then quickly gets up to watch again as his mother finishes her supplication to the Almighty. The night becomes a memory seared into his being.

August 27, 1842, Marietta, Ohio—the Beman and Betsey Gates Home

"She's beautiful, Betsey! Obviously takes after you! And she looks so healthy and calm! You have made me so happy, I could run out to the corner and sing the 'Hallelujah Chorus'! Are you all right? Can I get you anything? Just tell me. We are parents! Can you believe it? Mr. and Mrs. Beman Gates are parents!"

An exhausted Betsey Sybil Shipman Gates, lying weak but peaceful now in her bed, smiles at her husband and replies, "Yes, dear, I very well *know* that we are parents." Her sister, Joanna Bosworth, sitting nearby and herself drained of energy almost as much as Betsey, laughs at the response. The suffering and anxiety just endured had miraculously produced a first-born daughter—and a niece. Joanna cannot blame her brother-in-law Beman Gates for being ecstatic.

They name the little girl Mary—Mary Beman Gates in full. "Mary" after a sister of Beman's who had recently died, and the middle name "Beman" for himself, that name deriving from his mother's maiden name. Mary will be blessed to have parents such as Beman and Betsey who, at the time of her birth, are ages twenty-four and twenty-five, respectively, and had been married only ten months before.

Beman was born in January 1818 to a large family, his father a Massachusetts Congregational minister. His whole family comprised the church choir, and Beman's singing talent was so impressive he was given solos in Boston's "Messiah" performance when only nineteen. He studied a year at Amherst but had to leave due to a very tight family budget. Seeking to make his own start, he and a relative left Massachusetts for New Orleans. Along the way his companion fell sick on the Ohio River journey, tried to recover as the two laid up in Marietta, and finally died. This left Beman, not yet twenty, alone and penniless in a strange town. His singing, and musical talent with the flute, caught the attention of prominent members at the local Congregational church, including parishioner Charles Shipman. They urged Beman to stay and organize a singing school. Having no other prospects and feeling comfortable with the community and its friendly inhabitants, he agreed. His intellect and character soon expanded his activities in Marietta, and in 1839, he was named editor of the local paper, the triweekly *Marietta Intelligencer*. The paper had a wide circulation in southeast Ohio with little competition, and Beman's insightful editorials, especially during the political campaign of 1840, soon earned him a reputation as a young man of considerable intellect and rising influence. He met, won over, and, in October 1841, married one of Mr. Shipman's daughters, Betsey.

The Shipman family had moved to Marietta from Athens, Ohio, in 1837, when Betsey was twenty-one years old. She attended schools in Athens and Marietta and studied music for a time in Lancaster. Betsey was a beautiful, intelligent young woman and soon caught Beman's eye. She was described as a young lady with "delicate features and sparkling eyes" and a "bubbling spirit and keen wit somewhat subdued by shyness," all producing "a rare combination of refinement and vivacity."

Above all, her cheerful disposition is grounded in a strength of character. A love of music, using voice and instrument, is a mutual passion of Beman and Betsey. Her family had the luxury of owning one of the few pianos in pioneer Athens, and she learned to play at an early age. She now sings in the Congregational church choir with her husband, the director. Both parents possess personalities that foster a relaxed family household filled with wit and humor.

The Gates family expands with the addition of a son, Charles (Charley) Beman, on October 3, 1844. Their little caboose, Betsey (Bettie) Shipman Gates, arrives on February 24, 1853.

Betsey Sybil Shipman

Beman's position as editor allows him to influence public thought, and even at the time of Mary's birth, he is already recognized as an intelligent community leader. In 1850, he moves his family into a new and comfortable home at the corner of Fourth and Putnam Streets.

Beman Gates becomes a strong advocate for public improvements. Construction of a railroad to serve southeast Ohio is a key passion, and in that endeavor, he often meets with a cadre of like-minded men, including William Cutler, Rufus's uncle. William had procured the original charter for the Marietta and Cincinnati Railroad in 1845 and became its president in 1850. Beman is owner of his newspaper by then, but he becomes increasingly focused on the railroad business.[7]

Tuesday, July 4, 1848, Constitution, Ohio—the Old Stone House

"The very silence seems eloquent of bereavement."

They all knew the day would come. Rufus is now ten, and Henry Dawes insists that the terms of the settlement be strictly followed. For the Sarah Dawes and Cutler families at the Old Stone House, this is a time of dread and sadness.

Sarah's thirty-four-year-old sister Julia, Rufus's aunt, neatly records the sad situation in her journal:

<u>July 4, 1848</u> Rose today with a heavy heart. Rufus is today ten years old. The day which for the last nine years we have looked forward to with dread, has now dawned—probably the most important era in that dear boy's life. It is no trifle for a child of his age, to be removed from the influences of a pious mother and placed in circumstances such as those which await him. The children had a picnic on the hill, and no one came for Rufus.

<u>July 15, 1848</u> Quite a number of little boys came to play with Rufus and make a parting visit.

<u>Monday, July 17, 1848</u> Rufus has been to-day visiting all his rural haunts, his heart seems to cling to this home of his childhood. He evidently feels his situation painfully, but bears it with a fortitude scarcely to be expected from a boy of his age …

<u>July 21, 1848</u> A letter today from Malta fixes two weeks from the seventeenth as the day for the removal of Rufus & the visit of all the children.

<u>July 27, 1848</u> Mrs. Dawes had quite a party of little folk this afternoon. It rained hard and most of them staid the night.

<u>Monday, July 31, 1848</u> Mr. Dawes sent his carriage for all the children except Catherine. They will start tomorrow.

August. 1, 1848 – This has been a sad day to us – The children left this morning and Rufus is not to return with the others. The very house seems desolate – no sound of little footsteps on the stairs – no merry voices ringing through the apartments! The very silence seems eloquent of bereavement

The time of dread is painfully realized the next day. Julia sadly records her thoughts following the children's departure. They will only see Rufus again during limited summer visits and will miss him terribly.[8]

1848—1856, Rufus Dawes in Malta, Ohio

Rufus is a congenial boy and soon makes friends at school in Malta. The town is much smaller than Marietta, maybe five hundred people at the most, so there is little entertainment. Not that his father allows him much time for that anyway. Rufus is kept busy at the store doing various chores, stocking shelves, and making deliveries. There are strict rules in Henry's house, punishment for breaking them, and little time to be wasted in frivolity. Rufus misses his family and friends very much, but, encouraged by his older brother, Henry M., he accepts his situation pragmatically. Six months after leaving his family, ten-year-old Rufus is permitted to write his mother:

My dear Mother

For the first time in life I take an opportunity to write to you. I think you have been slighted. ... I am now going to school ... and am studying Latin, English grammar and arithmetic and I have to speak tomorrow and I have to write a composition ... Give my love to all the folks and tell that I would like to see them very much.

Rufus[9]

The 1850 census takers arrive at Henry's store and home and record the names and ages of all three sons now living there. Henry gives Rufus the middle initial "R," and tells the census man to record ten-year-old Ephraim as "Daniel W." Henry, the vindictive father, still harbors the grudge against his father-in-law.[10] Life with their father is harsh, especially for Ephraim, the black sheep. Ephraim expresses this in a letter to his sisters:

Father thinks I ain't more than a dog to hear him talk. No one could be more than a dog to live with him all his life. You dare not express an opinion of your own if it is at variance with any of his.[11]

Rufus has turned fifteen when word comes to Malta that his grandfather, the eminent Ephraim Cutler, passed away on July 8, 1853, at the age of eighty-six. The burial was at Gravel Bank cemetery, about a mile north of the Old Stone House. The family laid him to rest next to the two wives who had preceded him in death, Leah and Sally.

In addition to operating his mercantile store, Henry Dawes serves as a business agent for men who purchase large quantities of grain and wool. He and several partners operate a warehouse near the river, filled with products destined for markets both north and south. It proves to be a profitable business. As he matures, Rufus helps his father and older brother tend the store and pack wool. He becomes interested in national affairs. The war with Mexico has recently been won, creating military heroes he reads about in the newspapers weeks after battles have been fought. The names and exploits of various army officers are often mentioned in these battlefield accounts—names he soon forgets. He has no way of knowing it, but someday many of those names will become all too familiar.

Slavery is the volatile national topic dividing the country, especially after Congress adopts the Fugitive Slave Act of 1850. That act infuriates the abolitionists, those ardent haters of slavery, because the law now states that citizens have the *duty* to expose and return runaway slaves, even in free states. Underground Railroad activity is now more dangerous. Secrecy is paramount, for even within the slave-free North, many people have little sympathy for the slave population, dismissing them as unequal citizens and worrying about job competition, just wishing the Negroes would simply stay where they are, slave or not. Some even favor the 1850 act since it had the effect of forcing escapees to exit the United States completely, with Canada being the most viable refuge.

1856, On to Wisconsin

Rufus cannot believe it is happening. His father had traveled west to Wisconsin, where Henry's two older brothers, William and George, had previously migrated with their families in search of land for a new start, much as their father, William Mears Dawes, had done in Ohio years before. Henry was gone over a month, leaving his merchandise store in Malta to the care of his sons, admonishing them to make sure spent ashes were discarded away from anything combustible. He wrote that he bought land "near the route to La Crosse ... fine land, mostly prairie with timber enough and lots of springs." The property is near the small village of Mauston. And he intends to send his sons to a fledgling prep school/ university in Madison.

This is a disaster, one that neither Rufus nor anyone on the Cutler side had ever anticipated. What possible future can Rufus or Ephraim have with this move to the backwoods, even though Madison is the state capital city? Wisconsin has been a state for only eight years. Malta, Ohio, is boring enough, but Wisconsin must be downright primitive! Rufus is now eighteen years old, and Ephraim (aka Daniel), just sixteen.

Rufus ("Rufe" to siblings and friends) always anticipated attending Marietta College. Older brother Henry M. had been able to do so, graduating the previous year. Uncle William has the same desire for his remaining two nephews. He is a member of the college governing board and is a longtime friend of its president, Israel Andrews. William cares deeply for his sister Sarah's children since, for years, he assumed the role of surrogate father. Marietta College has a very good reputation, all male of course, established twenty years previously with close ties to the Congregational church. It seems a perfect fit for the Dawes boys, but not in the eye of father Henry.

William is not able to influence Henry Dawes, but college president, Israel Andrews, makes an attempt. Andrews appeals to Henry Dawes for reconsideration via a letter mailed upriver to Malta. But Henry is obstinate and has control over the purse strings. No protesting by his sons, or appeal from a college president, will change his mind.

Young Ephraim writes Sarah a quick letter, short on punctuation but heartfelt, nonetheless:

Dear Mother

Before this reaches you I will probably be on my way to Wisconsin (we mail Monday) whether I ever get back again remains to be seen I would have written sooner but I never knew or even thought of going until tonight as soon as I get there and probably before if I can get out of his sight I will write you I don't want to go and will not if I can help it maybe he'll let me come back with him Rufe says don't worry about him if he don't come down the first of the term Pres Andrews letter came tonight. Write Rufe and tell him how the donation party went off can't write any more now

Your affectionate son Ephraim

PS can I come down & assist you if I stay down here don't write to me until you hear from me[12]

The letter, when received, breaks Sarah's heart. The whole family at the Old Stone House is uniformly depressed and saddened. They may never see these boys again.

But why send the two sons out west to Wisconsin? There are schools much closer to Malta with more to offer. If not Marietta College, why not Ohio University in Athens or a college back east? Those are questions most certainly asked and not sufficiently answered. Henry, the father, wants his sons to become acquainted with the people and surroundings near Madison for future business purposes. In doing so, it serves to spite his estranged wife and her family. For, if at Marietta College, his sons would be back with their mother. At Athens, they would be attending a college that owed much of its existence to his hated father-in-law, Ephraim Cutler, who had been a prominent benefactor and trustee of the school since 1820. Henry wants nothing further to do with the Cutlers. What is clear is that the boys are very much not in favor of the decision yet have little choice but to accept it.

1856–58—Students at the State University of Wisconsin

Ephraim is the first to leave for Madison in April 1856, enrolled by his father at the college prep school under his surrogate name, Daniel W. Dawes. On September 17, 1856, Rufus reluctantly starts his three-day westward journey to join his brother. Unknown to him at the time, the seventeenth of September is to be an uncannily ominous date.

Rufus arrives in Madison late on Saturday, September 21, and on the 23rd writes his mother a four-page letter. He describes his journey—by boat up the Muskingum to Zanesville, then a series of railroads with car transfers at Columbus, Xenia, Dayton, Indianapolis, Lafayette, Michigan City, Chicago, Milwaukee, and, finally, Madison and the college, to room number 26, North Hall—all accomplished successfully with his baggage intact. The train traveling past the south end of Lake Michigan (his first glimpse of a Great Lake) to Chicago was so crowded, he was forced to stand. On the run to Milwaukee, he interrupted the boredom by conducting a presidential election vote among fellow passengers, noting the results as "Fremont 43, Buchanan 16, Fillmore 7." (James Buchanan will win the 1856 presidential election in November.) More importantly, he informs Sarah about sixteen-year-old Ephraim (aka Daniel W.):

> I found Eph looking as shabby as a beggar nearly ... I recommend him to you as an object of charity. He has written Father time and again but all to no purpose. ... I found him buried in a book with an old coat on out at the elbows, an old vest which has been worn out some six months, pants too short by six inches hitched up by one suspender, an old pair of stogy shoes that the

worst clodhopper in Wisconsin would not wear. I gave him a coat and pair of pants and he begins to look more like a human being. But it is robbing myself, however he shall not go naked as long as I have anything on my back.

To the young Dawes brothers, Wisconsin State University is an initial disappointment, nothing much resembling the traditions, campus, and course of study at Marietta College. How could it compare? Madison's all-male university had been in existence for only a short time, graduating its first class of two young men just two years previously, in 1854. But what are they to do? It is take it or leave it, their father tells them. He will pay their way at Madison and expect them both back at his store when class is not in session. That store is still in Malta, Ohio, but Henry's plan is to relocate to his newly purchased land near Mauston, Wisconsin.

The campus consists of two recently constructed four-story sandstone buildings, North and South Halls, both functioning as student and faculty quarters, classrooms, and kitchen. The buildings have a primitive warm-air heating system using wood-burning furnaces, but it is still cold and drafty. Sanitary facilities consist of an outside well with a hand pump and several outdoor privies. Freshmen are initiated with a "baptism" under the well pump, and they are expected to bring in firewood for the furnaces and the kitchen stoves. The water from the well is bad, meals are up to the students to supply and make themselves, and entertainment or basic amenities are scarce. Icy winds fiercely blowing across Lake Mendota make for winter days that are far more bitterly cold than any the Dawes brothers have experienced in southern Ohio. Rufus describes the buildings and city of Madison in the letter to his mother:

> The buildings ... look like a pair of penitentiary's. They stand on top of a barren hill with not a tree taller than ten feet within one-hundred yards. I am also disappointed in Madison, both as regards the size of the place and the beauty of it. But I am much pleased with the State of Wisconsin generally, it is a fine country, the farms look nice, the people enterprising, the little towns neat and clean ...[13]

Madison itself had been incorporated as a city just several months before the arrival of the Dawes boys, although it had been a growing village for some twenty years, home now to 6,800 residents and the center of state government. The center of town is a mile away from North Hall, with virgin forest separating the university from State Street, which ends a half mile east of campus. Most of the students hunt game to supplement what food they can grow or purchase. One of them takes a shot at some quail while leaning out of a North Hall window, only to mistakenly hit and dispatch a chicken in the yard below. There was only one thing to do: cook the chicken and seek forgiveness later.[14]

North Hall today—University of Wisconsin at Madison

They are college teenagers away from home, and they have fun where they can find and afford it. Not that the Dawes boys can afford much; Henry keeps tight purse strings. In November 1856, two months after starting college life in Madison, Rufus writes his father asking for more money. Henry responds to them both:

> I now enclose $6 which use only for necessaries for both of you. Try to do with as little as you can until I sell some Wisconsin land which I shall probably be able to do next summer. If Chancellor wants you to join any society in college do so and pay your part. If this enclosure don't meet present needs let me know … You should be careful to tallow your shoes.[15]

Later that term, Rufus apologizes to sister Lucy for not replying to her letters, simply explaining that he has no money for stamps. Brother Henry offers to send some, which they accept, because, as Ephraim writes:

Father don't furnish us any more money than absolutely necessary and wants to know everything we get with it.[16]

The first term ends in mid-December 1856, and the students are given a
three-week break. Rufus and Ephraim stay at North Hall, and in a letter
to older brother Hen in Marietta, written the day after Christmas, Rufus
explains why: Father Henry, thinking the vacation was only two weeks,
delayed sending enough cash for them to visit a Wisconsin acquaintance
for the holiday until it was too late to go. They are still trying to survive
on the six dollars received some time ago. So the two spend the week of
Christmas eating "meal and water." With the money now in hand, they
intend to visit the nearby family for the remaining vacation time, Rufus
explaining, "[T]will be better than to stay here and starve on the grub
such as we had last week."

Rufus continues to vent his frustrations to Hen and comments on
family matters:

> I am getting mighty sick of staying out here and from the way
> Father writes there is not much prospect of relief. He talks as
> though he did not intend for either of us to come home on the
> long vacation [summer break]. It is really no college at all com-
> pared to Marietta College. ... There are in the college classes 35,
> in the preparatory department 15. ... Studying geography, arith-
> metic and grammar about 56, which shows the general character
> of students. ... [A]bout 25 to 30 ten-year-olds, they have a num-
> ber of the <u>sophomore</u> class not quite 13 years old.
>
> I was glad to hear that Father was not mad at Jane's plan [sis-
> ter Sarah Jane's intention to become a missionary]. I expected
> that when he heard of it he would ... scratch her name off his 20th
> will and do other diverse horrible things.[17]

Rufus and Ephraim eventually become acclimated to the academic
life in Madison and realize not everyone is a backwoodsman. Sons of
Wisconsin's prominent figures, young men their age, are in class with
them—youth with similar intellect and ambition. There are even a few
Southern boys. When able, they visit the capital when the legislature is in
session and keep up on the issues of the day.

One young fellow they bond with is William F. Vilas, or "Bill"
to his friends. Bill's father, Levi, had been a prominent politician in
Vermont and moved to Madison to open a law practice. He had served
one term in the state assembly. Bill is slated to graduate in 1858 at age

eighteen, and it is obvious he will have no trouble meeting his goal of becoming a successful attorney in his own right. Occasional dinner invitations to his Madison family home serve to introduce Rufus and Ephraim to local and state politicians of influence. Besides, Bill enjoys having a good time as much as anyone.[18]

July 4, 1857, Madison, Wisconsin

He had long thought about it and makes the decision on his birthday: He will keep a journal. Rufus Dawes buys a six-inch-by-eight-inch leather book containing a hundred or so blank white sheets of paper, blue-lined. He begins with a blend of self-confidence tempered with a touch of modesty and subtle humor:

Dear Journal-

I have resolved to commence, upon this my 19th birthday, to keep a daily journal of all that may occur which I think will be of interest to me in future time should I be permitted to remain as one among mortals for any length of time.

Rufus R Dawes, Saturday July Fourth, 1857.

At present time attending the Wisconsin State University and am just finishing my freshman year of study.[19]

It is the beginning chronicle of a young American, uncertain about his future, separated from most of his family, and a financial pauper, but possessing intellect, character, and all the hopes and dreams for living a respected and productive life in keeping with the high standards established by his prolific ancestors. At this point he has no idea how or where that might be accomplished or in what endeavor.

Following completion of their first year in Madison, Rufus and Ephraim stay in Wisconsin and work to help clear their father's land near Mauston. It is hard work with little social life, but their time together increases the bond between them. They can also earn money between terms by helping local farmers, who also provide lodging. Those farmers around the hamlet of Black Earth are especially in need of some strong hands. They seem to have a preponderance of daughters, a delightful situation the Dawes boys take full advantage of. They find the experience rather enjoyable, and the money earned is beneficial too.

Back again for the fall term, they join the student-run literary societies present on campus, each being chapters of parent organizations established in eastern universities decades before, precursors of modern fraternities. These societies, most often using Latinate names, are a key part of campus social life. The activities often include debates, orations, and essays on topical issues of the day, or poetry and music recitals. The two most prominent societies, the Athenian and the Hesperian, provide excellent training for men with aspirations for positions of influence. Exhibitions are organized and advertised to area residents, hopefully attracting some of the young Madison maidens.

In December 1857, a local audience enjoys this midweek exhibition, with Bill Vilas presiding and R. R. Dawes and younger brother D. W. (aka Ephraim) Dawes featured orators.[20]

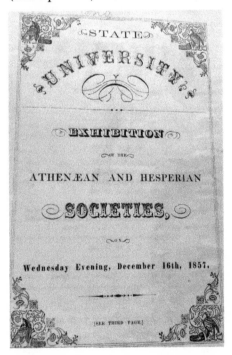

The 1850s, Marietta, Ohio—Gates and Bosworth Families

Mary Gates and brother Charley huddle together while their parents discuss the project with the studio photographer. The whole business of being able to capture a moment in time and preserve it on a metal or glass plate is now commonplace in America, but it is a new experience for the children. Beman and Betsey Gates have planned and paid for the sitting, and they want a positive result. But all the attention, fuss, and bother make Mary and Charley a bit nervous, and their expressions cannot help but display an appearance of unease.

About a year later, the Bosworths come along for another sitting. The Gates children recall they had survived unharmed from the previous experience, and next to cousin Frances (Francy), they are more relaxed. The parents coax them along: "Smile a little. Don't move for five seconds, or you will spoil it!" Finally, it is over, several images taken successfully, and the young folks can go home to change out of their fancy clothes.

Childhood in the Gates and Bosworth households is a place of music, singing, and laughter. There are sibling confrontations to be sure, but Betsey Shipman Gates and Joanna Shipman Bosworth make sure their children know right from wrong and make sure they follow the right path. The two sisters do so by example, with warmness of heart, a quick wit, and a cheery disposition. Mary feels close to her mother and comes to exhibit Betsey's combination of admirable traits. Every day is an adventure, and the world around her a fascinating place.

Beman Gates cuts a handsome figure: tall and distinguished, buoyant personality, entertaining companion. His first love is family; his second, singing. His deep bass voice is good enough to be a professional, his Boston mentor once told him. He and Betsey are dedicated choir directors at the First Congregational Church on Front Street. Betsey and Mary play piano and sing soprano, Charley does an acceptable violin, and songs and music fill the two large, connected parlors in the Gates

Charley Gates   Mary Gates   Frances Bosworth   Charley Gates   Mary Gates

Mother's Letters, DAA

home at Fourth and Putnam Streets, where friends and college students are often entertained.

Beman Gates sells his newspaper in 1854, feeling he can no longer give editing his proper attention due to railroad interests. He is soon elected vice president and superintendent of the Marietta & Cincinnati Railroad and travels considerably on business. Family, faith, local and national issues, music, railroads, and education fill his life. He serves many years as a trustee for Marietta College, whose buildings are on the rising ground just across Putnam Street.[21]

Thursday, September 3, 1858—Marietta College, First Day of Fifteen-Week Fall Term

Expect the unexpected! After two years in Madison, father Henry Dawes relents and allows his sons to return to Ohio and enroll at Marietta College. Henry has always been involved in politics, and his support of Republican Governor Salmon P. Chase is rewarded in January 1857 with an appointment as Morgan County notary public for a three-year period. That August, Henry is nominated for the Ohio legislature and is elected for a single two-year term. He now thinks it appropriate to have his sons in an Ohio college, at least while he is in public office.[22]

There is sadness at leaving their Wisconsin friends—friendships they will remember and try to maintain—but they are elated at being close again to family. Their mother, Sarah, and sister Lucy have moved into town with older brother Henry M., who, after graduating from Marietta College in 1855, studied law and has recently been admitted to the bar. He now has a local law practice with an elder partner. Uncle William and Aunt Julia are happy to have the Dawes boys return; in their minds, their nephews and nieces are the children they never had. It is fun rekindling past boyhood friendships and amazing how some of the girls have matured. The farm at the Old Stone House is close by, readily accessible via the new Union Railroad running southwest along the right bank of the Ohio River to Belpre, and they soon dive into the academic and social life on campus.

Rufus joins the oratory and debate societies, the chess club, and reads Shakespeare. Among his orations is an argument against the Homestead Bill, the controversial federal law that pits "free soil" Northerners, who want public lands opened to individual farmers, against Southern slave owners, who prefer large tracts for future plantations.

Marietta College Special Collections Library (MCSCL)

Author photo

Marietta College 1846   Erwin Hall today

His journal entries record evening and weekend adventures and parties with friends, both male and female, with an emphasis on the female. That October, he notes:

> Clifford and I hired a carriage and took a load of girls down to Newport. The ladies included Miss Temple, Miss Sallie, Rhoda Shipman and Mary Gates. We started around 8 o'clock AM and came back in the evening. We had a glorious time.[23]

All day with four girls at two-to-one odds! What could be better? If the young ladies (or their parents) had any qualms about the adventure (which was doubtful, given the characters of Rufus and Clifford), there was safety in numbers. Rhoda Shipman had brought along her sixteen-year-old cousin, Mary Gates. Rufus notes that she is shy but witty and quick to laugh. He is comfortable with most girls and enjoys gentlemanly flirting ... but this one, she is ... special.

Rufus sits on the campus hill thinking of Mary as he gazes at the Gates home on the opposite corner, hoping she might appear. The college students have already dubbed it the Corner, the reference clearly all about Mary. Rufus thinks it through ...

Our families have known each other for years. Mr. Gates and Uncle William have discussed railroad business at the Old Stone House many times. Our families have often dined together. My sister Lucy teaches little Bettie, Mary's sister, in school. She's become friends with Mrs. Gates and has gotten to know Mary too.

Mary was just a kid when I left for Wisconsin. This fall, it is different. She first caught my eye at church. Attendance at the First Congregational Church on Front Street is a requirement for our Deportment grade, and we all sit together in the right corner of the wraparound balcony. Of course, the balcony provides an open view of the pews below, and lo, that Mary

Gates has matured. She is a very attractive young lady! We all talk about her. Her blue eyes sparkle when she smiles; she is refined and animated. Sometimes there's a good view of her when she sings in her parents' choir. Her beautiful chestnut-colored hair is usually tied up or braided. I sometimes imagine her with it undone. Every time I glance up at her corner-room window, I think about that. All right, admit it! I can't get her off my mind! She is spellbinding, despite her age. Lucy thinks so, too, and keeps trying to push me in Mary's direction. If Lucy says to me one more time, "If I were a man, I would …," I think I'll … well, I don't know what. Older sisters can be such a pain! But I wish I could be as confident as Lucy says I should be.

Part of it is (at least, I tell myself) that Mary is so young. I've been to her home with the other students, all of whom hang around her like bees on honey. But will her parents ever respect me, despite their affection for my family? Who am I? Away in Wisconsin for so long. Son of a man Mr. Gates has opposed in his political editorials, no doubt due in large part to Father's dark history with my family. It's a small town; everybody knows the situation. Mother and sisters Kate and Lucy are barely getting by, essentially ignored by my father. It is a disgraceful situation we all have lived with for years. If I am ever to become serious with any woman of good account, I must be a respectable man, successful in my own right. For now, I am still in school, still obligated to him, by duty and by his insidious threat of total separation from family support should I resist him. Best to put any thought of this young girl out of my mind.

But, of course, that does not happen. "Who are you trying to kid, Rufus?" It is his junior classmate and good friend, David Chambers. "You're stuck on her, it's obvious! Of course, so is everybody else!" And that evokes laughter and shouts of "I am!" and "Me too!" from everybody in the room. About ten of them are together in the Kappa Alpha room, plotting the farcical Junior Class Exhibition to be presented in several weeks, the date set for Tuesday evening, March 29, 1859.

"Wonderful, thank you all very much!" Dawes says sarcastically.

"No, this is perfect!" Tim Condit chimes in. "I can see it on the stage: Old Railroad Rufus chugging by the Corner in hopes of making a pleasant stop at the 'Mary Gates Station,' and everybody else in the car wanting to hop off and join him!"

"Well, it couldn't be to impress her with his singing voice, certainly," contributes Chambers. "No offense, but Rufus, your vocal talent can only be admired by Mr. Newport here, who we all know emits a noise most approximating a farm animal, perhaps a braying sheep for comparison purposes, while your voice is more like that of a bear—tuneless and husky!" That breaks up the room, with mimicking animal sounds emanating from every mouth.

R. Marshall Newport protests in good nature, "Hey, I resemble that remark!"

The junior class puts on an entertaining show. The community audience, including the Gates family, chuckle over the clever humor evident in the playbill and thoroughly enjoy the show's satire.[24] They are sitting with Betsey's sister, Joanna; her husband, Sala Bosworth; and their daughter, Francy. Some parts of the show are a bit puzzling, inside jokes perhaps, over their head. Halfway through the program, Beman and Betsey Gates are amused but perplexed by an inane song titled "Who's Going to the Corner Tonight?" The solo features Mr. Dawes, billed as "Railroad Dawes," helped with a rollicking chorus from the whole class. His voice is dreadfully out of tune, and what is meant by the "Corner"?

"No candidate for our choir, certainly!" Beman whispers to Betsey. In the dim light of the audience seating, none but cousin Francy notice Mary's blushing cheeks.

DECLAMATION—Logan, Chief of the Mingoes, to Col. Cresap.

Court Marshal NEWPORT.*

(The biped Taurus, sulky as the animal himself, and twice as crooked in the legs.)

MUSIC—"I'm coming back in three years to take that Silver Cup."..Solo by NEWPORT.

CHORUS—"And I shall be his dad." (?)

[Entire audience expected to join in this chorus]

DISCUSSION—The Goose Question: i. e. Should the Gander set his turn.

Affirmative.............................Railroad DAWES.

Negative.................Clover Lummux CONDIT.†

MUSIC—"Who's going to the Corner to-night?".....................Solo by DAWES.

CHORUS—"I'm for the Corner—I, I, I."......................By the whole Class.

COLLOQUY—The Irish Wedding...Jo. SHAW.

SCENE, *An Irish Shanty on the Shannon.* TIME, *Midnight.*

DRAMATIS PERSONÆ:

Old Mither Flarnegin......................................JOHNSON.

Bridget, daughter of Mither Flarnegin...................SHAW.

Biddy, infant daughter of Mither Flarnegin............CHAMBERS.

Pat Murphy, successful suitor to Bridget.................GARRISON.

Jemmy Dougherty, ⎱ Railroad Mickies from Cork, ⎰ DAWES.

Dennis Mulligan, ⎰ disappointed rivals of Pat M. ⎱ NEWPORT.

Barney Flaherty, backer of Pat Murphy, Instructor of Shillelah fencing, and Champion of Erin's Isle...KING.

Patrick O'Brien, the Praest.....................................ALDRICH.

Johnny MacFinnegan, backer of the Corkonian Mickies and Diddler.......................................CONDIT.

REQUIEM—Sic transit *gal*-iria Junior Phizzle.

AIR—"Tune the Old Cow died on."

SHAW and DAWES	Air	Horn(et) Flute.
JIM KING	First Bass	Bass Viol.
CHAMBEERS	Tenor	Accordeon(ing) to Gunter.
CONDIT	2d Bass	*Conun-Drum*, invented per se.
NEWPORT	Falsetto	*Mal*-odious Organ, i. e. he'll bray.

* This young man has long cultivated the affections, and his amorous bump is now developing so much that it is thought that it will ultimately eventuate *in a horn.*

† "The earth hath bubbles as the water hath."—[Shak.

First Congregational Church
Front Street, Marietta, Ohio

A friend composed
this poem:

Oh, maiden so meek, pray
what do you seek, with those
innocent far-seeing eyes?

If you'd glance o're your book,
to a gallery nook, you would
start in blushing surprise.

A youth sitting there, with
soldierly air, is heeding nor
sermon or song.

His text is displayed in the
face of the maid. And none
of us think he was wrong.[25]

Church interior with wraparound balcony, where
students such as Rufus sat in the right corner.

Mary Beman Gates
Marietta, Ohio

Rufus R. Dawes
Marietta College

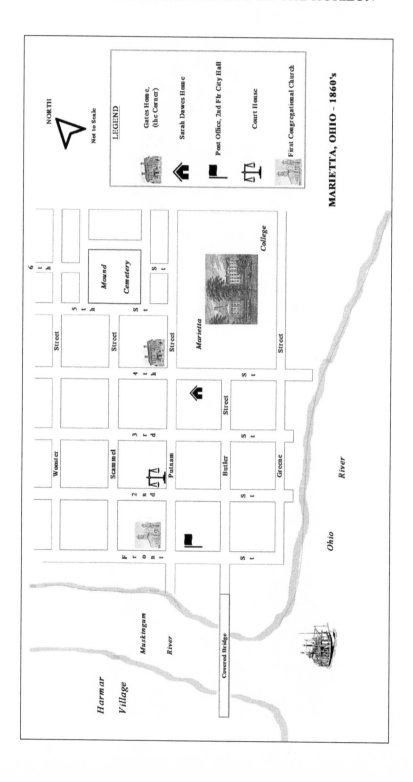

Endnotes

1. Dawes Arboretum Archives (DAA).

2. Ferris, Mary W. *Dawes–Gates Ancestral Lines: A Memorial Volume, Vols. 1 & 2.* (DGAL) Private printing 1940. And, Descendants of William Dawes Who Rode Association (DWDWRA) (website) http://www.wmdawes.org.

3. Wilson, Hattie Dawes. *The Search for Sarah and Henry Dawes. The Tallow Light* (magazine). Sarah and Henry Dawes court records. Marietta College Special Collections Library (MCSCL).

4. The slave-catcher scene witnessed by Rufus is fictional but plausible given the times and documented slave-related activity.

5. Baker, David. "November 12, 2015, David Putnam, Jr., Conductor on the UGRR. All Aboard!" Early Marietta (blog). http://earlymarietta.blogspot.com/2015/11/.

6. Burke, Henry Robert. "Abolitionist David Putnam Jr." Lest We Forget (blog). http://lestweforget.hatonu.edu/page.cfm?uuid=9FEC4E4F-A3C4-6825-FE2FD2153CFA7B9D.

7. Ferris, Mary W. *Dawes–Gates Ancestral Lines, Vol. 1 & 2.*

8. DAA.

9. *ibid.*

10. Washington County Public Library. Local History and Genealogy Archives. Marietta, Ohio.

11. Ephraim Dawes Collection. Newberry Library. Chicago, Illinois. (EDC-NL)

12. *ibid.*

13. DAA.

14. University of Wisconsin-Madison. Department of Political Science.

15. Ferris, M. W. *Dawes–Gates Ancestral Lines.*

16. EDC-NL. Letter to Henry M., October 1858.

17. DAA.

18. Wm. Vilas is to become a soldier, lawyer, politician, senator, cabinet officer, university regent, and philanthropist. Vilas Hall at UW Madison is named in his honor.

19. DAA.

20. EDC-NL.

21. Beach, Mary Dawes. *Mother's Letters: Mary Beman Gates Dawes.* Copyright 1940. See DAA for photos and family information.

22. Ferris, M. W. *Dawes–Gates Ancestral Lines.*

23. DAA.

24. Playbill from the EDC-NL.

25. Nineteenth-century photos courtesy of the First Congregational Church, Marietta, Ohio. Poem from *Mother's Letters* by Mary Dawes Beach. Today, a brass plaque is displayed in the woodwork above the church organ. It reads "IN MEMORY OF BEMAN GATES AND BETSEY SHIPMAN GATES," faithful and talented choir directors. Mary Gates photo courtesy of Peggy and Rich Dempsey (private collection). Rufus photo from MCSCL.

Chapter Two

A Son's Duty: a Reason to Hope

Monday, July 4, 1859, Marietta, Ohio—Sarah Dawes Home, Fourth Street

He celebrates his twenty-first birthday with the family at the home on Fourth Street, just half a block southeast of the Gates corner. For Sarah, it is wonderful to have her children together, and she and the girls prepare a nice late-afternoon meal. The Fourth of July birthday is always fun for everyone, a double celebration, with morning speeches, afternoon ceremonies, and evening fireworks. Independence Day has special meaning in Marietta—so many Revolutionary War patriots buried in Mound Cemetery, so many of their ancestors still living in the area.

"Happy birthday, Rufus," Sarah says, smiling at her middle son. "It's been so nice to have you back in Marietta. I'm going to miss you, very much." They had all kept quiet about it, not wanting to bring up the subject, but finally, she cannot resist her feelings.

Rufus replies, "I know, Ma. It has been wonderful. But I think it will be fine and turn out for the best." His response is a failed attempt at being upbeat about a situation that pains his mother and siblings. A confrontation with his father, Henry, just a week or so ago is quickly recalled in his mind: "Rufus, I need you to come with me to Wisconsin, and I need you soon," his father had said. "I'm moving the store to Mauston for good. I want to be there early enough in the fall so that winter weather won't interfere. We must pack everything up pretty quickly and have it shipped with us when we leave."

Rufus had begun to protest. "But, Father—" Henry cut him off, his voice rising, "Now, I know you have another year of college, and you can come back, but not for the fall term. You should be happy to know that if you come along now, Daniel can stay in Marietta at the college and, yes, I will pay his way again, though I seriously doubt whether he will ever make something of himself. But he's not that much good in my business, either. And, of course, there is Henry. What has he done for me? Left me as soon as he could! Hiding behind his mother's skirt! Gets involved in the Anti-Slavery Society! Sees himself as a big lawyer someday! Bah!" Henry's bitterness intensified as he continued. "You, on the other hand, *do* show some promise. I have worked very hard to grow the business, and there is so much potential in Wisconsin. I have aims to be involved in state politics, and you should become involved also! You have met some influential people there already, and we can help each other. If you apply yourself, you will see me reward you justly. But if you don't come, well, what reason have I to support two more sons who will have abandoned me, much less the women who did just that years ago?"

So, there it was, the familiar threat frequently brandished whenever Henry demanded obedience ...

Ephraim and Henry sit with their brother on the front porch after dinner, each chomping down on a basket of juicy melons while the ladies clean up. "Rufe!" Ephraim exclaims. "Tell the Old Man to go to Wisconsin alone. It's your life, you're twenty-one, he can't hold you if you don't want to go."

Hen joins in, not resisting an opportunity for a big-brother wisecrack, "Little *Daniel* here is actually right, Rufe—you certainly have every right to stay here and finish college. We can find the money to do that somehow, and legally he has no claim on you. You can live with us. We are cramped a bit, but we can make do. You'll just have to think a bit small!"

Rufus smiles and replies, "Believe me, I would like to do that. But I don't know; I have mixed feelings. On the one hand, I hate being away from all of you, and I don't want to miss my senior year and perhaps not graduate. On the other hand, he *is* our father, and I have been with him the longest, I know the business, and he does need the help. You may think it naïve, but I do feel a duty as his son to be where and when he needs me. Maybe I'm foolish. I know you may think that, but I think if I stick with him, it just might, over time, smooth his feelings toward Ma and the girls and to all of us."

"Ha! Fat chance of that happening!" Ephraim exclaims. "He will never change his ways, certainly not his opinion of me! He's hated me since before I was born!"

"Look, Eph, I know you have had it especially tough, and I don't grudge you at all for staying away from him. I also know there are business and political opportunities out there in Wisconsin, both for him and for me. He will be successful, I have no doubt. But after getting him established there, if I don't see myself or my future in Mauston, I *will* return here. And I will have done my best as a son and have a clear conscience."

"Hmm, what about that little Gates girl down the street, bro?" Henry kids.

"Well," Rufe replies, "that's another reason to come back—when she grows up a little and will then be more receptive to the affections of a mature, sophisticated, fine specimen of a gentleman like me! Besides, Fanny says her parents are likely to send her to school in the east, Massachusetts probably. She won't be around here anyway."

"Ha! Well, better hope nobody else jumps in ahead of you!" laughs Ephraim.

The Gates Home, Fourth and Putnam, the Corner

Mary Gates stands at her home's Putnam Street parlor window, looking down Fourth Street at the Dawes home, watching Sarah's three sons talking together on the front porch. *I wonder what they're talking about,* she thinks. *There's Rufus. He hasn't stopped by lately, though he makes me nervous every time he does. I never know what he's thinking. What does he want? He seems to like me. Charley says he must, and I can't help being flattered, but I'm not ready for a beau! Especially one who is four years older than me. He scares me a bit! Yet, still …*

His sister Lucy says he's going away to Wisconsin with his father. She can't understand why he would do it. So I suppose that ends it, whatever it is or was or could be. If he goes so far away, what use is it to think about him anyway? She contemplates that for a minute, the practical side of her mind at odds with the emotional side, then sighs, lets the curtain fall back into place, turns, and walks slowly away.

Thursday, July 28, 1859—A Wedding

Rufus hugs his sister Sarah Jane—just "Jane" or "Jenny" to the family—and smiles. "Mrs. Shedd! Congratulations! I wish you both all the best. I think, though, the both of us are making it tough on Ma. I'm going west again, with Father, quite possibly an unpleasant prospect. But you! You and John

Sarah Jane Dawes Shedd

JuliaCutlerJournal.blogspot.com, (JCL), MCSCL

heading to Persia! My missionary sister and brother-in-law! I know it's an admirable undertaking and you both feel strongly about it, but when will we ever see you again?"

"Thank you, Rufe," Jane replies. "I know you probably don't understand why, and maybe I should stay and do some missionary work with you! But it has been John's calling—*our* calling, I should say. And we have planned it ever since he graduated from Marietta College and then the Andover Seminary. His ordination next week will be the final step in our preparation to bring the gospel message to Persia. The people in that biblical land need to hear this so much. It's his life's work, and at twenty-six, he knows it's time to start on it. And it's mine too."

Rufus makes a small smile that is part grimace and kisses her on her forehead. "You're right; I don't completely understand. I do understand that we worry about you and will miss you. We will write and give you news that's probably going to be six weeks old when you get it! You better do the same."

With that lighthearted brotherly scold, Jane moves on to give her goodbyes to the rest of the family, with tears and sniffles and well-wishes intermingled.

Soon it is Rufe's turn for goodbyes. As the following week progresses, he confides to his diary:

Monday, August 1st, 1859. Eleven years ago today I went first to live in Malta. The first day of August 1848 is one of the memorable days of my life. This day and this week I spend in Marietta. Read Shakespeare all day in the Kappa Alpha Hall and called at Shipman's in the evening.

Wednesday, August 3rd. Went down to Warren [the Cutler estate, Old Stone House] in the forenoon. Rode on the cars to Scott's [train stop, where the Marietta & Cincinnati RR branches west]. Walked the rest of the way. Came back on the cars in the evening. Uncle Will assured me of assistance in any extremity.[1]

On Saturday, August 6, Rufus stops by the Bosworth home to enjoy an evening with Fanny. They have become close, and Fanny sometimes feels a tinge of jealousy over Rufus's infatuation with her younger cousin Mary Gates. They talk and laugh, and when it is time to leave, she gives Rufus a kiss. He responds with one of his own, holding her shoulders. The kiss becomes more passionate than either intends, and they both realize it at the same time. It ends with their eyes open, laughing at each other. "That was awkward," says Rufus.

Fanny smiles, gives him a hug, and says, "I'll miss you, Rufe. Take care of yourself."

That night in his diary, he notes:

> I hope this is not the last glorious time I shall be permitted to enjoy with our "dulce decus."[A]

> Sunday, Aug. 7th. Felt blue all day. Didn't know Marietta and Marietta folks had got so firm a hold upon my affections. ... Packed my trunk after church. Hen gave me his rifle.

> Monday, August 8th, 1859. Got up early this morning to get on the boat. Was very loth to tear myself away from the only place on Earth where I ever have been really happy. The trip up in the Lizzie Martin was dull and sorrowful. Reached Malta about the middle of the afternoon.

In Malta, Ohio

He is at work right away, with long, dirty hours helping his father pack goods for shipment to Wisconsin. It is "more of a job than I anticipated," he writes. On August 20, he and father Henry have a serious discussion about "future plans." His father "professes himself to do very liberally by me if my deserts are but moderate." The diary entry does not disguise his skepticism.

Meanwhile, Marietta College tries to change Henry's mind about Rufus's departure. President I. W. Andrews appeals in writing to Henry on September 7:

> Let me express my regret that your son Rufus is not to return to us. I cannot but feel that a young man of his abilities ought to have every advantage of education. If he lives he can hardly fail to make his mark in this world, and it seems a great pity that he should not enjoy the training that the last year of college would give him. ... He will do well as it is; he would do much better with another year's study.

[A] "Sweet beauty," from Horace, Odes, "Ode 1.1."

> I wish not to flatter you, but he is a young man of fine abil-
> ities, too fine to forego any ordinary culture. We should be very
> glad to have him here another year, and let him graduate with
> our class.[2]

Henry quickly reads the letter, then tosses it at Rufus. "Here, you can
read all the nice things your President Andrews says about you. Well,
that's all very fine, but what right has *he* to interfere with our family business? None! He sent me the same flowery letter three years ago when
we first went to Madison. He should be smart enough to know that if it
didn't work then, it won't work now!"

Rufus picks up the letter and reads it. *Yes, it is a nice letter*, he thinks.
*I'm impressed that Mr. Andrews thinks that highly of me. Maybe I can
come back and finish college here ... maybe not.* He folds the letter and
places it in his diary. It is perhaps worth a reread someday.

Before heading west, he decides to have some fun. Evenings are
spent with his Malta friends, attending parties and playing chess, whist,
and euchre. In the late evenings, he voraciously reads Shakespeare.
Rufus corresponds by mail with sister "Luce" and college friends Tim
Condit and Marshall Newport, all back in Marietta.

The local girls draw special attention. A Miss Williams from Lancaster,
who is visiting her cousin in Malta, catches his interest at a party. She
is attractive, a bit sultry, and a new conquest. She earns mention in his
diary on the sad day when she leaves for home. As he notes, "the 'Lilly of
Lancaster' departed this life and went home much to my dissatisfaction."
But there are others. A Miss Wheeler "is a rosy-cheeked lass of perhaps sweet sixteen. She has, moreover, been to Oxford." Then also Mary
Barker and a Miss Betty. Mary Barker, he notes, "is very much a lady."

But Mary Hall occupies his attentions most often (girls named
Mary seem to stimulate special appeal). Their time together on Tuesday,
September 13, merits this after-action report:

> This was a most beautiful moonlight evening. So, Billy and I,
> bent on better sport ... concocted a skiff ride. By a great deal
> of coaxing we persuaded Tip to go after Judy. We proceeded to
> operations, not however to skiff-riding. Since there was no skiff
> to be had, we took a moonlight walk down the river. Mary's a
> trump. Stayed on the stone steps rather unreasonably long.

He is having a good time, but it is temporary, and not the lifestyle he
desires:

I enjoy myself very much in the Malta society tho there is nothing to be learned and much to be forgotten. The "duckies" are generally speaking, unsophisticated, uneducated, and "untrained." Very pretty, open-hearted, and endowed with a large proportion of Mother-Wit.

Rufus and his father are getting close to embarking on the long trip west. Relations with Henry the elder, always volatile, explode one day after his father discovers that Rufus has traded the rifle brother Henry had given him to a friend—in exchange for a pair of pants. Rufus writes:

Had a terrible quarrel with Father this morning. It originated about an old rifle and waged about everything. It will be long remembered; indeed, it can never be forgotten. There was also an exhibition of character to be long kept in mind as a guide for future action.

On Again to Wisconsin

The trip begins with a ride upriver to Zanesville, again on the *Lizzie Martin*. It is another sad departure for Rufus. He is sorry to leave Malta, despite its "dingy houses and dirty streets, where for a short time I had enjoyed myself … and have certainly been treated with a great deal of politeness. The boys came down to see me off."

From Zanesville, they take a train to the state capital of Columbus, "a beautiful city, Gov. [Salmon] Chase's house struck me as being about the prettiest place I had ever seen." The next day it is on to Cleveland, booking their trip to Wisconsin via a Great Lakes steamship.

Saturday, 17th September 1859.

Three years ago today I started for Madison. Two years of that time were spent there, one glorious year in Marietta, and now I am again bound for the West. Where will I be three years from today?

If he had known the answer to that pensive question, he would have shuddered.

On Monday the 19th in Cleveland, perhaps to make amends for the "terrible quarrel," Henry buys Rufus a new hat. That afternoon they

(MCSCL)

board the propeller ship *Galena*, bunking in a good stateroom amidships. Rufus, his inquisitive mind always in use, notes that he had "never seen the screw method of propulsion in active operation before, and I was much amused at the little tugs scuttling around, propelled in this manner."[3]

The boat trip to Milwaukee takes four days, traversing Lakes Erie, St. Clair, Huron, and Michigan, with brief stops at Detroit, Glen Harbor, Manitowoc, and Sheboygan. There are other passengers, male and female, and good conversation to pass the time, at least when seasickness does not interfere. This awful malady hits all the passengers hard on the second day, when a fierce storm on Lake Huron tosses the small ship all about, waves crashing over the bow.

Fall 1859, Mauston, Wisconsin

They finally reach Mauston via train on the evening of Monday, September 28—two long weeks of travel with a dour father. Rufus spends the next day looking around his new town, describing it in his diary:

> A little Village split in two by a marsh. Contains several stores, three taverns, one good school-house, and perhaps 700 inhabitants. It will, I fear, be a dreary place.

Life in Mauston revolves around trading goods from Henry's store and clearing the land he had purchased south of town for plowing in the spring. To that end, Henry hires a half-dozen lumbermen at eighteen dollars per month and remains "in the woods" with them to make sure they earn their pay. Still, in Rufus's opinion, there should be "18 or 20 on the same terms," but he notes, "if he can't get them to work no one can."

It is a slow Thursday at the store on October 20. Rufus is reading the *Mauston Star*, the town's fledgling newspaper, while Henry's partner, Mr. Langworthy, is doing inventory. The top story grabs Rufus's attention. "Listen to this," he says to Langworthy and then summarizes the news story: "A radical abolitionist named John Brown, a native Ohioan who fought proslavery 'ruffians' in the Kansas territory, brought a band of twenty-two men, including three of his sons, to Harpers Ferry, Virginia. They attacked and seized the federal armory there, just four days ago, on Sunday. It says their intention was to arm slaves and lead them in revolt! Several people were killed, including the mayor. Virginia militia bottled the raiders up in a firehouse, killing several. The next day, President Buchanan called in US Marines. After Brown refused to give up, they attacked, and a few more on both sides were killed. Brown was wounded and captured, along with the rest of them. This says an army colonel named Robert E. Lee and his aide, Lieutenant J. E. B. Stuart, led the operation. I wonder why they were in charge. Anyway, they've got Brown in jail, and Virginia folks are all stirred up about it. What do you think about that?"

"I think this Brown sounds like a crazy man!" Langworthy replies. "Did any slaves revolt? Someday they will. Wouldn't you? How long can those Southerners expect to keep slaves? A damnable institution! But anyway, that's a long way from here."

"Well, it's not a long way from Marietta. Slaves have been trying to escape for years, and many people have helped them do it—that, I can personally attest to," Rufus responds. He thinks again of that sad Negro family in the boat and of his grandfather and uncle and the Putnams in his boyhood hometown, stations on the Underground Railroad.

As the weeks pass by, Rufus keeps up with the news stories about the raid's aftermath. The deed had been perpetrated on federal property; President Buchanan, however, allows Virginia Governor Wise to hold Brown's trial under state law. He chooses Charles Town, Jefferson County, as the venue. Lynching is feared, so Governor Wise calls in cadets from the Virginia Military Institute, under command of Major Thomas J. Jackson, to maintain security. Throughout the trial, feelings are intense on all sides. Juror's barns are torched, while Brown's letters from prison inflame supporters in the North and opponents in the South. Brown is charged and convicted on three counts and sentenced to hang, as are several others of his faction.

In Marietta, Ohio, 300 miles from Harpers Ferry but across the river from Virginia, the John Brown raid is major news, stirring all the passions of those on both sides of the slavery issue. Beman Gates, Mary's father, in Baltimore on business during the Brown trial, receives on-the-spot updates from an acquaintance who lives in Harpers Ferry, "no friend of Brown's, either." His friend conveys that citizen excitement is so feverish, violence is expected at any moment. Beman writes to his wife, Betsey, of his judgment on the affair. Betsey shares the letter with Mary and her fifteen-year-old brother Charley. Writes Beman:

> Nobody seems to care much about the other prisoners, but <u>Old Brown</u> is a <u>character</u>—some insisting that he is a fiend, others that he is a saint. For myself, although I don't approve of his acts, I believe that he stands a much better chance of going from the gallows to Abraham's bosom, than any of his persecutors do of resting in as comfortable a place as purgatory when they die …"[4]

Brown is hanged on Friday, December 2, before two thousand witnesses. Among them are VMI Major Thomas Jackson, forty-year-old poet and essayist Walt Whitman, and an actor named John Wilkes Booth, who has borrowed a militia uniform to feign authority and gain entrance. Jackson and Booth share the majority opinion of the crowd that justice is being done. Whitman is moved to write of the event in his poem "Year of Meteors (1859–60)":

YEAR of meteors! brooding year!

I would bind in words retrospective some of your deeds and signs,

I would sing your contest for the 19th Presidentiad,

I would sing how an old man, tall, with white hair, mounted the scaffold in Virginia,

(I was at hand—silent I stood with teeth shut close—I watch'd,

I stood very near you, old man, when cool and indifferent, but trembling with age and your unheal'd wounds, you mounted the scaffold …)[5]

John Brown's Harpers Ferry raid, his trial, and his execution spark passionate commentary on both sides of the Atlantic. North and South polarization become more intense. To Rufus Dawes, it seems that the country his forefather William had risked so much to help create is taking another step into a dark abyss. Where will it lead? How can it ever be resolved?

The Mauston weather is getting colder, and life there is boring, the society generally disappointing. Rufus is restless. Letters from his sisters and Ephraim are godsends, providing updates on family. Jovial correspondence from Marietta College classmates Condit, Newport, Metcalf, and Carver lift his spirits. He finds a copy of *Macbeth* to read. But these are temporary respites. Depressed, Rufus confides the following to his diary:

I never led so dull a life before. No excitement of any kind to relieve the dull tedium of this. Every day the same kind of an existence. May there be a good time coming! Have written to Bernard, Chancellor of the Wisc. St. University concerning my admission there next term. I must go or I will die off this winter.

Juneau County had been formed only two years before, and political competition between New Lisbon and Mauston for the county seat designation interrupts the local boredom. Dawes meets a local lawyer, John Kellogg, who has spoken at some of the meetings.

"So, you're the son of our new merchant," Kellogg says. "I thought I would stop by and meet you. I heard you're the one who passes out free merchandise to the Indians! John A. Kellogg is my name. I'm the prosecuting attorney here, so don't get into any trouble!" He laughs as he says it, a friendly laugh, but the initial impression made on Dawes is of a man not to trifle with, at least in a legal sense. Kellogg is visiting Henry's store, Dawes is checking inventory, and Henry is still out in the country.

"Well, my pleasure, Mr. Kellogg. I'm Rufus Dawes, my father's over-educated clerk. As you probably know, we came here from Ohio, but I studied at the state university in Madison for two years, plus four terms at Marietta College. Where did you study law?"

"It's 'John.' 'Mr. Kellogg' makes me feel older than I already am," Kellogg replies. "I studied in Madison also, a bit before you were there probably, but perhaps we have mutual acquaintances. I worked with Mr. Vilas—very bright lawyer. Anyway, originally from Pennsylvania, the family moved to Prairie du Sac when I was about twelve. Tried to make a living there as an attorney, then took this position in Mauston about two years ago. Got to support the family, you know!"

"Ah, so you're married! Any children? Sorry, don't mean to pry."

Kellogg laughs. "Ha, not prying, it's a small town! Yes, Adelaide and I have three little ones, all daughters. I think I'll give up trying for a son. Besides, I'm thirty-one, getting too old to be chasing after more of them. So what's behind that story I heard about the Indians, if you don't mind me asking?"

Dawes smiles and shakes his head. "All right, it really is a small town— word gets around. Here's what happened. I was new here, heard there was a large camp of Winnebago on the Lemonweir River, so I thought it would be interesting to visit them and see what their life was like. Well, they were all very friendly, gave me some water and venison jerky, but of course I couldn't understand a word of their language. Somehow, I made it known we had a dry goods store in town. I smiled and nodded a lot. The next day, about thirty-five bucks and squaws came to the store, single file, and I thought, *Well, I should repay their friendliness*. So I let them in. There were a bunch of them around me jabbering away when Mr. Langworthy came in and started to shoo them away with his cane. He scolded me with 'Young man, those squaws are taking off with half your stock under their blankets. Always do your business with them from the doorstep!' Of course, I felt like a fool, and there was hell to pay when my father learned of it."

Kellogg is laughing. "Don't feel bad, you're not the first one! Your father—it sounds as if he may have a temper?"

Dawes responds, "Well, don't get me started on that score."

"All right," says Kellogg. "Say, if you play chess, perhaps we can do a game or two sometime."

Dawes jumps at the chance. "Yes, that would be fun, just let me know when."

"Fine, we'll do it, then. By the way, I'm sure you've heard all about this county seat election business. I'm on the Mauston committee, and we're trying to sway folks in other towns to vote our way, and of course the Lisbon people are doing their best—or should I say *worst*—to do the same. Care to come with me to Germantown next week on an election-eering trip?"

Again, Rufus jumps at the chance to relieve the boredom, and the date is set.

Germantown, Juneau County, Wisconsin, North of Mauston

Kellogg and Dawes ride to Germantown for a debate with the New Lisbon delegation. Quite in keeping with its name, the farm-based community is primarily of German descent, and they love their beer. The audience and the debaters—excluding Dawes, who avoids alcohol—are feeling frisky almost from the start. A fellow from New Lisbon, arguing in favor of his town, goads his two college-educated opponents from Mauston into a fencing match against one of his friends, two against one. He boasts that his man cannot be touched. It is a daring challenge, and the local audience immediately voices their interest, urging Dawes and Kellogg to accept. A fencing match in Germantown! Not something they have witnessed before. Is this stranger that invincible, or will they witness a beating? Shame on these two Mauston dudes if they refuse. Small-town politics in the country!

"Have you fenced before, John?" Dawes asks his partner, sensing trouble.

"I've seen an exhibition. Seems you just need some good coordination. I can be a diversion at least while you go after him, since you fenced some in college, right?" Kellogg replies.

"Some, yes." Reacting to the crowd, he smiles, sighs, and looks back at Kellogg. There seems to be no way out. "Let's do it! The honor of our fair Mauston is at stake!"

The three contestants begin with a salute, tapping their fencing foils together—two wooden canes for the Mauston men and a hoe handle for the Lisbon hotshot, with the crowd loudly cheering them on.

Kellogg makes a thrust, which is deftly whacked away, as Dawes attacks. *Whap!* Before he can react, the Dawes thrust is parried, and a shot lands painfully on his left shoulder. Wincing, Dawes backs away, waiting for Kellogg to resume his diversionary attack, determined not to be caught again. *Whack! Wham!* Both Mauston men are hit this time, then must battle fiercely to fend off stroke after counterstroke from this stranger who quite obviously knows what he is doing. The man moves with amazing quickness and dexterity, skillfully landing blow after blow. After fifteen minutes of action, the Mauston men concede the match, battered, bloody in spots, and very bruised. The crowd cheers the Lisbon men, and any hope of Mauston being favored as the new county seat has disappeared from this group of Germantown folks.

The contestants shake hands, and Dawes and Kellogg learn the man's name. "Charles de Villiers," says he. "An expert fencer," says his crafty

New Lisbon partner. John has never heard of him, but Rufus recognizes the name, as de Villiers has earned a reputation in the Cincinnati area.[6]

Dawes and Kellogg, arms on the other's shoulders, walk gingerly toward their horses, wincing from their bruises and chagrined to know the joke is on them. Despite the beating, they chuckle at the circumstances. It is the beginning of a friendship. It will not be the last time they join in battle.

Christmas 1859, Mauston, Wisconsin

It is a disagreeable holiday. Rufus, bored and restless, homesick on this occasion especially, approaches his father and states his intention to leave Mauston for Ohio, to reenter Marietta College. He expects an ugly verbal confrontation, but to his surprise, his father agrees. "All right, Rufus. You have worked hard here, and I did say you could go back to college," says Henry. "Go make your arrangements."

That is it. Not the warmest send-off, but Rufus is delighted to be free of his father, and he looks forward to being back home in Marietta. He makes his plans, says goodbye to the Kelloggs, Mr. Langworthy, and a few others, then packs his bags.

January–March 1860, Marietta, Ohio

The trip back to Marietta during the cold first week of the new decade is all by train this time, via Milwaukee, Chicago, Indianapolis, and Cincinnati. He moves in with the family: mother Sarah, Henry M., Ephraim, and Lucy. Kate remains at the Old Stone House with the Cutlers. The small home on Fourth Street is only a half-block from the Gates residence and seventeen-year-old Mary.

Rufus enrolls in the senior class at the college. The twelve-week second term focuses on mathematics, intellectual philosophy, and political economy. His favorite, however, is rhetoric; it includes oration, composition, and discussion, both in class and with fellow students in his Hesperian Society. It is wonderful to be back among family and friends at the college. Ephraim is now in the junior class, and through him and the Society, he becomes friends with Bill Whittlesey—a young man of high intellect and ability, and son of the mayor—and with Russell Brownell. The popular Ted Greenwood has already graduated as valedictorian but is still close by, and longtime friends such as Tim Condit, Marshall Newport, and Dave Chambers are all here. They have a great time together in this, their final year of school.

Sunday, April 1, 1860—On Steamer Dr. Kane Bound for La Crosse, Thence to Mauston

Rufus Dawes, hands supporting himself on his dresser as he leans forward toward the wall mirror, stares at his reflection and ponders his decision. "What are you doing?" he slowly asks himself. His thoughts recall the past half year. *I missed the fall term in '59 going with father to Wisconsin. I came back to Marietta College for the second term—what a grand time! Now, with break almost over and all my friends returning for the third term, all the seniors looking forward to graduation, here am I, leaving this wonderful scene behind once again! I am supposed to be a bright student and a solid thinker. Yet here I am, turning my back on a good education, on my family, on my friends. None of them understand it. And I'm turning my back on Mary Gates.* "Are you sure you know what you are doing?" he asks his reflection.

Lucy had asked him the same thing just yesterday. "Rufe, why? Just a few months ago, you couldn't wait to get away from father and that place! Why go back now, before you graduate?! I know he wants your help back on his farm. But we all know him! He could turn on you at the drop of a hat!"

To Rufus, it comes down to two factors. First, a sense of duty his character will not allow him to deny. He skips this excuse in responding to Lucy, knowing she will roll her eyes over that reply. So he answers this way: "Luce, look, I want to make something of myself. I *need* to make something of myself. I see father as the most practical avenue. He has acquired large tracts of land, he's been a success at business, and he is already involved in Wisconsin politics. Those are doors that could open for me—at least, I hope so. On the other hand, if I don't go to Wisconsin, father will certainly shut those doors, providing nothing for me and thus nothing for Ma and the family. I can't let that happen."

Left unstated is Mary Gates. His thoughts are never far from her. But in his mind, Mary is just too young. *I don't think she's ready for anything serious. I don't want to scare her away. Plus, Fanny and Lucy have said that Mary is being sent east to a female academy in Ipswich, Massachusetts. She will be gone a year at least, maybe two. So, someday ... not now. If I can become successful and return when she is older, and I have more to offer, which right now is not much ... then, maybe then!*

For this trip he takes the longer, more leisurely route northwest, 1,400 miles on big river steamboats. First, down the Ohio River, then north up the mighty Mississippi. It is a relaxing voyage with stops at bustling river towns he has heard of but never seen. This is the golden age of steamboat travel on the wide rivers, and there are many boats passing both ways, passengers waving, whistles blowing, numerous grand boats docked at the cities, many people to meet, many sights to experience. He has plenty of time to think about his future, but it appears just as murky and uncertain as the rolling river waters passing beneath the bow of his steamboat.[7]

Rufus arrives in Mauston in early June. On the 10th, he writes a long letter to his sister Lucy, knowing, as always, that his correspondence will be shared with the whole family:

> My circumstances and situation are precisely what I expected them to be when I consented to come west to try to <u>save</u> a fortune. That I was embarking on an enterprise both unpleasant and uncertain I well knew before I left Ohio, but my purpose was formed then, and I have no word of complaint or regret to utter now. On the contrary, I find much encouragement ...

To Lucy, he notes that their father is skillfully managing his plan to create a profitable estate. Not doubting his father's ultimate success, he writes:

> [that] I may be able to secure an independence from it I still have reason to hope—"for which hopes sake" I undergo my present unpleasant <u>but not unavoidable</u> privations ...

He summarizes his life in the backwoods, working to clear 750 acres of woodland for farming. He comically describes the hired help: strong young men but woefully uneducated. Long hours are spent brush grubbing, burning logs, and splitting rails. There is nothing else to do, no "society" in the woods. "I verily believe I can give Old Abe, the prince of rail splitters, a pretty good race at his favorite employment," he writes home.

Rufus and his father take room and board nearby at a Mr. Stewart's, and he provides Lucy a sketch of the Stewart family's simple home: three rooms plus a sleeping loft. Each room is multitasked out of necessity, and his sketch plan notes with humor that:

> "B" denotes <u>our</u> bedroom, <u>their</u> sitting room, Parlor and Laundry, g and f are our beds, and + + represent their children, of which there are 10!

Lucy loves reading letters from Rufus. She bursts out laughing while visualizing her well-educated brother attempting to endure the ludicrous situation he has gotten himself into. Sharing a room with father must be a trial by itself, but she cannot imagine how her brother can withstand the lack of privacy in the incredibly crowded Stewart family home!

The National Scene

1860 is a presidential election year, and national political issues have never been more volatile. The issue of slavery and its extension to new states and territories has been festering for years, but this election has brought the issue to a crescendo of debate and division. In April, the Democratic Party Convention held in Charleston had dissolved in a philosophical split over the issue. Two parties are then formed: the

Northern and Southern Democrats, each holding separate conventions and each choosing separate candidates for president. Stephen A. Douglas, the famous debate antagonist of Abraham Lincoln, is chosen by the Northern party; Vice President John C. Breckenridge of Kentucky by the Southern party.

Politicians of the fledgling Republican Party realize the Democratic Party breakup provides an opportunity, and after several ballots, Abraham Lincoln of Illinois is nominated at the Chicago Convention held in mid-May. He is considered a moderate, and the party platform favors keeping new territories free of slavery. No changes are proposed to slavery in existing states, and there is no mention of reversing the Fugitive Slave Law or the Dred Scott decision. Abolitionists think Lincoln and his platform too soft; those in control within the slave states think him too radical and do not trust him. If Lincoln takes office, they believe, he will be a threat to the Southern way of life and to its agrarian economy.

To complicate the election, a fourth candidate is placed on the ballot, John Bell, representing a relatively small "border" faction whose platform is to keep everything status quo, essentially meaning continued turmoil but, it is hoped, no explosions.

On the farm near Mauston, WI—Rufus Dawes Diary Entry:

Monday June 25th, 1860—"Once more into the breach dear friends." I am again in the backwoods of Wis. and I fear almost inextricably entangled in them by the wishes of circumstances. … Attended a meeting of citizens … for the purpose as stated … of "gittin up a 4th of July." A delegation was dispatched to the "Mr. Daweses." A more ignorant assemblage of men I never got caught among before. Father and I made speeches which were evidently not understood but highly appreciated.

Thursday 28th—Commencement day in Marietta. How differently my classmates fare today. Wonder if they will give me a degree. "A. B." stands for a backwoodsman as well as the other thing—a title which I now have a right to assume.

Wednesday July 4th, 1860—Twenty-two years old today. Something of a day too. I introduced the speakers, read the Declaration of Independence, and marshalled the celebration. Father read his Marietta oration. The number of people present was possibly 700. The people of this settlement sadly need someone to lead.

The people are pleased to have Henry and Rufus among them—men who have direct family ties to the revolution, men who are educated. But after the holiday speeches, it is back to the farm, clearing land, and "breaking plow."

Then, heartbreak. It comes via telegram to Mauston. Mr. Langworthy rides up to the Dawes farm and delivers the news. He approaches his partner Henry, who is giving instructions to the timbermen, with Rufus splitting rails nearby. "Henry, this came for you and Rufus this morning. I am afraid it is bad news."

Henry looks at Langworthy, grasps the small telegram, reads it, and lowers his head. Rufus knows this signifies something dreadful. He quickly comes over and takes the slip from his father. "Henry M. died today ..." The paper freezes in his hand, and his tears blur the rest of the short message.

Older brother Henry Manasseh—intelligent, passionate, recently engaged to be married to Mary Nye, respected by all his siblings—has been struck down by cholera. He suffered the profuse diarrhea and vomiting associated with the waterborne infectious disease and died within days. The family at home is crushed. They had nursed him, watched him suffer and breathe his last. The doctors do not understand the bacterial cause, much less how to prevent or treat this common killer. That night, Rufus records a sad entry: "Brother Henry M. died on the 13th day of August 1860, ½ past two P.M."

Soon after Hen's death, Rufus writes to his surviving brother, twenty-year-old Ephraim:

> My dear brother—I have been trying to write a letter to Ma but I could not. Whenever I think of Hen I am completely unmanned. I laid down in the country this forenoon and for the first time I cried like a child, but it brought no relief. Bound together as our family has been with so many ties of a painful nature, it is terrible to have every bond burst.
>
> Oh Eph, I hope you will narrow yourself up like a man to take his place. You <u>must</u> do everything you can to make Ma & Lucy & Kate happy. God never blessed the earth with better hearts than theirs, and upon you and me rests the duty of making smooth their pathway through life.

He provides Ephraim with advice, committing himself to helping the family when he is able, and again explains his own situation and purpose for staying in Wisconsin:

> Next year, if I cannot succeed in getting anything from F [Father] to establish myself, I expect to have to fall back on the good name I am trying to make now for support. … I am engaging in politics not because I expect or want office, but it is the best way in the West to get acquainted & to make a reputation. With which as you know comes the opportunity of making a living in a case of necessity.

Henry Manasseh Dawes
1832—1860

Thursday, August 16, 1860—Gravel Bank Cemetery, Southwest of Marietta, Ohio

"Sarah, Lucy, Kate—I am so sorry for your loss. Henry was a fine young man. May God give you comfort in your sorrow. Please let me know if there is anything we can do for you." Betsey Gates gives the three grieving ladies, each dressed in mourning black, a firm hug as she addresses them. Beman and Mary follow in turn, clasping hands, murmuring condolences. They then repeat their concerns to young Mary Nye, Henry's fiancé. Faces are marked with tears and perspiration as the hot sun on this sultry August day is stifling, the black umbrellas to shield the rays helping just a little.

The Gates family and the Nyes, plus a goodly number of other friends and acquaintances, have all made the several-mile ride along the river road to attend the short graveside burial service, with Rev. Wickes presiding. Some have taken the train and hitched a ride for the short trek from station to cemetery. They lay Henry to rest close to his Cutler grandparents, Ephraim and Sarah. Ephraim's first wife, Leah, and several of their children, are in nearby graves.

Monday, August 27, 1860, Ipswich, Massachusetts

"Good morning, Mary. And happy birthday! I can hardly believe my little girl is now a young lady of eighteen! I am feeling a bit older myself just thinking of it!" Beman and Mary are in Ipswich, with Mary about to begin classes at Rev. John and Mrs. Eunice Cowles' "Female Seminary." The Gates parents are progressive thinkers, and they want their daughter to experience the best education available for young ladies of the day, and that means "back east."

Father and daughter had traveled to the Boston area earlier that summer, the home of most Marietta founders and of Beman himself. There are several schools of choice north of the city, and he still has family in the vicinity. Thus, it is the logical direction to go. Mary was impressed with the Bradford School in Haverhill on the Merrimack River. Beman preferred Ipswich, closer to the sea, and, as head of the household, his opinion won out.

The family has an early birthday celebration in Marietta for Mary, and then she and her father head east by train. Betsey feels the pains of her daughter going away to school, Bettie cries at the departure, and even Charley is a bit emotional at the thought of "Sister" missing from the home. Mary misses her family immediately and writes a letter home from New York, where they have stopped to visit Beman's brother:

Astor House, August 23, 1860

> Aunt Ann gave us such a warm welcome last night that I shall make no objections to visiting them this winter on account of being a country cousin. We had a delightful ride in Baltimore, and in Philadelphia we went to Independence Hall. I couldn't help feeling glad that I had succeeded in dragging through the life of George Washington.[8]

Beman leaves Mary at her Ipswich boarding house close to the school
and then proceeds to travel elsewhere in New England on business. The
next day, he suffers an attack of parent guilt and sadness, and pens a
letter to his daughter:

Topsfield, August 29, 1860

My dear Mary—

    I confess that the quarters in which I left you were less
inviting than even I expected, although I well know that the
best rooms that you would find at any school would not present
much of a home look. ...When I was a boy in New England I
never had as pleasant a room as the one which I left you in. ...

    There was really no occasion for writing this morning and I
have done so more to relieve my own heart than with any expectation that you needed cheering—for to be frank I never felt the
desolateness of homesickness so thoroughly as when I left you
last evening. But enough of all this. We will both cheer up and
with smiles address ourselves to the duties and labors before us.

Goodby my dear girl, your most affectionate father,

Beman Gates

Mary is homesick, too, but soon comes to know her classmates—
mostly girls from New England—and quickly admires and respects
Rev. and Mrs. Cowles. They are a unique and impressive pair. The
reverend is crotchety, blind, and an albino, no small shock at first
meeting. But he is exceptionally bright and remembers everything. He
is the "right from wrong" spiritual and philosophical leader, strongly
supported by his spouse. Mrs. Cowles, a dignified-looking woman
with a resonant voice and strong character, soon makes an impression. "Young ladies, in what lies the difference between the civilized
and uncivilized?" Not waiting for an answer from her one hundred or
so students, she exclaims, "Soap!"
    Letters stream back and forth between Mary and her Marietta family,
and with cousin Francy Bosworth, Mary's best friend growing up. These
are written in September:

My dear Mother,

When I took the three studies I have now I did not know of their being so hard or I should not have taken them all. We have to go to bed at half past nine and consequently I find it absolutely necessary for me to get up at five and these cold mornings I find it particularly disagreeable.

My dear Francy,

The school here at Ipswich is what you and I would call a little one-horse establishment. There are a great many fruit trees in the yard, but we are only allowed to have the fruit that is on the ground, however we can look at an apple or a pear so long sometimes that it falls.

A good many of the girls are very common looking but there are quite a number who I should think are born ladies. Georgia Parsons brought her guitar in here after tea and we had a nice time singing.

My dear Mary [from father Beman],

Last evening Bettie received yours of the 18th and before I was done reading it she was crying and sobbing at a sad rate. She "can't wait so long without seeing Sister." This morning she has taken the letter to Grandmother's and Auntie and is now at Mrs. Dawes with it.

Fall of 1860, Juneau County, Wisconsin

Father and son Dawes are Republicans, and they actively campaign for their party candidates. In northern states such as Wisconsin, the presidential contest is a race between Abraham Lincoln and Stephen Douglas. Rufus takes to the road around the county and beyond, making at least fourteen stump speeches and campaign stops, jotting quick notes of each in his diary. He has quickly earned the respect of the local townspeople and is selected at age twenty-two to be delegate to four county or state conventions. On the local level, Rufus campaigns for his father with success, as Henry is elected as one of three Juneau County commissioners, as county coroner, and as Republican county chairman.

In October, Rufus writes his mother:

I hope to get a good start in the world from Father as soon as he is able to give it to me. <u>He is not at the present</u>. ... Now you know him well enough to understand that faithfulness to his interests, labor for him or devotion to him will establish no claim to his gratitude, that he will not cast away at a trifle. ...

We are now building a house on the farm, this shape—

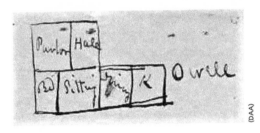

(DAA)

Two stories 11 foot—main part 36 x 28—wing 26 x 18. Neat, large and substantial. The day may come years hence when you & Luce & Kate & I can spend some happy hours over here.

Fall of 1860, Ipswich, Massachusetts

Mary Gates discovers that "my money did not go as far as I thought it would" and hesitatingly writes home about it. It comes as no surprise to her parents, and Betsey responds to her daughter:

Dear Mary

You seem to be rather downcy out of cash out of credit and all such ills. You need not feel so at all; your father expects you to go to Mr. McCloud[B] whenever you want money and I don't want you to miss a sight or a gratification that it is right you should enjoy for the want of it.

Never mind what Mrs. Cowles says about your being a ninny. I know you are not and I am as capable as judging as she is and

---

[B] A cousin of Beman Gates, living nearby.

my opportunities in your case are far greater than hers. You may rest assured you are nobody's fool if you are my daughter.

You affectionate Mother

Mary comments about the "net" Mrs. Cowles has devised "to entrap poor spellers." Three hundred words to spell correctly, and she admits to missing thirty-five at the first attempt, but quickly notes that was not as bad as some other girls. She confesses to be not the greatest student, but thinks Mrs. Cowles likes her anyway:

> The girls all try to get me to go to Mrs. Cowles if they have some permission to ask … comforting if I am discouraged about my studies. I have always thought that I had rather be a little wildish and a good scholar than a fool and one of these <u>proper</u> young ladies.

When her father writes that he will take it upon himself to correct grammar and spelling in her letters home—for her own good—she cheerfully responds to him:

> I am glad you have taken the arduous task of correcting my letters upon yourself. I want you to but don't want anyone else to. I must confess the commas and capitals bother me beyond measure. I have no idea where they belong.

Mrs. Eunice Cowles

Ipswich Female Seminary, Winter Scene

The girls at Ipswich are not immune from politics. A letter addressed to her father mentions the Pennsylvania election results in October, with schoolgirls both Democrat and Republican at odds with each other:

> I did not make a demonstration, for a wonder you might say. There were only about four girls in the school but wore some badge or other and it has made a deal of unpleasant feeling and I can't see that the discussions have done us any good.

Beman writes to Mary agreeing with her decision to avoid political demonstrations "where offense will be taken." As will be seen, however, advice is easier to proclaim than to practice.

Saturday, November 24, 1860, Marietta, Ohio

The November 8 election creates a terrific combination of excitement, emotion, and angst, but the Republican preelection calculations prove to be correct. Although ten Southern states keep Abraham Lincoln off their ballots, he wins the election in the electoral college by a two-to-one margin over Breckinridge. Over 82 percent of nationwide voters (free white males only) cast a ballot, and though he wins decisively, Lincoln's total vote share is less than 40 percent. The results portray a fractured populace, with deep sectionalism, North versus South.

The Gates family and most Mariettans strongly support the Republican platform and ticket. An elated Beman Gates mails Mary a vivid description of the local celebration of Lincoln's victory, poking fun at the primary Northern challenger, vertically challenged Stephen A. Douglas. He and son Charley, with artistic help from brother-in-law and professional artist Sala Bosworth, have celebrated by decorating his prominent corner home at Fourth and Putnam. Beman attempts to mask his jovial, almost boyish nature at the end of his letter, but he clearly enjoys the fun:

> My dear Mary
>
> Perhaps I can give you a little idea of the looks of town, in Marietta—made the finest show, because the windows [at the Gates home] by copying the mottos on half of one of them:

He then sketches the windows and the signs placed on them.

The towers, which were brilliantly lit up, could be seen all over town—both houses, as you know, occupying commanding positions.[c] But our house was, in some respects, the center of greatest attraction, because we had something so different from anybody else. From the attic window, on Putnam Street, we had a large national flag, suspended from a long pole on the end of which was a beautiful set of deer's antlers. Another large flag, inscribed "Lincoln & Hamlin," floated from the balcony on 4th Street.

While the procession was passing, Charley fired rockets and roman candles from the front yard—and we had the handsomest fire-works ever seen in Marietta.

Each pane of glass in the windows on Putnam and Fourth Streets, was covered with tissue paper alternately red, white, and blue, on which mottos were printed in type large enough to be read across the street, for you know our glass is large—14 by 20 inches.

The lower sash was filled with a transparency painted by Uncle Bosworth. It was a portrait of Douglas, with the skirt of his coat dragging on the ground, and this inscription (being a remark of T. H. Newton) printed over him: "Mr. Douglas, sir, can never be President, sir. His coat tail, sir, is over the ground, sir." Another window was filled with inscriptions of the majorities given to Lincoln, in each of the Free states. On the whole, we had a pretty good time—though I do not altogether favor such demonstrations.

Joanna Bosworth laughs and claps at the festivities and elaborate decorations while standing outside during the parade that marches past the Gates home. Her husband's window paintings, the deer head on the flagpole (looking like some giant arrow sticking into the Putnam Street attic), and nephew Charley's fireworks. It is a sight to see. She turns to her sister Betsey and asks, "Who do you think is having a better time? Our children or our husbands?"

Betsey loves a festive moment more than most ladies, and she laughs with her sister. "That's a good question. I think it's a tie! It's too bad Mary is missing all this." In the back of her mind, however, is the nagging

---

[c] The "towers" refers to the Douglas Putnam and John Newton homes, both impressive structures, each built with prominent "lookout" towers.

concern, *Those Southern folks are already so upset, talking treason even. What will they do now?*

The Gates family reads Mary's letter of November 30, written during fall break while staying with the McClouds in Topsfield, Massachusetts, their daughter Helen being Mary's classmate:

> Yes, Charley I am glad Lincoln is elected but Mrs. McCloud is so positive that his election is going to bring destruction upon the country that I can't help being silly enough to tremble a little. I believe Abraham Lincoln is a good man and so far as I can understand I believe republican principles are right.

December 1860—Dawes Farm, South of Mauston, Wisconsin

Work on the Dawes farmhouse has progressed to the point that Henry and Rufus can move into two rooms of the home's wing in early December, and thankfully say goodbye to the Stewarts and their full squad of children, plus the various dogs. The daily routine involves hard work on the land and the trial of living with father. Rufus writes his sister Kate about his:

> domestic tempest perpetual, never lulling, that rages around me when in the evening I return from my daily task. Ugh—what a life some people are doomed to.
>
> Since my introduction to this house divided against itself I am almost inclined to give ear to the doctrine of a "hell on earth." The father of this family adheres to it. Who can wonder?

Colder weather curtails outside work on the farm, and Rufus uses some spare time to organize a lyceum: a meeting place for discussions, lectures, and concerts. Mr. and Mrs. John Kellogg appreciate this sliver of refinement in Mauston. They approach Rufus after his lecture on The Ohio Company, the Marietta-founding organization his Cutler ancestors had helped to create.

"Rufus, well done, young man! Very interesting. You've got an impressive heritage," John says to Rufus as the audience files out.

"Yes," says Adelaide, "I really enjoyed your presentation. You express yourself so well! I didn't see your father here, though. Is he not well?"

Rufus smiles. "Thank you very much. I'm glad you enjoyed it and happy that I didn't put you to sleep! As for Father, he is doing well, and let's just say he's heard the Marietta story before."

John grins and says to his wife, "I'll explain later, dear. Anyway, Rufus, we are glad you are among us and have taken the time to give our community some enlightenment. Lord knows it could use some sophistication! I've heard many townspeople say how impressed they are with you. You've made a good name for yourself in a short time. Of course, they must not have heard about that humiliating fencing match! Let's keep that quiet!"

Betsey Shipman
(Mrs. Beman) Gates

Beman Gates

The Gates Home at the Corner
Fourth and Putnam

Sarah Cutler Dawes

Lucy (Luce) Dawes

Ephraim C. (aka Daniel W.) Dawes

L. Catherine (Kate) Dawes

Endnotes

1. Unless otherwise noted, diary entries are from the DAA.

2. Unless otherwise noted, letters quoted are from the DAA.

3. The 193'x30'x12', 709-ton *Galena* was built in 1857. It would be lost with all hands in September 1872 off Thunder Bay during a Lake Huron storm. www.boatnerd.com

4. Beach, Mary Dawes. *Mother's Letters*. DAA.

5. Wikipedia.com (website).

6. DAA.

7. The *City of Memphis* is one of the steamboats passing by Rufus Dawes, guided by a twenty-four-year-old pilot named Samuel Clemens from Hannibal, Missouri. He will turn to writing in a few years and adopt the pen name Mark Twain, a sounding call signifying safe water depth of 2 fathoms (12 feet).

8. Unless otherwise noted, Gates family letters are from Mary Dawes Beach's *Mother's Letters*. DAA.

Chapter Three

A Patriot's Legacy: Citizen Soldier

Winter 1861, Ipswich, Massachusetts

It is a new year, perhaps a significant year, and Mary decides to keep a diary. She buys a small booklet, preprinted with three days to the page, only big enough to make short notes. She notes the bylaws of Mrs. Cowles's school on the flyleaf and the names of her two roommates at Mrs. Morley's boarding house. Both are from Maine—Georgia Parsons of Kennebunk and Cyrene Robinson of Waterford. The simple bylaw rules are numbered:

1. Read Bible 3 chapters a day, 5 on Sunday

2. Avoid falsehoods of any kind

3. Do not speak ill of others

4. Do not buy confectionery of any sort

5. Try to rise at 6 ½ o'clock, Sundays excepted

6. Do not waste time

7. Put up our books at 9 ½ o'clock p.m.

8. Do not leave for the future what should be done at present

It does not take Mary long to be "wildish" and break a rule, as she dutifully records:

Tuesday, Jan. 1, 1861 Broke our fifth rule this morning by lying in bed beyond the appointed time.

Wednesday Jan. 2 Broke Rule No. 3.

Saturday Jan. 5 Broke Rule No. 5.

Friday Jan. 11 News came today that S. Carolina fired the first guns of civil war. Had oysters and crackers for dinner.

Sunday Jan. 13 Georgia and I had a falling out and I had a real cry this evening.

Tuesday Jan. 29 Mr. Cowles spoke half the morning. Dry as dust.[1]

Beman Gates no longer owns a newspaper, but his opinion is respected, and he is invited to write editorials for several papers in Ohio, with some of the editorials appearing in New England publications. He is a liberal on women's issues and urges his daughter to keep herself and her roommates informed about national events, especially the overriding issue of secession. In February, he urges her to spend some money and subscribe to the *Boston Evening Journal*, which he recommends "because it is not so strongly partisan as most of the Boston papers." In response to Mary's question about his views on secession, he writes:

I think it a great folly and a great crime. What the results are to be I think no man can tell, though I am hopeful that there will be a reaction at the south which will put Union men in charge of the affairs there and overwhelm the traitors ...

Mary shares her concern about it all—politics and her studies:

Georgia Parsons has uncles and a brother in Savannah, Georgia, from whom she hears often. The last news was they were drafting everyone into the service and Georgia's uncle has been chosen captain, or general or something else. Woe is me, tomorrow we begin spelling again.

Early 1861, the National Scene

The Republican presidential victory is unacceptable to firebrands in Southern state legislatures. They have made it clear they will not tolerate any interference with their lifestyle and are convinced the Republicans, with Lincoln as president, will ultimately undermine their institution of slavery. South Carolina is the first to rebel, voting to secede from the Union five days before Christmas. Like falling dominoes, six other Southern states take the same radical course, and in February 1861, these seven states formally create the Confederate States of America. Former secretary of war Jefferson Davis of Mississippi is elected its president. This all occurs before Lincoln departs from his home in Springfield, Illinois, and arrives in Washington. No president-elect has ever faced problems so challenging—the nation literally falling apart before his eyes.

Standing under the uncompleted dome of the US Capitol Building on March 4, 1861, the structure itself seeming to symbolize a nation in disarray, the newly inaugurated president addresses the nation. Lincoln focuses his remarks to the people of the South. He states his resolve to protect federal interests in all states, North or South. He argues that the Union is not dissolvable and that secession from it is not an option. He makes clear his resolve to use whatever means necessary to preserve the Union—that the central government will not be the first to use force, but if attacked, it will respond to quell any rebellion.

Rufus Dawes in Juneau County, Wisconsin, and Mary Gates in Ipswich, Massachusetts, and some millions of fellow citizens all read the inaugural address in the papers. To Rufus and to Mary, it is a masterpiece: eloquent, passionate, and correct. Lincoln's closing words are hopeful but haunting:

We are not enemies but friends. We must not be enemies. Though passion may have strained, it must not break our bonds of affection. The mystic chords of memory, stretching from every battlefield and patriot grave to every living heart and hearthstone all over this broad land, will yet swell the chorus of the Union, when again touched, as surely, they will be, by the better angels of our nature.

Friday, April 12, 1861, Charleston Harbor, South Carolina

Whatever angels South Carolina governor Pickens may listen to, they are not the "better angels" Lincoln has in mind. His state militia has already seized several forts around the harbor and Charleston's federal arsenal, capturing scores of cannons and twenty-two thousand weapons. This occurred in December, and, as Mary Gates noted on January 11, shots fired from South Carolina artillery kept a Fort Sumter resupply ship from entering the harbor. Thus emboldened, Pickens demands evacuation of this federal military installation. He regards the fort as not consistent with the "dignity and safety" of his state. No matter to him that the fort was placed in the harbor for coastal defense purposes and thus is wholly consistent with the safety of the citizenry.

Lame-duck president Buchanan does little in response. He ignores the surrender demands, but also seems to ignore the Sumter garrison. Running low on rations, the troops assigned there are essentially under siege.

Taking office in March, Lincoln soon organizes a US Navy relief squadron and notifies Pickens they are on their way, the intention simply being to resupply a federal facility. Confederate president Davis and his cabinet now take charge, deciding to prevent any resupply and to demand the fort's surrender, using force if necessary. The arrival of the first relief ships spur the Southern commander, CSA General Beauregard, to open a bombardment against the undermanned, outgunned, but resolute Sumter garrison. US Army Major Robert Anderson surrenders the battered federal island fort the next day. The brazen attack pushes the nation over the edge of a cliff.

President Lincoln agonizes over the situation on the weekend. He does not recognize this new confederacy, believing the Constitution binds all states into one Union. It is his obligation as commander in chief to restore federal property and put down the rebellion. The tiny sixteen-thousand-man United States Army, however, is spread out over the country, mostly in the far west. Many of its Southern-bred officers and men are resigning. He has limited legal authority regarding use of state militias, but feels it is necessary to use this authority to the maximum allowed. On Monday, April 15, he signs a proclamation calling forth seventy-five thousand men from state militias to serve for a three-month period. The secretary of war sends quotas to each state governor for infantry regiments of 780 men each. The more populated states of New York, Pennsylvania, and Ohio are called on to produce about half of the total.

Force is being met with force. Wisconsin, less populated and far from the nation's capital, is tasked to organize just one regiment.

Tuesday, April 16, 1861, Mauston, Wisconsin—Office of John Kellogg, District Attorney

"John, I'm sure you've heard! The president has called for seventy-five thousand volunteers but only one regiment from Wisconsin. I told my father this morning I must go. He wants me to stay and work on the farm, but I don't care. Everybody I've seen this morning is crazy about this. Just think of it! The stars and stripes being dragged through the streets of Charleston! I'm sure a whole company of men could be enlisted here in a few days. What do you think?"

John Kellogg stands up from his chair. The look on his friend Rufus's face is the same he has seen all morning from the townspeople on the street. Every man is angry and ready to fight. Every woman is subdued and worried.

"I'm mad as hell about it!" John responds. "Those damn idiots in Charleston and that traitor Davis have gone too far! Lincoln has no choice now. Buchanan did nothing. Thank God he's gone! I tell you what, you are the best man here to get a company organized. You know the people, they have heard you speak, and they listen to you. You've shown that patriot spirit; it's in your blood. I say do it and get started now. It won't be long before men from all over the state will be signing up, that's for sure. I'll help all I can. I've a mind to sign up myself!"

Thursday, April 18, 1861, Constitution, Ohio—the Old Stone House

Julia Cutler notes that people in Ohio, especially those near the Ohio River just across from Virginia, are in a "state of great excitement" over the Fort Sumter affair and over reports that Virginians are moving to seize the arms contained in the armory at Harper's Ferry. This latest news seems like John Brown's raid, now eighteen months past, is happening all over again, although for altogether the opposite purpose. For the Cutler family at the Old Stone House, there are additional and much more personal concerns.

William Cutler had taken over the family farm upon his father Ephraim's death, but is often away on business as vice president of the Marietta and Cincinnati Railroad. He had married neighbor Lizzie Voris, twenty years younger than he, while Rufus lived in Malta with his father.

Lizzie and William became parents several times but had suffered the loss of two of their very young children: a boy Willie and girl Ephie. There are three remaining: Annie, eight; Sarah, five; and their youngest, baby Jennie, who lies deathly ill while the nation is on the brink of war. Aunt Julia records the scene in her diary as she and Lucy Dawes, Rufus's sister, help Lizzie tend to the child:

> The Doctor came on early train, he thinks she will live through the day. He will telegraph to William at Chillicothe that her symptoms are alarming.
>
> A little before ten o'clock A. M. she ceased breathing as she lay upon a pillow on Lucy's lap. ... It is a very severe affliction to Lizzie to lose this lovely little babe so soon after burying Ephie. She took the dear little one upon her own lap and with many tears washed and dressed her for the burial. She was laid out in the crib & placed in the parlor, the third of her children who have lain there. She looked beautiful, her eyelids and lips a little parted as if she were just falling asleep, her little hand clasping the delicate forget-me-nots. ... We sent George to town to make arrangements for the funeral. ...
>
> William said today that in view of the troubles impending in our own land, he thought the next generation would pass through such scenes as the world never saw. Perhaps the little one now at rest was taken from trouble to come.[2]

Saturday, April 20, 1861—Ipswich Academy

"Georgia, what do you think of all this? It seems everything is snowballing into such a mess!" Mary Gates and her roommate, Georgia Parsons, have just read the latest Boston paper. The news about Sumter's surrender and President Lincoln's call for volunteers dominates everything. Rumors fly about Southern troops ready to take over the nation's capital.

Georgia is just as worried, if not more so. "I'm just trying to make sense of it all, but how can I? How can anybody? It's just crazy! I can't understand what those people in South Carolina are thinking! My own family members! Everyone here in the North is just livid! The president will not have any trouble getting volunteers; thousands of our boys are going to sign up the first chance they get. And then all those Southerners will respond, and ... I just can't believe this is happening! How did it get this far?"

Mary cannot concentrate on anything but the war. The fear of conflict, with Marietta being right on the border, consumes her thoughts as she writes in her diary that evening:

> News came this morning that Jeff Davis is within 24 hours march of Washington. Bridges burnt. Telegraph wires out and much excitement generally. Money and letters from home. Felt so bad I went down to see Mrs. Cowles. Have written I want to go home if they have war.

Thursday, April 25, 1861, Mauston, Wisconsin

Rufus Dawes does not need much convincing from John Kellogg. He posts a notice seeking "patriotic and ambitious young men" for military service, in response to the "trouble to come" referenced by his uncle back in Ohio. He then drafts a volunteer sign-up sheet and stops at John Kellogg's office to see if his lawyer friend approves of the wording.

He had thought about the three-month term of service and Wisconsin's disappointing quota for only a single 780-man regiment. *There is probably no likelihood to be part of that one regiment; many larger towns, especially Milwaukee and Madison, have existing militia companies that are better positioned to join. And despite all the rhetoric being displayed by certain politicians, I can't see how the North can quell this rebellion with only seventy-five thousand men in three months. It's likely to take many more men and much longer to accomplish. And if the state does not need us, we should be ready to go anywhere, to serve on our own if necessary, wherever we are needed—perhaps even in my border town of Marietta, Ohio!*

He has therefore drafted a simple one-sentence pledge statement:

> We, the undersigned, agree to organize an independent Military Company and to hold ourselves in readiness to respond to any call to defend our country and sustain our Government.

Dawes plops the paper in front of Kellogg and says, "John, here, see what you think of this. Two words are key: 'independent' and 'any.' Meaning, if we don't get the call from Madison, or if the government needs us for longer than three months, this says that we agree to serve anywhere and for any term, however long it takes. What do you think?"

Kellogg looks it over, rubbing his chin. "Hmm, yes I see that. A very simple yet very bold statement, Rufus. Whoever signs this must first be clear on those points. I think … it's fine. I like it. In fact, I like it so much …" Kellogg picks up his pen, dips it in the ink bowl, and signs his name. "There," he says, smiling, "your first recruit!"

Dawes is shocked. "John, what are you doing? You're married, you have three children, and you are ten years older than me. This is for younger single men. Not that I don't appreciate your willingness to go— it's admirable, but … Now, come on, don't do this on impulse. Just strike your name off. Better yet, I'll draft another on a fresh sheet. What would your wife say, anyhow?"

"I've already discussed it with her. She's not excited about the idea, I'll grant you, but finally, she said, 'Go, if you must go!' And so I am going. I will not hide behind this desk and let everyone else own the glory and satisfaction of crushing those Rebels. This is my chance, and I'm not going to lose it. Unless you refuse me, my name is staying on that paper."

Dawes cannot dissuade him. His original intention of enlisting only single men is foiled at the start. Leaving John, he gets busy, riding everywhere to enlist as many volunteers as possible, making sure they understand the terms. By nightfall, forty-eight men have signed the pledge.[3]

Tuesday Evening, April 30, 1861, Mauston, Wisconsin—Langworthy's Hall

Rufus Dawes calls the meeting to order, and the loud and excited conversation soon subsides. "Now, I wish to welcome you all here this evening and to thank every man here who has signed our pledge to sustain the national government!" Cheers and applause break out from the seventy-eight men who have by now agreed to serve, plus other onlookers who are present.

"We have a fine representation from our county and even beyond, patriots every one of you. God have mercy on those Rebels when we get into action—because we will not!" Louder cheers ring out. "I want to recognize several people … shall we say, some who have more than our average maturity." Laughter and cheers. "The honorable John Kellogg here, our district attorney, who collared many of you and assisted admirably in recruiting perhaps the best of the lot, or so he claims!" Laughter again, cheers and lighthearted jeers competing. "And we have former constable Rueben Huntley of Necedah here." Dawes points him out. "Perhaps some of you have met him before under embarrassing circumstances! A married family man, as is Mr. Kellogg, yet still will not be denied the opportunity to defend our country!" More cheers as the thirty-seven-year-old lawman-turned-lumberman Huntley meekly waves. Dawes adds, "And I must also proudly note that Mr. Huntley's wife and I share the same ancestor: my great-grandfather, William Dawes, who rode on that fateful night with Paul Revere, calling out to the minutemen to protect our nation, just as we are being called tonight!" That stimulates loud cheers, men rising out of their seats, strong right arms extending above heads.

The meeting gets down to the business of electing three officers and the requisite number of enlisted non-coms, the assembly taking on the resemblance of a mini political convention. Rufus Dawes and John Kellogg are quickly named captain and first lieutenant, respectively. John Crane, a popular Irishman, takes longer to win enough votes for second lieutenant. Five men who have earned respect in their civilian capacities are selected sergeants. They are David Quaw, Linnaeus Westcott, Eugene Rose, Harrison Edwards, and John Ticknor. Rueben Huntley is chosen as one of the eight corporals.

Then, like all other volunteer companies being organized everywhere, it is necessary to devise a dashing company name. After numerous suggestions, the men decide on the "Lemonweir Minute Men." The name of their local river will remind them of home, says one convincing voice. Dawes prefers simply "Minute Men," but so be it.

Rufus Dawes is prouder than he has ever been, unanimously elected captain of a volunteer infantry company he has organized. He has accomplished it on his own merit, independent of his father. On May 3, the governor's office makes it official: Rufus Dawes is appointed captain of the Lemonweir Minute Men and made part of the active Wisconsin militia.

Friday, May 10, 1861, Mauston, Wisconsin

Captain Rufus Dawes cannot wait to share the news with Kellogg, his second in command. "John, this is the day! We now have a hundred men ready to sign the muster roll. More came in the past week. Corporal St. Clair works at Stoddard's place, and yesterday he persuaded three farm boys in the neighborhood to join up. You know, I met Old Bill Stoddard on my recruiting rounds. I remember being introduced to his buxom daughter, who I could see had an obvious soft spot for young St. Clair. So maybe our corporal thinks matrimony by shotgun is on his horizon, and he sees the army as a better option!"

Kellogg laughs at that thought, but then sobers a bit at the thought of his own marriage, soon to be tested by separation.

Looking at the roster, Dawes continues, "Anyway, St. Clair brought in Rescun Davis, James Barney, and a James Sullivan, who cheerfully told me I should call him 'Mickey,' just like everyone else does—for Irish 'Mick,' I guess. I told him I would call him 'Private Sullivan.' I'm not sure about him. St. Clair says he is a hard worker and is almost eighteen, but he looks younger, and he's short, maybe five feet five. Of course, Lieutenant Crane vouches for him—'countryman' and all—but I wonder if little Mickey will be able to carry a full pack and keep up on a march."

Kellogg responds, "Well, we certainly have all sizes. That local man, Butterfield, must be six feet four, and that young kid with the round peach-fuzz face, Yates, may be shorter than your Irish Mick. But maybe they will surprise us, and we need the numbers, regardless."

"You're right," Dawes responds. "Time will tell. But we do have a bunch of tough lumbermen and farm hands and mechanics who know hard work. They are having fun with the drills we've started, not taking it seriously yet. Even sergeants like John Ticknor, who looks more like a soldier than just about anyone, seems to see it as a joke. But if we can get to Madison and join a regiment, and they see what other soldiers look like, our boys will straighten out, I'm sure of it."

President Lincoln realizes that seventy-five thousand volunteers for three months will not be adequate. Army General-in-Chief Winfield Scott advises him to expect a long and difficult conflict. In early May, Lincoln calls for forty-two thousand more volunteers to serve for three years unless discharged earlier. The prescient pledge drafted by Rufus Dawes for "any call" is validated.

The supplemental volunteer call, and the resulting militia quotas sent to all state governors, force the legislators of borderline states to declare their position. Will it be Union or secession? By May 20, Virginia, Arkansas, Tennessee, and North Carolina vote to join their seven Deep South neighbors in the Southern Confederacy. Marietta is now on the frontline. Several hundred yards of river separate them from rebellion, though Union allegiance is strong in the western Virginia counties, and there is serious talk about that region leaving Virginia to form their own state. The name Kanawha, after the prominent river, is suggested by many. The papers cover stories about pro-Union residents in cities of the South being persecuted and driven out by secessionists. Debts owed by Southern companies to Northern banks are being refused. The whole nation is in constant and ever-increasing turmoil.

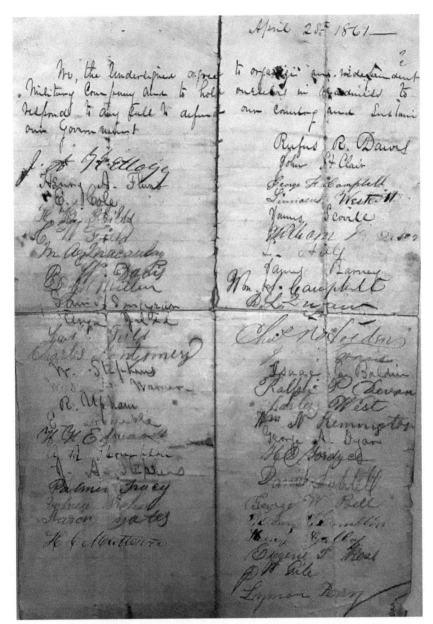

April 25, 1861—Pledge Sheet, Forty-Eight Signatures

Seventeen of these men had second thoughts before the enlistment date of May 10, for they are not listed on the official company roster. Most of these, however, enlist in other Wisconsin units formed later in the war.

The majority keep their pledge to serve in the Lemonweir Minute Men, suffering untold hardships in the rugged life of a Civil War soldier. Many will suffer wounds, some requiring amputations. At least five will die in combat or from disease.

Thursday, May 16, 1861, Massachusetts—Ipswich Female Seminary

Georgia comes into their room to find Mary engrossed in reading a letter. "Is that a note from home, Mary? What's the war gossip?"

Mary places the letter on her lap, shaking her head. "Well, this is from mother, and Charley wrote a few lines too. Here's the latest from Marietta—of course it's all a week old by now. Mother says the city council sent Father to Columbus to see Governor Dennison about sending troops to defend Marietta. Everybody is worried about a raid, Rebels from Virginia fording the river to burn the city ... all sorts of rumors. At first, Father was disappointed, thought Dennison was favoring other towns for political reasons ... Can you imagine! But now there are troops starting to come in on the railroad, even some from Indiana, and companies forming in town—boys all over the county signing up, and at the college too. Many of these boys are sick with the measles, and Mother and the other ladies have turned into nurses. Everything is changing day by day. Thank God Charley is only sixteen.

"Mother also sent the Marietta paper, and I notice that Rufus Dawes— you remember him, he was the college student who left midyear and moved to Wisconsin—well, it says he formed a volunteer company there and was elected captain of"—Mary looks again at the paper—"they are calling it the 'Lemonweir Minute Men.' I have no idea what a 'Lemonweir' is. Charley looks up to him and his brother Ephraim, who is also a senior now, and Mother really likes their mother, Sarah. I always noticed Rufus smiling at me in church. Now he's a soldier. I don't suppose he will be coming back to Marietta now."

Georgia grins at her roommate. "Hmm, I think I see a bit of disappointment, Mary." But she has war concerns affecting her own family on both sides of the conflict. She slowly confides, "Mary, I don't think this is going to end peacefully. There is too much passion on both sides. At some point, there is going to be shooting. I don't like to think about it!"

Mary shares her friend's concern. "I know. I don't, either. But I can't keep it off my mind."

Friday, June 15, Madison and Mauston, Wisconsin

Military companies from all over the state are being marshalled at the old fairgrounds near Madison, with barracks and tents quickly erected to accommodate them. The camp is named in honor of the governor,

Alexander Randall. He and his staff are busy organizing each unit into regiments, ten companies per regiment. The governor has authority to appoint the field officers commanding each regiment, subject to legislative approval. Men with prior military experience and training are sought-after, and many of them stalk the capital halls to make their own case, political favoritism inevitably involved. It is a typical process in every state, North and South. Selections are not always based on what a prospective officer knows, but *who* they know.

Rufus Dawes is having a hard time keeping everyone true to their enlistment pledge, and he rides all over the county to keep in touch and to recruit replacements when someone withdraws their name. He writes to his brother Ephraim that their mutual college friends from the state university, "Old (George) Bird and (William) Vilas are looking after my interests in Madison." He is not seeking a higher position, but rather to get his company assigned to the first regiment available.[4] It works. On June 14, Rufus receives a telegram from the Wisconsin military secretary: "Reply with a date that your full company can meet a mustering officer."

He responds immediately.

Thursday, July 4, 1861, Constitution, Ohio— the Old Stone House

In the quiet of the evening, Julia Cutler writes the following in her daily journal:

> I thought today of the living and the dead absent from us. Of Rufus, who is today twenty-three years old. He would have graduated at Marietta in the class of 1860, but his father took him to Wisconsin a few weeks before the close of his college course. The faculty conferred his degree upon him at the last Commencement. He is Captain of the Lemonweir Minute men. He and his company have been received into the sixth Wisconsin Regiment under Col. Cutler. Rufus has talent and principle. He is not tall but firmly built and very athletic. He has a very bright intelligent countenance and I think will be popular with his men. He always makes warm friends. May our father's God "bless the lad."

The Same Day, Ipswich, Massachusetts

Mary is smiling from ear to ear and gives her mother and eight-year-old sister, Bettie, warm hugs. "Oh, it's so good to see you! I was beginning to think I would never be able to!" Mother and Sister have made the trip to Ipswich to bring Mary home for the summer, with family visits and sightseeing to be part of the trip.

Betsey Gates writes home about her impressions of Ipswich before she and her two daughters begin a month-long visit in New England:

> Mary passed a very good examination, and everybody seems to like her very much and Mrs. Cowles is very anxious to have her come back.

Saturday Morning, July 6, 1861, on the Train from Mauston to Madison

"Rufus—I mean, *Captain*," Kellogg draws out the word, "listen to this and see if it makes any sense to you. I'm a lawyer, and I thought we were the experts at confusing people."

Dawes looks up from his letter, which he is trying to read as the railroad car rocks back and forth. "What? Sorry, I'm reading Kate's letter about Ephraim's graduation from Marietta College. She says he gave the best speech. And the faculty voted to award a degree for me too! Very nice of them. Maybe me going to war helped."

Kellogg responds, "They should have done it last year, in my opinion—you deserve it. You're almost as smart as me! But listen to this from old General Scott's *Tactics* manual." He holds up a worn copy of the 1835 booklet. " 'A column, by platoon, left in front, will form on the left in line of battle, according to the same principles, and, by inverse means, applying to the second platoon what is prescribed for the first, and reciprocally!' " He gives a puzzled look to his captain. "Now what the hell does that mean?"

Dawes laughs. "I don't have a clue. Hopefully, they won't expect us to do it when we get off the train in Madison!"

But they do. Finally arriving that evening at the east gate of Camp Randall, newly minted Captain Dawes and his stumbling crowd of backwoodsmen, haphazardly attired in a variety of homespun clothing and battered hats, are met by an impeccably uniformed officer on a spirited charger. Smartly saluting, the man announces, "Captain Dawes, I presume. I am Adjutant Frank Haskell. Colonel Cutler desires you to form your company by platoon and march to headquarters. Hibbard's Zouaves shall escort you."

Captain Dawes peers through the gate. A feeling akin to appearing unprepared before a board of college professors overcomes him. Beyond the fancy-uniformed Zouave company, with their red fez hats, short blue vests, and baggy red pants, all full of brass buttons and gold stripes, there are arrayed the other nine companies of the Sixth Wisconsin, standing at attention in perfect order, commanders and staff mounted in front, all awaiting the arrival of this last segment needed to complete their organization. Behind him, his backwoodsmen are craning their necks and gawking at the majestic scene.

"Good afternoon, Lieutenant," Dawes finally manages. "I should be glad to comply with the wishes of the colonel, but"—looking back at his company, then again addressing Haskell—"it is simply impossible for us to do so." So they "march" at their own gait to the assigned spot, escorted on both sides by the Zouaves, whose commander proceeds to shout out all sorts of orders, prompting his highly drilled soldiers to perform a variety of maneuvers and musket-shifting gyrations, all to the wonderment of the country boys from Juneau County.[5]

Colonel Cutler, an older gentleman with silver hair visible beneath his hat and a silver beard to match, welcomes them with brief remarks. He notes that they are now designated Company K, being the last company assigned to his Sixth Regiment. Lt. Col. Atwood is next, giving quite a long speech about patriotism, duty, etc. Finally, Major Sweet, a former state senator, now unfettered from legislative rules of time limitation, proceeds to invoke a variety of dictionary words meant to awe his audience. His attempt at humor sticks in the craw of the new Company K men, however, when he mentions that instead of being named Minute Men, perhaps Hour Men might be more fitting, due to them being the last company in camp. The soldiers of the regiment's other companies, amused by it all, soon dub the new arrivals Company Q.

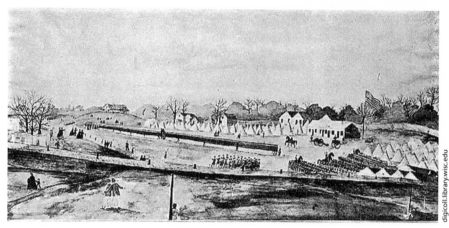

CAMP RANDALL IN 1862

July 1861, Camp Randall, Madison, Wisconsin

"We are going to have the best-drilled, best-disciplined soldiers, and cleanest company street in this whole camp, and it's up to us to see that accomplished!" Captain Dawes is speaking to his leadership cadre, Kellogg, Crane, and First Sergeant David Quaw, gathered by lantern light in his small barracks office that night. "There's a lot for us to learn, and we are going to spend all the time it takes to make the colonel proud of us. Here's the daily schedule I received from Adjutant Haskell." He reads from his notes:

- Reveille and roll call at sunrise.
- One hour of company drill.
- Fifteen minutes of preparation, then fall in and march to breakfast at the mess hall.
- Sick call and fatigue call. ("That means clean the company quarters and street.")
- Guard mount for those assigned that duty.
- Two-and-a-half-hour company and squad drill.
- Noon meal. ("We fall in and march there, as for every meal.")
- One o'clock, fall in and conduct three-hour battalion drill with the whole regiment.
- Supper.
- Dress parade.
- Nine o'clock, tattoo and roll call (" 'Tattoo' means our horrible band tries to play a tune," Dawes says.)

- Fifteen minutes later, taps. ("Then we go to sleep and do it all again the next day.")

Captain Rufus Dawes relishes his new role as company commander. In a light-hearted mood one evening, he writes Ephraim, mentioning fifty-four-year-old Colonel Lysander Cutler (no relation):

> Our colonel is a nice old man. He is not a Cutler in the full sense of the term—still I like him. Tell Ma to write me and send me a paper whenever you can. I am just as anxious to hear your gossip at home as ever. I don't expect to be shot and have no mournful message to send in anticipation of that event.
>
> Your Aff Bro, Rufe[6]

The regiment is issued good-quality Wisconsin militia uniforms, gray in color, but no weapons. The federal government is supposed to supply them later, and they are in short supply. On July 16, the 1,045 men of the Sixth Wisconsin Volunteer Infantry Regiment are mustered into federal service for a period of three years, unless sooner discharged. Company K musters in ninety-two men, having lost several who could not or would not sign on for three years. The Fifth Wisconsin, training at the camp with the Sixth Regiment, does the same. It is assumed they will both be assigned to the "western" theater of operations, somewhere down along the Mississippi, perhaps even fighting their way to New Orleans.

Then, five days later in Virginia, comes the much-anticipated first major battle of the war. It will be named Bull Run after the creek near Manassas Junction, 25 miles or so outside Washington, D.C. The first editions of the Madison and Milwaukee newspapers boast of Northern success. Unfortunately, these are soon dispelled as much gloomier facts are reported.

Dawes reads how Union General McDowell's inexperienced troops performed well in the morning, but stiff Confederate resistance under former VMI Professor Thomas Jackson, hereafter to be known as Stonewall Jackson, plus reinforcements arriving by train, turned the tide for the South in the afternoon. The battle turned into a disastrous rout for the North. The soldiers at Camp Randall read news accounts of their sister regiment, the Second Wisconsin, which had fought bravely while serving in a brigade commanded by a colonel named William T. Sherman. The gray-clad Badger Boys had been shot at by both sides; some Union troops mistaking them for Rebels.

It is shocking to read the casualty lists. The Second suffered over 150 casualties in the fight, including twenty-four killed outright. Many in camp recognize friends, even relatives, who have been lost or were wounded or are just "missing." It is a sobering wake-up call to these new citizen soldiers. This war is much more than parade ground drilling. It will be bloody, many young men will die, it will not end quickly. And, somebody had better get us out of these gray uniforms and into Union blue.

July 23, 1861, Madison, Wisconsin—Camp Randall

Corporal Rueben Huntley writes home to his wife, Sarah, using new Camp Randall stationary. The letter is penned by a friend who offers assistance to the spelling-and-grammar challenged corporal:

My dear Wife

The disastrous result of the Battle of Bull Run has entirely altered our arrangements here. We are under marching orders so shall leave this week. I shall not be able to come home. ... I will send my wages as soon as received. You need not write to me until you hear from me again. God bless you ... Good bye, Your husband.

R Huntley[7]

Colonel Cobb of the Fifth Wisconsin and Colonel Cutler of the Sixth receive their orders: "Your regiments are needed in the east. Report to Washington, D.C." Both regiments are placed on passenger trains heading toward the war by the end of the month.

The train cars are hot and cramped and noisy. The slow and steady chug-chug-chug of the locomotives contribute to the boredom and discomfort. On the other hand, the soldiers are treated like heroes along the way, cheered by the citizens and stuffed with food by the ladies of Milwaukee, Racine, Chicago, and Pittsburg. On August 1, camping a few days near Harrisburg where two companies are issued big, clumsy Belgian rifles, Rufus sends his sister Lucy a letter. Notable among the trip highlights he shares is a meeting in transit with Major Anderson and his family—he of Fort Sumter fame. The hero's family includes several daughters, one of whom took a fancy to the young captain:

The oldest of his daughters is a very handsome young lady of perhaps eighteen. The enclosed "sprig" please keep for me until "the wars are over" as it was presented to me by Miss Anderson.

The regiment's next stop is Baltimore's Patterson Park near the bay and Fort McHenry. Baltimore is a heavily secessionist city, and the men are attacked and fired upon one dark night by Rebel sympathizers. For Company K, the only casualty is Lieutenant Kellogg, who falls into an open latrine hole during the confusion. The superficial wounds he suffers are rather disgusting and cause a severe blow to his dignity, but woe to the man who ever mentions the incident in his presence.

By August 8, the regiment is in Washington, D.C., and bivouacs at Camp Kalorama near Columbia College, which is now converted to a hospital for soldiers wounded at Bull Run.[8]

Tuesday, August 9, 1861, Marietta, Ohio

Mary finally returns home via Buffalo, Cleveland, Columbus, and Cincinnati, and writes in her diary, "So thankful. Glad to see everybody and everybody glad to see us."

Among the "everybody" glad to see her are the students at Marietta College, right across the street. "Have you heard? Mary Gates is back." A steady line of competing young men are anxious to spend some time with the pretty local girl who has become more mature and womanly while away in Massachusetts. Mary has always been on the shy side, but free now of the woman-only atmosphere and rules set by Mrs. Cowles, she is happy to enjoy the company of her friends and the attention of all these handsome college men. Ephraim Dawes is one of them, and attending parties, he begins to take a fancy to Francy Bosworth. These are good times in the friendly musical parlors of the Gates home. It is a pleasant and enjoyable late summer and fall for Mary. She enjoys the comfort of being home with her family, the fun at parties, and engaging with the college men who seek her attention. There are walks along the river and carriage rides through the countryside. Mary records some outings in her diary:

Went to ride with Mr. Greenwood. ...

George Gill spent most of the evening here. ...

Invited to Mrs. Adams again. Went with Mr. Cochran. Had a regular grand time but offended Mr. Aleshyre's dignity.

The war news is always being covered in the papers, but since the debacle at Bull Run, there seems to be a general calm only interrupted by occasional skirmishes. The fear that Marietta and the Ohio River might become a battleground has subsided, and though many local boys are in the service, they have seen little action. Mary helps at the church, preparing kits for the soldiers, and Father is busy coordinating army supplies, but the college classes continue, student activities thrive, and civilian life is not too different than before this secession thing ever happened.

Saturday, August 13, 1861, Washington, D.C.—Camp Kalorama

Rufus Dawes writes to his mother and sisters using fancy stationary that depicts a bird's-eye-view portrait of the Capitol Building and surrounding city. Now that he is earning a captain's pay, $128.50 per month, he notes that:

> both of us [he and Ephraim] making a little money and applying a share to paying up your debts, the day I have long looked forward to is not far off, when the family (Ma & her children) can be placed in a position of honorable independence. ... [I]n one year I can easily place you out of debt and not impoverish myself at all. And I want to do it.

August 1861, Constitution and Marietta, Ohio

There is much activity at the Old Stone House. William Cutler has been elected as the US congressman for his southern Ohio district. He is traveling both to Washington and around southern Ohio on railroad business. William is also using his influence to organize a Washington County regiment of volunteers, the Thirty-Sixth Ohio, with prominent Marietta attorney Melvin Clarke and college professor E. W. Andrews as second and third in command. The colonel's commission to command the regiment has been offered to a thirty-year-old Ohioan named George Crook, a West Point graduate and US Army veteran of Indian fights out West.[9]

Ephraim, twenty-one now and a new college graduate, begins to manage many of the farm activities for his busy uncle. Troops heading south on the railcars pass by the Old Stone House, toward Belpre and the ferry there across the Ohio River, thence through Parkersburg to join Union forces being marshalled in western Virginia under General Rosecrans. Ephraim's aunt Julia keeps a running account of domestic activity at home and major war news. She writes in her journal:

> Ephe seems determined to enter the volunteer army. This is to me a great trial. I cannot bear to have him go. Henry is dead, Rufus in the army beyond recall, and now Ephraim!

Then, a more distressing event: William contracts typhoid and is very ill at home, with wife, sister, and nieces taking turns nursing him. The illness typically lasts six weeks or more, producing fever and delirium, and is often fatal.

William's sickness forces Ephraim to put off a call seeking his service as adjutant of a new unit, the Fifty-Third Ohio Volunteer Infantry. He often takes the short train ride between Marietta and the Cutler home to check in with William, sometimes bringing friends like Tim Condit with him.

Tuesday, August 23, 1861—Camp Kalorama

Rufus writes a lengthy letter to sister Lucy in Marietta, here in part:

> My 1st Lieutenant John A. Kellogg is a prince of good fellows. He is shrewd, worldly, talented, well informed, ambitious, and very fond of beer. Father insists that I must call on S. P. Chase.[D] If S. P. Chase wants to see me <u>he</u> will call. That's my philosophy. ... Tell me what has become of the old boys. Where is Tim Condit? And Benny Safford, where is he?
>
> Miss Anderson, who you are pleased to refer to as having "struck me," is interesting certainly, but only as the daughter of the old hero of Fort Sumter, and I do not know that my old <u>flame</u> Mary will suffer at all by comparison. This silly letter is for my sister Lucy only.

Wednesday, August 24, 1861—Camp Kalorama

Rufus pens a message to brother Ephraim in Marietta, including the following:

[D] Former Ohio governor, now treasury secretary in Lincoln cabinet.

Captain Bragg[E] is by odds the smartest man among our officers. He is as keen as a whip. … It's enough to make a dog laugh to hear his experiences. Our Colonel [Cutler] is an efficient commander. He is stern and unflinching in the performance of his duty, and I believe will be of determined courage. Frank Haskell is a first-class Adjutant. I am getting fat on this life, weigh 165 pounds.

Monday, September 8, 1861—Camp near Chain Bridge, on the Potomac River

The boring routine of drill, training, and grand troop reviews at Camp Kalorama ends, and the Sixth is marched around to several locations for picket duty. Captain Rufus Dawes provides an update to sister Kate:

> [W]e have been moving about from one place to another. … [W]e left everything but one woolen blanket and one oil cloth. We sleep on the ground with nothing above us but the canopy of heavens. To intensify our discomfort the weather has been cold and rainy. Rather a "hard road to travel" but I keep healthy, hearty and happy. … Our regiment has been doing picket duty along the Potomac River from Chain Bridge to Falling Waters along the Maryland side. My company has been deployed along some four miles. The rebel pickets & cavalry could be occasionally seen across the river. … [T]here was just danger enough to make it romantic.
>
> The scenery along the Potomac is very fine. The boys have fared sumptuously, every pig was pronounced secessionist and burned at the stake for his treason—turkeys and chickens stand the same miserable fate.

Tuesday, September 23, 1861—near the Chain Bridge

Washington is literally on the front line. Except for construction noise, however, it is a quiet front line, and young but perceptive Captain Dawes provides this assessment to Kate:

> The same masterly inactivity is still the order of the day. Beauregard is strenuously preparing himself for an attack by McClellan. McClellan keeps thousands of men building fortifications to resist an attack by Beauregard.

[E] Commander of Company E, from Fond du Lac. Lawyer and past delegate to the Democratic National Conventions.

Monday, October 7, 1861, Constitution, Ohio—the Old Stone House

Ephraim runs out the front door with a large shawl over his head to greet and cover up Mrs. Betsey Gates, who has come down to the Cutlers' home on the noon train. "Hello, Mrs. Gates, what brings you out in this rainstorm?"

As she enters the home, Betsey replies, "Well, hello, Ephraim. Two reasons: first, to see how your uncle William is doing, and second, to give you a little something before you leave. Your mother told me you've been appointed adjutant of the Fifty-Third Regiment. Am I correct that you leave tomorrow?"

Before Ephraim can answer, Aunt Julia enters the foyer and, giving Betsey a hug, responds to her question: "Yes, Betsey, we are afraid our Ephe reports to Camp Dennison tomorrow." Looking sadly at Ephraim, she adds, "We couldn't keep him away any longer. So here he is, as you can see, looking quite the soldier with his new uniform. And William is much better, thank you. Here, let me take your wet coat to dry."

Betsey, getting organized, looks at Ephraim, smiles, and shakes her head admiringly. "Ephraim, you do look very handsome, I must say. Beman and I both wish you God's protection. And for Rufus, also. You both have a special place in our hearts. Our Charley talks all the time about enlisting when he turns eighteen, but that's a year away, thank goodness, and I hope this awful war is over by then! But here, I knitted a pair of socks for you. I hope you can use them."

Ephraim takes the bundle, thanks Mrs. Gates, and begs forgiveness for having to leave. He has an appointment in Marietta at Cadawalder's Studio to have his photographic likeness taken while dressed in his uniform. Lucy and Kate have pestered him to schedule it before he leaves. Betsey and Julia move to the parlor chairs to chat.

Betsey begins, "Sarah tells me about Rufus, also. Julia, I feel so sorry for your sister. Her oldest, Henry M., gone just over a year, and now her other two sons going to war. Lucy struggling to make a living with her teaching in that small school room ... I don't know how she bears it."

Julia replies, "Yes, we've been keeping up with Rufus through his letters. He writes such good letters. Fortunately, he hasn't seen any fighting, but he says camp life and parades and picket duty are so monotonous. Of course, Sarah and all of us prefer that to fighting! But it does seem our General George McClellan has dawdled the time away with all those troops he's massing! Winter is fast approaching, and nothing is happening in Virginia."

"Yes, General McClellan," Betsey answers. "Beman knows him well from the railroad business. I met him once when he came through Marietta. George was only thirty-two, I think, when president of the Ohio and Mississippi line. And he had a lot of good experience in the army before that—West Point training, the Mexican War, surveying, a military observer in Russia, and so on. When McClellan was named commander of our western district, he asked Beman to help him by organizing and delivering supplies for the troops. Even made him a 'Captain of Commissary.' Remember when Beman commandeered that river steamboat on questionable authority of a telegram he received from McClellan? I thought my husband would get into trouble over that for sure! But it turned out all right. Beman always thought the general to be a solid organizer but also intensely full of himself. He was surprised when those few small victories in western Virginia got him elevated to where he is now, one of our top generals."

"Well," Julia says, "William tells me it was our own Dennison and Chase who bent the president's ear about McClellan, after McDowell lost so badly at Bull Run. Plus, he says old General Scott is about ready to retire, so that would put McClellan in complete control. As for McDowell, Rufus says he now commands the division that his Sixth Wisconsin is in. I pray for the best, but also wish I had more confidence in these generals."

Betsey responds, "Yes, I agree. And listen to us: Six months ago, who would have thought the topics of generals and war and young men going off to fight would be so acutely on our minds? I've written to Mary about Rufus and his Wisconsin company. Now we will be mentioning young Ephraim too. I worry so much about all these young fellows we know who are joining up to fight."

Julia sighs. "Yes, I know. Soldiers are passing by here on the cars all the time. Some of these boys are so young. The ones on patrol along the river often stop here asking for something to eat. They appreciate anything we give them. And already, many have gotten so sick in the camps that some have died, so far from their families at home. Before even seeing a Rebel! I have so much empathy for them all!"[10]

Letters Home from Captain Rufus Dawes

Camp on Arlington Heights, Oct. 28, 1861

Dear Kate—A military life unless occasionally interspersed with a battle is the most monotonous in the world. It is with us in this camp the same routine over and over again every day, brigade drill one day, brigade inspection the next, brigade review the third. Rufe

Arlington Heights, Nov. 21, 1861

Dear Kate—Last Saturday got a pass to the city. Called on Dave Chambers who prevailed on me to spend the night with him. Sabbath day we attended Dr. Gurley's church. There we saw Mr. and Mrs. Lincoln. A very long and homely man, with a very short and homely wife. I was entirely satisfied by his appearance that the President is no fool, though not a beauty. I am sadly disappointed in Mrs. Lincoln, she does not look smart at all, but rather gave me the impression of a little fat fussy woman, with a face as expressionless as dutch cheese. Rufe

Arlington Heights, Nov. 29, 1861

Dear Kate—One of my men, Harrison H. Edwards, died day before yesterday. This is the first death in my company. I caused him to be buried with full military honors, and in more respectful manner than any before in the regiment. This camping out in such weather as November always brings in our latitude, is beginning to tell upon our Army. Disease is making sad inroads in our ranks. Rufe[11]

The Chain Bridge over Chesapeake and Ohio Canal and Potomac River, 1861 (view toward the Virginia shore). VA Hwy. 120/123 today.

General McDowell and Staff
Arlington House, 1862.

November–December 1861—Marietta and Ipswich

Beman and Betsey Gates sit down with Mary in the parlor one early November evening for a parent/daughter discussion. Beman begins, "Mary, we have been thinking that you should go back to Mrs. Cowles's school at Ipswich to complete your studies. We love having you here with us, I'm sure you know that, but this next term will certainly benefit you in the long term, and I know Mrs. Cowles feels the same."

Mary is not caught by surprise at the proposal, as it has been brought up in the past. In fact, she and Francy and other friends have talked about her experiences in Massachusetts several times. There are limited opportunities such as this for young ladies, or parents willing or able to provide their daughters with a higher education. She understands that and appreciates it. Still, it is a trial to be away from home, and she missed her younger siblings a great deal last year. But to be truthful, there is not much except church activities to occupy the time during winter in Marietta.

She responds, "I've been thinking of it too. I think I will like to go back to good old Mr. and Mrs. Cowles. If only I wouldn't miss Charley and Bettie and you both so much. I hope perhaps you can visit—at least you on business, Father, though I know this term will not be as long as last year, when all that sudden war news just bothered me so much."

By mid-December she is back at Ipswich, much to the satisfaction of Mrs. Cowles and friends from last year. And this time, she brings three friends from Marietta. Joining her are cousin and best friend Frances (Francy) Bosworth, plus two Nye sisters, Maria and (later that month) Calista, both younger siblings of Mary (the widowed fiancé of Henry M. Dawes). As is common practice, Beman arranges a gentleman escort for their rail trip, in this case a somewhat elderly and bumbling Dr. "A."

Ipswich, December 15, 1861

Dear Father and Mother

Francy and I are rooming with Miss Eddy and we don't like it much either. If I had come alone I should have liked to room with her, but as Francy is with me it is a real restraint on us both.

Now I will tell you of our journey. Dr. A much to my surprise got us girls and our trunks through Boston safely. ... [W]e met with no accident (owing to good luck not Mr. A) you will please not say but that we were completely satisfied.

All three of us girls enjoyed the trip hugely. Maria Nye says she was never so happy in her life as she was between Wheeling and Pittsburgh, excepting for a few minutes when Dr. A left us and an old drunken man came up and told us we were drunk and offered Maria his ring etc. etc. It was while we were in a depot and as there were no gentlemen in the car or near we were somewhat frightened.

Mary

Life for Mary is soon filled with the routine of the academy, plus occasional social functions with her friends and fellow students. There are the sometimes-annoying attitudes of a few of her Yankee classmates, but having Francy with her this year, a family member and best friend, and a western girl, makes her time at Ipswich much more fun.

Helen McCloud—Maria Nye—
Rebekah Nye

Charles B. (Charley)—Betsey (Bettie)—
Mary—The Gates Siblings

William P. Cutler
Son of Judge Ephraim Cutler
Farmer, railroad executive, congressman, college trustee, abolitionist.
Married neighbor Lizzie Voris, twenty years his junior.

Julia P. Cutler
Sister of William P. and Sarah Dawes
Avid letter writer, war journal author,
family historian. Intelligent, insightful, pious.
Faithful sibling and aunt, friend to many.
Unmarried.

Brothers-in-Arms, 1861

Captain Rufus Dawes, Commander,
Co. K, Sixth Wisconsin Volunteers

2LT Ephraim C. Dawes, Adjutant,
Fifty-Third Ohio Volunteers

Endnotes

1. Unless otherwise noted, Mary's diary entries and family events are from Mary Dawes Beach's *Mother's Letters*. DAA.

2. Unless otherwise noted, quotes from Julia Cutler are from Peggy Dempsey's blog, "Julia Cutler's Civil War Journal" (JCJ). http://juliacutlerjournal.blog-spot.com.

3. The pledge sheet is preserved at the DAA (copy reproduced herein).

4. R. Dawes letter to brother Ephraim, June 10, 1861. DAA.

5. Dawes, Rufus R. *Service with the Sixth Wisconsin Volunteers* (SWSW).

6. Unless otherwise noted, letters from Rufus are from the DAA.

7. All R. Huntley letters quoted in this book are from the University of Wisconsin Digital Collections Library (UWDCL). http://digital.library.wisc.edu/1711.di/WI.Huntley.

8. *SWSW.*

9. Thirty-Sixth OVI facts obtained from JCJ and http://www.ohiocivilwar.com.

10. Conversation topics and facts derived from JCJ and Mary W. Ferris's *Dawes-Gates Ancestral Lines: Gates Family*, p. 27.

11. These three letters are recorded in *Dawes Journal, Book 1*. DAA.

Chapter Four

New Year, New Commander, New Promotion

**Tuesday, January 7, 1862, Wheeling (Western) Virginia—
Hotel Dining Room**

"Theodore, old friend, it's great to see you!" Rufus says as he and former collegemate Ted Greenwood sit down to have a late breakfast. "I'm glad you could break away from counting up barrels of salt pork or whatever and get me caught up on your activity."

"Ha, very funny, Rufus, Captain, sir! Although I don't have to 'sir' you, because I'm still a civilian, you know. I'm just using my brains for the government, making sure all you soldiers get your hardtack and blankets, and everything else you all lose or throw away! So you're on your way back from furlough in Marietta? I'm sure it was good for you to get back after all this time. Must have been a cold boat trip upriver here to Wheeling."

"Oh man, it was nasty and cold getting here! There's a lot of ice, and our boat kept getting bumped and jammed by it all. Plus, it was crowded with soldiers and a bunch of delegates to the West Virginia Constitutional Convention. That's an amazing situation, isn't it? Union men in western Virginia meeting to secede from a state that has seceded from the Union! I wonder what my great-grandfather William would think about all that is happening now," Rufus responds. "But as to my visit home, I got to the house at about ten at night on New Year's Day, and it was a complete surprise for Ma and my sisters. Even Eph was there; he got a few days off from his regiment. That adjutant work is keeping him busy; I warned him. It's been almost two years since I left Marietta. I never imagined that my means for coming back would be caused by a war, me being in

101

a soldier's uniform! Hen's death leaves such a void, though. I can see it aged Ma quite a bit. And Mary Nye—she's just so sad and lost, even after eighteen months since Hen died. Henry and Mary would have made a wonderful couple. She still stops to see Ma and Aunt Julia. A real sweetheart. I feel sorry for her."

Theodore tries to lighten the mood. "So, who did you have a chance to see?"

"Well, besides the family, I went to the college and visited with President Andrews and Professor Evans, and Kendrick too. The Seventy-Seventh Ohio is being organized there. Ben Fearing is the major and Cochran is adjutant, so I had a nice visit there, comparing experiences. Then, of course, I stopped at Shipman's, and guess where else? The Gates Corner. Mr. G. was not there, but I had a nice chat with Mrs. G and Charley."

Theodore stops eating and looks up. "Oh, really? Uh, was Mary there?"

With a sad smile, Rufus replies, "Miss Mary, unfortunately, was not there. You know she and Fanny are in Massachusetts at that female seminary. Mary went to school there last year, and Fanny decided to join her. Eph says he's taken a liking to Fanny, and I heard that you called on Mary last fall."

"Yes, I did, several times," says Greenwood. "There were several parties and outings. She is so ... nice. I must say, I enjoyed her company very much. But she's a girl who is hard to get close to, if you know what I mean. I'll be honest, Rufe, I certainly wanted to get more serious. If she hadn't gone to Ipswich and if this war had not started ... who knows. Now here you are, and I know you have a crush on her too. You always have." There's an awkward pause. "Well, you know, so does Condit and a lot of others. Who wouldn't? So, what now?"

"Mrs. G. did give me Mary's address," Rufus warily responds.

Greenwood smiles at his friend. "What the plan? Desert, then stalk her in Ipswich?"

"Very funny. No, I think I'll start by sending her some news clippings about our unit. You know, just to keep me on her mind a bit. Not trying to scare her away. But I've been gone such a long time. I didn't have the chance with her like all of you did." He senses immediately that the comment came off wrong. This is getting unsettling.

Greenwood leans back. "That sounds like the cautious approach your commander McClellan would support! Has his army—*your* army—done anything newsworthy that would interest her?" *Well, that was nasty,* Ted thinks. *Uncalled for, really.* "I'm sorry, Rufe, just being sarcastic.

Whatever you are doing is far more exciting than my job here at the quartermaster office. So, I guess I should say good luck, old friend." He changes the subject. "What's the latest news with you and your Wisconsin regiment? The last thing you wrote about was your colonel getting rid of a bunch of the officers."

"That happened near the end of October. I lost my second lieutenant, an Irishman named Crane, who I thought was going to be a fine officer. The men respected him. Colonel Cutler thought otherwise. Maybe it was the Irish thing, or maybe because Crane was having a love affair with a girl from Georgetown. I'm still not sure. Anyway, that opened his slot for my first sergeant, named Quaw—an Indian, by the way—a good man, gave up a good business to do his part for the country. Then in December, my first lieutenant, John Kellogg, filled a captain vacancy in Company I. So Quaw moved up, and I promoted another sergeant, John Ticknor, to fill the second lieutenant opening. He's another solid man—has a great tenor voice, by the way. He and another good friend, Captain Ed Brown from Fond du Lac, make a pretty respectable singing duet. Mr. Gates would approve—probably would want them in his choir! Then, before all that, Captain Bragg ... short and wiry, smart. He and Ed Brown were law partners ... a War Democrat, you would like him ... He was promoted to major after Lieutenant Colonel Atwood resigned.

"Confusing, isn't it?" Dawes continues. "It happens like that through every regiment. Some officers can't cut it and resign. But a lot of the Irish boys are upset that most of their officers were forced out. Some changes were needed, but I question the colonel on others. Still, he's the commander. Best to shake things out now I suppose."

Rufus changes the topic. "So, what are *your* plans? Maybe a transfer to the quartermaster office in Washington? Marshall Newport got a commission and is in that office, but since he's your cousin, you probably know that. I've seen him and Dave Chambers in the capital a few times."

Greenwood responds, "First, thanks to your uncle William's influence, I got this job, closer to the action than at the training camp in Marietta. General Rosecrans has his headquarters here for the western Virginia operations. So I see him often, and he's complimented me on my work. I'm trying to get an officer commission and a position on his staff. I'm pretty sure I can. I want to get into some action. If that happens, maybe we'll both see some fighting this year!"[1]

Sunday, January 12, 1862, Marietta, Ohio—the Gates Home

It is late afternoon at the Gates home, with Sunday services and Bible study at the First Congregational Church over for the day. Betsey sits in the parlor, taking a few minutes to read yesterday's papers, with a copy of the weekly *Home News* in hand. She chuckles at a short article describing a minor skirmish that occurred the past week in Ohio:

> A couple of female rebels—shame upon a disloyal woman!—recently crossed the Ohio from Belleville, Virginia, to Reedsville, Meigs County, sporting the rebel flag in the form of aprons. The sight was more than three of our loyal Buckeye girls could stand, and they forthwith captured and confiscated the aforesaid contraband goods, despite the resistance of the rebels. Bravo for the Meigs girls. The aprons were divided and sent to the boys from that county in Camp Putnam, and also to the Marietta Editors, as the Telegraph says, but they failed to reach the latter.[2]

Betsey is just about to make a comment about it when daughter Bettie comes into the room and cries, "It's not fair, Mother!"

"What's not fair, dear?" Betsey replies.

Bettie mournfully explains, "You and Papa and Charley get to write to Sister all the time, and I can't do it yet. It's not fair." Little eight-year-old Bettie feels left out.

Betsey answers with a soothing voice, "I know, sweetie. You are getting better at your spelling, though. Let's do this: I will write for you! You tell me what you would like to write Mary, and I will put it on the paper. That's called 'dictation,' and your father does it all the time at his office. It will be just like you did it, and you can sign it at the end."

Bettie is happy with that idea, and the two of them begin (with Mother editing considerably):

My dear Sister

Miss Lucy[F] commenced her school again last week. She had to quit because fifteen of her scholars had the measles. Rufe was at home last week and he looked right handsome in his soldier clothes, but Mother says he would look better if he had a handkerchief tied around his knees to keep them a little more together. Tell Francy that Eph's regiment has been ordered into Kentucky.

[F] Lucy Dawes, sister of Rufus, who operates a small local schoolroom.

Mary enjoys Bettie's (and Mother's) letter, and she responds right away, telling Bettie all about a dress-up oyster party her friends had one Friday evening in Maria Nye's room, as she dressed up to impersonate Confederate "traitor" Jefferson Davis. She writes a side note to her Mother: "I have had two or three papers from Rufus Dawes since I have been here."[3]

Sunday, February 3, 1862, Arlington Heights, Virginia

Corporal Rueben Huntley, former Necedah lumberman, writes home to his wife, Sarah. Homesick but resolute, he struggles with spelling and grammar:

> Dear wife I receved your leter yesterday and was glad to here from you. ... [I]t must make you feel very lonely now but you must bare up under your aflition nobley as I have to do. ... I am glad Albert is a good boy. ... I shall not be likely to com home until the war is over unles something takes plase for I want to see this thing through sens I have been here so long it is very stormy wether here now there is no frost in the ground here and that makes it very muddy we have to go out on picit but there is no danger there is no rebels nere[4]

Saturday, February 22, 1862, Marietta, Ohio

The nightmare scene Sarah Dawes has always dreaded is here, at her front door. She did have warning. Her oldest daughter, Kate, had gotten the surprising, troubling letter five days ago. It was from Henry, still Sarah's legal husband, though the separation has been in effect for over twenty years. He has returned to Malta on business and now proposes to have his daughters return with him to his farmhouse in Wisconsin! *Has he gone mad?!* Sarah thinks. *Does he think we can ever forget what all of us have gone through? After all this time, he expects Kate and Lucy to leave their home, to leave me, leave their friends, and keep house for him in the backwoods? I have not slept but a few hours each night since Kate placed that letter in front of me.*

Still, Sarah opens the door, her heart in her throat.

"Hello, Sarah, it's been a long time."

She gazes at the man she married over thirty years before, shocked a bit at his physical change. *Of course, I have aged, too, perhaps more than he*, she thinks. *He still has the deep voice. Still the cold eyes.*

Henry interrupts her thoughts: "You look well, Sarah. Your home looks ... comfortable." There is an awkward pause. Henry senses he can dominate. "Won't you let me in to talk?"

Sarah lowers her eyes and lets him enter. They move to the small parlor, and Sarah takes a chair.

Henry begins, "You know I have missed the girls. The boys, they are off to the army now. I suppose we should be proud, but they were silly for joining infantry units—Rufus especially. I told him to get in touch with Salmon Chase, to get a staff job under Stanton. They are both cabinet members working right under the president! Rufus could do much better than marching around with those lumberjacks. But he refuses. I don't understand why. I got Rufus involved in Wisconsin politics, you know. We have made respectable names for ourselves there. It is quite evident his move there was for the best. I knew it would be. Now I think Kate and Lucy could benefit themselves by moving there, as well. And I have built a substantial new home, large enough for them."

Sarah has tried to prepare herself, to imagine the words she would say. She decides to be direct. "Henry, Kate shared the letter you sent. They are not here now; they don't want to be. They don't want to go with you to Wisconsin. They will not go. You want them ... now? For what purpose? To be your maids? Why do you think they would agree to that?"

Henry is ready also. "Because they are my daughters. Because their prospects here, with you, are dismal to say the least. It would be of mutual benefit to them and to me. What have you to offer here? They have not married. Lucy tries to be a teacher; Kate just stays with your Cutlers, leeching off them. Jane's in Persia! I can offer much more. I think in a short time there, they would realize it would be well for them. I have built a profitable estate and will be able to—"

Sarah sits up in her chair and interrupts. This man has struck her before, and if he wants to do it again, so be it! She will not put up with this selfish, stupid nonsense. "What can you offer? Can you now offer love and care for them after years of neglect? They are women now, Henry, not little children. They know you. Anything you say now is meaningless! Would you come here now if Henry or Rufus or Ephraim were here by my side? Have you even been to poor Hen's grave? Shame on you, Henry Dawes! I don't expect any more money from you. I'm sure your plan is to hold that against me. But don't bother. I will get by without you and be much happier for it. I ... I do pity you. You have not changed. You have never understood what is good and important in life. I have nothing more to say to you. Now, please leave my home."

Henry quickly rises from his chair, a menacing scowl on his face. "Do not pity me, woman!" He has not expected such a quick and forceful rebuttal from the woman he dominated all those years ago. Sarah remains seated, staring at him, daring him even, but resolute despite whatever he will do. Henry pauses, dons his coat in silence, and walks out the door, not bothering to close it behind him. Sarah watches through the window as his carriage disappears down Fourth Street. She feels a shiver of emotional release and, with shaking hands, wipes a tear from her cheek.

Henry Dawes leaves Marietta two days later. He will never return.[5]

Saturday, March 29, 1862, Washington, D.C.—Dining Room, Willard's Hotel

The former Marietta College classmates shake hands and sit down at a corner table. It is three years to the day when they had joined together for the farcical junior class production at the college. Back then, R. Marshall Newport opened the evening program with a song titled "I'm Coming Back in Three Years to Take that Silver Cup," followed later by Rufus Dawes bellowing out that thinly veiled tune about Mary Gates, "Who's Going to the Corner To-night?" Those fun college days are over. No silver cup tonight, and the Corner is hundreds of miles away.

They are now both captains in the United States Army, and the nation is in civil war. Newport, serving in the Quartermaster Corps, Washington, D.C. office, has made dinner reservations for his old friend at one of city's best hotels. The room is full of officers in uniform, politicians and government staff in suits, and ladies dressed in the latest fashion. Conversational buzz and laughter make for a lively background, and wisps of cigar smoke rise toward the high ceiling.

"Well, Rufe," Newport begins, "I'm happy you got a pass to visit the capital and deposit some of your hard-earned pay with your uncle William—and, of course, to see me. But what has old McDowell been doing with you lately to crush this rebellion?"

Dawes laughs. "We are becoming the best picket-duty and parade-ground army ever assembled! I understand that here in Washington they call us the 'Pendulum Army,' moving back and forth, back and forth. My only casualty worries relate to measles and other more serious diseases, of which, unfortunately, there are too many. But generally, my men are healthier than most. You should break away from the QM office and visit."

Newport is not too excited about that invitation and simply responds, "Where are you posted now, exactly?"

"We built huts for the winter in a great spot, all over Arlington Hill overlooking the Potomac toward Washington. A very impressive mansion there with a great view, with big front pillars and a wide portico. It used to be the home of that Rebel General Lee, but you probably know that General McDowell set up his headquarters there. I served on a court-martial board that met in a room off the main hall. We all think taking over the place is justice due for Lee resigning his army commission and going with the Rebs. On Washington's birthday, our whole brigade—over 3,600 of us—lined up en masse on the lawn in front of the steps. General King, our brigade commander, gave a speech and had his adjutant read the farewell address Washington gave to his troops. Then each regiment fired a salute. *That* was inspiring. And right on Lee's front steps!"

Dawes savors a bite of steak, then continues, "This meal is terrific. You have no idea what they give us to eat—but wait, maybe you do, Captain QM! Anyway, back to my military saga. Ten days ago, we all thought we were shipping out with General McClellan to Fortress Monroe for the big push to Richmond. But as you know, Washington could not be left undefended! The president and Secretary Stanton would not let McClellan do that! General McDowell was promoted to corps command with three full divisions under him and told to stay put, to defend the capital. One of the divisions is ours. General King has been moved up to command that, and Colonel Cutler is now in command of our brigade. We have the Second and Seventh Wisconsin, Nineteenth Indiana, and our Sixth Regiment— the best brigade in the army, if you ask me. McDowell has twenty-five thousand men, but so far, aside from occasional marches back and forth chasing ghosts, we've seen no action, just an occasional Reb cavalry outfit off in the distance. We do have fancy troop reviews; he's big on that.

"The boys in our brigade are pretty disappointed. We've been around Washington since last summer and have not fired a shot at the enemy! And besides that, we're now camped in these leaky dog tents all around Fairfax Seminary, a couple miles southwest of Alexandria. It's cold, rainy, muddy, smoky ... We feel like pigs in the muck. No wonder they made a hospital out of the seminary buildings. Maybe you could pull some strings and send better tents our way. There's nothing worse than a cold, windy night sleeping under a wet blanket in a tent that constantly drips water on you."

Newport grimaces and says he will check into it.

Dawes ends the war talk and asks his friend, "So, you just came back from Marietta? How are things at home?"

"Yes, had a nice visit," Newport says, "the college is not the same. Mostly prep boys there now. A lot of the college students have joined the army or are talking about it. Charley Gates is a sophomore, and he's in the college militia company. Condit was still home, but he's left his seminary training to join the First Ohio Cavalry and will be sent off soon. He'll be riding to war instead of walking, like you."

Dawes smiles and nods his head. "That's why he was valedictorian—smarter than the rest of us. You mentioned Charley Gates. Did you happen to talk with him or Mr. and Mrs. Gates? When I was home New Year's week, I got Mary's address at her school in Massachusetts, and I've been sending her news clippings written about our division. She's sent me back some articles about things out east. She's not a McClellan admirer, which bothers me. She even addressed one of her short notes to the 'Army of the Potty Mac.' But I think McClellan is getting the army organized the right way. The food is better. The troops think he's a great leader. He's moving on Richmond soon. I guess she's been reading all those eastern editorials about the phony war and lack of progress. So there's that disagreement. Before you ask, yes, she's still on my mind. She's nineteen now, you know."

Newport briefly looks at Rufus, who is aggressively working on his steak, then hesitantly responds, "Rufe, I did not see the Gates family personally, but I'll pass on what I have heard about Mary. My understanding is she's engaged to be married or is about to be. I, uh, I can't say who the lucky man is—maybe someone we know, maybe someone in Massachusetts." He avoids the look of surprise and disappointment on Rufe's face. He simply says, "I'm sorry to break the news."

Rufus just stares at Marshall for a few seconds, then responds, "I, uh, I had not heard that. This is ... a surprise. Someone from the college? You said you don't know. Well, I'll have to give this some thought. It will take ... some getting used to." He drops his napkin over his unfinished meal. There is no longer an appetite. "I ... I guess things happen when away for a long time."[6]

Tuesday, April 8, 1862—Island No. 10 on the Mississippi River

A few members of the Sixth Wisconsin see battle action in a different arena. Corporal Rueben Huntley is one of them, assigned to temporary duty aboard the Mississippi River gunboat *USS Cincinnati* during efforts to capture the Confederate stronghold on Island Number 10. He had been sent there in February with several others, including Richard Upham of Rueben's Company K, and on this day of Union victory, he pencils a letter to his wife Sarah and son Albert:

> Dear sarah I have some news for you this time for we have got 10 island without fiting much last knight they sent a boat up to us and gave themselves up to comodor foot you can beleve we are glad for today we was again to fite them and we have news of a victory at Corinth in Tenisee so you can regoise with us for victory is with the right and god is on our side if nothing happens I will be home yet so wate a little longer with patents and you shall be rewarded.
>
> Dear son you appear to be glad to here from me it is the same with me but o Albert it is awful to here the howl of canon ball as they pas ore and to se our mortar shells waing 215 lbs burs high in the are in the knight its pretty to look at but awful to think of. Rueben H

Friday, April 11, 1862—Camp near Bristoe Station on the Orange and Alexandria Railroad[G]

Rufus Dawes crawls out from under his dog tent dragging his wet wool blanket and proceeds to hang it over a low tree limb in the hope it will dry out, at least a little, in the damp, cold air. The weather matches his mood. Around him the regimental camp is arranged in rows of small tents, the same as his. The rain has stopped, and the temperature is warm enough that snow is not probable. It has been a miserable few days in this muddy camp. Two days before, Jake, his contraband servant, had deserted him just after being paid $10 dollars, also taking with him the gold dollar coin Dawes had put in his hand for buying some dinner. It would be so nice to be back on the picket duty his Company K conducted the previous week, with his headquarters being inside a vacant little Episcopal chapel named St. Stephens, near Fairfax.

The blanket now steadily releasing its collection of rainwater, he sits on a box near the smoky campfire and begins a letter to Lucy:

> We are just now situated like toads in a puddle, waiting as always for the rebels to get ready for us before we advance ... with only

---

[G] See Northern Virginia map at end of chapter

hardtack, camp coffee, and ham apparently cured with creosote[H] to eat. We get no mails or papers either. All this however we might cheerfully endure if we did not feel that we had been put in a department where the prospect of accomplishing anything is small

Just then, Major Bragg strides up in his fast-paced, hurried fashion. "Rufus, I've just come from General King's headquarters. There's a telegraph there, and word came in about a major two-day battle the first of this week near a place called Pittsburg Landing on the Tennessee River. First reports are heavy casualties, but that the Rebs retreated. I know your brother is probably there in Sherman's division, so I thought you would want to know."

Dawes looks up with concern. Ephraim is in an all-Ohio brigade— one of the two other regiments being the newly arrived Seventy-Seventh, filled with many Washington County and Marietta boys. None of the troops have seen action, much less had adequate time for drill. But he knows that if there is a fight, Sherman will be in the thick of it. "Thanks, Ed. So, it finally happened. Ephraim wrote about trouble brewing near Corinth for weeks." His thoughts are with his younger brother, wondering how he fared, hoping for the best, dreading the worst. Getting back to Lucy, he quickly finishes his letter:

> I have just now heard of the awful battle of Pittsburg Landing. Let me know at once what you hear from Eph. God grant that he is safely through.

With this last hasty note, he hurries over to General King's headquarters. King, seeing the concern on his young captain's face, graciously gives Rufus permission to use the military telegraph. As Dawes watches, the operator clicks out a message to Washington, D.C., to his uncle, Congressman William Cutler, asking for any information available about Ephraim's well-being.

At the Old Stone House, Aunt Julia records the family concerns in her journal about her nephew as the long week transpires:

> Apr 13, 1862. Charles Gates came down and brought a dispatch from Mr. Gates saying that Dr. Hart and Mr. Curtis had gone on to Pittsburg Landing but that the others were not permitted to

---

[H] Coal tar oil used as wood preservative

do so. Great numbers of nurses were volunteering to go but were not permitted to do so; but the sick and wounded were being brought away as rapidly as possible.

April 15, 1862. Kate went to town to learn if anything was known about Ephraim. I begin to feel very anxious for his safety. He always writes promptly and a letter has had more than time to come. The suspense is awful. It seems more than we can bear. I am so thankful that Dr. Hart is there.

Apr 17, 1862. Lucy came this morning and to our inexpressible relief brought a letter from Ephe. Thank God, he is safe and did his duty. He was under fire from six o'clock Sunday morning until Monday night and did a little fighting on Tuesday. Wednesday morning, he wrote home but the letter had been delayed. He says he escaped with his life but lost everything else. But we take joyfully the spoiling of his goods since he is himself spared. Widow Fleming of Barlow lost a son killed and the other wounded. Young Porterfield of Marietta was also killed and young Booth. ...There is lamentation and weeping because of those who will return no more, Lieut. Wm. Scott was shot through the breast, wound very severe. Many of the 77th wounded are coming home on the steamer, War Eagle.

Thursday, April 24, 1862—Camp on Heights Opposite Fredericksburg, VA, near Falmouth

Dawes and Captain Edwin Brown stand on a muddy elevation next to an artillery battery, guns pointing south across the Rappahannock River toward the quaint town of Fredericksburg on the other side. Behind them is the large bivouac of their division, thousands of tents set up the day before after several days of wretched marching in rainstorms from Catlett's Station.

"Rufus, have you heard from your brother yet about the battle down in Tennessee?" Brown asked.

"I got a letter from him yesterday, finally," Dawes replies. "He was lucky to get out of it without a scratch. The Rebs surprised them, came at them en masse, and his colonel ordered a retreat, which became pretty much a rout, and then the colonel, Jesse Appler, just took off, panicked, and left his regiment! The other officers, including Eph, had to work hard under fire to try and rally the men. Can you imagine! If the commander is scared off, how do you keep the men from running away? Well, they finally got a new line restored, but they got pushed back about a mile and had their camp overrun; he lost everything he had."

Brown shakes his head and replies, "That's incredible. Sounds like they need a new commander. But it was their first fight, right? I sometimes wonder how I will react when we get into a battle, if we ever do! I like to think I will stand fast and do my duty and all of that, but when the bullets start flying around and men go down … I don't know. Do you ever have those thoughts?"

Dawes gazes back to camp and replies, "You'll do fine. We all will. At this rate, maybe we'll not have to worry about it. McClellan is on his way to Richmond, while we're going back and forth through all the mud. I know the boys are just looking for some real action, but 'Be careful what you wish for' is my philosophy. I'd be happy to see Little Mac end this whole thing, so we can all go home."

Glancing back at the camps, Brown changes the subject. "Look at all the slaves coming toward our camps! It's like a migration! Everything they have is bundled on their backs. I wonder what's going to become of all of them. And where are they going to go? You can't help but marvel at how they all want to get away but don't have a clue about where to go or how they will live. Clearly a miserable outlook, but they still must see it as the better option than slavery, which is all they have ever known."

Dawes replies, "I know; it's pitiful. I've seen slaves take great risks to be free. For years, my family in Marietta helped them escape north. This is the abolitionism people have written and talked about for so long, put into better effect than any legislation. There's no civil authority behind us anymore, and the slaves know it. They just want freedom. The army has no system in place to take care of them, but we also don't care a bit about the slave owners getting them back. Just after this morning's rainstorm, I saw an owner and his overseer trying to pull away some of their slave women from a big group getting handouts from Augur's brigade. Some of the New York boys took offense to that and literally kicked those two out of camp. They got a little carried away with it too. The provost guard had to be called out to save them. It seems to me that the great question of liberty is working its own solution."

Sunday, April 27, 1862, Ipswich, Massachusetts—Mary Gates, at Her Boarding House

Dear Mother

I saw in last night's Journal that Eph Dawes' regiment had its colors taken from them and had been sent to Fort Donalson.[1] Can it be possible poor Eph had to go? What does he write? Do you know whether Rufe Dawes is with McClellan, or is he still guarding Washington? He sent me Washington papers the first of the winter but stopped very suddenly. Love to all, your daughter, Mary

Monday, April 28, 1862—Destroyed Railroad Bridge over Potomac Creek, Four Miles Northeast of Fredericksburg, VA

"Colonel Haupt, this is Lieutenant Quaw and his company commander, Captain Dawes. Dawes here vouches for his lieutenant's construction abilities. So I'm putting him in charge of our detachment to assist in rebuilding this bridge, as ordered by General McDowell." Colonel Lysander Cutler, looking at Quaw and pointing his finger, continued in his usual blunt fashion. "Quaw, the general told me Colonel Haupt knows all about railroads and bridges, so you do just what the colonel here says for you to do." Looking around at the wide chasm of Potomac Creek and the mass of destroyed and blackened beams from the old bridge, Cutler concludes, "Dammit all! The Rebs have really made a God-awful mess of this! Why in the hell didn't we have some guards here? It looks to me like this job's going to tie up my men for a long time. What do you think, Colonel?"

The bearded Henry Haupt—forty-two years old, West Point educated, and a tunnel and railroad civil engineer from Pennsylvania—had recently been appointed by Secretary of War Stanton to command the military railroad system. Reconstruction of this 400-foot-long, 80-foot-high railroad trestle is his first major task. He is a busy man and does not have time for conversation. "Thank you, Colonel. It will get done as soon as we all get to work. Lieutenant, you can take your men over to those wagons and issue them shovels and picks and have them help clear out all the debris."

Haupt starts to turn and walk away. Lieutenant Quaw stops him. "Excuse me, sir, let me offer a suggestion."

---

[1] This proved to be a false report about the Fifty-Third Ohio Regiment's experience at the battle of Pittsburgh Landing (Shiloh).

Dawes turns his head toward Quaw with a "What are you doing?" expression.

Colonel Cutler eyeballs his young lieutenant with a look more menacing. Before either can tell the brash lieutenant to shut up, Quaw addresses the visibly annoyed Haupt. "Sir, begging your pardon, but I've been watching those men over in the trees trying to cut and work that timber."

Haupt sighs and looks in that direction. "Yes, so what? That's a brigade of New Yorkers we've already assigned to that job. There's plenty of men there already. So just do—"

Quaw interrupts. Dawes grimaces as he thinks, *Quaw! Put a lid on it and do what he says!* Colonel Cutler's expression portends an explosion. Dawes has witnessed these before.

Quaw quickly explains, "Colonel, that's my point. I can plainly see that those New York boys don't know what they're doing. We've got a bunch of lumbermen in the Sixth Wisconsin, and I've been in the business of making beams and ties. Put us in charge of the timber work, and we'll get all the beams you need three times faster than you will ever get them from those city boys."

Dawes, feeling he must support his man, decides to chime in. "Sir, I've seen my men at work in the backwoods before the war. I've split rails a bit myself. Our boys know what they're doing. We just want to be placed where we can do the most good."

Colonel Haupt looks at Quaw and Dawes, then at the New Yorkers off in the distance. Maybe this Quaw fellow has a point. "All right, Lieutenant. God knows we need to speed things up here. We're going to need at least a million feet of timber for this job. It's massive. So if you think you can do that, then head for the woods, and I'll send my assistant to reassign those other fellows." He pauses and looks at the trio of Wisconsin officers. "Don't let me down." With that, he strides off to another sector before anyone else can interrupt him further.

Cutler, locking eyes with Dawes and Quaw, shakes his head. "Don't let *me* down either!" he says.

The Sixth Wisconsin boys came to fight, but so far have had only rare glimpses of angry Rebs—the armed ones in uniform, anyway. Chopping trees and cutting beams is preferable to pointless marches through the red Virginia mud, however, and for the next week and a half, they take to their new task with spirit. Colonel Herman Haupt proves up to the monumental task. Using inexperienced volunteer infantrymen and freed slaves, the engineer reopens the supply route from the Potomac River to Fredericksburg. He and his workers complete the reconstructed bridge in just nine days, a marvel of nineteenth-century engineering and make-do construction, relying on local materials.

President Lincoln visits the bridge site on May 28. He is amazed at the accomplishment and describes it in his unique country style: "That man Haupt has built a bridge, four-hundred feet long and one-hundred feet high, across Potomac Creek, on which loaded trains are passing every hour, and upon my word, gentlemen, there is nothing in it but cornstalks and beanpoles."

One evening before taps, during the busy days of the "cornstalk and beanpole" bridge-building activity, Rufus Dawes notes an anniversary in his diary:

> May 3rd, 1862. One year today since I was commissioned Captain of the "Lemonweir Minute Men." One year in the military service has entirely satisfied me. I sincerely hope the "war will soon be out." Lt. Ticknor returned today. His return makes things much easier.

Then, in the following days, he records matters of importance regarding the leadership of the regiment and brigade:

> Thursday May 8th. Brigadier General John Gibbon takes command of the brigade. Colonel Cutler takes [back] command of the regiment to the great satisfaction of the men who do not like Lt. Col. Sweet.
>
> Sunday May 11th, 1862. There was a disagreeable altercation between Colonel Cutler and Major Bragg at dress parade.
>
> Camp Opposite Fredericksburg, Va. May 12th, 1862. Colonel Cutler has placed both Lt. Col. Sweet and Major Bragg under arrest and, it is said, has preferred charges against them for trial by Court Martial. Since their removal from duty, I have been ordered to act as field officer. In case of a vacancy in the field officers of the regiment[,] my chance for promotion would be good.
>
> Tuesday May 13th. Bad state of things in the regiment. General McClellan presses steadily on to Richmond. We are left out in the wet.

Wednesday May 14th. The country around here is desolate and deserted. Beautiful homesteads all around us abandoned and ruined. War is horrible.

Friday May 16th. Was introduced to General Gibbon. He was Captain of the Fourth US Artillery. He is a rather young-looking man. He seems punctilious in all matters of military etiquette, and will be, I take it, a rigid disciplinarian.

Saturday, May 17th. The Regiment was supplied with <u>white leggings</u>, and new hats with feathers, supplied also with white cotton gloves. These decorations were received with great merriment, but we are all proud of the splendid appearance of the battalion.

Friday May 23rd. General Augur's brigade and our own were reviewed in the afternoon by President Abraham Lincoln and E. Stanton Secretary of War. The brigade marched and appeared finely.

The four western regiments, wearing their distinctive uniforms most readily identified by their large black Hardee hats, have become the proudest, best-looking, best-drilled unit in McDowell's corps. They are now led by a commander, Brigadier General John Gibbon, who seems to be a hardcore regular, West Point Class of '47, and who understands the importance of esprit de corps.

Gibbon himself, who just turned thirty-five, is a novice when it comes to infantry, however—especially a unit this large. He was still a captain of artillery just a month ago, despite fifteen years of peacetime army service. He brought Battery B from a post in Utah to join the war and was assigned to General McDowell, then commanding the division. The battery soon became familiar to the western troops when Captain Gibbon pilfered over a hundred Wisconsin and Indiana volunteers to serve in his understrength six-gun unit. After good service, General McDowell recommended his promotion to general. McDowell has shortcomings, but he recognizes military talent. His appeal is directly to Secretary of War Stanton. West Pointers are needed in positions of authority; there are too many politically appointed volunteer officers. Gibbon's North Carolina background causes some delay. Indeed, he has brothers serving in the Confederacy, and there is no "Introducing Senator" from North Carolina anymore. But Congress finally approves Gibbon's four-step jump to brigadier general, and here he is.[7]

Gibbon has been impressed with the westerners. These volunteers are different than the regular army in a good way. Intelligent, better attitudes, but independent thinkers. They just need common sense direction, discipline, and unit pride. Gibbon makes his expectations known immediately and instills a spirit of unit competition for excellence. He recognizes and rewards individual exemplary performance, thus encouraging peer pressure to shame slackers into conformance. His leadership will forever be recalled and admired by his western volunteers.

Proud soldiers of Gibbon's brigade, black Hardee hats and white leggings

Monday, June 9, 1862, Ipswich, Massachusetts—the Oakes Boarding House

"Writing home about our trip, Mary?" Francy asks her roommate.

"Yes, this is to Charley. I owe him at least one," Mary answers. "He's such a ... well, I don't know how to say it ... a younger brother, but a friend. I can tell him things I would never mention to Father or Mother. We just have become so close. I miss him—and little Bettie, too, of course. But the big graduation is not that far away! We will soon be back in Marietta. I can't wait to be home with all our friends."

The "trip" was an excursion by the four Marietta girls to Andover, about 20 miles west of Ipswich. It was all approved by Mrs. Cowles, of course, and by Mr. McCloud, whose daughter Helen was part of the group. Francy arranged for 2 one-horse, two-wheeled chaises, and they left at 5:00 a.m. on the way to Helen's home in Topsfield, "taking the long way" and arriving at 8:00. Here, they needed to "do up their back hair and array ourselves in go-to meetin' clothes," when just then, as Mary describes it in a letter to Charley:

> [T]he bell rang and Sidney Augustus and Arthur Merriam and James Cleaveland were ushered into our presence. After a having a pleasant call they invited us to ride in their wagon, for it was like a wagon more than anything else. They took out the seats and we eight accordingly sat on the floor. I think I never laughed harder than I did that night. The boys behaved awfully and I expected they would shock Maria out of her senses but she joined in and seemed to enjoy it full as any one, and behaved full as badly as anyone.

Mary paused before continuing about the girl's trip the next day from Topsfield to Andover, another 12 miles west. Their prearranged guide, "Lottie Perkins' lover," could not come, so "Mr. McCloud marked the route on a piece of paper":

> As a matter of course we lost our way but as we all enjoyed riding and were sure of coming out in Andover sooner or later this little adventure rather added to[,] rather than took away from[,] our pleasure.

They found the Mansion House Hotel and the man who Mr. McCloud had arranged to give them a tour of town, including the theological seminary and the home of Prof. Stowe and his wife, Harriet Beecher Stowe.[1]

> We saw where the Stowe's live, saw Prof. Stowe, who is a very funny looking old man, and one of his daughters as homely as a mud fence. Mrs. Stowe who we wanted to see most we did not catch a glimpse of. ... But I must stop and expatiate on Prospect Hill. It is the highest point in Essex County. From it can be seen 25 or 30 towns. ...[W]e could see the smoke from Boston. ... It soon began to rain and we lost our way again, though this time we did not get far out of the way. ... [W]e could not find the words to express our enjoyment of the trip. ... Now then

---

[1] The famous author of *Uncle Tom's Cabin*, an emotional anti-slavery story published in 1852, selling hundreds of thousands of copies, becoming a major influence on public thought in the North, ridiculed in the South.

Charley, haven't we had a good time and don't you wish you were with us?

Monday, June 16, 1862

Major Bragg salutes Colonel Cutler in passing without comment. It's been a month since Bragg and Lt. Col. Sweet were released from arrest, but there is still no love lost between the major and his commander. Cutler's conversation with Adjutant Frank Haskell and Captain John Kellogg quiets down as the major walks by, and Bragg senses Cutler intends to keep their topic private.

Bragg's destination is the headquarters tent of Company K, Captain Rufus Dawes commanding. He finds him under a tree nearby, playing chess with Captain Edwin Brown. Captain Werner von Bachelle, commanding the Milwaukee Germans of Company F, is nearby, observing the match while training his black Newfoundland dog. Dawes watches and laughs as the animal stands on his hind legs and brings his right paw up in salute. "Ya, das is gut!" Bachelle exclaims, then feeds his pet a half piece of hardtack for a reward.

As Bragg approaches, Dawes and Brown begin to rise in military respect. Bragg, however, waves his hand and tells them, "Don't get up, don't get up. I'm glad I found you both together. I've got some news. Sweet has had enough of our 'Old Gray Wolf' Cutler. He's submitted his resignation. I deserve the lieutenant colonel position he will vacate, and of course that means my major slot will then be open. Rufus, that should be you, as senior captain. But Cutler wants Haskell, and he's talking to him right now. Haskell is an excellent officer and is a terrific adjutant, but he's still a lieutenant and should not be allowed to jump a captain. That's not right. The colonel has convinced General Gibbon to side with him, and Haskell has lots of influential friends in Madison who will no doubt try to sway the governor. So we need to come up with a plan of our own."

Dawes responds, "Well, that's interesting. The colonel has called the four captains who have the same date of rank to his tent this afternoon to settle the seniority question. I was told the other three contested Sweet's appointing me as senior, which he made when he had temporary command. Now with Colonel Cutler back, they want a drawing by lot to determine it. So it appears that my seniority is only temporary—unless I win the drawing, of course. As for Haskell, I agree. He's impressive but should have no right to pass over a senior officer."

The senior-captain lottery is at hand, with Captains Dawes, Dill, Hauser, and Hooe in Colonel Cutler's tent. Cutler, hat in hand held high, watches as the four officers each reach in for a slip of paper. Cutler has placed four in the hat, marked 1 through 4. On order, the four officers unfold their slips. Dawes looks down and reads "1." He is the lucky man!

Colonel Cutler's preference for Lt. Haskell is not swayed by the lottery result. The next day he orders "an expression of the officers of the regiment" for the open major position, excluding the field officers (Bragg and Sweet) and three staff officers, all of whom support Dawes. Cutler then appoints Dawes as officer of the brigade guard, sending him out of camp. It is now time to lobby the remaining junior officers, who all understand how their colonel wants them to vote. Cutler has a surprising surrogate in this endeavor—Captain John Kellogg. Rufus Dawes feels betrayed. His Mauston friend and former executive officer is now working against him, using his considerable lawyerly skills to promote Frank Haskell. Major Edward Bragg, though he is not allowed to vote, lobbies hard for Dawes, as do Captain Brown and Lieutenant Quaw.

That evening the officer caucus is held. Confident in victory for Haskell, Cutler directs Kellogg to introduce a binding pledge to make the recommendation unanimous for the man receiving the most votes. On the final vote, however, it is Dawes 14, Haskell 13. Colonel Cutler is embarrassed. He delays the report and rescinds the pledge for a unanimous recommendation.

Haskell and Dawes meet and shake hands. They respect the other's professionalism and have no ill feelings. Dawes sends a letter to his Madison friend William Vilas describing the situation, asking him to see the governor. He also writes his uncle, Congressman William Cutler, to apprise him of the details. Bragg forwards a recommendation favoring Dawes to the governor, signed by every officer who voted for him, and by the field and staff officers who were excluded from voting at the officer caucus.[8]

Monday, June 30, 1862

Captain Dawes is sick in his cot with chills and fever, which had hit him five days previously amid all the tension of regimental politics and two desertions from his company. Privates Knapp and Garthwait are AWOL. Dawes tries to find them in Fredericksburg, becomes ill, then sends Lt. Quaw to Washington to scour likely hangouts. He is laying sick and exhausted, both physically and mentally, when Colonel Cutler's orderly comes with a message to see the commander right away. Cutler hands Dawes a telegram and asks him to sign a statement acknowledging receipt. The message reads that Wisconsin governor Salomon has appointed Bragg as lieutenant colonel and Dawes as major of the Sixth Wisconsin. Captain Rufus Dawes is astonished. *I've won my promotion!*

The military rumor mill works to perfection. Before Dawes can reach his tent, admirers from his own Company K and Brown's Company E mob him. "No! Don't do that! Put me down!" Dawes is protesting as two of the brawnier men in his company, now his *former* company, lift him on their shoulders as the other men shout in celebration. Abe Fletcher and Rueben Huntley both ignore their commander this one time as they happily lift him up and down in unison with three hurrahs.[9]

Monday, July 7, 1862—Mary Gates in Ipswich, MA

Dear Mother—

What do you say to engaging in a correspondence with your pious Mr. Hinkle of Yale College? Day before yesterday I had … quite a little letter from Thornton M. suggesting the propriety of opening a correspondence.

Tuesday, July 22, 1862—Ipswich Female Seminary

It is graduation day at Ipswich. Mary is one of ten graduates and is the only one not a New England Yankee. Beman Gates comes in from a business trip at Boston to attend, although at Mary's request, he skips the school's invitation to be present for her oral examination the previous day. After the ceremonies, he travels with Mary and Francy on a vacation, visiting relatives and the girl's friends from school: first to Helen's at Topsfield, then back to Ipswich to say a final goodbye to Mrs. Cowles. Mary writes her mother about it from Portland, Maine, with a touch of good humor mixed with nostalgia:

A few scattered rose leaves mark the spot of Francy's conquest over Sidney Augustus. Here was the scene of my brilliant career. I felt right badly when I came to turn my back on the old school for the last time. I have had nothing but a good time since I first set foot in Ipswich. … It was so late when we got to Portland last night that we could not go out to Cape Elizabeth but are going this forenoon sometime, then hurrah for fishing, swimming, etc.

The first week of August finds them in Quebec, Canada, then on trains back to Marietta. It is a very nice post-school trip, especially for young ladies during wartime.

Meanwhile, at the War ...

- General McClellan's five infantry corps and 105,000 men launch their spring offensive up the James and York Rivers peninsula from Fort Monroe toward Richmond. Confederate General Joseph Johnston opposes him, and his defensive strategy slows McClellan's always cautious dispositions. Johnston is wounded on June 1, however, and must relinquish command.
- The South's new general, Robert E. Lee, continues the defensive strategy, but then initiates a brutal and costly offensive against McClellan's forces beginning on June 25. In a series of battles to become known as the Seven Days Campaign, Lee unnerves McClellan as Southern forces push the Union army into retreat. Casualties are staggering for both sides: 23,000 Union, 29,000 Confederate.
- On June 26, Stanton's War Department reorganizes separate Union commands operating in other parts of northern Virginia into a new Army of Virginia. Major General John Pope, victor at Island No. 10 on the Mississippi River, is placed in command. General McDowell's corps, including King's division with John Gibbon's Black Hat Brigade, are now part of this army, stationed near Fredericksburg on the east end of Pope's strung-out command.
- Newcomer General Pope issues an arrogant statement, confidently pledging no more defeats in Northern Virginia. To many in his new command, it is taken as an insult. To Confederate generals Lee and Jackson, it is a challenge. As Union forces under McClellan are checked east of Richmond and eventually evacuate the peninsula by boat, Lee sends three divisions under Stonewall Jackson northwest to confront Pope's 51,000-man army before McClellan's returning troops can reinforce them. Jackson has only half as many men, but his fast-moving corps of veterans have the confidence of past achievements against these same Union troops in last spring's Shenandoah Valley campaign. The Virginia Central Railroad between Richmond and Gordonsville is his lifeline to Lee.
- Disrupting the Virginia Central Railroad to isolate Jackson from the other half of Lee's army becomes a Union objective. The attempts

to do so are limited in size and scope, however, plagued as usual by poor Union tactical intelligence and timid senior commanders.

2:00 a.m., Tuesday, August 5, 1862—the Frederick's Hall Raid

During a period of intense heat, Gibbon's 2,800-man brigade embarks on a mission to cut the Virginia Central Railroad at Frederick's Hall Station, 40 miles southwest of their encampment at Fredericksburg. Their orders require a risky raid deep in enemy territory with a relatively small force. It is the first significant mission assigned to the Sixth Wisconsin. Major Rufus Dawes will directly serve under a commander who opposed his promotion.

Gibbon splits his force, sending 650 men of the Sixth Wisconsin and a cavalry squadron on a track farther west, under command of Colonel Cutler. After 15 miles, Gibbon's cavalry clashes with Rebels, and he halts his column. The next day he hears of a large Rebel cavalry force under General Stuart arriving on his left and decides to fall back. At the urgings of Bragg and Dawes, Cutler continues his part of the mission in the brutal heat, despite the risk of being cut off by Stuart's cavalry. The Sixth reaches the railroad near Frederick's Hall, destroys 2 miles of track, and burns various rail facilities and stores. They finally return to Fredericksburg safely, marching 90 miles in three and a half days under a broiling sun and oppressive humidity, not losing a man.[10]

Saturday, August 9, 1862—Fredericksburg Encampment

A tired Colonel Lysander Cutler sits in his hot headquarters tent writing his after-action report to higher headquarters. He recounts details of the grueling Frederick's Hall expedition and its accomplishments. He notes that his men "suffered severely from heat and fatigue, but were ready at any time to execute any order given. The only murmurs I heard were those of disappointment at not meeting an enemy." He pays specific tribute to several officers, including Lieutenant Colonel Judson Kilpatrick of the cavalry and newly minted Major Rufus Dawes, "for the prompt and faithful manner in which they caused all my orders to be executed, and also for valuable suggestions which I received from them." Rufus Dawes successfully passes his first test as a field officer during a challenging assignment and earns his commander's respect.[11]

The mission itself was foolhardy, however. Gibbon's brigade was ordered to venture far forward, between the superior forces of Jackson's infantry and Stuart's cavalry. They could well have been surrounded. Pope rendered a weak jab rather than a left hook. The Sixth Wisconsin is fortunate to return from its mission exhausted but otherwise unscathed. Fifty-nine of their Wisconsin and Indiana comrades are not so fortunate. Stuart's Rebel troopers captured these exhausted troops as they tried to return to base. Gibbon's brigade was left out on a limb on its own. Should they find themselves in a similar situation once again, thrust forward without adequate support, the consequences could be much more severe.

On This Same Evening—the Old Stone House

As the Sixth Wisconsin's commander is writing his report, Julia Cutler sits in the Old Stone House 300 miles away, faithfully recording events in her journal. Though far from the sound of cannon fire and musketry, the war brings trauma and distress to many of her neighbors, as she notes in her journal:

The 92nd regiment is recruiting or rather is being formed at Marietta. The quota for Washington Co. is three hundred. If the regiment is not full by the 15th, men will be drafted to fill it up.

This drafting brings the war home to every fireside. Women tremble for their husbands and sons. Men feel reluctant to be drafted. If they go at all they prefer to volunteer. They come to talk the matter over with William and to leave their families in his care. There will be five or six such families on our place. Mr. A., a good Union man, has an only child, a boy of very delicate constitution totally unfit for the hardships of the army. It is said that he has taken him & his nephew and gone to Canada where he now has a brother living.

I am afraid that the order of the Secretary of War arresting persons going to Canada to avoid Military service in to-days paper may give them trouble. I pity those who are obliged to go. War is a terrible scourge. Still we should put aside these selfish feelings, stand in our lot and do our duty.

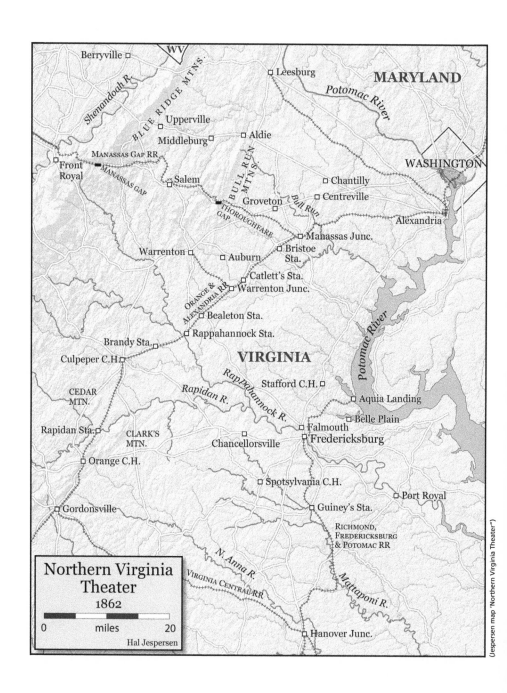

Northern Virginia
Theater
1862

0   miles   20

Hal Jespersen

(Jespersen map "Northern Virginia Theater")

Henry Dawes, Father

Reece Marshall Newport

Theodore Greenwood

Timothy Condit

Fredericksburg Virginia, 1863
View from north side of Rappahannock River

Potomac Creek Bridge–Aquia Creek Railroad built by US military railroad construction corps in nine days from standing timber (Lincoln's "cornstalk and beanpole" bridge).

John Gibbon

Lysander Cutler

Edward Bragg

John Kellogg

Photos from Library of Congress (LOC); Kellogg from Dawes Journal 2, DAA

Endnotes

1. Details of furlough and conversation with Greenwood derived from *Dawes Diary, Vol. 2. Wisconsin Historical Society* (WHS). http://content.wisconsin-history.org/cdm/ref/collection/quiner/id/31847. Further diary quotes in this chapter are from the same source.

2. Historical Marietta, Ohio (blog). http://historicalmarietta.blogspot.com, accessed Feb. 10, 2016.

3. Unless otherwise noted, Gates family letters and events are from Mary Dawes Beach's *Mother's Letters*. DAA.

4. UWDCL.

5. Julia Cutler's journal notes Henry's visit and Sarah's concerns. Further Julia Cutler diary quotes from JCJ.

6. Newport's role in diverting Rufus's attention from Mary is derived from letters in the Rufus Dawes Collection, WHS. Condit's service is from *Marietta College in the War of Secession, 1861–65.* (MCWS) https://ia902604.us.archive.org/32/items/mariettacollegei00mari/mariettacollegei00mari.pdf.

7. Gibbon, John. *At Gettysburg and Elsewhere: Personal Recollections.*

8. Dawes journal. DAA.

9. *ibid.*

10. Gibbon's report. *Official Records (O. R.) Vol. XII, part 1*, p. 122.

11. Cutler's report. *O. R. Vol. XII, part 1*, p. 123.

Chapter Five

"A Terrible Ordeal": the Iron Brigade

Monday Evening, August 11, 1862—Cedar Mountain Battlefield, a Few Miles Southwest of Culpeper, Virginia

"My God! This is sickening!" Captain David Noyes, Company A commander, holds his forearm over his face as he speaks in a vain attempt to quell the stench. Major Rufus Dawes and Captain Edwin Brown are with him, grimacing as they survey the scene of brutal conflict that occurred here two days prior.

Major Rufus Dawes, 1862

The two-division Union corps, led by General Nathaniel Banks, had boldly attacked Stonewall Jackson's three divisions, led by Generals Ewell, Winder, and A. P. Hill. Banks caught Jackson unprepared and initially drove the Confederates, killing Winder in the process. Jackson heroically rallied his men and sent in A. P. Hill's troops to rout the overmatched Federals. Union army commander John Pope, himself barely escaping capture, summoned his other two corps, Sigel's and McDowell's, to converge on the scene. By the time Dawes and his men, part of McDowell's corps, can arrive after a two-day, 42-mile march, it is far too late. Jackson has retreated to safety farther south, behind the Rapidan River. The horrible aftermath is left on the battlefield: corpses decomposing and grossly distorted in the sun and heat, a buzzing background noise produced by hordes of flies.

Thirty-year-old Captain Brown, already weak with stomach trouble and exhausted after marching 130 miles in oppressive heat over the past six days, turns and walks away. "I think I'm going to be sick," he says.

Dawes shakes his head as he sees hands, arms, and every fragment of the body thrown over the field. "It beggars description," he sadly responds. "I talked with one of the staff officers. There's over 300 dead they had to leave on the field, and 930 wounded. Plus, hundreds missing, probably on their way to a Reb prison. And that out of only 6,000 engaged! So much for General Pope's bombastic 'Where I come from, we always see the backs of the enemy' message!"

Noyes and Dawes follow Brown and leave the scene as a group of soldiers, many with faces covered with handkerchiefs, moves forward with shovels to bury the fallen soldiers. The detail includes many black contrabands who have followed along on the march, looking for work in exchange for food. Sergeant Howard Pruyn, of Noyes's Company A, has a teenage boy with him, a light-skinned contraband who latched onto Pruyn during the Frederick's Hall Raid.

Noyes addresses Pruyn. "Sergeant, I've told you: Enlisted men are not allowed servants while on the march. Tell him that he has to leave."

Pruyn responds, "Yes, sir, I know. He's so young, though, I don't know what he's going to do. But I'll do it now," and he turns to the lad.

Dawes, standing near, interjects, "Wait a minute, Sergeant. Last night my contraband 'dun got out,' as they say. The scoundrel deserted me just like Jake did before him. So I need to find a replacement. Do you think your boy would be able to fill my needs?"

Pruyn knows that officers use their subsistence allowance to pay for extra food items and require a servant who is capable of cooking and is a reliable scrounger. For a field officer like Major Dawes, who shares a mess with the surgeons, there are utensils and tents and baggage in the regimental wagons to be responsible for. Not to mention the horses these senior officers have that require feeding and attention. Pruyn responds hesitatingly, "Well, sir, I'll be honest: He doesn't know much. He's fresh off running away from a plantation down near Spotsylvania. He spent all his days working the fields."

Dawes studies the boy, who is standing nervously nearby. He tells Pruyn, "Well, right now I have nobody, and at least he's stuck with you, right? So maybe I can try him out. What's his name?"

"Billy—Billy Jackson," says Pruyn. "And thank you, sir. I hope you'll like him. He's been trying, seems grateful to be with us."

Dawes walks over to Billy, who stands barefoot and wears an old pair of pants held up by one suspender, along with a dirty shirt with holes in it. Dawes pats Billy on the shoulder and says, "Billy, I'm Major Dawes. I need a good servant, cook, and horse tender. That's my mare, Katerina, over there. She's held up well on our marches but is a little frisky. So I hope you know horses. Anyway, I'll tell you what you need to do and pay you a fair wage if you do a good job. I expect you to be faithful and not run off. I'll treat you kindly in exchange for loyal service. Are you agreeable to that?"

Billy is so nervous, he can manage only a stuttered reply: "Ye-yes, sah!"

Dawes responds, "Well, fine. Once you are done with your detail here, the sergeant will bring you over to my tent. We'll have to get you some better clothes and some shoes. Sergeant, these poor boys lying here probably have some items they will never need again. See what you can find for Billy until I can cajole the quartermaster for some new duds."

Captain Noyes walks with Dawes toward camp and asks, " 'Katerina'? Is that a sweetheart's name back in Wisconsin?"

Dawes laughs and replies, "No sweetheart—not in Wisconsin, anyway, or probably anywhere just yet. 'Katerina' is from Shakespeare, The Taming of the Shrew. Reading Shakespeare helped to keep my sanity while in the backwoods with my father." Dawes adds a comment about Billy: "I've got low expectations regarding my new boy. I wanted to help out Pruyn and the poor kid, but I expect Billy will probably run off right after I pay him, just like the other two, or skedaddle if we get into a fight."[1]

Wednesday, August 27, 1862, Marietta, Ohio—Gates Home

"Happy Birthday, Mary!" the family exclaims in unison.

"Now hurry up and blow that candle out!" says Mary's little nine-year-old sister. "Let's have some cake!"

They all laugh, and Mary does her duty. Little Betsey, whom they all call Bettie, grabs the first piece.

"Well, big sister, twenty years old today. Imagine that. You're getting old. Just don't think you can tell me what to do, though," brother Charley kids her as he takes the next slice.

"I'll tell you what to do," Mary retorts. "Stay in school and don't think about joining the army!"

It is a touchy subject in the household, and Beman and Betsey Gates glance at each other. Charley is still in school, but he will turn eighteen in six weeks. He often brings the topic up about "doing his part like everyone else."

Please, Charley, not today, Betsey thinks. She can't bear the thought of her only son heading off to this terrible war.

After cake, the adults head to the parlor. Betsey's sister Joanna and husband Sala Bosworth ("Uncle Bozzy" to the Gates siblings) join the Gates parents for some conversation, coffee, and tea. Betsey and Joanna soon sit together at the piano and play some duets, just like they did as young girls back in Athens. Beman and Sala stand and enjoy it, and as they watch their talented wives, they are reminded again that they are two lucky husbands.

Sala is always good for community gossip. Being the Marietta postmaster now brings him into contact with the public every day, and he hears a lot of local news. His failing eyesight has curtailed his art career, but influential friends whose portraits he has painted in past years helped him secure the federal government job. President Lincoln signed off on it, probably part of a batch of appointments handed to him by his secretary, in response to one of those White House lobbyists Old Abe always complains about.

Charley heads out the door to see friends, Bettie heads upstairs, and Mary Gates and her cousin Francy head outside to the swing under the big shade tree. Across the street and up the tree-studded hill is Marietta College. It's still summer break, but the fall term begins in ten days. Looking at the college, Francy sighs and says, "Mary, it's all changed here so much. When we were in Massachusetts, the war didn't seem so close. Back here now, so many of the boys we know—I should say 'young men'—are off to the army. The ones we used to see all the time ... so many of them. And some are dying. Mr. Buell's son, a captain in the artillery, was just killed last week. I know you're worried about Charley going someday. I sure don't blame you."

Mary grimaces a bit and replies, "I know! If only there was some hope that there's an end in sight! We hear all this bad news. That blowhard McClellan getting beat back outside Richmond ... I never thought much of him. And we seem to have another blowhard in General Pope. Now that awful battle at Cedar Mountain. Lucy Dawes told me about the letter she got from Rufus. He got promoted to major, you know. He told her about coming upon that battlefield after it was over and seeing all the maimed bodies. Terrible! I wonder why he shared that? It can't make Lucy—or his mother, especially—feel very comfortable."

"Well, I sometimes wonder why any man says or does a lot of things," Francy replies. "I suppose, though, Rufus has been in the army over a year, everything coarse and rough, seeing the things he's seen. Maybe he's gotten a bit hardened. This war changes people." She looks at Mary and asks, "You haven't heard from him, have you?"

"No, I haven't," Mary said. "He stopped sending newspaper clippings when we were still at Ipswich. I'm not sure why. Of course, it must not be easy to write while marching all over Virginia, though he does write his sisters. Lucy shared that he sends money for Mrs. Dawes. I think that's nice, don't you?"

Francy replies, "That *is* nice. I'm not surprised. The war must be having some effect on him. How can it not? But Rufus is and always has been a good man."

5:45 p.m., Thursday, August 28, 1862—on the Warrenton Turnpike near Gainesville

The orders are to proceed northeast to Centreville as fast as possible. Stonewall Jackson has struck a surprise blow, conducting a 54-mile flanking march in thirty-six hours through Thoroughfare Gap. His troops hit the Orange and Alexandria Railroad at Bristoe Station in Pope's rear and moved farther up the line to seize and destroy the huge Union supply depot at Manassas Junction. That was yesterday, the 27th. Pope calls his troops back from the Rappahannock River line to deal with Jackson, who he believes is now isolated and vulnerable to destruction. His problem? He has no clear idea of where Jackson's three divisions now are. They have disappeared.

King's division is ordered to move out again after dinner, heading east toward the old Bull Run battlefield on the Warrenton Pike, a main thoroughfare bordered by rail fences on both sides. The troops are tired of marching but are well-fed with fresh beef killed for them that afternoon. They expect an evening march before going into another bivouac somewhere up ahead. Hatch's brigade is first in column, then Gibbon's Wisconsin and Indiana Black Hat Brigade, then Doubleday's and Patrick's. Sixteen regiments in all, plus four artillery batteries, about nine thousand men total.

General McDowell, the corps commander, expects no trouble ahead and leaves his command to find and meet with General Pope. He ends up getting lost. General King, the division commander, falls ill, his staff says with an epileptic seizure. Thus, the two senior Union commanders are now incapacitated or missing, a worrisome situation. Nobody expects trouble, however, especially this late in the day, with sunset only an hour away.

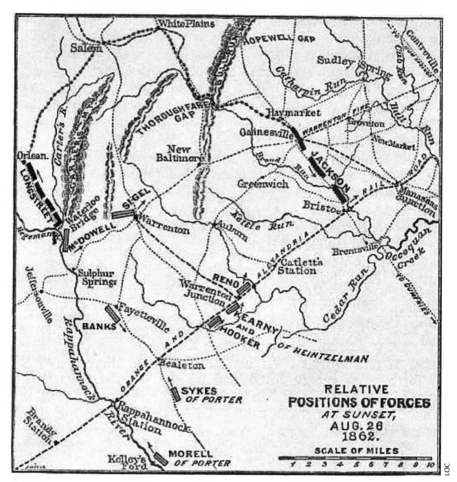

RELATIVE
POSITIONS OF FORCES
AT SUNSET,
AUG. 28
1862.

SCALE OF MILES

Notes:

1. Union general John Pope's Army of Virginia is composed of three corps led by Generals Banks, McDowell, and Sigel.
2. The Sixth Wisconsin is part of McDowell's corps, in Gibbon's brigade of King's division.
3. Divisions shown "of Heintzelman" and "of Porter" are arriving from General McClellan's Army of the Potomac, back from the failed Peninsula Campaign, and ordered to reinforce Pope.
4. Confederate General Jackson's 23,000-man wing has completed its surprise flank march to Bristoe Station, the route traced as shown. The next day (Aug. 27), he will seize and destroy Pope's supply base at Manassas Junction. He will then conceal his forces north of Groveton.
5. General Robert E. Lee leads General Longstreet's 28,000-man wing following behind Jackson.
6. The August 28 Brawner Farm Battle site is between Gainesville and Groveton, north of the Warrenton Turnpike (modern US Route 29), and is now preserved by the National Park Service.

But trouble *is* waiting for them. Stonewall Jackson has crammed his twenty-three thousand men into woods on a slight ridge a half mile north of the Warrenton Pike. He watches this federal infantry column unsuspectingly pass along and decides to attack. He knows that Lee and Longstreet are coming up behind him with another twenty-eight thousand troops. Lee's combined forces will still be outnumbered by Pope's army, now slowly being reinforced by troops from the chagrined General McClellan. General Lee feels his only chance is to defeat Pope before all of McClellan's troops can arrive, called back from their failed Peninsula Campaign. Jackson, therefore, decides to reveal his position, inviting Pope to battle and, in so doing, rough up, rout, or even capture this unsuspecting Yankee infantry column. He has no idea who these northerners are, nor does he care.[2]

Rufus Dawes is mounted on his bay mare Katerina in the major's place, moving serenely along at the rear of the Sixth Wisconsin column. It now numbers 504 men in ranks, as the grueling marches of the past month have placed many men on the disabled list. The Sixth is leading Gibbon's brigade, and Dawes has noted a line of skirmishers out ahead and left of the road: the Fourteenth Brooklyn Zouaves[K] of Hatch's brigade, their distinctive red pants standing out against the green fields. Everything is normal as they move along, just coming out into the fading sunlight after enjoying a stretch of welcome shade from woods on both sides of the pike.

Suddenly, the subdued buzz and shuffling and clanking of troops on the march is interrupted by BOOM! BOOM! BOOM! in quick succession. Instantaneously, artillery shells scream overhead and explode in the trees on the right side of the road. "What the ...!" Dawes hears Colonel Cutler's voice yell out a command: "Battalion, halt! Front! Load at will! Load!"

The men jump at the order, ramrods rattling cartridges down musket barrels as BANG! BANG! BANG! More rounds come in, overshooting again but one cannonball killing a spare horse, knocking it end over end against the roadside fence.

Cutler orders his regiment to lie down against the north bank of the roadway for cover, and Battery B, Fourth US Artillery, General Gibbon's former command, comes galloping down the pike. Tearing away the fences, they go into position in the field and start firing at the Rebel battery. Word comes down that General Gibbon is sending the Second Wisconsin off the road to attack what is suspected to be a Rebel cavalry

---

[K] The 14th Brooklyn's official designation is the 84th New York regiment, but the "14th Brooklyn" name was commonly used throughout the war.

detachment with several supporting guns on the left. Cutler, sitting on Old Prince, his dark bay, calmly comments to Dawes, "We'll probably be delayed a few minutes while the Second bags that squad over there."

The few minutes pass. Then, CRASH! The tremendous sound of volley musketry from many rifles! Additional artillery shells crash through the tree limbs all up and down the road. This is more than some cavalry! One of Gibbon's staff officers, Captain J. D. Wood of the Nineteenth Indiana, comes galloping down the road and yells an order for Cutler to bring the Sixth forward. As he rides back to Gibbon, Wood's passing words to officers he knows spreads quickly through the ranks: "The Second is being cut to pieces!"

Dawes spurs his horse, and she leaps over the fence as the Sixth moves through an open grain field in line of battle, colors front and center. Colonel Cutler is mounted in the center behind the banners, Lt. Col. Bragg is to the right on his white horse, and Dawes is in place on the left, just like the parade-ground drilling practiced many times before. This time, this *first* time, there is an enemy ahead who will shoot at them.

The Second Wisconsin is firing back at the Rebels coming at them out of the woods, but they are grossly outnumbered. Gibbon is a fighter and orders the Nineteenth Indiana and Seventh Wisconsin forward for support. The Rebels continue to reinforce and extend beyond Gibbon's line on the left. Intervening woods hide all this from Dawes as the Sixth moves forward on the far right of the brigade, but the gunfire noise is incredible! So far, as the tense soldiers of the Sixth move onward, they are not being fired on. Dawes feels a corkscrew sensation rise in his chest. Every part of his body is alert, and thoughts of what will come next scare him beyond anything ever experienced.

The Sixth clears the north edge of the timber, and Dawes can now see to his left what he has been hearing: his brigade comrades in line on rising ground, firing at a Rebel line that is also blazing away, not 100 yards separating the opponents. A sinking red sun is visible through the gun smoke, and many a soldier on both sides are sinking to the ground. The noise is deafening!

The Sixth moves down into a shallow swale. A line of confederates ahead, moving obliquely to strike the Second Wisconsin in the flank, apparently do not detect the Sixth's presence. Through the din, Colonel Cutler orders the Sixth to fire. Every rifle in the Sixth cracks at once. The Seventh Wisconsin comes into line among their comrades of the Second and fires a volley of their own. Dawes can see the appalling effect: The once-solid Rebel front is blown apart. Those lucky not to be hit fall back in confusion, and the Wisconsin boys respond with gusto to Lt. Col.

Bragg's call for three cheers. He is running on foot back and forth behind the line, his horse apparently shot or maybe just scared away.

"Well done, boys, well done!" Dawes shouts as he rides along the rear rank during the short lull that follows. It is by now becoming dark, and even though the firing on the far left is still raging, Dawes shouts to Bragg, "Do you think they quit?"

Bragg yells back, "I doubt it!"

He is right. The enemy returns with a rush and a yell—the Rebel yell. Whoop! Whoop! Whoop! All coming from several thousand voices, making for one continuous, bloodcurdling shriek. Soldiers on both sides are loading and shooting like madmen in the darkness. Hundreds of muzzle flashes allow Dawes to make out both friendly and enemy lines, more like opposing mobs than lines, as the carnage continues. He thinks, *It seems our boys are getting pushed back a little on the far left.* There, the Nineteenth Indiana, over a half mile away, is being outflanked and overpowered, and getting mauled by Rebel artillery pieces firing into their flank.

There is a 250-yard gap between the Sixth's left and the Seventh Wisconsin. Gibbon has been sending couriers to division headquarters and the other brigade commanders for help. Hatch does not respond. Patrick's troops never move forward to fire a shot. Nobody seems in command. Finally, General Doubleday sends two of his three regiments forward to fill the gap: the Seventy-Sixth New York and Fifty-Sixth Pennsylvania. They arrive just in time to help meet the new Rebel onslaught.

Dawes rides behind the line encouraging the men and comes up to Colonel Cutler in the center, calmly sitting on his horse. He yells at Dawes, "It looks like we're going back on the left, don't it, Major?"

"Yes, sir," replies Dawes, "that's why I'm telling our men to keep up the cheers."

Cutler begins to say something when Dawes hears a distinct -TCHUG!- Cutler claps his hand on his thigh and, in a clear voice, shouts, "Tell Colonel Bragg to take command! I am shot." He turns his horse toward the rear to find medical aid. All along the line, wounded men are doing the same. Others lie still on the ground. The men in line keep up a continual effort of fire!–load!–fire!

The arrival of Doubleday's regiments inspires Gibbon to move his men forward with a cheer. The Rebels momentarily fall back, then come on again with their yell. It results in more casualties but no clear advantage either way. For another half hour at least, the two sides blaze away, neither the rugged westerners or the veteran Confederates wanting to give in. Darkness, exhaustion, and severe losses gradually cause the firing to finally ebb away after eight o'clock.

Bragg orders backward steps while keeping alignment to match the slow retreat of the brigade. The line halts, and Bragg orders the men to fire in the darkness toward the Confederate position. The Rebels do not respond, and on Bragg's order, the men shout three loud cheers. A line of skirmishers is sent forward to warn of a counterattack, while the rest of the exhausted men drop to a knee to rest but with arms at ready. Bragg tells Dawes, "Ride over and check our left flank."

Dawes hears nothing on the left and can see even less. "Easy Kat," he says in a low voice as he slowly guides the mare toward where he thinks the Pennsylvania regiment ought to be, weaving through trees maybe 120 yards into the darkness. He comes upon a silent line of moving troops, and before he addresses them, he realizes these are Confederates! Keeping quiet, he quietly turns his horse before being challenged, and, with heart thumping, reports back to Bragg.

Gibbon sends an order for Bragg to hold his line, and the Sixth does so until past midnight. All this while, soldiers on both sides try to locate the moaning wounded and drag the killed to a collection point. Surgeons are at work in the woods south of the pike. It is a gruesome scene. Shrieks and groans from hundreds of suffering young men permeate the darkness. The Sixth suffers eight dead, and they are hastily buried. Sixty-one are wounded; three are missing.

This is the fight that Gibbon's brigade has been yearning for, for so long. For at least two hundred men, it is their last—either killed outright, or doomed to die soon, or maimed for life, never to serve again. The year of drill and discipline has paid off, however. They fought with skill and courage. The account of their brave performance will become known to the officers and men of the army. No more "Band Box Brigade" insults. The cost to earn their fighting reputation is horrific, however, and the men will be under no illusions when battle calls again.

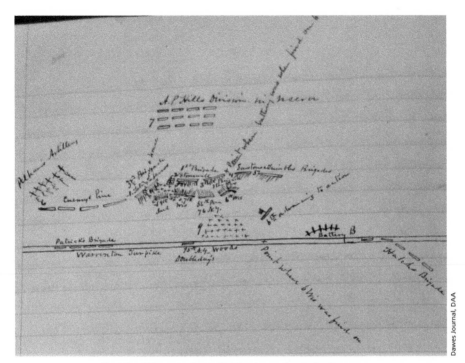

Sketch of Brawner Farm Battle drawn by Rufus Dawes

Sunday, August 31, 1862—the Old Stone House

Julia Cutler vents her frustrations regarding the Union army leadership[3]:

> What country ever raised such a volunteer army as ours, intelligent, brave, self-sacrificing—a million of men under arms to sustain the government and put down the rebellion. This army comprising the flower of our youth, our educated men, the pride and hope of our country, presents the strange spectacle of going into the struggle, with no talented competent leader. For a time, the national hope and faith was in Gen. Scott who "never lost a battle," then Gen. McClellan "the rising young hero" was hailed as a deliverer. In vain. We cast our eyes longingly upon Fremont, Buell, Halleck, Pope. No man equal to the exigencies of the times has arisen. William says, "[I]t is not men for the ranks but brains for the generals that we need."

Corporal Rueben Huntley writes his wife, Sarah Dawes Huntley, about the Brawner Farm Battle[4]:

Dear wife in accordance to my promis i will tell you about our fite on Thursday. Just before dark we met them and commenced the fite and it lasted one hour and a half and it was a hard fite i tell you. ... i suppose Weston is discouraged about me but i could not help it so be of good chear

Rite often and let no how you git along tel me about the children i will agane soon let you no how i am i have no more this time Rueben Huntley

Friday, September 5, 1862—Upton's Hill, near Washington

Lt. Frank Haskell, who General Gibbon assigned to his staff on April 14, is in the camp of the Sixth this Friday night, grouped around a campfire with many of his Wisconsin friends, Rufus Dawes included. There are bitter feelings toward Generals Pope, McDowell, and King. The Union army has been resting near Washington for five days, following its second bitter defeat near Bull Run.

Rufus Dawes and his fellow soldiers have had time to digest what they endured and have been lucky enough to survive. They are trying to mentally deal with the scenes of violence and death playing over in their minds. Many close friends are dead or painfully wounded.

Haskell begins, "The newspapers are referring to the battle as 'Second Manassas.' Our standup fight against Stonewall Jackson the evening of August 28 was just the opening round, and I really have not seen much written about it. I suppose it might be called 'Gainesville,' because that was the last town we passed before the fight. Or maybe after the farm there. I heard the name 'Brawner' as the family that skedaddled when Jackson's corps showed up on their land. They may not be back soon. The Nineteenth Indiana held the line right by the farmhouse, and they and the building got shot up pretty bad, plus there's all the carnage ..." His voice trails off.

Haskell regroups and continues, "Gentlemen, whatever they name that battlefield, the fact is that our four regiments took about 1,800 men into the fight against Jackson's two divisions! General Doubleday's two regiments came in to help us, maybe 500 men there. But, just for our brigade, we took 750 casualties—42 percent!—over 130 killed outright and dozens who have died of their wounds since then. The Second and

Nineteenth are just really shot up, the Seventh almost as bad. I know the Sixth fought hard, but the terrain, I think, helped to at least keep our losses lower than the rest."

Captain John Kellogg adds his thoughts: "I'm thinking of our field officers who were killed and wounded ... Seven of our twelve! Colonel Edgar O'Conner of the Second and Major Isaac May of the Nineteenth Indiana, both gone, both hearty comrades who we had come to know and respect. And the other three regimental commanders—our Colonel Cutler and Robinson of the Seventh, both shot in the legs. Meredith of the Nineteenth had his killed horse fall on him."

Haskell responds, "Yes, and to me, there is little consolation that the Rebs must have suffered even greater loss. We have heard that both their division commanders, Generals Ewell and Taliaferro [he pronounces it 'Toliver'] are wounded. In fact, word is that Ewell lost a leg in front of our boys in the Sixth. Bully for us!"

Dawes comments, "But to leave behind badly wounded men when we retreated! And to give up the ground that we had saved and won, while Jackson was separated from the other half of Lee's army ...What a waste! I'll never forget that agonizing 6-mile move overnight to Manassas Junction. I don't know how some of our boys made it. Doc, you know, it was awful. All of us so beat and exhausted when we finally stopped and dropped near the tracks at daylight for a couple hours' sleep."

Dr. Abram Preston looks at Dawes and responds, "I'll never forget it. It was the worst night of my life. Performing amputations that morning without sleep. How those boys could suffer along on that walk and then face losing a limb at the end ..." His voice trails off, and he looks at Dawes. "If not for you, Major, Captain Marsh would have been picked up by the Rebs. His knee should recover. You put him on your horse; that saved him."

Dawes nods at Preston, then addresses Haskell: "Frank, I'll say it: It seems to me that General Gibbon bit off more than we could chew that night. Why were we out there on our own?"

Haskell responds, "The general is mad as hell about it! General King was nowhere to be found until it was all over! He later said he had a seizure ... I'm not so sure it wasn't made in a bottle. McDowell, well, we've all heard about our lost corps commander! Hatch and Patrick would not budge without orders, while we were getting hammered right in front of them. And Sigel's whole corps and Reynolds's division ... They were only a mile away. They heard the firing. Why didn't they do something? It's disgusting! General Gibbon is sure to put it all down in his report. Maybe that will result in some changes now that the president put McClellan back in command."

"Here, here!" the group responds. None of them ever favored Pope, and they are very happy he is gone. "I'll risk censure," Captain Edwin Brown chimes in. "General McDowell should be cashiered, as well. We all know what most of our men think—that he's incompetent or a traitor."

Dawes adds to the agitated discussion: "Let's not forget our fiasco of an attack on Saturday, the 30th. Patrick's brigade ran back on us, the regiment behind us skedaddled, and we were stuck in that woods with Jackson's Rebs coming at us, all by ourselves again! We lost good men there. I'll never forget poor little Bicklehaupt shot through the lungs, trying to mutter a message for his folks." He pauses, looks sadly at Dr. Preston, then in a cracking voice, says, "We had to leave him to take his chances with the Rebs. It would have killed him to carry him back. I hope it was the best thing to do. There was no time. Others were being shot there."

A sad, uncomfortable silence falls among the group, most of them looking down or absently poking logs in the fire. Edwin Brown breaks the silence, looking at Haskell: "General Gibbon—and you, too, Frank—stayed with us there, all the way back to our lines across that open field. I'll never forget that: you both staying with us under all that fire. It means a lot."

Haskell responds, "Well, thanks for that. And, Major Dawes, you are right. It does seem such a waste. It's apparent our leader, General Pope, was not prepared or was misled or is just plain stupid. When Longstreet's juggernaut hit our left flank, it was all over in his mind. Then, even with all our losses, General McDowell chose our brigade as rear guard for the retreat. But why retreat anyway? There were more troops coming on from McClellan's army. A true *commander* would have recovered and hit back. I remember General Kearny—may he rest in peace—coming up to General Gibbon while we protected the turnpike by the Robinson House, so bitter about the whole situation!"

Dawes speaks: "Let's face the truth. We have too many senior commanders who don't have the confidence of the men. And for good reason. Here's an example: That Saturday night, after dark, when we were on the hill supporting Battery B and there was firing on both sides of us, up walks General Shurz, a division commander. He asks Colonel Bragg if we can come over and help his men, who are under attack. Bragg tells him, 'Certainly we will, if they let us leave here,' and he points him in the direction of General Gibbon. But he did not go there! Nor did he leave us until Bragg very emphatically gave his views as to generals leaving their command when engaged with the enemy! What do you think of that! I may be doing him an injustice, but we all thought he had pretty thin motives for staying with us so long. We need more fighting generals like Phil Kearny, but now he's killed at Chantilly. It's just discouraging, to say the least."

In his tent after the group breaks up, Major Dawes writes home:

Dear Mother—I have tried in several ways to let you know of my safety ere this. We have had a terrible ordeal—in battle almost every day from Aug 21st–31st. ... Our brigade has lost <u>800</u> men, our regiment near 150. How I have escaped without injury is beyond my comprehension.

Your Aff Son, Rufe[5]

* * * * *

McClellan quickly reorganizes the army. Both Pope and his Army of Virginia designation are gone. McDowell, too. His corps is now commanded by General Joseph Hooker and designated the First Corps of the Army of the Potomac. General King is replaced as division commander by General Hatch. These changes are all welcome news to Rufus Dawes and his fellow soldiers.

There is little time to reflect. Confederate General Lee decides to maintain his army's momentum by invading Maryland. His intends to further discourage an already demoralized Northern populace, perhaps to the point of capitulation. Crossing the Potomac will cut the Baltimore and Ohio Railroad, a key Union supply line. Maryland may also be ripe territory for new recruits to the Southern cause.

Like pieces on a chessboard, Union troops are soon put in motion to intercept the Rebel army.[L]

* * * * *

Lisbon Maryland Sept 12th, 1862

My dear Mother

Our army is moving up to the battlefield for I feel convinced that they intend to fight us. Probably before this reaches you the

---

[L] See Maryland Campaign map at end of chapter

great conflict will be over. If so you will know that I was there. My health is good and I am ready to take my chances. Do not feel that our task is easy, or sure of successful accomplishment. The battle will be desperate and bloody, and on very equal terms. Give my love to all. If I am badly wounded I would like Lucy to come to Washington or Baltimore. If I am killed I want no more honorable grave than the battlefield. Your aff son, Rufe[6]

An exhausted Captain Edwin Brown, Fond du Lac pre-war lawyer and best friend of Rufus Dawes, also takes time to write home from the Lisbon bivouac site, 30 miles north of Washington:

Dear Ruth

I have just time to write you a line—nothing more. You are doubtless informed of the defeats of our army, which explains our being here. Three times has my life been in jeopardy, where danger was in <u>every inch of space</u>. You can say to your friends that your husband was <u>no coward</u>, where so many showed "the white feather." The troops had no confidence in Pope or McDowell therefore many behaved badly. The only troops that really maintained a good name for themselves <u>everywhere</u> was Hooker's and Kearny's divisions and Gibbon's brigade.

They have more confidence in McClellan, none too much in him however. Rebels are in force in Maryland, we are massing to meet them. I am weary and sick. If the enemy were off our soil I should go to Hospital. Honor requires that everyone who has any patriotism left should meet the insolent foe. Should I live to see them driven out of this state and away from Washington—I will have some rest. I received a letter from you & sister Ann two days ago—was glad to get them.

My love to all, your relations and my parents in particular. Let them see this, I shall have no time to write them. Kiss the babies for their war worn father.

Good bye, E. A. Brown[7]

Confederate General Robert E. Lee has once again directed his two wing commanders, Jackson and Longstreet, to split up. To Jackson is assigned the task of capturing the Union arsenal and thirteen-thousand-man garrison at Harpers Ferry, nestled below surrounding heights overlooking the confluence of the Shenandoah and Potomac Rivers. Longstreet's command concentrates at Boonsboro, 15 miles farther north. Lee counts on a typically slow reaction from McClellan.

Fortune falls on the Union side, however, when Indiana soldiers discover a misplaced copy of Lee's order outlining Confederate unit dispositions. Realizing Lee's vulnerability, McClellan sends his troops via several routes toward Boonsboro, planning to smash Longstreet while Jackson is occupied at Harpers Ferry. They must first pass through several gaps in the South Mountain range. Lee tasks General D. H. Hill to plug the northern gaps and delay the Federals until Jackson can reunite with Longstreet. The North Carolinian has five brigades in his division. He counts about five thousand men under his command, many regiments depleted due to straggling. In his favor is the terrain. The high and rocky passes are strong defensive positions.

Daniel Harvey Hill is a staunch secessionist and a tough, aggressive commander. Five years previous, his wife's sister married Stonewall Jackson. Fifteen years previous, he married the daughter of Davidson College's first president. Among his groomsmen was fellow Tar Heel and fresh army officer John Gibbon.[8] Here on the green slopes of South Mountain, Generals Gibbon and Hill, close friends in younger days and happier times, will approach each other again. They epitomize the nation, split apart by differing allegiances, and are now preparing to lead their soldiers into violent combat, one against the other.

11:00 a.m., Sunday, September 14, 1862—National Road, Five Miles West of Frederick, Maryland

Lt. Col Bragg and Major Rufus Dawes pause on their horses at the side of the road as their soldiers of the Sixth Wisconsin march past, stepping lively and full of good humor on this beautiful morning. Dawes comments, "Can you believe that reception we got in Frederick? What a scene! Everyone waving flags, giving us food, cheering ... No wonder our boys are feeling good."

Bragg responds, "It was a sight to see, that's for sure. I don't think Bobby Lee is going to get many Reb recruits in this neck of the woods!"

Dawes gazes west across the valley. Another beautiful scene has burst into view from here, on the ridge crest of Catoctin Mountain. In the valley about 3 miles away is the little village of Middleton, with the South Mountain range maybe 8 miles distant. But the scene is marred by the scars of battle nearby, and smoke from combat is rising from South Mountain.

Bragg says, "There was a cavalry fight here yesterday between Jeb Stuart and our boys under Pleasonton. I talked to one of the town councilmen. He says they call this Fairview Pass and told me that George Washington and British General Braddock took this route to Fort Dusquene almost a hundred years ago during the French and Indian War. Now, here we are. Makes one wonder. Maybe somebody will mention us in a history book someday too!"

Sunday Evening, September 14, 1862—on the National Road, Turner's Gap, South Mountain Range

"Forward, Seventh! Forward, Nineteenth!" shouts General John Gibbon in a loud, clear voice, sitting on his horse at a high point on the road. On his left is the Nineteenth Indiana and on his right, the Seventh Wisconsin, both in line of battle proceeding steadily up the mountain pass. They have crossed through cornfields and orchards delineated by low stone walls. Fresh apples now fill haversacks. The terrain ahead appears to be open fields and rocky grazing land, with forested slopes rising to the mountain crests on both sides. Just as at Brawner Farm two weeks ago, this battle unfolds as the sun is soon to set over the mountain crest, about to bring closure to what had otherwise been a beautiful September day. For many soldiers, it is the last sunset of their lives.

-Crack!- -Crack!- The sounds of rifle fire continue to echo ahead. Artillery shells scream in from a Rebel battery posted near the mountaintop.

Major Rufus Dawes is commanding half of the Sixth Wisconsin, five companies composing the right wing. Lieutenant Colonel Edward Bragg commands the regiment in the absence of the wounded Colonel Cutler but is now directly managing the left wing. Both are dismounted as the regiment moves in double column up the mountain pass, fifty paces behind the Seventh Wisconsin's long line. The pass is becoming bowl-shaped as Gibbon's brigade moves steadily upward. The Seventh's left is at the road, its right flank ending uphill almost to the edge of the virgin hardwood forest that covers the steep slope all the way to the top.

Dawes keenly looks ahead through the smoke and fading sunlight as the skirmishers out in front fight their way upward. Captain Rollin Converse and Lieutenant John Ticknor are up there with Companies B and K. *Good old Company K*, Dawes thinks. The boys are working hard, going after it, exchanging shouted curses with their opponents, and taking casualties. The soldiers dodge left and right; trees, rocks, and fences provide cover as they fire at the enemy ahead. It is a deadly game of fire and maneuver, trying to pick off an opponent with the chance of being picked off yourself, always pushing ahead. Every barn and deserted

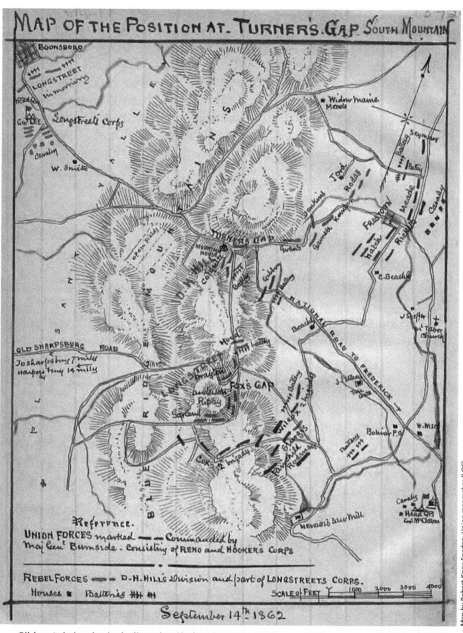

Map by Robert Knox Sneden, Union mapmaker (LOC)

Gibbon's brigade, including the Sixth Wisconsin, is shown in the center about to attack Colquitt's brigade of Confederate troops at Turner's Gap. The National Road is now designated US Route 40.

farmhouse or shed conceals the Rebels, but they are being steadily rooted out. A two-gun section of Battery B under Lieutenant James Stewart is in the road, blasting rounds into buildings and other Rebel hiding places, in support of the skirmishers up ahead.

Lieutenant Frank Haskell is on horseback behind his general, grouped with fellow staff officers Lt. Hildreth and Captain Cutting. Cutting serves under Army Wing Commander Ambrose Burnside, and he has stuck around after conveying his general's order to Haskell's boss.

General John Gibbon immediately realizes what Burnside's order requires. To paraphrase, "Detach your western brigade from the rest of Hatch's division and attack to seize Turner's Gap. Reno's and Hooker's corps are also attacking uphill on Rebel positions a quarter mile left and right. But your brigade will make this attack in the middle, up a steep mountain pass, all by yourself. My cavalry has made a probe, but we have no idea how many Rebel soldiers will oppose you. Despite all of that, the crest must be carried tonight." Gibbon asks himself, *Why would my former West Point classmate single out my brigade? He must trust me to comply. I am a career soldier. I will carry out the order.*

Captain Cutting yells to Haskell as a case shot from Battery B shatters part of a farm outbuilding, sending Rebel soldiers flying: "General Burnside says you western boys know how to fight! Now I can see it for myself!"

Haskell dutifully thanks the captain for the compliment, but he is worried, and says so: "These are just their skirmishers. I'm sure we're going to run into their main line pretty damn quick! There's a lot of woods and walls ahead for perfect cover and concealment. Colonel Meredith's men took some prisoners; they're Georgia troops, Colquitt's brigade, five regiments! So there's plenty of Rebs up there. And it's getting dark, hard to see. Who's behind us for support?"

Cutting shouts back, "Gorman's brigade of the Second Corps, I think."

Just then, heavy rifle fire explodes ahead as the skirmishers run back and the Seventh Wisconsin fires at Rebels behind a stone wall to their left. As the Seventh's right companies move up to get in an oblique fire, they are hit from the right and rear by a volley from a Confederate line hidden in the dark tree line. Soldiers in the Sixth watch in shock as they see about fifty men in the Seventh go down.

"Dammit!" yells Bragg.

From the Seventh up ahead, Captain Hollon Richardson runs back shouting, "Sixth! Come forward and help us!"

Immediately, Bragg's clear voice rings out, "Deploy column!"

Dawes gets his right wing on line in a field. On the right is the enemy in a tree line with rising ground. "Right wing, ready! Right oblique, aim, fire!" The loud volley cracks from some 150 rifles toward the muzzle flashes coming from the woods. "Right wing, lie down! Load at will, load!" Dawes shouts again.

His men comply, and over the top of them runs the left wing. Bragg gives his soldiers the same firing command. The two officers continue the leapfrog fire-and-load advance, two repetitions each, all the while being under severe fire front and side, taking casualties all the way. There is heavy firing on both sides of the road as all four of Gibbon's regiments are now in action, attacking Colquitt's Georgia troops in the growing darkness. Following an order from Gibbon, Bragg and Dawes struggle to move their men up the steep, rocky slope and into the trees to flank the Georgians. Shooting flares at close range in the dark, men shouting and cursing in the bedlam of battle. The Georgians pull back.

The firing dies down as ammunition is almost gone. The fifty rounds each man carried has been fired, and leftovers from the dead and wounded have been collected. Rifle barrels are hot and fouled with carbon. General Gibbon reports there is no ammunition resupply available: "Hold the position at the point of the bayonet." But the Rebels do not counterattack. They seem to break off in silent retreat over the pass, and Bragg orders three cheers for the Old Sixth, lustily shouted by the worn-out survivors of the regiment. Volunteer skirmishers probe ahead to be sure it is clear. They stumble over rocks, tree limbs, and bodies in the darkness.

All lie exhausted on the cold, rocky ground. Occasional shots ring out. Dead and wounded men in blue and gray lay scattered up and down the battlefield. Moans and groans and cries for water are heard in the darkness, and soldiers warily move low to the ground, searching them out. Canteens are empty, and several soldiers of the Sixth die thirsty. Dawes watches as Sergeant William Lawrence slips away in agony with a bullet in the gut. Dawes quickly scoots down the line looking for water for the doomed soldier. John Kellogg, Lawrence's company commander, is doing the same. It is fruitless, but Lawrence sees and tries to acknowledge their efforts for him despite his misery. Lawrence fades, his comrades cling helplessly to him, and as Dawes and Kellogg watch in grim silence, this brave Union soldier from the small Mississippi River town of De Soto gasps his last breath. Stretcher bearers finally climb up, find, collect, and carry the severely wounded downhill to the field hospital.

* * * * *

The evening fight on South Mountain has attracted high-level spectators. About a mile behind the fighting lines, Generals Burnside, Hooker, and McClellan watch from an open vantage point near the National Road as their Union troops battle up the slopes. Directly ahead and above them fight Gibbon's brigade, doggedly advancing against Colquitt's Southerners in the waning light and into darkness.

They witness a spectacular light show: the deadly Rebel gunfire volleys tracing like lightening in the sky, Wisconsin and Indiana rifles flashing in response, artillery shells arcing red-hot trails in both directions, exploding in red-and-yellow bursts, the crashes and booms echoing down to the valley below—and can that be the faint sound of cheers we are hearing in this cool night air? On clear display, the awesome fury of combat involving thousands of men carrying out their orders. Awe-inspiring. The generals cannot contain their enthusiasm, acknowledging with admiration the incredible bravery being displayed on this magnificent stage.

McClellan and Hooker have seen many units fight battles, most recently during the Peninsula Campaign. The fighting quality of these western soldiers has been mentioned after Second Manassas, but never witnessed. Now they have no doubt. These soldiers under General Gibbon are tough, tough as iron, and they say so. Newspaper reporters hear of the remarks and report them in glowing prose. Their readers gobble up copies to read about a rare Union victory. The name sticks. Nobody is sure of the exact conversation between the two generals, both tending to exaggerate (and the reporters even more so), but everyone is sure that Gibbon's brigade earned their name, forever after the "Iron Brigade," in the bloody darkness on the slopes of Turner's Gap, along both sides of the winding National Road, on a Sunday evening, September 14, 1862.

8:00 a.m., Monday, September 15, 1862—the Turner's Gap Mountain Slope

No relief came for the Sixth Wisconsin during the chilling cold of night. Lt. Col. Bragg had sent Adjutant Edward Brooks back to General Willis Gorman to hurry them up and offer himself as guide. Gorman refused, stating, "All soldiers are cowards in the night." He would not send his men forward till sunrise. At 8:00 a.m., daylight having shone on the shivering Wisconsin soldiers for almost two hours, Gorman sends the Second New York State Militia Regiment to take over. By that time, they are not needed. A company of the Sixth has already been sent to the top of the pass, securing it near the Mountain House traveler's lodge.[M] Some dead and wounded Confederate soldiers are discovered, but the Rebel main body has retreated down the other side of the mountain toward Boonesboro.

The eleven dead soldiers of the Sixth Wisconsin have been collected for burial in a shallow trench dug in the rocky ground at first light. Multiple bullet hits scar the nearby trees. Captain John Kellogg stands next to Major Rufus Dawes to observe the solemn scene. The distasteful promotion episode three months past has not been forgotten but now seems so petty, so insignificant after what each has seen and endured together since Brawner Farm. Friendship and respect between Kellogg and Dawes has been reestablished under the common bond of battlefield warriors.

Lieutenant John Ticknor joins them, and the three officers, all original members of Company K, stand respectfully to pay final homage to the fallen. Ticknor informs Dawes that his former company, sent forward early as skirmishers, have suffered two fatalities, with several seriously wounded. Short of stature but brave as they make them, George Chamberlin, the former circus boy, is laid to rest. His skirmish team of Corporal Frank Wilcox and Privates Ephraim Cornish and Mickey Sullivan are all lying wounded in the field hospital. Chamberlin is placed in the common grave near the body of Sergeant Lawrence.[9]

The second fatality is hard for Dawes and Ticknor to accept. Corporal Rueben Huntley, the thirty-eight-year-old former Necedah lumberman and constable, was killed in action on the slope and lays here now. Huntley's lifeless form is carefully placed next in line, and Kellogg speaks in a low voice: "I remember that night in Mauston when you singled out Corporal Huntley for being a family man. He's married to your distant cousin, as I recall. Last fall he asked me to write the state office for him, to get his wife some money from the Volunteer Aid Fund. I have this thought of her now, back in Wisconsin, not knowing her husband is gone, and her children no longer having a father. I'm sorry. He was a good soldier."[10]

Dawes responds, "His wife, Sarah Ann, and I have the same great-grandfather: William, the patriot who rode with Paul Revere. I met the family when I first came to Mauston, but we saw each other only on rare occasions. But I got to know Rueben well this past year. He was the first of us to see real action, remember? He volunteered for six months' temporary duty on that Mississippi River gunboat, part of the Island Number 10 victory in April."

[M] Today the "Old South Mountain Inn"

Ticknor adds, "I remember him talking about it after coming back in July. The gunboat USS *Cincinnati*. We were all so anxious to hear what a battle was like, especially as seen from a gunship. He wrote letters to his wife and boys, and sent money home whenever the paymaster would get around to finding us." Tough John Ticknor looks to Dawes with tears in his eyes. "I never saw better work on a skirmish line than old Huntley was doing, then I saw him fall. Emory Mitchell, his tentmate, saw him go down, too, like he was dead before he hit the ground, didn't make a sound. Mitchell found him this morning, and they brought him here for burial."

Dawes adds a final tribute: "He was a quiet and modest man but true as steel. He told me several times that it was his duty to be a soldier despite his age and being a father, and I never heard him utter one word of complaint about hardship or danger. I'm proud of this brave man. Proud of all these boys. They have given up everything for this cause."[11]

Kellogg thinks of his own family, his wife and three daughters at home. As the burial detail finishes and forms in line for Lieutenant Colonel Bragg's final words, Kellogg says, "At least Corporal Huntley leaves behind a legacy; he has children to carry on. These other boys here will never have that satisfaction."[N]

Dawes walks over and pats Captain David Noyes on the shoulder. His Company A has been hit hard: three men—George Miles, Jacob Langhart, and John Weidman—lie here in the trench. Twelve more have been wounded, some severely, including Privates Aldridge and Rice, who are in very bad shape. Noyes points to the body of Private Miles, a red stain on his breast. "I can't get over Miles. The boys came up to me yesterday afternoon and told me Miles was sure he was going to be killed, that he could not be talked out of it. Everybody liked him, including me. Great attitude, a fine soldier, the life of the company. I told him to stay behind with the wagons, but he refused. We began our advance up the mountain, and he was the first man shot. He fell and gasped out, 'Tell my father I did my duty,' then died." Noyes pauses. "I should have insisted. He wouldn't be lying here ..."

Dawes interrupts: "David, stop. There is no way you could know. He made the call, God bless him. It's not your fault." But when the casualty lists are printed in Baraboo, there will be anguish in the Miles home and throughout Sauk County.[12]

Time only for a brief prayer, then Dawes, Kellogg, and Noyes walk toward the road. Captain Ed Brown is seen sitting with his back against

---

[N] Someday a great-grandson will make a name for himself in news reporting, becoming prominent in a communication medium none on this battlefield can imagine. His name will be Chester "Chet" Huntley.

a boulder, head down and coughing into his folded arms. Dawes and Kellogg stop to talk with him, and Dawes puts a hand on his friend's forehead. Instantly, he feels the high fever. Kellogg looks on with shared concern, and they both recall the conversation they had with the shivering Brown last night on the cold mountain slope, urging him to go downhill to the surgeons and the hospital.

Said Brown that night, "You're right, I am too sick to be here, but I will not go away from the regiment." He paused at that point, looked at his two close friends, then said, "I can't seem to get over this notion that I'm going to get killed. It's a phantom fear, I know, and it would be a coward's way out if I left my company now. So, as long as I can stand, I will stick to my post."[13]

Now, fresh with the story of Private Miles in mind, Dawes addresses Captain Brown again: "Ed, you've got about as high a fever as I've ever felt. You need to get back and take care of yourself."

Brown responds, "Thanks, but I'll be fine. Nothing has changed since last night. I'll not leave the men." He is adamant.

Dawes and Kellogg reach the road as Lt. Col. Bragg is mounting his horse. Dawes decides to relate the situation to Bragg. Says Bragg, Brown's former law partner in Fond du Lac, "It sounds like Edwin. There's nobody with a keener sense of honor. Let me handle it," and he walks his horse toward Brown, who is rejoining his company.

As Dawes mounts his own horse, he overhears Bragg addressing Captain Brown: "Captain, you are not well enough to be at your post. I want you to get in an ambulance and ride, at least until your fever breaks, or we can get you to a hospital." As Brown starts to protest, Bragg cuts him off with, "That's an order, Captain!"

Brown, now having no choice, salutes, turns command of Company E to Lieutenant Marston, and slowly walks toward an ambulance wagon in the rear.

As Bragg and Dawes ride together, they receive the final casualty report from Adjutant Brooks. The regiment entered the fight last evening with four hundred men. In addition to the eleven killed in action, there are seventy-nine wounded and two missing, the last probably laying wounded in another unit's field hospital or possibly lying dead and unfound somewhere on the wooded slope. The ninety-two casualties equate to 23 percent of the regiment.

Gibbon's whole brigade has suffered 319 casualties, a rate of 25 percent, the worst hit being the Seventh Wisconsin, with 147. There are ten brigades in Hooker's First Corps, yet Gibbon's casualties account for over one-third of the total corps losses. The brigade's exceptional performance, this Iron Brigade, has earned praise and lasting tribute, but many western soldiers question why General Ambrose Burnside ordered them to assault Turner's Gap alone.

The brigade marches downhill on the road they had fought over last night. They pull over into a field to cook breakfast and make coffee, so badly needed since few slept that cold night on the line. But almost as soon as fires are started, word comes to "Advance back up the road and report to General Hooker at the Mountain House on top." Men moan with growling stomachs and sore bodies as their companies form in column to trudge back up the mountain, once more viewing the battle scene, once more thinking of last night's battle and of friends lost forever.

* * * * *

Union success in forcing open the mountain passes has made Lee's South Mountain defense line untenable. He orders Longstreet's units to retreat toward Sharpsburg along the upper Potomac River, and either await Jackson's arrival from Harpers Ferry or recross the river, thus abandoning the Maryland excursion. The course to be taken depends upon how quickly McClellan advances. If McClellan dallies, allowing scattered Confederate units to unite, Lee is confident his troops will once again defeat the attack he expects McClellan to eventually launch.

3:00 p.m., Monday, September 15, 1862—North of the Boonsboro Pike, East of Antietam Creek

Rufus Dawes is worn out. Last night spent on the cold slope of Turner's Gap without sleep after a hard fight and among the dead and wounded, then a march through Boonsboro chewing hardtack for breakfast. Our boys were buoyed up by the happy and cheering residents there, then a left turn onto the Sharpsburg Pike, through little Keedysville, and now to here. General Hooker ordered Gibbon's brigade to lead his corps this day, a place of honor, and it was accomplished without incident as cavalry screens in the advance gobbled up Rebel prisoners by the fifties, the sick, tired, and wounded stragglers from Lee's army.

As soon as the column tops the first ridge west of Keedysville, Rebel gunners near Sharpsburg spot them and fire. Their artillery shells fall short, and the Sixth keeps going for a while, then are directed off-road for cover behind a ridge. The hungry men of the Sixth break the fence rails for firewood. Coffee and sizzling salted pork are soon being cooked despite artillery rounds dropping or exploding close by, the Confederates firing blind, but the soldiers too hungry to care.

"Heah, sah," Billy says, "got some coffee fo yah. Look like yah be needin' it."

Dawes takes a sip, pauses, then takes some more. "My Lord, Billy, this is splendid! I don't know where you found this batch, but I hope it's not the last of it!"

Billy smiles. "Weall, sah, dat be mah secret."

Two artillery batteries come galloping up the pike, turn onto the ridge, and rapidly wheel into position. Within minutes they are booming away at the Rebel guns, a long-range artillery duel. Refreshed by the coffee, Dawes rides up the ridge for a better view. To the left, several thousand men of Richardson's division are being formed. In the distance, beyond the trees lining Antietam Creek, he can plainly see Rebel infantry formed in lines over the rolling fields and woodlots, extending for over a mile.

Toward evening, Hooker's corps is ordered to move north up the east side of Antietam Creek and go into bivouac. General Doubleday has now been moved up to command the four-brigade division, which includes the Sixth Wisconsin, as General Hatch was wounded last night at South Mountain. Doubleday is the third commander of the division in the past three weeks.

Rufus Dawes checks on Edwin Brown and finds him buried under a blanket in the ambulance. He nods approvingly, and with duties now done, enters the tent Billy has set up, eases himself onto his low folding cot, and, like the rest of the regiment's exhausted men, is soon asleep.

Tuesday, September 16, 1862

The day is spent in loud artillery duels, with thousands of soldiers like Rufus Dawes as spectators. There is a fine view from a hill behind their bivouac. McClellan dallies. Lee uses the time to hurriedly call in his dispersed units. He arranges his troops and positions artillery.

Finally, around four o'clock, Lt. Col. Bragg walks quickly to his second-in-command. "Major, let's get everyone moving. In column, over Antietam Creek with the rest of the brigade. The good news is we are not first in line for a change; that's to be the Pennsylvania Reserves in Meade's division. The bad news is they get the bridge while we get wet crossing at a ford."

Major Dawes sits on his mare in midstream as his Wisconsin troops gingerly wade in the waist-deep stream, holding cartridge boxes, haversacks, and rifles high enough to keep them dry. As he responds to greetings and banter from the young soldiers, he thinks, *The morning report lists almost three hundred men present for duty. We had twice that number a month ago.*

Meade's troops are already up ahead with some cavalry, moving slowly toward an enemy they know is out there somewhere in the countryside. Once across, the movement becomes the familiar start-stop-wait-start-again process. This westerly hike goes on for over a mile across the gently rolling farmland and woodlots, passing occasional homes and barns. Supply wagons have been slowed on the clogged roads, and haversacks are nearly void of rations. As orchards are passed, the men quickly pick apples and peaches to replenish.

About dusk, sharp rifle fire erupts to the left. As Dawes rides next to the column, someone makes a loud comment: "Sounds like the Reserves done woke the animals up!" The overcast sky hastens the darkness. Visibility is near zero when, at nine o'clock, a staff officer informs Lt. Col. Bragg to stop. "Sir, hunker your men down for the night right here. No fires, no noise, keep rifles ready. There's another brigade to the south on picket. Orders for tomorrow will be coming." The young officer is unfamiliar with the topography, can't see much beyond his own hand, and is troubled with uncertainty. A mistake is made. It will not be discovered until dawn.

Lt. Col. Bragg and Major Dawes struggle in the darkness to arrange their men in columns by division, a series of two-company lines parallel with the nearby Hagerstown Pike. The post-and-rail fences bordering the road are dimly visible to their right. Anyone desiring to travel the road straight south toward the tidy town of Sharpsburg would soon pass through Union pickets and then be rudely introduced to Stonewall Jackson's troops, the old foe from Brawner Farm.

Lieutenant Joe Marston slowly walks along the twenty-eight men of his depleted Company E, all lying prone on rubber blankets or shelter halves, quietly arranging themselves for the night. A figure slowly approaches in the darkness, using what looks to be a sheathed sword to feel his way. Closer now ... then, "Captain Brown, what are you doing here? I thought Colonel Bragg told you find a hospital." Several men in the company overhear and prop themselves on elbows to see their captain back among them.

"I'm fine, Lieutenant. Don't worry about it. The rest in the ambulance did wonders."

Brown's response is not convincing to Marston. He clearly sees the gaunt outlines of Brown's face in the dimness. "Sir, I can handle this. I don't think you're—"

Brown cuts him off: "I said I'm fine, Joe. I'll not hide in the rear while my company goes into action, that's for damn sure! So that's it. I'll share this blanket if you let me share your ground cover."

Brown knows he should not be here—he is still under orders not to be here—but he will not let his men go forward without him. He thinks of his family and tries to suppress the dark phantom.

Around midnight, the unmerciful clouds produce a persistent drizzle and fog. There can be no warming fires, no candles to light the drafting of a last message or to read a letter from home. Soaked to the skin, they try to sleep, knowing what the morning will bring.

Two columns away, near the flags designating regimental head-quarters, Major Rufus Dawes suddenly realizes that tomorrow's date is September 17. It has become a peculiar triennial milestone in his life. Six years previous, he first left Ohio for Wisconsin. Three years previous, after "one glorious year in Marietta," he found himself "again bound for the west," wondering at that time where he would be in another three years. Here he is. In a Maryland farm field, surrounded by soldiers as nervous and miserable as he, on a wet and dreary night, dreading the pending summons to combat.

Brigade adjutant Frank Haskell finds Lt. Col. Bragg near the flags as the rain comes down a little harder. "Sir, General Gibbon just received orders from General Doubleday. Our brigade will spearhead tomorrow's attack for the First Corps. Colonel Phelps's brigade will follow us. The advance will be south along this side of the Hagerstown Pike. Your regiment will lead the way, the Second Wisconsin will be on your left, and the Seventh and Nineteenth in support behind you. Ricketts's division is to move forward also on our left. Expect to move forward at first light."

Bragg nods in grim acknowledgement. Turning to Major Dawes, Bragg makes a caustic comment: "I'm sure our General Doubleday presented it this way ... General Gibbon, you will be pleased to have the honor of leading our whole army in this glorious attack against the foe. God be with you!"

Dawes cannot help but grin and shake his head. Leave it to Bragg to cut the tension with sarcasm. Still, the prospects of surviving tomorrow are dim. Bragg and Dawes both know it. It is a long, solemn, damp, and dismal night.

Dim Light of First Dawn, Wednesday, September 17, 1862°

Major Rufus Dawes is stirred awake by the sound of a galloping horse and shouted orders: "Get these men moving now! You are in open range of the enemy batteries!" General Doubleday is dashing on horseback along the roadside fence, aides following. Bragg and Dawes quickly rise to their feet and start giving orders. The men are wet and groggy. It takes shouts, kicks, and shaking to get them up and moving. The mistake made unknowingly last night is now obvious: They were positioned on the wrong side of a hill—the side facing Confederate artillery posted on high ground to the west. They are a big target.

Bragg knows he must get the men out of there, and he shouts orders to realign the two-company "columns of divisions" so that they are facing south in five successive lines, the right end of each line near the fence line of the road. Behind the Sixth, Lt. Col. Tom Allen of the Second Wisconsin is doing the same.

Dim sunlight streaming through the foggy patches has now made it quite light. The massed regiment moves forward, travels maybe 15 yards, and then -Whizzz ... BANG-! An artillery shell explodes overhead. Then another and another! Then -BLAM!- A percussion shell explodes in the moving mass of Wisconsin soldiers. Major Dawes, riding on his horse in front of the last line, witnesses the instant carnage just in front of him. He feels the concussive blast and sees Captain David Noyes on the ground screaming, his right foot torn off. His Company A is decimated once more. Two men are instantly killed; eleven others are blown down with ugly shrapnel wounds. That's Private Young with both arms in shreds!

"Keep moving! Keep moving!" shouts Bragg and Dawes as the following lines step around the ghastly scene. They both understand the need to get out of the artillery bracket. Dawes looks back to see litter bearers from the rear sprint forward to pick up the pieces. *My God, what a beginning! Thirteen men out of action in one shot!* The regiment quickly moves across the field and into a strip of woods, passing through a line of troops from the Pennsylvania Reserves among the trees who have manned the front line all night. From this point on, it will be all enemy.

In the woods, Bragg and Dawes dismount. Billy Jackson is there, withstanding the shelling as well as the veterans, and takes the horses back north, out of the fight. Bragg orders the regiment into a line of battle and sends Companies C and I, under Captains Hooe and Kellogg, forward as skirmishers. The Second Wisconsin moves in next to them

---

° See action map, 0600-0730 hours, at end of chapter.

on the left. Solid shot and shells are shrieking in the air going both directions, some smashing into the tree limbs above them. As soon as the skirmishers reach the south edge of the woods, Rebels sheltered ahead among farm buildings and orchards open fire. Rounds whizz by and smack into trees. With a shout, the skirmishers make a dash across the green field, which slopes down to the right toward the road. Kellogg quickly leads his company up the slope to the left, flanking the Rebel skirmishers, shooting some down and pushing the rest farther south as the main battle line moves forward to follow. Captain Hooe's company lags behind, and Bragg shouts, "Move forward that skirmish line on the right!"

Their axis of advance and the roadway converge a bit, causing the right wing, led by Lt. Col. Bragg, to merge against the fence. Dawes has his own problem on the left. They come up to the farm buildings and a large garden bordered by a picket fence, too tall to jump over. Dawes shouts, "Everybody, pick up that fence and knock it over, all at once now!"

The men try, but it is sturdily built and will not budge.

"By the left of companies, through the gate, double-quick!" Company E is on the left. As Dawes watches and shouts for everybody to hurry through, he spots a familiar figure. That's Ed Brown by the gate! Looking on, he sees Brown wave his sword and urge and push his men through the small opening. Suddenly, -zzipp!- A bullet shoots into his open mouth and pierces out the back of his neck. Dawes watches in shock and horror as he sees his best friend instantly fall backward to the ground, killed before his eyes. The deadly phantom that Captain Edwin Brown has stubbornly resisted with courageous sense of duty has ruthlessly struck him down. Dawes is frozen, emotion rising in his throat. His impulse is to run to Edwin, to his close friend. His mind tells him, *No, I can't! Snap out of it! We've got to keep moving!*

The crashing booms of opposing cannon fire is tremendous, and the air above is filled with shrieking shells going in both directions. Explosions and air bursts are all around. The left-wing companies rush through the garden, smashing plants and vines and flower beds, and confront the picket fence on the far side. The posts are not as strong, or the adrenaline is flowing faster; the men knock it over and keep going, into a peach orchard left of the farmhouse. Dawes runs through the low branches to a rail fence on the far side. A bullet hits a fence post and ricochets past his head with a screeching whine. His men come up and fire at the Rebel skirmishers ahead, dropping a couple before the Rebs disappear into a cornfield on rising ground 100 yards away, the green stalks standing thick and tall. His men are now even with the right wing, but the Second Wisconsin is not yet up on the left.

Bragg yells across to Dawes, "Move forward into the corn!" He is not waiting.

Dawes gives the order. The skirmishers rejoin the regiment as they advance in line up the sloping green field toward the Rebels in the cornfield. Bragg's right wing lacks the room. The three right companies, Kellogg's Company I now one of them, are crowded onto the turnpike itself, having rushed through the farm access openings in the fence line. The road is a shooting gallery, and Bragg runs over, ordering the company commanders to move their men into a field just right of the road. Dawes looks that way and spots the regiment's color guard, with the national and state flags flying, in position near the roadway fence. The whole line moves forward, most of the regiment now entering a corn maze taller than the soldiers. The sea of green leaves restricts sight distance, and everyone expects a sudden flashing volley to erupt on them at any moment.

The line steadily continues to the middle of the cornfield, the high point, where the ground starts to gradually slope south. There is nobody to their left. Dawes is thinking, *We have come up too fast. The Second Wisconsin is still behind us. I don't want to get shot at from behind by our own men!* Just then, sharp firing breaks out on the right. Through the din of the artillery and small-arms fire, Dawes hears shouting and curses in that direction.

Confederate infantry in the woods to the right have unleashed a volley uphill into the flank of the three right companies. Dawes can't see it happening through the green stalks, but, sensing trouble, he orders his wing to lie down. A man comes running up through the corn. "Major Dawes, Colonel Bragg wants to see you quick, at the turnpike."

Green stalks smack his face as Dawes runs to the fence. He sees Bragg, who turns to him and in a strained voice shouts, "Major, take command, I'm wounded," then falls to the ground.

Dawes sees a tear in Bragg's coat. *God! He's shot in the body!* "You two men, get a shelter tent and carry the colonel to the rear!"

The three right companies are in line behind the rail fence on the far side, facing west and firing at the Rebels in the woods. They are taking casualties from return fire. As his commander and friend is being carried away, Dawes realizes what just happened: Bragg must have ordered the change of front after being hit in that first volley. He stayed on his feet until he was sure his regiment had a proper alignment to meet the new threat.

Dawes also realizes he is now in command, tasked with leading the point of attack amid the growing bedlam. And the fight has just started! He feels a huge weight of responsibility. It is terrifying. His mind races with multiple thoughts: *What do I do now? I don't want to make a mistake! … Calm down! We are out in front of everybody. Stay put and wait a bit for the support to come up. Then we can move out together.*

"Keep firing!" Dawes shouts as he stands near the turnpike fence, scanning ahead through the smoke. "Give me your rifle!" he yells at a soldier. He lays it on a fence rail and fires at a cluster of mounted Confederate officers he noticed maybe a couple hundred yards away. Other soldiers get in the act. Their commander is on the firing line! Loaded weapons are handed to Dawes, and he fires six shots in succession. "Did you drop any, Colonel?" a man asks. "I can't tell, but they sure did skedaddle!" Dawes shouts back.

He tries to keep watch on both wings. Confederate bullets are zipping through the corn stalks, hitting the fence, smacking with muddy spouts into the plowed furrows of the field. Rebel artillery is screaming in from the front. Union artillery is firing in response from behind, and some rounds are falling short. An air burst nearby shoots shrapnel in all directions. One jagged piece strikes Lieutenant Bode of Company F in the head. He is killed instantly. Minutes later, an exploding shell wounds another friend, John Ticknor. As Ticknor is taken to the rear, bleeding and seriously hurt, Dawes angrily realizes that the artillery bursts are coming from the rear! Nothing is worse than being fired on by your own people!

More troops in blue are coming on line to the left! "Yes!" Dawes shouts as he spots Lt. Col. Allen just behind the first line of the Raggedy-Ass Second, one arm in a sling, the other with a sword pointing forward. Allen is manifestly the man in charge. Dawes sees Allen waving his sword, motioning for the Sixth to join his line. Dawes yells out the order: "Attention, battalion! Forward guide left, march!" They stride through the corn again, alert to anything coming into their restricted view, heading on a slight left oblique to keep in touch with the Second Wisconsin.

Sergeant Major Howard Huntington is nearby. Dawes grabs his arm, points toward the pike, and shouts in his ear, "Tell Captain Plummer that if it's practicable, to move the right companies in line with the left wing." After a few minutes, Huntington returns and shouts, "Captain Kellogg is in command and desired me to give Major Dawes his compliments and say that it is impracticable—that the fire is murderous!"

" 'Compliments'!?" *That sounds like John: cool under fire no matter what, taking charge. All right, then, but we are getting separated.*

The Sixth Wisconsin line keeps advancing, and a second blue line is close behind. That's Colonel Phelps's small brigade of New York troops. They were shot up at Second Manassas and South Mountain and now have only about 425 men left—regiments the size of companies. But Phelps has two companies of green-uniformed men of the Second US Sharpshooters, both recruited from Vermont. They are armed with .52-caliber breech-loading Sharps rifles, and Phelps splits them off from his own line to plug the gap near the turnpike fence.[14]

Dawes can't see the sharpshooters, though, and he's still concerned about Kellogg and the three isolated companies on the right. They must be under a hot fire, and he's thinking, *it would be good to have John with me now.* "Sergeant Major, go back to Captain Kellogg again, and tell him he can get cover in the corn and to move forward and join us, if it is possible."

Huntington takes off again and is quickly lost in the stalks and gun smoke. As Huntington runs toward Kellogg, a spent bullet hits him and knocks him down. Grunting with pain but realizing he's not hurt too badly, the sergeant major moves out again and finds Kellogg hunkered down behind the fence, the seventy-five or so men with him firing away, laying on their bellies or kneeling behind the posts for cover and better aim. They are in a tough spot, with fire coming from the woods to the west and down the road from the south. Wood rails are constantly taking splintering hits, and bullets are kicking up stones in the road behind them.

Grimacing with pain, sweating profusely, and panting, Huntington yells over the gunfire, "Major Dawes says you could move into the corn for better cover and to join our line!"

Kellogg looks at him incredulously, thinking, *I just told him the fire is murderous! But he's in command, so ...* "Right wing! In line, cross the road and through the fence into the corn. March!" The men look at him wide-eyed, then rise to a crouch and start to run to the other side of the road. Instantly, at least seven of them are shot down in their tracks by fire coming from two directions.

"Get back! Get back behind the fence!" cries Kellogg. He crawls over to one of his wounded men and pulls him over to the rail fence, the young soldier in bad shape, shot in the back. Several others lay in the road, not moving. "God dammit! I told him so!"

Dawes can't see the disaster at the turnpike. His command is approaching the end of the cornfield. A low rail fence at the edge comes into view, and as the two-rank line ahead of him reaches it, they finally see the enemy line of battle. A long row of dirt-colored Rebel soldiers rises from behind a low line of jumbled fence rails. In unison, they raise their rifles. At the same moment, Wisconsin company commanders shout, "Fire by file! Fire!" The opposing soldiers blast at each other simultaneously.

Bullets slam into Wisconsin soldiers just in front of Major Dawes. Men get knocked backward and go down by the dozens. But the survivors are as mad as hell! The rear rank men close the gaps. The hundred or so red-legs of Brooklyn from the line behind run up and fire into the Reb line, too, and the whole mass goes crazy. "Let's go! After them, God dammit to hell! Charge!" Wisconsin and New York boys are mixed together, angry and wild, shooting through the gun smoke into the gray line, loading as fast as they can on the run, flags swinging back and forth, no parade ground now, just a ragged throng of pissed-off soldiers caring for nothing but to take those bastards in front of them! Dawes and the other officers and non-coms are yelling encouragement the men can't hear. The soldiers are shooting and loading furiously with total disregard for personal safety until they are hit, then they slump to the ground in death or in pain, the latter looking helplessly for assistance or staggering back toward the cornfield. The blue mass slowly dwindles under the Rebel fire and, by some common impulse, falls back to the low fence, hits the dirt, and keeps firing while trying to keep themselves as small as possible.

A new rifle volley erupts to the right, and the men hear three cheers—Union cheers! There is help coming in over there! "Bully for the right! Up and at them again! Let's go!" Dawes yells. "Forward, men, forward!" The ragged line moves out again, screaming and laughing and shooting. He can't see it happen, but Kellogg now seizes this moment to move his fence-line survivors up in line on the right.

The decimated Confederate soldiers in front of them can't take it any longer. They break for the rear. It is a long way to safety in the woods by the little white church to the south, probably 500 yards. The woods to the west are closer, and scores of them run in that direction. But the post-and-rail turnpike fences are in the way. They are tall and sturdy, and both must be climbed to reach the trees. The retreating Rebel soldiers are easy prey as they clamber up five rails and over, cross the road, and try to do it again. Many never make it, shot in the act, falling forward or backward all along the fence line.

Dawes sees Captain Converse nearby leading his men, all fight in every fiber of his being. One of his soldiers gets hit. The man stumbles and turns to Converse, a look of shock and fear on his black-smeared face: "Captain, I'm killed!" Converse can't help him now and yells back, "Well, get to the rear, then, if you can!" Then he continues to urge his company forward. The captain takes a few steps, then -THUNK!- A bullet bores through both legs. Dawes sees him spin, hears him shout, "Dammit! Hyatt, take charge, I'm shot!" He hobbles to the rear himself. Such is happening all up and down the line as Major Dawes runs right and left, shouting for his men to keep up their fire and advance, all amidst the incredible noise and roar of battle.

Half way across the field, they steadily move forward shooting and yelling, the little white church visible in front, running over downed Rebels, a couple of enemy battle flags picked up, victory in their grasp. *We are winning!* Dawes and his dwindling survivors are ecstatic, but they are running out of steam. The rifles barrels are becoming fouled with black powder residue. Cartridges boxes are near empty. *Where is our help? Where is the Second and Twelfth Corps? We need them here right now ... We could run the enemy into the Potomac River!*

Then Dawes sees a new line of Confederates emerge from the distant woods at double time on both sides of the road, at least ten battle flags flying, heading straight for them. The Wisconsin and New York soldiers see it too. They no longer resemble a solid line of battle. Their irregular line is now broken into squad-size groups because of all the casualties. Dawes at once realizes, *We do not have enough shooters left to take on this new force!* His men fire off a weak volley, then frantically try to reload. It is taking too long! Persistent, hard pounding on ramrods is required to push the cartridges down dirty gun barrels. Frustrated soldiers are trying to hurry, nervous fingers putting percussion caps on rifle nipples now, but feeling a gut-wrenching sensation of disaster, of impending death. Fear quickly replaces the thrill of victory.

At the 150-yard range, the gray line halts, raise their rifles, and -BLAM-! Their volley cuts down black-hat and red-leg Union soldiers all along the line like a scythe going through grain.

The survivors, including Major Rufus Dawes, know they cannot survive another volley, much less stop this assault. *We are going to die if we don't get the hell out of here!* "Battalion! Retreat!" he yells. There is no other choice, but some of the men do not want to give up the ground. Tomlinson of Company B turns around with a look of total disappointment and yells at Dawes, "God! You ain't going back, are you!?" But they do go back—in a hurry and in disorder. It's save who can! *Ouch!* A sting on his leg, like a strike from father's hickory stick, shocks Dawes into running even faster. Over the low fence, into the corn, downhill through the trampled stalks, over dead bodies in blue and gray, and out the north end. Behind them, the Rebel yell is keeping pace. Fear of death has taken over every thought..

Into the low field now, the farm buildings and orchard ahead, where Edwin Brown lies dead, killed a half hour ago. *Am I going to run over his body like a coward?* The thought is instantly repugnant. *I would rather die! We will not be routed! Not my men! Not Wisconsin soldiers!*

A soldier runs near, carrying the blue Wisconsin state flag. Dawes yanks it away from the man and starts to wave it crazily back and forth, using it as a staff to stop the herd of running soldiers, calling on them to face the enemy. "Attention! Attention, men! Rally on the flag! Rally on your flag! Wisconsin soldiers, get back in line! Rally here on me! Wisconsin men, follow me!"

Surviving officers and non-coms hear the orders, more like frantic pleas, from their commander. When they hear "Wisconsin soldiers" and "Rally on your flag," it hits home. *We are better than this! We will not shame the name of our regiment, of our brigade, earned so dearly by our comrades in the past month of fighting.* They grab their men, any men, all struggling with the churning inner conflict—fear of dying versus duty and honor.

Scared soldiers wearing black hats remember who they are. They will not allow themselves to be consumed by fear. They stop, they pull their friends back to join them, they load their rifles, they stand fast behind the brave leader who is waving their state's flag. These survivors of the Sixth and of the Second Wisconsin, maybe two hundred in total, the pride of the west, will continue the fight! *We are not running back any farther! We will do our duty.*

From uphill along the turnpike fence line, General John Gibbon looks behind him to the north and spots a group of Union soldiers forming around a waving blue flag. He is looking for help, and this is the only help he can see. He runs down the road shouting at the officer waving the flag, recounting in his mind what has just transpired around him in the past twenty minutes:

To support the Second and Sixth Wisconsin men fighting in the cornfield, he had ordered a two-cannon section from Battery B into position in a field 30 yards west of the turnpike, across the road from the cornfield hillcrest and in front of several big straw stacks. Lieutenant James Stewart's two guns blasted rounds at the Confederate troops, did a lot of damage, and helped to finally relieve Captain Kellogg's three companies trapped along the turnpike fence. They paid a high price: Fourteen men in the two-gun section were shot down in ten minutes of action.

Captain Joseph Campbell brought up with the battery's other four cannons, going into line to Stewart's left, the left-most piece planted on the road. All six guns fired at Rebel batteries in the distant field near a small white church, then at the retreating gray infantry. But then, on came the Rebel onslaught that had blown back the Union troops, now all gone in retreat through the bloody cornfield.

The front line at this moment is here, at Battery B, and whooping Confederate infantrymen are after them. Men and horses go down as gray troops rush and shoot their way into the south end of the cornfield less than 100 yards away. Campbell orders canister rounds to blast them, then he is shot through the shoulder and goes down. Lt. Stewart takes command of the battery amidst the horrendous chaos—cannons blasting, roar of musketry, horses screaming, rearing, and falling, sergeants shouting orders to cannoneers, men all around crying out in pain as they are hit.

Gibbon witnesses this disaster unfold as bullets constantly whizz by. He is mounted in the turnpike, centered on his command, just as he had positioned himself on the National Road three days before at South Mountain. But his artilleryman's eye sees the left-most piece being aimed too high. He screams at the men, but they cannot hear him. Dismounting, he runs behind the twelve-pounder Napoleon, turns the elevating screw up to lower the muzzle, aims at the roadway in front of the corn stalks, and yells "Fire!" -BOOM-! The canister round blows away fence rails, corn stalks, and Confederate soldiers in a cloud of smoke, mud, and dust.

Stewart's men are working frantically amid the carnage, low crawling to bring rounds from limbers to loaders, loaders and cannoneers bending down or on their knees in a pitiful effort to avoid the hail of bullets. The stubborn foe in gray is still picking them off. Gibbon has seen at least twenty more men go down. His worst fear seems imminent: *The guns, the guns of my old battery, the battery I commanded less than five months ago, to be lost to the enemy!* It would be the most shameful disaster to befall any artilleryman. Death itself would at least be honorable.

Major Rufus Dawes is heartened; soldiers from both regiments have rallied around him. *But half our men must be down. Where is Colonel Allen?* Then he hears "Major Dawes, Major Dawes!" He looks toward the road to see General John Gibbon running toward him, face grimed with black gunpowder, sword dangling crazily, yelling in desperation, "Major, move your men over if you can, and let's save these guns!" He points uphill to Battery B on the other side of the road, a smoking, fiery cauldron. "If you can" does not sound like Gibbon. *He must understand what we have already gone through—and what he is now ordering us to do.*

Dawes does not hesitate. "Right face! Forward march!" he shouts to his makeshift command. He runs uphill toward the road, the fences, and the field beyond, still carrying the state flag, Wisconsin soldiers following. Gibbon is next to him, all excitement, shouting up to his old battery even though they cannot possibly hear him, "Here comes the Sixth, boys! By God, they won't have these guns!"

Rebel infantry have come down through the shattered cornfield on the left, and they open fire on these moving blue targets. Dawes looks back to see several men go down, then his wood flagstaff takes a bullet strike between his hands. A second later, another sharp sting snaps at his leg. More bullets cut through the linen, constantly tugging the staff in his grip. The realization hits him: *Our color guard has already been decimated carrying the flags. I can't possibly survive this. I am going to die here!*

As he runs up toward the booming cannon of Battery B and the crashing gunfire ahead, his mind is instantly filled with burning thoughts and emotions triggered by the presence of death. Flashing before him, he sees his mother and Lucy and Kate and Jane at the Old Stone House, his brother Henry's confident laugh, brother Eph in clodhopper clothes, grandfather Ephraim, Uncle William, Aunt Julia, Vilas, Condit, Greenwood, and all the college friends, Brown, Bragg ... his life in panorama. But the most burning emotion is a tremendous feeling of sadness— love unrealized, killed before it had a chance to bloom. *Mary! Mary! My only love, Mary!*

A ragged cheer from sweating and grimy survivors of Battery B brings him out of his thoughts. They are at the battered battery, the enemy just ahead. He sees Rebel soldiers pop up, shoot, then drop down for cover to reload. His men fire back whenever they see a gray form at the top of the hill through the smoke. Dawes recklessly runs forward waving the flag through the feverishly working gun crews, over a body lying between two cannons, the noise and bedlam incredible! He is shouting at his men now, almost crazed with thoughts of death and duty, "This is it, men! Save these guns! They will *not* take them!"

Then, -BOOM!- Cannoneers working the gun just 10 feet to the right pull the lanyard and fire. The double-charge canister explosion rocks the heavy Napoleon back on its trail. The tremendous crash stuns him, he feels the heat flash, and choking white smoke envelops him. *There is no sound! I see explosions, men shouting, men shooting all around. But there's no sound!* He goes down on a knee, holding the flag staff to steady himself, mouth opening and closing. Then ... a great ringing noise. He is thinking, *Stupid! I got too close! Stupid! I can't hear!*

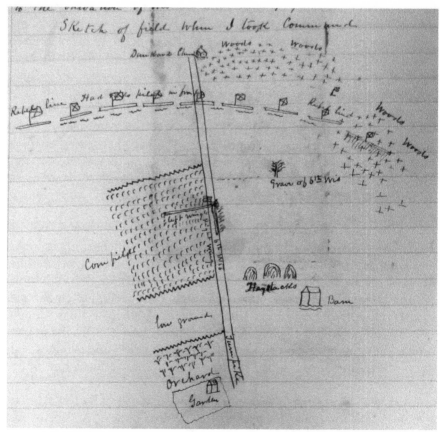

"Sketch of field when I took Command" by Major Rufus Dawes[15]
(North is to the bottom)
Dunkard Church
Rebel line had rails piled in front
Left Wing—Position of the 6th Wisconsin—US and State flags—Right Wing
Cornfield—Grave of 6th Wis Woods
Haystacks—Barn (D.R. Miller farm)
Low ground—Orchard—Garden—Farmhouse—Turnpike

He comes up dazed, sees a line of Union blue, stars and stripes fly-ing in the center. They are charging uphill from the trees to the right, cheering and firing at the Confederates behind the fence at the corn-field. "Hurrah!" *They are Black Hats! Must be the Nineteenth Indiana or Seventh Wisconsin, driving into the enemy flank, shooting them down, chasing the rest away from us. God bless them!* Dawes shouts in jubilation but cannot hear himself or anything else. There is only loud ringing and the sensation of shaking hands as he loosens his tight grip on the dam-aged flag staff. He realizes that somehow, he is still alive.

9:00 a.m.—in the North Woods, North End of Miller Farm

His ears are still ringing, but now he can at least hear the words and shouts being uttered around him. His survivors and Battery B have been ordered out of the fight to the relative shelter of the North Woods, which they had passed through in early morning.[16] Bank's former corps of two divisions, about seven thousand men, many in brand-new regiments and now designated the Twelfth Corps, have been battling in the same dese-crated cornfield, woods, and farmlands over which Hooker's First Corps and the Gibbon's Iron Brigade had fought from dawn to 7:30 a.m. The Twelfth is led by fifty-eight-year-old General Joseph Mansfield, a career officer with no recent combat experience. Mansfield is killed early, but his troops drive the Confederates back toward the Dunkard Church, where they stop, exhausted and depleted, short on ammunition. Sumner's Second Corps is now attacking in a third wave, with Sedgewick's divi-sion moving into action. It is another in a series of piecemeal attacks that allow Lee to scramble enough troops to hang on and counterattack through the smoke and woodlots. Sedgwick is wounded, his division ambushed in the West Woods and routed, and fighting north of Dunker Church ends in stalemate. The seesaw fighting strews thousands of dead or wounded soldiers on bloody fields.

The roaring sound of that battle is being heard to the south. Major Rufus Dawes is the only field officer remaining in what is left of the Iron Brigade, perhaps 400 here with him out of 1,100 who entered battle at dawn. Junior officers and sergeants are taking head counts to see who is missing. It has been a bloodbath.

"Major Dawes!" Captain Kellogg, striding purposefully toward Dawes, is almost shouting to be heard over the cannon and musketry noise. He approaches Dawes, dismisses military courtesy now that he is close enough that nobody else will hear him, and says, "Rufus, why did you order us away from the fence that second time!? I had already told you that the fire was murderous, that we could not do it!"

Kellogg's forcefulness takes Dawes by surprise. "What? What are you talking about?"

"Huntington came up that second time and gave me your order to move into the cornfield! We tried, and at least seven of our men were instantly shot down in the road. Damn, Rufus! I had told you before that we couldn't do it!" Kellogg cannot hide his anger.

"No! No, that's not what I told him. I told him you should move 'if it was possible'—I meant that you be the judge. I know what I said. He must have misunderstood!" Dawes is stunned. "God, I'm sorry, but that's not what I meant." But he knows it is too late for "sorry"; the men are dead or badly wounded, and the damage cannot be mended. It was one of his first orders upon taking command, and it resulted in disaster. Dawes turns to look toward the battle and thinks of it. *I should not have sent Huntington that second time. It's my fault. It's my responsibility.*

Kellogg can see the shock and sadness in his friend's face. He lets out a breath, recalls that Huntington had been hit just before making it through the hail of bullets to reach him. Kellogg thinks: *The pain, the stress ... The sergeant major could have misunderstood or made an error. Who could blame him?* "All right, Rufus, all right. I think I see what happened. It was a mistake. In all the noise and confusion ... I could have refused the order, but I didn't. There's nothing to do about it now. It's been a horrible day for everyone. We've both seen too many good men go down this morning. Edwin ... Bachelle ..." He pauses, then adds, "We did the best we could."

They have no time now to contemplate their actions as Lt. Hildreth of General Gibbon's staff rides up. "Sir," he says, addressing Dawes, "General Gibbon instructs you to move the brigade farther to the rear, north of the farm, where we bivouacked last night."

Dawes passes the order to the three captains now in charge of their regiments: Ely of the Second Wisconsin, Callis of the Seventh Wisconsin, and Dudley of the Nineteenth Indiana, who tells Dawes that Lt. Col. Al Bachman is killed. The depleted command moves north, behind a row of artillery batteries. Just as they are settling into the field, about noon but seemingly much later, an officer walks toward them from the north. "Colonel Bragg!" is shouted by a host of soldiers as they recognize their commander joining them, left arm in a sling.

"It's great to see you, old friend, sir!" Dawes exclaims as the two shake hands. "We thought you were ..."

Bragg finishes the sentence: "Dead or dying? Well, not yet. Not yet. No, the Reb marksmanship needs some improvement, apparently. They clipped me in the arm. It bled a lot but didn't hit a bone. Hurts like hell, though. I couldn't take the butchery at the field hospital, had to get away, and here you come, back where we started." Pointing toward the hillside, Bragg adds, "I think that's where we slept together last night, Rufus." Bragg becomes quiet, though, as he scans the pitiful remnant of his regiment and brigade.

Dawes shakes his head and almost grins for the first time today. Bragg's sarcasm has eased the mood once again, at least temporarily. *It is good to have him back. It is amazing to see him alive and walking, and it is amazing that I am alive and walking. I saw Edwin shot down, and so many others. Why them and not me? Why am I still alive?*

General McClellan's hesitation to attack the scattered Confederate army on the 16th proves costly. Robert E. Lee and his outnumbered troops fight desperately on the 17th to somehow withstand the morning Union onslaughts on their left flank. Timely troop movements orchestrated by Stonewall Jackson, and the toughness of their soldiers, save them—but at great cost. The Union army is fought to a draw here, and the blame rests with George McClellan. His piecemeal, poorly coordinated attacks doom the brave efforts of his troops by allowing the Confederates time to react. The three Union corps that took turns attacking Lee's left flank contained a combined force of more than 43,000 men. Stonewall Jackson controlled about one-fourth that number. McClellan also had 38,500 infantrymen available on other parts of the field. Had these forces been aggressively committed in support of each other at the same time, it is probable that Lee's army would have been driven to the Potomac River and crushed.[17]

These high-level mistakes are not yet clear to Rufus Dawes and the Iron Brigade as the long day nears an end. They have nobly followed orders and fought heroically but have been decimated in the rolling killing fields along the Hagerstown Pike. The exhausted survivors simply know that many friends are missing from their ranks. The Sixth Wisconsin took 286 men into battle this morning; 152 have been killed or wounded. The other three Iron Brigade regiments lose almost 200 more, bringing the total brigade loss to over 30 percent. Four brutal battles in the past three weeks have devastated the proud western unit. And Rebel soldiers are still out there.

Twelve-Pounder Napoleon Cannon, Limber, and Caissons at Antietam National Battlefield Park.
Dunker Church is in the background.
Battery B, Fourth US Artillery, fought with six such Napoleons 1,000 yards north of this location.

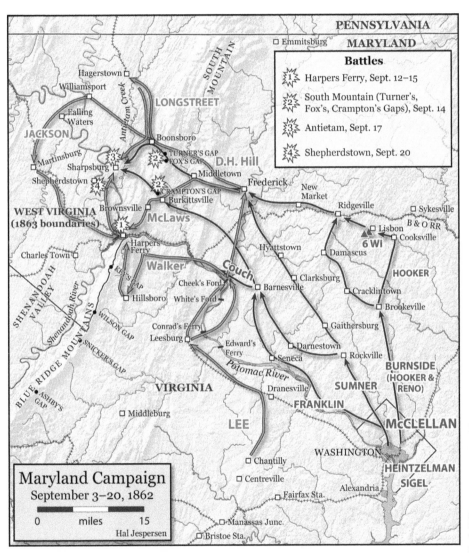

Maryland Campaign, September 1862.

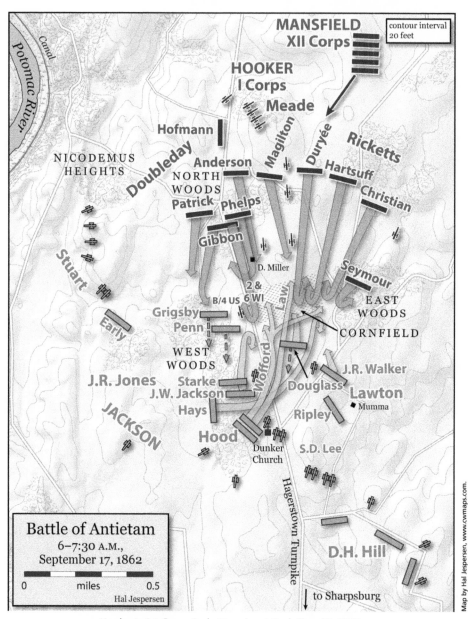

Hooker's 1st Corps Early Morning Attack Sep. 17, 1862

View looking south from the North Woods toward the D. R. Miller farmhouse and barn. The Sixth Wisconsin advanced under fire toward the farm at 6:00 a.m., Sep. 17, 1862.

Georgians of Lawton's brigade exchanged fire here with the Sixth Wisconsin as the Black Hats emerged from the cornfield.

View north up Hagerstown Pike from Battery B's position. Miller barn is left of road; farmhouse and cornfield on right. Major Rufus Dawes rallied Wisconsin survivors and led them up the road with General Gibbon to save the guns from capture by Confederates of Hood's division.

South front of the D. R. Miller farmhouse after the battle. Major Rufus Dawes led the Sixth Wisconsin left wing assault through a garden and orchard on the right, moving toward the camera position. Captain Edwin Brown was killed at the Millers' garden gate.

Famous Alexander Gardner photo taken two days after the battle, view to north, shows dead soldiers from Starke's Louisiana Brigade along the west side of the Hagerstown Pike.

Author and photographic researcher William Frassanito concluded that the Sixth Wisconsin and Second US Sharpshooters "caused many of the casualties" lying here.

Captain, husband, father, friend— Commander Edwin Brown, Company E, killed in action at the Miller Farmhouse at age thirty.

Captain Werner von Bachelle, killed in action on the Hagerstown Pike near the Bloody Cornfield.
Buried in Antietam National Cemetery, his pet dog at his side.

LTC Alois O. Bachman, Nineteenth Indiana, led the rescue of Battery B and Sixth Wisconsin. Killed in action south of the cornfield.

Endnotes

1. *Dawes Journals, Books 1 & 3*. DAA. Events, battle details, and sketches by Rufus Dawes in this chapter are from this source unless otherwise noted.

2. Nolan, Alan. *The Iron Brigade*, and Civil War Trust (website). http://www.civilwar.org.

3. Julia Cutler diary quotes in this chapter are from JCJ.

4. Rueben Huntley letters are from the UWCDL.

5. Dawes letter. DAA.

6. Dawes journals. DAA.

7. Edwin A. Brown Collection. WHS.

8. Nolan, Alan T. *The Iron Brigade*, p. 121.

9. Beaudot, William and Herdegen, Lance. *An Irishman in the Iron Brigade: The Civil War Memories of James P. Sullivan*, p. 61.

10. R. Huntley letters. WDCL. Contains an Oct. 1861 letter to Mrs. Huntley regarding the aid fund.

11. Huntley recollections from a letter by Dawes to former Co. K comrades in Juneau County, WI, printed in a January 1886 Mauston newspaper, no identifier. EDC-NL. See endnote ii in chapter 6 for soldier burial information.

12. Miles's premonition from Pionton, Mair and Cheek, Phillip, *History of the Sauk County riflemen*, p. 47. (HSCR). Available online at http://content.wisconsinhistory.org/cdm/ref/collection/quiner/id/44929.

13. *Dawes Journal, Book 3*, p. 117. DAA.

14. Phelps's report. *O. R. Vol. XIX, pt. 1*, p. 233.

15. *Dawes Journal, Book 3*, p. 120. DAA.

16. The battery lost nine killed and thirty-one wounded, including Captain Campbell—a 40 percent casualty rate—plus 26 horses killed. Two medals of honor were awarded to Battery B soldiers in this action, one to fifteen-year-old bugler Johnny Cook. *Hell for Battery B, 4th U S Artillery at Antietam*. http://goldenanchorsharon.blogspot.com/2013/03.

17. Based on the Official Records, Hooker's First Corps early morning attack had 8,288 soldiers engaged. The corps suffered 2,500 casualties, including 400 killed (30 percent total loss). Stonewall Jackson's opposing forces numbered 6,980. They suffered 2,825 casualties, including 510 killed, a 40 percent casualty rate.

Chapter Six

Recovery, Defeat, Disappointment

Thursday, September 18, 1862—Antietam Battlefield

Captain John Kellogg walks behind the Sixth Wisconsin survivors lying on the wet ground in line of battle, so small a group now that the regiment stretches no more than 70 yards end to end. It had been a restless night for everyone—too much to remember, too much picket firing. He just had some coffee with several company officers, much of the conversation subdued as the men recounted their experiences. Fellow officers Brown, von Bachelle, and Bode are known to be killed, and four lie wounded in makeshift hospitals set up in Mr. Poffenberger's farm buildings. The enlisted ranks are devastated.

Lee's battered army is still in place around Sharpsburg, all Union efforts to break them yesterday having minimal success because of poor coordination and with an awful cost in life on both sides. *Are we going to go at them again today?* Kellogg approaches headquarters, Major Rufus Dawes and Lt. Col. Edward Bragg standing under a tree with their horses saddled and ready.

"Good morning, sirs," Kellogg quietly greets them. "Any word?"

Bragg turns and winces with the sudden movement, his arm still in a sling, pain throbbing from fingers to neck. He should not be here, but nobody says anything. There are others in the ranks who are banged up. Rufus Dawes answers, "Not yet. If there is an attack, we think it must be by the Fifth and Sixth Corps. They were hardly engaged at all yesterday. At least, that would make sense, which doesn't always seem to matter. Our corps is in bad shape. Colonel Hoffman's brigade is the only one that didn't see much action. They were sent over to cover the right flank while we went through the meat grinder, lucky for them."

"Well, Rufus," Kellogg responds as he munches on a piece of hard-tack, "if we do go in again, Converse and Plummer say they would like to stand next to you or me. They think we must have some mystical power to deflect oncoming missiles, claiming as evidence the shell fragment that tore into the oilcloth we shared last night, smack-dab right between us, and somehow didn't give us a scratch! Splattered mud all over me, though."

Bragg glances at the dirty coat and laughs. "They may have a point! That *was* amazing! If the quartemaster doubts your story, I'll vouch for a new oilcloth!" The gallows humor helps to soothe the anxiety, but each man knows he could absolutely be lying cold and bloody on the battle-field right now, facing his Maker and whatever judgment is deserved. They also know that everyone here has the same thought, so why dwell on it?

The day wears on with no word of pending action. Dawes decides to write a quick letter home telling Mother that he is safe, so far. Newspaper reporters are around, and maybe one who is trustworthy can mail it safely. All he has handy in the saddlebag is a pencil and some plain paper. He sits down under the tree using two ammunition boxes for chair and desk. He has always confided in his mother, and his thoughts flow freely onto the paper[1]:

Before the enemy near Sharpsburg

Sept. 18th, 1862

Dear Mother

I have come safely through two more terrible battles, South Mountain and the great battle yesterday.

Our regiment is almost gone—we have lost near <u>400</u> men in killed and wounded in the late battles. Seven out of twelve officers in the last battle were shot. We are now under Hooker and will probably be annihilated before he & our Brigadier will let our Brigade be relieved. The men have stood like iron and been worth any two eastern brigades in the army. Lt. Col. Bragg was wounded yesterday. I commanded the regiment and was obliged at one time to carry the color to keep the men up to save a cannon—it was <u>riddled to ribbons</u> in my hands, but bless them, every boy from the Badger State in sight rallied around me and

we saved our battery. We lost 160 men out of 400 in the fight—
the battle may be renewed any moment.

Your aff. son, Rufe[P]

Friday, September 19, 1862—Antietam Battlefield

The Rebel army is gone. They left during the night across the Potomac
River, hundreds of wagons carrying wounded soldiers, hundreds of their
men with severe wounds left behind to the care of Union surgeons and
citizen relief agencies such as the US Sanitary Commission. Union skirmishers are followed by whole brigades probing forward to investigate.

The Iron Brigade, as it is now being referred to in several Northern
papers, moves past the fields of their battle two days past. A vast sea
of human destruction meets their eyes. It is simply indescribable.
Rufus Dawes sits on his trusty mare as the Sixth walks slowly down
the Hagerstown Pike, in between the sturdy rail fences that border the
road. The stench of death is everywhere, as the fences are lined on
both sides with dead bodies in every grotesque position imaginable.
His horse is jumpy, hard to manage, covered in sweat—unnerved by
the smell. Every man present will never forget the sight. The task now
at hand is to find, identify, recover, and bury their comrades, who lay
where they fell more than forty-eight hours ago, mixed up with other
dead soldiers, friend and foe. Exposure to the elements makes body
identification difficult. Personal effects and uniforms must be used in
many cases. It is always a stomach-turning duty.

Slowly, carefully, respectfully, the survivors of the Sixth collect their
dead, as soldiers from other units do the same around them, taking
care of their own. There is no Graves Registration unit. Dawes passes
the cornfield on his left, then Battery B's position on the right, then up
the rise to the point of their farthest advance on Wednesday. He knows
that Edwin Brown's body has already been collected and brought to the
rear on Wednesday by stretcher bearers. Lt. Col. Bragg, even though
wounded himself, has hastily arranged for Edwin's body to be placed in
a casket for shipment home to Wisconsin.

There! On the side of the Hagerstown Pike they find Captain Werner
von Bachelle, commander of the Milwaukee Germans of Company F,
his body riddled with bullet impacts. He was shot when the Sixth's line
moved forward after initially breaking the Confederate line. His trained

---

[P] His letter does not arrive in Marietta until September 22, eight days later. It is shared among the family
with a combination of relief, thankfulness, and dread.

Newfoundland dog is lying next to him, obviously having stayed by his fallen master's side until it, too, was killed. Bachelle had served in the French Army and spoke with a heavy accent but was all military, respected by officers and men alike. Now his men ask Dawes what to do with his body. Should they send his corpse to the rear, where it might also be sent home?

"As far as I know, he has no family," Dawes quietly responds. "His dog was the only living thing he ever talked about. I think he would prefer to be buried here with the men he led and fought with. And let's place his dog next to him too."

Sergeant Major Huntington, limping from his own wound, directs the burial detail to an elm tree in a field west of the pike.[Q] Twenty-six Sixth Wisconsin soldiers and one Newfoundland dog are buried there in two rows, the men using boards and wooden box tops to mark the names.[2]

As the men finish their sad work with a parting rifle salute, Dawes replaces his hat and notices a black buggy parked off the road south of the cornfield. Two men are moving a bulky piece of equipment mounted on a tripod. He is familiar with the instrument, this camera, but has never seen it used outside a studio, especially on a battlefield. Someone is taking photographic likenesses of the carnage along the turnpike. Most of the remaining dead are Confederate, the last to be buried, plus there are multitudes of horses lying everywhere and the scattered debris of battle. At first, he is repulsed and is ready to shoo them away. But no. *Let them do it. Let people see what war is really like. Let them see what we have gone through. That these men will make money from it is distasteful, but let them do it. Let people see the horror.*

There is no system for next-of-kin notification. Tens of thousands of wives and parents learn of casualties through newspaper lists, if at all. There often are errors. Some get short messages via telegraph. Letters take weeks. Sometimes, no word is ever heard—the loved one disappears.

Behind the Antietam battlefield where the hospitals are, dead bodies are lined up under blankets, and amputated limbs are heaped in piles. Young men are suffering, and doctors and nurses are swamped in their efforts to help, among them a forty-one-year-old civilian named Clara Barton. In that horrible arena, a harried surgeon tells Sergeant Andrew Miller, Company I, to escort a casket carrying a senior officer from the Sixth Wisconsin to Hagerstown. The name of the dead occupant is misidentified. In Hagerstown, Miller sends a short telegraph message

---

[Q] See chapter 5 for the Rufus Dawes sketch of the battlefield showing an approximate grave location. The US Burial Corps removed the bodies four years later and reinterred them in the Antietam National Cemetery. Some were not identifiable and are marked "Unknown."

to Fond du Lac, attention Mrs. Edward Bragg: "Your husband, Lt. Col. Bragg, is killed. The body is on its way home."

10:00 a.m., Saturday, September 20, 1862, Marietta, Ohio

Sarah Dawes walks to her front door in response to the bell. She is home alone, Lucy being at her school and Kate at the Cutler's Old Stone House. Looking through the window, she sees it is Mr. Stephen Newton, a neighbor, with a troubled look about him. She opens the door, and he addresses her: "Hello, Mrs. Dawes. I am sorry to bother you, but I am afraid we have bad news."

News of the great battle in Maryland has been on her mind, but information is scanty. Sarah's heart skips a beat, her knees become weak, and she wails a mournful, "Rufus is dead!"

"No, no," Mr. Newton replies, immediately chastising himself for the stupid way he addressed her. "That's not why I came. I have no news about Rufus. I'm so sorry to scare you; I wasn't thinking. But word has come by telegraph that Lieutenant Colonel Melvin Clarke *has* been killed in Maryland with the Thirty-Sixth regiment. Mrs. Clarke does not yet know, though some boys in the street are already running about with the news, and I hope she has not heard it from them. My purpose is, Could you break the news to her? I know you and she are friends, and it would be better coming from you than from me. I know it is a lot to ask. I've sent word to Reverend Wickes."

Sarah needs a few moments to recover. She is in constant fear for her two sons. *Thank God it is not Rufus—or Ephraim! But I fear what I do not know. And poor Mrs. Clarke and her family ... Another good and true man, a leading citizen, struck down by this war! How can I tell her?* "Mr. Newton, you scared me half to death! I know how she will feel. But yes, I will go to her. Please give me the telegraph message, and I'll leave now." *May God help me be strong for her*, she thinks as she closes the door and walks with Newton up Fourth Street.[3]

Sunday, September 21, 1862, Fond du Lac, Wisconsin

Mr. Isaac Brown, father of Edwin, is worried and troubled about the accounts of the great battle in Maryland and by events relating to it at home. He decides to communicate with his thirty-year-old son, knowing it could be two weeks waiting for a reply[4]:

> Dear son—I write to express to you how anxiously we are waiting to hear the reports of casualties to our men in the late battles

and yet are almost afraid to hear—our earnest prayer is that you have gone through the deadly contest safely.

The excitement has been intense here since Thursday evening caused by the report that Lieut. Col. Bragg was killed on Wednesday—it was a dispatch direct to Mrs. Bragg by Sergeant Miller—which stated his body would be sent home by express— great exertions have been made to learn more about it but up to this time that simple dispatch is everything that can be learned, and strange to believe there seems to be a disposition to believe it is a hoax, we all <u>hope</u> it may be, but it is almost hoping against hope. If Bragg is really dead the war party will be deprived of its most available candidate for Congress. ...

I note in your last letter to Ruth that you complain of being worn down by hard service, and that unless you could get rest soon you were fearful that you would give out. I suppose ... it is difficult to get a furlough or a resignation accepted. But my advice is to try to the utmost to get one or the other rather than sink under the loads from sheer exhaustion. I think by now you have proven your courage and patriotism. ...

May our ruling Providence continue to watch over and protect you.

Your affectionate father

Isaac Brown

A committee of Fond du Lac citizens, friends, and colleagues of Edward Bragg in the local Democratic War Party try to console Mrs. Cornela Bragg and her family, and offer to meet the train that carries his body. They do so this day in Chicago, locate the casket, and open it to pay last respects to a brave companion. The sight of this lifeless body in a stained uniform, straight from the battlefield, shocks them ... But it is not Edward Bragg! Despite being four days dead, they all recognize Bragg's law partner, Edwin Brown, as being the poor man being sent home.

My God! What to do? Mrs. Bragg needs to know right away ... But poor Ruth Brown! J. T. Conklin, the party leader, decides he must send the stunning news: unbelievable relief for one family, dreadful shock and sorrow for another. He telegraphs a message to Fond du Lac:

The body is E. A. Brown instead of Bragg. Will be home tomorrow. *Chicago Times* reports Bragg wounded in arm.

The shock hits the Ruth and Isaac Brown families hard. Two little boys and a girl lose their father. Mr. Conklin telegraphs later in the day from Milwaukee—the body is decomposing rapidly; the burial must occur immediately upon arrival. The very thought is repugnant and adds to the pain. The town converts the respects planned for Lt. Col. Bragg to Captain Brown, with the militia honor guard and band and fellow lawyers of the bar there to meet the train on Monday afternoon. The procession down Main and Sixth Streets to the Brown home sees respectful citizens lining the streets along the route. As daylight fades, they reach the small Pier family cemetery on Ruth's father's farm. Eulogies are spoken at the well-attended graveside service, and the heartbroken family says goodbye to their husband, father, and son. It is the best they can do.[5]

Sixth Wisconsin Headquarters Tent, North of the Antietam Battlefield

Lt. Col. Edward Bragg is unaware of the tragic misunderstanding and terrible drama unfolding at this moment for family and friends back in his hometown. As Isaac Brown writes his son and the stunning telegraph is sent from Chicago, Bragg sits at his field desk writing the required after-action reports for South Mountain and Antietam. As he nears the end of the South Mountain account, he recalls the cold night after the battle, lying on the mountain slope without ammunition and without relief, and writes this sarcastic paragraph:

Soon after daylight my regiment was relieved by the Second New York, of Gorman's brigade, who had been lying in the field, under cover of a stone wall, at a safe distance in the rear, refreshing themselves with a good night's sleep, after a long and fatiguing march of some ten miles.

Bragg then writes the Antietam account, using information supplied by Major Dawes for the period after he left the field, wounded in the arm. He gives his second-in-command recognition for his actions that terrible day, this in part:

While advancing into the cornfield, Captain Edwin A. Brown, Company E, a good officer and genial gentleman, fell, instantly killed by a musket ball. The portion of the line in the cornfield was under the immediate command of Major Rufus R. Dawes, who discharged his duty in watching and guiding its movements with signal courage and ability.[6]

Rufus Dawes is called in to review the drafts for accuracy. He chuckles and heartily endorses the cutting remarks about General Gorman. It is highly unusual commentary, criticism of a senior officer in an official report, and he wonders if it will survive scrutiny from Generals Gibbon or Hooker. He thanks Bragg for the Antietam compliments, but in reading it, silently relives in his mind the awful carnage, and of Edwin's death, which haunts him every night.

Sunday, October 5, 1862—Sixth Wisconsin Camp at a Bend in the Potomac River, One Mile North of the Antietam Battlefield

The army under McClellan has been resting dormant for the past two-and-a-half weeks. The troops appreciate it, but President Lincoln is frustrated with the inactivity and McClellan's constant call for resupply and reinforcements, still in the belief that Lee outnumbers him. Lincoln understands the problems but knows Lee must be much worse off. Still, he has used the Confederate withdrawal back to Virginia as victory enough to justify issuance of the Emancipation Proclamation, which, incidentally, McClellan personally opposes. The president visits McClellan in the field to encourage some action and to review the Northern troops who have so recently been involved in severe battle. Lincoln is once again disappointed in McClellan's lack of urgency and in his attitude, which clearly seems to say, "It's *my* army, not the country's." The president confides his impression of the visit to an associate—McClellan acts as if the troops are his "bodyguards" rather than the nation's fighting force.[7]

* * * * *

"Well, Rufus, I better get back to my quarters pretty soon. Today has been a revelation for me, that's for sure." Captain R. Marshall Newport had spent much of the day with his old college friend touring the battlefield, discussing the state of the army, and talking of home. They sit together now in front of the Sixth Wisconsin headquarters tent, located within a nice view of the river and surrounding farmland.

Major Rufus Dawes responds to Newport, "I'm glad you stopped by, Marsh. It's a little different atmosphere than what you are used to. If you can do something about replacement uniforms and shoes, that would be great. Some of our boys are barefoot."

"I'll try," say Newport, "I'll try. You know, I just can't get over the level of destruction. It's stunning, awful. I'm still shocked by our visit to the Thirty-Sixth Ohio camp. Going there intending to say hello to Colonel Clarke, and then finding out he had been killed, shot through both legs by a cannon ball. God, I still can't imagine how his wife and family are taking it. And then Friday, at that big troop review by President Lincoln and General McClellan. I've seen the president in Washington many times, but I've never seen him so careworn and sad-looking. I watched him clearly as he reviewed your brigade, your soldiers so battered and so few in the ranks. As he scanned your men standing there, it just seemed to me that he was visualizing all the poor fellows who are gone."[8]

Yes, thousands of soldiers are buried in fresh, shallow graves at Antietam. But hundreds of miles away, there is another acquaintance gone, and neither Dawes nor Newport are aware of it.

Wednesday, October 1, 1862, Marietta, Ohio

Beman Gates comes home from his railroad office a bit early for lunch, surprising Betsey and Mary. They both recognize immediately that his mood is dour, and he moves slowly to a chair in the parlor. He has been saddened much lately, with close friends and associates William Nye and Lieutenant Colonel Melvin Clarke, both prominent Marietta lawyers, having died in the past ten days.

"Is there something wrong, dear?" Betsey asks. Mary is looking on from the hallway opening, recognizing that her father's expression is not normal.

Beman leans back in his chair, hands grasping the armrests, a pensive, sad expression on his face. "Yes, I'm afraid so. General Rosecrans telegraphed me this morning at the office. We worked together bringing him supplies, I'm sure you remember. Anyway, this was not about provisions. Theodore Greenwood, who has been serving on his staff, passed away last evening. He wanted me to pass the news to his family."

With that statement, Mary gasps, and Betsey brings her apron up to her face as she responds, "Oh no! No! What a fine young man! His poor parents! How many times has he been here in this very room, having a good time with the other students. Oh, this is so, so awful!" Betsey thinks of the crushing loss now being felt by Mr. and Mrs. Greenwood and almost breaks down. She turns to Mary and instantly sees the impact on her.

Mary stands with both hands over her mouth, tears welling in her eyes. *Ted ... Such a gentleman, so smart. I liked him very much. He and I ... Ted wanted to court me, but ...* The sadness and loss overwhelm her. She turns and runs up the stairs to her room where she falls on her bed and breaks down. *Dear Ted! I'm so sorry! Forgive me!*

Theodore Greenwood had obtained his captaincy on the staff of General Rosecrans, just as he had hoped. But he was not used to the rigors of field service and became seriously ill from some unknown ailment. Everyone around Marietta knew him and his parents. Aunt Julia notes the sad saga in her journal:

Sunday, September 28, 1862. Mr. & Mrs. Greenwood sent a note requesting prayers for themselves and son who is lying dangerously sick in Mississippi.

Monday, September 29. Kate ... called at Mr. Greenwood's. They are in great trouble. Mr. G started for Jacinto where Theodore is. He is a most talented and estimable young man, a graduate of Marietta College, one upon whom great hopes have centered.

Tuesday, September 30. Theodore Greenwood is dead.

Wednesday, October 1. Kate went with Mrs. Bailey to see Mrs. Greenwood and Julia. They are almost heartbroken. Mr. Greenwood has gone hoping to find him alive. Gen. Rosecrans, on whose staff he was, telegraphed Mr. Beman Gates. He had sent to St. Louis for a metallic coffin, the body being preserved in ice until his arrival.

Sabbath, Oct. 5. Theodore E. Greenwood's funeral was attended at eleven o'clock today. President Andrews conducted the service and made the address. ... [H]e was much affected as were many who heard him. Kate took up a beautiful bouquet of white flowers which Lucy had arranged, and by his mother's permission, laid it upon his coffin.

Thursday Evening, October 9, 1862—Sixth Wisconsin Camp near Bakersfield, Maryland

"Major Dawes, I will say it because you know it to be true: I do respect and enjoy Col. Bragg very much, but it is nice to have a little more room while he is back home in Wisconsin, and I think I will sleep better without him, because when he drinks his whiskey, he snores all night!" Dr. Oscar Bartlett and Rufus Dawes sit comfortably under the fly of their wall tent, enjoying the pleasant early fall weather. Their portable stove keeps them quite comfortable at night, and Billy has been doing a great job in keeping their mess chest well-stocked.

Rufus laughs and responds to Bartlett's comment, "Well, I have to agree with you on that, but will deny I ever said it. He may be gone permanently if he wins the election for Congress back in Fond du Lac. I think his election is pretty sure, and it would be a great reflection on his service here, but you never know. Say, what about you? What's the latest with your promotion over to the Third Wisconsin? You could be gone from us pretty shortly yourself."

Bartlett replies, "So far, no word from the governor, but that could happen, yes, and very soon. The Third needs a chief surgeon badly, and it would be a good move for me. But I would be sorry to leave the Sixth. Sorry to leave your company, in particular—except for getting beat at chess constantly!"

"And I will miss not being able to say that finest of all pronouncements: " 'Checkmate!' " Dawes laughs. "But, with that, I better get back to my letter to my sister."

"All right," Bartlett responds. "You know, you mentioned her last to you, and that you learned of losing a friend serving with Rosecrans. I'm sorry, Rufus. It must be especially difficult for you, what with just seeing Edwin fall. I have so many fond memories of him, and I know you two were very close."

Thoughts of Edwin and Ted are reopened with Bartlett's condolences, and the void left by their deaths is again felt deeply. "Thanks, Oscar, I appreciate that. I ... I have thought about it often. Why them? Two of the most intelligent and honorable young men I have ever known. I can't rationalize it; it can't be rationalized. My conclusion is ... that when we decided to join the army, to put on this uniform and go into harm's way, we must now think in terms of not surviving. Just do what is necessary and not think about it, and what happens ... happens. Otherwise, these thoughts and worries become all-consuming and can make one too timid—or worse, a coward. Edwin and Ted were dedicated to the cause.

I certainly don't want to see their loss go for nothing or dishonor their sacrifice by not continuing the fight. If it is to be me the next time, so be it."

Dawes continues, "I consider it an honor to be part of this regiment, and to lead them in battle is the highlight of my life. Look at these men. We have wounded and convalescents coming back every day, wanting to return. We have every man accounted for. Every man! Nobody missing without cause! In fact, General Gibbon tells me that the *whole brigade* has no stragglers or unaccounted-for men! That's incredible compared to the rest of the army, or even our corps, especially after the fights we've been through. He told me that the First Corps nearly doubled in strength between the day after the battle and the head count made four days after. Almost double in four days! Why? Because a bunch of them were stragglers, those who disappear somehow during a battle. Not our brigade! Nobody here wants to let the others down. Nobody wants to tarnish the name and reputation that's been earned with the blood of so many of our friends. General Gibbon's letter praising us to the governors, along with General McClellan's stirring endorsement that was passed on to all of us—those have sealed it. These boys are battered but so proud to be recognized, and they will follow those two men anywhere."[9]

He pauses, a bit embarrassed by this soul-baring to his tent partner, and glances up to see Bartlett intently focused on him, absorbing his every word. Bartlett breaks the brief silence: "Someday, I hope to cure a lot of sick people and never have to patch up another gunshot wound. But, Major, I will never forget having served with you and with the Sixth Wisconsin."

Major Dawes resumes his reply letter to Lucy, and after assuring her that he has "never [been] more healthy in my life," he writes of his good friend Ted Greenwood:

> I communicated to Newport this morning the sad intelligence of his cousin Greenwood's death. He feels very badly. You say rightly that Greenwood would have succeeded well. There was strength of purpose and clearness of intellect. How the young men of my circle are being cut off. There was Dick Green just the other day—really as promising a young man as I ever knew, and an intimate friend.
>
> Greenwood's death is indeed a great blow to his parents. I know he was his "father's pride." Had he lived I should have expected of him the most brilliant and successful career of any

young man of our college generation. He had the industry and perseverance to achieve almost any success, had he not possessed half the talent.

General McClellan's forte is organization, and he spends six weeks on it. The summer campaigns have been rough on equipment, and many changes are needed to replace leaders who have fallen. This is especially true in the Iron Brigade.

Of course, the delays do not go over well with the president and Congress, and the frustration is made all the worse when Confederate cavalry commander J. E. B. Stuart leads 1,800 of his bold and confident troopers on a 125-mile three-day sweep clear around the Army of the Potomac, causing havoc and doing "gentlemanly plunder" all the way to Chambersburg, Pennsylvania. Stuart deftly avoids poorly coordinated Federal units giving chase, and he returns completely unscathed to Virginia very tired but with 1,200 captured horses, 30 civilian hostages, wagons full of supplies, and jubilation at their accomplishment. It is the second time Stuart has ridden around McClellan, the first during the Peninsula Campaign last June, and the embarrassment for the Northern leader and the army is intense. McClellan blames the worn-out horses of his cavalry command and asks Union general-in-chief Henry Halleck for more mounts. A frustrated Lincoln telegraphs McClellan directly: "Will you pardon me for asking what the horses of your army have done since the Battle of Antietam that fatigue anything?" McClellan still has the confidence of the rank and file, including Rufus Dawes, but not of the president.

The Iron Brigade regiments need replacements or reinforcement, and Dawes complains that the governors are slow in providing the former. Four days after the battle, Rufus writes Lucy that the Sixth went from seven hundred strong on August 21 to less than two hundred after Antietam. The brigade suffered 1,593 casualties in that same period. General Gibbon requests help and receives McClellan's promise to assign a new western regiment as soon as one is available. His preference is another Wisconsin or Indiana unit, but when he returns on October 14 from a visit with his family in Baltimore, Gibbon finds that McClellan has assigned him a "western" regiment from Michigan. It is the Twenty-Fourth Michigan Volunteer Infantry, mostly recruited from Detroit, and they are brand new. Their full ranks are about equal in number to the other four regiments combined. When the brigade is drawn up in formation to meet the newcomers, their new colonel, Henry Morrow, launches into a speech saying how proud his men are to be part of the brigade, along with other patriotic declarations. He closes his oration with the normal expectation of hearing, at the very

October 1862, the army rests—General John Buford third from left, General John Gibbon, Iron Brigade commander, at far right.

least, some polite applause, perhaps even a good Union cheer. What he gets is silence.[10]

Rufus Dawes writes his sister that the Michiganders appear to be a "good regiment—raw." To the tanned and tough veterans in the ranks, however, these new soldiers—dressed in brand-new standard-issue uniforms, small kepi hats, brass still shiny—are soldiers in name only. *They are coming into our elite fraternity not having proven themselves worthy*, many think. *Let's see how they perform.*

Thursday, October 16, 1862, Warren County, Ohio—the Old Stone House

More bad news is happening back home. Uncle William Cutler has been involved in a nasty political campaign to retain his seat in Congress. He is a strong Union man, and many in Ohio favor the Democratic party platforms, which seek peace talks with the South, essentially acquiescence, and which oppose Negro emancipation. Lies and innuendo about William abound in the newspapers, congressional boundary redistricting places him at a disadvantage, and hundreds of soldiers who would likely vote for him are off to the war. The voting returns compiled on this day are not official but are certainly against William. His sister Julia writes of the situation in Ohio:

The paper tonight says but four Union congressmen are known to be elected in this state. One of these is Schenck, the opponent of the traitor Vallandigham. I am glad that he is defeated as he deserves to be. I am sorry that our good state which has sent to the battlefield more than 100,000 of her sons must fall into the hands of the enemies of liberty and of the government, because her <u>true</u> men have gone to fight and are not here to vote.

Saturday, October 25, 1862—Sixth Wisconsin Camp near Bakersfield, Maryland

The time spent in camp provides the soldiers an opportunity to reflect and to pay respects to fallen comrades. Ordnance sergeant Jerome Watrous writes a letter to Mrs. Ruth Brown:

Mrs. E. A. Brown

Having been a member of Company "E" (your Husband's company) it is with feelings of deepest sorrow that my memory wanders back to the many happy and profitable hours I have passed in the company of my noble, generous and brave Captain, and your kind and loving husband; to the 17th inst when the noble fellow along with thousands of others patriotically and heroically gave up his life in defense of the Country, and flag he loved, as well as honored.

I can hardly believe myself, but it is too true that Captain Brown is no more for this earth, and you Mrs. Brown are not the only one who feels his loss. The men who have been in his company mourn his loss. All his men loved him and feel that a dear friend has been taken from them. Be assured that you have the heart-felt sympathy of every man of Company "E."

Your husband never flinched from a duty and but few of his rank have fought more manfully or bravely in any company of the world.

With great respect

J. A. Watrous

Ord Sergt

McClellan finally gets the army moving the last week in October. The troops cross the Potomac and head south, following the east slopes of the Blue Ridge Mountain range, with most of Lee's army on the other side, in the Shenandoah River Valley, matching the Yankees stride for stride. But then Lee steals a march on McClellan once again and gets troops in front of the Federals, protecting the route toward Richmond.

By early November cold weather arrives, and the men suffer accordingly. Lincoln can suffer no more of slow-moving McClellan and removes him from command on November 7, appointing a reluctant General Ambrose Burnside in his place. It takes Burnside awhile to review what is going on with troop locations and plans. This adds to the delay and allows Lee more time to counter the Federal moves. Burnside is under pressure from Washington and vocal newspaper editors to attack, to use his large army to defeat Lee decisively. It is altogether another dangerous situation for the soldiers of the Army of the Potomac.

Along the way, other changes in leadership occur, and Major Rufus Dawes comments on them in letters home. He cannot hide his bitterness toward a multitude of continual military failures and of the misguided opinions expressed in the press. He is one whose life is on the line with the decisions made by higher authority, and despite his duty to serve and obey orders, he sees through the stupid rhetoric pushing the army toward another disaster. Despite these crucial concerns, thoughts of his family are always on his mind:

Near Warrenton, Va. Nov. 7, 1862

Dear Lucy—After some heavy marching, we are stopped by a snow storm at a familiar spot. The enemy moves along about ten miles ahead. It is terribly cold and disagreeable campaigning now. Col. Cutler has returned not fit for duty and is in command of the brigade. Gen. Gibbon has been given command of Rickett's division. We are sorry to lose him. He is a brave and skillful officer.

Warrenton, November 9th

Dear Lucy—We are still waiting for something to eat. ... The new regiment of Michiganders have been bawling "bread, bread!" all day like a pen of pigs. I would try to stop them if I was boss over there.

Stafford County, Va., In the pine brush,
ten miles from anywhere,
Nov. 20, 1862

Dear Mother—Last night we lay without tents in a terribly cold and driving rain storm. Today we are in camp drying off. We are now in the grand division of General Franklin; the orders say on the left of the army. I believe you will agree with me in hoping that we will be <u>left</u> when any more bloody fighting has to be done. Col. Bragg has returned to the regiment. He was badly beaten in his race for Congress. All because he is a "war man." They are for peace in his district. I was very glad to hear of Timothy Condit's promotion.[R] He is a most excellent man and has seen the roughest part of the service.

Camp near Fredericksburg, November 25, 1862

Dear Lucy—I am glad Eph has been so fortunate to get a flying visit home. I should surely enjoy such a one myself, but I don't expect to be able to visit home this winter. As soon as I get my pay I intend to send you $100. We have been so long without pay that we have to live on borrowed money, which is intolerably expensive.

Old Sol Meredith is now Brigadier General and is to take command of our brigade. Col. Cutler will come back to take command of the regiment, and Lt. Col. Bragg says he will resign. Bragg, who with faults as all men have, is the most talented and bravest officer belonging to the regiment.

Camp near Brook's Station, Dec. 1, 1862

Dear Kate—Our great army once more has come to a halt. For how long nobody knows, I presume not even Burnside. Meanwhile all (except the old soldiers) are shivering and suffering in their little dog kennels. The Country demands an advance. "Richmond must fall!" Lee's army must be "bagged," there must be a bloody battle, at least ten thousand of our brave soldiers must be killed

---

[R] College classmate Timothy Condit was promoted from sergeant to lieutenant in the First Ohio Cavalry, serving in Tennessee.

and wounded, nothing short of this will appease the bloodthirsty appetite of our people, our valiant "stay at home rangers." How credulous and gullible our people are! And how wickedly criminal those lying newspapers who continually overrate our army and over praise every movement.

I did not make a fool of myself at the time of McClellan's removal as many officers did. I do not know that the army has suffered for the change (further than the delay which, I fear, has been almost fatal). I acquiesce as a soldier should. But I fail to see the propriety of the removal. In this matter, we of the army have a right to feel deeply—our lives depend upon it. Three hundred of our comrades, our everyday associates, many our dear friends, lie cold under the sod of that bloody field of Gainesville. Victims of Gen ——'s want of system, and ignorance of the situation. ... [A]nd for this wholesale murder no advantage results to our cause. We want to feel that such things are not likely to recur.

I want to go to Washington, but it is mighty hard to get a chance—perhaps after we get our pay I can get there for a day or two. We have been five months without pay. I shall send Ma what I can when it comes which will probably be soon now.

Lucy is doing bravely with her school. I think by all of us uniting we can bring our beloved Father to a realizing soon that his despotic rule is gone by forever. He was badly beaten for the distinguished position which he aspired and no doubt got the ill will of half of the little community. Give my love to Aunt Julia and all the family.

Brook's Station, December 5, 1862

Dear Lucy—Our Grand Division (Franklin's) is on the move again. We had just got comfortably fixed for winter. Gen. Meredith is now commanding our brigade. As for the matter of deserving promotion, if that was ever taken in consideration in our system of appointing Brigadier Generals, four or five men in our brigade would have had a star before Old Solomon.

Sunday, November 30, 1862, Warren County, Ohio—the Old Stone House

Thanksgiving is just past, a wonderful dinner enjoyed with friends, but many of Julia's family were missing: Sarah and Lucy are ill, Eph and Rufus toil with their regiments. She is thankful that the year has seen her nephews safely through danger—so far. But today she records the dismal outlook for her beloved country:

> So ends the autumn of 1862. Rebellion still uncrushed and boasting itself of Northern Democratic sympathizers. The national heart bleeds and tears flow from the eyes of thousands of mourners who weep for the beloved ones who will return no more. What further miseries are still in store God only knows. With southern rebels and northern traitors at home, and all Europe down upon us we do seem to be a God forsaken people. More than a million loyal men bear arms in this land today, but where are the leaders?

Thursday, Christmas Evening, December 25, 1862—Winter Camp near Belle Plain, VA

"Merry Christmas, gentlemen!" Rufus Dawes announces to his dinner companions. He dramatically uncovers a large can of peaches and proclaims, "After a fine dinner—thank you, Billy Jackson—we all deserve a treat. These are from my sister Kate and Aunt Lizzie, wife of Congressman William Cutler. You are fortunate I have the gift of willpower, because there has been many an occasion where I was sorely tempted to make a frontal attack on these all by myself."

After receiving accolades for the surprise, Dawes hands the can to Billy for dispensing to the party cozily seated inside his unfinished log hut, portable stove providing some heat, and temporary canvas roof doing its best to keep out the rain. With him are the regimental surgeons comprising his regular mess: Doctors Andrews, Preston, and the newest addition, John C. Hall, who replaced Dr. Bartlett in November. Lt. Col. Edward Bragg is an invited guest.

After dinner, the five men sit at the table and chat about home. It is Christmas, after all, and they all wish they were enjoying the holiday with loved ones far away. But the talk quickly turns to the dispiriting situation facing the Army of the Potomac and the nation. The Sixth Wisconsin and the Iron Brigade have passed through another humiliating defeat two weeks past, the bloody fiasco at Fredericksburg on December 13. Although being subjected to relentless enemy artillery fire while positioned on an open plain on the army's extreme left flank and suffering greatly for three nights in the December cold, they had been fortunate to serve only as witnesses to the carnage that befell other Union soldiers. The regiment suffered only four men wounded.

Dr. Hall reflects, "Gentlemen, I am the newest man to join your circle, but let me make an observation: This reminds me of Valley Forge. After this latest disaster, I don't know how you two commanders are able to carry on. Before the battle broke open, I thought you both too pessimistic about our chances against Lee at Fredericksburg, and quite frankly, I was concerned about your motivation to lead our soldiers. But afterward, I saw that you were correct. And I know you both take no comfort in that, but remain here, still dedicated to the cause and ready to go at it again. I salute you."

Lt. Col. Bragg takes the lead in responding, "The only success the army achieved was again won by our corps: General Meade's and General Gibbon's divisions. They fought hard and broke through Jackson's line, but where was their support? General Franklin kept his old Sixth Corps completely out of action! What was the point of sending our boys in at all? They fought and died for nothing!"

Rufus Dawes contributes, "Over four thousand casualties in those two divisions, including General Gibbon wounded, while Franklin had six more divisions, including our own, who spent the whole battle simply being target practice for Rebel batteries, lying on that frozen ground, no protection whatever! General Doubleday relieved Old Sol for moving us too slowly—embarrassing for Meredith, yet I understand it. But who will deal with the generals who put us all in that fix to begin with?"

Bragg, feeling the effects of medicinal whiskey provided by Dr. Andrews, decides to redirect the frustrating conversation: "Dr. Hall, thank you for your compliment. I'm very glad you are with us tonight, for I heard of your plunge over the riverbank when your little horse broke away under that artillery fire!" Everyone laughs at Dr. Hall's expense, knowing the story of the good doctor's panicked reaction when experiencing an enemy artillery barrage for the first time.

John Hall smiles and nods, taking in the humor, though recalling that the incident referred to scared him to death, and for good reason. But he understands the intent of Bragg's comment and instantly realizes that this type of humor employed by veteran soldiers such as Bragg and Dawes is their way of dealing with the incredible danger they face. Rather than being miffed at being singled out, he respects them even more for what they must endure. "Yes, well, at that moment, I felt the urgent need to attend to official business in the rear."[11]

The men at the Christmas dinner leave unsaid their disgust at the bloody, senseless piecemeal charges made by General Burnside's other troops at Fredericksburg under Generals Hooker and Sumner. The frozen fields in front of strong Confederate positions on Marye's Heights were strewn with bodies in blue. President Lincoln realizes it was his order that placed Burnside in command and his directives that pushed his loyal but inept general to make a move. He had hoped that the man would use his army's numerical superiority to advantage, but when hearing of the butchery, Lincoln breaks down in misery, declaring, "If there is a worse place than hell, I am in it!"

By contrast, the armies of the west show some promise for Lincoln and the Union. Confederate General Bragg's Army of the Tennessee is forced to retreat by Union forces led by General William Rosecrans after a horrific three-day battle near Stone's River and Murfreesboro, Tennessee. It occurs December 31–January 2 and results in more total casualties than Antietam, with a higher loss percentage of those engaged than any battle in the war. A good part of the Union army is routed on the first day but enough held on, thanks to stiff resistance by Union troops led in part by a pint-sized general named Phillip Sheridan.

It was a Union victory by the slimmest of margins. Rosecrans withheld his beat-up army from pursuing the Confederates—another frustration for the president. Still, it is a victory and helps to ease the pain and gloom of Fredericksburg. The appalling casualty lists break hearts in many homes as the new year begins, however, and Marietta, Ohio, is not immune.

Thursday, January 8, 1863—the Old Stone House, Julia Cutler's Journal

Lieut. Timothy Condit, a graduate of Marietta College, a talented & worthy young man, was killed at Murphiesboro [*sic*], Tenn. His body expected home today. A very sad case—His mother a widow, & mainly dependent on him is lying very low w Typhoid fever also his sister.

Julia Greenwood, sister of the late Capt. T. E. Greenwood, is reported to have gone deranged.

Rufus Dawes receives this latest appalling news and, on the 18th, sadly writes his sister Kate:

> I have just heard of the death of my classmate Timothy Condit.
> All of our good men are going down.

Rufus Dawes contemplates the loss of four close friends in the past four months: Edwin Brown, Dick Green, Ted Greenwood, and now Tim Condit. Their families are devastated. *When will it end? Who is next? Will it be me?*

No! I will not allow myself to think like this! It does not do me nor anyone else any good. It serves no useful purpose. Perhaps I have become hardened. Yes, that is certainly the case. I have seen scores of men killed around me, seen thousands of dead on the battlefields. But for as long as I have my life, I will live it honorably and productively. I will enjoy what I have. I will look forward to happier times, peaceful years. I will defend my family and fight to preserve this country. If I can ever get a furlough home, I will approach Mary Gates finally and determine if there is any chance with her. If that is still possible, then my life—if I am permitted to have the life that my dear dead friends have been denied—will be determined. To be with her—that is the hope for my future. If that is not to be, then I must move on without her.

7:00 a.m., Tuesday, March 10, 1863—Camp at Belle Plain Overlooking the Potomac River

"Rufus, have some more eggs. You better have a big breakfast, because you might not get much to eat on your trip home." Dr. John Hall pauses, takes in the looks of his young cabinmate, and exclaims, "I have to say, you are the happiest-looking fellow I have seen around here in months! I am so glad your leave came through! Fifteen days! There isn't a soldier in this army who deserves it more."

"Thanks, Doc," Rufus Dawes replies, "I can't believe it finally happened. Thank you, General Hooker! When he took over from General Burnside, the furloughs started to open, and I'm lucky enough to get one. Maybe he favors his old First Corps soldiers. Whatever the reason, I am out of here and can't wait! It's been a year since I've been home, and they don't know I'm coming."

It is a dreary, cold, and rainy day, and Dawes waits for two hours at the Aquia Creek supply depot for his boat. He does not care. After surviving countless miserable days in the field, including the army's infamous

"Mud March" in late January—the fiasco that led the president to fire Burnside and appoint General Joseph Hooker as the latest army commander—he can deal with this minor inconvenience.

There is a bright spot here that lifts his spirits even more: The warehouse office posts a notice of officer personnel actions and listed there is Lysander Cutler's promotion to brigadier general, finally approved by the Senate! *Good for Cutler! He deserves it ... and it allows Bragg's promotion to be our colonel—and me for lieutenant colonel. Cutler has already told me that he will recommend such to the governor, that he will not intercede for Haskell. And with General Cutler gone from us, probably to a brigade command, Bragg will stay put and not resign, as he has continued to threaten. This is a great day!*

The steamer bound for Washington, D.C., leaves Aquia Creek landing around 10:00 a.m. filled with drunken officers spitting tobacco juice and relieving themselves over the side. *No matter. I'm used to that, and I'm on my way home.* The slow boat steams all day up the wide and white-capped Potomac River to reach the city after dark. Then an hour's wait at the train relay house, boarding the 9:00 p.m. westbound on the Baltimore & Ohio Railroad next to two quartermaster officers who are endless bores, with their competing "war stories." *Ha! Paper cuts, perhaps.* Finally, curling up in a dirty sleeping berth bouncing along the winding track as dreams of the slaughter in Antietam's cornfield roil in his subconscious mind once again.

It is after midnight when the conductor deposits in his berth a dirty soldier's overcoat filled with humanity to match. The man's snoring is enough to convert the Antietam dream to a team breaking plow on Father's Wisconsin farm, a recollection scarcely more pleasant. *Nota bene: Always take a full berth in a sleeping car.* The day's trip through the mountains to Grafton in western Virginia offers a scenic panorama. At one viewpoint is witnessed a snow storm, rain storm, and sunshine at the same time. A bed in town is found and allows a few hours of catch-up sleep before boarding the cars on a cold 2:00 a.m. train to Parkersburg.

It is now Thursday, and reaching the city at 8:00 a.m. tired and stiff, there's a hurry to catch the miserable little steamboat that ferries across the Ohio River to Belpre, Ohio. From there it is familiar territory, taking a Union Railroad train northeast to Harmar. The Old Stone House is passed at Constitution Station, looking less like the house of his youth, but all the surroundings eliciting many happy memories. Jumping off the train, walking fast over the Muskingam River on Harmar Bridge and then up Butler Street, a turn on Fourth Street, the Corner and the college buildings visible through the bare tree limbs, to Mother's home. A ring of the bell, a movement inside, the door opens, and a long hug from an astonished mother, tears down her cheeks, the tough veteran infantry officer a bit misty-eyed, as well.[12]

Lucy is away "down to Warren" at the Old Stone House. Passed her by without knowing—so a food-filled, happy day is spent with Ma. Then back on the Union Railroad for a visit with Lucy, Kate, Uncle William, and Aunt's Julia and Lizzie—all surprised at the sudden appearance of a longtime-missing brother, nephew, soldier. Aunt Julia's comment catches his attention: "Rufe, your mother and I and some other ladies had dinner just last night at Mrs. Gates's home. Everyone asked about you and Ephe, and now here you are! How wonderful!"

There is so much to catch up on, so many questions to answer. Aunt Lizzie is nearing full-term pregnancy and does not stay with the group for too long. Mary Nye happens to be there as an overnight guest, everyone treating her as a sister/niece, as she would have been if Henry M. was still alive. Time flies in warm conversation, the night is spent in his old boyhood room, and Friday the 13th is certainly a lucky, happy day at the old home before a cold train ride back to Marietta with his sisters. To Rufus Dawes, such pleasant occasions come but few times in one's life. *If only the mission with Mary Gates proves positive, I could not ask for more.* The prospect of failure, however, is an awful thought. His mind tumbles with the fear of rejection.[13]

Monday, March 16, 1863—the Old Stone House

The weather is warmer but rainy as Rufus and Kate arrive by train for a day visit, the only day that Uncle William is home this whole week, having appointments and meetings all down the line of his railroad. William and Rufus sit by the fire in the same parlor Grandfather Ephraim sat with an angry Henry Dawes over two decades past in circumstances far less pleasant.

William addresses his nephew: "Rufus, thank you again for your letter of February 24. I passed it along to many of my Republican colleagues, all of whom were very impressed and encouraged by your observations and opinions. We in Congress often do not hear the truth, and since I am no longer going to be there, it was especially important to circulate it then."

Rufus replies, "I was happy to write it and meant every word. We are all happy about the conscription law so that our old regiments can be filled up, rather than each state continuing to send in raw units with no experience from top to bottom. Hooker is reorganizing the army, increasing furloughs as reward for good service. He's created a new system identifying each corps with distinctive insignia badges, and it's surprising how much it has already improved morale. I see good progress."

"Your point about conscription is important," says William. "So many members in Congress have taken considerable abuse for supporting the draft. And I hope General Hooker's organizational and leadership skills will translate to battlefield success. Based on the past ... Well, I won't dwell on McClellan. But your comments on slavery and emancipation, I thought, were brave and bold. Here again, many congressmen have taken heat at home for supporting the president's Emancipation Proclamation."

"I have seen the Southern slavery culture firsthand," says Rufus, "and I can say without hesitation that there can be no understanding between the North and South as long as that cursed institution of slavery remains. I want no peace until that is destroyed. Taking their slaves hurts them more than crops or horses or even casualties. It strikes at the core of their economy and upsets their subjugation society that's been ingrained there for generations."

Warming to the subject, Rufus continues, "We did a raid to Northumberland County last month at the mouth of the Potomac. They have been untouched by the war, and there is a lot of smuggling across the wide river there to Maryland. About eighty slaves of all ages and both sexes wanted to come back on the boat with us. Their owners, a wealthy doctor and his daughter, pleaded with them to stay. To the slaves, it was the only place they had ever known. But to a person, they all came with us. The proclamation made it possible for us to do that. But I will say, our expedition commander, Col. Fairchild, was against taking them. Lt. Col. Bragg and Dr. Hall and myself argued for it long and hard against Fairchild and many other officers. In the end, the slaves were allowed on board, and we brought them back to Belle Plain. God knows how those poor folks are getting along now, but they all chose freedom. On the boat going back, that slave owner told Hall and me that he respected our antislavery convictions and expressed contempt for any Northern officer who did not share it. His reasoning was that any Northern soldier who opposes emancipation is nothing more than a thief, robber, kidnapper, and murderer for invading his property and seizing his goods, if that's all they came for."

Lucy came in on the evening train and brought Rufus an invitation signed by several Marietta town leaders, including Professor Evans and Rev. Wickes of the First Congregational Church. "Rufus," Lucy says, handing the paper to him, "they would like you to make a speech giving your views of the army and the country. Ma thinks it a great honor. You could perhaps read from your accounts of the battles that you wrote for us. We are keeping them safe in a file box like you asked us to."[14]

Rufus reads the request. "Well, that *is* an honor, though I would just as soon be allowed to sit around and relax instead of preparing a speech. This isn't rhetoric class; it's real people wanting to hear real facts. But I suppose this former student shouldn't disappoint them! I'll need some time to jot down my thoughts, and I must leave on Friday or Saturday at the latest. Thursday would be best. I'll let them know tomorrow."

Aunt Julia gives her nephew some advice: "Rufe, you talk with us about the war in such an honest and forthright manner. Just give your speech the same way that you talk with us, and the people will listen with complete interest."

Thursday Evening, March 19, 1863, Putnam Street, Marietta, Ohio—Washington County Court House

The courtroom is packed with townspeople, the room well-lit with lamps ringing the walls, and the space is buzzing with conversation. Rufus surveys the audience, nods to family, grins at friends, and looks for Mary Gates. He sees Charley standing along the wall with other college students, but where is … *There!* Sitting with her parents and the Bosworths, along with Fanny. Rufus and Mary lock eyes briefly before she shyly looks away.

Mr. R. E. Harte calls the meeting to order, and Rev. Wickes offers a prayer giving thanks, supplication for the nation, and pleas for the safety of loved ones far away. Rufus collects his thoughts and reviews his notes as Mr. Hart provides a short introduction. Then, as applause greets him, it is time. He focuses, knowing all eyes are fixed on him. *Speak from the heart,* he thinks. *Take command.*

"Ladies and gentlemen, good evening. I am honored to be here with you tonight. It is such a pleasure to be back home once again, if only for a brief time. As I meet my friends in private, the questions most frequently asked are something in this wise: How does a battle seem? How do you feel in battle? What is it like? Is the Army of the Potomac really demoralized? How does the army like General Hooker? How does the army like the Emancipation Proclamation? How do they like the conscription law? What does the army think of the so-called Copperheads?

"So far as is proper for me with regard to my obligations and duty as a subordinate officer in the service, I shall offer the conclusions on these topics to which I have been drawn by actual observation in the army, together with such incidents in my own experience in camp and field as may perhaps serve to illustrate what a battle is—what your own dearly loved friends in the army are undergoing in their efforts to crush this rebellion."

Rufus Dawes proceeds to recount his experiences in battle at South Mountain and Antietam. He has his written account in front of him but does not need it. The memories come back, his words recount the action as it happened. The room is hushed, the audience mesmerized. His family has read his summary, but hearing him describe it now, certainly avoiding the worst of his memories, makes the heart beat faster. It is frightening, exhilarating, shocking, saddening. *Rufe, what you have endured ... We can't express it.*

He answers the questions that are posed in a complete and positive manner: "We are not demoralized. Discipline and efficiency standards are high. The paymasters have finally arrived. We like General Hooker because he is our commander and we expect him to lead us to victory—and he has given us onions and potatoes and furloughs. We like the conscription law because it fills our ranks and commits the nation. If anyone does not like the proclamation, he keeps quiet about it. The Negroes view us as liberators everywhere we go. They run away given the chance, and that hurts the Rebels. Copperheads and those who give aid and comfort to the enemy deserve their fate."

He explains each issue in detail, provides responses that make sense, and speaks with the authority of one who has been there and is going back. The presentation lasts over an hour, with the audience intent on every word. Here is a young man, one who grew up among them, who has witnessed and lived through all the events that have affected their nation for two years. He knows what he is talking about. They are not listening to a reporter or editor or politician who may not have all the facts—or worse, who may have ulterior motives. As Rufus Dawes finishes, the audience stands with sustained applause. Mr. Harte asks that a copy of the speech be published, and the audience votes loudly in favor. Let this be an answer to the Copperheads and those who would let the Southern Rebels break the Union!

Mary Gates stands and applauds with the rest. She has not seen Rufus for over three years. He is lean and handsome in his uniform. And what a wonderful speech! Everyone here must take heart that the military situation is not so dismal after all, with soldiers such as Rufus in the ranks. What did he say about the leaders, though? "The fighting of an army depends more upon the courage and good faith of subordinate commanders than seems to be understood throughout the country." No person in this room can doubt that he excels in those standards.[15]

I wonder ... Well, it is time to head home. He is surrounded with people now. I think Lucy said he leaves tomorrow night. Perhaps ... a goodbye gift, something he could use in the army. I'll talk with Francy. It would be a gift from friends.

Lucy, Sarah, and Rufus Dawes walk home from the courthouse bundled up to fight off the chill. The citizens have finally allowed him to leave after many handshakes and well-wishes. Lucy turns to Rufus. "Rufe, did you see Mary Gates? I thought you would go over and talk with her. You are leaving tomorrow, you know. Even her little sister, Bettie, asked me yesterday in school if you were going to call again. That girl is wiser than her years, that's for sure."

Rufus Dawes, hardened combat officer, is being nudged as always by his older sister. "Yes, Luce, I know I'm leaving tomorrow. I was swamped tonight, couldn't get away from the people. And I have gone over to say hello—three times—but each time Fanny or Charley or Mrs. Gates is there, and Mary seems to keep them close to her for protection. I'm very happy to find out that she's not engaged. I guess I should have asked you about that a long time ago. But she gives no indication that she has any interest in talking with me, at least privately."

Lucy responds, "Rufe, what about that comment you made tonight? 'Courage and good faith of subordinate officers,' I think you said. It seems to me a little of that is needed with regard to Mary, and you are running out of time."

Midafternoon, Friday, March 20, 1863—the Gates Home at Fourth and Putnam

Mary looks out her bedroom window and sees him walking up Fourth Street. He's heading here! And Francy and Charley are gone. *What should I do? I know he has an attraction for me, but I'm just not sure how I feel. He is years older, away in the army for who knows how long, and certainly heading into a spring campaign. I just don't want to think about that, after hearing him describe the battles he has survived so far. Francy and I did go to town this morning and buy him some sheepskin gloves. They are gauntlets that cover the wrists. She was going to take them over to Mrs. Dawes this afternoon, wrapped up with our little notes inside. But now he's here!*

Major Rufus Dawes, photographed in Marietta, March 1863.

The bell rings, and Betsey Gates opens the door. "Rufus, hello, it's so good to see you. Please come in." She turns to call her daughter: "Mary, Major Dawes is here." A pause. "Mary, we have a guest, and I suspect he came to see you. Am I right, Major?"

Rufus Dawes feels an embarrassing blush form on his cheeks. *Why am I so uneasy? Mrs. G. knows why I'm calling, but where is Mary?*

"Hello, Mrs. Gates, how are you? Uh yes, yes, I would like to see Mary if that's all right, I mean, if she is available, rather, if she would like to." *Oh, brother! I must sound like a real dope. If Eph could see me, he would be on the floor laughing. Where is she?*

Betsey Gates smiles at his nervousness and tries to put him at ease. "Rufus, we were all so impressed with your speech last night. My goodness, you have been through so much! But the positive reassurances you made were so wonderful. We all came away much relieved about the condition of the army." Turning, she shows him to a seat in the parlor and goes to the stairway to call again, "Mary, are you coming?"

Rufus sits down, but then quickly pops up again as Mary enters the parlor, very shyly offering her hand in greeting, then sitting on the sofa across the room. "Hello, Rufus, or is it proper to address you as *Major Dawes?*"

She looks wonderful. Am I staring? What did she ask? "Yes, that's the proper title ... But no, that's not what I meant. Please call me Rufus or Rufe, if you please, just like always. It's good to see you, Mary. I am leaving this evening and I have been wanting to express ..." He pauses to choose the proper words, which he has already thought of but are not coming out right now, and Mary, who has been nervously looking at his boots, takes the opportunity to initiate a diversion.

"Mother, won't you come in to visit? Rufus is leaving soon." The ploy works, as Betsey arrives thinking, *My, this was a short visit, very strange,* as she brings in the wrapped gift. "Mary, don't forget this."

Rufus, frustrated at the interruption of privacy, stutters a few words ... He did not mean he had to leave *right now*, and how is Mr. Gates, and how is Charley doing at college, and some other gibberish. All the time he is thinking, *What I really want to do is tell Mary I love her and will she write to me and give me a chance to earn her love in return, but here is her mother sitting here and ... This is going all wrong!*

Betsey Gates realizes what is happening. She can tell from his expression that this young man, Sarah's son, cares deeply for Mary and wants to say so. But Mary controls the situation, and it's not a mother's place to push her daughter either way. So they chat for a short while, and Mary presents the gift. "Francy and I purchased something for you. We hope you can use it, and I'm sorry she's not here now. But she says you should not open it until you get back to your regiment. We both wish you the very best, Rufus. Please be careful."

Rufus accepts with thanks, promises to abide by their wishes, and says goodbye. He wants to say so much more, to tell her how he feels about her, but ... it is too late. The opportunity is past. *I have failed.*

It is a quiet and somber officer who boards the train to Belpre that evening. Ma and his sisters shed tears at his departure, certain that his mood reflects a sadness at leaving family and friends. For Rufus, that is certainly true, but it is not the primary cause of his depression. *Will I ever have a chance with Mary again? Why didn't I just tell her when I had the chance, face-to-face? Could I have been any more dull and stupid?* The disappointment is his own fault, and he is angry at his ineptitude. As he sits on the seat and feels the cars sway back and forth, he glances into his valise and the package inside. *At least I have this.* [16]

Aquia Creek Landing—Union Supply Depot—Stafford County, VA
Starting and return point for a furlough home, March 10 & 24, 1863.

Union soldier burial detail, Sept. 19, 1862—Photograph by Alexander Gardner.

Researcher William A. Frassanito determined that this view looks north toward the Miller barn, barely visible on the far right. The Sixth Wisconsin buried their dead comrades on this day in this same field west of the Hagerstown Pike, about 100 yards behind Gardner's camera location.

Endnotes

1. Dawes letters. DAA. Quoted Dawes letters are from this source unless otherwise noted.

2. The US Burial Corps removed the bodies four years later and reinterred them in what would become the Antietam National Cemetery. A committee of concerned citizens led the Maryland State Legislature to adopt an act securing the land. Northern states made contributions based on population for the "humane and praiseworthy undertaking" to locate, remove, identify, and rebury the bodies of soldiers killed at Antietam, South Mountain, and other Maryland sites, plus those who died of wounds in hospitals. The cost was estimated at $5 per head. Best efforts were made to identify the bodies using uniforms, letters, etc. By October 1866, 4,667 bodies were orderly buried in sections by state, or in an officer section, or in a large "Unknown" section. Twenty-seven marked graves of Sixth Wisconsin soldiers are in the Wisconsin section, most killed or died of wounds at Antietam. Some are marked "Unknown." No Wisconsin bodies were recorded as from South Mountain; however, seventy-seven "Unknown" bodies were recovered from that site. It is assumed that the Iron Brigade soldiers killed at South Mountain, including Reuben Huntley, are in the "Unknown" section of Antietam National cemetery. "History of Antietam National Cemetery." http://www.whilbr.org.

3. Recorded by Julia Cutler. JCJ.

4. Edwin Brown Collection. WHS. Other letters quoted in this chapter relating to Brown are from this source.

5. *Dawes Journal, Book 3*, p. 135. DAA. Transcript of a Fond du Lac, WI, newspaper story of the sad event.

6. *O. R. Vol. XIX, pt. 1*, p. 254.

7. Goodwin, Doris Kearns. *Team of Rivals*, p. 454 and others. The "bodyguard" description from "Abraham Lincoln and George B. McClellan" (referencing Rafuse, Ethan S., *McClellan's War*, p. 395). The Lehrman Institute (website). http://www.abrahamlincolnsclassroom.org/abraham-lincolns-contemporaries/abraham-lincoln-and-george-b-mcclellan.

8. *Dawes Journal, Book 1*, p. 44. DAA.

9. Gibbon, John. *At Gettysburg and Elsewhere: Personal Recollections*, p. 74.

10. Nolan, Alan T. *The Iron Brigade*, p. 159, and Gibbon, John, *Recollections*, p. 76.

11. Derived from Dawes journals (DAA) and transcripts of Dr. John Hall's journal, EDC-NL.

12. *Dawes Journal, Vol. 2*. WHS.

13. JCJ.

14. *ibid.* and Dawes journal, DAA.

15. The speech and scene are recorded in the *Dawes Journals, Book 1*, pp. 67–75. DAA.

16. The scene is recreated from letters between Rufus and Mary written after the fact, preserved at DAA and WHS.

Chapter Seven

Are You Willing?

Saturday, March 21, 1863—Washington, D.C., Train Station

A tired and gloomy Major Rufus Dawes walks slowly along the crowded ramp to the station. It has been an uneventful and efficient trip, the nation's capital reached in less than twenty-four hours. As he enters the building, a voice ahead of him calls out, "Colonel Dawes!" He looks over to see none other than First Lieutenant Frank Haskell approaching him.

"Well, hello, Frank! This is a surprise. Are you coming or going? And, so that you know," as he taps his shoulder insignia, "I'm not a lieutenant colonel yet."

"Ah, but you are, sir!" Haskell replies. "I've just come from Madison, and the governor has issued the promotions for you and Colonel Bragg. Also, Captain Hauser to major. I think he made it effective March 10, if I remember correctly. Congratulations!"

They chat for a while and then go their separate ways—Haskell back to General Gibbon's staff and Dawes heading to town for a couple nights' stay with Marietta College friend Dave Chambers and family. As he heads toward a livery carriage, he is thinking, *Haskell still being a first lieutenant is a shame, but such is the plight of staff officers—limited rank advancement. My promotion brightens the day, but I would give it up for another chance with Mary in Marietta.*[1]

The Next Day

"Well, Marshall, you were mistaken about Mary Gates. She's not engaged as you said. I found that out for sure during my leave in Marietta last week." Rufus Dawes, Marshall Newport, and David Chambers are sitting

217

together at the Chambers home, talking of old times and current events. Rufus is referring to the dinner he had with Newport a year ago.

"Ah, well, what do you know," Newport responds, blowing some cigar smoke away. "So, does that mean you two got together for a good time, which, knowing you both, might mean some piano or chess? Or is she still Little Miss Shyness?"

Newport is a longtime friend, but he can be a bit annoying. This is one of those moments when Dawes wonders about him. *I'm not so sure that he didn't steer me away from Mary for a reason. I think I'll keep any details to myself.* "Any time with her doing anything would be a good time. But yes, we did get together. She and Fanny gave me a gift package. I'm supposed to wait till I get back to camp."

"Ha!" chimes Newport. "I hope it isn't perishable. Dave, just like old Railroad Rufus to dutifully keep a promise. I would have opened it on the train."

Chambers keeps it neutral. "I think you two have different attributes, I'll say that much. And thanks for the wine, Marsh. French wine to boot. Very nice."

Newport laughs. "Nothing but the best for my two old college mates. On second thought, at least you and I can enjoy it, Dave—unless Rufe, you've acquiesced and now joined our army of liquor drinkers. If not, you must be the only officer I know who doesn't enjoy a drink, at least now and then. That's how things get done, you know. Promotions are sought, deals are made, favors called in ... over a bottle or at a bar. It frees up discussion. We have suppliers coming to us all the time in the quartermaster office, and I bet most of the contracts are sealed with a handshake at a bar. That's just how it's done here. Besides, it's also a good way to forget about the all discouraging army news that we hear all the time."

Chambers glances at Rufus, afraid that offense has been taken. He is close friends with both, but Newport can be a bit snobby. He should know better than to goad Rufus about alcohol or the army, especially after what he has been through in battle. There's a reason for his abstinence, and it goes back to his youth. *So just leave it alone, Marshall.*

Dawes smiles at Newport and responds, "What you do is your business, Marsh. I just don't see the need for it. But you're right: I get kidded about my whiskey avoidance all the time. Usually it's cheap whiskey, by the way—none of your French wine available in the field! If meetings at a bar are an effective way to do government business ... then fine. I do have to say that we in the army appreciate the better food coming our way. Potatoes and onions ... Our boys are happy for just that.

You are obviously doing well. Every time I've seen you, that uniform is immaculate!"

The dinner conversation is less contentious. Rufus shares experiences in the field and recent news from Marietta. David and Marshall tell stories of Washington politics. Theodore Greenwood and Timothy Condit are remembered with fondness and regret. Those fun-filled college days seem so distant now.[2]

Tuesday, March 24, 1863, Belle Plain, Virginia—
Iron Brigade Camp

Lt. Col. Rufus Dawes makes it back to the regiment's camp before the end of his leave, transported again by a Potomac River supply boat. Bragg and he exchange promotion congratulations, and the colonel brings his second-in-command up to date. As soon as he can get away, however, Dawes heads into his cabin to open the package from Mary.

He rips open the wrapping and finds a pair of sheepskin gauntlets. *Nice! That is something I can use. No more scratches and cuts from shoving away tree branches while on my horse. Very thoughtful.* There are two notes inside. He reads the one signed by Fanny Bosworth first, and chuckles. They have been friends for a long time, have always kidded each other, experienced a moment of something more, just as quickly realized that was not them, and became even more comfortable with each other, almost as brother and sister. Fanny offers her best wishes for his safety but closes with a few humorous references of youthful times together, including that awkward kiss.

Now ... for Mary. He received no encouragement from her last Friday, so her note is opened with apprehension. It is friendly, encouraging, formal. She writes well. She mentions his family and how much she and her parents enjoy their company. She feels sorry for Mother, who worries about her two sons in the army. There are congratulations again on the speech: "Your words captivated Charley, I dare say the whole community," she writes. Then, "We hope these gloves serve you well. Sincerely, Mary Gates."

Well, nothing very personal there, he thinks, but she did not say to stay away! He feels stupid but can't resist holding the letter up to his nose. No, nothing there. The gloves go on, and he admires them. Perfect fit. *We would be a perfect fit, too, Mary, if only I can sway you somehow. My face-to-face effort failed miserably. My only remaining opportunity is a thank-you letter. I must not be dull and stupid this time*[3]:

Miss Mary B. Gates

Positively I did not open that box till I was "in camp," though my fingers itched sorely.

Accept my thanks for the token of sympathy and encouragement—for I infer from it that you are "hand in glove" with me in the good and glorious cause, and that you desire me always to "throw down the gauntlet" to its enemies. My compliments and thanks to "Miss F. B." with the assurance that I am as penitent for past transgressions as becomes a soldier.

He sits back to review. *Very witty, I think. Always break the ice with humor. But now, "into the breach!" What do I say next? How do I say it? Be serious and get to the point. I have nothing to lose, everything to gain.* He dips his pen and continues:

The indications here are of hard work very soon. Encouraged by the sympathy and sound doctrine I met with among the people at home, I shall go into the struggle cheerfully and hopefully.

I hope you respond to this note. It would give me a great deal of pleasure to correspond with you. Are you willing?

Very Respectfully,

Rufus R Dawes

He places the letter in the mail, his thoughts focused on Mary. It will be a long two weeks, at least, waiting for a reply—that is, if a reply is made at all …

General Hooker has initiated changes in the army beyond the furlough system and food enhancements. Each corps is provided with a unique badge to be worn on the hat, a different color for each division. For Major General John Reynolds's First Corps, the patch is a full circle, which for the First Division, including General Meredith's Iron Brigade, is solid red in color. The badges provide immediate unit identification, and for the soldiers, they quickly become important symbols, inspiring unit pride. Their actions will reflect on the whole unit. No longer will stragglers get lost in the crowd. The provost guard will know who they belong to. This side benefit of the badge system certainly factors into the idea.

Of special note for field officers such as Bragg, Dawes, and Hauser, regiments are issued two pack mules for stowing their gear. In theory, it will provide more mobile and reliable transportation in rough terrain—provided, of course, the mules cooperate. Lysander Cutler, the Sixth Wisconsin's original commander and now a brigadier general, is assigned command of the Second Brigade of James Wadsworth's First Division, so he will be a close neighbor.

Wadsworth is a wealthy fifty-five-year-old politician from New York granted a general's star despite no military experience. He was kept in the background by McClellan and ran for New York governor and lost. But with Little Mac now gone for good, he uses his influence to take division command from General Abner Doubleday. Doubleday, in turn, takes command of the Third Division, formerly commanded by General Meade, who has moved up to command the Fifth Corps as reward for his fine showing at Fredericksburg. These are but a few of the leadership changes, common in any army, but for the Union side, the frequent turnovers following failed campaigns are a continual detriment to overall coordination and efficiency. Promotions and assignments do not always reflect good service and competency. Political influence often plays a large factor.

Wednesday, March 25, 1863—Camp at Belle Plain

"General Wadsworth, the officers of the Sixth Wisconsin have come to pay you their respects. If it pleases the general, I will introduce our officers and staff." Lt. Col. Dawes has marched the regiment's officers for a courtesy call on their new division commander, the little band leading the way as they keep step to the music. It's a longstanding tradition performed by every unit. "General, this is Major Hauser." A shake of the hand, and Wadsworth replies, "Major Hauser, how do you do?" Then the next, and the next, all down to the lowest second lieutenant.

Finally, through the line, Wadsworth announces, "Gentlemen, won't you please step over to the table and enjoy some of my whiskey." The officers gladly comply, all except Lt. Col. Dawes. He stands back with Doctors Preston and Hall. "Well, doctors, it's whiskey time, as always. What do you think of our New York general?"

Dr. Preston is sampling the general's liquid refreshment, so Hall answers first: "He's an impressive-looking gentleman, that's for certain. Clayton Rogers speaks favorably of him, and he should know, since he's stayed on the general's staff, though he admits it's too soon to tell. The general does seem to have a true interest in troop welfare, which is certainly a good thing."

Dawes replies, "I am told he has no battle experience, no military training before the war. But on the other hand, we have all seen West Point officers fail us miserably. We have four fine brigades in our division. Let's hope he is smart enough to keep us all out of a big ambush."

Captain John Kellogg has wandered over, glass in hand, and overhears the last comment. "I agree with that! And I'm sure we will find out soon enough."

Wednesday, April 1, 1863, Marietta, Ohio—the Gates Home

His letter arrived this morning. "Are you willing?" His question has been on Mary's mind all day. She thinks, *What should I do? Everyone knows that formally corresponding with a man is tantamount to engagement, and I am certainly not ready for that—with Rufus Dawes or anyone else. That boy in Massachusetts wanted to do the same, and I turned him down for the same reason. Rufus is a fine gentleman, as good as any of those Yale men. I can't think of anyone better, really. He obviously wants to court me, but I really don't know him well. He's been away in Wisconsin or in the army since before I went to Ipswich.*

I do feel bad about his visit. His last time home for a long time ... perhaps forever ... and I acted so childish! He has seen so much fighting already, and his unit—the papers now call them the "Iron Brigade"—will certainly see more bloody battles. That is part of it too. To become involved with a soldier ... I have seen the weeping and sorrow of widows and girlfriends. I wept and mourned horribly at poor Theodore's funeral. I want to marry and have a family someday, and a man like Rufus would be the kind of husband any woman would want. He seems so much like father—well, except for singing or music. Charley looks up to him. Mother likes him and his family. Father is not here now, and I'm not sure how he feels. I would like his thoughts. Of course, Bettie kids me about Rufe's bowed legs.

I'm sorry, Rufus, I just can't. Not now. Not with you and our whole country in such turmoil and uncertainty. I hope you will understand. I am honored that you show such interest in me, and I will always hold you in high regard and pray for your continued safety, but I must politely and respectfully decline your request to correspond.

She composes a reply letter to that effect and mails it the next day. It does not please her to do so, and she feels a burden of sadness when thinking of the disappointment her message is likely to bring, a sting of cruelty to a man already facing cruelty and danger in the country's service.

Wednesday, April 15, 1863—Camp at Belle Plain

Lt. Col. Rufus Dawes has been in an uncharacteristically sour mood for a week. There is much to supervise with getting the regiment prepared for the new spring advance against Robert E. Lee's Army of Northern Virginia, and he has supervised everything relentlessly, cutting no slack for anyone. Doctor Hall has become a close friend—living together in a small cabin all winter either makes friendships or ends them—and he has seen the abrupt change in mood. Conversation is limited, and there is no interest in chess or any amusement. Rufus uses his spare time to ride alone.

Rufus did share the first letter he received from home last week. It contained the sad news that his aunt Lizzie and uncle William lost the pregnancy. The baby she had been carrying turned out to be twins. They were delivered prematurely and died the same day. Rufus naturally feels badly for Lizzie and William; they have suffered far more than any parent should. These twins bring to five the number of young children they have placed in a grave.[4]

But another letter came a day later, and he does not talk about it. It obviously is having an impact, and Hall believes it must involve that girl in Marietta. As they finish a quiet meal this evening, he decides to pry: "Rufus, pardon me asking, but you've been in a pretty dour mood lately, ever since that last letter came. I'd be happy to talk about it if it would help."

Dawes looks up at him with a vacant stare. The lively look from his dark eyes is not present tonight, and there is no response.

"It's about that girl in Marietta, isn't it?" Hall persists.

Dawes sighs, leans back, and is tempted to bark a rebuke. But John is a friend, and he's trying to do what friends do. Finally, he relents. "Yes, it's about 'that girl.' Mary Gates. I can't stop thinking of her. I asked her if she would correspond. Her letter said, 'No, thank you.' Expressed very nicely, but, 'No, thank you.' So that's it. I'll have to get over it, but ..."

John Hall makes a face and ponders the situation. "Well, that *is* tough. Disappointing, obviously." He thinks it over a few moments and then asks, "If this is bothering you so much, which it certainly is, then you must care for her very deeply. Does she understand that? I mean, have you told her? If your feelings are strong and sincere, which I'm sure they are, I think she would need to know. Besides, I have not seen you give in to disappointment or tactical reverses without coming back on the offense. Lord knows I see it all the time on the chessboard!"

"So you're saying try again?" Dawes asks. "That could really turn her away, annoying her even more. She's never indicated any feeling for me at all, except for sympathy and good wishes."

"Well, Rufus, it seems to me you have nothing to lose. If she becomes annoyed by someone liking—no, *loving* her—then maybe she is best left alone. But what is worse: a hurt to your pride or avoiding a chance to win her over? If you give up, you may regret it for a long, long time."

Dawes is silent for a while, and Hall leaves him alone. The words the Doc used—"If you give up'"—strike home. He thinks of his family. They are not prone to give up in the face of challenge. *I am the same. Mary, my feelings for you are sincere and absolute. Whether you accept it or not, I will tell you so. I will* not *give up without another attempt.* Still, as he dips his pen, his hands tremble a bit with trepidation:

6th Wis. Vol., 1st Division, 1st Corps, April 15th

Miss Mary B. Gates

Almost a week ago I received a paper from you in acknowledgement of my note. My inference was that you wished me to understand that you politely declined to accede to my request to correspond. With this view it is perhaps even impertinent and ungentlemanly for me to address you again. I have hesitated long whether to venture to or not. Tomorrow, under our present orders, we are to commence our active campaign, and I may not have another opportunity, so I have at last, at the imminent peril of placing myself in a character most galling to my pride, concluded to tell you plainly <u>why</u> I asked you to correspond with me.

It was because I <u>love</u> you—because by the strongest and holiest impulses of my nature I am drawn to you as the only woman I ever loved, or it seems to me, I ever could love. I am by no means so egotistical or presumptuous as to assume, as a reason for addressing you thus, that I have inspired a like sentiment. Indeed, if I have interpreted rightly, the indications are that so great a blessing is not in store for me. If, in the face of such circumstances, I am making a fool of myself by declaring a hopeless passion, I can't help it. If I had not found it utterly useless to try to help loving you, I never should have written this letter. However you may regard my suit, I am sure you will find sufficient in this letter to excuse me for writing it.

Rufus R Dawes

On this day also, Major John Hauser is traveling back to Wisconsin on leave of absence. He took with him the tattered state flag and staff, the same one carried by then major Dawes to rally broken Wisconsin survivors outside of the cornfield. Dawes had given it one last pensive look as he passed it to Hauser, instantly recalling the gut-wrenching minutes when he felt sure he would be shot down at any moment. On April 17, the *Madison Journal* recorded this article:

> Major Hauser, of the 6th Regiment delivered today at The Executive Office, the old regimental flag of the gallant Sixth regiment, worn and torn, and tattered in the fierce conflicts of Gainesville, Bull Run 2nd, South Mountain, Antietam, and Fredericksburg. It will be replaced by the Governor with a new flag under the law passed by the late session.[5]

Thursday, April 23, 1863, Belle Plain—Sixth Wisconsin Camp

"Billy, the word is we will be moving out soon. We need you and Jake to stock up a ten-day supply of food for our field officer mess. Here's the list we've made up, and the money you will need is in this envelope. Now don't let that Sutler cheat you. I'll read it to you, but you can keep the list." Billy has proven reliable—is, in fact, now an integral part of the behind-the-scenes essentials for the regiment's senior officers—but Lt. Col. Dawes wants to be sure no mistakes are made.

Dawes reads as Billy holds the paper in his hand. "All right. Let's go down the list. First, at the commissary, two hams, twenty-five pounds hardtack, one dollar's worth of coffee, and fifty cents' worth of tea. Then, at the Sutler, one can prepared milk, five pounds of soda crackers, and five loaves of soft bread. Have you got that?"

"Ah, yas, sah!" Billy says. "Don't yah worry, sah. I'll git it all and take that ol' stubborn pack mule ta carry it. Ah got us sum empty ammunition boxes we goin' ta sling over dat mule fo it all. It'll be jes fine. Ceptin' when dat mule jes don't wanna go. He jes sits down and don't move."

Dawes laughs, but the joke could be on the officers if that mule doesn't keep up on the march. Aside from the food, the animal will be carrying blankets, oilcloths, woolen shirts, extra boots for each officer, and a wedge tent, plus a bag of feed corn.

While Billy takes care of that, Dawes helps supervise the regiment's preparations for the spring campaign. Indications are that General Joseph Hooker will get them moving before May 1, so weapons, uniforms, and equipment are all inspected to make sure everyone is ready to go. Ten days' rations must be carried per Hooker's orders, ammunition supplies obtained, uniforms put in good shape or replaced, and unnecessary items removed from knapsacks. The troops are old soldiers now, so they know the drill. A scattering of new recruits from Wisconsin arrive, and they are unceremoniously ushered into the routine by the sergeants.

At the end of the day, Col. Bragg, Lt. Col. Dawes, Major Hauser, and surgeons Preston, Andrews, and Hall sit around the campfire outside the headquarters cabin, reviewing the regiment's readiness. The morning report shows almost four hundred men present for duty.

Colonel Bragg asks Dr. Preston for a health status, and Preston responds, "Sick call hasn't been too busy, and the regiment is generally in good health, a lot better than most units. There shouldn't be many on the 'weak squad' that we will leave behind. The wounded men who have come back over the winter are in pretty good shape; they should all be able to march and perform. Even that Irish scamp, Mickey Sullivan—

Private Mickey Sullivan, Co. K

from your old Company K, Colonel Dawes—he says he's ready to go. That fellow is a bit of a wonder, isn't he?"

"Little Mickey," says Dawes, smiling. "He was wounded at South Mountain, had an operation on his foot, was discharged last fall, couldn't stand being home, and then reenlisted! He came back even though he was the only man left from his skirmish team—or, as the infantry manual so formally terms it, 'comrades in battle.' Mickey always jokes about that term."

Dr. Andrews injects a comment: "Sullivan! I remember him! I tried to extract that ball out of his foot the morning after the South Mountain battle, but it was wedged between the bones, and I couldn't grasp it with the forceps. It hurt him like hell, and he used every profanity I ever knew and some I didn't—but not at me, at the Rebs! Afterward, he was cracking jokes and keeping everyone's spirits up in that dirty barnyard we had for a field hospital. He's one tough Mick."[6]

Dawes responds, "Sullivan and George Chamberlin were the two littlest men in the company and always getting into mischief. It seemed like I was always putting them on some sort of punishment. But they are both brave as they come—well, *were* in the case of Chamberlin. He's dead on that mountain. But Sullivan is as witty as ever. I was over in K today, and as Ticknor and I walked by Mickey, I asked him how his right foot was, because they took off his second toe and a good-size chunk behind it. He said, 'Sure and it'd be fine, sir, but 'tis now a half-boot-size smaller!' I talked with Ticknor, who just got over his own wound from Antietam, and we recalled the names of those in the company who are gone from a year ago. Six have been killed, and five discharged due to wounds. Two were wounded and taken prisoner at Gainesville. In all, about thirty have been shot. I'm sure it's the same in your old companies too." He turns toward Bragg and Hauser, and they nod in agreement, with Bragg holding his left arm up and pointing at it in jest as a reminder to his staff that he is a wounded convalescent too.

Colonel Bragg then sums it up: "The four hundred we do have are fat, healthy, and contented, and they know how to fight. I wish we had more, but we will make a good showing with these boys, I'm sure of that. We've talked about this before. It's a dark hour for our struggle, with so much disappointment and peace-mongering at home. General Wadsworth and I can personally attest to that, as otherwise we would both be elected and not be here! The army needs to strike a great blow for the cause, or else the cause, and our country as we know it, could well be lost."

Sunday, April 26, 1863—Camp near Belle Plain, Virginia

The mail arrived yesterday afternoon. There were three from Marietta, one each from Lucy and Kate, and ... one from Mary Gates! He had torn open Mary's letter first—so anxious and nervous, his fingers were shaking:

"Dear Lt. Col. Dawes"

Hmm, very formal. Too formal? Reading on ...

"I must say that I was shocked not a little by your expression of love for me. For aside from the newspaper clippings you sent me over a year ago, which suddenly stopped coming, I had no idea that you were even thinking of me. Until your visit home last month, it has been three years since we have talked face-to-face when you were at the College. However, I do feel and believe that your expressions toward me are sincere. I cannot honestly say that I share the same feelings toward you, not having had an opportunity, or likely will have an opportunity soon, to come to know you better. Of course, I have thought of love and of the man I would someday marry. I use my own parents as an example of love and devotion to each other. I see it every day in their actions. I would be very blessed to someday have a love for someone that is more than life, a love that shall last through time and eternity.

I sincerely appreciate your continuing sacrifices in defense of our country and will forever be flattered and honored by your sentiments toward me. I do care for you and will certainly keep you in my thoughts and prayers with the earnest desire for your continued safety. But, I cannot say that I have love enough to commit to a permanent correspondence and engagement. Perhaps when you return on leave, or, God willing, this war is over and won, we may then have time to engage in a proper acquaintanceship. Sincerely, Mary B. Gates

"Disappointment" is an insufficient word. He is crushed, the feeling of emptiness, loss, uncertainty, and gloom. *I have felt this before,* he thinks. *Leaving the family to live with Father when I was only ten. Leaving Ohio for Wisconsin. Hen's death. I need to reflect. When I felt this way in the past, my brother and sisters were always there, they with their own demons, all brought on by the stigma of a broken family, but we have always had each other. I have so hoped that this time there would be acceptance and a chance at obtaining a much-longed-for treasure: a happy life with Mary.*
Today, Lt. Col. Rufus Dawes is assigned to command the brigade picket line, and there is considerable downtime in this duty that allows for drafting response letters to the family. *I will not have a chance to do so much longer,* he is thinking. *Should I mention anything about Mary in my answers to Lucy and Kate? No. Certainly, there is nothing assured with Mary—quite the opposite it appears—and much to be embarrassed about if my suit of her becomes a failure:*

Dear Lucy

We are under orders "to move" and have been for a week. Next week we must go, it seems to me, if it is the intention to go at all. Our boys have got their pay. They are fat, happy and valorous. That terrible dread that seemed to settle like a pall over their spirits after the slaughter in the Antietam Cornfield, has given away to more cheerful feeling. Expeditions are going out continually to harass the enemy. Their doings are carefully concealed from the newspapers. The 24th Michigan, of our own brigade, went to Port Royal on the Rappahannock the other day. They crossed the river in boats at night, in face of ten thousand rebels, drove in their pickets, captured several prisoners, destroyed much valuable property, and ran away again before the rebs could organize to pursue and destroy them.

Your Aff Bro, Rufe[7]

He looks again at the captured "Last Will and Testament" found in a Rebel skirmish camp by the Twenty-Fourth Michigan. Lt. Col. Mark Flanigan had brought it by as a curiosity. Dawes reads the second paragraph, written by a John Cooper of Carolina County, Virginia:

Secondly, I do hereby emancipate and set free my beloved wife Charlotte and my daughter Nancy, and such other children as may be begotten on the body of my wife Charlotte.[8]

Rufus shakes his head and thinks; *His wife is a black slave girl! If this does not expose the immorality of the Rebel cause, nothing else does! Yes, this war is about preserving the Union. But it is also about ending this appalling institution of human slavery. It dooms both slave and master. Now, to answer Kate, who has told me about the passing of a neighbor near the Old Stone House:*

Dear Kate ... I am sorry to hear of the death of Mrs. Slocomb. Really, I may be permitted to say she was a long time getting ready. Death is a word so familiar in the Army that it scarcely strikes us with that solemn awe that it's occurrence was want to at home.

Where he is most near he seems least regarded.

My love to everybody, Rufe

Lt. Col. Rufus Dawes contemplates his next message, the all-important one to Mary Gates. *Her letter does not indicate a desire to correspond and certainly makes no corresponding expression of the love I declared to her. Therefore, should I dare to address her again? Yet, she did respond! And she writes that she believes me to be sincere. But she probably thinks I am a lonesome soldier living an infatuation fed by circumstances of war and danger. She is partially correct in that, for once we meet the enemy again, I may never have a chance with her—or anything else in life. This is a fact I am fully aware of. For that reason, the fact that I may never have another chance, makes it altogether mandatory that I express to her, as fully as I can communicate by letter, exactly how I feel about her. If not now, perhaps never again:*

6th Wis Vol's, 1st Div, 1st Corps, Army of Potomac, Apr 26th

Mary B

I have received your letters and hasten to avail myself of your permission to write to you again. I must tell you candidly that there is but one subject upon which I can find it in my heart to address you, so long as I may do so without offense or impropriety. I approach it more readily because I <u>have</u> found hope in your letter—a hope which, slender as it is, I would not give up for all else I hope for in this world—a hope that has almost made a coward of me for fear there <u>will</u> be a battle before I can know that it will be realized, or that I must give it up forever.

I am very grateful to you for believing me to be sincere. I know very well that I can add nothing of force to what I have already said by argument or protestation, but I will assure you that my love is no transient or hastily conceived passion. Do you find anything inconsistent with weak human nature in my conduct toward you while in college when I tell you that it was <u>there</u> my constant effort to crush my love for you [began] because I believed it was a hopeless love. Hopeless, because it was unrequited—hopeless, because without any fixed aim or object in life, and with a very doubtful future, I had no right to ask you to return it. When you know this, I do not think it will not seem impossible to you that I might have thought of you sometimes during that "three years"—I did many times.

I will tell you once where I thought of you. It would seem very silly to anybody else, and it may to you. Shortly after the battle opened at Antietam our Colonel was shot. I succeeded to the command, becoming with my life and honor responsible for the good conduct of my regiment. You have heard the story of how we were broken to pieces and driven back in confusion, more than half of our numbers bleeding or dying on the field. Orders, exhortations, entreaties were vain to rally my men over-come with the terrible fear of Death.

I took the Wisconsin State flag in my hand, and swinging it over my head, and calling every man from Wisconsin to follow me, I turned back into the open field. When I took up that color in my hand, I gave up all hope of life. It did not occur to me as possible that I could carry that flag into the deadly storm and live (four men had fallen under it). I felt all that burning throng of thoughts and emotions that always comes with the presence of Death. I had no right to think of you there. For what reason should I? Why did I? I would have died with your name on my lips.

The spark was smoldering. Do you wonder that the flame burst out when I saw you this winter so much? Has it not lasted under auspices most unfavorable?

I would not say more than I mean. With the sentiments I have professed for you, and the kindness and candor you have treated my suit, I would deem myself worse than a villain to assume any false character, or say anything I would not sustain with the best effort of my life.

Notwithstanding what you have said I shall await anxiously for an answer to this letter. Surely if you can find it in your heart to look with favor upon my love so freely tendered, there can be no harm—I hardly know how to fill out this sentence. But if there is no ground whatever for the hope I am indulging, I beg of you to tell me so plainly that I can't mistake. It will be better for me. The earliest hour that honor and duty will allow,

I will get a leave of absence and come and see you, if in the plainest words, I can feel that there is any use.

God has in this world no higher blessing for me than the realization of my <u>hope</u> that that day will come when you "know that the love you have for me is more than life, a love that shall last through time and eternity."

R. R. D.

PS—I write this on a soldier's desk—a drum head. I am field officer of the picket.

Late Morning, Tuesday, April 28, 1863—Belle Plain Camp

Rufus Dawes dutifully makes notes in his pocket journal. The letters to Mary and his sisters were posted yesterday. Who knows when he might receive a reply. Today, it is all business, as he notes in his journal:

All hurry and bustle this morning. Orders to march at 12. Has the grand movement begun at last? Or will we be fooled again, and subside once more into a state of chronic expectation.

Rumor says the 11th & 12th Corps moved yesterday and the booming of cannon this morning toward Port Royal proclaiming that <u>somebody</u> is stirring.

I think perhaps Gray-back is somewhat in the dark this time as to where the belligerent Joseph means to come down upon him. Reconnaissance to Port Royal—reconnaissance's to Culpepper—demonstrations right in front—have obfuscated <u>us</u> if nothing else.

I fear there is a storm brewing for us this afternoon. Rain is coming down. These fine showers are bringing out the spring flowers. How many of us poor soldier boys will never see their return?[9]

* * * * *

Joseph Hooker's appointment as Union army commander came on January 25. The president was at best pragmatic in his selection and in a very direct letter to Hooker the next day made known his reservations regarding Hooker's reputation as a braggart and backstabber. Lincoln's letter read in part, "I have heard, in such a way as to believe it, of your recently saying that both the Army and the Government needed a dictator. Of course, it was not for this, but in spite of it, that I have given you the command. Only those generals who gain successes can set up dictators. What I now ask of you is military success, and I will risk the dictatorship."

In the months following his appointment, Hooker has reorganized and reinvigorated his army. There are now seven infantry and one cavalry corps, each commanded by a major general. Artillery batteries are assigned to each division within the corps for better support and direct control.

On the Confederate side, Lee's army has the same organization and senior leaders as in the summer and fall campaigns of 1862. General Longstreet and two divisions of his First Corps, however, are in southeast Virginia scouring for provisions because by this period of the war, northern Virginia has been ravaged. Lee's depleted army is outnumbered by over 50,000 men.

To achieve the military success Lincoln asks for, Hooker believes he has devised an ironclad plan to defeat Robert E. Lee's Army of Northern Virginia. He has kept the plan secret, even from some of his seven corps commanders. Spring rains have delayed the start and have disrupted the planned first phase—a cavalry raid around Lee's army to confuse and divert the enemy, and to serve as payback for Confederate General J. E. B. Stuart's successful sorties around the Union army last year.

The role to be played by Rufus Dawes and his Iron Brigade comrades in Hooker's grand plan is to be a diversion and blocking force. The Union First Corps will cross the Rappahannock River on pontoons south of Fredericksburg, followed by the Sixth Corps near the city itself. It is familiar territory—the site of General Burnside's disastrous defeat less than five months past. The river crossing should serve to hold Stonewall Jackson's forces near the town, while the bulk of the Union army, fully two-thirds, cross the Rappahannock and Rapidan Rivers at upriver fords some 20 miles away. This main force will attack Lee's left flank from the west, being the hammer to smash Lee on the anvil of the First and Sixth Corps. That is the plan. The initial problem for First Corps commander General John Reynolds is how to cross the river in the face of Confederates from Early's division waiting on the other side, ready to contest it.

Daybreak, Monday, April 29, 1863—Reynolds's First Corps Approaches Fitzhugh's Crossing on the Rappahannock River, Five Miles South of Fredericksburg

Colonel Edward Bragg, hands on hips, is shaking his head as he addresses his second-in-command, Lt. Col. Rufus Dawes: "This is a real fiasco if I ever saw one. And it's likely to get us all killed!" They are both watching dozens of braying mule teams with cursing drivers and engineer troops attempting to maneuver and drop their loads of wooden pontoon boats at the river's edge. The thick fog, the darkness, and the slippery slope are making a mess of things.

Despite the ruckus, Dawes yawns deeply before replying. The regiment has been up all night moving toward the river in the darkness and under rain showers but has been impeded by the late-arriving and lumbering pontoon detachment—a wet, muddy stop-and-start march that has been frustrating and miserable. "It reminds me of the cackling geese that saved Rome, only here we have a hundred mules that have no doubt woken up the Rebs across the river. So much for our nighttime surprise crossing! If we and the Twenty-Fourth Michigan have to cross now, it will be daytime. The fog is starting to lift too."

"That's still the order," Bragg says, his noted sarcasm in full evidence. "'Secure the crossing by taking the enemy rifle pits on the far side so that the engineers can build their bridge for crossing the rest of the division feet-dry to the other side.' I'm sure you are as honored as I am that General Wadsworth selected us. 'Full faith and confidence,' and all that. But I'll admit to a bad feeling about this. Looks like they've got maybe twenty boats at the water, only half done."

Dawes shares the same thought. He thinks again to last evening, just before pitching the tent in the bush and snugging in for the night, then promptly getting orders to move out for the awful all-night march here. He had placed Mary's two letters in an envelope addressed to her in Marietta. He inserted a short note, sealed it, and walked over to Dr. A. W. Preston. The two had messed together for a long time and had come to know and respect each other over those long discussions during and after evening meals. "Here, Doc," he said. "I have a favor to ask. We're about to start the new campaign, so it's time to do my part and take my chances. I'm not worrying myself sick about it and don't have any premonitions, but just in case I don't come back, would you please see that this is sent? I would appreciate it."

The doctor looked at Rufus and, with the solemn pledge of a friend, said he would be honored to fulfill the request if it became necessary, but he would also be happy to return it to Rufus upon his safe return.

"Well, of course that's what I'm hoping for," Dawes said. "I just don't want these to get lost. They mean a lot to me." The two shook hands, and Preston placed the envelope in his saddlebag ...

Now it appears that this mission will be much more perilous than first thought, and the river looks ever wider as the opposite shore slowly becomes visible through the gray mist. Dawn is coming late but not late enough. Dawes thinks of home. "It reminds me a bit of the Muskingum or Little Hocking Rivers back in Ohio," he wistfully mentions to Bragg. "About the same width, maybe some 150 yards, with that steep, tree-lined bank on the other side."

Bragg turns to look at him as he chews an unlit cigar. "Really? Well, I bet back home you didn't have someone shooting at you." Just as the words come out of Bragg's mouth, -CRACK!- -CRACK!- Shots are fired from the other side into the mass of mules and teamsters. Then more shots in quick succession. A mule goes down, shots ping off the big boats, drivers shout, officers wave their arms, and the whole mass starts to panic. They are not used to being on the receiving end of gunfire, and they are now excellent targets for Rebel sharpshooters. First one team, then another, then everybody—all make a grand skedaddle for safety up the slope, drivers whipping mules, boats dropping onto the ground, mud flying, wagons bumping into each other.

Dawes and Bragg run back to the regiment and see their men scramble to get out of the way of the maddened pontoon train. There are catcalls from the Black Hats, some laughter and whoops, a rather comical scene, but they all soon realize the impact: Surprise has been lost. *We are going to cross in open boats under the direct fire of the enemy, like ducks in a pond.*

9:00 a.m., Monday, April 29, 1863

The regiment is formed in a shallow ravine 300 yards north of the river. Colonel Bragg gives the men final instructions: "Boys, you know that our firing across the river this morning after the big mule skedaddle did not move the Rebs. They're too protected over there. So the general says we are the ones to clear them out by crossing over in the boats. Part of the Twenty-Fourth Michigan will join us on the left. The rest of the brigade will move down to the bank on both sides of us and fire across to provide cover. Colonel Wainwright has placed over thirty guns behind us to blast the Rebs too. When I give the order, we will march down in company columns to about 200 yards from the river, then 'by the right of companies,' double-quick to the boats, two boats per company, row like hell to the other side, and take those rifle pits. The general is counting on us, and he knows the Sixth Wisconsin is up to the task. We are from the west. We know how to handle boats, and we know how to fight! Let no man shirk his duty!"

Lt. Col. Rufus Dawes is standing next to good friend Dr. John C. Hall, listening to Bragg's instructions. When asked, John Hall tells Dawes that Dr. Preston has just been sent away on detached duty. Dawes nods and looks at the men in the regiment. Everyone is paying attention, and he can tell they share the same dread that he feels about the task before them. Everyone is already mud-covered from lying prone this morning on the river bank, shooting across at the Rebs—a futile effort since the enemy was well-protected in rifle pits. He had several close calls, bullets striking next to him, hearing the whizz of projectiles close by. Several men had been wounded.

But there is no way I am going to hold back now. This is the time to lead from the front. I will not let us fail, he says to himself as he checks his Colt revolver.

Dr. Hall has taken in the scene, and it churns his stomach. *Am I about to witness a hopeless slaughter as these boys get shot in the middle of the river?* He turns to Dawes and, with tears forming in his eyes, says, "God bless and protect you," as they shake hands.

In the distance, commands are shouted. The artillery in the rear opens a terrific cannonade, and the three supporting Iron Brigade regiments, plus the Fourteenth Brooklyn, trot forward toward the bank in line of battle. When they stop and open covering fire, Bragg yells out from his spot in the center of the line, "Forward, double-quick! March!" As soon as the regiment appears on the plain, the Rebels across the river open fire. At 200 yards from the boats, Bragg yells out, "Now for it, boys! By the right of companies, run, march!"

Dawes is in his place near the right column and runs forward as fast as he can. Rebel artillery fire is now coming in, and bullets are whizzing past or hitting the ground all around. The rifle-and-cannon-fire noise from both sides is deafening. Now at the boat! "Heave her off! Oars, oars!" Men have dashed up and into the boats, but some are hit and go down in the mud. The oars are in the bottom. "Get the oars up! Get off the oars!" They struggle to pull them out while others strain to push the big boats into the water and get on board. Bullets are flying in! -WHIZZ!- -PING!- -SPLAT!-

Dawes pulls up an oar and is passing it back to an enlisted man, when -WHACK!- A bullet smacks into it, sending splinters flying. Men shove the boat off and clumsily hop in, then begin to furiously pump the oars. Other men are shooting at the shore. The water around is churning. Dawes looks back and sees a soldier, Hoel Trumble from his old company, helping to push a boat away, then get hit in the head by a bullet. Trumble's hat flies off, and he drops into the water face-first, disappearing.

"Row! Row!" Dawes stands up in the bow, all excitement now, urging his men on, sword waving. The brush-lined bank is getting closer. His boat is the second to hit the shore; others are close behind, men shouting and firing. His men jump over the sides into the waist-deep water and claw up the slippery bank, grabbing bushes or getting shoved up by the next man behind. Shots ring out as the men go crazy in their quest to shoot or capture any Rebel soldier they see in their rifle pits. Dawes fires his pistol at Confederates running up the slope as Black Hat soldiers all around scramble up and about, coming at the Rebels from every direction. A sharp clip pulls on his sleeve. He looks down and sees a tear in his new left-hand gauntlet, a close call. Dawes spots Oliver Fletcher, a Lemonweir boy he recruited two years ago, attack a rifle pit, shoot a Confederate soldier in a one-on-one gun battle, grab a rifle from a wounded comrade, and capture two more Rebel soldiers in the next trench. Bravery and disregard for individual safety is displayed all around. He sees Rebel soldiers fall, more throw down their rifles. Here and there up the slope, Wisconsin and Michigan soldiers lay fallen in the slippery red-clay mud.

General Wadsworth gets caught up in the excitement as he stuns his staff by jumping in a boat himself, holding his swimming horse's bridle behind him, cheering his men onward. Dawes is focused ahead and does not see this sight, but the men in the First Division certainly do, or soon hear of it. Wadsworth forever earns their respect. First Lieutenant Theron Haight of the Twenty-Fourth New York, part of the unit tasked all night to move up the pontoons, is now a witness to the river assault: "It was a splendid sight to see the little blue-coated crowd rush up the bank along with the white-headed general, and a few moments afterwards to see the rebels swarm out of their rifle pits into the open, chased hotly by the vigorous boys from the west." [10]

Dawes climbs up through the smoke and bushes into smoke and gunshots among a platoon of Sixth Wisconsin soldiers. A smattering of bullets from the rear smack into the ground and chunk into tree limbs. Several men fall. Charles Conklin is hit in the knee, and Corporal Gabe

Ruby of Company I goes down hard with a shot in the middle of his back. Dawes turns him over to check and sees a blank stare—Ruby is killed. *It's coming from our own men, maybe the Seventh Wisconsin, across the river! They can't see us! We're going up faster than they think.* He spots the color bearer, runs to him while sheathing his sword, and grabs the flagstaff. *I've got to let them know we are near the top—to stop firing across the river!*

Panting now as he climbs toward an opening near the top so he can be seen, he raises the star-spangled banner and begins to swing it back and forth.

General James Wadsworth

Artist Depiction of the Fitzhugh's Crossing Assault

Doctor John Hall, hands over his ears, watches the river crossing from a protected spot near Battery B, their Napoleons booming fire support over the river. Seventh Wisconsin soldiers are down the slope near the river, firing at the Rebel rifle pits on the other side, over the heads of the boys in the pontoon boats. Hall is trying to locate Rufus and spots him in a leading boat as the ragged flotilla hurries across. "Rufus, get down! Why are you the only man standing?! Get down!" he cries out to himself amid the crashing noise. He loses sight of Dawes as soldiers in blue with their black hats land their boats and attack up the opposite bank, dodging and shooting amidst the brush and timber that is all torn apart by the artillery preparation. *There he is! I can see him! He's got the flag out in the open!* "Rufus, stay back!" The Seventh Wisconsin is still firing. Gun smoke obscures his view. Then Hall hears cheers from the other side, the Seventh ceases fire, and the crashing explosions subside, just sporadic shots from across the river. *Cheers from a thousand voices now on our side! Our boys have done it! Where is Rufus? I can't tell where he went.* A sickening feeling washes over him. *No, don't let it be him,* he thinks as he rushes down to the shore to cross over with the Nineteenth Indiana to set up an aid station and help patch up the wounded.

Wednesday Morning, May 6, 1863, Marietta, Ohio

Mary Gates has not slept well the past two evenings, ever since receiving the letter from Rufe Dawes dated April 26. The beautiful letter. *No one has ever ... I am struck speechless by his sincerity, his eloquence, his plea, his love for me. I had no idea! Is this real? I have read it many times over. It still makes my heart beat fast. What should I do? It's my turn now; I must respond to him.* "Tell me *so* plainly," he wrote. *God, what should I say? I do care for him very much. But "love" is such a strong word. He has used it, plainly and openly. Can I?*

I have not shared this with anyone. Not Mother or Father or Francy or Charley. Maybe I should, but what can they say? It all comes back to me. How do I feel about him? How do I feel? And now, news of a great battle happening near Fredericksburg again. Reynolds's corps the first to be involved again. Why is it always him? I find myself worrying about him now. I never did before, but now ... God, please keep him safe! He is such a good man, and he loves me!

These thoughts and more scurry through her mind as she walks down Putnam Street from her home, heading to the post office on Front Street. She passes people she has known since girlhood along the way, doing business in the stores and shops or at the courthouse. As she turns the corner onto Front, she realizes she has acknowledged nobody along the way. Her mind has been so focused on Rufus Dawes. *Gosh, they must think me terribly rude today.*

"Hello, Uncle Bozzy!" she says as she enters the second-floor post office.

"Well, hello there, Mary! Back again for the mail? I usually don't see you here so often!" says Uncle Sala Bosworth with a wink and smile. "Today's mail just came in, a bunch of soldier's letters needing the three cents due on pickup. Pretty lucky to get this batch too. Mosby and his bandits have been stealing the Virginia mail for weeks now. But here's an envelope for you, and I'll cover you on the three cents."

"Thanks. You're a sweetie!" says Mary as she sees that the envelope is from Rufus. *Another letter already and a thick one, at that. What could he be sending me that could twist my thoughts any more than he already has? Maybe some newspaper clippings.* She walks over toward the door and sits down in a chair to open it. Uncle Bosworth is in the back room now, sorting letters. She is alone.

Opening the envelope, she finds ... the two letters she had sent to him. The first, declining his request to correspond, and she remembers how difficult it was to write. The second, her response to his expression of love for her—her careful, cautious, respectful reply. *The one that prompted him to write me the beautiful letter I am still pondering. But why is he sending these back now? Is he afraid of losing them on the march? Or has he changed his mind about me?* She looks again in the envelope and sees another paper, and unfolding the six-by-ten sheet, she begins to read the short note written in Rufe's neat handwriting:

April 28th, 1863

We are advancing upon the enemy. I doubt not that we must have a bloody, desperate battle. I leave this where I have perfect confidence it will be sent to you in case I am killed—and only in that event.

Mary's heart skips, and she feels a sudden loss of breath as if someone has hit her hard in the chest! *My God, no!* Hands shaking, she begins to read the first words of the second paragraph through misting eyes, then breaks down in sobs as it ends—ends forever!

I loved you dearly, <u>sincerely</u>, and I am sure my dying prayer will be that God will bless you always and make you happy. I don't believe you will ever think lightly of the love of a man, who if he had few other merits, gave his life freely for his country and the right.

Rufus R. Dawes

His last words "ever think lightly of the love ..."! "Gave his life freely for his country ..." *Rufe! Not you! Not now!*

I want to go home! I've got to get home! Sobbing, crying, staggering under the grief and shock, she heads down the stairs and runs out the front door onto Front Street. *I can't let people see me; I don't want people to stop me. I just want to go home!* She turns the other way, away from the busy shops on Putnam Street, toward Butler. It's a longer route, but she must avoid contact. She turns up Butler Street and is soon slogging through mud created by the recent rains. A good part of the town center drains this way. She tries to run, gets bogged down, her dress spattered now with mud, shoes weighted down, holding the envelope, sobbing incessantly, thinking of him lying dead somewhere, while she continues to slog along for three long blocks to Fourth Street. A left turn on Fourth, the college to the right up the hill, spring sunshine and flowers of no comfort. *Oh no! I am passing Mrs. Dawes's house! Should I stop there? No, I can't do that! I just want to get home!* She cuts across the corner at Putnam, slams open the front door, and runs exhausted, sweaty, unmindful of dress and shoes so soggy and dirty to collapse on the bed in her parents' room. Now free to let her feelings fully explode, she cries uncontrollably.

Beman and Betsey Gates are in the dining room enjoying a quiet breakfast as the door slams open, and they hear running footsteps coupled with the sobs of their daughter. They both move swiftly across the hall to their bedroom. Betsey sits and reaches out to her daughter. "Mary, dear, what's wrong?! What's the matter?"

Mary cannot control her grief, and the words cannot come out through her sobs. She reaches toward her mother with the envelope in her hand. As Betsey reads it, with Beman looking over her shoulder reading also, the words strike their hearts with shock, confusion, and sadness. "Oh, my Lord in Heaven!" cries Betsey. "Oh no!"

Beman reads the note, face hardened, brow furrowed, not sure what to say. Finally, he asks, "Does Mrs. Dawes know? I have not heard any news. She lives right down the street. We should have heard something. Perhaps she does not know. Betsey, we must go see her—to see if she knows, to show her the letter. Mary, I'm so, so sorry."

It is half hour later at the Sarah Dawes home. "I don't believe it! No, it can't be true! Rufus is not dead! I won't accept it!" A shocked and grief-stricken Sarah Dawes sits in her parlor with Betsey Gates. Beman has stayed home with Mary, who is too distraught to face Mrs. Dawes. Betsey sits with a pained expression, burdened with the task of breaking the horrible news. "No," Sarah says again, "I believe anything Rufus would tell me except that he is dead. It cannot be, it just can't."

Lucy Dawes is there, too, her school dismissed after Beman Gates dispatched his house maid with a note: "Lucy, please come home at once. It's about Rufus."

"We had no idea that Rufus and Mary are—I mean, *have been* ... having any kind of relationship," says Lucy, tears running down her face. "It's all so confusing, so surreal. I just can't believe this is happening! I need to get word to Aunt Julia and, somehow, to Kate. She's away with Uncle William to Baltimore."

Aunt Julia unexpectedly receives the word when she happens to meet a saddened Lucy later that day at the Scotts Landing station. Julia is there to send off her visiting half-sister, Clara, back to her home in Illinois, while Lucy takes the train to inform the Cutlers.

Meanwhile, Beman Gates sends a telegraph to William Cutler with the news, suggesting that William make inquiries to the war department using his government connections. At the end of the day, family and close friends are crushed; sick with an awful, empty feeling of loss, and all are very concerned for a mother and sisters who are now plunged into sorrow and confusion. Julia Cutler makes a day-ending note in her journal, a notation she has always dreaded might one day be necessary:

> There is a note that Rufus was killed in battle, but I cannot believe it true. They all have been in great suspense & trouble.

The next day, Julia provides more detail to her journal:

> Upon inquiry I find that a package of letters has been received by Mary Gates, which were not to be returned except in case of his death—I don't wonder they all feel alarmed and distressed— But somehow, I can't help believing <u>he</u> <u>is</u> <u>alive</u> & have tried to inspire Lucy with the same confidence.

The sad news spreads quickly through Marietta College and the townspeople. No, not another fine young man gone! His presentation just weeks ago so inspiring, his attitude and soldierly bearing so impressive. Now this word. It is too much. The poor family!

Thursday, May 7, 1863, Marietta, Ohio—the Gates Home

Mary has suffered through a long night of fitful sleep and teary outbursts. By nine o'clock she has recovered enough strength to come downstairs. Father has left for his office, but the rest of the family is in the kitchen. Betsey and Bettie give Mary a hug as she enters, as does Charley, who is now heading out to class at the college. "Let me know if you want to talk later," he quietly says in her ear.

"Mrs. Dawes is convinced he is safe," Betsey says soothingly to Mary, "and Julia Cutler feels the same. I don't know how or why, but I just feel they are right. I think we all need to think positive until we hear some certain news. You should try to keep hope, dear, and you should eat something. You didn't have anything yesterday."

"I'll try," says Mary as Bettie slides a plate with buttered bread slices toward her. Mary manages a smile toward her little sister, warmed by the obvious look of care and concern showing in the ten-year-old's face.

The past twenty-four hours have been such a rush of emotions. *I will be twenty-one in August*, she thinks, *and I realize now how sheltered I have been. I've met boys and enjoyed their company, and Fanny and I have talked about this one and that one so many times. And Theodore Greenwood was so very special, he could have been the one. His death was such a dreadful loss. And now Rufe Dawes! Is it because of me? I didn't want him to affect me so deeply. But he has! His awkward visit. His letters. Just three of them, but so beautiful! His* love *for me! So openly given, so honest and sincere. Then, suddenly, yesterday's note! In his own handwriting, like an apparition from the grave. I can't stop thinking of those words. Those* last *words! A love gone before I have a chance to return it.*

Mary suddenly breaks down, sobs wracking her body as she sits at the table, head in hands, Betsey scurrying over with a comforting embrace, Bettie staring at her sister in shock.

Friday, May 8, 1863, Marietta, Ohio

Lucy has cancelled her school again and apprehensively walks to the post office to see if the morning mail has arrived with any news. Sala Bosworth is fully aware of the awful message his niece Mary received here the other day, and he shares everyone's concern about Rufus. He has spotted a letter addressed to Lucy, and it's from the Sixth Wisconsin! Seeing Lucy come into the room, he quickly hands it to her. Fearing its contents but anxious to know, she tears it open and reads the short message from a Doctor Preston: "My dear Madam—Your brother, Lt. Col. Dawes of the 6th Wis. is <u>alive and well</u>." It goes on to explain that he was holding a letter for Rufus at his request, and he had either lost it or it was sent by accident. He forgot who it was addressed to and assumed it was Rufus's sister. *Thank God!* She hugs Mr. Bosworth with tears of joy on her face and scurries out to pass on the great news to her family and that of Mary Gates.

"Thank the Lord, Lucy! Such wonderful news! Mary! Rufus is safe! It was a mistake. Lucy has a letter from a doctor with Rufus's regiment." Betsey Gates is ecstatic—happy for the Dawes family, so happy for her daughter.

Mary rushes into the parlor, eyes red from continual tears. "Please, Lucy, can I see it?" As she reads Preston's short message, she is still apprehensive. "I've been so hoping and praying … Can we believe it? What if this is another mistake?" She can't help the tears that fall once again. She knows now that her life has changed. The thought of Rufus gone—*a good, kind, brave man who loves me deeply ... I could not bear the loss. And now he's seemingly back from the dead! I don't want to lose him again!*[11]

That Evening, the Old Stone House

Sarah Dawes is staying with Julia, seeking comfort from her younger sister in the old house where they grew up. She is clinging to the hope that Rufus is not dead, that there has been a mistake, but she fears the worst and is in anguish over the uncertainty. It is after dark when William's telegraph message arrives. His inquiries to Washington have wound their way through army channels with a response. Lt. Col. Dawes of the Sixth Wisconsin is not reported killed, wounded, or missing. The short message sent to the Constitution Railway Station and hurried over to Julia's home reads, "<u>Rufus is safe</u>!" Great news! Sarah and Julia thank God for mercifully answering their prayers. It is beyond words to describe the relief.

But still, they remember Rufus recounting the awful Edward Bragg and Edwin Brown identification mistake after Antietam. Could this be another? *God, if we only could know for certain!* Sisters Kate and Lucy have tried to find out by mailing anguished letters of inquiry to Rufus's friend at the Sixth Wisconsin, Dr. John Hall. It will seem an eternity waiting for a reply, but it is all they can do.

April 30–May 6, 1863—the Battle of Chancellorsville

About the same time on May 6 that Mary Gates sits in the post office and begins to read the awful letter, "to be sent to you in case I am killed," Lt. Col. Rufus Dawes is among one hundred thousand wet, tired, and discouraged Union troops slogging through the mud after retreating to the north side of the Rappahannock River via the United States Ford pontoon bridge. Dawes is sick. A severe thunderstorm had plunged down on the men at 5:00 p.m. yesterday as a prelude to an all-night cold-soaker. As he rides slowly along with the dispirited column, his body shakes with chills.

General Hooker's spring campaign against a grossly outnumbered Confederate army has turned into disaster. It had all started well. While Dawes and the Iron Brigade fought successfully to secure a bridgehead south of Fredericksburg, Hooker's main force surprised Lee by outflanking the Confederates far upstream. The surprise soon became negated as Hooker's troops were forced to take narrow roads entangled in dense woodlands known locally as the Wilderness. Their easterly advance slowed enough to allow General Lee time to scramble his spread-out troops. Confederates under Stonewall Jackson's command pushed west to meet and blunt the Northern army, using the almost impassable terrain to advantage.

Then, on May 2, Jackson and Lee concoct a bold plan. Jackson will take his twenty-eight-thousand-man Second Corps on a daytime 12-mile end-run using back roads to strike the Union right flank. Lee takes a huge gamble. He has only two divisions, about thirteen thousand soldiers, to keep Hooker's seventy thousand men at bay while Jackson makes his move. Hooker cooperates by timidly maintaining a defensive posture.

The Iron Brigade and Reynolds's corps have essentially been left alone, and with Hooker's main force being blunted farther west, their role as "the anvil" is negated. They remained idle for three days until Hooker recalls the First Corps on May 2, ordering it to join the main army and reinforce the right flank. It is too late to help thwart Jackson's late-afternoon attack, which crushes Howard's Eleventh Corps and throws Union forces back over a mile. During a night reconnaissance, however, Jackson is accidentally shot in three places by his own troops and is rushed to the rear, gravely wounded. Lee places aggressive General J. E. B. Stuart in temporary command. Hooker still outnumbers Lee on May 3, but orders movements that unintentionally favor Lee's plans, giving up high ground on which Lee masses artillery. Lee attacks again on that day and, with the key artillery support, forces Hooker to order a fighting withdrawal.

Heavy fighting near Fredericksburg at Salem Church, between Sedgewick's Union Sixth Corps and several Confederate divisions, ends in stalemate, but when Hooker keeps his troops on the defense on May 4, Lee turns loose more men against Sedgewick's isolated corps and forces him to retreat over the river early on May 5. Hooker holds a council of war with his senior commanders. Most prefer to continue the fight, knowing they still have a numerical advantage. But Hooker, knocked unconscious for an hour on May 3 by an artillery shell that hit the house pillar on which he was leaning, has had enough. He orders a full retreat, back across the Rappahannock. He has squandered his advantages, failed to capitalize on early success, frustrated his subordinates, and lost his nerve. It is another in a series of gross failures committed by the various commanders of the Army of the Potomac.

us — To be shot like sheep in a huddle & drown in the Rappahannock was the certain fate of all if we failed, of many if we succeeded

Battery   1st position of 6th   Battery
_____   # #

| | | | | | 6th Wis. double quick into boats —

14   75.   N. Y. Troops
Boats — | | | | | |

River   High Bank   River
Rebel rifle pits
Brick house

Bowling Green Road

The plan was simple — Troops were moved down along the edge of the river and batteries planted on the hills back to fire at the Rebels as hard as they could, while we ran into the boats, rowed them across the river, scrambled up the banks and drove the rebels out with the bayonet, or held ground if we could until the boats could bring more troops to help us —

Letter and sketch to sister Lucy describing the April 30th Fitzhugh's Crossing assault, written the next day, May 1, 1863. The "Brick house" was the Smithfield Plantation, now the Fredericksburg Country Club.

Endnotes

1. The meeting with Haskell is mentioned in the *Dawes Journal, Book 3*, p. 174. DAA.

2. The time with Chambers and Newport in D.C., along with the "snob" remark, are from a Dawes letter to sister Lucy, March 25, 1863, preserved in the Rufus Dawes Collection, WHS. Letters quoted are from this source unless otherwise noted.

3. The "dull and stupid" remark is by Dawes in his journal. DAA.

4. JCJ.

5. This flag and many others are carefully preserved at the Wisconsin Veterans Museum, Madison, WI, and can be viewed on their website.

6. Beaudot, William and Herdegen, Lance. *An Irishman in the Iron Brigade*, p. 63.

7. Dawes journal, p. 81. DAA.

8. *SWSW*, p. 134.

9. Diary entries. Rufus Dawes Collection. WHS.

10. https://dmna.ny.gov/historic/reghist/civil/infantry/24thInf/24thInfArticle-HaightAmongPontoons.htm

11. The remarkable account of the Chancellorsville campaign, Fitzhugh's Crossing, and the trauma of Rufus's letter mailed by mistake is documented in several sources and weaved together for this narrative. Sources are: First, daily journals kept by Dawes of the actions between April 28 and May 6. Originals are at the WHS, and transcripts are in the Dawes journals, DAA. Second, Dr. Hall's journals, transcripts of which are in the EDC-NL. Third, Rufus's letter to Lucy Dawes of May 1, 1863, WHS. Fourth, Mary Frances Dawes Beach's *Mary Beman Dawes*, chap. 3, pp. 48 and 49, MCSCL.

Chapter Eight

To My Best Girl

Friday Morning, May 8, 1863—Sixth Wisconsin Camp near White Oak Church, VA

He had managed to eat a little breakfast, still aching and with a fever. A staff officer from the division comments on a Rebel raid on the B&O Railroad that captured mail and says no mail has gone out or in since the campaign started. Dawes moans at that news, thinking, *What if my last letter to Mary didn't get through? It was sent about that time. All that I wrote about the depth of my love for her will then be unexpressed; she will have no reply to her hopeful letter.* He walks back to his tent feeling miserable and depressed and begins to compose a new letter to Mary. He just wants to sleep, it's a struggle to focus, but he tells himself, *I need to get this off today.* He addresses it to "M. B. G."

Rufus pauses to look at the letters "M. B. G." *Hmm,* he thinks, *M. B. G., meaning Mary Beman Gates.* He smiles as he visualizes her. *"M. B. G.—to me it also means My Best Girl! Those initials will always mean she is MY BEST GIRL!*

He blinks a few times and thinks, *Rufus! Focus! I won't mention my "I am killed" letter. She probably didn't get it. I hope not. I just want to know if she got the other one, my "tell me so plainly" letter of April 26.*

He begins to write, struggling with dizziness caused by dehydration:

I am much troubled lest you may have not received my letter. The thought is intolerable, that by accident, you may have reason to suspect that I failed or delayed to write to you. ... I will not repeat but only more fully declare the sentiments of my first.

He pens a few lines about the battle, then:

I was scratched a little in my left hand but regret to say not enough to make an honorable scar. Inspired by the <u>hope</u> I have found in your letter I have striven to bear myself through this terrible struggle as <u>you</u> would be proud to have me. R. R. D.[1]

Billy is called in to place it in the outgoing mail. Strained by the effort, Dawes is soon asleep.

"You did *what*?" It is three hours later, and Rufus Dawes is curled up under two blankets in his wedge tent, suffering with chills and a fever, a bucket close to his cot.

"I'm so sorry, Rufus," Dr. A. W. Preston responds as he sits inside the tent. "I don't know what happened to the envelope you gave me. I was sent over to the Eleventh Corps that next day, and when the Rebs overwhelmed everybody in that awful evening attack, we all skedaddled and got so mixed up. I lost other papers too. I'm so sorry; I'm sure it's lost. And even if it was mailed somehow, we've heard that the Rebs probably captured our mail. But just in case, four days ago I sent a quick letter to your sister in Marietta to let her know that you are safe and healthy."

"Oh no!" groans Dawes. "Doc, how did this happen? I trusted you to keep it safe! And the letter wasn't to my sister. She's going to get your note and wonder what's going on! I can't believe this! What if it *did* go through?"

Preston apologizes again, and Dawes waves him off, anger and frustration mixed with a need to throw up.

There's only one thing I can do, he thinks. *I need to write Mary again, to tell her what happened, just in case she gets that letter. I can only hope now that the Rebs* did *capture it.* For the second time that day, a sick Rufus Dawes struggles to write an acceptable letter to his "Best Girl":

You can scarcely imagine my embarrassment, regret and indignation on learning this afternoon that a letter I had left to be sent to you if I was killed, and "only in that event," had been permitted to get in the mail.

Explaining Dr. Preston's involvement and chagrin, and with his head pounding and his fever rising, he concludes:

What an intensely annoying situation! I cannot tell you how much I have been troubled by this mistake. I said nothing I am ashamed or sorry to have you know. I did not wish to destroy your letters, and it was only under the circumstances a matter of honor to send them back. I shall be very anxious to know if you got the letter or not. R. R. D.

Sunday Evening, May 10, 1863—Sixth Wisconsin Camp

"Rufus, Rufus!" Dawes is shaken awake by a persistent nudging on his shoulder. He's been in solid sleep for several hours and wakes slow and groggy with an enormous headache. He is still sick. "Huh? What? Who is it?" he angrily mutters.

"John Hall. Sorry, Rufe, but I need to show you something. It can't wait."

Dawes groans as he rolls over, aching all through his body. He feels worse now than he did yesterday. What could be so important? "Are we moving?" he asks.

"No, no," Hall says, leaning close. "I received these letters today from your sisters. They think you've been killed. The letter Preston says he lost ... well, apparently it was sent and received."

"What?!" Dawes instantly sits up, knocking his sick bucket over, its vile contents spilling out. He doesn't care, but Hall stands up with a disgusted grimace. His head throbbing, Dawes grabs the papers in Hall's hand and begins to read the anguished words written in Kate's and Lucy's handwriting. "Oh no, no!"

He is too sick to write now. As Hall leaves him, Rufe's mind is wracked with despair. What the family must be going through! And what of Mary? *When she finds out I'm safe, what will she think then?! This the worst thing that could have happened! Preston! What have you done to me?*

The Same Evening, Marietta, Ohio—the Gates Home

Mary has been thinking of him all day, all week. Today's sermon by Rev. Wickes went unheeded, her mind totally fixed on Rufus Dawes. She had glanced up at the student balcony with tearful eyes. Such a whirlwind this past week! So many emotions—his beautiful letter of love, the complete shock and grief over his death message, then being risen again—joy mixed with confusion mixed with impertinence. *No, he would not do that on purpose! To plunge his family into grief on my account? No, he would not do that. His message was sincere; he wanted to make a last expression of his love. It had to have been sent by mistake. The terrible impact was awful. Still, I can't deny how it has affected me! I can't imagine feeling this way about anyone else.*

It is time for self-evaluation as she thoughtfully analyzes her feelings. *I think I loved Theodore Greenwood. I didn't realize it until he was gone. He was such a good man, with such a great future ahead of him. I always felt I wasn't good enough for him, but I cared for him, deeply. A first love, never fully realized, perhaps not a true one. I will never know. This is so crazy. Father and Mother will think me impetuous and emotional. But I know Rufe loves me, and after this week, I know I love Rufus Dawes! I tremble thinking I may lose it, that this war will cut it off from me again. I must tell him so plainly that he will not mistake, just as he pleaded me to do! I don't want him to have any misunderstanding about it. I do love him, completely.*

She sits at her desk and begins the most important letter of her life. It is to "Lieutenant Colonel Rufus Dawes." He is, she now realizes, the man she truly loves.

Monday Morning, May 11, 1863—Sixth Wisconsin Camp, White Oak Church

M. B. G.

I never was more shocked in my life than at receiving letters from my sisters last night written in all the anguish of believing me killed or desperately wounded. I had very little idea that you would really get the letter for I believed Dr. Preston had <u>lost</u> it, and I was feeling very bad about <u>that</u>.

I shudder to think of the pain and suffering this most unfortunate mistake has caused my Mother and Sisters. I feel so grossly outraged by the carelessness of Dr. P that I can scarcely speak to him, though he has always been one of my best and truest friends in the Army—and deeply regrets his blunder though little dreaming of its consequences.

I am much distressed lest by this matter you have been placed in a position very embarrassing and painful to your feelings. I am told you were affected by the letter. I cannot deny that it gave me a great thrill of happiness to know that you cared something for me. But I know as a <u>friend</u> you would have been shocked and pained, and I would scorn to assume anything more unless from your own assurance.

I should feel very bad to think anyone would believe me capable of taking advantage of such a time.

It is with the greatest difficulty that I can sit up to write. I cannot collect or arrange my thoughts as I would.

It was impossible for me to have telegraphed to have reached Marietta so soon as [the] several letters [that are] on their way.

I am too sick to write and must give up.

R. R. D.

There. It's the best I can do. "Billy! Billy, come here please! A letter to mail."

Billy enters the tent and takes the letter from his boss. "Ya lookin' bad awful, sah! Ah'm gettin' the doc."

"No! No doctors! Not now! Just let me sleep." Dawes falls back on his cot, miserable in body, mind, and soul. The following six days pass dismally with no further word from Mary and no change in his miserable physical and mental condition.

Sunday, May 17, 1863—Sixth Wisconsin Camp

Her letter came last night. She had written it the same day he had sent her the letter expressing shock and consternation about the awful "mistake," so concerned that she would think him a scoundrel for taking advantage by such a means. He begins to read, fearing a scathing response, but thank God! *It is much more than I have hoped for! Mary Beman Gates, My Best Girl, has written that SHE LOVES ME!* "Struck dumb with the realization" *is how she put it. I can't stop reading it! I'm worthless right now because of it and so glad to still be on sick call, no duties to call me away. I'm the happiest sick man in the army! I would give anything to be with her right now! A letter is all I can do. There is so much to express!*

My <u>dear</u> Mary

I too am struck dumb with the greatest joy of my life. I cannot express a tithe of my feelings. God bless you, my <u>dear</u> Mary, for what you have said in your letter, and may He help me that you never have cause to repent it. I have read your letter over and over again, and great hardened soldier that I take pride in being,

> I have cried over it almost like a baby. If in all my sinful life I was ever thankful to God for anything, I am for this, the crowning blessing of my life ... I want you to know all about me.

The words flow out of him. He tells her all that he can think of that she should know. His spiritual thoughts. His abstinence from drinking and smoking despite all the temptations in the army to do so. His financial net worth, the situation with Father, and his duty to support Mother and his sisters.

He responds to Mary's mention of the late Theodore Greenwood and of her past feelings for him. As soon as he reads her admission of a love lost with Ted's death, he realizes that it was Ted who Marshall Newport had referred to about Mary being engaged. Mary's relationship with Ted Greenwood had never reached that level of commitment, however. *So at the time, last March, why did Newport tell me otherwise? At best it was misinformation; at worst, deceit to bolster his cousin Ted's chances with Mary by keeping me away.*

As he puzzles over Newport's motives, he cannot think unkindly of Greenwood, who was in love with Mary and had pursued her. *Ted had the same desire to share his life with her as I do. How can I be resentful of him for that? Besides, I cannot believe that Ted had any part in a plot to steer me away. He was too much of a gentleman to resort to deception*:

> I was deeply interested in what you told me about Mr. Greenwood. I love you more dearly for so generously confiding to me this, your great sorrow. You may be sure it will always be sacred to me. It was on account of what I had been <u>told</u> about him, that I was afraid to go to call on you sooner when I was in Marietta. Greenwood was a noble, honorable fellow, he would indeed have made a great and good man, but so far as agreeing with what you say of <u>yourself</u> in his connection, I think you are a great deal too good for him, or me either.

He confesses his trepidation at writing that first letter, believing himself unworthy of similar feelings on her part. He briefly describes the river crossing at Fitzhugh's, a battle he takes great pride in being part of. He discusses the army's likely movements and discusses the slim chance for a furlough. He is sorry for the poor stationary, and finally concludes:

What a place to carry on courtship. God bless you for what you have told me of your love. You are more to me now than anything else in the world, more than <u>life</u> itself.

Your dear lover, Rufe

Monday, May 18, 1863—Sixth Wisconsin Camp

Rufus is finally feeling healthier and reminds himself that sisters Lucy and Kate need a response. Dr. Hall wrote them when Rufus was in bed sick, but today he wants to respond to Kate's nice letter himself. She needs to be reassured. He intends to let the distress created by Preston's blunder subside before he tells Kate about Mary:

Dear Kate—

I am quite well again now, and have almost recovered my equanimity—not quite. I am very much obliged to you for your very <u>sensible</u> as well as kind and affectionate efforts to find out about me. I was so sick I could hardly hold my head up when I got your first letters, which did not help to cool my fever. ...

Lucy says Father has not yet sent his money. I hope we will not have trouble with him. Perhaps he is hard up—<u>I</u> know nothing about him. He is reaping his reward. I wonder who he can make his mind to leave his property to. ...

Well Eph has got Henry's[S] debts almost cleared. How strange that he should in his time clear Hen's honor. Haven't we had a romantic history? And I believe the last chapter, will very properly, tell of justice and right rewarded and wickedness and tyranny punished. Your share of suffering has been great. Greater and longer than any of us have had, but I hope happier times are in store for us all. Be assured anyhow that you have the love and respect of your brother. Rufe

[S] Brother Henry Manasseh, who died in 1860.

Monday, May 25, 1863, Marietta, Ohio—the Gates Home

"Finally, Francy! Two letters from Rufus. His letter of the 11th came almost a week ago, and I answered right away, last Tuesday." Mary and Francy are in Mary's second-floor room, and Mary is a bundle of nerves. Happy with the realization she is in love, concerned for her sweetheart's safety, puzzled and concerned with the long delays in hearing from him. "What if he has changed his mind or is so sick that he's in the hospital? I can't stop trembling sometimes thinking of all the bad things that could be happening right now, and there is no way to know."

"Mary, I'm sure he hasn't changed his mind! You need to calm down and realize how slow the mails run to and from the army. Sometimes, they don't go through at all. What are the dates on these two?" Francy asks.

"The 17th and 18th," Mary replies. "Seven days to get here! I understand what you are saying, but the uncertainty is so hard to bear!"

She cannot know that Lt. Col. Rufus Dawes is, at that moment, part of a five-day Federal expedition into Virginia's King George County, east of Fredericksburg. The Sixth Wisconsin, Nineteenth Indiana, and Twenty-Fourth Michigan regiments have been chosen to reconnoiter and to rescue the Eighth Illinois Cavalry, which had been cut off after Confederates burned a bridge behind them. Colonel Morrow of the Twenty-Fourth is in command. Dawes, still not well from his long bout with fever, has been stationed with 160 men to guard a crossroad. It is enemy country, and he directs his command in preparing fortifications. He also tries to prevent them from embarking on unauthorized pig-and-poultry raids. It is hot, he is very weak, and the burdensome duties over five days exhaust him. He had sent off a short note just before leaving on the reconnaissance, written to Mary at 3:00 a.m. on the 21st, so that she would understand the absence of correspondence for a time. He had drafted a long letter to her during the time at the crossroads, but upon a report of an imminent enemy attack, had burned it rather than have it read by a Rebel should his unit be overrun and himself captured or killed.[2]

Francy leaves for home, allowing Mary a chance to read her letters from Rufe in private. As she closes Mary's door, Francy calls out, "Please give my love to your Rufe also; he's got a special place in my heart too. But don't worry cousin—he's safe with you! Maybe his younger brother will come back someday. That would be nice."

Mary sits at her desk and writes:

"My dear Rufe, I am willing to cast my lot with you. Your lovely letters only serve to reinforce my conviction that you are the man for me. I only desire your love and enough for us to live on. I know that you will always look to my welfare and protect and defend me from anything that might arise. I don't need great wealth or fame. That is not too much to ask, is it? I wish so much that we could be together now. Receiving your wonderful letters and sending you my poor messages in return is such a provokingly slow process. I have received your letters and felt that I was behind in answering. Please don't be impatient for my responses, for it is the mail and not my reluctance to respond that is the reason for delays."

Rufus is so cute! His letter has this list of his personal traits, things he wants me to know. His paragraph about his religious beliefs is a bit shocking: "I am not a Christian," *he writes, and then frankly expresses his fear that he will* "suffer very much in your respect by this confession." *Then he admits he should have resolved the question of his faith while at Marietta College*: "<u>Then</u> there was everything to encourage, <u>since</u> then, until <u>now</u>, there has been everything ... to discourage, and turn my thoughts away from such things, except the continued and earnest prayers and pleadings of my Mother and sisters, and, I ought not to forget, my merciful preservation through great peril. I have not any excuses." *He is so honest and sincere, and I love him for it. This is something we will deal with together, for as he writes,* "I hardly dare say that I am completely <u>settled</u> in my religious faith."

Mary writes him back, expressing her own hope that he can become "settled" with the Christian faith. She pledges her support and writes, "The special way our love has been sealed must be due to Divine Providence, come to us in the form of the good Doctor Preston."

She writes a few more lines, passing on well-wishes from Francy and Charley and those at the college, and she mentions that story Lucy shared about him standing up in the boat during the river assault. She writes, "Why would you do that?! Would you please remember me before doing anything so foolhardy?"

That evening at the dinner table, younger brother Charley teases his sister about her correspondence. It is a well-meaning tease, for he knows now that she is in love, and he likes and admires Rufus Dawes, a Marietta College man who has become a senior officer in one of the most respected regiments of the Union army. But teasing is what brothers do. "Come on, Mary, why don't you share his letters with us? I, for one, would like to hear what he has to say, wouldn't you, Bettie?"

Of course, Bettie responds, "Oh yes, that would be fine! I don't know much about this Mr. Dawes."

Mary turns a shade red and frowns at Charley, but before she can retort, her mother quickly interjects, "Now shush, Charley! And don't get your little sister involved too! How would you like to read letters you might get from some local girl, though I can't imagine what kind of girl would *initiate* anything so brash."

Beman Gates chuckles at the whole situation. Here is his fun-loving son, Charley, trying to stir things up a little, Mary about to retaliate, Betsey stepping in. He catches Betsey's glance, though, clears his throat, and enters the conversation: "Now, Mary, of course you don't need to share your letters. They're your private property, and, Charley, you know better. But that being said, if Rufus has mentioned some things about the army or the military situation as he sees it, especially after this latest disaster, I would certainly like to hear his analysis. He was so open about expressing his opinions at the courthouse speech last March. Would that be too much to ask?"

Mary relents and is excused from the table to retrieve the letter Rufus wrote on the 18th, and she gives Charley a little fist to his shoulder in the process. She returns to the table and begins to read excerpts about the Chancellorsville defeat and his war strategy evaluation:

I don't think the Rebellion is to be crushed here. Unless we may annihilate the great Army in front of us, the varying fortunes of battle in Virginia may little affect the general result. When the Rebels have exhausted Virginia as a battle ground, there will be another general evacuation, a la Corinth, without so far as I can see, any crushing loss to them. The capture of Richmond, and the crushing of the army in Virginia, will end the war, but the capture of Richmond without the Army would be almost as barren a conquest as Moscow to Napoleon. By opening the Mississippi, by rigidly enforcing the blockade, by possessing and holding, if possible, such important points on their R. R. communication as Chattanooga, etc., by continual forays to prevent the growing of crops and cotton, by stealing their negroes, we may exhaust and crush them[—]rather than by trying to annihilate their armies[,] by fighting on equal terms. There—what kind of general do you think I would make? Would you go for me for Commander-in-Chief?

Mary pauses and is smiling as she continues to look at Rufus's letter, reading other words that she will keep to herself. Her family is impressed. Beman has been listening intently and comments. "I think he would make a very good general, better, I shall say, then many we have already suffered with."

Tuesday, May 26, 1863—Camp at White Oak Church near Fredericksburg

Two wonderful letters from Mary, dated the 11th and 19th, are waiting upon his return. Her last one is special, such a heartfelt assurance of her love! *She must now have my letter of the 17th in response to her first. I need to write her now and wait no longer to express what has been on my mind for so long.* Mindful of the sincere concerns she expressed so earnestly in her most recent letter, he makes a point to address them, and decides, *Now is the time*:

> My dear Mary, I have been entirely, abundantly satisfied with all you have written to me. Your letters have all made me very happy, and filled my heart with love for you. Oh Mary, don't "tremble" for my love. It is yours forever, yours with all the strength and earnestness of my nature, and it only grows stronger … Let us define our relationship that there can be no "misunderstanding," and if you answer as I hope, may God forbid any possibility of "estrangement." <u>Will you be my wife?</u> I am ready to pledge myself to <u>you</u> for life by the most solemn and sacred tie of Earth. I <u>know</u> my happiness is bound up in you, I haven't a doubt left.

There! I've said it! I wish so much that I could ask her in person! But there is no chance now that any leave of absence will be granted. The annual summer campaign is looming, and the army is being weakened by so many regiments reaching the end of their enlistment period, leaving us all the time. He continues the letter, discussing the dismal prospects of getting home, writing:

> Col. Bragg asked for six days to go to his little daughter lying at the foot of death, but was refused. He threatens to tender his resignation again. … Tell me how you feel about this, and how long you can wait if I can't get away. I know you would have me act honorably in everything, and in good faith with the service I

have entered, and the cause to which I have dedicated my life if it is needed.

As to that last possibility, he confesses that he would rather be killed than severely maimed, for her sake. It is a callous remark made by a hardened soldier who has seen the cruel wounds suffered by many of his soldiers. He knows that doctors seem to have little to offer these men; they are mostly on their own in dealing with the loss of an arm or leg. But he immediately regrets writing it and assures Mary that he is again in good health, "immune to the hardships of campaigning," and has a "more than ordinarily strong and active body." Except for one thing:

> By the way, I still suffer from deafness in my right ear. I don't see as it is any worse, but I fear that it will never be any better. I believe that is my only physical infirmity.

He tells Mary that he is happy that she has always acted so warmly to Lucy, for his sister is "the kindest, most generous, most self-sacrificing sister ever there was in the world." But it is obvious from Mary's letter that Lucy feels some angst toward Mary, as one who may be taking her younger brother away from the family. He pledges to convince Lucy that Mary will prove to be "the tie that should keep me near her and my mother for life. If you had rejected my love I never could or would have gone to Marietta to live ..." Using Mary's words again, he writes:

> Nothing can shake my faith in "Special Providence" after this. It seems to me that God intended us for each other. Think of me loving you almost from the first time I saw you, but from force of cruel circumstances not daring to ask for your affection, trying to crush my hopeless passion, always trying to forget you, and then after so long to find I loved you more than ever. Did you ever care anything about me before this winter? I shan't be displeased if you say you didn't.
>
> It is almost midnight and I did not sleep one wink last night. Ran a picket for three miles in strange country and visited it twice in the night. Good night and God Bless my dear Mary. I have asked you the most important question of my life, but I feel as

though I know what your answer will be. I couldn't give you up now.

Yours, Rufe

Thursday Evening, May 28, 1863—Sixth Wisconsin Camp

Dr. John Hall walks up to Lt. Col Dawes, who is sitting under his tent flap with papers and pen. "Colonel Dawes, how are you feeling? Physically, I mean. I haven't seen you too much lately, what with our excursion down the peninsula and then you on picket duty. I'm happy to hear that your grumpy mood after Chancellorsville has completely changed for the better. By the way, Dr. Preston tells me that he is very pleased and relieved that you suddenly seem to forgive him for his mistake, but he's really puzzled by all the smiles and jovial greetings you are now giving him. A complete reversal! Something very good must have happened."

Dawes responds, "I'm fine, John. I'm feeling back to normal. As for Dr. Preston, I'll let him wonder for a while, but I'll tell you a little secret. You know about the letter he sent off by accident. And thanks again for writing my sister that it was all a mistake. But that letter went to a girl back in Marietta that I am writing, not my sister, and ... well, I'll just say it ... a girl I'm in love with. And horrible as it was for everybody at home for a few days, the letter made her realize that she loves me too! I can't tell you how happy I am! But, again, that's just between you and me for now." He does not mention the proposal; it's too soon for her response, and he can't be *certain* what it will be.

Hall smiles in response. "Rufus, that's amazing! What a story! Good for you! I suppose you're writing her now, and I'm interrupting."

"I've been writing every chance I get!" he says. "Yesterday was my brother Ephraim's twenty-third birthday, and I told her about that and how much she will like him, and I told her I'll be twenty-five on the Fourth of July, and then I asked her how old she was. I don't even know her birthday."

"No, you didn't ask her that, did you?" Hall asks, laughing.

"Yes, I did. I thought I should know, and besides, she is a few years younger anyway. But I did have second thoughts about asking, so I quickly wrote that if I was with her, would she box my ears for asking? Right now, though, I'm writing to my father. I've told you about my family's long story with him. Anyway, he heard the report of my death from a friend in Ohio and wrote Colonel Bragg asking for particulars.

We haven't corresponded for a long time by his choice, and I'm sure he has since found out that I am safe, but I'm writing anyway, just to thank him for his concern."

Hall nods and smiles, and as he leaves, says, "I'll leave you to it, Rufe. I'm very glad for you, and you are a good man for reaching out to your father, despite everything in the past."

Rufus Dawes pauses to look at what he has already written: "I am grateful for the solicitude on my behalf" and "regret deeply the pain." *Did it really pain Father?* "A provoking rumor of my death was by some means started in Marietta." *He does not need to know the real story about Mary Gates.* Rufe includes a description of his actions at Fitzhugh's Crossing, actions that he is proud of, a stirring success already reported in the newspapers. *Perhaps it might impress Father that his son has done something noteworthy.* He now closes:

> If it will be a pleasure to you to hear from me I shall be glad to write, but not receiving any answer to my last communication, I supposed you were so displeased with something in my conduct as not to wish to have any communication with me.
>
> Hoping for you the most abundant success and comfort in your old age, and pledging to you every proper assistance and support,
>
> I am your Son, Rufus R. Dawes

* * * * *

The month of May concludes in disappointment for Rufus, for he writes Mary, "No letter yet. Well, I can appreciate in my own trouble all you could have felt in not hearing for so long from me."

But May 1863 has been one of exciting activity in love and in war: the crushing Union defeat at Chancellorsville and the ongoing yet promising campaign in the West to conquer Vicksburg led by a general named Ulysses Grant, which, if successful, will secure the great Mississippi River. In the east no significant troop movements are happening, but everyone knows that Robert E. Lee probably has something up his sleeve.

In Marietta, Ohio, and around that part of the country, the seventeen-year cicadas are coming out of the ground, millions of them singing and screaming in gardens and trees.[3] Children like Bettie are amazed at the sight and sounds of them—adults, too, for that matter, though the girls cover up to keep the big, buzzing insects out of their hair.

For Rufus Dawes and Mary Gates, two young people who have found love amidst the chaos, it has become the most stressful-turned-happiest month of their lives. But lingering always is the uncertainty of what this terrible Civil War will bring tomorrow, or the next day, or the next month.

Tuesday, June 2, 1863—Sixth Wisconsin Camp near White Oak Church

Her letter arrived last night, just after Lt. Col. Dawes rolled in tired and dusty from another two-day division-picket-duty assignment along the Rappahannock. It's too soon to expect a reply to his marriage proposal, but what better way to come back from a mission? And he has been worrying about her reaction to his personal confessions. He writes her right away:

My dear Mary

I was "paid for waiting"—the first three words, "My dear Rufe." Well, Mary, I promise you faithfully never to get "impatient" (your word is best) again. Oh, my dear Mary, how completely you have proved to be the noble woman I believed you ... I look forward to the joyful day when you will be my wife. ... I would not ask you to marry me if I did not feel sure of my ability to secure our independence and respectability, though I cannot promise, and you don't care for, wealth and luxury. But I can "protect and defend" you, and make you comfortable and happy.

Now, Mary, I thought never to mention to you this "Ghost in our family"[T] because ... I can and will keep you clear of all connection with that trouble. ... Eph and I regard it as our sacred duty to champion the cause of our dear, patient, long suffering Christian mother.

Lucy would tell you that I was the most undemonstrative member of our family, but she didn't see me when I got your photograph.

[T] Father Henry.

You may give Francy, if you please, as much of my love as you can spare, for it's all yours you know. Maybe she won't like that type of return for her compliment, well, it's the best a fellow in my unfortunate situation can do.

I am in command now until our Col. gets well. The Major's horse kicked him in the foot a few days ago, and it is now a serious affair. He will probably have to go to a hospital.

Oh, I most forgot. There <u>was</u> a necessity for <u>some</u> field officer to stand up in that boat. Men going into the face of such appalling danger must have a <u>leader</u>. That is why I stood up. I am not <u>foolhardy</u>. Now that I feel that the bullet would hit two, I shall not forget the motto recommended by the one who loves me best. Life was never half so precious before. But God will spare us for each other. Don't you think so? You ask me to be a Christian. I can only say, pray for me that I may be.

Your love, Rufe

Wednesday, June 3, 1863, Marietta, Ohio—the Gates Home

Mary Gates is beaming! *His letter,* his proposal *asking me to be his wife, has come today! I think he knew how I felt about him, but God bless him for asking me so formally and, again, so beautifully!*

"Mother, Father, I am in love with Rufus Dawes, and he with me. He has asked for my hand, asked me to marry him, and I so much want to say yes! I want you to know, and I hope you are happy and pleased for me. And yes, I do want to be his wife, more than anything."

Betsey and Beman Gates have witnessed a jumble of emotions with Mary ever since Sarah's son Rufus stopped by the house in late March. Betsey certainly recognized the love Rufus felt for her daughter during that awkward visit. *The brief correspondence commenced, then that awful letter sent by mistake, the crushing grief, then to learn he was safe, and seeing the dramatic impact it has all had on Mary. It has been a whirlwind! But is this too soon, too sudden? Is this in some way a response to Mr. Greenwood's death, which saddened Mary so severely, more than we realized at first? Beman and I share these concerns. But she is a sensible young woman, and she is just so happy! How can we not be happy for her?*

Beman asks, "Mary, I ... I think we ... This is all very sudden." He looks at Betsey, who gives him a mother's knowing smile and short nod. "Well, we are certainly impressed with Mr.—I mean, Lieutenant Colonel—Dawes, and we trust your judgment and good sense, and so, yes, we are very happy for you, for you both."

Mary runs to Beman and, with happy tears, gives both Father and Mother a long embrace. "When will he be coming back?" chokes Beman. She responds, "He says he doesn't know and will try to get a leave of absence, but it is almost impossible now. Thank you, thank you both so much! He is a good man, and I know he loves and cares for me very much. I know you will like him. I'm going upstairs to write him right away!"

Beman holds Betsey by the shoulder and removes his wire glasses. "I did not expect to have this happen so suddenly. I don't know how to feel. Am I losing a daughter or gaining a son? And with the war and with the brigade Rufus is part of ... Betsey, I just hope that—"

"Don't say it, dear," Betsey interrupts. "We all know the dangers he faces. We must pray every day that he is kept safe and that Mary and Rufus have a future together. It's all we can do."

In the privacy of her room, Mary begins to write her response to the most important question ever asked of her, sniffles and tears of joy welling up as the words pour out:

"My dear Rufe—I was never so happy in my life than to receive your proposal. Of course, Rufe, don't you know that I will be your wife? My answer is Yes! I long for the day when we can be together forever. I am sorry to hear that General Hooker is not normally willing to listen to a sweetheart's plea for her man's leave of absence! But no matter how long it may take for us to marry, be it years even, I will be here for you. I realize and appreciate the responsibilities you have before you, but as soon as you can honorably obtain a leave I trust you will do so. I so much want to see you and plan our next steps together. I pray for you daily. You write that you are deaf in your right ear. Well, I will share something -- I am deaf in my left! So, we share that in common! I am, your love, Mary."

She responds to his checklist of faults, confessions, and fears, giving him strong assurances that these mean nothing in comparison to her love. Mary then hurries to Uncle Bozzy's post office for mailing. In complete contrast to her anguished trek in the opposite direction just four weeks ago, she is a happy, bouncy, smiling young lady. Those who notice her are thinking she looks more beautiful than they have ever seen her.

* * * * *

Warning orders to march are received and then countermanded the first week of June. Robert E. Lee *is* up to something and Rufus suspects a Confederate move north again, perhaps even into Pennsylvania.

Lt. Col. Dawes is now "in charge of the family" since Colonel Bragg has been sent to a Washington hospital to mend his seriously injured foot. The extra responsibility is time-consuming for Dawes, but he confesses to Mary, "I like it." On one occasion, to allow himself time to write her, he orders Major Hauser out with the whole command for battalion drill, only to be promptly foiled by three interruptions involving various dispatches and paperwork. He usually writes at night in his tent, sometimes dozing off after spending a hot day in the ever-increasing Virginia heat and humidity, his candle leaking wax as it flickers and dies.

Sunday Evening, June 7, 1863—Sixth Wisconsin Camp

My Dear Mary—

We are back in camp again after literally roasting for two days in the line. Our movements are very "mysterious." I cannot pretend to conjecture the situation.

If I am Colonel, you be Colonel too, and I assure you, Colonel Mary shall always have that deference to her wishes and opinions to which her equal rank entitles her. I don't expect ever to have a project or a plan in business or anything else without consulting you about it. Now what do you think of that?

I'll tell you what I think. Half the domestic misery in this world is caused by want of openness and confidence between the man and wife.

I have a great anxiety that we shall be one of those remarkable and happy pair who love each other more and more as they know each other better and live longer together. I don't see how it's going to be possible for me to love you any more than I do now though. I think I love you more than I do myself. What I wouldn't give for "one quiet evening together" of consultation, plan making, and affection. And it will come, before "this cruel war is over" too.

I got such a good letter from Lucy last night. She is feeling very much happier now. One thing, Mary, my friends are all very much pleased with the prospect of my getting "so good" a wife. Eph says "I always knew Rufe had a sneaking liking for her, and I think it's a mighty good thing." My Uncle Wm. Cutler, who looks on me almost as a son, told Kate he was "very glad of it, and Rufe couldn't do better if she made as good a woman as her Mother." My Mother sends me her congratulations and entire approval. It is not very pleasant to have them all know of our affairs, but as the Cat has got so woefully out of the bag, it's pleasant to know they approve.

Wednesday, June 10, 1863—Sixth Wisconsin Camp near White Oak Church

Rufus Dawes has only one thing on his mind this morning: Mary's letter arrived last night, and *SHE SAID YES! Where is my wonderful Doctor Preston? I want to give him a bear hug!* Rufus is awake well before dawn to draft a buoyant six-page reply to Mary Beman Gates, My Best Girl, the girl who has now pledged herself to be his wife:

My dear Mary—

I wonder if when we become dignified, respectable old people we will laugh at our love letters of today. Well, at the imminent risk of furnishing a joke for twenty years from now, I must tell you that, if I had only had you after reading the letter that came last night, I should just had taken you in my arms and drawn you so closely to that heart that will never, never have an emotion in which you are not concerned. I don't know as it made me feel "weak" to read your answer to my question, but it made me feel more like crying than laughing.

Hold fast to your faith that I will come to you just as fast as I "can honorably," and we will not mourn any more over the cruel fate that keeps us apart. ... You are just being mustered into the service now Mary, and for the rest of my time you will have your trials and hardships as a soldier, and I doubt not that they will be harder to bear than mine, for, you see, you are a raw recruit. Your love, Rufe

On June 12 the camp life ends. Confederates under Robert E. Lee are on the move north, and the Union First Corps is ordered to give chase. The commander of the Sixth Wisconsin, Lieutenant Colonel Rufus Dawes, veteran combat officer, understands that this is the prelude to a bloody battle somewhere, sometime soon. He is awake after midnight to hastily pen a parting letter:

1 A.M., June 12th

My dear Mary

We are to march this morning positively, no postponement on account of weather or even rebels. ... I think the whole army is going, for the order is from Gen. Hooker. If so, it will be your second time "under fire" to search those dreadful lists. My regiment will go out strong and cheerful, and always determined to vindicate its glorious history. It has been my most ardent ambition to lead it through one campaign, and now the indications are that my opportunity has come, and if I can do anything "glorious" I want you to be proud of me.

I must go to attend to the business of getting my "command in readiness." Good bye my dear Mary until—well, as soon as possible. I wish you could feel, and I guess you can, how much it made me love you when you say you wouldn't "for the world marry any man with two arms" if Rufe Dawes had only one.

Your lover, Rufe

The regiment is on the move in the hot and humid weather, suffering through "suffocating clouds of dust." Rufus writes and mails loving letters to Mary whenever he can; as usual, however, incoming mail while on the march is sporadic at best. A letter he does receive merits a prompt response while at a night bivouac:

Sunday, June 21, 1863—near Guilford Station, on the O&A RR

My dear Mother

I was very much gratified to get your letter. I wanted to hear you say yourself just what you did. I cannot tell you how deeply

I have felt the importance of this step I have taken. ... To hear my dear, good mother tell me that I have chosen wisely is a great gratification. ... I want you to get some opportunity to see Mary and get acquainted better with her.

Why does Father not send all the money due? I got a letter from him last night. Poor, weak, powerless old man. Still striving by foolish inaction, rebukes, and flimsy hypocrisy to reach a Son who has almost grown to despise him for his weakness. To think I ever cringed before such a man. He is fairly on his knees to me to come back to him. ... It makes my flesh fairly weep to think this, we, all of us, so immeasurably above him, should have been ground down by his tyranny. But the shackles are off me, and I can never, shall never, return to this house of my humiliation. He shan't ever set foot in my house.

Get $50 from Uncle Wm. Show him this and he will take it for an order. Has Luce got the title to those RR bonds yet? I would advise her to turn them into money if she can. The M&CRR will have track destroyed by the Rebs this summer. See if it don't ...

Don't be surprised of a big fight here soon. You aff son, Rufe[4]

Monday Evening, June 29, 1863, Marietta, Ohio—the Gates Home

Charley Gates has been pestering his older sister for two weeks, asking her to share some of the information she has received from Rufus as he and the army are on the move. General Hooker has been ordered to keep his forces between Lee's Confederates and Washington, and he wants to know where the First Corps is heading. Charley's admiration for Rufus Dawes has been amplified upon reading a published account of his daring river assault at Fitzhugh's Crossing. The letter Dr. John Hall had sent to Lucy described it in detail, and she had sent it to the *Marietta Intelligencer*. Now the whole town knows about it.

"All right, Charley. I've gotten letters here written up to last Wednesday. I'm surprised that one got here so quickly. So I'll share where he is writing from and other things about the situation, but don't expect any more than that!"

"That's all I want to know," Charley responds. "You can keep all the mushy stuff to yourself! I've got a map here, not a very good one, and I'll try to trace his line of march."

"Let's see," Mary says as she arranges Rufe's letters in chronological order. "He wrote this one on June 5. Oh yes, they had been ordered to move, packed everything up, then had it cancelled. Then he writes about the college commencement and Newport and Chambers and his friend Birney. Then he mentions his visit here, and ..." She stops talking and smiles as she rereads a paragraph to herself, it being Rufe's comments about their awkward last meeting in March, in this same parlor:

> Do you remember that call of mine the afternoon I came away? I came very near telling you I loved you then. I think I <u>should</u> have found sufficient courage before I left, if you had not called your Mother in. I have a curiosity if I <u>could</u> have said anything worth listening to then. I can't remember a word. I felt miserably afterward that I did not do it. How ridiculous it would have been though!!! I wonder if you women realize what power you have over us, no matter how proud and independent we try to be, when we begin to love you.

"Mary! Wake up and read that later, will you!" Charley complains.

Mary blushes and says, "Sorry, he writes such nice things, and I probably *should* read this one part to you, but you're right. Let's move on. It's not until the 12th, and he wrote it at 1:00 a.m., when they broke camp and marched away. He says the heat and dust were awful. I think that was the day a soldier in the Nineteenth Indiana was to be executed for desertion. Rufe wrote two days prior that he was ordered to detail two lieutenants and twenty reliable men to serve on the firing squad. The men he had to assign detested the duty; he did too. How awful! I can't imagine it."

She continues, "That night they camped at Deep Run, then after the next day, Bealton Station, and when he wrote on the night of the 15th, they were near Centerville. His next letter was written on the 18th, near Leesburg. Here he says, 'If there is a battle look to see if Gen's Reynolds or Wadsworth figure in it. By them you can trace me.' "

Charley is nodding as he scans his map, marking circles around the towns being mentioned. Mary scans the remaining letters and says, "The next one was written on the 19th at Broad Run, about 10 miles from Leesburg. That night he mentions it was raining and leaking through his tent. It looks like they have stayed there, because his letters from the 21st and 24th are both at Broad Run again. Charley, this should tell you how rough it is in the army, all this marching and camping in all sorts of weather. You need to think about that before you go off again, talking about enlisting!"

Charley responds. "Yes, yes, I know, but men like Rufus are doing it. I'm just sitting here behind the scenes, going to school, sleeping in a warm bed, while he is out there making a difference!"

Mary has heard this before. "I know, Charley, but you are an only son, and you worry Mother and Father, all of us, with your talk about joining. But never mind now. Let me read this part for you that he wrote on the 24th. He mentions a young boy brought in who was caught sleeping at his picket post—another firing-squad offense. This poor private—Rufe calls him a "fat cheeked, inoffensive boy as ever lived"— had filled up on a supper of "rebel chicken" and dozed off. Rufus says he "couldn't do it" and released him, even though he could get into some trouble himself. The young man was "scared to death," but when he was released he was so grateful, he told Rufe that he "would remember the Lt. Col. to the last day of his life." Isn't that nice? I'm sure Rufe felt badly about that soldier who was executed and couldn't stand to see another one."[5]

Charley silently contemplates the daily toil, stress, and responsibility being placed on the twenty-four-year-old officer who is in love with his sister. *Will I be able to handle that if I do enlist and become an officer, like I am training for at the college?* "Rufus did a good thing, a difficult thing, Mary," he says. "Broad Run on the 24th. That's five days ago. I wonder where he is now."

* * * * *

The six-week lull after the Union's demoralizing defeat at Chancellorsville has been a period of reorganization for both the Army of the Potomac and the Confederate army of Northern Virginia. For the Northern side, General Joseph Hooker is kept in command, at least for the time being, even though his failure of leadership had resulted in an embarrassing defeat at the hands of a foe one-half in size. Finger-pointing and blame had been tossed back and forth between the army's corps commanders and Hooker, while President Lincoln and Secretary of War Stanton are at a loss at what to do next. Over the short span of seven months, Generals McClellan, Pope, Burnside, and now Hooker had all grossly underperformed when matched up against Robert E. Lee. Is this army forever doomed to march forth with great numbers and superb equipment to do battle in Northern Virginia, only to come limping back wounded and dejected? How long can Lincoln expect Northern citizens to support the Union cause, be it ever so just and necessary?

Poor leadership is not the only problem for the Union army. A significant number of volunteer regiments have been leaving the service at the expiration of their enlistment term. Veteran regiments and commanders are seen marching away almost every week. A few new volunteer regiments are arriving, but these units are composed of green recruits led by inexperienced officers.

On the Southern side, soldiers and citizens are never prouder of their battlefield achievements. Chancellorsville has perhaps been Robert E. Lee's most impressive victory, but it cost him and the Southern cause its most bold and brilliant field commander: Stonewall Jackson had been shot down by friendly fire while returning to Confederate lines after a nighttime reconnaissance. He lost an arm to amputation, suffered severely for a few days, and finally succumbed to pneumonia.

Lee knows that Jackson is irreplaceable, but he has complete confidence in the fighting prowess of his army. And his tough Southern soldiers believe themselves to be invincible under Lee's leadership. Jackson's death and the arrival of additional units scraped together from the diminishing Southern manpower barrel require a reevaluation of the army organization and command structure.

Lee is up to the task. He reorganizes the Army of Northern Virginia into three infantry corps, artillery attached, each with three divisions, all but one containing four to five brigades. General Pete Longstreet, Lee's "War Horse," still commands his First Corps. General's Richard Ewell (back in action after having a lower leg shot off by an Iron Brigade soldier at the Brawner Farm fight last August) and A. P. Hill are promoted to command the Second and Third Corps, respectively. General J. E. B. Stuart retains command of his superb cavalry corps.

By June 1, the effective strength of Lee's army is up to seventy-five thousand. It is a compact and powerful force led for the most part by experienced commanders. The regiments comprising most of the brigades have served together for two years and are often from the same state. They know each other well and feel they can whip any ten Yankees sent against them.

With the blessing of Confederate president Jefferson Davis, Lee is now taking the fight to Northern soil, intending to decisively beat the Army of the Potomac on its own ground and win the war for the South. He knows that now is the time, a time when his Confederate army has reached its zenith in terms of numerical strength and self-confidence, while its opponent, the Union army of the Potomac is shrinking and in turmoil at the top.

The Iron Brigade and the Sixth Wisconsin experience the organizational ramifications very quickly. Their First Army Corps, commanded still by Major General John Reynolds, has lost a net of seven infantry regiments and five artillery batteries, and changes have thus been necessary. The corps retains its three infantry divisions and the three general officers commanding them, but each is reorganized with fewer brigades. The divisions are now significantly smaller than before, in fact being about half the size of the typical Confederate infantry division.

For the Iron Brigade soldiers, there is some bit of good news in all of this: General James Wadsworth's First Division has been cut from four brigades to just two. But Wadsworth has designated General Solomon Meredith's five western regiments as the First Brigade. The Iron Brigade Black Hat westerners take great pride in the fact that they are now the First Brigade of the First Division of the First Army Corps of the First Army of the Republic. If ever the whole Union army were to be arrayed on one huge field, the Iron Brigade will have the place of honor, being on the far right, first in the reviewing line.[6]

Each Iron Brigade soldier feels that the fighting reputation they have earned, their distinctive uniform, and their unique all-western makeup have all now been fully recognized and rewarded by the army brass. The soldiers read about their reputation in the papers, and in letters home they make sure their families know about it, as well. They will not let down the army, the country, and, most especially, their brothers-in-arms. None will ever doubt their devotion to duty in the face of the enemy.

Mary Beman Gates is painfully aware of the pending confrontation that her fiancé, Rufus Dawes, is marching into. Newspaper reports of the Confederate incursion into Maryland and southern Pennsylvania seem to magnify the peril with every edition. Rufe's letters arrive irregularly, and she worries continually for his safety. His unit always seems to be the first to fight.

Endnotes

1. Rufus Dawes Collection. WHS. All letters quoted herein are from this source unless otherwise noted.

2. Dawes journals. DAA.

3. Mentioned by Julia Cutler in her journal. JCJ.

4. Letter courtesy of Rich and Peggy Dempsey Family Collection.

5. The letters are also transcribed (minus, in most cases, Rufus's personal comments toward Mary) in the *Dawes Journals, Books 1 and 3*. DAA.

6. Nolan, Alan T. *The Iron Brigade*, p. 224.

Chapter Nine

Gettysburg

Tuesday, June 30, 1863—Bivouac along Emmitsburg Road at Marsh Creek, Five Miles Southwest of Gettysburg, Pennsylvania

It is early on a gray, overcast evening, and Dawes walks slowly along columns of two-man shelter tents that seem to lend a semblance of order amid the hustle and bustle of hundreds of noisy soldiers. He nods approvingly as he glances down the rows of neatly stacked Springfield rifle muskets, four in each stack, arranged along the company tent lines. His men are cooking meals with messmates, scraping mud off their worn boots, comparing all the pretty girls they had passed by, writing letters, relaxing … an army of young soldiers in the field.

He passes by his old Company K, the backwoodsmen from around Mauston who he had recruited to serve two long years ago. Less than half of the original number are left. The Irish kid, Mickey Sullivan, feisty as always, is telling some tale that has his messmates laughing. Albert Tarbox seems to be the butt of the joke, and he is smiling with the rest, something about a young maiden with flowers who this morning had taken an obvious liking to the handsome young sergeant. Tarbox is a lady-killer, Dawes knows, only eighteen when he signed up, leaving his folks and lumberjacking near Necedah behind to help quash the rebellion. Dawes does not interfere.

As he walks on, he cannot help but smile, acknowledging the occasional "Good evening sir," and drifts away toward his own tent near the road.

It has been a busy day. The cheers and applause the troops received yesterday as they marched proudly through Emmitsburg, Maryland, were seconded today at every farmhouse and crossroad they passed. Men cheered and shouted encouragement, ladies passed out baked goods and water, teenage girls waved American flags and smiled as waves of boys in blue whistled and stared while marching past. The local citizenry was elated to see that the thousands of troops marching by their homes and farms were wearing blue uniforms, not gray and butternut. News of Lee's invasion has spread quickly, and everyone understands that unless protected by Union soldiers, their barns, shops, and livestock will be fair game for thousands of hungry and ill-clothed Southern soldiers. They shudder to think of their peaceful, rolling countryside becoming the same war-ravaged wasteland that is now northern Virginia.

The campsite had been neatly set up midmorning by each of his companies in a wet clover field. Bivouac on the march is once again a well-practiced routine experienced many times before. This site is better than most. Good water and wood close by, and the site well-drained. Smoke from hundreds of campfires drifts low in the warm, moist air. Almost as far as he can see, on both sides of the full-flowing creek and on both sides of Emmitsburg Road, about half of General John Reynolds's First Army Corps is settling in for the night, probably 4,500 men all told. The rest of the corps must not be far away, farther south somewhere along the highway.

This morning's march from their bivouac in Maryland began under a persistent light rain once again, but compared to the frenetic pace of the past several days, the hike today was an easy trek. The men were in a festive mood as they made a leisurely march of only 3 miles to their current site next to Marsh Creek, just off the puddle-filled flinty thoroughfare leading northeast to the road junction town of Gettysburg 5 miles away.

Brigadier General Solomon Meredith's Iron Brigade was at the head of the First Corps column today, and it was the Sixth Wisconsin's turn to be first regiment in the order of march. The Sixth thus became the first infantry unit from the Army of the Potomac to cross into Pennsylvania, the state line just behind them now, with Lt. Col. Rufus Dawes riding at the head of his regimental column. It is also the Mason-Dixon Line, and how refreshing it is to be in Northern territory once again.

Today being the end of the month, and pursuit of the enemy notwithstanding, it is payday for the troops. But it is also the end of the fiscal year, and every unit commander has a host of forms to complete reconciling clothing, ammunition, equipment, and rations. Ever since the halt, company and staff officers have been busy nonstop with the pay musters, paperwork returns, food ration distribution, and equipment inspections. By midafternoon the men had time to attend to personal business and cook their meals without being interrupted. And what meals! Despite what their pursuit of Lee ultimately portends, how wonderful to be in bountiful and friendly Pennsylvania! Farmers have brought in all sorts of food donations and items for sale. Dawes notes chickens, pigs, and geese being served up over numerous cook fires, courtesy of kind Pennsylvania farmers. *But some undoubtedly obtained surreptitiously by our expert foragers, despite orders to the contrary.* Dawes smiles. He is glad the men are enjoying a good meal for a change. Thinking of that, Dawes wonders what Billy has in store for the field officers' mess tonight. He is famished.

Everyone knows they are getting nearer to a confrontation. Buford's cavalry division is scouting up ahead somewhere, and the word is that several Confederate divisions are concentrated west and north of Gettysburg. The three depleted divisions of First Corps comprise the vanguard of the Army of the Potomac's pursuit of Robert E. Lee's Pennsylvania invasion. Two other corps—the Eleventh under Howard, and the Third under Sickles—are several miles behind. General Reynolds has been given command of all three corps, the vanguard "wing" of the army, almost one-third of its total strength, and that places General Abner Doubleday in immediate command of the First Corps. The troops know little of all this high-level stuff. They follow orders, pass around rumors, and go where and when told to go.[1]

Given the Rebel army's bold aggression, the eventual clash of these two veteran armies will certainly involve a pivotal battle. The late-night consensus over campfire discussions is that, worst case, Lee could consolidate his nine large divisions and pounce on the fragmented portions of the Union army that are now chasing him from various directions. This could mean defeat in detail and a potential rout of Union forces, worse than the defeat at Chancellorsville just eight weeks ago.

All of this has filled the Northern papers and been the talk of the army. It also fills the mind of Dawes as he walks along, deep in thought. Editorials are chastising the Lincoln administration and army generals for allowing Lee to get so far north. Southern Pennsylvania is in a panic. The Rebels are said to be near the state capital at Harrisburg. The governor has called out the home militia, a weak force to be sure that will be no match against any veteran Rebel unit. General Hooker, the latest in a line of failed army commanders who have been embarrassed by Lee, has been roundly criticized throughout his own officer corps. Many know that "Fighting Joe" himself admits he lost his nerve and desires to be relieved. There is not a complete understanding of where Lee's army is located. Lee knows where he is going, and he always seems to show up where least expected. *Our cavalry up ahead is trying to scout things out, but they are lightly armed and spread out.*

Then, just two days ago, we learned that President Lincoln relieved General Hooker! Here we go again! General George Meade, the relatively unknown head of Fifth Corps, is now our latest army commander. The president ordered Meade to assume command of the army even as our scattered troops are moving toward battle. And we are told that the order was much to Meade's surprise—he was awakened in the middle of the night by a courier. One staff officer told us that Meade at first thought he was being arrested!

Well, thinks Dawes, *shaky leadership or not, our Army of the Potomac is moving after Lee anyway. As far as our regiment, our brigade, our division, and our corps are concerned, we will not hesitate to pitch into the Rebs and make them pay for bringing the war to northern soil. We know the rest of our army feels the same… Well, at least most of them. We have no confidence in the "Flying Dutchmen" of the Eleventh Corps. They were blown away at Chancellorsville, resulting in the partial rout that caused Hooker's confidence to crumble. What is left of them are now our nearest backup. They have some good units, but overall, we don't trust them. I worry if we must rely on them.*

This was the topic of much serious discussion among the brigade officers last night. None of us know much about Meade, though none have reason to doubt his courage. He has been with the army a long time, wounded a year ago outside of Richmond, bravely led First Corps divisions in hot action at Antietam and Fredericksburg, but few of our boys would recognize him if he rode by. Perhaps Meade will prove to be a leader who is less on show and more on substance. Dawes pauses, looks upward, and mutters to himself, "God, I hope so," and then resumes his walk toward dinner.

His mind cannot get off the subject. *This change in army leadership while we are underway to meet the enemy is awkward at best. And besides, Meade has made less than a favorable first impression. The boys took a very cool demeanor today when, as ordered, I read to them the general's first message to the troops. Our new commander stated the obvious when he wrote, "The whole country looks anxiously to this army to deliver it from the presence of the foe." But when I read his parting words—that "Corps and other commanders are authorized to order the instant death of any soldier who fails to do his duty at this hour"—I could hear the murmurs. Better he could have noted our past sacrifices and courage and devotion to duty as assurance of our success! But I read it and made no comment. Our boys know what to expect and what to do. They just hope the generals do, also.*

Dawes pauses as he arrives near the road, leans against a tree just above the creek, and lets out a tired sigh. His day is nearly done. Adjutant Brooks has performed his usual efficient job in coordinating the month-end paperwork. Dawes has reviewed it all and signed off as regimental commander. The rolls show that 340 officers and enlisted men are present for duty in the Sixth, and here they are, arrayed around him. If a battle is soon in the offing, it will be his first as their commander from start to finish. It has been his ambition to be in this situation, yet a shiver suddenly runs through his body. A shiver brought on by wet clothes, but also a shiver reflecting immense pride, burnished with the weight of responsibility for the lives of these fine young men—a shiver reminding him of the crashing violence that pending battle will certainly bring, whenever and wherever it will come.

"Dreaming of that girl back in Ohio again, Colonel?" The words shouted in jest startle him and bring him up straight as he steps away from the tree. He looks toward the road to see Lt. Col. William Dudley on his mount, second-in-command of the Nineteenth Indiana, smiling broadly at him while slowly leading a good part of his regiment up the Emmitsburg Road, heading north. Young Dudley, dark hair and moustache, with a deeply tanned face, always carrying himself as someone older than his years would suggest. Yet he has proven to be tough and fearless in every battle and has been promoted over other officers who are senior to him. A thought quickly flashes in Dawes's mind: *Dudley always makes me feel old! I'm almost twenty-five; I don't think he's yet twenty-one!*

Dawes smiles and shouts back, "Ha! Now that you mention it, I do think it would be nice to be back in Ohio just now! Besides, it looks like you have in mind to take on the Rebs all by yourself. You probably don't need me. Where are you going?"

Dudley laughs and reins his horse over to the roadside. "Picket duty, our turn, I'm sorry to say. We're going to set ourselves up a ways to the north, so all you Badger Boys can get a good night's sleep without worrying about Bobby Lee or Jeb Stuart sneaking up on you in the dark. I thought I heard some of the boys talking about getting acquainted with some friendly Union chickens, too, but I am probably mistaken on that."

Dawes leans forward, quickly slaps his knees, and comes back up laughing his response: "Well, I know from experience that I wouldn't want to be anywhere close to the Nineteenth if I were a chicken! Don't get the farmers angry now. Our boys are looking forward to a triumphal march through Gettysburg tomorrow, and it would be nice if these folks tossed sandwiches at us instead of feathers from their missing hens."

"You always manage to look at the totality of the issue, Rufus! I'll see you tomorrow; I'm looking forward to Gettysburg—I hear it's a college town. Hopefully not a boy's school or a convent!"

"Well, you can check it out before we do. It's going to be our turn to bring up the rear. At least with all this rain, we won't be eating your dust, just slogging through the puddles like everyone else."

"Too bad, Rufus. That means you'll get last dibs on any peach orchards we might pass!" With that, Dudley canters up to his troops and is soon out of sight as the Nineteenth passes by a stand of trees farther up the road.

What a fine officer, thinks Dawes. *What a tough bunch of soldiers! Not as disciplined as my Sixth, certainly, but rugged fighters.* The carnage at Antietam flashes through his mind. *These same Hoosiers saved our bacon on that horrific morning last September when we were shot to pieces and being chased by Hood's Texans. They paid the price for stopping Hood, with many killed and wounded, including their commander and my friend, Major Al Bachman. When Al was killed, Dudley stepped in and took command, despite being the youngest captain in his regiment* [2] *If we get in a fix again, they will be there for us, and vice versa. There is an unbreakable bond, a brotherhood, among all of us in the brigade. We have a proud reputation to maintain. We will not let each other down ...*

It is dusk. The dinner with his small mess—Major Hauser, the surgeons, Adjutant Brooks—has been wonderful, the conversation lively. Harris and Ticknor have stopped by, Harris playing his harmonica, Ticknor's clear tenor voice singing a few lively camp songs, Billy keeping time with hands and feet. Billy has set up a nice camp and served up fresh beef steaks, potatoes, and best of all, peach cobbler ... courtesy of some Maryland farmer's orchard. And the biscuits from real flour, with sugar topping he scrounged from somewhere ... *Delicious!*

It's later now and dark, the night air punctuated by occasional laughter interrupting the steady backdrop of frog, cricket, and flying insect noises. The others have wandered off, leaving Dawes alone at the small fire, Billy squatting close by, cleaning up the pots and utensils. Dawes looks at Billy in thought. "Say, Billy, that was a fine meal tonight."

Billy looks up and smiles. "Whiah, thank ya, sah! Not bad if'n Ah says so mysef!"

"Billy, we passed into Pennsylvania today, crossed the Mason-Dixon Line. Do you know what that means?"

Billy's pot scrubbing slows down, and he looks again at Dawes, his smile broadening a bit. "Oh yes, sah! Dis ain't Virginny no mo'ah. Dis be land where der be freed slaves, sah! Swear Ah could feel de air bein' fresh and clean as soon as de wagon passed dat sign. De other boys says de same thang."

"Billy, you know I would hate to lose you, but if you have a mind to, you can walk away from this army and find a place up here in Pennsylvania where you could work and earn a living and make a new life. I'm sure there's any number of free blacks doing that very same thing not far from here, certainly."

"Sah, bein' 'spectful fo you sayin dat, but where would Ah go? A'hm jes a know-nuthin, got-nuthin. Ceptin y'all soldier boys, most ob y'all anyways, da only white mens Ah ever knowed jes treat me like so much dirt. Might be de same eben here up north if Ah took off on mah own. 'Sides, Ah needs to git mah mammy an mah sistah out of Virginny. They's still down in Reb country, still slavin' fo some no good massah. Ah can't do it lessen y'all win dis wah. No sah, dis here Missah Lincolm's army mah home now."

"Billy, you've said before that you want to be a free man, to make your own choices. This war will be over some day, and after all we have been through, I hope that means we have kept the Union together and that slavery is abolished for good—everywhere. I just feel you should take hold of that freedom, now that you can have it."

Billy sits for a few seconds, puts down the pot, and slowly responds, "Sah, jes sayin' Ah be free don't make it so. I guess most ob us maybe don't know how to *be* free. Fo' now, Ah'm a thankin' you fo keepin' me, thas fo' sure. But Ah'm a worried 'bout yah, sah, cuz you be headin' off to a big fight agin. And you boys alez seem to get in a big tussle ebry time, and you ridin' up der on dat big ole mare ... Ah don't wanna think 'bout it. All those Reb white boys wantin' nothing more than to knock you off dat horse. Den what? You a young man wid a lady friend waitin' and all. And where be Billy den?"

Billy's response catches Dawes by surprise, but he knows his servant's blunt assessment is true. Commanders on horseback are lucrative targets, just as much as color bearers. How many times has he felt the bullets zip close by? *Billy needs us, he needs me, and he needs to get his family out of bondage. If I'm gone, what does become of him? Maybe Bragg or Hauser or Converse will keep him on, maybe not.*

Dawes responds, "You mentioned your mother. And I know your father was sold off years ago and is ... well, who knows where. Do you think your mother knows where her Billy is now? Would she want you to stay up north?"

Billy smiles, a sad smile nonetheless. "Well, sah, Ah sees your point. But Ah can't do it. And ya know, sah, my mammy alez called me Willyum.

Willyum Jackson. She alez say 'Billy' be a slave name dat da massah like to use cuz it be easy to say. 'Willyum' be what she wants me to ansah to ... Ha! But 'Billy's' fine, sah. 'Billy's' jes fine."

It takes only a second for this response to sink in. Dawes studies Billy for a moment, forms a small smile, and nods. As he rises to head to his tent, Dawes pauses, looks back at Billy, and says, "Very well. You served up a fine supper tonight. It really hit the spot. Good night ...William."

Both William and Dudley have reminded him of that special some-one in Ohio ... not that he needs reminding. It has been three days since his last letter to Mary. *I finally have time now,* he thinks, *and between all the paperwork, she has been on my mind with every free thought!* Once inside his tent, he removes his hat, sword belt, and revolver, sits on a wood box at his folding table, opens his correspondence box, dips his pen into the inkwell, and begins to write on a new sheet of paper:

Bivouac in <u>Penn</u>. 6 miles from Gettysburg, June 30, 1863

My dear Mary

I am afraid it will be a long time before you get this letter, and, in fact, I am not sure the Rebels are more likely to read it than you. I hope that you have got the letters that I have written since the campaign opened.

We left South Mountain in great haste on the 28th, and marched to Frederick city through a drizzling rain as usual. Next day we moved from Frederick to Emmitsburg, Md., and to-day we came here, where we are having a muster for pay. I don't think I ever knew at this time of year such a long continued, misty, driz-zling storm as we have been marching through since crossing the Potomac. I have not heard anything from you for ten days, and very little hope of any mail soon. I am so afraid that you are sick that I don't have any patience to wait. I can only most earnestly hope that you will be brought safely through any danger. This would be to me such a blank, miserable world without you.

We have marched through some of the most beautiful coun-try I ever saw. It is refreshing to get out of the barren desert of Virginia into this land of thrift and plenty. ... [E]verybody, great and small, is perfectly overjoyed to see us coming.

The rebel stealing parties are running away ahead of us and I presume the whole rebel army is concentrating to give us battle. We see no papers and can gather only from rumor the probable position of affairs.

I am kept full of business on such hurried marches as this, scarcely from morning to night getting a moment I can call my own, so I can't write you such letters as I would like. But I will have a good long time to tell you sometime.[3]

"Colonel, beg your pardon, I have a message, sir!" It is Sergeant Major Cuyler Babcock outside the tent.

Dawes answers, somewhat annoyed, "Yes, what is it?"

"General Meredith wants to see all the regiment commanders at his headquarters right away—plans for tomorrow and the latest information on what the Rebs are up to."

Dawes breathes a heavy sigh and thinks, *I knew this would not last.* He shouts out to Babcock, "All right, I'll be right out and on my way over. Please inform Major Hauser where I'm going."

"Yes, sir," comes the reply.

Dawes packs up his writing box and folds the letter into his coat pocket as he mutters to himself, "I hope Old Sol keeps this short for a change."

7:00 a.m., Wednesday, July 1, 1863

He had returned last night from the commanders' meeting tired and wet from a steady, drizzling rain, and after giving orders for reveille to be sounded at dawn, he had fallen asleep in his tent almost immediately. This morning the men make their coffee and munch on hardtack and dinner leftovers, despite being bothered again by a passing shower. The overcast sky is a little brighter to the west, however, and to the experienced weather eye of Rufus Dawes, he is thinking, *We might have a dry day for a change!*

General Reynolds, with his staff and cavalry escort in tow, splashes down the road as dawn is trying to break through the gray clouds. Word soon comes for Wadsworth's First Division to move out and follow the general to Gettysburg. Reynolds is obviously in a hurry to get his troops moving north, but Dawes knows his regiment is last in line today, so he has a little time. He pulls out the letter he had started to Mary last night and jots a quick line:

"Pack up, be ready to march immediately." Finish the first chance.

He places the unfinished letter in the inside pocket of his frock coat and heads toward his horse, leaving William to pack his tent and small kit into the regimental wagon.

7:30 a.m., Marietta, Ohio—the Gates Home

Mary Gates comes down the stairs and enters the kitchen. Sunshine breaks through the open windows and lights up her little sister's face as she sits at a small table combing her doll's golden hair. "Well, good morning, Mary," her mother says as she continues putting away clean silverware. "I hope you slept better last night. Father left you something in the parlor."

"It's a big new map!" ten-year-old Bettie blurts. "Father says you can use it to follow where the army is going."

Mary's mother smiles, shakes her head a bit, and says, "There, that surprise didn't last very long! There are biscuits and peaches for breakfast. And I think your father is just as interested in the army's progress as we all are."

Mary smiles pensively and responds, "Well, I'm not too hungry right now, maybe a peach a little later would taste good. Bettie, let's look at the map! That was nice of Father. But the news is so slow getting here that it's impossible to know where they really are right now. I have not heard from Rufe for days, when he was still in Virginia. His mother and Lucy haven't, either. The newspapers seem to get everything wrong. It's just so difficult to know what is happening!"

"Well, Mary, you know he's very busy with the regiment. But there has been no news of any battle, and I am sure he will write when he can. But we know that with Lee and his Rebel army between us and Washington, it may be difficult to get news reports and mail through in our direction."

As she watches her daughters walk to the parlor, Betsey Shipman Gates turns to finish her kitchen chore. But her mind is with her twenty-year-old daughter and on that young officer—no, the young local boy she had seen grow to a man, who is approaching, or perhaps is already swept into, another bloody battle. And that young officer in the middle of this terrible war has become her daughter's sweetheart, the man she wants to marry. Betsey thinks also of Sarah Dawes, her two fine surviving sons serving with infantry regiments in harm's way and far apart. *Boys Charley's age are dying every day in the army. We are so happy he is here at home, attending college, safe from the horrible battles. But Beman and I know he wants to go, to do his part, feeling guilty that he is not among the young men in blue serving their country.*

Dear God, she thinks, *how many sweethearts and wives and mothers are agonizing at this moment over the same worry or are already in grief over their loss? And now thousands of these boys are marching toward another battlefield. What if Rufus's farewell letter, mistakenly sent after the last battle, comes to Mary a second time and proves to be true? The pain will be horrific. How much longer, Lord? How long must this misery last? Please, watch over him, over all of them.*

Mary comes back, places a biscuit and peach on a plate, and, turning to go upstairs, says, "I'll take this with me, thanks. I just feel a need to write Rufe right now and be able to send it today."

Betsey smiles, trying to mask the emotions from her daughter.

7:30 a.m.—Emmitsburg Road

The brigade ordnance wagons pull up, and Dawes oversees the issuance of additional ammunition to the regiment. Orders are for each man to carry sixty rounds today. The cartridge boxes hold only forty, so the extras are busily stuffed into pockets and haversacks.

Dawes turns his attention to the road as the five New York and Pennsylvania regiments of General Lysander Cutler's Second Brigade begin to march past. Cutler and his staff trot on horseback at the head of their long column, and Dawes salutes his grizzled old former regimental commander, who responds with a nod and quick touch to his hat brim. Right behind Cutler ride his several staff officers, among them Captain John Kellogg, who makes a show of recognizing his Mauston friend by standing up in his stirrups, removing his hat, and bowing his curly haired head in Dawes's direction, almost losing his balance in the process. Kellogg comes back up smiling, and Dawes cannot help but chuckle as he returns the salute by raising his hat.

Cutler's troops are immediately followed by the noisy clatter of a hundred-plus horses pulling along the caissons, limbers, and six 3-inch ordnance rifles of Captain James Hall's Second Maine artillery battery. The troops and battery form a column more than a half-mile long. They are taking the lead today for Wadsworth's Division as the other half, Meredith's Iron Brigade, wait for the rain-soaked pickets of the 19th Indiana to come in. Dawes thinks: *By the time we finally get going the road will be churned into a muddy mess.*

Dawes mounts Katerina and moves at a walk toward the head of his regiment, which now, at 8:00 a.m., is finally filing onto the Emmitsburg Road in column of fours. Ahead of them, in a long column, are the four other regiments: Second Wisconsin leading, then Seventh Wisconsin, Nineteenth Indiana, and Twenty-Fourth Michigan. The recently formed one-hundred-man brigade guard, made up of twenty soldiers from each of the five regiments, brings up the brigade rear. From end-to-end in long columns four-men wide, about 1,900 Black Hats of the Iron Brigade are on the move north. *It is always a sight to see,* thinks Dawes, *rifles at the right shoulder, daylight gleaming on the barrels, young men marching with a steady gait, appearing so much taller wearing those big black hats.* He feels an immense pride in being part of this famous brigade of veteran western soldiers, the best troops in the army.

His own men in the Sixth are in a jovial mood. They all expect an easy 6-mile march today with a bivouac close to the friendly townsfolk of Gettysburg. The Germans from Company F soon start one of their Hessian marching songs. Few except them understand the words, but the whole regiment takes step in time. Then his old Company K gets into the act with a favorite oddball marching ballad about a heifer gone wild, and he can hear Captain John Ticknor's clear tenor voice leading the refrain after each crazy verse: "On the distant prairie, hoop de dooden doo," followed by cheers and whistles.

It is fun stuff, a good day on the march. Dawes gets caught up in it himself. At a brief stop when the column ahead becomes bunched up, he calls for the little regimental band to come up front. "Play something patriotic," Dawes tells the drum major. "Let's come into Gettysburg with some style!"

"How about 'The Campbell's Are Coming'?" R. N. Smith asks.

"Perfect," says Dawes. "Maybe the townsfolk will take it to mean 'The Rebels Are Running' when they see us march in!"

The fifers and drummers strike up the tune, and the whole regiment takes up the march again, keeping step to the fighting song of the Scottish clans. Dawes passes word for the color guard to unfurl the stars and stripes. *There, this is the way to bring the old Sixth into town! It is exhilarating, marching in step with brothers-in-arms, band playing, flags flapping in the breeze, through the rolling countryside, past farm buildings, grain fields, and orchards.*

Surgeon Preston rides up next to Dawes and smiles his approval, silently thankful again he is back in good graces with his commander. He now knows that his awful mistake had served to open the heart of that girl in Ohio. Preston's commander is now one happy man to be around.

"Good morning, Rufus—I mean, Colonel. This ought to bring out the citizens! It looks to be a memorable day."

The column marches along for a time, looking forward to a pleasant day, until suddenly, the feel-good atmosphere abruptly ends. A rider comes dashing toward them from up ahead. It is Lieutenant Woodward of General Meredith's staff. "Sir, the general directs that you stop the music, furl the colors, and close up. There is action ahead."

Dawes is surprised, especially for the "furl the colors" order. "We've never done that before," he mutters to himself. As Woodward rides off back up the road, his horse smattering mud and pebbles along the Twenty-Fourth Michigan troop column, Dawes commands his small band to stop playing and fall back to the rear. *I'm going to pretend I did not hear the "furl the colors" order*, he thinks, and as the Sixth marches forward, the national and state flags are kept flying.

Yes, sure enough, with the little band now silent, both Dawes and Preston can distinctly hear the distant -crump!- -crump!- of cannon fire. They pass a farmhouse and orchard off to their right and, reaching a crest in the road, can see their four sister regiments up ahead picking up the pace. Farther up the road, maybe a mile away, he discerns Gettysburg rooftops. It looks like the last regiments of Cutler's brigade off in the distance, perhaps a half mile ahead of the Iron Brigade, are filing left off the road and hurrying cross-country to the northwest, heading toward the rising sound of gunfire and wisps of white smoke rising over intervening woods. That pleasant march through the friendly streets of Gettysburg might not happen after all.

A lone rider, an officer, walks his horse slowly toward them, passing the troops of the Twenty-Fourth Michigan going the other way. As he comes closer, Dawes recognizes Lt. Col. George Stevens, second-in-command of the Second Wisconsin. *A bit strange*, he thinks, *since the Second is leading the brigade, and here is George making his way to the tail end.* Dawes hails him: "George, what's happening up front? Do you have some news for us?"

Stevens stops and then turns his horse to ride next to Dawes as they proceed on. He does not answer at first, seemingly deep in thought.

Dawes tries again. "George? Are you feeling all right?"

"Oh, hello, Rufus ... Hello, Doctor. I'm sorry, just not quite myself. I should be up front with the regiment, but ... but, I tell you, I keep seeing my wife and kids in my mind, and I, I just ... I just feel a little gloomy right now ... Actually, more than a little ... And it's strange, you know, it started just when we heard the firing up ahead, and I had to get away— get away from the men, I mean. I didn't want them to think I'm ... well, you know." There is a long, uncomfortable pause. "I've got to get my head into this business we seem to be getting into, but I just ... I just have a feeling ..." Steven's voice trails off, another long pause, then he looks at Dawes, sees the concern, says, "I'll be all right. I'll just go along with you for a bit, if you don't mind." Stevens is looking straight ahead as he speaks, avoiding eye contact, his depressed mood out of character, not the confident, experienced officer Dawes has come to know and respect.

Dawes makes a quick sideways glance to Dr. Preston, who is studying Stevens with a concerned look. "Sure, George, sure. This thing is probably some of Buford's cavalry running up against Jeb Stuart, or maybe some infantry probing. Cutler's brigade up ahead ought to be enough to help them out." The three ride together in silence for a few minutes. Soon, up ahead, they see the Second Wisconsin leave the road past some farm buildings and head cross-lots through the muddy fields after Cutler's brigade. They all know what this means. It is not just Cutler's brigade being summoned to assist Buford's cavalry—the Iron Brigade is heading that way too.

The column marches on, by now perhaps 4 miles from last night's bivouac, and each regiment in turn is heading off-road. General Meredith has pulled his brigade band aside, and they are playing "Yankee Doodle" as Dawes leads his men past a substantial barn and an attractive two-story red-brick farmhouse on their right, then takes a left-oblique onto the muddy track to follow the Twenty-Fourth Michigan. The noise of gunfire ahead increases, and now they can see the Second Wisconsin, still in four-man column like all the rest, take off at the double-quick. The Seventh and Nineteenth follow suit in turn. Stevens stiffens in the saddle, turns to look at Dawes, hesitates a few seconds, and with a forced smile, says, "Looks like I better catch up! Good-bye, Rufus ... Doctor. Good luck!"

Dawes and Preston watch him ride off after his regiment. Preston speaks first: "Rufus, have you ever seen him like that? It seems to me that Colonel Stevens is suffering from a premonition of ... Well, it's obvious he's very depressed. I've had soldiers tell me about these before. They usually don't amount to anything. Just superstitions. Don't you think?"

Dawes is thinking just the opposite. His mind immediately recalls Antietam and Edwin Brown's premonition of death, which proved to be brutally accurate. The brutal scene from last September flashes again before him: Brown shouting the order he had just given him, Dawes watching in horror as a bullet zips through his open mouth and out the back of his head, his best friend killed before his eyes.

Dawes pauses, blinks a few times to clear his head, and turns to Dr. Preston in response to the man's question. "I'm sure you're right, and it bothers me to see him agonize about it. I know for sure he's a brave man. Hopefully, it all turns out to be nothing, and we can kid him about it tonight." But his face is frozen with the grim look that Preston has seen in him before and clearly recognizes: a steely-eyed battle face.

Riding on, Dawes glances back at his nearest soldiers and locks eyes with Lieutenant James Converse of Company G—from Beloit, Dawes recalls. The young lieutenant's face and those of his soldiers reflect a mood that is no longer jovial. *At least we are coming up as the last regiment in the division*, Dawes thinks. *Maybe we can stay out of this one for a change.* The five hundred Michiganders just ahead start jogging forward, their new black hats bouncing up and down. Dawes turns again in the saddle and shouts toward his men, "Sixth Wisconsin! Forward, double-quick! March!"

Dr. Preston waves and rides back toward the wagons at the rear to look for Dr. Hall. If there is to be a battle, the surgeon's services will be needed, and a place must be found to perform their bloody work.

There is no letup. The column is running nonstop through openings in fence lines made hastily by Cutler's troops now far ahead, over a wet gully, through a muddy field, up rising ground into and then through a stretch of woods mostly cleared of underbrush by grazing cattle, swerving around the trees ... all jostling knapsacks, canteens, and pouches bouncing on hips, clattering tin cups, muskets swaying over shoulders at each jogging step ... everyone panting now, sweating in the rising mid-morning heat, some falling behind. The sound of artillery and rifle fire grows louder as they press on, and Dawes can now smell the gunpowder smoke in the sultry air.

Just out of the woodlot now, following the other regiments over a crossroad, he can see the other units of the brigade, each forming quickly into battle lines, colors front and center, then heading across a golden wheat field toward the dark-green wooded crest of a low ridge off to the left, to the west. The regiments are moving forward as soon as they are ready, not waiting for the regiment behind them, and he can see their steady blue lines in two ranks moving forward, rifles over their right shoulders, colors centered and waving in the slight breeze. *Just like the parade field*, thinks Dawes, *but now heading toward an enemy we cannot yet see.* Things are happening quickly, and Dawes feels that familiar knot form in his stomach.

A strung-out line of dismounted cavalrymen is falling back through the gaps, remounting, then heading left to cover the flank. Several hundred yards away, Dawes spots Rebel skirmishers fire shots and then run away over the ridge. He looks quickly to the north and as he does, -Blang!- -BLANG!- The crashing sound of deadly musketry volleys where Cutler's brigade must now be, maybe a quarter mile in that direction. Dawes clenches his teeth. *This is much more than a Rebel probe. We are in a fight!*

General Meredith's aide, Lieutenant Woodward, comes galloping toward him once again. "Colonel, form your line and prepare for action!"

Dawes stands in his stirrups and loudly shouts over the rising noise of gunfire, "Sixth, by companies, into line!"

Each company commander repeats the order, and the men scuttle in unison, as they have done in training and battle many times before, from columns of four into two-rank company lines, each behind the one in front of them. That maneuver completed, Dawes then shouts, "Forward into line! By companies, left half wheel, double-quick! March!" Despite the excitement of the moment, Dawes cannot help but feel pride as his soldiers complete the maneuver that transforms their long column into a line of battle-facing soldiers perpendicular to where they had started. They move forward, heading west toward the ridge, just like their sister regiments have already done ahead of them, Dawes riding in front, centered on the colors, as he shouts an order for his men to load their rifles while on the move.

Artillery fire is now bursting into the area. Then -CRASH!- -CRASH!- Unmistakable, violent musketry volleys erupt 300 yards ahead in the woodlot on top of the ridge where he had seen the Second Wisconsin enter seconds before. Another staff rider dashes toward him—boyish-looking Lieutenant Marten, eyes wide and intense, coming close to shout over the noise: "Sir, General Doubleday directs that you halt your regiment! You will be the reserve for the First Division."

Dawes reins up and turns in the saddle. "Sixth Wisconsin! Halt! Lie down!"

The gun noise and artillery fire is growing in intensity. Ahead, the other four regiments of the Iron Brigade have disappeared over the crown of the ridge into the distant trees, and from the noise, Dawes knows immediately that they are clashing with the enemy. The gunfire is nonstop, no commanded volleys but men firing at will, distant shouts and the shrill Rebel yell. He knows it is all violence there, yelling, smoke, and shooting. *Men are killing and being killed just out of our sight! We are the first to get into it again … just like at Antietam.* The thought of that tightens the knot in his stomach. Soon, scattered numbers of wounded men from the other regiments come struggling out of the woods, back from the violent action just beyond the distant ridge, trying to get help toward the rear.

His own men are winded and sweaty after their 1,300-yard run. Most are gulping water from canteens and adjusting equipment. Others are flaked out in the grain, chests heaving. Panting stragglers come up and dive into their places as they catch up with the regiment. All of them are wondering what is next.

Lieutenant Harris, one of two officers leading the one-hundred-man brigade guard that has followed the Sixth on their sprint, runs up to Dawes, breathing heavily. "Sir, what instructions do you have for us?"

"Well, the other regiments are already engaged. We are in reserve. I'm not sure about you." Dawes pauses to think, then, "Split the guard into two companies and form them on each end of our line. You'll be with us for the time being."

Harris, catching his breath, nods, "Yes, sir, I'll take the left company, and Lieutenant Showalter of the Second Wisconsin will take the right."

"Very well, I'm glad to have you back with us, Lloyd." *And I'm glad for the extra one hundred men*, he thinks without saying it. Dawes looks northwest through the mounting battle smoke, trying to see what is going on. Every other regiment of Wadsworth's division that had marched ahead of them this morning is hotly firing at an enemy force he still cannot clearly see. The noise is constant, and plumes of white gunpowder smoke drift slowly across the fields. Peering above a band of trees not far away to the northeast, he recognizes what looks to be a church steeple or small cupola rising from a multistory brick building. It stands out to him, and as he looks back west, he thinks back to his college days in Madison and Marietta. *That big building looks like it belongs on a college campus.* He pulls out his pocket watch. The hands show 10:15 a.m. Dawes takes a long drink from his canteen, pats the sweaty neck of his steady horse, and then draws his sword.

Another horseman, a staff lieutenant, comes riding up fast. Pointing north, he shouts, "General Doubleday directs that you move your regiment at once to the right!"[U]

Dawes rises in his stirrups, points his sword, and cries out, "Sixth, on your feet! Right-face!" Each company shifts accordingly, now facing north. Dawes shouts again, "Double-quick! March!" He trots Katerina to the head of the column, the 420 men under his command running behind him. The firing to their left from the hidden Iron Brigade is heavy.

Two more staff officers on horseback ride up and join him. Captain J. D. Wood of General Meredith's staff yells out through rising musketry

---

[U] See map end of chapter

noise, "Our boys are blasting the Rebs, but Cutler's brigade is in trouble! If they break, our line on the left is out-flanked!"

Lieutenant Clayton Rogers of the Sixth, now serving as a staff officer for Division Commander Wadsworth, also passes on Wadsworth's command to support Cutler as Woods gallops ahead to get a closer look. The Sixth keeps moving forward, running through a wheat field in a shallow valley between the two ridges, with enemy artillery shells streaking through the air and stray bullets hitting around them. They pass the college building on their right and look with morbid curiosity at a small group of officers and soldiers crossing in front of them, struggling to carry off the body of an officer in a blanket, left arm hanging and limply bouncing up and down. Who it is, they cannot see.

Captain Wood rides up again with a contorted face and reins his horse as Dawes passes. "Go like hell! It looks like they are driving Cutler!"

Dawes mentally takes in all that is transpiring in front of him as they jog closer to the cauldron ahead. About 200 yards to his left front are two small Union regiments. *Must be from Cutler's brigade … Yes, there's the red pants of the Fourteenth Brooklyn, exchanging fire with a distant line of screaming Rebels coming toward them.* The Union troops are falling back to a fence line bordering a roadway as an artillery battery is driving down that road to the right, heading helter-skelter away from the enemy, under fire from Rebel troops swarming after them. *That must be Hall's Maine Battery. They are in trouble!* Horses and men are being shot down, men cutting away the leather traces to clear the guns and limbers, trying to save their guns, horses rearing and plunging. *They may not get out of there*! But worst of all, hundreds of Cutler's Union troops, about 300 or 400 yards ahead and beyond the road, are in full disarray and retreating to the right with a hoard of Confederate infantry in fast pursuit, shouting their shrill Rebel yell, shooting Yankees down as they run. His mind racing, Dawes quickly thinks, *How could things have gotten into such a mess so fast? If these Rebs aren't stopped, they will turn and roll right into the backs of the Iron Brigade, fighting hard now in those woods, and completely cut our boys off!*

But he also sees a chance. The strong Rebel force is disorganized in their chase of Cutler, and it looks like they have not yet noticed the Sixth's approach. The irregular Reb line will soon pass farther to the right than he is now leading his column. *We need to form into line and fire into their flank,* he quickly realizes and immediately reins up to shout another order. "File right, march!" His veterans react instantly, the head of the column runs to the right, each company following in order. In less than a minute, they are all trotting parallel to the turnpike in the same direction the Rebel horde is moving on the other side. Then Dawes shouts, "By the left flank, double-quick march!" At this command, every man pivots to the left, forms into a standard two-rank line of battle, and heads forward at the double-quick to the north, toward the enemy right flank, trotting closer and closer to the turnpike fence. The colors are flying in the center, and Lt. Col. Rufus R Dawes, mounted on his brown mare, is leading them in front, sword pointing toward the enemy. "Forward!"

This gains the attention of Rebel officers closest to the turnpike. The Sixth is not a narrow column any longer; it is a battle line over 100 yards wide, running straight toward them. Sharp commands are shouted, and Rebel soldiers stop, wheel to their right to face the new threat, aim their weapons toward Dawes and his oncoming Black Hat Union line, and fire.

-Hiss!- A bullet screams death past his head. Chunks of the wooden fence rails 50 yards ahead splinter off. Dawes looks back to his right and sees several of his men hit the ground as the rest run on, loaded rifles still on their shoulders, leaning forward into the fire as if it were a rainstorm.

He turns back and then -THUNK!- Katerina suddenly rears and plunges. Dawes spurs the animal to regain control, but she falls heavily forward, head dropping and flinging him onto the damp ground like a slingshot. His disciplined line of men passes around him as they keep heading for the fence line. Adjutant Brooks runs toward him, but Dawes quickly takes stock, feels like he is all right, the soft ground absorbing much of the blow but sticking mud to his uniform and face. He instantly realizes how lucky he is that his horse did not fall on top of him. He struggles to his feet. "I'm all right, boys!" he yells as he chases after them. The soldiers nearest their flying flags just ahead let out a cheer, even as one man takes a hit and falls to his knees with a painful cry, clutching an elbow just destroyed by a Rebel bullet. Dawes glances back. His mare is hobbling away on three legs, obviously wounded or injured in the fall, or both.

No time to think about it. His men are up to the stout post-and-rail fence line on the south side of the turnpike, rifles on the top rail, drawing a bead on the surprised Rebel soldiers across the opposite fence line and in the field beyond, wanting to shoot in the worst way, but waiting for the command. Soldierly discipline at its finest. Dawes catches up and quickly notes that it's a wide road and the fence is five or six rails high. Recalling his review of the area maps the night before, he realizes that the roadway is the Chambersburg Pike. *No matter. Let's nail those Rebs!* "Fire by file! Fire by file!" he shouts, and the company commanders immediately echo the call. The two soldiers at the extreme right of each company line, both front- and rear-rank men, fire simultaneously at the ragged line of Rebel soldiers. Immediately, that touches off a rolling wave of flame from each company, his men aiming and firing in sequence with muzzle flashes erupting down the whole line from right to left, men instantly reloading after they fire and continuing to fire at will.

Dawes is at the fence line, in the center next to the color guard, and through the white sulfur smoke, he sees the devastating punishment that his veteran troops are inflicting. Rebel soldiers wheel and fall. Those not hit fire back and then run back north and ... almost disappear! *What is happening?* Dawes and his men find out in a hurry. The Rebels have found some sort of cover maybe 150 yards away, jump into it, and are now firing back as quickly as they can load and shoot. Wisconsin boys are firing back, all shooting and gunfire, rails splintering with hits in front of them, bodies along the line absorbing crushing, bloody bullet impacts.

We can't withstand this! We've got to move! "Over the fence, boys! Over the fence!" His men start to clamber over the high fence or work together to yank the horizontal rails out of the posts. Under intense fire, they scramble into and cross the road to the stake-and-rider wood fence on the far side, firing back at the Rebels through as much cover as the fence offers. "Keep going!" Dawes shouts, and his men, despite the intense fire coming at them, clamber over or through the fence and into the open field beyond, firing back at will. Some of them do not make it. Dawes can see several of his men hit as they try to negotiate the fence, hanging head-down over a rail or writhing on the ground after being hit by Confederate fire.

His men move forward into line, firing at the line of smoke and fire ahead. Dawes and his men can see the Rebel battle flag and a line of heads aiming their muskets at them and firing, with spurts of yellow flame and clouds of smoke billowing. Bullets are whistling past or hitting with a sickening -thunk!- into friends nearby. "Charge! Charge!" his men are calling. They know this cannot be sustained as is. Dawes looks frantically about for some help. Looking left, he sees a thin line of Union soldiers, and he runs over to the nearest officer. It's the Ninety-Fifth New York, Major Pye, maybe a hundred men.

"Move forward aligning on me, Major!" Dawes yells.

"Charge, it is!" responds Pye, and Dawes runs back to his own line, shouting, "Forward! Charge! Charge!"

His men do not hesitate. They run into the storm of gunfire, slowing down to aim and shoot, then moving out again to reload on the run, all care about maintaining a line gone, each man trying to keep up with their American flag being borne by the color-guard heroes, who themselves are being shot to pieces. The men are crazy with anger and desire to reach the Rebels and crush them. All around them, friends and tentmates are falling, hit by enemy fire. Ahead, looming ever closer, is the enemy, shooting at them from a defilade position, a ready-made trench of sorts. "Come on, you cowardly bastards! Stand up and fight like men!"

Dawes runs behind his men, sword in one hand, revolver in the other, exhorting his men with "Forward! Align on the colors!" Everyone's blood is up, minds steeled to the fact that their next step could be their last but pressing on with a maniacal fury into the muzzle flashes of the enemy, trying to keep up with the man next to them, stepping over and around those who have caught a bullet and are curled up on the ground with painful wounds and plaintive cries. He glances behind and sees men who have been hit lying still or hobbling back to the fence line. His glance captures an officer, sword still in hand, stumbling, turning, looking up, falling like a limp doll, lying still. *It's John Ticknor! I'm sure of it!* "God!" he cries, but he can't stop now. Just ahead, his men are closing in on the Rebels, shouting, cursing at their foes, shooting, running forward. They are crazy with the fury of battle, incensed that these Rebels are shooting at them, wanting to pitch into them and get even. To his left, Major Hauser is yelling, "Forwarts! Forwarts!"

Dawes keeps up behind the color guard and sees the flag fall once, get picked up, moved forward, then down again, this national symbol leading the attack drawing furious enemy fire. Dawes runs up and leans down to scoop up the fallen flagstaff when he is wrestled aside by one of his men, surely a survivor of the color guard, who does his duty and runs forward, carrying it aloft again.

A young soldier, hat gone, hair matted and face sweaty and pale, in obvious pain, stumbles into Dawes out of the smoke and battle noise. Dawes catches him with his arms and lowers him to the ground. A thought flashes through Dawes: *I know him! A kid from some small town on the Mississippi—Prescott, I think. It's Private Kelly, Company B, the Color Company.*

Kelly looks up at Dawes, blood on his lips, and, with shaking hands, rips open his shirt. Dawes can see the bloody hole in his chest, can hear the air in Kelly's lungs bubbling through with every panting breath. Kelly stares at Dawes with eyes wide open, and with painful, halting words as he gasps for air, says, "Sir, it's bad, I'm gone! I know it!" He cries out in pain, "Please tell my folks I died a soldier! Please, please ..." He leans his head back and grits his teeth in agony.

"I will, Kelly, I will, I promise, I promise." Dawes must leave him. He quickly lowers Kelly's head to the turf and runs forward after his strung-out mob of soldiers. They are no longer in a well-ordered line, but rather a winged V formation with the colors, and Dawes just behind, at the point.

To his right, he sees an officer. It looks like Lt. Remington, plus several of his men, madly making a rush toward the Rebel battle flag, which is stuck in the ground at the Rebel trench 50 feet away. It is obvious his men aim to capture it. The Rebs see them, and an even heavier flurry of gunfire erupts, hitting almost every Wisconsin soldier mid-stride, knocking them down. Others spring forward, and there is terrific fighting, thrusting, screaming, stabbing, and swinging as North meets South in brutal hand-to-hand combat.

To his front, his men reach the edge of the Rebel trench shooting and shouting. Muzzle flashes crash in both directions, men go down, and Dawes rushes through an opening and fires his pistol at gray shapes in front and below him. Instantly, he realizes what he sees. *It's a railroad cut—a wide swath dug through the ridge for a railroad but with no rails. Not finished.* The depression is about four feet below grade where he is, but it gets much deeper to the left where the right-of-way runs through the ridge. And it is filled with Rebel soldiers! Hundreds of them! His first thought is *My God! There are more of them than there are left of us!*

There is more firing now on his left as the Sixth's left-wing companies and the Ninety-Fifth New York catch up. They overpower and eliminate the Confederate men at the top edge and then fire down at the Rebels massed in the deeper part of the cut. The Rebels here are trapped, the slope of the cut too deep and too steep for them to use it as an effective fighting trench. Off to his right, a blast of gunfire erupts down the cut and into the Rebel soldiers. A dozen wheel and fall under this fire as the melee around their flag is raging on. *Yes!* He realizes what just happened. *We've flanked them on the right, able to shoot down the cut lengthwise!*

His men begin to yell out all along the line, "Surrender! Throw down your muskets! Throw down your muskets!" Some Rebels raise their hands, begging for quarter, while pockets of close-range shooting, thrusting, screaming, and falling bodies rage at spots along the depression.

Instantly, Dawes sees the situation, thinks, *I must take charge! Seize the moment! Maybe they can't see how few we really are.* He shouts down to the horde of Rebel soldiers, "Who is the colonel of this regiment?"

A gray-coated Confederate officer with stars on his collar, moving among his men, looks up and shouts back, "I am. Who are you?"

Dawes shouts, "I command this regiment! Surrender, or I will fire!"

The Confederate officer quickly takes in his situation amidst the muzzle blasts, shouting, and chaos around him. He is exhausted from the tough fighting against Cutler's routed troops, has just taken over from his wounded commander, and is in a bad spot. A hundred rifle barrels are pointed down at his men from above. To his left, Yankees on top of the steep cut are firing down on his men, some of whom are running for the rear through the cut to the west, others raising arms and yelling, "Quarter!" The brutal struggle around his regiment's flag is over; his men there are overpowered. Yankee soldiers on his far left are straddling the cut at the end of his line, poised to fire again. He drops his head, lets out a sigh, quickly strides forward, unbuckles his sword, and, reaching up, hands it to Dawes. "We must surrender, sir. My sword," he says with subdued voice. His shocked men, tough soldiers that they are but disciplined as well, begin to drop their rifles and raise their arms all along the line.

Not all of them, though. Confederate soldiers on the back fringes, not wanting a trip to a Union prison, clamber up the far slope of the cut and take off across the field to the north. Then, farther down the deeper end, a gunfire blast erupts from the top of the cut into the surrendering Rebels. Scores of Confederate soldiers fall as many survivors take off out the west end of the cut, trying to avoid another volley, trying to escape death or surrender. "What the—!" Dawes shouts and sees that it is the Fourteenth Brooklyn, catching up with the charge, firing a volley into the cut when they first arrive over it, apparently not realizing the surrender is happening ... or maybe not caring.

Dawes hears several of his men shout, "They're getting away!" And he watches as squads of his men chase after them into the opposite field, unceremoniously shoving surrendered Rebels out of the way. He spots a running Rebel officer fire back at the Yankees with his revolver, men in blue and gray ducking as rounds whiz past. John Kilmartin of Company G quickly takes aim, fires, and drops the officer dead in his tracks.

Dawes looks away. *We've done it! Somehow, we've done it!* He jumps into the cut with his men and soon becomes the recipient of several more swords tendered to him by other chagrined Rebel officers, their ingrained honor and chivalry maintained even in this bloody scene. Adjutant Brooks comes over and takes the clumsy sword bundle out of his arms—all except that first one, which Dawes still holds. Face sweaty and breathing fast from the intense action, Dawes addresses his opponent. "Who are you, sir? What unit is this?"

The answer is made with a deep Southern drawl: "I am Major John Blair, sir. Our colonel was wounded and taken from the field before we engaged you. We are the Second Mississippi Regiment. There are North Carolina troops mixed up with us, also, I am sure."

Major Hauser now comes over to this impromptu introduction of opposing commanders. "I am Lt. Col. Rufus Dawes of the Sixth Wisconsin Volunteers. Fall your men in without arms on this side of the cut. Major Hauser, here, my second-in-command, will take charge and lead an escort, taking you and your men away from the field as our prisoners." The two officers salute each other, one the victor, the other a dejected, chagrined prisoner of war. Blair's parting, pensive words strike Dawes as odd: "Wisconsin. Thank God you are not a New York regiment."

Dawes turns his attention to his men. Details are sent out to assist wounded comrades lying in the field of their charge. Captain Converse is leading a group who are pulling and pushing a recaptured cannon owned by Hall's Maine Battery back to the turnpike. Some of his men are trying to attend to wounded Rebels, and Dawes sees a Black Hat soldier half-carrying a badly wounded and crying blond Southern boy out of the grisly bottom of the cut. *One second we are killing each other, and the next ...* He orders his surviving officers to get the rest of the men organized on the north side of the cut and be ready for further action. The Rebs might be coming back.

Lieutenant Goltermann leads a volunteer skirmish line toward the next ridge in case the Confederates decide to counterattack. One of these volunteers is Corporal Frank Waller, who comes up to Dawes with the captured battle flag of the Second Mississippi. There is nothing more treasured by both sides than a captured battle flag, and a bunch of officers and NCOs crowd around to look at the bullet-riddled, square-shaped banner with its star-filled blue bands running corner to corner, the names of four past battles stitched into the red triangular spaces in between.

"Sir, what should I do with this flag?" Waller asks.

"Give it to me, Corporal," Dawes replies. "Well done!"

Waller does so, but the normally stoic NCO takes a moment to say a few words, his face smudged with black gunpowder, features still taut from the brutal fight, his voice quick and emotional: "There were others who were shot trying to get it before me ... Drummer Eggleston, Bodley Jones, others still lying just over there. Lieutenant Remington went down too. I want you to know that." He then turns away to join the skirmish line.[5]

Dawes knows he needs to get this prize to the rear, but he cannot spare a healthy soldier, so he walks over to Sergeant Evans, who has been wounded in the leg and is now starting to hobble toward medical help near Gettysburg. He is trying to use two Rebel muskets as crutches, so

Dawes opens Evans's uniform coat, tears the banner off its staff, and ties it around Evans's waist. "Here, Sergeant, take care of this and keep it safe, and get yourself patched up."

"I'll do it, sir. Thank you for the honor."

Major Blair's sword is a burden, but it is a trophy he wants to keep. Dawes hands it to the wounded corporal going to the rear with Sergeant Evans and says, "Find Dr. Preston and tell him to keep this for me."

Evans and the corporal painfully join scores of other wounded Badgers on their way toward medical help in Gettysburg.

As Dawes is securing the captured flag, the crowded cut is busy and noisy with activity. His men in the prisoner detail are shouting and shoving the Confederates, trying to push them into a controllable bunch, adrenaline still rushing through their veins and wary of all these tough Rebels who probably outnumber them, hundreds of loaded weapons still lying at their feet. As Dawes joins his survivors lining up on the north side of the cut, another Rebel soldier runs away, trying to escape to an old fence line across the undulating field to the north. Two of his men fire at the man, who falls, and Dawes's men trot toward the downed soldier to investigate.

Dawes yells at them, "Take a look around up there," and then continues to check on his men. His two soldiers soon return to report that the Rebel was badly wounded. It was a hard thing, but they could not help him. The bleeding Reb is left on the field. Dawes grimly nods. *Such is war*, Dawes thinks, *a very hard thing.*

Just then, two shots ring out from the direction of the fence line. Dawes and everyone around him instinctively duck, but he still sees the impact. His remaining color bearer, undoubtedly the man who had shoved him aside during the charge, Corporal Charles Mead, is hit directly in the head, his blood and brains exploding out from under his black hat, which flies off as Mead drops, killed instantly. The Sixth's flag hits the ground as several of his men fire back and take off with vengeance to clear out whatever Rebs were responsible. There will not be any mercy shown.

Dawes struggles to control his emotions, but he is shaken. Mead was the last man standing in the Sixth Wisconsin's eight-man color guard. In their fifteen minutes of intense action, Mississippi gunfire had hit every member of the color guard. Lieutenant Hyatt asks a few men if they will assume the duty. Not surprisingly, there is hesitation. Then Corporal Isaiah Kelly, a bloody rag tied around one knee, steps up: "Sir, I'll carry the flag."

Dawes looks Kelly in the eye, nods, and says quietly, "All right, Corporal, if you feel up to it." As he walks slowly down the line, Dawes can't help but think, *Have I just condemned this man too?*

As he walks through the bloody human wreckage and discarded equipment at the bottom, he stops in his tracks at seeing the handsome face of Sergeant Albert Tarbox, the twenty-year-old lady's man, now staring up with sightless eyes in a final expression of shock. "He was shot in the back by a Reb," says tough Mickey Sullivan, bleeding badly from a shoulder wound, "as he stooped down ta see aboot me." Dawes closes his eyes and shakes his head.

Lying dead nearby is rugged Corporal Abe Fletcher ... never to see the forested hills of Mauston again. Corporal William Evans of Company B is quickly carried by on a stretcher, moaning from an abdominal wound. Fitzhugh's Crossing is immediately recalled: *The shouted warning from Evans that saved me from a sniper's bullet.* And so many others: Mead, Kelly, Pearson, Stedman, Armstrong ... Eyes close tightly as Dawes recalls Private Armstrong, he the fat-cheeked young boy recently arrested for sleeping on picket duty, a capital offense. Dawes had mercy, simply scolding and releasing him. Young Armstrong, so profusely thankful, vowing never to fail again. Dawes recalls the boy's parting words: "I'll remember the colonel for the rest of my life!" How short that life! He is now lying dead and bloody on the trampled field in front of the cut.

His mind is quickly routed elsewhere as a mounted courier from General Wadsworth rides up with a congratulatory message on the Sixth's successful counterattack, plus an order to fall back about 200 yards to a wooded area on the right of the unfinished railroad at the next ridge east. He calls it Seminary Ridge—the same ridge that extends south past the road and on which sits that big college-looking building. Dawes, suddenly very tired, looks southeast at the building cupola. "So that's a religious seminary. Right in the middle of this battle."

The young corporal looks down at this mud-spattered officer, notes a smear of blood on his coat sleeve, and, not knowing how or if to respond, replies simply, "Yes, sir," before leaving Dawes to contemplate the irony.

Dawes leads his survivors in column along the railroad bed to the trees. Behind them, the railroad cut and the field in front of it are littered with the discards of battle, hundreds of muskets, and dead soldiers in blue and gray. Young soldiers full of life twenty minutes ago are now gone forever, left on the ground where they have fallen. Numbered with them are some desperately wounded Confederates who could not be tended to or moved. The orders are immediate; they will try to get them help later. For some it will be too late. It is an awful, bloody landscape.

Once in the trees and protected somewhat by the brow of the ridge just north of another railroad cut, the shattered Sixth Wisconsin pauses to reorganize. Shattered companies are consolidated under surviving officers. Brooks and Babcock walk the thin line to tabulate who is present and who is not. The company roll calls are sad affairs, as names are called, and survivors respond with what they know about missing comrades.

"Harland, John." No answer. Then, from a survivor, "He's killed, I'm sure of it. I saw him shot through and fall down into the cut when he was going for that flag." Such is an all-too-typical response in each company formation.

Discovering that both officers leading the brigade guard, Harris and Showalter, have been wounded and have gone to the rear, Dawes decides to disband the sixty or so survivors and send them back to their respective Iron Brigade regiments. He thanks them for their service; he will certainly note it to their commanders. And he thinks, *How fitting! Every regiment in the brigade was represented in our charge. They knew what it meant. Not one of them flinched.*

Dawes pulls out his pocket diary book and opens a new page. It is time to tabulate. He listens as Adjutant Brooks runs down the results of the roll calls. He methodically transcribes in pencil the hurried casualty list for each company. From Company A down to Company K, his old company, he jots down the grim numbers below three columns he heads with "Killed," then "W" and "M" for wounded and missing. Then, adding the numbers in his head, he records the sickening summary at the bottom of the page:

Killed 19 — W – 126
Loss   145
Missing   6
                      151

One hundred fifty-one lost out of three hundred forty! My God! It is Antietam all over again, in what? Fifteen minutes? Our proud regiment! Cut to pieces! One casualty for every yard between the pike and the railroad cut. Two of his officers are dead, and six are wounded. Captain John Ticknor, jovial singer, friend, comrade—*I recruited him two years ago. We laughed and sang together just last night. Silenced forever. Orrin Chapman, young, recently promoted, full of promise—gone.* His mind fills with images of the others, other young men he had known well for two long years.

Lieutenant Colonel Dawes does not realize that his math is wrong. His wounded total is in error, ten more than the company numbers add up to be. Under the trying circumstances, he can be excused for the mistake. He also does not know that before the battle is over, the final number under the "Killed" column for his beloved Sixth will increase by eleven.

It is a sad half hour under the trees of Seminary Ridge, with Dawes, the commander, awed by the courage of his men, exhilarated by the success of the charge and its impact on the overall battle, crushed by the suffering and loss of life, humbled by the responsibility. It is a hard thing. He is at the same time proud of himself and his men but sickened by so much violent death—violent death to his comrades, men he had led in the fight. He realizes the day is not over; it is just beginning.

And now it comes. Another congratulatory message from General Wadsworth but with orders to advance back to the ridge next to the bloody railroad cut. The Sixth will extend the line of the Iron Brigade and three Pennsylvania "Bucktail" regiments arrayed to the left-front, to support an artillery battery being placed where Hall's battery had been positioned earlier that morning. No matter that there is open ground ahead and to the right, dominated by Rebel batteries on high ground to the north and west. *If that's what is needed, we will do it.* He sees that more Union troops, the 2,500 men of General Robinson's Second Division, are filing off to the right, going north of Cutler's survivors to extend the line in that direction. *There must be more of Lee's army out there! We will be in the middle.*

The 190 men who are left in the Sixth Wisconsin are now reorganized. Surviving officers combine depleted companies into provisional commands. The men are strained and hurting over the loss of so many comrades. They are thirsty and hot and sweaty and grimed with black powder. But it is time to go, as ordered. In line of battle, Dawes orders his men forward down the slope and toward the ridge ahead. They are instantly under fire from enemy artillery less than a mile away. -WHOOSH!- -BANG!- -BANG!- The screaming shells find the range! Dawes, running behind the colors in the center, hears a crash and screams to his left. A solid shot has just plowed into a man in the rear rank, somehow missing the soldier in front. A sergeant quickly runs over, but it is a bloody mess, the man killed instantly, not sure who right now. Then, an air burst! A couple more men drop.

The men keep running. Up to the ridge finally, they fire on Rebel skirmishers and push them back. More artillery comes down. "Lie down!" Dawes orders, and the men try to bury themselves into the ground. Dead bodies from Cutler's earlier fight and defeat lay splayed out around them, some being further maimed by shell hits. But the enemy infantry does not come. The Sixth lies under the brow of the ridge for cover and waits. It is midday, with hot, sultry, bright sun. They wish they were anywhere else but here. If the enemy attacks in force, they know they will be in big trouble out here in the open.

But now it is almost quiet. The enemy must be deciding on their next move. With Lee, there is always a next move. The men munch on hardtack and wait. Time drags by. Through couriers, Dawes learns of the morning success of the Iron Brigade. Their quick assault into the woods had smashed the Rebel attack on Buford's cavalry, but they had taken severe casualties, especially in the Second Wisconsin, the first of the Iron Brigade to crash into the enemy. Among these is Lt. Col. George Stevens, hit badly in his midsection in the first Rebel fire, less than twenty minutes after leaving Dawes and Preston, taken to the rear in agony. It does not look good. *Poor George! His premonition proven true, his wife in Fox Lake to be a widow, his children fatherless. Horrible.* Dawes recalls the look on George's face as they rode together that morning. *He* knew *his fate, and he went forward anyway. That is courage. That is duty. But it is chilling.*

Stevens is not the lone officer casualty, of course. Most shocking is the report that General Reynolds was killed at almost the same moment, just as the infantry fight commenced. It was Reynolds whose body was carried across their path as they ran toward the railroad cut. Despite its own awful losses, however, the Iron Brigade, including the Sixth, has severely cut up two Confederate brigades and swept up at least five hundred Rebel prisoners. Among them is General Archer, one of the Confederate brigade commanders, a terrific coup. The Iron Brigade now holds the woods a quarter mile off to the left of the Sixth Wisconsin, with Stone's brigade of three Pennsylvania regiments—about 1,300 men—lined up in between. It does not look like a strong, defendable position. Dawes can see the whole field. The Iron Brigade in the woods and Stone's men near farm buildings between the woods and the Chambersburg pike are several hundred yards in front of the other Union troops. Stone's 1,300 men are in their first real fight, and they are formed in an L-shaped line, facing both west and north, each wing subject to enfilading fire. Dawes wonders why Doubleday does not consolidate the corps onto the next ridge to the east, to Seminary Ridge, which is higher and has open ground to its front over, which the enemy would have to advance.

Major Hauser returns from his prisoner detail and provides the tabulation of surrendered Rebel soldiers turned over to the provost guard. He smiles as he tells Dawes, "230 of dem, by Gott!"

Dawes is glad to see him. It is good to have him and the prisoner detail back. But what is happening? This feels like the calm before the storm. Dawes pulls out his journal book as he is lying on the ground, diligently intending to keep up with his record of events. This has become part of him, part of what he feels is important. *Perhaps it is foolish. Who will care? Who will ever see it? Maybe it will all vanish in the millisecond of an artillery shell explosion, all these notes flying about in the wind like so much confetti. Or later today some Rebel soldier scrounging among dead Yankees might pull it out of my pocket and throw it away.*

But Dawes is compelled to record it. He has had time to compose himself, to be ready for what comes next. He is a hardened veteran commander of an elite unit. This important event should be documented while it is still fresh. So, sitting on the ground with his back to his line of soldiers, he begins to transcribe what has just happened, as neatly as his rough pencil allows, following the blue-lined paper of his small journal book:

Battle Field near Gettysburg
July 1ˢᵗ 1863 2.P.M.
Bloody desperate fight.
Crowning glory of the Old Sixth!
Major Stone of the 2ⁿᵈ Miss. Infantry surrendered his sword and regiment to me—230 men.

He does not realize he misidentifies his captured opponent. The Mississippi commander's name is Blair, not Stone, a fact lost in the mind-numbing blur of violent combat. It does not matter now. A shudder shakes him. *"Crowning glory"? "Surrendered ... to me"? What am I writing? "Crowning glory of the Old Sixth!"* He is appalled at how cold and self-serving that sounds. *What glory is there for Ticknor, Chapman, Tarbox, and the rest? This is not about glory! Almost half of my men are dead or painfully wounded!* He takes his pencil and strikes out the "Crowning glory" line.

He pauses to think of the grim task ahead. *The battle will certainly resume. I may be dead in an hour!* A tightness in his gut forms, his body tenses, but he continues:

If I am killed today let it be known that ...

The emotion comes over him, and his face contorts with a rush of guilt and sadness. *Mary, I do love you! I did love you!* Tears well up in his eyes. His hands shake, and he is barely able to keep control. But he must go on. He made a promise. He begins again, but he can no longer neatly follow the blue lines, all he cares is to record it as he had promised. He now keeps that promise, but it is finished in a nervous, emotional scrawl, outside the lines and increasingly at an awkward angle. He is just barely able to complete it:

Corporal James Kelley of Company B shot through the breast, and mortally wounded, asked to tell his folks he died a soldier.

The last word, "soldier," is almost illegible.

July 15, 1863, photo looking northwest from town down Chambersburg Pike. In the afternoon of July 1, the Sixth Wisconsin is positioned in the trees to the right (north) of the distant Seminary/Oak Ridge railroad cut, facing attacking troops of Hill's and Ewell's Confederate corps on the opposite side. They support Stewart's Battery B, Fourth US Artillery, split on both sides of the cut on the west side of the crest.

The railroad cut, July 2016, view southeast toward Seminary Ridge. At 10:30 a.m., July 1, 1863, the Sixth Wisconsin charges from right to left into the Second Mississippi, positioned in the incomplete railroad bed.

Later, under fire, Dawes leads his men down the bed to the wooded ridge in the background (it was then far less dense). In midafternoon, Confederate infantry will charge across this ground into rifle fire from the Sixth Wisconsin and double-canister discharges from six cannons of Battery B, Fourth US Artillery.

Battle flag of Second Mississippi. Soldiers from both sides died trying to protect and seize it.

SGT Albert Tarbox, killed in action in the railroad cut, July 1, 1863.
Buried in Soldiers' National Cemetery.

Major John Hauser

Unidentified Corporal, Co. A, Sixth Wisconsin

Midafternoon, Wednesday, July 1, 1863

The Confederate assault soon renews. Lee's original plan was to engage the Union army only after he could completely consolidate his spread-out divisions. But now his available troops far outnumber the Federals, and he cannot resist an opportunity to chew them up. Besides, Heth's division had been surprised this morning and was badly mauled by the Black Hat Brigade of western troops. A. P. Hill wants to retaliate, and Lee knows he must regain the initiative. He must allow his soldiers to restore their Southern honor.

The remaining two brigades of Heth's division are brought forward, plus General Dorsey Pender's 7,500-man division. To the north, the powerful division led by Confederate general Robert Rodes is about to hit the Second Division of the Union First Corps under General Robinson, whose 2,500 men are outnumbered almost four to one. Elements of the Union Eleventh Corps are arriving in the fields north of the town, making a very loose right-angle connection with General Robinson's right flank. They are about to be assailed by General Jubal Early's Confederate division of General Ewell's Second Corps, coming in from the northeast. Out of the distant dark-green woods, the long lines of Lee's crack infantry advance. Their intent is to crush the woefully outnumbered Union First and Eleventh Corps, occupy Gettysburg, and seize control of the surrounding high ground before Union reinforcements can arrive.

Union artillery fires at them, Rebel batteries answer, and the air and ground are filled with whooshing, screaming projectiles and bursting shells. The artillery battery on the south side of the railroad cut that Dawes and the Sixth Wisconsin are supporting, four guns of Lt. John Calef's Battery A, Second US Artillery, are getting hammered by several Confederate batteries both north and west of them. Shrapnel is hitting men and horses as they fire back in response. It becomes too much, and Calef is forced to limber up and retire.

Then, to the far right, Ewell's corps attacks and Cutler's survivors, who are next to the Sixth in diagonal lines facing north, retreat as Robinson's division next to them becomes involved in desperate charging and countercharging. To the front and left, Hill's Confederates in long lines assail Stone's Pennsylvanians and the Iron Brigade, who are mostly hidden from view in the woods. The fighting there is furious, nonstop, crashing musketry.

Dawes, lying in the middle of his line, watches Calef's battery scramble away. He has received no orders. He runs bent over to the left and dives down next to Hauser. "I think we've been forgotten. There's no artillery left to support. We're too exposed. We need to get out of here!"

Hauser ducks his head as a shell whooshes past and replies, "Ya, I tink so!"

Dawes leads his men on a dead run single file down the railroad bed toward the trees from which they had advanced earlier. After running under a gauntlet of artillery fire southeast along the unfinished railroad bed, but without casualties, the Sixth is now lying down on the reverse slope in the shade of the trees.

General Wadsworth orders Stewart's Battery B, Fourth US Artillery, into position. Stewart's 6 twelve-pounder Napoleon smoothbores are split into 2 three-gun sections on both sides of the Seminary Ridge railroad cut. Stewart stays with the right half; Lieutenant Davison commands the left. The Sixth Wisconsin supports the artillerymen from the trees on top of the ridge.

The Iron Brigade and Stone's Pennsylvanians are under viscous attack by A. P. Hill's screaming infantry, outflanking the Northerners left and right. The shooting is furious, men going down in droves, but the Rebels are paying dearly for every foot of ground. Dawes hears furious volleys and the Rebel yell to his right. He knows that soon, it will be their turn. Sweating in the mid-80-degree heat and high humidity, young Wisconsin soldiers in blue watch grimly as more than half of Lee's infantry come after them.

Kneeling with Lieutenant James Stewart 20 yards behind three brass Napoleon cannons and their sweating cannoneers, Dawes covers his ears. *I'm not getting too close this time!* -BOOM!- -BOOM!- -BOOM!- The twelve-pounders roar and recoil right to left at an oncoming line of charging Confederate infantry 200 yards away, in line on both sides of Chambersburg Pike. Through the smoke he sees sickening gaps in the enemy line, soldiers blasted away by Stewart's canister rounds. Incoming artillery and small-arms fire are crashing and zipping through the air. Cannoneers and horses are hit occasionally, the big animals rearing, drivers trying to hold them steady, men working the guns with a frenzy. His own soldiers are to the right, firing at the Rebels from the cover of the tree line. The Badger boys are yelling, "Come on, Johnny, come on! Get closer, Johnny, and we'll send you to hell!" The noise is terrific! The Rebel line retreats over the ridge.

Dawes runs left to the edge of the deep cut and watches as Union troops in thin, ragged lines several hundred yards away, his friends in the Iron Brigade and Stone's tough Pennsylvanians, slowly retreat from the woods and farm buildings across the fields on the other side of the

Chambersburg Pike. They are under heavy fire, being overwhelmed. *My God!* he exclaims to himself. *There were 2,500 men there this morning— so few are left!* He can see bodies littering the landscape. *There is Holon Richardson, still on his horse, carrying the flag of the Seventh Wisconsin.* Dawes watches the blue line receding like a wave breaking on a beach. Men are diving with their rifles behind a low barricade of fence rails among scattered trees in front of the Seminary buildings, these hastily put in place by reserve troops earlier in the day. They lie on their bellies, among maybe fifteen pieces of Union artillery placed there also, making a last stand. Thousands of Confederates from Pender's division pause a few hundred yards away to regroup, but everyone knows they will come. It's the Alamo!

"Here they come again!" the shout rings out. Dawes runs back toward his men. The Rebels are steadily advancing again, shooting as they come this time, bullets zipping past all over the place. Stewart's artillerymen keep firing as fast as they can, his Sixth Wisconsin men shooting from cover also, all noise and shouting and violence. Just then, Clayton Rogers dashes up on horseback, spies Dawes, and leans over to him: "The orders are to retreat at once beyond the town. Keep good order!"

Dawes is incredulous. "What?! We can stop them!"

Rogers quickly points toward the town, and Dawes looks northeast behind him through the tree trunks. His heart sinks. Over the open fields, he sees masses of scattered blue infantry and artillery rushing madly toward the rear. Thousands of gray soldiers—flags flying, sun shining on steel rifle barrels—are chasing them in long lines, shouting the Rebel yell. *The Eleventh Corps has caved in! We are about to be cut off!*

From north to south, the First Corps troops realize they are in big trouble. If they retreat now with all their speed, exhausted though they are, disaster, death, and capture might be avoided. But it will be close.

"Battalion, about-face! Forward guide center, march!" Dawes leads his men on foot at a fast pace toward Gettysburg, along the north side of the unfinished railroad bed. Ahead and to the left, toward the Eleventh Corps disaster, Ewell's Confederates are streaming toward the same objective. Dawes can clearly see them coming on a converging course through the fenced fields and around some large buildings at another college campus. Behind them, Hill's Confederates are yelling and shooting. Everyone picks up the pace to a run. They are all hot, exhausted, scared. Dawes is leading them and in control, but says to himself, *I've got to get us out of this!* He shouts back to his men, "Keep up! Keep going!"

Breathing hard and sweating profusely, they finally come to a cross street in town running north and south, but it is swept by Rebel gunfire from the left. Some of his men fire back. *Where are we to go?* thinks Dawes. *I have no idea.* Up ahead at the next street are wagons, ambulances, and caissons plunging wildly to the right. Dawes takes the cue: *Move to the right, to the south, away from Ewell's Rebel soldiers.* But first they must cross this street.

He spies a board fence on the other side. Several planks there are missing, and there looks to be a vacant lot behind it. "Follow me, single file, double-quick!" He runs across, through the narrow opening, and shoves anyone who gets stuck out of the way to keep those behind from getting caught in the open. Two men are shot running across, the next men dragging them through, helping them as best they can. Now in the lot, they reform and head toward the next street that leads south. It is jammed with hundreds of soldiers, horses, artillery batteries, and wagons in a stampede trying to get away. Southern artillery shells are crashing into buildings, bricks flying, all is bedlam. Some of the mob in blue return fire; others simply run into buildings for cover or to await surrender, many of those with the Eleventh Corps crescent moon emblem on their caps.

His mind racing, Dawes tells himself, *I will* not *let my men get caught up in this!* But everybody is prostrated with heat and thirst. His men are at a breaking point. He yells at them to form two ranks, has them hug the building wall, and keeps them there a few minutes to let most of the mob pass by them. Rebel soldiers appear up the street and open fire, bullets zinging and smacking against the walls. His troops fire back, but some start to break. Dawes jumps on a building stoop and cries out, "For God's sake, boys, stand up to it! We are bad hurt but not a bit scared! We captured a whole Rebel regiment today! Now three cheers for our Old Sixth Wisconsin!"

It is dramatic, some would say absurd, but in the tenseness and terror of the moment, it is exactly what is needed. His men respond. They have lived through a horrific day, beaten their foe, once again earning the respect of the army, and they are not about to quit now. Their cheers are loud and clear—they will get out of this somehow! As if on cue, they are rewarded by a gray-haired citizen who comes struggling along with two buckets of water! The men crowd around to dip cups and canteens for a quick drink. The refreshment comes just in time. Dawes leads them on at a trot, the rear company firing to keep the Rebels at bay.

The Sixth is moving quickly now, down the road for about half a mile amid the mass confusion of the broken Union army, past homes and buildings, then up rising ground at the southern outskirts of town. Dawes sees a steady line of battle ahead wearing blue uniforms. *Thank God!* They run through it, and the exhausted, sweat-soaked Rufus Dawes approaches the nearest officer: "What unit are you? Do you know where Wadsworth's division is?"

"The Seventy-Fifth Ohio, Steinwehr's division, Eleventh Corps," the man replies. "All the stragglers are forming in the cemetery, up there," and he points uphill.

Dawes is quick to respond, "We're not 'stragglers'! We are the Sixth Wisconsin!" He then turns and leads his men uphill into the cemetery. Everything and everybody around them is in a state of noisy disarray and confusion. "A cemetery! What a place to reform," he tells Hauser. "Keep the men together. I'm going to find out what's going on." Babcock hurriedly walks with him. The men of the Sixth collapse among the gravestones, exhausted.

Dawes searches for someone in charge, then comes across a dispiriting scene. General Rowley, commanding the First Corps, Third Division, is on horseback, wildly shouting conflicting orders to every group he passes. "Is he drunk?" Babcock asks.

"I don't know," Dawes replies. "Maybe, or maybe hit in the head. It's not a good thing either way!"

Another rider approaches Rowley. It's Lieutenant Clayton Rogers of Wadsworth's staff, and Dawes is close enough to hear: "Sir, General Rowley, I must place you under arrest by order of General Wadsworth!" Rogers commands several soldiers to grab the reins of Rowley's horse, who, mumbling in protest, does not resist.

General Wadsworth on horseback now comes over himself, having spotted Dawes and his regiment, one of the few here that is still a cohesive force. "Colonel Dawes, take your command to the east toward that wooded hill. Report to Colonel Robinson."

"Yes, sir!" Dawes replies, and Wadsworth moves on, looking for more of his scattered division, allowing Dawes no chance to ask the obvious question: "Robinson? What happened to General Meredith?"

He leads his men around headstones and scattered soldiers, through the arch of a two-story brick gatehouse, toward an open area and the hill beyond. Two generals and their staff are on horseback in the road they cross; it looks like Howard and Hancock. Dawes is immediately encouraged. *Hancock! That is great! If the Second Corps is up, we can hold after all, and he is a fighter.* They pass a battery going into position, four brass Napoleons pointing down the road toward town, men busily shoveling protective earth mounds in front of each cannon. He recognizes

Lieutenant Stewart and Battery B! *Thank God, they made it here! His boys won't let any Rebs come up that road!*

5:30 p.m., July 1, 1863—Culp's Hill

Dawes finds Colonel Robinson in the rolling, rocky fields heading up to the hill—"Culp's Hill," he says. It is a sad and solemn sight to see the skeleton of what is left of the brigade. A few surviving officers come over to shake hands, and he hears about Meredith, hit by shell fragments, his horse also, both going down with the horse on top of Old Sol, injuring him severely. There is more, much more, but there is no time now. *My God!* thinks Dawes. *There are maybe five hundred men left in the brigade besides us, strung out in a line facing the town. Two-thirds of our proud brigade are missing! Hurt bad as my Sixth is, we are in the best shape of them all. Look at the Twenty-Fourth Michigan! There are fewer than one hundred soldiers there, and that's a captain now in charge. They marched just ahead of us this morning five hundred strong! Where are Morrow and Flanigan?*

The woefully thin brigade is positioned on the military crest of the rising ground up Culp's Hill. Dawes and the Sixth Wisconsin are on the far right, facing north toward the town in timber interspersed with boulders, looking down a steep slope. The wooded hill gets higher to his right, but there are not enough men to cover it. Dawes turns to Major Hauser: "They better send more help up here, quick."

Hauser responds in his booming voice, "Ya, dat is for sure. Mine Gott! How ve going to hold dis place?"

The regimental headquarters wagon appears, and William Jackson hops off, approaching Dawes like a lost puppy coming home. "Mah God, sah! Ah'm glad to see y'all, but Lordy, y'all jes lookin' awful! Dis bin a bad fight! Ah neber seen thangs as bad as this afor!"

"William, thank God! I was afraid you got caught in town. Get some help to break out these shovels and spades for the men to use. Sergeant Major, get the men working to dig a breastwork line up the hill."

A Rebel attack is expected at any moment. The men, exhausted as they are, take turns with the shovels and use felled logs and limbs to form a low protective wall through the trees and boulders. They work hard at it for almost an hour when Dawes sees a column of soldiers coming up the hill. At the head is Colonel Ira Grover, commanding the Seventh Indiana, part of Cutler's brigade.

"Hello, Dawes!" Grover calls out, "You've had a hell of a day. I heard about the charge—well done! But my God! The whole division is

Culp's Hill photo taken late July 1863. Left is north to town, occupied by Ewell's Confederates. The Iron Brigade defense line is visible on the distant slope, the Sixth Wisconsin just inside the trees. Earthworks in foreground mark positions of five 3-inch rifled cannons of Reynolds's Battery L, First New York Artillery.

just so cut up! I can't believe it. We just made it here from wagon-train guard-duty back in Emmitsburg. We heard about the fight going on and waited for relief or some orders, but finally I couldn't stand it anymore. So I left the trains, and we got here as fast as we could. I met General Wadsworth up by that cemetery, and he sent us here to extend the line to your right. They'll probably court martial me for leaving without orders, but what the hell."

Seeing the digging, Grover asks, "Do you have orders to build breastworks?"

"No, but I would advise you to do it," Dawes replies. "There are a lot of Rebs out there, and I think they will want to take this place. How many men do you have?"

"Four hundred and thirty or so," replies Grover. "So I thought we would be needed."

Dawes smiles. "We are going to need every man and more. This is a big hill, and most of it is empty. I for one am awfully glad to see you!"

The Hoosiers begin to cut trees and dig in. Grover and his men are solid, and Dawes begins to feel better about the situation. He finds a large boulder near the center of his line for his headquarters, then walks downhill, stopping at each regiment of the Iron Brigade, or what is left of them, to find out about friends he does not see. It is sickening. Fourteen brigade field officers left the Marsh Creek bivouac this morning. Only four are now present unhurt, Dawes and Major Hauser of the Sixth being two of them. George Stevens is known to be mortally wounded or dead already. Fairchild, Flanigan, Callis and Dudley—Dudley, we joked together last night—were all hit badly in arms or legs, probably each suffering amputations. It is hard to know for sure. Most of the hundreds of severely wounded are missing, agonizing in makeshift hospitals at the Seminary or in town, all now being held by the enemy, including the surgeons who stayed behind to care for them. The proud Iron Brigade has been decimated trying to hold those two ridges west of town. They inflicted huge losses on the Rebels today, but they had been forced to get out when the right flank caved in. Accounts of personal bravery are too numerous to tell, unbelievable almost, the color guards especially. Everyone has lost close friends, messmates, even relatives. It is a sad and solemn evening on Culp's Hill.

Thursday, July 2, 1863—Culp's Hill, Gettysburg

Dawes spends a restless night with his men, exhausted, hungry, woken constantly by startling nightmares and gunfire from the picket lines. Beams of sunlight are now angling down through the trees, and he thinks of Mary. *Maybe she is thinking now about me.* He pulls out the letter he had started to Mary thirty-six hours previously. To Dawes, it seems much longer. So much has happened. During those hours, so many brave and true young men have been lost. He adds this update with a slightly shaking hand:

July 2nd 8 A.M., dear Mary

God has preserved me <u>unharmed</u> through another desperate, bloody battle. Our regiment lost 150 killed and wounded. I led my men in one of the most glorious charges of the war. Major Stone comd'g. the 2nd Mississippi Reg't. <u>surrendered</u> his <u>sword and regiment to me</u>, 230 men. There are no communications now with the North but sometime I hope you will get this note.

Good bye, my dear Mary.

Rufe

Early in the morning, the troops on Culp's Hill watch as General Cutler's New York and Pennsylvania survivors trudge up the slope to join the Seventh Indiana. Units from General Slocum's Twelfth Corps already occupy the rest of Culp's Hill, anchoring the Union right flank, and all now seems secure. The men spend the day behind their breastworks, mindful of Rebel sharpshooters, thankful that Lee's Confederates have not attacked again with any force. The brigade position offers an excellent vantage point, except for the eastern third of the compass, that area being blocked by trees and the hill crest. Dawes watches Rebel troops moving to his right until they are lost to sight, and with his field glasses, he can see the lengthened Union line and left flank, ending probably 2 miles to the southwest. He spends hours laying on his back behind the headquarters boulder, gazing at the sky, remembering, contemplating, listening, dozing.

Marietta, Ohio

Dispatches arrive of a major battle happening at Gettysburg. Marietta College commencement ceremonies are this evening, but this war news diverts all attention. Mary Gates is at her father's former newspaper office, next to the telegraph operator, and an early message reads: "General Reynolds Killed."

What did Rufe write? "If there is a battle, look to see if Gen's Reynolds or Wadsworth figure in it. By them you can trace me." Mary is near panic. Immediately she thinks: *If the corps commander is killed, what of Rufus?*

Culp's Hill, Gettysburg

The relative calm lasts until 4:00 p.m. It starts toward the southwest. A thunderous storm of musketry and cannon fire erupts on the army's left flank, reverberating all the way to Culp's Hill and beyond. Rebel skirmishing nearby then picks up, and Rebel artillery from somewhere to the north crashes all at once. Their targets are Union guns posted on Cemetery Hill and on the saddle leading to Culp's Hill. The Union guns reply, and a furious artillery battle rages, multiple booms every second from cannon shots on both sides. The ground shakes, shells shriek through the air from both directions, incoming rounds impact all over Cemetery Hill, and ammunition limbers, sometimes taking direct hits, blowing mangled horses and men in all directions.

The shelling continues, but since it does not seem to signal an attack up Culp's Hill, and since the Confederate target is not his position, Dawes and those around him become distant spectators to the furious battle raging far to the southwest. Union troops are seen retreating in great numbers, and the Rebel yell can be heard increasing in volume even at this distance. If the Rebels break through, they could roll up the whole Union line. Finally, long blue lines of infantry are seen, at least twenty battle flags flying, charging into the smoke and chaos. The musketry noise intensifies, and it becomes apparent that the counterattack will succeed. The Rebel juggernaut will be stopped. It is a huge relief.

Around dusk, the Confederates attack the Union right flank, and that is Culp's Hill. "Get ready, boys! Keep your eyes peeled! The hill is steep, aim low, aim low. Wait for the command, steady now!" Dawes commands as he runs in a crouch behind his men, the company commanders echoing his words. Musketry crashes from Union rifles to the right, and they hear the Rebel yell. The men of the Sixth are ready and waiting, but no attack is being launched on their front.

In the darkness now they wait, all the while listening to the roar of rifle fire on the east side of the hill. "Colonel Dawes! Colonel Dawes!" comes a staff officer on foot through the trees.

"Here, here I am."

"Sir, take your regiment to the right and report to General Greene!"

"Where is he?" Dawes asks.

"Right over in the woods where they are attacking."

A quick thought flashes: *Oh, no! Not again! Not like yesterday!* But he does not say it. Instead, he stands and shouts, "Attention, battalion! Right face! Forward by file right, march!"

He leads his men up the dark hill, around the trees, stumbling over roots and rocks and limbs, heading for the muzzle blast reflections that light up the branches, running toward the rising noise of battle, looking for a general he does not know, not sure how or where to find him. He approaches a mounted officer who points them farther up the hill. The woods are crowded with wounded men heading to the rear. Pressing on, Dawes dimly sees several mounted figures just in the trees. "Where is General Greene?" he shouts over the din of the rifle fire.

The closest man shouts back, "Right here!"

Dawes has found Greene. The old man's face, what can be seen hidden behind a huge moustache and full gray beard, is sporadically illuminated by gun discharges.

Greene peers down at Dawes and asks, "Who are you?"

"Lieutenant Colonel Dawes, Sixth Wisconsin, reporting for orders!" is the shouted reply.

Greene tells him to form a line of battle, and Dawes gives the orders. Once that is done, Greene rides over to Dawes, points toward the gunfire, and commands, "Now, Colonel, I want you go forward into those breastworks as quick as you can and hold them!"

Dawes gives a quick salute with a "Yes, sir!" He quickly calls his commanders over. "The general wants us to go into his line of breastworks. Once we go over the hilltop, we will be right in the line of fire. Now here's what we're going to do: I am going to order, "Forward, *run*, march," and when I do, we all run forward as fast as we can. Tell the men to keep going till we're there—don't stop for anything. But have them keep quiet! No shouting or shooting! There's no sense in drawing fire."

With that, he gives the order, and off they go through the darkness, over the hilltop and through the trees. The only sounds they make are running feet through low brush, panting breaths, and rattling equipment. Many of the soldiers soon outpace Dawes as the ragged line quickly moves forward to the unknown. Then, suddenly, the first soldiers come up to the back side of the breastworks. They're occupied! These are Rebels! "Fire! Fire!" A rattling volley erupts from Wisconsin Springfields point-blank into the equally surprised Confederates. Shouts erupt along the line, and those Rebels who are not shot, shoot back at these dark figures with the tall hats. One loose volley is all they can do. Shocked by the suddenness of the encounter, they scramble over the breastworks and run downhill. Reloaded Wisconsin rifles continue to fire at the dark moving shapes retreating through the tress. "Cease firing!" Dawes yells several times. It is all over in less than a minute. A sudden, unexpected charge, a violent close-quarters gun fight in the darkness.[V]

Then, off to the right comes another line of soldiers. It's the Fourteenth Brooklyn, filling the now-empty breastworks over there. To Dawes, the whole situation is now obvious. *The Twelfth Corps men were hard-pressed, Greene sent for the nearest help, and General Wadsworth sent us and the Fourteenth Brooklyn. Again. Just like yesterday morning at the railroad cut. Greene probably did not know the breastworks were full of Confederates—at least, he didn't mention it!*

The Rebel fire has died down, and he can tell they are far below them now. But it is also clear that the Confederates hold former Union works farther right. *That's for someone else to take care of,* he thinks as he moves

---

[V] See Culp's Hill map end of chapter

down the line to check on casualties. There they are, two of his soldiers, already collected and lying dead side by side in the shallow trench. He recognizes the faces, knows the name of one, young John Durant from Bragg's old Company E. Kneeling over them, Major Hauser and the sergeant major look up at Dawes. "Both killed up close," Babcock says quietly. "You can see the powder burns. Nobody else is hurt too bad. We got a bunch of them too. One wounded fella says they're from the Virginia Tenth. Maybe so—he's not talking much."

Dawes keeps his men alert for a counterattack, but except for scattered distant shots, it is quiet in front. Then, behind them, a whole line of troops comes up through the night, all shouting and cursing and making a huge racket. They plop themselves next to and on top of the men of the Sixth, many of them shouting in German, and then begin to wildly fire their muskets. Dawes is incredulous. *What in God's name are they doing? It looks like most of them are drunk! They're laying down, shooting over the top without looking, mostly hitting tree branches. It's crazy!* He seeks out the commanding officer—it's an Illinois regiment from the Eleventh Corps—and tells him to stop shooting. Dawes is ignored. "Let them shoot off some steam," says their commander. They all keep firing, and Dawes does not see how his men can respond to any attack with these numbskulls among them. Finally, he sends Brooks off through the woods to locate General Wadsworth.

Soldiers of the Sixth display looks of anger and disgust, but as the wild shooting and shouting continues, Dawes thinks, *What can I do, really?* Finally, shadows of horsemen appear. It's General Wadsworth, General Cutler, and several staff officers, including John Kellogg, who appeals to the Illinois commander to order a cease fire. But the whiskey is enough to make the man obstinate and insulting to this staff officer, forgetting he is representing two generals. Dawes can see Kellogg arguing with the officer, and then, in a flash, John has had enough and loses his Irish temper. Kellogg draws his sword and smashes the flat of the blade on the commander's hat, knocking him down immediately. "Now, dammit! Stop the shooting!" he yells. General Cutler quickly comes up before things escalate further and orders another Illinois officer to take command. This man, suddenly sobered, obeys, gives the orders down the line, and the shooting gradually ceases. It is a bad scene to be sure, especially in the face of the enemy! Dawes is glad it's over. What idiots to give them all that commissary whiskey!

Friday, July 3, 1863

The Sixth Wisconsin defends the breastworks for a few more hours, no further action involving friend or foe forthcoming. Around midnight, Twelfth Corps units relieve them, coming back to the positions they had left in response to General Meade's order for left-flank reinforcements. As it turned out, they had not been needed. Longstreet's violent afternoon attack had been stopped by Second and Fifth Corps troops. But the absence of these soldiers from Culp's Hill had almost resulted in disaster for the Union right flank. Greene's fourteen-hundred-man brigade was left alone on the east slope. Confederate general Johnson's division, six thousand veterans originally led by Stonewall Jackson, had attacked with a fury. General Greene was a tough old West Pointer and civil engineer. His men had held, thanks to their tenacity, their strong defensive position, and the timely help from the Sixth Wisconsin and other hurried-up reinforcements.

The Sixth brings their two dead comrades back with them to their previous line on the north slope. Just before daylight, a shallow grave is dug behind the line, and the two Wisconsin heroes are buried by their comrades, their names carved into ammunition box covers stuck into the mounded rocks and dirt. There they lay, far from unsuspecting family members somewhere in Wisconsin, never to be seen by them again. *At least they are respectfully buried. Our fellow soldiers, close friends, killed on Wednesday morning, are still lying exposed on the bloody field in front of the railroad cut.*

Fighting rages again on the east side of Culp's Hill all morning, but the Confederates cannot dislodge Twelfth Corps troops from their strong position. A lull occurs on the hot, sultry day, until two cannon shots on the Rebel side signal the unleashing of a terrific two-hour cannonade, followed by a massive midafternoon Confederate assault on the Union center. The Sixth is not involved, except to share in the intense anxiety as to the outcome.

The grand attack, to be remembered in history as Pickett's Charge, is aimed directly at General Hancock's Second Corps, at a division positioned on Cemetery Ridge that is led by the former Iron Brigade commander, John Gibbon. Lee's massive, gallant assault withers under heavy rifle and artillery fire, but still they come. Fighting is furious, and a breakthrough is checked by reinforcements fed into the melee by Gibbon's best staff officer, the Sixth Wisconsin's Frank Haskell. The human wreckage at what becomes known as the high-water mark of the Confederacy sees both Hancock and Gibbon down with wounds, along with thousands of men on both sides. As the Confederate survivors limp back to their lines, it is obvious that Lee's army is clearly defeated—barely, but decisively.

Saturday, July 4, 1863

An exhausted Rufus Dawes takes a chance and lights a small candle behind his boulder in the first dark minutes of this new day. He adds a quick update in his letter to Mary:

> Saturday, July 4, 1863 12 Midnight

> I am entirely safe through the first three of these terrible days of this bloody struggle. The fighting has been the most desperate I ever saw. ... O Mary, it is sad to look now at our shattered band of devoted men. Only four field officers in the brigade have escaped and I am one of them. I have no opportunity to say more now or to write to anyone else. Tell mother I am safe. There is no chance to telegraph. God has been kind to me and I think he will yet spare me.

On this day, his birthday, as Rufus Dawes writes his message, General Lee orders the overnight withdrawal of his battered troops to a defensive line along Seminary Ridge, west of town. About five thousand Union prisoners are taken with him, but those who are severely wounded are left behind at various makeshift hospitals in and around the town, almost every sizeable building being utilized for the care of thousands suffering every kind of wound. Union surgeons are generally left to their work, including the three from the Sixth Wisconsin: Andrews, Hall, and Preston.

Word comes soon after the warm break of day that the Confederates have pulled back. Units are sent out as skirmishers, and orders come for the Sixth and other regiments to seek out wounded and bury the dead.

The wounded Sergeant Evans has managed to return to the regiment with the captured Second Mississippi battle flag. He had been sheltered in town by a caring family, the lady of the house hiding the banner from Confederate soldiers who searched her home. Dawes decides to walk the captured flag to General Meade's headquarters, intending to present the prize to the Union commander. Meade is gone; everyone is busy. Dawes keeps the flag and takes a return route that passes along the mangled ground held by Union troops of General Gibbon's division, who repulsed the Confederate's desperate, gallant assault the day before. He talks to officers about the fight, learning now that Gibbon and General Hancock were both wounded, but should recover. These officers quickly realize that this lieutenant colonel is with the Iron Brigade and treat him with deference and respect. Everyone knows about the first day's action and the decimation of the brigade. They also tell him of the heroics displayed by a Wisconsin officer on General Gibbon's staff, Lt. Frank Haskell, who did more than almost any man to bring in reinforcements under heavy fire, actions so critical to stopping the Rebel charge led by Pickett's Virginians.[6]

The carnage lies everywhere. Rebel dead and some wounded men are still scattered thickly on the field. As Dawes solemnly walks through the battlefield with the flag over his shoulder, a weak voice nearby cries out, "You have got our flag!" It is a wounded Rebel sergeant of the Second Mississippi, whose survivors had been part of Pickett's failed assault. He is a member of the color guard and had narrowly escaped capture by the Sixth Wisconsin at the railroad cut on Wednesday morning, only to be among the thousands shot down on Friday afternoon. Dawes kneels next to him, offers his canteen for a drink of water, and seeks assistance from nearby Union ambulance corps men, overwhelmed as they are already. Dawes wishes the soldier well before leaving, never learning the poor fellow's name. The man's face, however, joins an ever-expanding mental photo album of maimed young soldiers, a troubling catalog compartmentalized in a dark corner of his mind, its existence resisted, but always there.

Dawes finds a mount and rides into reoccupied Gettysburg. He finds that the Adams County Courthouse and the railroad station now shelter most of his wounded soldiers and surgeons. Andrews is sick himself but still working. Preston and Hall are exhausted, taut, bloodstained. Preston confesses to Dawes that the captured sword entrusted to him has been lost, reclaimed by a Confederate officer two days ago as the man scoured the aid station amidst the suffering, seizing walking-wounded as prisoners.

Later on that stormy, overcast, dismal day, Dawes manages to send a brief telegraph dispatch to his mother that "I am safe tonight." He also begins a letter to Mary:

In line of Battle before Gettysburg

July 4th, 6 P.M.

What a solemn birthday. My little band, now only two hundred men, have all been out burying the bloody corpses of friend and foe. No fighting to-day. Both armies need rest from the exhaustion of the desperate struggle.

Evening, July 4, 1863, Marietta, Ohio

Mary Gates feels compelled to write to Rufus at the same moment he is writing to her:

Your birthday, and I have been all the time anticipating so much pleasure in writing to you today, but it is only tonight that I felt I could write to you at all. … I shall not undertake to tell you how slowly and sorrowfully the last few days have dragged along. The first news we had of the battle was that the First Army Corps was engaged, and General Reynolds killed. About noon today we began to feel more hopeful, that you had gotten safely through again, but this afternoon we hear the 1st Corps is engaged again. When will they ever let you rest?

…I am very, very thankful for the assurance of your safety after the first day's battle, and now Oh! to know you are safe tonight. I shall watch oh so anxiously for tidings this week, praying that God in his mercy may spare you.[7]

At about this same moment, Julia Cutler expresses the thoughts and prayers of everyone:

Wakened by the Parkersburg Cannon firing National Salute. I feel too anxious about Rufus to think much of anything else. He is 25 years old today. May God have him in his holy keeping.

The horrific, historic battle of Gettysburg is over. On the night of July 4, Confederate general Lee's army retreats from Gettysburg after sustaining 30 percent casualties. The Confederate ambulance train is a 17-mile long rolling nightmare of misery. The most severe cases are left behind for Northern surgeons to care for, if they can. Many will succumb to their wounds. During the three-day battle, over seven thousand soldiers

*Now Gettysburg College. Photo taken on July 15, 1863, by Matthew Brady, view looking east. (LOC)

Pennsylvania College* Unfinished Railroad Sheads Residence and Peach Orchard Gettysburg

Lt. Col. Rufus Dawes led the Sixth Wisconsin in a hurried retreat toward town along the railroad bed shown above, as Ewell's victorious Confederates converged on Gettysburg from the left.

The Chambersburg Pike (right center) became the primary escape route for the decimated First Corps. The Seventh Wisconsin took heavy casualties covering the Union retreat here. Iron Brigade survivors made their way through the streets of Gettysburg to Cemetery Hill, at the tall tree on the horizon. They reorganized to defend Culp's Hill, the taller mound in the distance. The Sheads home in the center was a year old during the battle and still stands today.

from both sides are killed outright, and at least thirty-five thousand suffer wounds. Thousands more are headed to dreaded prison camps. Decomposing bodies of soldiers and several thousand horses, plus the scattered debris of damaged weapons and equipment, grotesquely deface several square miles of the landscape.

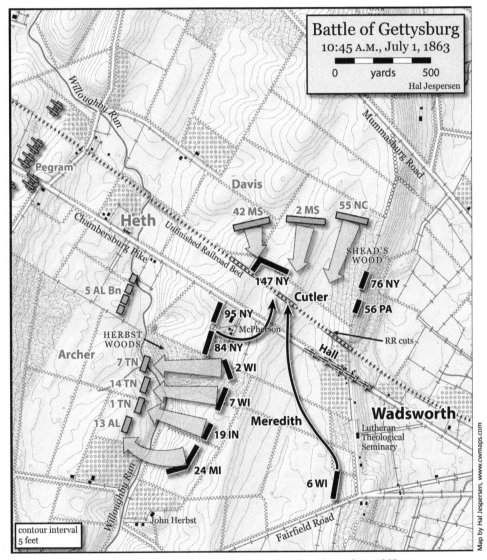

Sixth Wisconsin and Iron Brigade Action, Morning July 1, 1863

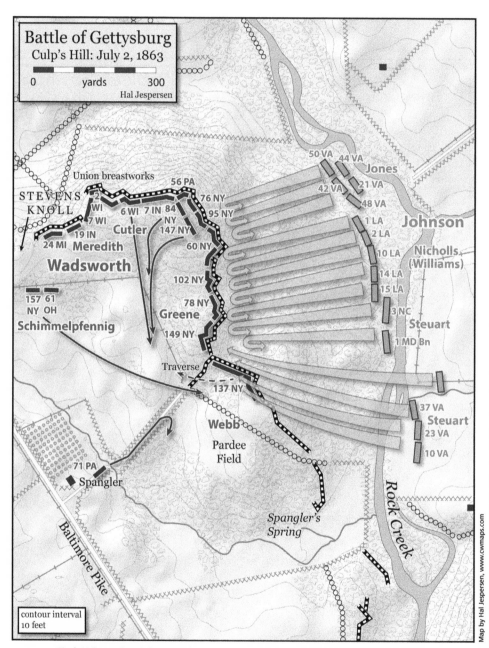

Battle of Gettysburg
Culp's Hill: July 2, 1863

0   yards   300
Hal Jespersen

Union breastworks
STEVENS
KNOLL
56 PA
76 NY
95 NY
2 WI
7 WI
6 WI 7 IN 84 NY
147 NY
19 IN
24 MI
60 NY
Cutler
Meredith
Wadsworth
102 NY
157 61
NY OH
78 NY
Schimmelpfennig
Greene
149 NY
Traverse
137 NY
Webb
Pardee
Field
71 PA
Spangler
Spangler's
Spring
Baltimore Pike
contour interval
10 feet

50 VA 44 VA
Jones
42 VA 21 VA
48 VA
1 LA
2 LA
Johnson
10 LA
Nicholls
(Williams)
14 LA
15 LA
3 NC
Steuart
1 MD Bn
37 VA
Steuart
23 VA
10 VA
Rock Creek

Map by Hal Jespersen, www.cwmaps.com

Sixth Wisconsin Night Attack to Restore Right Flank of Culp's Hill, July 2, 1863

Endnotes

1. General Doubleday's report. *O. R. Vol. XXVII, pt. 1*, p. 243.

2. Nolan, Alan T. *The Iron Brigade*, p. 141. Also, Dudley's Antietam report, *O. R. Vol. XIX, pt. 1*, p. 251.

3. Rufus Dawes Collection. WHS. Letters quoted herein are from this collection unless otherwise noted.

4. This chapter's accounts of the battle are taken from the *Dawes Journals, Book 3*, p. 215–253, which include a section titled "Incidents and Personal Recollections of the Charge." DAA.

5. Francis Waller will be awarded the Medal of Honor for capturing the flag. He is the Sixth's lone recipient of this award.

6. Lt. Franklin Haskell wrote a lengthy but stirring account titled *The Battle of Gettysburg*, which was published in 1908. It is well-known to historians and was republished by Forgotten Books in 2012.

7. *Dawes Journals, Book 3*, p. 218. DAA.

Chapter Ten

Distant Engagement

Tuesday, July 7, 1863, Marietta, Ohio

Northern citizens mourn the dreadful losses but celebrate the Gettysburg victory. They are further heartened by General Grant's capture of Vicksburg, Tennessee. Thirty thousand prisoners were taken there, and the Mississippi River is now open to Union navigation. As Lincoln eloquently proclaims it, "The Father of Waters runs un-vexed to the sea!"[1] Finally, after two years of continual frustrations, Northerners see meaningful accomplishments. But in Virginia, Lee's wounded army is still the powerful force keeping the Southern Confederacy alive:

Dear Rufe

I am beginning to feel I could write to you again, and how happy I am. Not quite sure you are safe yet but taking heart from the fact we have no bad news, and we have the list of killed and wounded in the 6th Wisconsin up to Thursday evening.[W] ... If only you are safe how we shall rejoice! Don't you suppose I was proud of you and the 6th Wisconsin last night when I read of your regiment, the 14th Brooklyn and the 95th New York, capturing a whole brigade! There has been greater rejoicing over your victory in Pennsylvania than I've ever known, and within the last half hour dispatches have come saying that Vicksburg is ours. "Great Babylon is fallen!" I do not know how, as a nation, we are going

---

[W] July 2.

to bear our successes, but I know as an individual, I can't bear much more of anything.

All my love, Mary[2]

President Lincoln urges an aggressive pursuit, hoping for elimination of the defeated Confederate force in one last decisive battle. Lee has been forced to dig in on the north side of the Potomac River, which is swollen and unfordable. It is a situation eerily similar to Lee's retreat after Antietam. Union General Meade and the tired survivors of the Army of the Potomac follow Lee cautiously through persistent rainstorms. At night on July 9, Rufe uses a pencil to write Mary:

> Almost half of our regiment has marched barefooted for a week … I am just about worn out. … [Y]ou can hardly know the strain such as those three days at Gettysburg. I have not slept in a dry blanket or had dry clothes on since crossing the Potomac.[x]

In Marietta on Friday, July 10, Kate and Sarah Dawes (Sarah sick in bed the last few days) finally receive the dispatch sent six days ago from Rufus that he is safe! Kate rushes up Fourth Street to share the news at the Gates home. Lucy describes that scene in a letter to Rufe: "Kate went immediately to tell Mary, but Charley had seen the dispatch and the news. She found Mary crying for joy!"[3]

Sunday, July 12, 1863, near Hagerstown, Maryland

Meade is under pressure from General-in-Chief Henry Halleck in Washington to attack Lee's wounded and seemingly trapped army. Meade knows he still faces a formidable opponent, depleted but defiant, with ample ammunition to riddle the Northern enemy. He fears that his own battered force might suffer a bloody Pickett's Charge in reverse. Union soldiers anticipating the assault, including Rufus Dawes, certainly do not feel "safe yet," as Mary hopes. In fact, they expect a bloodbath:

Line of Battle near Hagerstown July 12th

My dear Mary

---

[x] June 25.

We are again facing the rebel army, and another awful struggle seems certain. Under such circumstances it is <u>hard</u> for me to say anything to you. I have been waiting, and hoping for a long time for a day of rest that I could make up to you what I owe for your good, kind, cheering letters. I feel I am a long way behind. But I <u>can't</u> write today more than I am tonight alive and well, and have all your letters up to July 4th. This battle must end our campaign for the present, and then, if God is kind enough to spare me, I will come home to see you.

May God bless you dear Mary. Good Bye

Rufe

Meade postpones the attack. Overnight the river recedes, and Lee's soldiers escape to Virginia. Lincoln is dismayed, feels that an excellent opportunity has been squandered once again, and authorizes Halleck to send Meade dispatches that reflect the president's "great dissatisfaction." Meade is offended and requests to be relieved of command. Lincoln realizes his recently appointed commander has stopped the invaders and likely saved the Union and is being highly praised in the press for doing so. He accepts the short-term success despite fretting over the long-term impacts. Meade is kept in command, and grateful thanks are rendered.[4]

Mary Gates writes Rufus almost every day. He does the same at every opportunity, using "all sorts of contrivances to get my letters in the mail." He thanks her for her "good, kind, encouraging letters." The First Corps mail wagon cannot arrive too often or too soon.

The remnant of the Iron Brigade is constantly on the move, often without adequate shelter, suffering in heat and stormy weather, part of the cautious chase of the Confederate army heading back to Virginia after its defeat at Gettysburg. On days when the army does pause, Rufe serves as an appointee to a general court-martial, his "head filled with hearsay evidence." He is burdened with command duties and writes his letters late at night. These provide updates on his activities and convey concern for Marietta citizens in the path of a Confederate cavalry raid into Ohio being led by General John Hunt Morgan. Every letter expresses in loving prose his complete infatuation for his fiancée, Mary Beman Gates.

He writes Mary on July 18, after crossing the Potomac River at Berlin and now bivouacked in Loudon County, Virginia:

I am desperately struck after a young lady in Marietta. Hoping that after these few lines will find you with the same great blessing. Oh Mary, won't you send me another photograph. I want to see you in all your phases. ... The one I have was in the battle and on all the marches I assure you, and Mary, death would have come very splendidly for me to have taken one last look.[5]

On July 21, with "205 men present for duty now," Lt. Col. Dawes has his:

boys (they are all older than I) living at the expense of the aristocratic Rebels of Middleburg. I make them board my men whenever they are sent to guard. The boys are living high. I had a long talk with a lady of the place. ... [S]he had "lost all she had to live for." I cannot tell you how bitterly this woman felt and expressed herself toward us. ... General Cutler commands our division now, General Newton our corps. We are honored with the advance again. ...

When I was in that awful charge at Gettysburg, so horrible now it's over I can hardly think of it, you were writing me a letter, <u>thinking</u> of me if not praying for me.

Wednesday, July 27, 1863, Warrenton Junction, Virginia

The First Corps has reached this familiar beaten-down landscape, "a terrible place for water and wood," near the Orange & Alexandria Railroad supply depot.[6] Two days are spent reclothing and shoeing the ragged troops, many of whom have been marching barefoot. Dawes finds time to perform an obligation that military service has not permitted to date. On a hot evening, pestered by mosquitoes, he carefully and neatly writes to Mary's father:

Beman Gates Esq.

My dear Sir

Mary told me some time since that you know of our correspondence, and I am assured that you know of our mutual love, and her promise to be my wife. I have not failed to appreciate what was due from me to you as her father, but feeling that if you had seriously disapproved of my attentions to her I should have known, I thought best that we should be entirely satisfied of our own hearts before I spoke to you on the subject. We solemnly believe now that our happiness for life depends on our being united, and I most earnestly desire your own and Mrs. Gates approval of our engagement.

I know, Sir, how solicitous you are for Mary's happy, prosperous settlement in life, and appreciate that, excepting her love, I have not all to recommend me as your choice for her husband. But this much I feel it due to myself to say. I never would have asked her to be my wife if I had not felt entirely sure of my ability, within a reasonable limit, to make her comfortable and happy.

Of my character, habits and prospects, I don't know that it becomes me to say anything, but within a limited circle I have, as all men, my standing and record, which, whatever they may be, I shall recognize your right to question. It is certainly my wish to be acceptable to you, and I shall spare no effort to that end. I shall esteem it an <u>honor</u> to be admitted as a member of your family, and can assure you always of my loyalty to its interests, and my duty as a <u>son</u>.

In our love for each other we have found the highest blessing of our lives, and we have no doubt left of our <u>duty</u>. Are you willing to give our union your sanction and blessing?

With my regards to Mrs. Gates and my most earnest hopes for your united approval.

I am very respectfully,

Rufus R. Dawes

There, I've done it, he thinks. *I believe we will have the support of Mr. and Mrs. Gates, but even if not, I know our love is sealed and safe between us. I'll write Mary to let her know:*

I wrote a short letter to your father today, which I tried very hard to write just as it ought to be. Now tell me if I said anything the wrong way. I shall feel very badly if I have made a mistake.

The First Division is now on picket duty for the First Corps, while the other two divisions guard the Orange & Alexandria Railroad. Colonel Bragg arrives in camp for a few days after recovering in Washington, mentions that chances are good for him attaining a general's star, then leaves for Wisconsin on extended sick leave, still due to his foot injury. He is the lucky one, or the one with the most influence. Major Hauser has also tried for leave—his wife deathly ill, his children in a sorry state, his property going to ruin, and himself sick. Army headquarters has rejected his pleas, and he considers resignation. Dawes thus sees no prospect for getting away anytime soon and thinks of Mary day and night:

> What a dream I had last night. I had just one day leave in Marietta, but you were in Belpre. I started down post haste on the cars, but you had gone back to Marietta. I set off back and just as I got to the "Corner," William stuck his head in the tent with "Kennel, your boots is blacked and breakfast's ready." And now, my dear Mary, good night. Rufe

General Briggs of Massachusetts has been appointed division commander, superseding General Cutler, who goes back to his second brigade. There is disappointment for long-time friend Cutler, but Briggs is also an acquaintance. He was president of the court-martial Dawes just served on and says he got his star through the influences of a distant Dawes relative in his home state.

The Sixth's home state, Wisconsin, sends a new national flag to the regiment, with battle names inscribed in the field of stripes. Dawes returns the "old color" for safekeeping with a message: "It can no longer be unfurled, and five bullets have pierced the staff. Its tattered folds and splintered lance bear witness more eloquently than words what has been the conduct of the men who have rallied around it from Gainesville to Gettysburg."[7]

August 1863

The Virginia heat is oppressive. A 12-mile march southwest from Warrenton Junction to Beverly Ford near the Rappahannock River railroad bridge results in numerous sunstroke victims. The troops are ordered to cross on pontoons and form in line of battle straddling the railroad. This stirs up the Rebels, who attack a cavalry screen out in front, but nothing more significant occurs. The territory is familiar ground. Just one year ago, the regiment was seven hundred strong and about to be baptized under fire at Gainesville (Brawner Farm).

Dr. John Hall returns from Gettysburg duty on August 4, joining the regiment south of the river. Dawes is happy to see him. *A congenial and intelligent friend brightens an otherwise dull camp life, plus a surgeon is needed if we get in a fight.* Hall brings updated news about brigade officers shot at Gettysburg. In the Nineteenth Indiana, young Lt. Col. Dudley has suffered two amputations on his shattered leg and is being discharged. Lt. Col. Flanigan of the Twenty-Fourth Michigan also is an amputee, while Major Wight has lost an eye. Both are lost to the service. Colonel Morrow was also wounded but should be back soon. In the Second Wisconsin, Colonel Fairchild has lost an arm, and George Stevens suffered a few days from his gruesome belly wound before dying. Major Mansfield is recovered. Colonel Callis of the Seventh Wisconsin likely will not return to duty due to his wound. It is a long, sad litany.[8]

The division pulls back across the river on August 8, but General Briggs assigns Dawes to remain in place, commanding a three-regiment, six-hundred-man fortified outpost. They get relieved four days later, crossing to the north side, but then on the 15th, Briggs selects him to command the south-side post again.

Sunday, August 16, 1863, Marietta, Ohio

Mr. and Mrs. Gates are off together on a business/sightseeing trip east, so Mary is "Mistress of the House." The parents depart after sending a warm and welcoming letter to Rufus, graciously endorsing their daughter's engagement to him, and Mary cannot be happier. Eighteen-year-old Charley is busy catching up with college studies, having recently gotten a sample of army campaigning when he joined volunteers to confront Morgan's raiders attempting to cross the Ohio River at Buffington Island.[9] Good friend Mary Moore is staying in the house to help with Bettie and to provide some adult female companionship.

Saturday, August 22, 1863—Sixth Wisconsin Camp, North Bank, Rappahannock River

On this torridly hot day with sickness rampant in the regiment, Dawes is relieved from his temporary outpost command duty. General Briggs is relieved, too, assigned to organize draftees in Alexandria. The round-robin of division command, vacated by General Wadsworth in late July due to sickness, now sees General James C. Rice in charge. Rice is also a Massachusetts native, Yale educated, but a New York lawyer at the war's outbreak. He entered service immediately and has served in battles since First Bull Run. He earned his star soon after Gettysburg, where, as a colonel, he took command for his fallen brigadier, Strong Vincent, and led the storied defense of Little Round Top on the second day of the battle.

Rufe writes to Mary about the army situation and about her father's response:

> Tell me how you are satisfied with your father's letter. I think it was very generous indeed to me, and good to you for him to write the way he did. I can only hope to be worthy of the confidence he so kindly expresses, and so richly favors in his willingness to trust me with your happiness.

He is interrupted by the mail wagon and the arrival of Mary's letter of the 16th. He reads her concerns and pens an immediate response: "How long will 'the folks' be gone? Not that I am afraid to come if your mother is home, but would enjoy surprising you."

A few days later:

> My dear Mary. Aug. 27th. Your birthday! I know it will be a pleasant day for you there. ... My twenty-first was a great epoch in my life. How much did you think one year ago that today you would be the promised wife of Rufe Dawes? ... Rufe had a very warm place in his heart for Mary Gates then. I have been wracking my brains for some token to send you today, but more than my true love I can't think of a favorable thing here in the army.

* * * * *

"Welcome back, Colonel! I gladly relinquish command of the Sixth Regiment." It is August 28, and Dawes is addressing Colonel Edward Bragg, finally back from his Wisconsin leave, where, in addition to healing his foot, he tried for the Democratic Party nomination for governor—and failed.

"Well thanks, Rufe, I guess. I bet you *are* glad. And well done, I will add. I've heard very good reports, not that I ever doubted, and the camp here looks in great shape. And, of course, there's Gettysburg. Courageous action—no better reputation for the regiment. I read your report and was proud to read about it in the papers. But so many good men gone. Ticknor and, from my old company, Durant, King, Leeman ..." He pauses a few moments. "But we can't become too pensive, can we? And damn, it's a lot hotter here than in Fond du Lac! So what's this about your engagement? You must have a likeness. Let me see it!" Bragg studies the photograph quickly produced by his second-in-command and exclaims, "Ah-hah! I can see why you are so stuck on her! A very pretty young lady! Congratulations."

"Thank you, she's special," Dawes says. "I can't tell you how much I'm ... Well, let's just say it's been a struggle keeping my mind focused on the regiment. But since you approve, you won't mind endorsing my application for a leave of absence!"

Bragg laughs. "That didn't take you long! I just got here. But yes, write it up, and I will forward it with approval. I don't blame you a bit. You deserve it."

September 1863

The request goes forward to the new division commander, and General Rice promptly denies it. Dawes complains to Dr. Hall: "I can't believe this! I have never slacked in any duty. Bragg is back now in command, so for what reason did he deny it?"

He seeks out General Rice and requests reconsideration. They meet, Dawes reviews his past service, and Rice relents: "Resubmit the paperwork, and I will approve it."

Yes! The application is resubmitted through the Iron Brigade headquarters, approved and endorsed by the division and corps commanders, then forwarded to army headquarters. General George Meade returns it with this note: "The Commanding General declines to grant leaves of absence at the present time for private considerations."

Rufe writes:

Dear Mary. I pity you so much I can hardly contain myself, and feel sufficiently miserable myself. General Meade refuses to allow me to come home to see you. ... I would give cheerfully anything I have in the world to see you if only one day. ... Talk with your father and mother and ask yourself if you are willing to be married next winter.

The "private considerations" General Meade has in mind have much to do with a planned offensive against Robert E. Lee's army. The Confederate command had transferred General Pete Longstreet and two of his divisions (led by Generals Hood and McLaws) to Georgia by rail, reinforcing Confederate general Braxton Bragg as a prelude to an attack on Rosecrans's Union army near Chickamauga Creek, south of Chattanooga. (Longstreet's Third Division, Pickett's decimated shell, is left behind). Lee's depleted force now numbers about forty-five thousand. Meade wants to take advantage by pushing forward toward the Rapidan River in a turning movement. A large Union cavalry force defeats J. E. B. Stuart's cavalry at the battle of Culpepper Courthouse on September 13, pushing them south across the Rapidan River. Two young Union generals of "high swagger" figure prominently: Dawes's acquaintance Judson Kilpatrick (from the Frederick's Hall Raid, August '62) and George Custer.

Meade orders his troops south from Culpepper, and they march through the wedge of well-worn countryside between the Rappahannock and Rapidan Rivers. They march on, despite the Union high command deciding to reinforce Rosecrans using troops from Meade's Army of the Potomac. Meade bids goodbye to his Eleventh and Twelfth Corps, sent west on September 24. His army's infantry force is now reduced from seven corps to five, for a resulting strength of about seventy-six thousand troops.

Out west in Georgia, General Longstreet's Confederate troops arrive before the Union reinforcements, and in a brutal three-day fight at Chickamauga, help to rout half of Rosecrans's Army of the Cumberland. Units under General George Thomas hang on long enough to enable a withdrawal to Chattanooga. There are over forty Ohio regiments in the battle, and citizens of Marietta and the surrounding towns are in suspense as casualty lists become published. There is shock and mourning once again for those who have been shot down. Major Ephraim Dawes and his Fifty-Third Ohio are fortunately not engaged.

Daybreak, Saturday, October 10, 1863—North Side of Rapidan River at Morton's Ford

The First Corps is massed for a fight in the fields south of the little village of Stevensburg. The Confederates are on the other side of the river. Orders came last night: "Charge across the river and attack the enemy in his entrenchments." The Sixth Wisconsin, veterans of the assault at Fitzhugh's Crossing, is selected to lead the attack across the Rapidan. To the Wisconsin men, it seems that no good deed goes unpunished.

General Newton, First Corps commander since taking over on the second day at Gettysburg, orders various troop movements to deceive the enemy and has his artillery fire away—to no effect. Dawes and his men anxiously await all day for the order, but none is given. The sky darkens, and new orders arrive: "Make a hasty march back north toward Culpepper."

Confederate general Lee, his mind always active for an offensive opportunity, decides to turn the Union right flank via the old Cedar Mountain-Sulphur Springs-Warrenton Pike route used successfully against General Pope fourteen months previously. Meade orders his troops back north across the Rappahannock to parry the move. The Sixth Wisconsin crosses at a familiar spot, Kelly's Ford, 5 miles downstream of the Orange & Alexandria Railroad, then marches northeast for 30 miles night and day to reach the heights around Centreville on Wednesday the 14th. Those shoes issued in late July are new no longer.

General Solomon Meredith

General James C. Rice

Rufus writes Mary a letter on the 12th. He must use a pencil because "I forgot to put my ink in my haversack when we started":

Night before last I got your <u>dear</u> letter, and although I marched through the bitter, chilly night fog, I was perfectly happy. ... I can never fail to love and be grateful to your parents for their generous confidence in me, and consideration for our feelings in everything. You "know" Mary, I will come to you this fall if I can possibly, and you know how hard I have tried.

It is my conviction that God intended us for each other, and our lives would be miserable without each other. I believe I loved you the first time I ever saw, and I am not sure but you loved me. You do <u>now</u>, and would then, I firmly believe, if we had better understood each other. But dear Mary, how <u>could</u> I, crushed by the tyranny of my father, in honor, ask you to give your life and happiness to my hopeless future. But thank kind Providence, the dark clouds have been swept away, and the silver lining of your love that was always before me has brightened into a clear sunshine.

It is once again a strategic chess match. The back-and-forth troop movements will be labeled the Bristoe Campaign. Several serious casualty-producing clashes occur that the Sixth Wisconsin is fortunate to avoid ("The Second Corps seems to do the heavy work now", Rufus writes Mary), but no significant advantage is gained to either side. Lee and Meade will continue the deadly game in the cold and mud of October and into November.

It is a rough campaign of marching and exposure. But as Rufe writes Mary on October 21, after a frosty march to Thoroughfare Gap in the Bull Run mountain range, the new camp offers a respite:

My dear Mary

You can hardly know how comfortable and home-like it seems to me tonight to get into my wall tent. Since the 8th we have had nothing above us but the open canopy of heaven.

I climbed this morning to the top of the highest peak and enjoyed the scenery. I wished all the time I had you to help me enjoy the ramble.

What a dinner we had today! Roast turkey! Honey! Graham biscuit!! It is no small epoch. ... Col. Bragg devoted his entire attentions to an oven of flat stones and a turn spit for the turkey, (who, by the way, paid to us, good and true Union soldiers, the penalty of his life for gobbling at one of our soldiers with all the venom and derision of a miserable <u>rebel</u> that he was) and, to his infinite satisfaction and pride, "in one hour and a half brought in a roast turkey that would have done honor to the table of a Lord." He gave me also a lesson in carving. Gen. Meredith was not assigned to command of the division, and has gone away.

"Lack of confidence on the part of the troops" was the objection raised by Gen. Newton. Pretty severe on old Sol.[10]

The regiment soon moves 10 miles south to set up camp at Catlett's Station on the familiar Orange & Alexandria Railroad, where Lt. Col. Dawes is "detailed as President of the Division General Court Martial which will probably keep running now all winter." His astute service while serving on previous courts, once as judge advocate, has earned him the burdensome duty, but he feels inadequately prepared for the responsibility. A trip to headquarters prompts General Rice to inquire, "Where did you practice law, Colonel?"

Dawes simply responds, "I never was in the practice, sir, not even a student."

Taken aback, Rice asks, "Have you any profession?"

The answer: "No, sir."

The two have a long and mutually respectful conversation. Lt. Col. Rufus Dawes develops a high opinion of Rice, for the general is obviously a "Christian gentleman ... who displays courage and zeal in his profession."

The war department is worried. It has seen the departure of many veteran regiments as enlistment terms expire. The next exodus is slated to occur before or during next spring's 1864 campaign— all those men recruited under the three-year muster of 1861. That includes all the Iron Brigade units, except the Twenty-Fourth Michigan. A means to avert this huge, pending veteran manpower exit must be found.

Secretary Stanton devises an idea to coax veteran soldiers into reenlisting for another three years, or for the war's duration: Pay a $402 bounty (the "catch" to be paid in installments) and earn both the title Veteran Volunteer (with a special chevron to be worn on the sleeve) and, most influential, a thirty-day furlough. Units that reenlist three-fourths of their members will be able to take the furlough together—and, very important to the soldiers, the regiment will retain its identity and not face consolidation into another unit.

As usual, the rules get tweaked and some confusion reigns, but the soldiers begin to think about it. Mary Gates asks her fiancé about what it means for him and what he intends. In early November, Rufe responds:

I am sure Mary, I have no present intention of reenlisting. I have got "enough" of it and I want to be with you for the rest of my life after this present term is over. I need not tell you that our house will have more charms for me than this miserable service of which the only attraction is <u>duty</u> to Country, to humanity, and to myself as a man of such stirring times. Even in my humble capacity as Lt. Col.[,] I am getting a small place in the history of these grand steps in the progress of civilization, that <u>we</u> will always be proud of, Mary.

Two other items of significance occur in the Sixth around this time. First, Mosby's Rangers capture adjutant Brooks, who is apparently betrayed by a pretty young lady seeking assistance for a property guard. William brought Lt. Col. Dawes the news this way: "The Adjutant dun got captivated!" Brooks is now walking his way to Libby prison, with some "ranger" on his horse.

The second item is much more positive—in fact, downright wonderful! Rufus Dawes wins an approved leave of absence! General Newton toys a bit with Dawes in reviewing this his third request:

Newton: "You state no reason."

Dawes: "Sir, what's the use? Every reason seems to be rejected."

Newton: "Have you another reason, one that has not been rejected?"

Dawes, with a look of hopelessness: "Sir, I have. I want to see my girl very much."

Newton, with a smile: "Hmm, I see. Well, you have given a reason not forbidden by my orders. Therefore, it must be good and sufficient." And with a stroke of his pen, "Here, Colonel, endorsed for ten days."

Dawes can't believe it but is on his way home before there is any change of mind or serious military action that would interfere. He leaves on Tuesday, the 17th.

Friday, November 20, 1863—on the Train to Marietta, Ohio

A very tired Rufe Dawes is near his destination. His train is approaching the Constitution Station, and, as always, he looks toward the small platform to see if anyone he knows is there. The family travels to and from Marietta frequently, and … *Yes! There's Ma! And little Annie beside her.* He runs toward the door as the train slows to a stop. "Ma! It's me, Rufe!"

The sight of the son she has not seen for eight long months startles Sarah Dawes. She has worried and thought about him every day. *That horrible time in May when we thought him dead, and then Gettysburg, and ...* "Rufe, son, oh my word, what a gift! Let me look at you!" Then a long, tight embrace and the tears that well up. Passengers smile, and a few applaud. It is good to see a warm, loving reunion. There have been too many grieving parents and widows these days.

"My plan was to surprise you at home, like the last time. But this will do! And, Annie!" Dawes says as he looks at Uncle William and Aunt Lizzie's oldest daughter. "Ten years old now! How you've gotten taller!" Then to his mother, "Where's Kate?"

Sarah answers Rufe's question about his oldest sibling, who lives with the Cutlers at the Old Stone House. "She's not been feeling well and is at the house with Aunt Julia. We don't think it's serious. Rufe, Lucy will be so glad to see you! Today is her school's last day for the term, so she will have time to spend with you. That is, if Mary can share! How long do you have, son?"

"I have to be back on the 26th, so I'll need to leave Monday night. That allows almost four full days here. I can't tell you how good it feels to get away."[11]

The trio arrive in Harmar and walk to Sarah's home on Fourth Street. Sarah prepares a lunch as Rufus unpacks and washes up. He's anxious to walk, rather run, up to Mary—and Sarah understands. After wolfing down the food, Rufus is relieved to hear her say, "Go on now, Rufe, go see Mary. Lucy will be here soon, but we can see you later." With a kiss and a hug, he is out the door.

The Gates Home at Fourth and Putnam (the Corner)

They have both been longing for this moment for months. In that span of time, they have sealed a love for each other and become engaged through the mail. Mary answers the door, and they embrace, a long, loving embrace, unmindful of anything or anyone else, not caring if anyone sees. Rufe releases her, smiling broadly at her teary-eyed, rosy-cheeked face, and they lovingly kiss for the first time. She melts in his arms. He feels so good, so strong, though thinner than she recalls. She does not want to let him go.

Betsey Gates can't help but shed a tear herself while gazing at the two of them as they walk into the front parlor. They are both so happy, her daughter so much brighter than Betsey has ever seen her. *God bless them!* They chat for a short while, Rufe describing the trip home and thanking Mrs. Gates for the wonderful marriage approval letter, hoping to see Mr. Gates too. "We must have you for dinner," Betsey says, "and your mother and Lucy and Annie too." She will send the cook with a note to Sarah.

"That will be wonderful," Rufus says, and asks Mary to walk the neighborhood with him.

Arm in arm they stroll the familiar streets and through the campus, enjoying the pleasantly warm fall afternoon. "Is anyone looking?" he says, and as she begins to glance about, he picks her up in a twirl and kisses her on the lips before setting her down.

"Rufe Dawes! Don't you do that again! What will people think?" But her face cannot conceal the joy, and Rufe says with a wry smile of his own, "I am sorry, my dear, but this old soldier must attack when he senses an opportunity! You don't know how long I've wanted to hold and kiss you!"

"Well, don't you do it again," she says, "at least, not for a little while," and they laugh and walk together in perfect contentment, touching shoulders and holding arms.

Up the hill and into the college campus now, Rufe's thoughts turn back to old friends. "Looking at that bench reminds me of Newport. He told me once as we were sitting there that he was stuck on a girl whose parents had a lot of money. Maybe that had something to do with it! But he didn't get her, obviously, since you told me he got married last month to Eliza Edgerton. I'm glad for him, hope he's happy. He certainly seems to be doing well in the Quartermaster Corps."

"You told me about how he steered you away from me, Rufe," Mary says. "I thought perhaps that he didn't like me, that being the reason, but now we both think it was because of Theodore. Whatever the case, I can see that, with you, it's all past, that we *are* together *now*, and best to look ahead. That's one thing I love about you, just so you know."

"And I love you for loving me, despite all my shortcomings," Rufe responds. "I will tell you a secret now, though, as walking here on campus and speaking of Ted and Marshall reminds me. Lucy told me about the time Timothy Condit had you and Francy penned in a closet. When I read the story while in Wisconsin, I just had to laugh, but I was also quite jealous. The secret is that he was another who loved you while in college—besides me, I mean. Did he ever tell you so?"

Mary replies, "No, he never said anything like that. I ... I never knew that. He was ..."

Rufe finishes her sentence: "Timothy was a true friend. He lived and died nobly."[12]

They walk on and soon change the subject to happier thoughts. It feels so wonderful to be with each other at last.

Dinner at the Gates Home

The food is wonderful, and eating at a real table in a warm room with Mary and both families ... *I cannot be happier!* The whole Gates family is present, including Beman, and between mouthfuls and trying to stifle uncouth army camp habits, he answers questions about the service. Little Bettie is a charmer, passing him second helpings with big smiles. Charley is a bit in awe, but Mary has told him not to pry about details, especially Gettysburg. Rufe asks *him* about his brief field service against Morgan's Raiders, nodding with interest and treating Charley like a veteran. Mary takes notice and loves Rufe even more.

Some details do come out. Beman Gates dominates the questioning, and Rufe respectfully responds. The fall campaign has been difficult—camping in all sorts of weather, many nights without a tent. But he doubts much will come of it. The most promising results will come from the western theater, at Chattanooga. As court-martial president, he was forced to try an acquaintance, Lieutenant Colonel Jordan, for dereliction of duty while in command of a picket line that was captured, including about forty from the Seventh Wisconsin. Another case involves a captain who shot his finger off to avoid Gettysburg.

Rufe notes that his own beloved regiment and brigade have not been immune to troubles. In fact, his leave came at a good time. Irascible General Cutler and obstinate Colonel Bragg have been feuding again, spurred on, in Rufus's opinion, by both being a slave to the whiskey bottle. Then General Meredith came back to reclaim division command from Cutler, immediately igniting controversy and threats of legal proceedings between the two. It is claimed that Cutler was the man who convinced General Newton that Meredith had lost the confidence of the men, thus causing his dismissal. Meredith has political friends, so who knows how that will end. And "General Cutler always calls me over, wants to confide in me, and I certainly do not want any part of it. So I'm happy to be away for that reason also, and I hope it's resolved before I get back."[13]

But he tries to avoid military talk and instead basks in the friendly atmosphere while gazing at his fiancée, Mary.

Saturday–Monday, November 21–23, 1863

Rufe, Mary, Lucy, and Annie take the train down to Constitution and the Old Stone House to spend time with the Cutlers and to visit with Kate. It is a pleasant surprise for Aunt Julia and Uncle William, and they are gracious hosts. They have known Mary since she was a child, and through letters shared by Kate and Lucy, they know that their cherished nephew is wildly in love. Everyone is happy for both.

Rufe asks Uncle William to sit down with him and Mary to discuss financial matters. "Uncle Will, by my records, and tell me if my figuring is off, I have $1,420 in my account with you. That includes my pay through October. I have property worth about $200, mainly my horse, and no debts." Uncle William concurs, so Rufe continues, "Now, I'm sure that I can send Mary $100 per month, and we can live within our means. And if I am wounded and in a hospital, my funds with you would certainly cover her travel expenses to see me. What I would ask you to do for me is to see if I can purchase a life insurance policy. I think that would give me some peace of mind."

Uncle Will notices Mary's concerned expression. He also is thinking, *Rufe, for a soldier, in your unit especially, that will be a difficult purchase.* "Sure, Rufe, I'll make inquiries from companies I deal with, and I'll let you know." Addressing them both, he adds, "You have a very good start here, and I'll do all I can to advise you and assist."

The Indian summer weather remains favorable the next few days, and Rufus and Mary spend hours together on carriage rides through the countryside, talking, laughing, hiking the hills, and making plans. They spend two nights at the Old Stone House, Rufe showing Mary all the animals, his boyhood haunts, the farm fields, and quarries. Old neighbors the Bailey's stop by, and the young couple visit the nearby Burgess family for tea. They visit Gravel Bank Cemetery to pay respects at the graves of his Cutler grandparents and brother Henry Manasseh.

Standing over Hen's grave, Rufe confesses to Mary, "Being here reminds me of the misery of my youth with Father. He had the cruel and absurd theory that children should always be kept at some form of work and never waste time with idleness or play. That term, 'idleness,' was always such a demon to me. Hen and Eph and I always had each other, though, and Hen always stuck up for his little brothers. What a difference when we could visit here in Warren."

Rufe and Mary discuss marriage. Being with each other now has assured them both that ultimate happiness will be as husband and wife. "I can't be sure when I will be back this winter. The veteran question is still not certain. If we get three-fourths to reenlist, then the regiment should be sent to Wisconsin for thirty days, either Madison or Milwaukee. I would divert to Marietta if possible, and we could get married then. But field officers must accompany the unit, so we would then need to travel right away to Wisconsin. You should think that over and discuss it with your parents. I certainly want everyone to agree to it."

Mary responds, "It sounds wonderful to me. I'll marry you anywhere and anytime. But I'll talk with Mother and Father."

The two evenings after dinner are spent in games of whist and Mary playing piano. Kate is still not feeling well, and Mary stays with her as the family goes to church Sunday morning. Monday morning, they take the train back to Marietta, and Rufe prepares to go back to the army. He says his goodbyes to the Gates family, then Beman and Betsey shoo out Charley and Bettie so Rufe can be alone with Mary. The two tightly embrace. Rufe dabs her eyes and says, "Don't worry about me—and write me all you can. I love you with all my heart."

She tries to say the words as the tears well up. "I love you, too" is all she can manage before a parting kiss.

Then he is gone.

Sarah boards the train with her son as Lucy gives him a hug and a "You better write more often" sister scold, giving him no excuse as she hands him a package of paper and envelopes. Trembling lips betray her feelings. Sarah leaves him at Constitution Station with hugs and kisses. As she steps off, planning to stay again with Julia, the Cutlers' hired man, John, climbs up to give Rufus a gift box. Canned peaches, he says, courtesy of Aunt Julia, Aunt Lizzie, and the Burgesses.[14] "Give them my profound thanks," Rufe says. "That's a rare treat for a soldier."

It is a reflective train ride back to the army. *What a thrill and emotional uplift to be at home with the woman I love and the family who cares for me so much! If only I could stay. Duty and honor require otherwise, but sometime this winter I will make Mary my wife, and I will be her husband. After that, I must take my chances and trust that I will come back to Mary for good next July 16 when my term expires. But I have no illusions. So much can happen in eight months.*

He reaches a relay house outside Washington on Wednesday afternoon. Here, he writes Mary a hurried note in pencil while waiting in a noisy, smoke-filled room:

[T]hose four days were a thousand times happier than any in my life before and I ought to be more consoled. … [I]t won't be long

and we'll never part again when we can get through our term. I
had to stay all night in Parkersburg and lost six hours at Grafton,
the train being late, and here I am delayed again. I am afraid I
can't get a photograph in Washington. I am very sorry for I fear
you will be disappointed. ... Be cheerful and happy as you can
for my sake, won't you? Do tell me if that jump down the hill has
made you very lame.

He reaches the city in the evening, safely deposits the box of peaches
at the National Hotel and spends a pleasant night with old chum David
Chambers. Chambers congratulates Rufe on his engagement, claiming,
"Tip and I always said Mary Gates was the prettiest girl in Marietta."

The nation's first Day of Thanksgiving, recently established by
President Lincoln, is observed the next day, Thursday the 26th. How
Rufus wishes to be dining on turkey and celebrating with Mary at his
side, instead of boarding the last train heading south to Rappahannock
Station. He arrives in the evening to find the regiment's camp empty.
They and the rest of the army are off on another campaign. He hops
a ride on a Fifth Corps mail ambulance and bounces along on a "cold,
dreary, freezing" nighttime search for the Sixth Wisconsin. Finding his
unit's wagons at Germanna Ford on the Rapidan River, he grabs a couple
hours' sleep, exchanges his travel clothes for his "battle armor" of sword,
revolver, and field kit, borrows a horse, and starts in pursuit of the Sixth
at first light on a cold and wet Friday the 27th. He finds them marching
in column at midmorning and is immediately in harm's way.

General George Meade is pushing his army in one last 1863 campaign. He intends to strike swiftly at General Lee's exposed right flank
south of the Rapidan. The weather is awful, and the plan, which depends
on speed, goes awry, as so often happens with the Army of the Potomac.
Just after Rufe reports for duty, heavy firing erupts ahead. The enemy
are Rosser's Rebel cavalry making a bold dash into the Federal column.
They succeed in capturing about twenty wagons and mules, killing and
wounding several teamsters, and blowing up several ammunition wagons, successive explosions rocking the woods.

The Sixth is "ordered forward on a double-quick ... deployed as
skirmishers, pushed through a thicket, and crack, crack, whizz the bullets were flying around our heads." Dawes locks eyes with a horseman
in a blue overcoat. In an instant, the man raises his revolver and fires.
The bullet just misses, clipping Rufe's hat brim as it zips by his face. *The
soldier is a Reb!* John Kilmartin of Company G quickly reacts and shoots
the man dead, the man's gray uniform revealed under the blue coat.

Dawes writes, "We very soon drove the enemy away, killing four and wounding several." Sergeant Isaiah Kelly of Company B is the only casualty, but the wound will cost Kelly an arm.

Bragg looks at the bullet hole in Rufus's hat and laughs. "Dawes, I don't think the Rebs can kill you! You've got to be the luckiest man in the army! Certainly in this regiment!"

"Well, I hope you don't jinx me, sir!" Dawes replies. "What a way to return to duty! Maybe my reaction time is off. Now that I'm back, it's good to see that you and General Cutler seem to have patched up your differences."

Bragg's face changes with the comment. "The old man gave that ridiculous order to hold our boy's pay for the property damage some-body caused—you know, punish everyone for the sins of a few—and I was not going to stand for it. He finally came around, so it's over, I think. Maybe his anger about the division command's squabble with Old Sol Meredith stirred him up. But Meredith is gone for good, 'unable to physically perform due to injuries,' the reason given. So General Cutler is set as division commander. But if I get my star—and the state agent says I'm next in line—I'll look to get a command out west and try to take the Sixth along with me. What do you think of that?"

Taken aback, Dawes responds, "Do you think the army would allow it? Maybe the boys would like it, I don't know. But going west ... serving near my brother ... that part is appealing. Never thought about it." *And,* he thinks silently, *I can't imagine splitting up the Iron Brigade.*

They march forward on Friday, then on Saturday morning, as he writes Mary, "[W]e moved in line of battle and drove the enemy in fine style for 3 miles when we were suddenly shocked by Ewell's whole corps at Mine Run. The skirmishing was very hot, but excepting artillery fire we were not engaged. Sunday, Monday, Tuesday we grimly faced the enemy, hourly expecting to be sent against his works. During this time, it was soaking rain and bitter cold. ... [W]ithout shelter, we suffered much."

Union delays have once again provided Lee enough reaction time. While waiting for a summons to battle on Sunday night, Rufe writes to Mary:

This is a different experience from our pleasant ramble last Sunday. What a change in sensations in a few days.

Then, at night on Tuesday, December 1, "[W]e retreated in great haste across the river." General Meade decides not to attack Lee in his entrenchments, much to the relief of his troops, who foresee a slaughter. Cold, wet, and exhausted, Dawes and his men trudge back north, recross the Rapidan at Mitchell's Ford, then the Rappahannock at Kelly's Ford, and are back in winter camp by December 4. The Mine Run Campaign is history, but Lt. Col. Dawes notes to Mary that "great toil and great suffering was undergone by our army." Reported Union casualties for the eight-day campaign are 1,653, including 173 killed and 380 missing. Confederate losses are estimated at 700. At the end, excepting those unfortunates, the two armies are back where they started.[15]

Upon returning to the Kelly's Ford camp, Dawes finds three "excellent" letters from Mary and struggles to find information about brother Ephraim, for, as Rufe arrived in Washington on November 25th, a great battle near Chattanooga was being fought and won in stirring fashion by Union forces under General Ulysses Grant. Eph's Fifty-Third Ohio was there under Sherman, and old friends from Marietta in the Ninety-Second Ohio were attacking Missionary Ridge as part of the Fourteenth Corps. Rufe writes Mary:

Eph surely must be safe if he is not on the lists. It is a great relief. Poor Whittlesey, cut short in the beginning. ... God has surely watched over and protected Eph and me, and why not for some good end? I ought to be a good man.

Eph is safe, as his regiment supported an artillery battery and thankfully avoided severe fighting. Not so the Ninety-Second Ohio. They are part of the heroic uphill charge that routs General Braxton Bragg's Confederate troops, thus relieving the Chattanooga siege and opening the way to central Georgia. Their commander, Lt. Col. Douglas Putnam Jr. of Harmar—son of the Underground Railroad operator and grandson of Israel, the Revolutionary War general— is severely wounded. Captain Wm. Beale Whittlesey, the only son of Marietta's mayor, and Adjutant George B. Turner are both killed in action while leading the assault. Putnam, Whittlesey, and Turner are all recent Marietta College alums and good friends of both Rufus and Ephraim Dawes.[16]

Knowing well the dangers he faces as an infantry officer in an elite unit, and mindful of the mounting toll of friends already lost—"the most promising young men of Marietta College"—Rufe is impelled to write Mary about marriage:

The strongest reason, Mary, though it is hard to say it right out, why I feel it best to marry this winter, is the <u>fearful risk of the spring campaign</u>. It's almost appalling to think I am the only single man of the hundreds of this Reg't. who has gone through <u>all</u> the battles entirely unscathed. I can't bear the thought of going into it without having you as <u>my wife</u>. … Enough for tonight with my most affectionate kiss. Please tell Lucy why I have not written—I will use her envelope tomorrow. My love to your Mother. I believe she will accept it from a dutiful son in futurum esse.[Y] My respects to your Father and Charley and a kiss to Bettie for so kindly expressing her approval of our arrangements. I always liked Bettie. Can you think why? RRD

December 16, 1863, Marietta, Ohio

Mary sits in the kitchen and thinks of Rufe. *His short visit home has sealed my love, no more doubts. But then he immediately gets into a fight, and I am scared again for his safety. Such a relief now, him safe in his cozy little winter cabin with good Dr. Hall, encouraging me to travel with Father on his business trip to Brooklyn. But now, Mother is badly sick, and I'm staying home to care for her.*

And she is not the only one ill. Everyone is worried about the Cutler's little Annie. Such a sweetie, the same age as our Bettie. I came to know her better during our two-day stay at the Old Stone House. Annie has been very sick all month with severe throat ulcers and fever. It's diphtheria, Dr. Regnier says. I've visited, and she is very brave and tries to smile, but her condition … It just lingers.

And now Rufe writes about marrying this winter, which I want to do so passionately, but he can't say when, and then he comes right out and says he wants it because he's afraid of being shot next spring! He wants a wife before that, and what of me then … a widow! Why does he write that? I know he loves me, and I can't help but love him, but I don't know if I can withstand worrying for his safety every day until next July! But his letters make me laugh too! I miss him so much!

[Y] Latin for "going to be."

Thursday, December 31, 1863, Village of Culpepper Courthouse, VA

"Tell Colonel Bragg that the regiment can stay here in these houses for the time being. It's too damn cold to have the men outside, except for those poor, miserable men on picket duty. But make sure there is no property destruction. These local folks have all left, and we're just borrowing their homes for shelter, but I want no damage. You understand?" General Cutler is addressing Dawes as he visits the two-story home acting as regimental headquarters.

"Yes, sir, I'll make sure of it."

Cutler leaves, and Dawes sighs in relief. He looks back on an awful Christmas week. The corps ordered out of winter quarters on the 24th to advance 13 miles along the O&A RR to Culpepper. It was the coldest day of the winter. Two freezing days and nights were spent on picket, the men without shelter until allowed to take over abandoned homes. Now in shelter, he has been working tirelessly to reenlist his men as veterans, explaining the issue, answering questions, trying to get the three-fourths necessary for keeping regimental identity. He feels it his duty as a patriot to keep the army as strong as it can be, though still intending to leave next July himself. The key to the whole veteran question is the promise of a thirty-day leave as a unit. Most soldiers have not seen Wisconsin for two and a half years. Colonel Bragg has been of no help until recently, drinking too much, even getting into a whiskey-fueled brawl with a staff officer. Rufe sums it up to Mary on New Year's Eve:

> We have two hundred ninety enlisted men. Tonight, we have one hundred ninety-five sworn in. We need twenty-three more men. I never felt more proud of the little band of true men. ... I will most cheerfully go out with them in the next last campaign of the war next spring. After using the influence I have over them to induce them to again volunteer, I regard it a matter of sacred honor to see them through the worst ...

Two nights later, the quota is met! Two hundred seventeen men plus six recruits have signed up. It is remarkable. Reflecting on it, a soldier writes, "Re-enlisted after two and a half years of suffering and privation; weary marches and disastrous campaigns; after passing through seven of the hardest fights and battles of the war. Re-enlisted for three years more in defense of the Union and to maintain the integrity of this Nation. More years of hardships and weary marching before them; the sacrifice of life itself, if required. Where is recorded a more exalted example of patriotism and loyalty?"[17]

It is a proud day, too, for Rufus Dawes, for he has "worked hard at this," and if Generals Meade and Lee cooperate by keeping things quiet, there is every prospect now of sending the regiment to Milwaukee for thirty days—and himself to Marietta for a wedding![18]

Back in Ohio, a much more pleasant holiday has been spent. Mary and the Gates family enjoy a merry Christmas with Beman and Betsey, who is feeling better, leading the First Congregational Church choir in joyful songs. Major Ephraim Dawes surprises his family by appearing on leave, bringing small presents for everyone. Their Christmas is celebrated with the Cutlers at the Old Stone House, with dinner's main course featuring a plump cooked goose. The only disappointment is for Annie, still too sick to enjoy the family fun. In the last few days of the old year, a bitter, tumultuous year for the nation, Julia helps nurse railroad men injured in a nearby derailment, while William and Lizzie once again care for a seriously ill child. Julia Cutler records her year-end thoughts:

This day ends 1863, a year that by the mercy of God has to our family been crowned with many blessings—But to our Country one of bitter sorrow—in bereavements unnumbered—May it result in redemption to the slave.[19]

Endnotes

1. Foote, Shelby. The Civil War: A Narrative—Unvexed to the Sea, p. 320.

2. Dawes Journal, Book 3, p. 218. DAA.

3. JCJ.

4. Foote, Shelby. Unvexed to the Sea, pp. 273, 274.

5. Rufus Dawes Collection. WHS. Further letters quoted are from this source unless otherwise noted.

6. Refer to maps in chapter 5.

7. Several Sixth Wisconsin national (US) and regimental (solid blue with emblem) flags are preserved at the Wisconsin Veterans Museum, Madison, Wisconsin, and viewable on the WVM website.

8. Nolan, Allen T. The Iron Brigade, pp. 266, 267. Lt. Col. George Stevens is buried in the Wisconsin section, Gettysburg National Cemetery.

9. Marietta College in the War of Secession, p. 60. John Hunt Morgan's twenty-four hundred raiders crossed into Indiana from Kentucky on July 8, 1863. Pursued by Union forces, Morgan's cavalry entered Ohio and attempted to recross the Ohio River in Meigs County at Buffington Island. Most of his force was captured there, but Morgan and four hundred escaped, traveling northeast past Marietta, intending to cross the Ohio again. Scaring the populace, but cut off, outnumbered, and exhausted, Morgan surrendered his force after a firefight near Lisbon, Ohio, close to the Pennsylvania line on July 26.

10. "Severe" because the six-foot-seven Meredith, despite military competency limitations, had been seriously wounded at Brawner Farm and Gettysburg and has always treated Dawes kindly. His men thought him twice as brave under fire, especially on a horse, because he presented twice the target.

11. The chance meeting on the train is mentioned in Julia Cutler's journal.

12. The comments regarding Newport and Condit are from Dawes letters to Mary. WHS.

13. Dawes mentions unit "politics" and feuds in his 1874 Draft Journals, Book 2. DAA.

14. JCJ.

15. O. R. Vol. XXIX, part 1, p. 8 for General Meade's report; p. 19 for Mine Run sketch map; p. 686 for Union casualties.

16. O. R. Vol. XXXI, part 2, p. 512 for First, Third, and Fourteenth Corps/Brigade report; pp. 524–526 for Ninety-Second Ohio report. For in-depth information

on Whittlesey and Turner, see Marietta College in the War of Secession, pp. 35 and 43, respectively.

17. Cheek, Phillip and Pointon, Mair. History of the Sauk County riflemen, p.85. WHS.

18. Veteran issue and duty in Culpepper from *1874 Dawes Journal, Book 2*. DAA.

19. JCJ.

Chapter Eleven

Happiness, Hopes, and Fears

Tuesday, January 5, 1864—Sixth Wisconsin Headquarters

"Did you get the order?" Colonel Bragg asks Dawes, who is shivering while changing clothes after the 15-mile ride through the snow and mud to and from army headquarters.

"No, General Williams wouldn't give it to me. I tried as best I could to explain all we've gone through to sign everyone up, that the thirty-day leave home was the key condition. But the A.G. says General Meade is holding things up, afraid too many men are leaving at the same time." Then, raising his head and looking directly at his colonel, Dawes adds, "And Williams mentioned hearing about a scheme that would transfer us west, out of this army."

"What?!" Bragg responds. "How the hell does he know that?"

Dawes is cold and frustrated, so he just says it: "Oh, I don't know, Colonel, could it be it was part of your big argument with Colonel Kingsbury the other night?" He almost includes the word "drunken," but holds back.

Bragg is silent for a moment. He knows. Sighing, Bragg responds, "I've got to watch my whiskey, I know. I wish I could. Let me see what I can do."

Dawes throws off his wet boots as Bragg leaves, angry with his commander, and thinking, *You're going to destroy yourself—and us—if you don't control it. And not just you! Even our corps leadership—General Newton, Colonel Kingsbury, the whole staff—they're all drunk every chance they get!*

Thursday, January 7, 1864

Army Special Order No. 4 is finally issued. The 226 reenlisted veterans in the Sixth Wisconsin and their command staff are sent off to Wisconsin on this bitterly cold afternoon. The same order sends thirty-one other units totaling 6,100 soldiers home on thirty-day leave. General George Meade has no choice but to comply with the war department's veteran furlough directive, but he dispatches his concerns to Washington. General-in-Chief Henry Halleck responds via telegraph on January 12th, assuring Meade that all Veteran Volunteer units "will return to their proper commands."[1] Bragg's intention to transfer the regiment out west is dead on arrival.

The Wisconsin men suffer from severe cold on the unheated train as it travels to Alexandria. There is a two-day delay in Washington waiting for a train, but Colonel Bragg stays sober and even takes the whole regiment to a theater performance. The experience is the first taste of art and culture for many, but to a man, they would rather be on the way home.

On the 9th, Dawes sends his mother a telegraph: "Regiment here waiting for transportation to Wisconsin. Look for me next week." He knows this dispatch will be shared with Mary right away, certainly arriving before his letter. *So*, he thinks, *she will know I am coming, and then we can be married! I'll stay on the troop train through Baltimore and Harrisburg to Pittsburg. I'll leave the regiment there and take a train to Marietta. The happiest day of my life is almost here!*[2]

January 1–13, 1864—the Old Stone House

1864 begins with single-digit temperatures, snow on the ground, and ice in the river. Yet the year seems to be starting with a bright outlook. Annie Cutler appears to be improving, the doctor says so, and parents William and Lizzie feel relieved. Ephraim is still home on leave from his Ohio regiment. The ladies are quilting for a pending Dawes marriage— not for Rufus and Mary Gates, that date still being uncertain, but for Rufe's thirty-three-year-old sister, Kate. She is to be wed next month to an out-of-town widower, the Rev. Samuel A. McLean. William and Lizzie's youngest child, little Sarah Cutler, celebrates

Sarah (7) and Annie (10) Cutler

her eighth birthday on Sunday, the 10th, enjoying cake and presents, which she proudly shows to Annie, who is still bedridden. The next day, William kisses his family goodbye and is off again to Chillicothe on railroad business. Then, in midafternoon, as cousin Kate sits with her, ten-year-old Annie wakes with a weak smile, sits up, tells Kate that daytime sleeping makes her tired, sips some water, moans slightly, and falls back, motionless. Kate rushes to her and screams for help. The family frantically tries to revive her, all in vain. She is gone. There is shock, disbelief, and grief unimaginable.

The snow around the family plot at Gravel Bank Cemetery is shoveled away on Wednesday morning, January 13, and Annie is laid in a cold grave beside the five siblings who preceded her in death. Little Sarah weeps beside her grief-stricken parents. She is the sole surviving child.[3]

Thursday Morning, January 14, 1864

It happens again. As Sarah Dawes slowly steps on board the train at Constitution Station, returning home to Marietta after attending Annie's solemn graveside service yesterday, she is greeted by, "Ma, it's me, Rufe!" He grabs her small bag and pulls her into his arms for a warm hug.

"Rufus! Oh, Rufus!" she exclaims and breaks down into a rush of tears, the soul-wrenching sadness of the past two days, combined now with the joy of seeing her son, simply overwhelming.

Rufus, not understanding the depth of emotion being displayed, says, "Ma, it's fine, it hasn't been *that* long since I've been away. Didn't you get my telegraph?"

Sarah wipes her eyes as they sit down. "Yes, son, I did get it, and we're so happy, especially Mary, of course, but… " She then explains the sad situation in the Cutler household.

"Oh my God!" he says. "I can't imagine it. Annie looked so cute and lively the last time I … Uncle Will and Aunt Lizzie must be devastated. I'm so sorry!"

On the short ride to Harmar Station, Sarah brings Rufe up to date: Lucy is still with the Cutlers, Eph is gone to Cincinnati until Saturday. Rufe hires a waiting buggy to avoid having his mother walk home in left-over snow and puddles resulting from warmer temperatures. He enjoys a short respite and lunch at home, then makes a quick jog up Fourth Street to the Corner! Mary sees him coming. "Rufe, thank God!" she exclaims, and they embrace, kiss over and over, then embrace again. The passion builds, and it is all they can do to release themselves in slight embarrassment as Betsey walks in, wrapped in a shawl, still not fully recovered from illness but smiling at the young couple anyway. "Rufus, it's *so* good to see you. We've been talking about the big day since Sarah showed us your telegram. But your poor family. We are heartbroken about little Annie."

With that thought, the young couple's passion subsides, and the three sit in the parlor to discuss the wedding. "We need to buy some things on Friday for the ceremony and my trip," says Mary.

"Yes, that's fine," says Rufe, "but I must pay respects and condolences to Uncle Will and Aunt Lizzie."

"Of course," responds Betsey. "God bless you for that. We've talked to Reverend Wickes, who says Saturday is not possible and he won't marry anyone on a Sunday, so Monday is the earliest day."

Rufe responds, "Well, it will have to be very early on Monday, and we'll then have to leave right after the ceremony, so I can return on time to the regiment in Milwaukee." He looks apologetically to Mary. "I'm sorry. It's because of my orders. It can't be helped."

"Well then," says Betsey, "we will have a nice early ceremony right here in our parlor, before dawn if necessary, with candles, but you must eat something before you leave, because in this weather, you never know what delays might happen on the train."

Betsey leaves them to be alone with each other but cannot disguise a measure of sadness. The two of them are so much in love, but looming ahead is the awful war and the mortal danger Rufe will face in the next campaign. If not for their sake, for the love she has for her daughter and for Rufus Dawes, she would yield right now to her conflicting emotions and tell Mary to wait. But, then again, they are young and in love and want to be together despite the war and the uncertainty. If the worst happens, if Rufus is taken from Mary, at least they will have experienced a measure of happiness. Betsey prays every day that they are both allowed a long and happy life together. She knows that Sarah Dawes—and the whole family, for that matter—feels the same.

That night Mary prepares for bed with thoughts of the evening and of her life about to be changed forever. They had a wonderful dinner here with Rufus and his mother. Afterward, they sat in the parlor to chat, Charley and Father asking Rufe all about the army and grand strategy. Then the evening had ended with a good-night kiss from Rufe.

Mary's head is filled with wedding details. She smiles and thinks, *What details? It certainly will not be the wedding I have imagined since I was Bettie's age. No church ceremony, no choir, no fancy wedding gown, no large audience, no elaborate party afterward. Instead, it is a rush to have it done, before daylight in the middle of winter, our "honeymoon" to be spent on a long train ride to a strange western city even colder than here, spent with soldiers and their wives, who I do not know.*

She looks out her bedroom window toward Rufus, a half block away. It is pitch black, and all she can see in the bedroom's dim lamplight is her own thoughtful reflection in the glass. *So be it! I am so happy! I know he loves me, and I can't wait to become Mrs. Rufus Dawes. Please, Lord, continue your protection. Let me live a happy life with him.*

Monday, January 18, 1864, Marietta, Ohio—Wedding Day at the Gates Home

It has been a busy three days filled with a variety of emotions—excitement, anticipation, warmth, and happiness opposed at times by sadness, loss, grief, and apprehension. Rufus, Kate, and Lucy train down to the Old Stone House, spending the day with the Cutlers. Uncle William, Lizzie, and Aunt Julia are always glad to see Rufe and hear about his adventures, but this visit is understandably subdued as they are in deep mourning over Annie's passing. The Cutlers will not attend the wedding, they say apologetically. William must travel on business; Julia must stay with Lizzie. "Please give this silver sugar basin to Mary as a bridal gift," says Julia, "and bless you both."

Rufe feels terrible for their loss. Lucy and Kate travel home with him after supper, with Lucy trying to brighten the mood, pestering both her siblings about their pending weddings.

Mary and Betsey and Sarah use Friday to shop for decorations and food and treats for Monday. Major Ephraim Dawes arrives home on Saturday, happy to see his older brother, kidding him about the marriage, shocked and saddened over Annie. Sunday services are attended at the First Congregational Church on Front Street, and wedding details finalized with Rev. Wickes. Mary and Rufus pack their bags in readiness for their post-wedding trip to Milwaukee.

Early Monday morning finds the Gates home decorated and candles arrayed. Betsey wakes early, helping Adaline, the family cook, in preparing the breakfast and treats to be served. Charley brings in wood and lights the fireplaces to warm the rooms. Beman follows orders and tries to stay out of the way, a headache developing already. Even little Bettie is up and ready to go, excited by the whole event, helping her mother with last-minute preparations. Mary dresses by lamplight after a fitful sleep. The Bosworths arrive to assist, with Francy going up to be with Mary. Soon after, the Dawes family makes the short walk by lanternlight and arrives at the same time as Rev. Thomas Wickes. Rufus and Ephraim look fine in their uniforms; their boots blacked, hair neatly combed. Ephraim is enjoying a chat with Francy Bosworth, who now is back downstairs, while Rufus fidgets, looking serious, as if he were sitting in a court-martial proceeding.

Beman knocks on Mary's upstairs door. "Are you ready, dear?" he says.

She opens her door, smiles, and gives her father a kiss on the cheek. "I think so, yes, I'm ready. Let's go."

At the appointed time, Beman escorts his daughter down the stairs and into the parlor as Charley plays "Wedding March" on the piano. Mary has never been one to call attention to herself, and her face reflects her nervousness. Beman passes her arm to Rufus, kisses his daughter, pats Rufe on the shoulder, and stands next to Betsey. Rufus and Mary hold hands and gaze at each other before turning to the minister. The family quiets, smiling for the happiness of the moment but apprehensive of what the future might bring when Rufus returns to war.

Rev. Wickes reads from Corinthians, makes brief remarks, offers the vows for recital, pronounces the two husband and wife, and introduces Mr. and Mrs. Rufus R. Dawes! The newlyweds embrace with smiles as the family and few guests applaud in congratulations. It is half past 5:00 a.m. There are handshakes and hugs, then time only for breakfast and brief conversation before it is time to catch the train. Ephraim must also return to

The Parlor of the Former Gates Home Today[4]

his regiment, so he will accompany the newlyweds on Uncle William's Marietta & Cincinnati Railroad to the track's current end in Loveland, then by coach to the Cincinnati rail station. From there, Rufus and Mary will travel northwest to Milwaukee and the temporary headquarters of the Sixth Wisconsin.

Charley brings up the carriage, and there are good wishes all around. Little Bettie is tearful, not wanting to let go of her sister—even just a month apart will be too long. Beman and Betsey and Sarah have that melancholy feeling all parents experience when seeing a child leave the nest. They hope that Rufus—and Ephraim, too—can return for a short visit before they both return to harm's way. Then the three are gone. The families retreat inside to warm up and chat, expecting well-wishers to visit later, each reflecting on the new family just begun.

The trio reaches Cincinnati after an all-day trip through southern Ohio, enjoying a packed lunch on the way. Ephraim leaves them with hugs for both and, winking to his brother, laughingly says, "Enjoy yourselves, and don't miss your train in the morning!"

Mary reacts with a blush as she holds Rufe's hand, watching her cheerful brother-in-law walk away, heading for his train and General Sherman's army. The couple checks into a downtown hotel and dines together before going upstairs to their room. They are both tired from the long day, but thoughts of this night have been with them for so very long. There is shyness and tentative approach, but their love for each other soon dispels all hesitation, leading to lovemaking with warmth and passion they never imagined possible.

It is early morning, and Rufe's internal clock wakes him. He is accustomed to early rising—indeed, to no sleep on overnight marches, camping often under a leaky tent or with no cover at all, enduring heat, humidity, insects, rain, wind, cold, mud, and snow. Some veterans say they cannot get a good night's sleep anymore in a soft bed. Not Rufus. He accepts whatever state he is in and makes the best of it. And he thinks the current situation must be like heaven. Mary is warm and soft beside him. Their bed is quiet and clean and calm. No bugles, no horses, no hundreds of men coughing and cursing and laughing and smoking. He watches Mary's slow breathing, her hair on the pillow, and does not want this to end. But there is duty—there is another train to catch. He looks out the window to see a white blur of snow falling heavily. Rufe wakes her with a soft nudge and a kiss. "Mary, dear, time to wake up. We need some breakfast before we go."

Tuesday, January 19, 1864

It is late afternoon, and Lucy Dawes is at home, intent on writing the newlyweds a letter, a greeting from Marietta they can read soon after their arrival in Milwaukee. She shares her family's excellent writing skills and has fun drafting it, realizing this will be the first correspondence Rufe and Mary receive as a married couple.

A snowstorm from the west is swirling across Indiana and western Ohio as Lucy is writing. Rufe and Mary's train takes all day to travel 24 miles, reaching little Hamilton Ohio, north of Cincinnati, near the Indiana state line. They must switch train lines in the morning to continue the journey, and they struggle to bring their bags inside the station. "Rufe, I'm cold," Mary says. "We need to find a place to stay."

He leaves her near the station stove, then heads into the snow to reconnoiter. He finds an upstairs room for rent in a nearby house, meals included with the deal, the lady having pity on this handsome officer with a new bride. The next morning it is back on the train, heading northwest across endless Indiana farm fields covered in white, with stops at every little town. The snow has ended, and they cuddle together, conversing with traveling citizens and soldiers.

"Where are you heading, Colonel?" asks the friendly old conductor as the train pulls away from Winamac, Indiana.

Rufe responds, "Milwaukee, to join my regiment there, the Sixth Wisconsin, on veteran furlough. From Valparaiso we'll take the Pittsburgh and Fort Wayne line into Chicago."

"Hmm, not now, I'm afraid," say the conductor. "The locomotive engineer union is striking that line. Nothing is moving till that's settled. Did you say the Sixth Wisconsin? You are part of the Iron Brigade, aren't ya? I know, because my sister's son, my nephew, is in the Nineteenth Indiana. Adam Juday, Company G, from over in Elkhart County. Maybe you know him. He was wounded in the left side at Gettysburg.[5] Were you there? Of course you were! We all read about the battle. Terrible, they lost so many!"

Dawes squirms a bit in his seat. "Yes, sir, I was there. I don't believe I know your nephew, but I knew … know many of his officers. They are a fine unit." He glances away and quickly visualizes May, Bachmann, Dudley, Hart, and others.

The conductor notices the reaction. He reaches toward this young officer with an outstretched hand. "Your name, Colonel?"

The response: "Dawes, Rufus Dawes. And," he says, smiling, "my wife of two days, Mary."

The conductor warmly shakes both hands and says, "An honor, sir, madam, and congratulations! Rookstool's my name. It is a pleasure to meet you both. Milwaukee, you say? Let me see what I can do about getting you there. Don't you worry. I'll be back with you soon." He leaves on a mission.

"Rufe, what do you think? How will we get there?" asks Mary.

Right now, he has no idea, but says, "We'll find a way. Let's see what Conductor Rookstool comes up with and take it from there."

Thursday, January 21, 1864, Northwestern Indiana

"Rufe, you certainly know how to arrange an exciting honeymoon! This is quite an adventure!" Mary clings closer to his arm, both bundled under a blanket, her cheeks rosy and smiling as her breath fogs the air. The sleigh they ride in slides down a small hill in the road, and they laugh at both the sensation and the whole situation.

"You'll find I'm full of surprises, Mary!" he claims, and they laugh again in the enjoyment of being together, sleigh riding across Porter County, Indiana, in the crisp air, deep snow covering the ground and blanketing the trees.

Rookstool *did* come back to them yesterday: "You'll have no trouble getting a room in Valpo," he said, "and I know a fella with a sleigh. He'll take you up to Porter in the morning, and then give this note to the station master there on the Michigan Central. I'll try him on the telegraph too. Now, that's a freight line mostly, so I don't know about the cars, but this note should get you on board, and it does go to Chicago. Good luck, best wishes, and God bless you both." Rufe and Mary thanked him warmly.

"Why, sure! We've got a spot for you two!" The smiling station master in Porter leads Rufe and Mary around the building and points to the Michigan Central freight train two tracks away. "Right there!" and he points to the last car.

"It's a caboose!" Mary exclaims. "Rufe, isn't it ... cute?"

"Well, if you like it, I like it," he laughs.

The freight train engineer walks toward them, and the station master makes introductions. "An honor to make your acquaintance," the engineer says. "The caboose is warm and fairly clean, there's coffee on the stove, and the crew will take good care of you. I've told them who you are and to leave you alone."

Rufe clasps the hands of both men in thanks and tries to offer payment, which is politely declined. "That's not necessary, Colonel," says the engineer with emotion. He is a Detroit man, and he knows of the carnage the Iron Brigade's Twenty-Fourth Michigan suffered last July at Gettysburg. Eighty percent casualties, and this lieutenant colonel was fighting there too. "It's I who am thanking you! Please, just relax, warm up, and enjoy yourselves now, and we'll get you to Chicago safe and sound."

A station boy helps the couple with their bags, and they step in, explore a bit, settle down, hot coffee in hand, and soon are off to Chicago. They travel across the white landscape, view icy Lake Michigan, talk and cling together, all leading to lovemaking in the caboose bunk under its woolen blanket. They are two young and happy honeymooners absorbed in each other, thoughts of war set aside.

Friday, January 22, 1864, Milwaukee, Wisconsin, and the Old Stone House

Rufus and Mary splurge in Chicago, with dinner and room at the Tremont House at Lake and Dearborn, notable as the Republican Party headquarters for the 1860 convention. They take the Chicago and Milwaukee Railroad through Waukegan and Kenosha to Milwaukee, arriving this evening. The regimental headquarters is at the Newhall House Hotel at Michigan and Broadway, and here Rufe reports in, salutes the officer of the day, and books a room. It has been a long and tiring but adventuresome honeymoon trip. Something to talk and laugh about in later years.[6]

DR. JOHN C. HALL.

On this same day, Kate Dawes receives a letter from Milwaukee—not from Rufus but from regimental surgeon and Rufe's friend Dr. John Hall. A bit surprised, even apprehensive, she quickly opens it. It's about the stirring reception the Sixth Wisconsin received in Milwaukee on the 15th. Hall thought she would like to know about it, and he includes a newspaper clip.

The soldiers had marched into the reception hall, rifle butts hitting the floor on command with a loud "thug." Welcoming speeches were made by a previous governor and by one-armed Lucius Fairchild, former colonel of the Second Wisconsin, now secretary of state. "A shame Rufus missed it," Hall writes, but he understands that "bright eyes" were waiting in Marietta. One of the speakers, however, credited Colonel Bragg as commanding in all the battles, including Gettysburg, a fight Bragg had missed. The captured Mississippi battle flag was unfurled during that account, making the moment even more dramatic. Hall felt that the speakers had "no right to falsify history," and he explained what he did to correct the record, because "it was in my power to do it." Kate reads his message:

> I felt indignant at this gross injustice to Colonel Dawes, and I was amazed that Colonel Bragg did not promptly disclaim this honor and place the credit where it properly belongs. Col. B. is a brave and efficient officer, but he has no right to wear the laurels that belong to another. ... I feel a sort of pain and disappointment when I find a brave man utterly selfish. I think perhaps you had better say nothing to your brother about this, as it might

give him unnecessary pain. ... I went to the Sentinel office in the evening and corrected their report of the speeches. ... [Y]ou will see that the proper credit is given him.

With great respect, I am John C. Hall[7]

Sunday, January 24, 1864, At the Old Stone House and in Milwaukee

Julia Cutler records her thoughts on this, her fiftieth birthday:

> This is my birthday, a sorrowful one to me for my heart mourns for dear little Annie whose young life gave so much fairer promise than mine, she so loved and cared for, with the elements of a noble character, certain of Christian culture, and a healthy mental development, with a prospect of wealth—how much good she might have done—how much happiness conferred—but she is taken, and I am left. But God is wise to determine our destinies and who shall call Him to account?
>
> Another cloud just now is Kate's contemplated removal. I hope and believe her happiness will be promoted & therefore acquiesce, but the loss of her society will be a sore one to me.

On this day also, Rufus and Mary end a weekend in Milwaukee, meeting officers who live nearby and wives of those who have them. The next day, Monday, an orderly brings up Lucy's letter of January 19. "Rufe, it's from Lucy, and she addressed it to me! She wrote it the next day after our wedding. How nice!" Mary begins to read it, laughs, and says, "Here, Rufe, I should read this to you; it's for both of us."

Rufe, who is perusing a newspaper, comes to Mary and, with his arm on her shoulder, listens as she reads Lucy's message:

> Mrs. Dawes, Dear Sister
>
> I am astonished to find myself in such a state of complete resignation under the "new designation." I hope you are equally calm and composy. I have spent most of the day with your mother, found her in a very comfortable frame of mind considering yesterday's raid and the capture of her daughter by a black Colonel. Bettie is much better. Your father escaped his headache,

he and Charley took their dinner down to the Point.[z] We dined on oysters, coffee, & wedding cake in the sitting room, discussing the fugitives & trying to see the silver lining of this cloud.

Well Mary, how do you like your new name? Sister, you and Rufe are <u>one</u> now so you will excuse my talking to both in one breath. I hope the roses have come back to your cheeks, for you looked as tho you were led to the "halter" rather <u>against</u> your will. I felt tempted to send for the Provost Marshal & have the Col. arrested, but he looked so terribly in earnest I did not dare interfere.

(This page is for the <u>better-half</u>)

It has been snowing all day and we fear you will be detained on the way. But Rufe is an old "soger" & ought to know how to take care of you. Dear Mary, I don't know of a girl who has a finer prospect for happiness than you. Not that you will find Rufe perfect, he has his faults (such as neglecting to answer letters!) but he has fewer than most young men—and of the positive good traits in his character is his love of <u>home</u>, and you will make him a happy home I know, and God will bless you for it—may it be a foreshadowing of a home in the "Better Land." We shall soon have more friends gathered there than here, and it is worth all the sorrows of this life to have an <u>assurance</u> of a home in Heaven. Thank God that his affections were fixed upon one who is activated by Christian principles.

I am aware that I am not writing a congratulatory letter after the most approved style, but it is not necessary for me to tell you how much I love you both and rejoice in your happiness, as you are fully aware of that.

I am afraid it will be harder to come home than it was to go away. I have some thoughts of having Rufe arrested and sent to jail.

I presume you found Eph very agreeable company. Did he introduce those officers? ... I forgot to kiss Rufe or say good bye—please perform that duty for your aff. sister. Luce

---

[z] Refers to the "Picketed Point" on the right bank of the Ohio River at the southerly end of Front Street— in pioneer days the site of a fortification for protection from Native Americans. A historical marker is located there today.

Mary sighs and gives Rufe the kiss with a teary-eyed smile. "Isn't that just a perfect letter?" she says. "And to think that, at first, Lucy seemed so upset about our engagement. Now she's made me feel so much a part of your family! I'm crying, I know it, but ... I'm just so happy she calls me 'sister.' It means so much!"

Rufe embraces her and responds, "You're Mrs. Dawes now, and I'm the happiest man in the world knowing that you are."

"Rufe, let's write a response to Lucy. She'll be so glad to hear from us."

"Not right now, Mrs. Dawes," he responds and pulls her close. Their time together is drawing ever closer to an end, and he dreads it, thinking, *Lucy can wait. She will understand. Besides, she says I don't answer letters anyway!* "I don't want to waste a moment that takes me away from you," he says and kisses Mary passionately. They are soon lost together in lovemaking.

Mary finally succeeds in convincing Rufus to begin a letter to Lucy the next day, Tuesday the 26th. They are doing things together constantly, and the four-page letter takes two days to complete:

Dear Luce

Mary will have me write something home this afternoon though I protest hourly. ... I shan't undertake to give you any account of our trip and experiences. ... I am not yet sufficiently restored to my equilibrium as a common mortal to undertake a letter. ...

Wm. J. Dawes, our Fox Lake cousin, is here on Gen. C. M.,[8] and has treated us very well indeed. I will send your land papers to Pr. Du Chien this week by a man of our Reg't. whom I can trust. We have neither seen or heard anything of Father. We are both as happy as we can be. Rufe

Mary then takes over:

Really, my dear Sister Lucy, this is the best I can do in the way of getting Rufe to write. ... We left Newhall House yesterday morning and got a very pleasant room at a private boarding house. ... I wish I could write as good a letter as we had from you yesterday. ... Friday afternoon Gen. Cutler & Capt. Dawes called, and in the eve. we went to hear Grace Greenwood's lecture, "Lights of the War Cloud."[9]

Saturday morn Rufe took me down to their Armory where I saw the muskets, knapsacks, etc. of the poor soldiers of the 6th Wis. And I saw Rufe's blankets, desk and cooking utensils. Well, I wouldn't have missed my visit there for anything, but—I couldn't enjoy it, and to think Rufe isn't through yet, it is too bad. I am hoping that Providence will intervene in some way, and save Rufe from any more battles, and spare him to us.

Mrs. General Smith is certainly very kind to me. ... She spent all Monday morning helping me select a dress, then going with me to the dress makers. ... This afternoon Rufe and I have been out riding ... most delightful drives around Milwaukee ... as beautiful a city as I ever saw. ... I like Mrs. General Cutler, and think her a kind and unpretending woman. ...

I was going to write Bettie a letter and enclose in this, but have not time. Please tell the folks that you have heard from us, and tell them I will write in a day or so. ... Please save the account of the reception for us, we are going to have a scrapbook. With much love, Mary.

Tuesday, February 16, 1864, Milwaukee, Wisconsin, and the Old Stone House

Rufus Dawes shouts to his mount, "Come on, Kat, let's have some fun!" He spurs his trusty mare at a gallop along Erie Street, nearing the end of an afternoon ride while Mary naps at the boarding house. The animal is fully healed from the Gettysburg bullet wound and enjoys the chance to run. But the Minié ball is still lodged under the skin behind her left shoulder blade, tender to the touch, and as Dawes braces his knees to take the corner at Broadway, he irritates the sore spot. Katerina reacts in pain, interrupting her stride, and loses her footing on an icy patch. Horse and rider go down onto the street and end up in a snow bank. Katerina struggles off Dawes, who is pinned underneath, and regains all four legs. Lt. Col. Dawes stays down, wet, muddy, and grimacing in pain, holding his left boot. "Ah, my ankle!" he groans and knows immediately he cannot stand.[10]

The Old Stone House celebrates a wedding ceremony and reception at 6:00 p.m. this day, as Kate Dawes weds Rev. McLean. Aunt Julia describes the event in her daily journal, noting the names of twenty family and friends in attendance and the food served, including oysters and six different cake choices. She also notes:

> Kate wore a brown silk very handsomely trimmed, a real lace collar with no ornament on her head but her own natural curls. ... Everything passed off very pleasantly. Kate looked better than I ever saw her. The supper was served early, the guests sitting around the table which was beautifully arranged by Lucy. ... [T]he glass & silver, of which there was much, looked well by lamp light, and the ornamentation of the cake with grapes & grape leaves made with frosting was particularly complimented. William gave Kate a $500 1ˢᵗ Mortgage Railroad Bond, for a wedding present.

Tuesday, February 23, 1864, Marietta, Ohio

"Be careful, dear, it's slippery here," Mary says to Rufus as he carefully steps down from the train, using crutches for support. It has been a week since the accident, and his ankle is still badly sprained.

Despite that, he is smiling broadly at his bride. "I know, I know, you keep reminding me. I wonder, though, if I fell again and made it worse, I might get to stay home even longer!"

"Well, I wouldn't mind that, as you know," Mary responds, "but I'm sure my Lt. Col. Dawes would never stoop to that sort of sly scheme." She turns, smiles even more brightly, and waves a greeting. "Hello, Charley, over here."

Charley Gates jogs toward his sister, and Mary greets him with, "Gosh, it's great to see you! And we can use the help, as you can see!"

Charley gives her a hug, then steps back to take a closer look. "Well, sister, you don't look too much older and maybe only a little larger, now that you're a married lady and all!"

Mary playfully swipes at his laughing face and responds, "Why, you stinker! You're lucky my husband is currently disabled, or he would defend my honor!"

Charley turns to address Rufus and shake hands. "We were all sorry to hear about the accident, sir—I mean, Rufe. I know you told me to call you 'Rufe,' but me being in the college militia and national guard soon, and you being a colonel ... It just seems a bit ... unprofessional."

Dawes laughs and says, "Well, Charley, don't worry about it. We're simply brothers now. If you ever get Federalized and we are both in uniform, then we'll observe the military courtesy. But right now, thanks for coming to help out this old cripple!"

Charley smiles and says, "I'm happy to do it. And I have to say, you both seem to be in great spirits. Married life must agree with you."

Rufe smiles and slowly strides over to talk to a man he recognizes, as Mary responds to Charley, "Rufe's accident was awful. He was lucky not to have been seriously hurt. But since he wasn't, we view it as all good fortune! He got a surgeon's approval for a thirty-day disability leave. His regiment is on their way back to Virginia, but Rufe will be away from the army and with me instead for another month! I wish it was forever, but it's better than we expected."

Charley notices the concern on Mary's face. They all realize that Rufe will face more fighting this spring.

Monday, March 7, 1864—the Burgess Home, near the Old Stone House

"Rufus, my boy, you've got many stories to tell. I could listen to you all night," says eighty-year-old Rev. Burgess. He and his wife have been close neighbors and friends to the Cutlers for years, and of course, Lizzie (Voris) Cutler is Mrs. Burgess's daughter.

Rev. Burgess is corrected by his wife: "Now, dear, Rufus is not a *boy* any longer. Far from it! He's a veteran officer, a married man now." Mrs. B. smiles at Mary. "We are so proud of you both—and of Ephraim too."

"Well, thank you, and thanks very much for this wonderful turkey dinner! It was delicious!" says Rufus.

Mary adds, "Yes, it was just perfect. I'll have to learn your recipe. Rufus may discover that my cooking skills are not yet fully developed."

Lucy Dawes chimes in with, "Oh, don't worry, Mary. If Rufe has gotten this far on hardtack and salt pork, he can eat anything!"

William and Lizzie Cutler complete the table, and everyone thinks it's good to see them able to socialize while still deeply feeling the loss of daughter Annie, gone almost two months now. William asks Rufus, "Rufe, I've heard from friends in Washington that the president is bringing General Grant to replace Halleck as general-in-chief. I've also heard Grant intends to have his headquarters in the field with the Army of the Potomac. You may have a new commander when you return."

Rufus can sense that Mary would rather keep the conversation away from war matters, but he must reply. "Yes, sir," he says. "I've heard that, too, but we are pretty used to having new commanders every year! I just wonder what that means for General Meade. He will be in an awkward spot. Say, how are the plans coming for the railway bridge at Parkersburg?"

Rufe successfully changes the subject, as William launches into a reply about his railroad company affairs. Mary silently thanks her husband by squeezing his hand, thinking, *Bless you, dear! We don't need to dwell on the war; it will come to us soon enough.*

Later, after dessert, Lizzie smiles at Mary and says, "It was so nice of you to bring Bettie along on your stay with us. She is such a sweetie, and our little Sarah needs someone to play with, now more than ever." Her last words become emotional, and Mary tries to soothe the moment. "Well, Bettie is pretty precocious, so I hope she is behaving for Aunt Julia. But the girls seem to be getting along well. Thanks so much for allowing Rufe and I to stay a few days with you. We really love it here, and Rufe has so many fond memories."

The pleasant evening with the Burgess family comes to a close, and the five head back to the Old Stone House, where Aunt Julia is entertaining, or is being entertained, by the girls, Sarah Cutler and Bettie Gates. On the short carriage ride, Mary thanks William and Lizzie again for their hospitality. "We'll take the train home in the morning," she says. "Mother is giving a party for us tomorrow night. We are both looking forward to it so much! There will be a chance for Rufe to see a lot of his friends. It will be just like college days again, won't it, dear?" She looks at Rufus.

Rufe smiles and says, "It will be fun. I'm looking forward to it—especially since I get to show off my bride to everyone!" But he remains quiet for the remainder of the ride, thoughts crossing his mind of those close college friends who will be forever absent—Greenwood, Condit, Whittlesey, Turner, others. *No, dear,* he thinks, *it will not be "just like college days." But yes, it will be fun, and I will enjoy it, especially having you beside me.*[11]

Friday Morning, March 18, 1864, Wheeling, West Virginia

The horse-drawn omnibus is approaching Wheeling with two despondent young passengers among its occupants. The time for separation is here. Rufus and Mary had left Marietta on the 15th, accompanied by Rufe's mother, Sarah, to visit with his newlywed sister, Kate Dawes McLean. Kate and her new husband live now in West Alexander, Pennsylvania, just east of that narrow sliver of newly formed West Virginia, whose west boundary is the Ohio River.

It was an awkward visit for Mary. Kate is ten years Mary's senior, and Rev. McLean must be at least ten years older than Kate! Mary loves her mother-in-law, but staying with her and Kate and Kate's stepchildren for several days in a strange and sparsely furnished small home ...

It was not her idea of how best to spend time with Rufus just before he returns to the army. But Mary understands that Rufus felt badly about missing Kate's wedding, and Kate's new home is somewhat on the way to Washington, and Sarah enjoyed the time with her daughter, so it all made sense—or so Mary tells herself. Rufe's mother, Sarah, had planned to accompany Mary back to Marietta, but today she has stayed behind at Kate's due to a sick headache. Mary is a bit relieved over that, though she is ashamed to admit it. *I can't help it,* Mary thinks. *At least Rufe and I can be alone when we say goodbye.*

Rufe looks at his young wife as they reach the packet boat wharf in Wheeling. Mary's expression is one of fear and pain. Passengers begin to exit, and Rufe steps out, but Mary seems paralyzed and hesitates. "Mary, dear, we need to go, honey. Can you come down now?"

Mary turns to him, her lips quivering. "I know, Rufe, I just don't want this to end. I'll be all right, though," she says and tries to smile. They walk together toward the small steamboat that will carry her downriver to Marietta. Rufe does not have much time. His train sits on the track a short distance away, and it leaves for Washington very soon. He pays a baggage boy to put Mary's luggage on board, then the two find a spot offering a modicum of privacy for goodbyes. They have dreaded this moment.

Mary promised herself to remain strong but feels weak at the knees and almost sobs her farewell wish. "Please, please take care of yourself, Colonel Dawes. No more flag-waving or boat-standing! Remember that I love you and want you home."

Rufe embraces her, feels a trembling in her warm body, and kisses her. "Keep a good heart, my love. I am coming out all right," he says, unable to utter anything more. He watches as she slowly walks up toward the ramp, slipping and almost falling as she steps up, then is out of sight inside the boat. He has a rush of pity for her and resists an urge to run onto the boat. But then Mary appears on deck, managing a smile, and waves her handkerchief.

Rufe waves back as his train whistles a warning, and he hurries with a slight limp to clamber on board. He finds an open window facing the riverboat, tries to catch a last glimpse of Mary, and is frustrated by obscuring engine smoke, but raises his hat up and down anyway in the hope that she can see him. The train pulls away and he is gone.[12]

Mary is quiet and reflective on the winding river trip back to Marietta, trying in vain to repress dark thoughts. She has been Mrs. Rufus Dawes for exactly two months.

Sunday Evening, March 20, 1864—Sixth Wisconsin Camp near Culpepper, Virginia

Lt. Col Rufus Dawes pulls into camp in an army ambulance. As he gingerly climbs down and starts to recover his bags, Dr. John Hall and William quickly come over to greet him. William grabs the luggage as Hall shakes Rufe's hand and says, "Welcome back, Colonel! It's great to have you back! How's the ankle?"

Rufus responds, "Thanks, but I can't truthfully say I'm glad to *be* back. At least it was a fairly comfortable ride from Washington, courtesy of General Cutler letting me ride along in his ambulance. The ankle is getting better every day. William, Mrs. Dawes sends her regards and a little gift for you. Check the outside pocket of my valise."

William sets the bags down, checks the pocket, pulls out a small box, and opens it to discover a new pipe. He looks up at Dawes with a smile and says, "Looky heah! Ain't dat so nice of Mrs. Dawes! Ah'll be tryin' it out fust chance! Ah thank her kindly. And, sah, Ah been lookin' and axin 'bout a new hoss fo yah, since ya sent ole Kat back to your fathah's farm."

John Hall comments, "William, you know, is now chief steward of our officer mess, appointed by Colonel Bragg. He's doing a great job. I don't know what we would do without him."

Dawes and Hall share information as Rufus unpacks in the tent they share. "General Cutler says Major Hauser is likely to have his resignation accepted," says Dawes. "His child died, and his wife is ill, so I hope he gets it."

Hall replies, "That's too bad. He's a brave officer, but I'm sure neither of us will miss his cranky outbursts. By the way, Colonel Bragg seems to be laying off the whiskey, at least while he's getting signatures for his promotion recommendation. How about recruits?"

Dawes answers, "The general says we will be getting about 125 very soon, all volunteers. I hope there's more coming. If Colonel Bragg gets the promotion to brigadier general he's been trying for, our regiment's strength probably won't be enough to warrant me being promoted to colonel, according to the war department rules."

Hall responds, "We've talked about that before, and it just stinks in my opinion. The more a unit fights and loses men, and the more experienced its officers become, the less chance there is for promotion! Rather than creating new regiments, they ought to be filling up the old ones with recruits who can learn from the veterans. You've said that's what the Rebs do, and I think it must be why they are always so tough to whip! But, of course, to do otherwise would mean our governors couldn't appoint new officers for these new regiments from their circle of friends!"

Rufus nods. It's an old complaint. "Well, you know I agree with all that. Here is one exception, though. Frank Haskell got his colonelcy in a new Wisconsin regiment, the Thirty-Sixth, which probably will be sent here to Virginia. He's *definitely* qualified to command. He's been General Gibbon's right-hand man for a year and a half."[13] Dawes then turns the issue toward Hall. "What about you, John? You said you applied for a chief surgeon opening."

Hall replies, "Yes, I did. I'd hate to leave you and the Sixth, but Dr. Preston is likely to stand in my way here, and I owe it to my family to make a little more money. We'll see if it pans out. Are you too tired for chess?"

Monday, April 4, 1864, Marietta, Ohio—the Gates home

Mary and Rufus have been sending letters almost daily since their parting in Wheeling, each anxiously awaiting the daily mail delivery. He caused Mary to cry with his first letter, penned on his arrival in Washington, as he closed with the words, "I miss you morning, noon and night terribly all the time."

Mary is the chief Marietta correspondent now, so she dutifully shares the nonpersonal parts of Rufe's letters to the families Gates and Dawes. The mail service is erratic, but Mary has gotten two letters today, and she has them ready at the family dinner table. "This one is dated March 25th, just a short one, so I'll just tell you about it. First, he got paid, and he sent me $160, so Daddy, I need to deposit that in your bank." She skips the part about Rufe wanting her to keep money on hand in case of emergency, meaning him being severely wounded and needing her to come to him. She continues, "And he spent $100 for a 'nice horse, better a great deal than my old one.' " She pauses and says, "You know he sent Katerina off to his father in Mauston after the accident. Then he says that his cousin, Captain William Dawes, had just left after a two-day visit … I met him in Milwaukee. He is a wonderful man—has a bad limp from a wound."

Mary unfolds the next letter. "This is dated the 27th, and Bettie, he wrote this part for you after I told him you were so worried for him sleeping in the cold."

Bettie stares, attentive to every word:

Your story about Bettie quite overcame me. Well, I just pull the blankets <u>over my head</u> and stay so all night. Poles & cedar boughs and woolen blankets are the component parts of my bed. We have got a little Sibley stove in the tent and manage to keep quite comfortable though the weather has been very cold, snowy and windy.

Bettie makes a face. She is not convinced. "Well, he can't keep that stove going all night," she says. "I think he should have a woolen cap!"

Her mother, Betsey, agrees: "I think that's a wonderful idea, Bettie. That's a project for us to work on."

Mary smiles and continues, "This news is more for Daddy and Charley":

We have had a complete reorganization of our army. Our old 1st Corps is submerged into the 5th Corps under command of Gen. Warren, whom you know I like. We are now the 1st Brigade 4th Division 5th Corps and you may so direct your letters. General Cutler will command our brigade, Gen. Wadsworth our division. Our drunken Gen. Newton is in merited disgrace.

Mary paraphrases other information: "Rufe is back on the court-martial board again as president. He hates it as such a bore; he's there from 10:00 to 3:00 every day. But they must respect his judgment and good sense, because they keep appointing him. Colonel Bragg says he will resign if he doesn't get his promotion. Rufe is really torn over Colonel Bragg. He has been a good friend, an able commander, and a brave officer. But Colonel Bragg continuously embarrasses himself and everyone when he drinks too much, and it puts Rufe in a very bad position with the men."

Beman Gates responds, "That *is* a very tough situation. Perhaps it *would* be best for Bragg to resign. How can he expect a promotion if he is drunk in front of his men? But I understand he would not be the first— look at that General Newton, for example. Hopefully, it soon resolves itself for Rufus."

Mary reads Rufe's parting message, except for last sentence, which she cherishes for herself:

Remember me to Charley—Give my love to Bettie, Your Mother and Father, my respects to all the family. A kiss and a blessing to you, my own dear wife. Rufe

Friday, April 8, 1864—Sixth Wisconsin Camp near Culpepper

"Sah, are ya happy wid yah new hoss?" William Jackson asks. "Ah like da name yah giv her. 'Bettie.' Dat's a nice name, easy ta say, not too fancy."

Dawes laughs and says, "I'm very happy with her, William. She's a fine animal, trots better than any horse I tried and runs like a deer. I named her Bettie after my little sister-in-law, who's eleven years old and a real cutie. I just hope this horse stands in a fight as well as Katerina did."

"Wayal, Ah'm not surprised yah wife's sister to be a cutie, if'n she's as good lookin' as yah wife, if'n Ah may say so, sah. As to da fightin', Ah'm a hopin' dat dis heah army will git south far enough for me ta git my momma an sistah away from dat nasty massah down near Spotsylvania."

Dawes responds, "Mary would certainly be pleased with your compliment, William. As far as the upcoming campaign, it seems to me that this army *must* succeed, otherwise the Confederacy is a fixed fact. If we are defeated, I'm afraid most Northern people will end their support for President Lincoln, and everything we've fought for will be for nothing."

Saturday, April 16, 1864—Sixth Wisconsin Camp near Culpepper

Thoughts of the upcoming campaign are on everyone's mind. Dawes often sees General Grant at a distance, since the building used for the court-martial board is across from Grant's quarters in Culpepper. The general looks very different from the preconceived idea Dawes had in mind. Grant seems very plain and unassuming, very much unlike McClellan or Hooker. Dawes knows that the man almost has the fate of the nation in his hands. Grant and the president have incredible burdens.

Dawes has a burden, too, as an infantry commander who will soon be in action again, this time with a young wife at home. His service obligation ends three months from today. He forces himself to look past all that might transpire in those ninety days by optimistically focusing on the future. He again asks himself, *What will I do when I am out of the army? I now have a wife to support. It's not too soon to think about a job.* He sits down and writes William Cutler:

Dear Uncle

I noticed that the B.&O.R.R. have purchased the North Western branch, and joined hands with you on the bridge project. ... I am greatly rejoiced at the brightening of your prospects. It has occurred to me that some opening for me at home might possibly be provided ... in the project you suggested when I was at home, or in some other way.

It is now my desire to leave the service at the expiration of my term, three months from today, provided I can step into some business that is respectable and reasonably profitable.

I see no present prospect for promotion in the service, and when I have completed[—]honorably and faithfully, the record will show[—]my contract as a soldier, I do not believe it my duty to subject my wife to the unhappiness and myself to the peril and discomfort of another three years' service.

I should be glad to have you write me what you think of the matter, and what the prospect may be for me at home. ... I cannot take my wife to Wisconsin where we should be subjected to the unhappy influences of my father, and where I am at best an adventurer.

Respectfully, your Aff. nephew, Rufus

Friday, April 29, 1864—near Culpepper, VA

Lt. Col. Dawes and Captain Rollin Converse, commander of Company B, ride together on this pleasant afternoon, heading back to camp from Culpepper. The respect between the two young officers is mutual, and they enjoy their chance to talk. Dawes does not confide in many subordinates, but Captains Converse and Kellogg are two exceptions. "You know, Rollin," Dawes says, "one year ago today we made that river assault at Fitzhugh's Crossing. About this time of day, we were lying on the ground, targets for Rebel sharpshooters. I remember finding a spot where I could get a good view. Then your Corporal Evans quickly told me, 'Colonel, there's a man shooting at your knoll!' I rolled over a little, and -smack!- A bullet hit the ground right where I had been. Evans saved me that day." Dawes pauses, then says, "His poor body is now buried in the national cemetery at Gettysburg."

Converse looks at Dawes and replies, "He was a good soldier. One of a hundred such good fellows I have had the honor to command. With the new campaign about to commence, I often look at those still here and wonder who might be next to fall. I know I shouldn't think that way, but I can't help it." Converse hesitates a moment before venturing this question: "Sir, what do you think of Colonel Bragg. I mean, it's no secret about his drinking. He's had several wild sprees, the worst being the time you had to take over for him at dress parade. The boys like him, but if we get into a fight, and he's ... Well, it's on a lot of minds right now."

Dawes sighs and responds, "I know—believe me, I know. He and I have talked about it, and he admits to it, straightens out for a while, but then ... He really let loose after losing all his money on that horse race in Strasburg a couple weeks ago, when our Captain Holloway's horse finally got beat. Don't repeat this, but the colonel confided the other day that our state representatives told him no promotion will be considered for a drunkard. That's when he came back from Washington and stayed clean for a while. But it's got him badly depressed, and I worry about his state of mind. I'll do what's necessary, but my hope is he'll be all right once we get away from camp."

"You look tired, Colonel," says Converse. "That and this court-martial business must be weights you don't need to carry."

Dawes nods in agreement. "Well, court today was especially trying because it involved two of our men, Jones and Kilmartin. You know they were arrested for sneaking out one night and entering a lady's private home to rob her at gunpoint. Well, we've been hearing the case all day. Jones is always a ringleader, and Kilmartin is a rough character, and the evidence is solid against them. I feel bad, though, because Kilmartin probably saved my life last fall by shooting that Reb cavalryman wearing the blue coat, and now it looks like he'll be sentenced to prison."

"Well, sir, it's not all bad news. Phil Plummer got back from recruiting in Wisconsin, and our new major looks fit and in high spirits. The men like him, and I'm sure he will be a much more agreeable fellow for you than Major Hauser was. And how about Brooks? Our young adjutant somehow doesn't look too bad after his time in Libby Prison, certainly better than most of the poor returnees I've seen. Still, I'm sure it was a bad time there. And too bad for Doctor Hall for not getting his promotion, but I know you enjoy his company, and he'll stay with us for the time being, at least."

Dawes agrees with all those points and adds another: "We've got the Seventh Indiana in our brigade now too. It's a change to our old makeup, but these Indiana boys are 'western' with a good record, and I know Colonel Grover is a solid commander. I feel good about our prospects in a fight with their addition and General Cutler in command of the brigade." Dawes has another favorable thought as the duo reaches camp: *I have a loving wife,* he thinks, *and it's time to write her a letter. We will be moving out any day.*[14]

Wednesday, May 4, 1864, Marietta, Ohio—the Gates Home

Mary is keeping house this week, as Father is off to Cincinnati and Mother is visiting relatives in Athens. Bettie is in Lucy Dawes's school, and nineteen-year-old Charley is at the college, so she spends time with Cousin Francy and keeps up correspondence with Rufe. There is news regarding Charley, however, and she jots a note to her mother:

> We are all going on in the even tenor of our ways excepting Charley who had another war fit, for which I don't blame him one bit. Judge Putnam offered him the position of 1st Lieutenant in the company which the student Woodruff is to be Captain. Charley told him he would not accept it as his father and mother were both away from home. I tried to talk him out of the notion of going but it was no use and he came home last night and wrote to Father. He is very cool about it and you need give no uneasiness on that score for he says he is not going to accept any position until Father gets home. He has been in his room every night when study bell rang.
>
>   Mary

Mary writes Rufe every day and reads his letters over and over. He's told her to spend their money if she needs to, and to travel with her father. This evening in bed she reads:

> Try and be of good cheer and hopeful. The danger to which I may be subjected may not be very great after all. You have been dreading the battle for so long I fear you will suffer very intensely

in your week of trial if it comes. Have we not great reason to be thankful …

He thanks the Gates ladies for the woolen cap and wristlets, which "came safely and are very acceptable," though she laughs as he confesses that "the cap seems to find a way of slipping off my head during the night." Rufe itemizes his pay and money on hand. It totals $1,680, which he says is "rather a small pile for an ambitious couple to be sure, but it's a 'little something.' "

But today, his letter of April 29 arrives. His handwriting is hurried, and he has closed with these words, both tender and ominous:

> I am kept very busy nowadays and write very poor letters, but my dear true loving wife, there is not a minute of my life that my heart is not full to overflowing of loving and longing for you. Your husband, Rufe
>
> I burned your letters yesterday. It was a hard task, but I felt there was too much risk in leaving them for any accident.

A tear runs down Mary's cheek as she contemplates the words "any accident." She knows what that means. What she can't know is that at this moment, her husband and thousands of his fellow soldiers are moving south toward the enemy.

Mrs. Mary Beman Gates Dawes   Lieutenant Colonel Rufus Dawes

Endnotes

1. Dawes mentions Col. Bragg's plan in a January 2, 1864, letter to Mary, Rufus Dawes Collections, WHS. Unless otherwise noted, letters quoted in this chapter are from this collection. See *O. R. Vol. 33*, chap. 45, pp. 357 and 358, for Meade and Halleck dispatches and summary of "Veteran" units sent home. The supposition of Bragg's plan being leaked to Kingsbury is the author's, though Dawes noted that altercation in a Dec. 27, 1863, letter to Mary.

2. A good account of the regiment's trip to Milwaukee is contained in the *History of the Sauk County riflemen*. The telegram is contained in the Rufus Dawes Collection, WHS.

3. See JCJ, created by Peggy Dempsey, for the events described. In poignant and painful prose, Aunt Julia describes Annie, the details of her tragic death, and the impact it has on the family and their Christian faith, which is tested but remains steadfast.

4. The photo is by permission of the Betsey Mills Club, Marietta, Ohio. Betsey Gates Mills is the young "Bettie" of the Gates family. See the club website for its history and current activities.

5. Adam Juday served in the Nineteenth Indiana, his mother's maiden name being "Rookstool." Biographical information from Findagrave.com, contributor Cindy K. Coffin. Juday's wound specifics from Wm. T. Venner's *The 19th Indiana Infantry at Gettysburg*, p. 173. Conductor Rookstool is fictional.

6. The modes of transportation on this snowy trip (including the sleigh and caboose), the route taken, and the dates noted are all from the *Dawes Journal, Book 2*, DAA. The Newhall House, a six-story "magnificent" hotel, was built in 1857 at the corner of Michigan and Broadway. It burned down with the loss of seventy-six lives nineteen years after the Dawes couple's stay (WHS).

7. The illustration is from *SWSW*.

8. William J. Dawes, son of William (Henry Dawes's older brother who had moved to Dodge County, WI, from Ohio), is then a captain in the Eighth Wisconsin Infantry (known for its famous mascot, the war eagle "Old Abe") and is apparently serving temporary duty on a general court-martial board in Milwaukee after being wounded in the foot at the battle of Corinth, October 3, 1862. He soon joined the Veteran Reserve Corps, comprised of wounded veterans serving light duty. See Eighth Wis. battle of Corinth report in *O. R. Ser. I, Vol. XVII*, pp. 202 and 203, and *SWSW*, p. 239.

9. Grace Greenwood, a trailblazing nineteenth-century female poet, author, journalist, and antislavery/women's rights activist.

10. Katerina's wound, the fall on an icy street, and the sprained ankle is recorded in the *Dawes Journals, Book 2*, DAA. The exact location of the fall and the date are suppositions.

11. The return date to Marietta, the Burgess dinner with attendees, and the Gates party are chronicled in Julia Cutler's journal.

12. Julia Cutler recorded the visit to Kate. The parting scene is derived from Dawes letters in JCJ and WHS.

13. Haskell was promoted to colonel of the Thirty-Sixth Wisconsin on Feb. 9, 1864, per *Roster of Wisconsin Volunteers*.

14. Conversational topics derived from letters in the Dawes Collection, WHS.

Chapter Twelve

Heart Like a Stone

General Ulysses S. Grant commands all Union army forces but has decided that Washington is no place for him. He is a field general, and he is placing himself where the foe is the strongest—in Virginia, where the Gray Fox, Robert E. Lee, has thwarted the Army of the Potomac for two years. General Meade still commands that ninety-three-thousand-man army, and he still gives the orders to the commanders of his four consolidated and reorganized corps. These are now the Second, Fifth, and Sixth Infantry Corps, along with a cavalry corps, under Generals Hancock, Warren, Sedgewick, and Sheridan, respectively. But Meade's orders come direct from Grant, who situates his separate headquarters close by. Rufus Dawes notes it is an awkward arrangement, one that adds a level to the chain of command.

General Lee's Army of Northern Virginia is organized in essentially the same manner as at Gettysburg and Mine Run, minus Pickett's shattered division. Lee's sixty-five thousand troops are south of the Rapidan River, ever watchful for the movements of their bulky Union opponents. Lee is outnumbered but knows Grant and Meade must enter the same countryside where General Joe Hooker was repulsed one year ago—the green scrub jungle named the Wilderness.

General Lysander Cutler's Iron Brigade is now one of three brigades in General Wadsworth's 8,153-man Fourth Division of Warren's Fifth (V) Corps. They march on May 4 from the Culpepper camp to cross the Rapidan at Germanna Ford, then head southeast on Germanna Plank Road to Wilderness Tavern, 5 miles past the river. The Orange Turnpike intersects there, heading southwest.[1] There is about a square mile of cleared land on the south quadrant of the intersection, with the two-story Elwood House, owned now by a Mr. Lacy, sitting there on high ground. Beyond the open fields is thick and tangled second-growth forest.

* * * * *

Thursday Morning, May 5, 1864—South of the Lacy House

William Jackson sits under a tree cleaning and loading the Colt revolver belonging to Lt. Col. Dawes. It is a bright and pleasant spring morning, the dogwoods are in bloom, and new green is everywhere. Interrupting the scene, however, are thousands of blue-uniformed troops, among them the Sixth Wisconsin. Dawes and several other officers lounge in the shade, enjoying small talk and jokes. Muffled gunfire noise erupts to the south.

"That must be Crawford's division," Dawes says. "Sounds like they found something." He expresses a disturbing thought: "I hope we don't get tangled up in this wilderness again."

The noise increases in intensity, and the officers rise as they see an orderly approach. "The brigade is moving forward," the man says. "Colonel Bragg directs that Company I should form as skirmishers."

Captain John Kellogg moans and says, "Not again!" Kellogg starts toward his company, absorbing wisecracks: "The colonel must like you, John—or not!"

Major Phillip Plummer jokingly asks, "What word shall we say to your wife?"

Kellogg shouts back, "Never mind about *my* wife! Just look out for Converse's girl!"

Now drawn into the banter, Captain Rollin Converse comments, "Ha! Plummer will get shot before any of us! Of course, Dawes is the only man they can't kill!"

The group laughs and disperses to their posts. It is time for business.

Dawes is smiling as William hands over the revolver with a comment: "Lawdy, sah, y'all jes a little ... Ah don' know what!"

"Just a little fun, William," Dawes says. "Keep Bettie for me. I'll go on foot; these woods are too thick for a horse." Dawes heads toward Colonel Bragg, and the two form the regiment in reserve behind the Seventh Indiana. The other brigade regiments form the front line.

"We're supposed to stay 150 feet behind them," Bragg says, "and guide right. Griffin's division is going up the turnpike on that side, and Stone's brigade is off to our left."

The low branches of scrub pine and oak, plus tangles of briar vines, frustrate the soldiers as the line moves forward for about a mile. Hot firing erupts ahead on the front line. It sounds like the attack is going well, but visibility is maybe 50 feet, and it is impossible to know for sure. The Sixth comes to a shallow ravine, and through the green leaves, Dawes spots Colonel Grover on his horse in the middle of the Seventh Indiana line. Dawes is wondering how Grover has managed to get his horse through the thickets, then more surprised when he hears Grover order, "Fix bayonets!"

Dawes is thinking, *Bayonets in this mess?*

The Sixth moves uphill to follow the Hoosiers, but when they reach the top, the Seventh is nowhere to be seen, and there is nobody visible to the right. The foreboding feeling of being lost or cut off prompts Bragg to run over to Dawes at the right end of the line. Bragg says, "Keep the men moving forward to catch up. I'll run to the right to find the line." Bragg is quickly lost from sight.

Dawes moves closer to the center as the 100-yard-wide Sixth Wisconsin line struggles forward for five minutes. Gunfire suddenly breaks out ahead, and Major Plummer shouts to Dawes, "Colonel, look there!" He points to the right.

Dawes peers low through the trees and spots a heavy, irregular line of Confederate infantry moving quickly past them, exposing their flank. Dawes thinks, *They don't see us, but they're heading right where Colonel Bragg just ran! There's a gap to the right, and the Rebs are into it!*

Dawes shouts orders: "Change front on the color company! Left wing forward. Major, take charge of the left wing! Right wing, about-face! Right wheel, double-quick, march!" Dawes moves as the right wing executes the order to face the passing enemy line just as a gunfire volley erupts to his left. He looks to see how the left wing is coming up to complete the alignment, but it has not moved! Dawes runs that way to find out why.

Captain Charlie Hyatt shouts at Dawes, "Major Plummer is killed! He was shouting the order to move, but we can't do it. There's a Reb line coming at us!" The Sixth's line is now an inverted L, with Rebel infantry approaching on three sides. Dawes orders "Fire!" The closing enemy does the same. Men go down all along the line. "We can't stay like this!" Dawes shouts to Hyatt. Everyone knows it is a bad spot, and they are loading and firing as fast as they can through the smoke and trees. Bullets are whizzing and smacking trees. The shrill Rebel yell is all around. Death or a prison camp seem moments away. Some of the new recruits are near panic.

Dawes is the only field officer present, and he has no idea what happened to the front line or where Colonel Bragg is. All he is thinking now is, *I've got to get the regiment out of this!* Grabbing one of the flags so he can be seen, he shouts, "Fall back! Fall back!" He then heads in a direction of least resistance. The Confederates smell blood and chase after them, shooting and shouting. Dawes rallies the men, ordering officers and sergeants to form a hasty line, and they fire several rounds to fend off the attack. They retreat again and repeat the desperate resistance two more times. The Rebel attack fizzles, and Dawes leads a brief counterattack to make sure. The men are exhausted; at least fifty are gone, most killed or wounded, among them Rollin Converse. He was seen to go down in a flurry of gunfire. The enemy was too close; his men couldn't get to him. John Kellogg and his skirmish company are missing. Dawes is panting and sweaty, but pauses to think. *We were lucky to get out of that trap, but where do we go now?*

Dawes lost his hat to a snagging branch during the hurried retreat and places a red bandanna round his head to blot the perspiration. He walks with the flagstaff over his shoulder, hoping to find the brigade. They come to a fence at the edge of a field and follow it to a narrow lane in the woods. He takes a chance on the path and, with great relief, joins a column of Union troops moving to the rear. A man comes up to him from the missing company. "Colonel," the man says, "Captain Kellogg is dead. I saw his body."

Dawes simply stares and nods as he leads the survivors in a silent trudge through the woods. He visualizes Plummer, Converse, and Kellogg. *An hour ago, we were enjoying a cheerful repartee under the tree. Now they are all gone.* Those parting words—"Dawes is the only one they can't kill"—replay in his numbed mind. Their advance has been shattered, lives lost. *For what? How did this happen?*

Dawes is suddenly shaken from his gloom by hands grasping his shoulders and a voice emotionally asking, "Are you badly hurt? Come here and let me see. Thank God you are not killed!" It is Dr. John Hall. The Sixth has reached the restored Union line, and Hall, seeing the red bandanna and dirty, sweat-streaked face, assumes Dawes has been headshot. It is good to see Hall, and Colonel Bragg, too, who made it safely here after being swept up with retreating troops on the right.

General Cutler is there near the Lacy House, and he's in a bad mood. "No damn place to have a fight," he snarls at Bragg and Dawes. "We were whipping them though! Ewell's corps. We took battle flags from two Virginia regiments, and our boys grabbed almost three hundred prisoners. But we must have drifted left in these woods, and the damn Rebs ambushed us in a gap on the right. Georgians, I think. Stone and Rice collapsed on our left, and we lost a lot of good men. No damn place to fight! Get your men building breastworks here. They might press us."

Bragg and Dawes shout the orders. The men work feverishly, anticipating an attack, but none comes. "Maybe the Rebs are as mixed up as we are," they say. The regiment itemizes the missing, draws ammunition, cleans weapons, munches on hardtack, and waits. In late afternoon, orders come for the division to move left in support of Hancock's Second Corps, which is attacking down the Orange Plank Road against A. P. Hill's Confederates. The Plank Road is about 3 miles south of the turnpike and roughly parallel to it. The land in between is the same low-visibility wilderness fought over this morning.

General Cutler's Iron Brigade forms the second line as Wadsworth's division moves into battle on Hancock's right. There is sharp skirmishing and firing throughout the advance as they drive the Confederates through the woods. Ahead is Stone's brigade, and part of them breaks for the rear until stopped by the Iron Brigade veterans, who take their place on the front line.[2] Darkness intervenes, and at 8:00 p.m., the men are ordered to halt in line overnight with skirmishers out front. The ground in the rear is strewn with Confederate casualties, many pleading for help and water. Dawes and his men do what they can to help. It is a cold, horrible night. Today's chaos and loss of friends hit home. Everyone realizes the fight will be renewed tomorrow.

The attack resumes at 4:30 a.m. Artillery shells rain down through the trees, but the brigade drives A. P. Hill's corps back. Union cheers ring out along the line. The Iron Brigade gets mixed up with Hancock's troops as the two converging lines meet, but the Rebels are pushed beyond the Plank Road and are on the run! Wadsworth reforms the division and moves forward in four lines with the Plank Road on the left. The strong Union advance is pushing the Rebels back, some Southern units breaking under the pressure. Suddenly, heavy firing breaks out to the right. The brigade on that end is flanked and breaks away. Through the trees and smoke, Dawes hears a new crash of musketry and the Rebel yell up ahead. The Union front line starts to roll up, and all is confusion. Dawes looks left toward the edge of a clearing nearer the road and spots General Wadsworth on horseback, riding through the lines of the 149th Pennsylvania, trying to restore order, leading a counterattack. Several hundred men are following him, flag waving. Then there is a flurry of action, and Dawes looks again, Wadsworth is down, troops fall back, and the whole Union mass retreats through the woods, followed by the Rebel yell.[3]

The Confederate counterattack smashing into Hancock's corps and Wadsworth's division is conducted by General James Longstreet, whose troops arrive on the field just in time to save Lee's right flank. But Longstreet is shot accidentally by his own men, and his attack is finally contained along the Brock Road. As Dawes and Colonel Bragg work to reorganize the regiment, a crestfallen Lt. Earl Rogers, serving on division staff, comes over with the stunning news: "General Wadsworth's gone," he says.

Dawes fires back in rebuke, "Why did you let him charge forward on his horse that way?"

A sorrowful Rogers replies, "My God, nobody could stop the old man!"

General Wadsworth had earned the respect of his whole division, and the soldiers feel his loss deeply.

Saturday, May 7, 1864—near the Brock Road

General Lysander Cutler replaces Wadsworth as Fourth Division commander, and he rides over to see Colonel Bragg. Dawes is close enough to hear. "Colonel Bragg," says Cutler, "I'm placing you in command of the Third Brigade, effective immediately."

Bragg is taken aback but says, "Uh, yes, sir. What happened to Roy Stone?"

Cutler looks annoyed and simply says, "Horse fell on him," then turns away.

Bragg looks at Dawes, and both men are thinking there is more to it. "Well, Rufus," Bragg says, "the regiment is yours again. Not how I pictured getting a brigade command."

Dawes reviews the situation after Bragg leaves. The Sixth has suffered sixty-three casualties in the past two days of combat, including three officers and five enlisted men killed. Fifteen are missing, including Captain John Kellogg. They are most likely dead or captured. The regiment is now reduced to 310 men, but they have fared better than their sister regiments. The Iron Brigade has lost over five hundred men killed, wounded, or missing. A cannon ball killed Colonel Williams of the Nineteenth Indiana yesterday morning. Colonel Mansfield and Major Parsons of the Second Wisconsin are prisoners, as is Colonel Grover of the Seventh Indiana. Colonel William Robinson's Seventh Wisconsin has been hit hard, but by seniority, he again assumes brigade command, as he did at Gettysburg. Many veteran noncoms, so important to unit effectiveness, are lost. Dawes does not know it, but that railroad conductor's nephew, Sergeant Adam Juday of the Nineteenth Indiana, was killed on Thursday, May 5.[4]

The whole army is beat up. Last night, Sedgewick's corps on the far right had been hit by another Rebel flank attack, a General Lee maneuver that Union generals cannot seem to detect or avert, with units routed and hundreds captured before darkness ended it. Lee's army has also lost heavily, but their tough veterans have blunted every Union thrust and counterattacked with fury. Officers gather around Dawes and debate various rumors. Last year, Joe Hooker called it quits after a similar drubbing. The question now is: What will Grant do?

The opposing forces both work to reinforce breastworks that extend for several miles like ragged scars through the woods. It is a nightmarish landscape. Wounded men caught between the lines suffer and die, some helplessly burned by fires ignited from bursting shells and gun wadding. There is sporadic skirmish and artillery fire, but no major action, as both sides lick their wounds.

"Forward, march!" Dawes shouts, and the regiment moves southeast in column on the Brock Road. It is 8:00 p.m. and Warren's corps is ordered to move toward Spotsylvania. There is no retreat north! Grant is moving around Lee's right flank and heading toward Richmond! Weary though they are, soldiers shout, "Hurrah!" But it soon becomes a stop-and-start all-night march. Speed is of the essence, but the advance is repeatedly slowed by cavalry actions ahead. Rufus Dawes shares the frustration of many in the Union ranks, thinking, *We never seem able to get where we need to be when we need to be there!*

The Union troops know this is the year victory must be earned, and they want to get on with it. But they do not now realize how different this campaign will be. The fighting will not be one "week of trial." The war is soon to become a continuous, brutal battle. Most of the participants will not survive it unscathed in body or mind.

Sunday Afternoon, May 8, 1864—behind the Fifth Corps Line, Opposite Laurel Hill

Lt. Col. Rufus Dawes watches as Second Lieutenant Huntington helps to lay the body of his company commander, First Lieutenant Howard Pruyn, into a red-earth grave near several pine trees along a narrow dirt roadway. Members of Company A prepared the spot, and they now pay silent tribute to their popular leader.

William Jackson feels the loss as much as anyone, and as the group heads back to their breastworks, he says to Dawes, "Sah, if'n it wen't fo Lieutenant Pruyn, Ah would not be heah. He was a good man. Ah'll nevah fo'git him."

Dawes nods and agrees, "Yes, he was a good officer and a good man. I remember that day near Cedar Mountain, when he was still a sergeant. He couldn't keep you, I needed someone, and here we are. I know he was happy to see you doing well."[5] *And here's another fine life ended*, Dawes thinks. He recalls the details of this morning's combat: Warren's Fifth Corps arrived near Spotsylvania too late. Confederate infantry and artillery blocked their path at a wooded rise named Laurel Hill, protected behind strong earthworks they seem able to erect on a moment's notice. Warren threw General Robinson's division at the Rebels, but they were bloodily repulsed, Robinson badly wounded. That was early morning. At 10:00 a.m. Warren sent Cutler's and Crawford's divisions in a second assault on both sides of Brock Road. The Sixth entered dense woods again on the far right of the line and were hit by an unexpected right-side flank attack, plus artillery fire from the left. The line broke in disorder, and Dawes worked hard to rally the men. Lt. Pruyn was directing his company when he was seen to fall forward on hands and knees, stagger back through the woods, then fall and die. Since then, the men have worked to improve fortifications, harassed continually by Rebel sharpshooters.

Monday Afternoon, May 9, 1864—Fifth Corps Line Opposite Laurel Hill

The quarter-mile-wide space between the opposing trenches is a scene of deadly sniping among the brush and trees and farm fences. The Southerners have reinforced their skirmish line and own the woods and higher ground. Soldiers in blue are being hit despite their log-and-earth barriers. Lt. Col. Dawes turns to Sergeant Major Babcock and says, "Pass the word: General Cutler wants the brigade to rout out those skirmishers. I need thirty volunteers to reinforce our picket line and get it done. The Seventh Wisconsin is sending men out too."

Five minutes later, Dawes has Lt. Goltermann and Sgt. Fairchild next to him, plus about thirty other volunteers. "All right, Lieutenant, I'll have the men fire into those trees limbs to keep Johnny's head down, then you take your men over the wall here and go after them. Good luck!" The firing commences, and the plucky little immigrant German leads Fairchild and the men into the field. Instantly, there is a smattering of return fire, and Dawes sees one man go down. The skirmishers are lost to sight, but gunfire and shouting increase through the trees.

Seventh Wisconsin boys nearby also run out into the fray, among them a group of Chippewa American Indians recruited over the winter. Dawes watches in amazement as they whoop across the field toward the enemy, and he sees some fall. The Rebels put up a fight, and several boys from the Seventh run back toward the lines. Several get hit and go down. Dawes can hear the wounded men moaning. "I need some volunteers to get the wounded!" Dawes shouts. Several men of the Sixth rush out and bring them back, joined by a few who had taken cover. One young soldier is in bad shape, with a bloody chest wound. His companion from the Seventh is clinging to him, pleading, "Bill, hang on! We'll get you back!" The man is hit too bad. He struggles briefly, then gasps his last breath.

Dawes witnesses another death. He grimaces and, in familiar routine, slowly reaches into the dead soldier's pockets for some identification.

"You're Colonel Dawes, aren't you, sir?" the sad-faced survivor says.

"Yes, I am," Dawes says, looking up at the boy.

"His name is William—William P. Dawes," the soldier replies quietly while nodding toward the dead soldier. "I'm a Dawes, too—Flavius is my name. Four of us brothers and cousins joined Company I of the Seventh at the same time in February. Two were wounded a couple of days ago, and now William is dead. I'm the only one left! Sir, I believe we are related."

Lt. Col. Rufus Dawes is stunned. "I had no idea!" he says. "I don't believe we have ever met. This is hard to comprehend." He looks at the glazed eyes of this dead young soldier, a distant cousin he does not know. He thinks, *I should be grieving, but there have been so many ...* "I'm very sorry about William here. I'll have a stretcher brought over. We'll help you carry him back to your company." He can't think of more to say. "I'm sorry we had to meet like this. You both did brave work out there today." Dawes shakes his cousin's hand—Flavius, the man said—and ducks low to check on his own skirmishers, to see if any of them are lost.[6]

Tuesday, May 10, 1864, Marietta, Ohio

The newsboy runs up Putnam Street and turns right at Fourth Street to the home of Sarah Dawes. She responds to the knock and opens the door as the boy blurts out, "A telegraph message, ma'am. I was told to get it to you right away!"

Sarah's heart is racing as she quickly gives the boy a coin, thanks him, and anxiously opens the envelope. It is from her brother, sent from Chillicothe:

To Mrs. S. C. Dawes, Marietta, 4th Street across from College

Morning papers contain list of casualties among officers. Rufus not among them. General Wadsworth killed. Lee retreating. W. P. Cutler

With a sigh of relief, she heads out the door to walk the half block to the Gates home and to Mary. Reports of heavy fighting came three days ago, and people at home have been in dread suspense ever since. This message is the first detailed word anyone has heard. Mary reads the note and gives her mother-in-law a long hug. "Thank you! Thank you! I've been praying and hoping. It's just so hard not to know what is happening. Father has been in Washington for the Ohio Relief Commission, and I'm hoping he can send some news soon." Mary's eyes are red from tears. The constant fear and uncertainty is agonizing.

William Cutler's telegram reflects news that is four days old, and Mary wonders where Rufus is now. *If General Wadsworth is killed,* she thinks, *then Rufe must be in the thick of things again!* She has tried to write him cheerfully, but in one of her last messages had admitted to being sad and lonely. Rufe's letter of May 1 came today, and he responded this way:

The hardships and discouragement are not all on my side. You, "weeping, sad and lonely," dreading almost to hear from me every day. ... Do not try to write a cheerful letter to conceal [an] aching heart. I do not wonder you have "a good cry" from sheer misery, trying to say cheerful things when your soul is in dread to have me in danger. I feel very confident and hopeful myself. I trust and believe the same kind Providence that has so often "covered my head" in battle will care for me hereafter.

Mary sits with Charley late that night. She can't imagine a better brother. Fun-loving, handsome, a friend to everyone, a teaser, but always there when she needs him. "Charley," she says, "I just feel so guilty telling Rufe how lonely and sad I am. He sees through my attempts at being cheery. And then he tries to cheer *me* up. And now you! You're going into the army next week! How am I going to manage with both of you in danger?"

Charley shakes his head. "You know I can't say anything about Colonel Dawes ... Rufus, I mean. He certainly knows how to take care of himself, plus you said he feels confident and hopeful. But, Mary, don't worry about *me!* My enlistment in the 148th is only for a hundred days. All we'll be doing is rear-area assignments, freeing up units for field duty with Grant. So, not very exciting and certainly nothing to worry about, though I'm looking forward to finally doing *something* for the country! Besides, now you won't have to put up with my 'war fits,' as you like to call them."

Mary laughs. *He always makes me laugh*, she thinks. She would not be laughing if she could see Rufe at this moment.

Wednesday, May 11, 1864—behind Entrenchments
Facing Laurel Hill, near Spotsylvania

Lt. Col. Rufus Dawes finally finds the time, if not the inclination, to write Mary a letter, his first since crossing the Rapidan seven days ago. It has been a week from hell with no letup in sight. Yesterday's attack failed miserably again. Lieutenant Oscar Graetz was killed. Remington and Timmons were wounded. The regiment got pinned down in a ravine with bullets whizzing just overhead. Little Aaron Yates of his old Company K was killed when Yates stuck his head up too far. Somehow, General Warren had come up to observe. Dawes had yanked on the general's yellow sash to pull him down, no doubt saving the corps commander from multiple bullet strikes. Warren got angry but thanked him later. To his credit, Warren now can now report firsthand that Laurel Hill is impregnable, if only Generals Grant and Meade will listen. Dawes writes:

My dear wife Mary

Through God's mercy I am yet alive, and besides the fearful tax on my energies mental and physical, I have nothing to complain of and everything to be thankful for. For six long days we have struggled almost continuously under musketry. Major Plummer, Capt. Converse, Capt. Kellogg, Lieut. Pruyn, and Lieut. Graetz are in their graves. Capt. Remington, Lieut. Timmons, and Lieut. Converse are wounded. The peril of the last week has been fearful. I cannot hope to pass thus safely through another such [battle]. ... Our loss is about one hundred and forty now. The battle must soon be resumed. I cannot write now. The frightful scenes of the last week make my heart almost like a stone. You know, my own dear wife, that ...

Dawes closes his eyes, tries to hold back the emotions, his thoughts in turmoil. *I tried to begin "confident and hopeful." But all these good men, good friends, even a cousin—gone! I keep thinking of John and his wife and three little girls. How can I forget that? I can't. I'm sorry, Mary. This is all I can do.* The sentence is left unfinished; he simply ends it with "Good bye," then seals the envelope, steels himself, and crouches along the line to check on his men.

The surviving troops feel the effects of three failed assaults on Rebel entrenchments at Laurel Hill. Each attack had been hopeless from the start. Casualties have been awful, the troops are exhausted, and trust in leadership is at a low. Dawes contemplates the situation: *Our Fifth Corps is being ground up by these assaults. General Robinson had a leg amputated, his division so mauled on Sunday that it's now disbanded, the shattered brigades split up among our division and Crawford's. General Rice, the fine gentleman who once sat with me to discuss law, a hero at Gettysburg, was killed yesterday. That attack was suicidal. Even General Sedgwick, commanding the Sixth Corps, is killed. The eighty or so men left in the Second Wisconsin were pulled out of the brigade today, assigned as provost guard. More important to me, my brave boys of the Sixth Wisconsin are being cruelly whittled away.*

11:00 a.m., Saturday, May 14, 1864—Spotsylvania Battlefield

Today, as his men keep low behind new breastworks, an exhausted Rufus Dawes writes a letter in pencil to Mary, briefly describing the past two terrible days. He is barely able to function. Thursday, May 12, was the most terrible twenty-four hours in his three years of military service.

His division was ordered to make a morning assault on Laurel Hill again. Adjoining units refused to move. Colonel Bragg sent an order for the Sixth to advance, hoping their example would inspire others. Dawes wondered why Bragg had authority to send the order, him being the junior brigade commander, but he complied and led the Sixth forward.

The attack had no chance. The Rebel positions grow stronger every day. The men know it; the generals don't seem to care. Company H was in an exposed spot and suffered at least five killed and many wounded. Among others severely wounded were the two convicted home invaders, Jones and Kilmartin. They had been sentenced to three and five years, respectively, in Sing-Sing Prison, but when marching orders came May 3, they both pleaded to join their comrades. General Wadsworth, now himself killed in action, had granted the request.

Attacking Union troops hit the ground under withering fire and then melted back. Dawes got his soldiers out the best he could and approached Colonel Robinson's headquarters to report. He was shocked to find his brigade commander cowering behind the breastwork. William W.

Robinson—a brave veteran of many battles, previously wounded, solid disciplinarian, a good man—had broken under the strain. Colonel Bragg had been forced to take charge.

That afternoon, the Sixth marched 4 miles to the left to support a Sixth Corps attack. They built breastworks, then moved right 2 miles, then came back in a driving rainstorm and entered the ghastly killing zone ever after known as the Bloody Angle. They were told to fire at the enemy all night in the dark, in the storm, shin-deep in mud, with bodies everywhere. It was hellish. The Rebels retreated to another prepared line, and in the morning light, Dawes viewed a scene of horrific carnage: bodies and parts of bodies sticking out of the mud, trees mowed down by the volume of bullets fired. He led his men into the woods to get a few hours' rainsoaked sleep on the 13th, marched back to their old positions at Laurel Hill, then marched again *all night* to the extreme left of the army. The foggy night was pitch black, the mud thick and endless. Soldiers dropped from exhaustion all along the cross-country route. They dug in before daylight and now find themselves just north of the Fredericksburg Road: the Union army supply lifeline to the northeast.

Grant has side-slipped his troops to the left again, abandoning the Laurel Hill line, but Lee matches his move. The two armies now face each other in parallel lines meandering roughly north-to-south. Dawes knows little of the strategy, but he does know that about a mile southwest down the road, where it tees into the Brock Road, sits the Spotsylvania County Courthouse. From the courthouse in both directions are enemy infantry and artillery firmly entrenched. General Burnside's Ninth Corps (he responsible for the Fredericksburg disaster in December 1862) had squandered Grant's best chance to defeat Lee's army by miserably failing to take the key courthouse intersection four days ago when it was only lightly defended.[7]

Now, another cruel mistake. General Cutler heard an erroneous report from a wounded Sixth Wisconsin soldier that Lt. Col. Dawes had been killed in the May 10 assault. Cutler sadly made the report before learning it was untrue. Correcting it came too late. The New York papers printed it.

"Not again!" Rufe vents at Captain Cowdrey at division staff. Cowdrey apologizes, but Dawes is angry that Mary will see the report. He writes her not to give up despite what she reads, as there "are often mistakes." But he tells her it is not probable for him to "come out safely." He mourns the Sixth's one hundred fifty casualties incurred so far, "many of our best and truest," but his willingness to endure hardship and loss for the cause is still strong. He ends with:

If we may only finish this horrible business here our lives are of poor account in comparison to the blessing to humanity.

I know you are praying for me, and suffering as only few can know, but I can't write false hopes of escaping forever. Good bye my own dear wife. May God give you comfort and happiness if I am taken away. Your loving husband[8]

Others beside Mary are concerned about Rufus. Beman Gates has been in Washington coordinating donations from Ohio. The supplies include medicines, vegetables, lemons, lint, bandages, and tobacco. It is difficult to leave obligations at the bank he now manages in Marietta, but he wants to be of service. He fights off sickness to scour hospitals, seeking information about his son-in-law, questioning wounded soldiers recently arrived from the battlefield. In letters to his family yesterday and today, Beman assures them that Rufus is well by all information available. Several wounded from the Sixth tell him of the bravery displayed by their commander, mentioning Rufus taking the flag to rally broken troops. (Mary will shudder when she reads this.) There are over seven thousand wounded men in Washington, but the worst cases are still at Fredericksburg "depot hospitals." He will try to find out more.

Wednesday, May 18, 1864, Mauston, Wisconsin

Henry Dawes stops the buggy in front of Langworthy's, ties his son's retired army horse, Katerina, to the post, and walks up the steps. "Hello, Langworthy," Henry says. "How's business?"

Langworthy gives Henry a pained look and silently walks up to his old partner with this morning's *Mauston Star* in hand. The paper is folded open to a front-page article. "I'm sorry, Henry, very sorry. If you had not come into town, I would have ridden out to your place. "

Henry takes the paper and quickly reads the article: "Lieutenant Colonel Rufus Dawes probably killed. —The *Chicago Tribune* ..." Henry lowers the paper and closes his eyes.

Langworthy attempts to offer hope. "Read on, Henry. The Chicago paper named him 'Dana,' not 'Dawes.' Perhaps there is a mistake."

Henry reads the article and sees that the Sixth Wisconsin is specifically mentioned. "There is no other lieutenant colonel in the Sixth," Henry says. "They must mean Rufus."

"I know it seems that way," Langworthy says, "and there must be awful, terrible fighting. The paper says that John Kellogg is missing and presumed dead, and other boys from around here too. I feel so sad for

Adelaide and her children. But, Henry, you should find out for sure about your son. Don't give up hope."

Henry knows someone of influence who might help. Why not start the inquiry at the top? He mails a letter, including the news clip, to an Ohio politician who should remember him and who is now in Washington. He asks Salmon P. Chase, secretary of the US Treasury, to use his influence in tracking down his son.

Thursday, May 19, 1864—Sixth Wisconsin Breastwork near Spotsylvania Courthouse

Sergeant Major Cuyler Babcock finds Lt. Col. Dawes looking through field glasses at the end of the line. "Sir, there's a gentleman here to see you—a civilian. He says he's your father-in-law."

A startled Rufus Dawes runs down the trench to see the smiling face of Beman Gates! "Sir, Mr. Gates, what are you doing here?! I can't believe it! It's great to see you! How is Mary? We haven't gotten any mail."

The two warmly shake hands, and Beman gives Dawes a big bear hug. "That hug is mostly from Mary!" he says, stepping back to examine his son-in-law. What he sees is a man who has aged beyond his years, dark eyes sunken, five-foot-nine body thinner and dirtier than Beman has ever seen him. But Rufus is seemingly healthy and alert. "How I wish Mary could see you! We've had so little news. She's … concerned about you, as I'm sure you know." "Concerned" does not fully describe Mary's state of mind, but Beman avoids adding more pressure to his war-worn son-in-law.

"Sir, I would give anything to see Mary, but obviously not here or right now. We've had a couple of days' rest, but I'm sure it won't last. Tell me: How in the world did you get here?"

Beman summarizes, "Well, I took the boat with our supplies down the Potomac to Belle Plain on Saturday. Sunday, I walked the 10 miles to Fredericksburg, the last four in a huge hail and rain-storm. My supplies finally were delivered on Wednesday. The suffering there is inconceivable. Every building, barn, or shed is a hospital. I got a pass to the front while I was in Washington, and after distributing my supplies, I connected with some reporters in Fredericksburg who I knew from my newspaper days. One of them loaned me a horse, not much of one, but it got me here."

"That's wonderful, sir! I'm sure all your work is greatly appreciated." Dawes shouts down the line for William, who comes running. "Sir, this is William Jackson. William, Mr. Gates, my father -in-law. William, can you make us some coffee?"

"Yassah," William replies and nods to Beman. "A pleasure, sah."

"Thank you, William," Beman Gates responds.

Rufus and Beman spend twenty minutes discussing Mary and the family. Beman does not have much time. "Mother and I gave Charley our blessing to join the 148th Regiment. We really didn't want to, but you know how he feels. He wants to do his part for the country, and Betsey and I felt that if we denied him, it would crush his self-esteem. He's scheduled for muster this week as first lieutenant in Sam Knowles's Company A. They're supposed to leave Marietta next Monday. I may not get home in time to see him off, but I hope to meet him in Washington."

"I understand," Dawes says. "But that horse you have looks awfully shaky. I'll give you mine and send a man with you to bring her back. I named her Bettie, you know."

Beman replies with a laugh, "Yes, I know! Your little sister-in-law is so proud! Rufus, thank you. May God continue to protect you. Mary will be thrilled when I telegraph home about our meeting." Mr. Gates and drummer boy Arthur Gaubatz head north up the busy Fredericksburg Road, with Beman thinking, *I'm saying goodbye to* both *my soldier sons this week. If I was young enough I would join too!*

Beman Gates and drummer Gaubatz ride past wagons and ambulances going both directions, but after only 2 miles, Beman looks left across the fields and asks, "What troops are those heading this way?"

Gaubatz turns, and his eyes bulge. "Mine Gott!" he shouts. "Those are Shonnies! Ve got to go!" He spurs the old plug horse forward, and Beman does the same to Bettie. Shooting starts, and Beman hears the Rebel yell as he and Gaubatz gallop north toward Fredericksburg. The two get out of the way just in time as Union troops advance to meet the enemy's surprise attack. Heavy firing explodes behind them.[9]

Friday, May 20, 1864—Breastworks North of Fredericksburg Road

My dear wife—

I was very much rejoiced yesterday to see your father for a few moments. It was very good of him to come out to see me, and it did me a great deal of good to see him. Our hearts were rejoiced this morning by receiving our mail. I got five letters from you. I won't try to write my dear Mary how my burdens are lightened by your dear loving letters.

Belle Plain Landing, May 17, 1864, three days after Beman Gates landed
with supply donations.
James Gardner Photo

Jericho Mill and pontoon bridge over the North Anna River, May 1864.
Photo by A. & J. Gardner

Tell me what you hear from Eph. I doubt not that he has been in battle. I was very much concerned about your father. There was a battle on the road to Fredericksburg directly in our rear.

Your letters came to me timely when "I was sick with the horrors of war." ... [T]he assurance of your "undying love" and that you are well and hopeful never came so sweetly to me than this morning. I do live now in the joy I look forward to with you. I could hardly bear myself as a man without that prop.

God bless my dear wife

Mr. Gates makes it back safely, reaching Washington as Rufus is writing to Mary. Beman sends a telegraph message to his wife, Betsey, which is received in Marietta at 4:00 p.m. on the 21st:

Left front today. Rufus well. Shall be home Tuesday. Beman Gates

* * * * *

General Grant is coordinating multiple Federal campaigns via telegraph. General William T. Sherman's army advances toward Atlanta from Chattanooga beginning May 7. Major Ephraim Dawes and his Fifty-Third Ohio regiment are part of the onslaught. A series of battles erupt as General Joseph Johnston's Confederates try to counter. In Virginia, Grant gives up trying to crack Lee's lines around Spotsylvania. That two-week meat grinder has inflicted eighteen thousand Union and fourteen thousand Confederate casualties. The soldiers have never experienced anything so brutal and exhausting. Grant and Meade devise another southeast flanking maneuver beginning May 21. Most of the depleted Union army reaches the North Anna River after two days and 45 miles of hard marching.[AA] General Warren's Fifth Corps, including the Sixth Wisconsin, crosses on pontoons near the Jericho Mill on May 23, before Confederates can fortify the south bank.[10]

Monday, May 23, 1864, Marietta, Ohio

First Lieutenant Charles Gates, Company A, 148th Ohio Volunteer Infantry, is dressed in his new uniform and ready to leave the house

---

[AA] See Overland Campaign map at end of chapter

just past midnight. He sneaks into Bettie's room, gives his sleeping little sister a kiss on the cheek, and heads down the stairs. Betsey and Mary are waiting to see him off.

Charley and Mary hug, and he kisses her forehead. "Goodbye, Mrs. Dawes," he says with a smile. "I'll be back about the same time as your husband, so you better plan a big party for us!"

"I can't wait for that day!" Mary replies.

He then turns to Betsey. "I know, Mother, I'll be careful. But there's nothing to worry about. The most we'll be doing is filling the dull trenches where Butler's army is bottled up outside Richmond."

Charles Beman Gates (Age 19)

Betsey Gates does worry, of course, as she hugs him and kisses both cheeks. "You know your father wanted to be here, but he might meet you on his way home. Be sure to write. Adaline packed some food for you; I put it in your knapsack. God bless you, Son!" She tries to hold back tears, but they form anyway.

Charley reaches in his vest for a pocket watch and says, "I've got to go! It won't do for an officer to be late. My company is on the first car down to Belpre."

Mary and Betsey lean on each other in the doorway, acknowledging his wave and familiar smile from the corner. Then, walking with his easy gait down Putnam Street toward town, he is quickly lost to the darkness.

William Cutler is awakened before dawn by pounding on the front door of the Old Stone House. "Mr. Cutler, there's been a derailment just south of here, and it's bad. It's the train carrying Colonel Moore's regiment from Marietta. He sent me to get you. Several cars are off the track, and there's some bad injuries!"

William is at the scene by daylight, and it's a mess. He sees the tender (coal car) and four other cars off the tracks down an embankment, but the only car severely damaged seems to be the first one. Soldiers have pulled out three bodies, now covered with blankets, and several injured are being tended to. Colonel Moore and Engineer Morse approach.

Moore says, "Mr. Cutler, thank you for coming. It's a tragedy, horrible. Only 5 miles from starting, and this happens! Jeremiah Stuckey of Company A was killed, plus two students who only came along for the ride to Belpre, John McKinn and young Nugget—can't recall his first name."

William sadly shakes his head and looks at Morse. He asks, "Pierce, what happened?"

"The rains must have weakened that section," Morse says. "The track caved as soon as the engine passed. There was nothing I could do."

"All right, I can see it," William says to the distraught engineer. He knows him to be a capable man. "We'll have to get this track realigned to higher ground as soon as we can."

The three head toward the disaster for a better look. William recognizes Charley Gates resting under a tree in obvious discomfort. Charley and his little sister, Bettie, have been frequent visitors to the Old Stone House for years. "Charley, are you hurt?" William asks.

Lt. Gates painfully rises and salutes the colonel as he replies to William Cutler, "I got slammed into some seats when we tipped over. It hurts a bit, but I'll be all right. My watch got the worst of it, though," he says with an attempt at humor, holding up his mangled timepiece.

Colonel Moore says, "Lieutenant, you better have the surgeons look you over. You may need to go back with the other injured."

Charley responds quickly, "Sir, I'm all right, a bit bruised is all. I don't want to leave my company just over that."

Moore hesitates and then relents: "All right, if you feel up to it. We'll be marching the rest of the way to Belpre pretty soon, so if you can, see to your company."

Charley salutes and gingerly walks away, his chest in more pain than he let on. He thinks, *I might as well get rid of this watch. We'll pass the McClure house. I'll ask them to get it back home for repair.*

Tuesday, May 24, 1864, Marietta, Ohio

Julia Cutler enters the Gates home at Fourth and Putnam, greeted by Mary. "Hello, dear," Julia says, "it's so nice to see you. I hope you are coping with all this anxiety."

Mary's furrowed brow and sorrowful demeanor readily provide an answer. "Well, Auntie," Mary says, "I am trying to cope, but it is *so hard* imagining what Rufus and Ephraim and now Charley are all facing right now. Every day, the paper lists the casualties from Virginia and Georgia, and there are *always* soldiers we know. Sometimes, I just cry, and I'm not ashamed to say it."

"Oh, I know, dear," Julia responds. "I feel the same. We are so thankful Charley survived that terrible wreck! Your mother-in-law and I stopped at the site today. It was awful. Those poor boys! Mrs. McClure lives close by, and she gave me Charley's watch to return to your mother. He thought perhaps it can be repaired. Here it is."

Mary looks at the dented metal and shudders. She thinks of her brother and what might have been.[11]

Friday, May 27, 1864—the Old Stone House

Julia Cutler continues to record both pleasant experiences and worrisome war news:

> Lizzie & little Sarah went to town with William. He came back on the 11 o'clock train, and went back on the three o'clock to bring them home on the cars in the evening. Lizzie got Nancy a pretty black calico dress for helping her do the wall papering. An old man called and wanted to tell fortunes. I told him No! Our fortunes came to us fast enough.
>
> Ephe is twenty-four years old today. How little we expected for him such a life of peril as he is now enduring. Sister Sarah [Dawes] sent down a letter just received. He passed safely through the battle of Resaca, Ga. His regiment lost 47 killed and wounded and were highly complimented. He writes "they were perfectly wild with enthusiasm." Sherman's advance has been thus far a perfect success. … Ephe's horse was shot under him.

Saturday Afternoon, May 28, 1864—Fifty-Third Ohio Line of Battle near Dallas, Georgia

Whooping Rebel troops clad in gray and butternut emerge from the woods 25 yards away with two battle flags waving and officers cheering their men forward. Major Ephraim Dawes is behind Company C as the enemy makes a dash for his regiment's breastworks. The Ohioans fire, many Rebels go down, but the remainder are shouting, cursing, and shooting back. Led by their color bearers, a mob of them keep coming. Major Dawes seizes a rifle from one of his men and fires at the nearest flag, throws it back, and draws his sword. Ephraim yells, "Never let that flag cross the road! Shoot that dirty scoundrel with the flag!" He turns to order a charge over the works, aiming to capture their flags. Instantly, a bullet pierces through his face like a red-hot iron. Blood spouts over his chest, and he drops face-first into the dirt, sword and hat falling off.

Before touching the ground, he thinks, *I am killed! … But no! I can hear the noise and see the bullets striking.*

He crawls on hands and knees 20 yards to the rear while coughing up dirty blood and gasping for breath, waving off a man coming to help, then reaches a sapling he uses to prop himself upright. His uniform coat is wet with his blood. As bullets continue to zing past him, his hand moves up to assess the damage. In shock, he feels his shattered lower jaw. The chin is torn and hanging down, the lower lip and all the lower teeth but two are gone. His tongue hurts and must be partially cut. But his upper jaw angles are intact, and that provides some mental relief. Still, he knows it is a horrible wound, and the pain is excruciating! He can barely breathe through the gruesome mess that is his face.[12]

Sunday Afternoon, May 29, 1864, Marietta, Ohio—the Gates Home

Betsey, Beman, and Mary Gates take time after dinner to write Charley, now with his unit at Harpers Ferry, Virginia. The family has heard more train-wreck details and are thankful Charley was spared. The dented watch, however, is indicative of a nasty chest bruise, at the least. Mary pens this to her brother:

> The folks are all writing to you today. As Mother writes to "her all" you will no doubt count her letter a little better than the rest, but this you must know Charley, my letter is actuated by pure disinterested love.
>
> No doubt all the letters today will tell you … we do miss you. Adaline the cook has lost an important prop. … [H]er pies and cakes dry up for want of someone to eat them. Bettie misses you at all times … and the young autocrat … sees you still in her dreams. But Mother, "Oh if these lips had language!" And Charley … I miss you "boat nights," to do this, to stop doing that. … I guess you never thought I would think of you so many times in a day and wish you would come in and make me laugh. … And so it goes, we all talk of you and plan for your coming home. The empty chair on the other side of the table, the old ragged hat … the "boy's room" darkened. The old familiar things that you left behind all remind us of what might have been and call out a heartfelt "Thank God" … while three at your side were hastened to eternity.

I suppose Father tells you in his letter of going to the front and really seeing Rufus and shaking hands with him. And did he tell you the whole of Ewell's Corps passed him …?

Nineteen-year-old First Lieutenant Charles Gates undoubtedly knows how much his family misses him, and today, he longs for his home and now-darkened room. He has dutifully attempted to march, drill, and camp without tents since suffering the chest injury, not wanting to leave his company. But he has developed a deep cough with sharp pain and breathlessness. The surgeon is finally called. He is shocked to see a huge chest bruise with probable rib damage. But worse still, he diagnoses pneumonia. Charley is moved into a Harpers Ferry boarding house. Soon, an urgent telegraph message is sent by his long-time friends to Mr. and Mrs. Gates.

Tuesday, May 31, 1864, Marietta, Ohio

Mary sits at Uncle Bozzy's post office and quickly reads two letters from Rufus, dated May 24 and 25. Rufe writes, "I got the gloves and am very thankful for them now—I wear them much." *Good,* she thinks, then reads on and is immediately worried for her husband. He writes of a battle on the 23rd "which for an hour raged with great fury."[AB]

Two divisions of confederates under A. P. Hill made a surprise evening attack, almost succeeding in driving the Union Fifth Corps into the North Anna River near their pontoon crossing at Jericho Mill. General Cutler had ordered Rufus' Sixth Wisconsin to anchor the connection with Griffin's division on the left. On came whooping confederates of A. P. Hill's Rebel corps, breaking most of Colonel Robinson's Iron Brigade who were about to make supper They could not form in time and were chased in disorder toward the pontoon bridge. Rufus kept his Sixth Wisconsin together and, with supporting regiments and Captain Mink's battery, fought and stopped the Rebel onslaught, then joined a counterattack to drive the Johnnies away. The Sixth lost two killed plus eleven wounded, among them Lieutenant John Beely with a bullet in his chest.[13] Mary's chin quivers as she reads:

I wonder if a man can go forever without being hurt in battle. My escape almost appalls me sometimes. It does seem as though your prayers were shielding. Pray for me my dear wife. I firmly believe God hears and answers your earnest entreaties.

[AB] See North Anna map at end of chapter

With my whole love and earnest sympathy for you in our hour of trial and a kiss. Rufe

May 25th, 1 p.m.

My dear Wife

We are again closing for a desperate battle. The bullets clip the green leaves over my head as I lay in the breastworks writing. I thank you for your good, cheering letters, and pity you more than I can write.

I am very willing to write Lucy, and should as soon as you asked me, if the campaign had not completely taken my time, thoughts, labor, everything from all but the work before me and you. I have had no full night's sleep since May 7th when I took command of the regiment. Day after day and night after night we have fought, marched and dug entrenchments. I have not changed my clothing since May 3rd. I have not the composure with bullets clipping, and [the] poor bleeding, dying soldiers around me, to write as I could wish. But with my warmest love for your good kind loving letters. I am, Rufe[14]

Mary slowly walks home, deeply feeling sadness and guilt for telling Rufe of Lucy's disappointment in not receiving any letters. *With all he is going through! He is so depressed!* She is sharing all this with her mother when an urgent knock is heard at the front door. The telegraph message from Harpers Ferry arrives: "Your son C. Gates deathly ill. Advise come immediately. Mrs. Hartshorn boarding house, H. F." The Gates family is suddenly plunged into unimagined fear and panic.

A distraught Mary must stay with eleven-year-old Bettie as Beman and Betsey Gates rush to be at their son's bedside. Suspense and helplessness madden them all. But the train trip that begins that afternoon is agonizingly slow. First, traveling the same track Charley took a week ago, past the accident scene to Belpre. The river ferry across to Parkersburg. Then the Baltimore and Ohio Railroad east to Harpers Ferry, over 300 miles of winding track and twenty-five stops in between. Mr. and Mrs. Gates have traveled this scenic line before on worry-free business trips and to visit Mary in Massachusetts. On this night, the trip is an excruciating eternity. Beman and Betsey cling to each other and pray for their son.

This Same Tuesday, May 31—Boarding House of Mrs. Louisa Hartshorn, Harpers Ferry

It is 7:30 in the morning, and Captain Knowles and Darius Towsley visit Lieutenant Gates at the boarding house. They are shocked to see Charley obviously failing. His breath is raspy, and he is very weak. Towsley stays and does what he can, and he writes notes that can be given to Charley's parents. After a while, Towsley asks Charley if he wants to say a word for his family.

"Tell Father and Mother and my two sisters I bid them goodbye. I am ready to go."

Towsley says in response, "Lieutenant, you have done your best for your country."

Charley weakly replies, "I want to do my duty for my country." Then, "I would like to speak to a minister." A chaplain from a New York unit is summoned and prays with Charley, who responds, "Amen, amen."

Charley drifts in and out of consciousness during the day. Captain Knowles returns and tells him that his father is arriving by train. Charley asks what time and, not being sure, Towsley says, "1:00 p.m."

Charley responds, "There won't be any chance of seeing my father." He lingers and is encouraged to hang on for his father's arrival. "I don't give it up yet," he says, but then soon wakes again and mutters, "I won't live that long. I don't want to be buried here."

Lieutenant Colonel Kincade and Sam Shipman, a cousin, have come to his side, and they promise Charley he will be sent home. It is just after 5:00 p.m., Towsley dutifully records, that Lieutenant Charles Beman Gates "turned on his back and died without a groan, or moving a muscle." Charley will never see the cheerful and heartfelt letters his family wrote to him on Sunday. His exhausted and grief-stricken parents, Betsey and Beman Gates, cannot arrive in time to tender love and comfort or to say goodbye.[15]

Thursday, June 2, 1864—the Old Stone House

Julia Cutler has recorded the war's tumultuous events for three years. She sometimes reflects upon becoming somewhat inured to the continual tragedies. Today, however, tragedy has hit home:

Lucy came on evening train. Ephe is wounded, lower jaw shot off. They received the dispatch from William who is in Chillicothe, also one from Ephe June 1st from Kingston "I leave for Nashville today." …

We are extremely anxious about Ephe, but thankful he is alive.

Lucy & I went to Marietta on the extra train which took up Mr. & Mrs. Gates and poor Charlie's lifeless body. Several persons from Marietta were on who went to Belpre to meet them. We went in the omnibus to the Gates' house—it was a sad scene.

Major Ephraim Dawes manages a rail car seat for an agonizing train journey heading north this day. His face is wrapped in a cloth. He is in extreme pain, gasping for breath, choking, miserable, still wearing his blood-soaked uniform. If not for his black servant Wesley, a newspaperman friend named Hayden Smith, a helpful medical steward, and money borrowed from an officer he does not know, he would not be here. The surgeons advise staying away from army hospitals, where infection is rampant. They tell him to go to Cincinnati. There is a doctor there named Blackman who might help him. It will be a long and excruciating trip.[16]

Friday, June 3, 1864, Marietta, Ohio

The whole community shares in the grief being experienced by the Gates and Bosworth families over Charley's death. Mary, already in constant worry about Rufus, is now in complete despair. She knows she must be strong for her parents and for Bettie, but life will never be the same without the son and brother they all loved so much.

The *Marietta Register's* Wednesday edition reported this:

> Died: It pains us to announce the death of Charles Beman GATES, First Lieutenant of company A, 148th Regiment. He died after a short illness at Harper's [sic] Ferry, Tuesday of this week—May 31st—only eight days after leaving Marietta, in his usual health. His age was about 20. Lieut. Gates was the only son of Beman Gates, Esq., of this city. He was a young man of a good deal of promise, of fine talents, a pleasant and agreeable associate—and beloved by all who knew him. He was a member of the Junior Class in Marietta College. Mr. and Mrs. Gates left for Harper's [sic] Ferry Tuesday evening, but too late to see their cherished son alive. They are expected to arrive home with his remains this [Thursday] night.[17]

The funeral service at the First Congregational Church on Front Street begins at two o'clock. The church is full as Marietta College president

Israel Andrews offers a heartfelt address. Rev. Wickes, heartbroken for the family who has led the congregation in joyful song for many years, prays now for their strength and comfort. It is a short journey to Mound Cemetery, where the crushed Gates family tearfully mourns as their beloved Charley is lowered into a grave.[18]

Many of these same townspeople call at Sarah Dawes's home before and after the service to inquire about Ephraim, expressing their sympathy and regret. Lucy Dawes and Julia Cutler split time there and up the street at the Gates home. Later, the two ladies meet the Cincinnati train that brings William Cutler. He has no news except that Ephraim is wounded very badly and is headed to Nashville.[19] Almost lost to mind is Rufus.

Monday, June 6, 1864—Union Entrenchments on the Cold Harbor Battlefield

Lt. Col. Rufus Dawes is lying behind his log-protected headquarters trench, contemplating the past week. The army had made another southeast maneuver, crossing the Pamunkey River at Hanover and reaching the Cold Harbor crossroads 17 miles east of Richmond! Elated troops praise General Grant for bringing them this close to victory without a major battle. But a narrow window of opportunity to isolate Robert E. Lee's army from Richmond disappeared when Union forces were too exhausted to take advantage. Tenacious Rebel soldiers worked all night to again build a strong defensive line. Grant ordered a massive assault on June 3 anyway. It was a disaster. Thousands of Northern troops were slaughtered in the ill-conceived attack. Dawes can only be thankful his men were not involved. The opposing armies now face each other behind entrenchments, trying not to become a target for sharpshooters.

A flurry of Rebel bullets zip overhead. Dawes looks up to see William Jackson running zigzag toward him through the scattered trees behind the trench. William crawls the last 30 feet to avoid the shots, and Dawes pulls him in. Panting and sweaty, William hands his boss a letter. It is from Beman Gates and is marked "Deliver Quickly."

Dawes reads, "Charley died at Harper's Ferry on Tuesday." Rufe closes his eyes, says, "Oh no, not Charley," and immediately feels immense concern and pity for Mary. He recalls last January and Charley's plaintive question to him: "You are part of the Iron Brigade! How do you think I will feel for taking no part in the war and being in the same family?" Rufe thinks of the inexplicable irony: He, spared through so many battles, while poor Charley is suddenly gone before having a chance to serve.

Rufus mourns his brother-in-law but is still unaware of his other brother's situation. In Marietta, Uncle William receives a message sent by Ephraim from Nashville, dated yesterday. It reads, "Leaving for Cincinnati tomorrow—Wound doing well." William and his niece Lucy Dawes will meet him in Cincinnati via the railroad, and all will then meet with Dr. George C. Blackman.

Thursday, June 9, 1864—Bivouac near Railroad Bridge over Chickahominy River, Virginia

An approaching Colonel Edward Bragg shouts out, "I almost can't believe it, Rufus, great news today! Kellogg is alive! The Rebs declared him a prisoner. I'm not sure where. And today, General Cutler says there's been no casualties in the whole division, the first time in a month."

Dawes's face lights up. "John back from the dead! Are you sure? Thank God! Great news for his family!" Then, thinking of a Rebel prison, Rufe says, "He must be having it tough right now. But still ... I'll write his wife right away!"

Bragg sits down and says, "Amazing, isn't it? We gain one back, but so many others lost. I'm sure you've heard about Haskell, killed last week at Cold Harbor. But now that we are away from the constant firing ... it feels strange. My mind is numb. I'm too stupid to write my wife and tell her anything more than I am alive and well."

Rufus replies, "I know. My senses are totally blunted. I just learned that my wife's brother has died while with his hundred days' regiment! I can hardly believe it, such a fine young fellow. I don't know what to write Mary. She's devastated."

Bragg responds, but with little expression. How many "fine young fellows" has he seen die? "I'm sorry to hear. By the way, that reminds me ... You will be interested in this. I answered for you, so you don't need to see Surgeon Beech." Smiling, he hands Dawes a folded paper, marked up with a series of chief surgeon endorsements seeking information from every command level between Washington and brigade headquarters, five of them, plus notes from Secretary Chase and War Secretary Stanton!

"What is this?!" Dawes exclaims. He then sees the attached letter from his father. "Oh no! This is humiliating! That crazy man will do anything to keep his family bowed down in shame. To think this passed through so many hands, being laughed at!"

"Oh, I don't know, Rufus," says Bragg. "Maybe going to the top reflects his concern."

Rufus responds, "You don't know him. This is all political influence show-off and personal ego."

"Well, regardless," says Bragg, "I have more news. There's another organization change. My Pennsylvania brigade is being transferred to Griffin's First Division, to be commanded by Colonel Joshua Chamberlin, the Gettysburg hero. And, old Gray Wolf Cutler wants me to replace our Colonel Robinson. Officially he is 'sick,' but you know the situation. You've had to take command for him yourself lately. So this resolves it, and I'm back with the Iron Brigade!"

A kaleidoscope of emotions fills Rufe's mind as he writes Mary. Yes, he feels refreshed with a creek bath, change of clothes, a basket of fresh strawberries, and even a shave. Yet the past month has been gruesome. Kellogg's resurrection is wonderful, but there is so much violence and scenes of blood and screams seared into his brain. Now poor Charley is dead, and the Gates family is grieving and inconsolable. To add worry, William Jackson is sick, maybe with smallpox. The ambulances won't take him, fearing contamination. It is too much. Discontent and bitterness creep into his psyche[20]:

My dear Wife

I was distressed last night not to hear from you, for I know it is because you are overwhelmed with sorrow that you can't write. Dear Mary, I would give the world to be with you to help and comfort you. I can hardly wait to hear ... how you are, and your poor mother, and Bettie and your father.

All is quiet here. The pickets are friendly. A few moments ago, the enemy tossed a shell toward our camp ... a sort of evening salutation.

We have heard from Capt. Kellogg as alive, well & a prisoner. I wrote a note to his wife. I know such tidings of me would be blessed news to you, and believe they will to her.

Col. Bragg now commands our brigade. Col. Robinson is sick. He is a Rip Van Winkle and a coward anyhow. Dr. Preston has come back full of his oily manners. ... Lt. Harris has proven a shirk and a coward.

I have felt very miserable all day in foreboding of evil to you. I hope and trust the next mail will bring me some word of cheer.

As this evening closes back in Ohio, Julia Cutler sums up an eventful and emotional day. Her nephew Ephraim Dawes (still her "Ephe") has arrived at the Old Stone House to convalesce. All agree it is the best place—away from the city, quiet, and cooler. Sarah Dawes is both thankful to see her son and heartbroken at his ugly wound. Julia writes:

> Ephe, accompanied by Lucy and Wesley his colored servant, arrived on the evening train, Mrs. Dawes met them at Scotts Landing and came with them. The Major though very tired was in good spirits and his wound, a ghastly one to behold, is said to be doing well. Wesley has been taught how to cleanse it with a syringe & to dress it properly. Ephe has such wonderful fortitude—he never complained or makes ado about what he has suffered & is still suffering.

> Dr. Blackman told him that by next October he thought, he would be well enough to have an operation performed. A new under lip will have to be made, a new jaw and teeth inserted - after which he thinks the disfigurement will not be great.

Saturday, June 11, 1864—near the Chickahominy River

Mary has finally felt capable of writing. Rufe is elated but is shocked as he reads of Ephraim's wound for the first time. Similar wounds he has seen are awful, but usually not fatal. He quickly responds:

> I have just got a dispatch from Uncle Wm. that Eph is at Cincinnati & doing well. I hope it is not so bad as I had feared.

> I am going to get Wm.[AC] into a hospital I guess. Poor, faithful fellow, he shall not lack for care if I can help it.

> Tell Luce she <u>must</u> take $25 anyhow from you. I have not got any money here to send. I know she can't afford to pay for a trip[21] out of her own money. I should be mad if she don't take it. Army is on the move and so is the mail. In great haste—Your loving Rufe

---

[AC] William Jackson.

Wednesday, June 15, 1864—South of the James River, East of Petersburg, Virginia

"Finally, Babcock, we're away from that lousy water at the Chickahominy! Look at this pontoon bridge! Almost a half-mile long, and all the boats. It's a sight! Reminds me of the Ohio River at Marietta."

Acting adjutant Cuyler Babcock responds to Dawes, "And we've got our wagon, which means a chance for a tent and better meals. Was that General Gibbon I saw you with?"

Dawes replies, "Yes, and he's *Major General* Gibbon now. It was good to see him. I told him I was sorry to hear about Colonel Haskell. The general's division was badly mauled at Cold Harbor, and Frank's death was an especially tough loss for him. They were close. The general told me we are stealing a march, that Grant's got Lee wondering where we are going. If the Eighteenth Corps can seize Petersburg before Lee gets there, we can isolate Richmond without a fight. I hope he's right. Gibbon shook my hand and then said, 'By all the ordinary chances of war, Dawes, you should have been dead long ago!' How's that for a parting word?"

Babcock simply shakes his head. They both know Gibbon is right. Thinks Dawes, *If I can survive only one more month ...* [22]

7:00 a.m., Sunday, June 19, 1864—Petersburg Trenches

My dear Wife

I had not time to read your good, long letters and one from Eph last night. ... Yesterday afternoon another horrid massacre of our corps was enacted. We charged over half a <u>mile</u> over an open field on entrenchments that <u>could not be</u> climbed by the men if they got there. ... We are now lying in rifle pits from which it [is] almost sure death to raise your head. It is awfully disheartening to think we have Generals who will send their men to such sure destruction.

It is very sad to think of Eph so terribly wounded. Don't you think he is a brave man ...?

There is a sudden disturbance on the line. Dawes investigates and returns. The pencil drifts downward as he writes:

(A poor fellow was just now hit at our breastwork, killed)[23]

Death is ever-present; soldiers have become hardened to it. The Fifth Corps had taken another brutal beating. General Cutler reported losses in his division at one-third of those engaged. In Griffin's division, Colonel Joshua Chamberlin took a bullet through his body hip-to-hip. Doctors think his outlook is grim.[24]

The letters from home do much to relieve Rufe's stress, however, and he chuckles reading Ephraim's attempt at grim humor:

The Johnnies pinked me at Dallas, Ga. two weeks ago today. … It makes a terrible looking wound and will disfigure me considerably I think. The doctors seem to think they can easily fix it. … Have concluded to quit smoking, and singing, and whistling and all such frivolous amusements. Came pretty near concluding to quit talking and eating the first few days. I nearly died, couldn't scarcely swallow …[25]

Tuesday, June 21, 1864—Petersburg Trenches

Rufus Dawes sits in his "four feet deep, eight feet long, three feet wide hole, shielded by green boughs" 400 yards from the enemy. He again writes Mary about the most recent failed attack, that of Saturday, the 18th:

I have lost fifty-five men before Petersburg, six killed outright … less than any regiment in the brigade. I saved one man's life that I am sure of. A man of the 19th [Indiana Regiment] was shot in the arm. … It cut the main artery so that he would bleed to death in five minutes. I held the artery in my fingers until I had no strength left in my hands and finally got a towel twisted by a bayonet on his arm so as to stop blood running. All under musketry. Our brigade was simply food for powder in the assault. …

I wish I had some facilities for answering your letters. If I only was home, I'd _more_ than realize your dream in the way I'd hug and kiss you. Rufe

The dull time in the hole, dangerous though it is, provides an opportunity to respond to Ephraim:

I felt very much concerned about your voice. But Mary tells me it is very little injured and when the doctors manufacture for you some teeth, lip, jaw bone and I forget what else, it will be good as ever. But seriously I am very glad to know your voice is not injured, for we all know you have talents oratorical and for music. ...

We have been fighting very philosophically. As the boys have it, "fighting like the devil when there was a fight to win and running like the devil when there wasn't." If it had not been for my sprained ankle I should have run faster. ... Every boy rallied every time at the colors and was ready to go again.

Rufe also responds to several letters his father, Henry, has written. Rufe begins with a polite thank you. Then, family business. Henry needs his estranged wife, Sarah's, agreement to sell an Ohio land parcel:

For your earnest solicitude for me and efforts to honor my memory when I was believed dead, I am sincerely grateful. I have thus far been wonderfully preserved through the deadly storm of battle. ...

[B]efore I consent to influence my Mother (who will probably do what I say) to sign this deed ... [is the property] all upon which she has tangible, unobstructed security for her alimony? If it is, she can only sign the deed on condition of ... right of dower upon such other property of yours ... equivalent and available for her yearly allowance of three hundred dollars. Or better, upon condition that by payment to her of an agreed amount you be released from the claim to alimony.

I lay these conditions because life-long experience has shown me that your unrelenting effort to keep your property clear of her legal claims has not been for the sole purpose of facilitating your business, but because you did not want her or your daughters to have any more property than you could help.

I expect, if alive, to leave the service in about three weeks. ... I have prospect of a reasonably lucrative position in Ohio which I am inclined to accept.[26]

There, Rufe thinks. *I am no longer under his thumb. It is time to be blunt. I will not let my mother be taken advantage of, and I will never live near him again.*

The day ends with another distasteful duty, besides trying to stay alive: He is summoned to appear before a Fifth Corps board of inquiry evaluating Col. Robinson's fitness to command the Iron Brigade. It is a loathsome task. He has served with Robinson for three years. A board member directly asks, "Do you think Col. Robinson qualified to command a brigade in an active campaign?"

Dawes pauses and then answers, "In my opinion, he is not well-qualified," clarifying under questioning that Col. Robinson has displayed a "lack of energy."

Col. Robinson is present to defend himself and asks Rufus eleven consecutive questions. Dawes provides straightforward answers to these and others posed by the board members. Left unmentioned is Robinson's state of mind on May 12, and Dawes does not volunteer that unseemly incident. The board is left to read between the lines and question other witnesses.[27]

Colonel Bragg is outside the headquarters, and the two discuss the command situation. Says Bragg, "I've got my nomination as brigadier general! That will put you in complete command of the Sixth. Now we'll need to get your promotion to colonel!"

Dawes extends his hand. "Ed, that's great! Congratulations, finally!" *And*, he thinks, *lay off the whiskey!* "But they won't promote me now. The Sixth doesn't have enough men to warrant a colonel, and besides, I'm getting out next month anyway."

Bragg answers, "I'll see about the promotion. Lucius Fairchild is on our side in Madison, with his office next door to the governor. He knows you deserve it, so the rules be damned. I'll get up a petition and endorsement. Besides, General Cutler will approve it too. You know he doesn't want to lose you. I've heard he has some ideas up his sleeve."

The last comment creates some uneasiness. *Something to be wary of*, thinks Dawes.

Thursday, June 30, 1864, Marietta, Ohio,

The Gates home has lost its vibrancy since Charley's death. Mary's parents remain sorely depressed, everyone still in mourning dress. The piano sits unused. Adding to the stress is an attempted burglary. A night watchman shouted at the thief and fired a shot that scared him away. Mary shared the news with Rufus. Tonight, on this warm evening, Mary Gates and Francy Bosworth chat in the backyard.

"Francy," says Mary, "two letters from Rufus arrived today, and with all the chaos and violence around him, he still writes such encouraging words to me. I asked him about mourning clothes, and he says, 'Don't you remember I most admired you dressed in black? A man who objects to his wife dressing in any way she chooses is generally a mean huzby. By all means, dress as becomes your mourning for the loss of a dear brother.' How can I not love him more for that!"

Mary continues, "Then he mentions his servant, William Jackson. William was sick with the measles, and Rufe got him into an army hospital—not an easy thing to do, him a contraband and all. Rufe writes, 'I shall try to bring him home with me. He wants to go with me. I shall give him a chance for a common school education if I can.' William has been so faithful! I met him in Milwaukee and like him very much. Every day, he sneaks up to the front line in the dark before dawn to bring Rufe his daily meals. But now another worry! Rufe mentions possible trouble getting out of the army! Something about new rules to prevent veteran officers from leaving the service!"

Francy tries to soothe her cousin's mood: "Well, if anyone can argue a case, it's Rufus. Let's not worry about *paperwork* dangers."

Mary understands her meaning; those flying metal projectiles are of most concern.

Francy shifts the subject: "It was nice to see Ephraim the other day. Lucy sounds confident in what the doctors say, and everyone is amazed at his courage and positive attitude. Lucy dislikes his lady friend, though. What do you know?"

Mary replies, "Her name is Ella. I don't know much about her or where she's from. He's infatuated, proposed marriage, I think, but I'll put it this way: Her words and actions don't reflect a wholesome or caring nature. Mrs. Dawes feels the same, but neither she nor Lucy want to butt in while he's dealing with that terrible wound. It's very awkward."

Francy responds, "I hope everything turns out well. He's vulnerable right now, and he deserves someone who really cares for him."

Mary knows Francy better than anyone and realizes there is more to her cousin's comment than just friendly concern.

As Mary and Francy talk, Lt. Col. Dawes sits in his sultry trench, writing to his wife. The front line is quiet but dangerous. One man was instantly killed last night by a random shot fired in the darkness.[28] Rufus deals with that, then delves into jumbled month-end paperwork exacerbated by missing company officers. But there is another struggle, this one with the war department: Secretary of War Edwin Stanton rules that officers of Veteran Volunteer regiments who "accepted" the thirty-day veteran furlough with their reenlisted men thereby signaled an intention to "re-muster" themselves for *three years*! This includes Dawes and eleven other Sixth Wisconsin officers whose terms expire on July 15. None of them ever stated an intention to reenlist, and besides, the officers were *ordered* to accompany their regiment back home. The illegality and unfairness of it all breeds indignation, as Rufus writes:

> [I]t is a hardship to have a shadow thrown over honorable service just at its close ... an iron hand upon the men who came [into the service] freely three years ago and whom they have in their power. It is mean beyond measure.

Lt. Col. Rufus Dawes is not a man to retreat from a just cause. He will engage in a formidable defense of his right to return home after three years of honorable, truly *heroic* service to his country. His prolific ancestors William Dawes, Manasseh, and Ephraim Cutler would have done the same.

Monday, July 4, 1864—Petersburg Trenches

> My dear Wife—I feel so stupid and languid and good for nothing today [that] I can hardly write. It's rather the stalest birth day of independence and myself I can remember. There are great rumors tonight of a great explosion under the enemy's works. General Cutler is full of projects to get a Colonel's command of 840 men for me, but aside from my objections ... there are not enough men left in the 2nd, 5th and 6th to do it.[AD]

> I got a letter from Eph with a line from his girl enclosed. She writes very prettily—tell me all about her when you have seen her. I got a letter from Kate also. I am afraid she has hard times.

> The boys who go out on the 16th are getting very anxious. Twelve days only is short, but much history may be made in that time here. I trust Gen. Grant has more sense than to assault their works in front again. With my love & a good kiss. Rufe

---

[AD] General Cutler's idea to consolidate these three regiments and place Dawes in command.

Friday, July 8, 1864—in a Wooded Bivouac behind the Petersburg Trenches

Lt. Col. Dawes submits a formal request to Fifth Corps headquarters requesting he and his fellow officers be allowed to muster out of the service on July 15. He writes Mary of this "first shot" and notes that his brigade commander and old friend, General Edward Bragg, will "lend us every help in his power." Bragg's boss, however, Division Commander General Lysander Cutler, "will do what he can to put obstacles in the way." Those two have butted heads before.

The drama unfolding near Petersburg is almost matched at home. It involves Ephraim's love life. Lucy sends Rufe a letter questioning Ella's suitability as a wife for Ephraim, thus drawing him into the controversy. He penned this to Mary yesterday evening:

> I don't know what I can say or do about Eph. What _can_ be done? Only to try to make Ella better when she becomes our sister? I cannot think Eph would be carried away with a woman about whom there is anything <u>very</u> wrong. But I have unlimited faith in Lucy's and your own intuitions of this young lady and I feel troubled. It is said a woman's intuition of character is better than a man's judgment. What a misery it would be to find one was mistaken when too late. Let us thank God again, my own dear wife, that every day we live strengthens the faith, confidence and happiness we have in each other.

Sunday, July 10, 1864—Back in the Petersburg Trenches

Two long letters from Mary revive Rufe's spirits, even though the brigade is back for their turn in the hot, dusty, dirty trenches. But his men bring ice from a house on the skirmish line, and the Rebs don't shoot much anymore except for occasional "shrieking and howling" artillery shells. The nearby Ninth Corps area, with a division of colored infantry, sees no respite, however. Both sides shoot at each other all the time. Dawes remains hopeful that July 15 will see him return to Mary, despite silence from headquarters, but he confesses to her:

> On many accounts I shall regret to leave the regiment. ... The reg't. very much regrets to have me go. Not specially on account of personal popularity. But because they know I am <u>on hand</u> in a pinch, and because I am the best man left, in plain words.

I think your suggestion [regarding Ephraim and Ella] very good. It will be a most unhappy task to say anything despairingly to him of one to whom he is engaged, but if I may avert the calamity of an awful marriage I am willing to try in the way you suggest. It must have been a great trial for Ma to speak disapprovingly of Ella to him.

Monday, July 11, 1864—Petersburg Trenches

"Congratulations, Colonel! It's official! Here's the letter from Lucius Fairchild announcing your promotion! No one deserves it more." Gen. Edward Bragg smiles as he hands Rufus Dawes the envelope.

Dawes accepts the news with stoic gratification: "Thanks, General, I appreciate your efforts. The army probably won't muster me as such, though, if I decline to serve another three years, which I won't do. But having command of the Sixth Wisconsin, the best regiment in the army, is all I have aspired to attain."

Back in the trenches, Dawes assures his officers that the promotion does not alter his intention to leave the service. That is disappointing to those staying and comforting to those intending to depart—Dawes is their strongest advocate.

Cuyler Babcock hands Dawes a Rebel newspaper obtained on the friendly picket line. It's a story about the capture of former adjutant Brooks. Brooks had somehow convinced higher headquarters to give him thirty men from the brigade, arm them with Spencer rifles, mount them all, and place him in charge of a behind-the-lines raid to cut a railroad line. The Rebel paper proudly tells the story of how a wounded Rebel captain and six civilian neighbors bluffed Brooks into surrendering his whole band.

Dawes shakes his head. "Well, Cuyler," he says, "our man Brooks certainly made a mess of the 'secret mission' he bragged about. Now they're all on their way to a Georgia prison. I thought it was a bad idea from the start, and he not the one to lead it."[29]

The day is quiet, and Dawes responds to his sister Kate McLean's letter, in which she had sent more sad news:

Dear Kate—

I met Johnny McLean[AE] near Hawes' Store. I enjoyed his visit very much. I remember it was Sunday, and of his speaking of the

---

[AE] Kate's twenty-one-year-old stepson since her marriage to Rev. McLean, a private in the 100th Pennsylvania regiment in Burnside's Ninth Corps.

pleasure it would afford him to attend worship quietly at home. He seemed very cheerful, hopeful and brave. He must have been killed near Hawes' Store or Bethesda Church. Burnside was on our right until the 3rd of June, and ... had a heavy battle near Bethesda Church on June 2nd.[30]

Friday, July 15, 1864—behind the Petersburg Lines

First Sergeant Erastus Smith shakes the hand of his former company commander and says, "Colonel Dawes, it has been an honor to serve under your command. Good luck to you, sir."

Lt. Col. Rufus Dawes returns Smith's salute and then shakes his hand with a reply: "First Sergeant, my respects for your selfless service. The honor has been mine. My best wishes for you always."

The goodbyes continue as Dawes moves among those men mustering out today at the expiration of their three-year term. Five of his old "K" men depart for homes they have not seen since 1861, most bearing scars from bullet wounds. General Bragg is there, too, sending off men from his old Company E. The whole group departs with Captain Plummer in charge, he also leaving at his term's end but without his brother Phillip, killed in the Wilderness.

Dawes turns to Bragg after the men are gone. "Ed, thanks for your endorsement yesterday on my letter to General Williams at army head-quarters. That was my second shot. Today, I'm submitting this, the third, and I ask your endorsement again."

Bragg reads the document handed to him and says, "Your resignation, request for honorable discharge, and refusal to re-muster for another term. Whew! We've talked about this, Rufus. The army has already dismissed officers who would not re-muster, even slandering it as 'in the presence of the enemy.' It's shameful, staining their service that way for life. They could do that to you."

Dawes says, "I've got no choice but to risk it. I tried going to Washington to plead my case at the war department, but General Cutler wouldn't allow it. I've done my duty faithfully for three years, and the government should do the same. Mary and I have looked forward to this day, and yet here I still am, literally a prisoner of war. My duty now is to my wife."

Bragg sighs, "All right, I'll endorse it. But I'll note again that legally, your being mustered out due to term expiration is more proper and appropriate than a resignation. You shouldn't have to do that."

Dawes smiles and says, "Thanks, 'Counselor.' Always nice to have a good lawyer on my side—and a general, to boot!"

Rufus seeks additional counsel and advice from a man he has always respected, Uncle William Cutler. William is no longer a congressman, but his reputation is impeccable, and his political influence is significant. Rufus explains the matter and summarizes:

> My situation is very peculiar. I am not properly in the service and cannot get properly out. ... I have suddenly become a representative of a large number of old [veteran] officers in the same predicament.[31]

Saturday, July 23, 1864, Marietta, Ohio

Beman Gates sits alone at the Point, overlooking the broad Ohio River. He recalls the times Charley sat here with him, enjoying the view, pointing to the boats, talking of current events and the future. Beman and Betsey have spent many tearful moments since Charley's death, many nights holding her close as she cries herself to sleep. If not for their faith and the support of family and friends, it would be unbearable. But now there is another burden. Mary is sick with worry over Rufus. Both fear the inevitable bullet or shell that will cut down their life together, and now when he is expected to escape the peril, obstacles are thrown in his path that keep him in danger.

Beman now apprehensively opens the letter received today from Rufus, fearing bad news. Mary and Rufus have faithfully corresponded. *So*, Beman is thinking, *what message does he want to convey directly to me?* Beman reads as Rufus vents about his ongoing legal battle with the army. As a former newspaper editor, Beman realizes the depth of his son-in-law's anger, with terms such as "monstrous tyranny," "breach of faith," and "trickery" sprinkled freely in the text. Yet finally, this:

> I am much distressed about Mary when she learns the posture of affairs. To be illegally and forcibly detained ... is very trying. But I shall bear it as becomes a man, and do what is <u>right</u> before my own conscience.[32]

Beman folds the letter with misty eyes. *I did not lose my only son*, he realizes. *I have been blessed and honored with a second.*

* * * * *

The opposing armies are in stalemate. Lee is outnumbered, but with his men sheltered in formidable trenches, the odds are in his favor. Lee has sent General Jubal Early with fifteen thousand troops up the Shenandoah Valley to threaten Maryland, Pennsylvania, and Washington, D.C., itself. Grant answers Lincoln's call for help by sending the Sixth Corps hurriedly north to defend the capital. Lee's diversion borrows time. Grant does not have the strength now to make a strong move.

Or, possibly he can. Pennsylvania troops, miners in civilian life, believe they can dig a tunnel, plant explosives, and blow up a Confederate fort and trenches lying on high ground 500 feet from the Union line. The resulting gap could then be seized by armed assault, blowing a hole in Lee's lines that could split his army. The Pennsylvanian's corps commander gives his approval, assault details are planned, and troops are trained for the key mission. Grant and Meade are skeptical but eventually authorize it. Then, as always seems to happen with the Army of the Potomac, leadership failures gum the works. First, the corps commander is General Ambrose Burnside, he of woeful ability and judgment. Second, politics intervene. General Meade learns that Burnside's choice for leading the assault is a division of colored troops. If they fail and are massacred, Meade would face criticism for relying on and/or sacrificing black soldiers. "Pick another division," he tells Burnside.

"But it's the day before, and they are ready to go," Burnside protests.

Meade is adamant. A competent general would choose his next-best unit. Burnside decides to draw straws. Thirty-two-year-old Division Commander James Ledlie, in command for less than two months and claimed to be a drunk and a coward, is chosen under the lottery. It is a recipe for disaster.[33]

Saturday, July 30, 1864—Petersburg Trenches South of the Mine

Fortunately for General Bragg's Iron Brigade, they are not part of the actual assault. Their mission is to provide fire support for the attack, which will be triggered by the early morning mine explosion. Rufus Dawes feels the ground shake and looks up in time to see a tremendous blast that obliterates the Rebel fort. He describes the ferocious battle in today's letter to Mary:

> Our men gained the enemy's works, broke their line, and the advantage held would have defeated the rebel army. But history now stands with the enemy who by most desperate valor drove our men out and regained all they had lost. The pile of dead

around the ruins of the fort is the largest I ever saw. I had three men wounded … on the skirmish line.

I hear nothing from the Secretary of War. God bless you, and keep you, my dear wife. I am well and feeling as brave as I can, but it almost looks like I am doomed to suffer—a victim of military despotism. Your loving husband.

I have no stamps, and can't get any.

As hundreds of dead and wounded of the shattered Ninth Corps litter the brutal battle scene hereafter named the Crater, orders come for the Iron Brigade to move out of the trenches and head farther south. Dawes walks the trench line to coordinate the move with General Bragg and officers of the other regiments. He walks by soldiers digging a grave behind the Seventh Wisconsin sector. It is not an unusual sight; men have been killed every day by sharpshooters. Returning some time later, he sees that the grave has been filled and a headboard posted. Pausing out of curiosity, he is stunned to read, "Dawes, Flavius, Co. I, 7th Wis." In his numbed mind, he visualizes the action on May 9 at Spotsylvania, the tragic irony of an introduction over a cousin's dead body, and this young man's sorrowful words, "I'm the only one left."[34]

Now, Rufus Dawes thinks, *I am the only one left.*

Sunday, August 7, 1864—Extreme Left Flank of the Petersburg Trenches

Were it not for Dr. John Hall's company and the similar plight of other officers held against their will by the army, the frustration and anger Dawes harbors would be more distressing. The regiment is now on the army's extreme left, away from the filthy and dangerous trenches at last. No time for slacking, though, as Dawes issues orders governing camp layout, cooking times, and even police calls. His headquarters has a shady bower to shield the oppressive heat, and a cow that gives milk, courtesy of the chaplain, who wandered upon the lost animal and determined to save it.

No word has come from army headquarters or the war department about his discharge. He sent another written request to General Warren yesterday. Five officers of the Sixth, all with expired terms and away from the unit recovering from wounds or illness, have been honorably discharged. That being the case, he argues, all officers whose terms ended on July 15 should be granted the same.[35]

Hall has just returned from assisting in the Ninth Corps hospitals. "Rufus, thank God our men were not part of that mine explosion attack. I've never heard such gruesome stories of the fighting there. A fiasco! Such poor leadership! Those colored troops were thrown in at last and were caught in a massacre. The Rebs just slaughtered them, taking few prisoners. A court of inquiry started yesterday. Everyone thinks General Burnside will be relieved."

Dawes responds, "I saw it happen at a distance. The Rebels were vicious, but *they* obviously had leaders! Our generals let a great opportunity escape us again. They should *all* bear responsibility, more of them than just Burnside. How many times have we been ordered to charge against hopeless odds? Our dead testify to it. We haven't been paid in four months! The war department and army headquarters lie and cheat and keep us here illegally, then threaten disgrace if we don't agree to serve three more years! How can our army expect to win this struggle with such villains running things? Maybe we don't deserve to win at all!"[36]

John Hall is quiet as he contemplates the state of mind displayed by his friend and commander. The bitterness revealed is profound. Hall has not seen any slippage in command efficiency or devotion to the regiment's welfare. No, Rufus would not let that happen. This is an officer who demands maximum effort from himself and has always been duty bound to a fault. There is no one braver. But despondency can lead to a breakdown or recklessness. Either could be fatal to his life or his reputation. Hall concludes to himself, *My friend must get out of here.*

The Same Sunday Afternoon, Marietta, Ohio

My own dear Rufe

Another quiet Sabbath day and you away from me and in danger. It has been so long since I have seen you and known you that I am almost forgetting you. I don't mean that I don't think of you and long to have you with me, for I think of hardly anything else from morning till night, but somehow, I can't remember how you look and more especially how you act.

I dreamed of seeing Charley last night. Mother and I were standing in the front door and we saw him coming up the street, looking as he always did, his step ringing clear and loud. I was not at all frightened but thought we had made a mistake in supposing him dead, but Mother said, "You have come to us from the dead." "Yes," he said, "I have come for—" I reached out my hands for Mother and said, "Charley don't say Mother!" "Yes, I have come for Mother, I want her to be with me." And then he came up and kissed me and I can almost feel his soft warm lips on my cheek now. ... I sat on the floor holding on to him and crying because he could only stay until Mother was ready, and telling him how we missed him, and that the piano has never been opened since he died which is really true.

It is foolish I know to repeat dreams, much more so to write them out, but it has come up so often and so vividly today I can hardly look at Mother without choking up.

Mary has also been under severe stress these past months. Charley's death has devastated her family. Tens of thousands of Union soldiers have fallen all around her husband. She desperately wants Rufe away from the danger and back home with her. She needs him to get out of there.

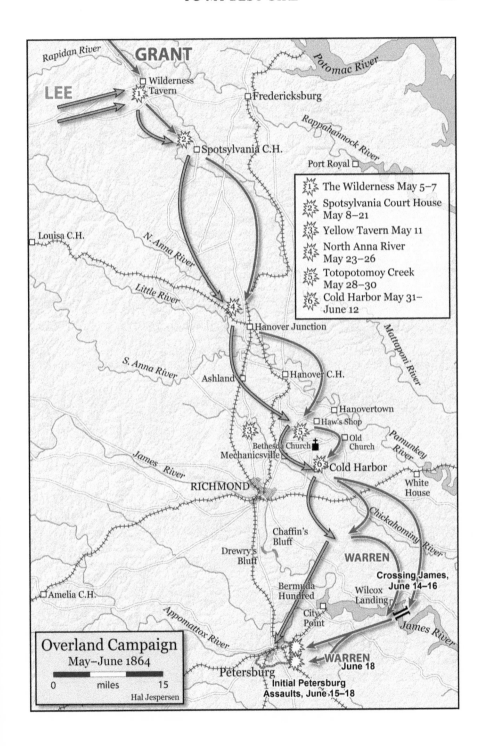

Rapidan River

GRANT

LEE

Wilderness Tavern

1

Fredericksburg

Potomac River

Rappahannock River

2

Spotsylvania C.H.

Port Royal

1 The Wilderness May 5–7

2 Spotsylvania Court House May 8–21

3 Yellow Tavern May 11

4 North Anna River May 23–26

5 Totopotomoy Creek May 28–30

6 Cold Harbor May 31– June 12

Louisa C.H.

N. Anna River

Little River

4

Hanover Junction

Mattaponi River

S. Anna River

Ashland

Hanover C.H.

Hanovertown

Haw's Shop

3

5

Bethesda Church

Mechanicsville

Old Church

Pamunkey River

James River

RICHMOND

6 Cold Harbor

White House

Chickahominy River

Chaffin's Bluff

Drewry's Bluff

WARREN

Crossing James, June 14–16

Amelia C.H.

Bermuda Hundred

Wilcox Landing

City Point

James River

Appomattox River

Overland Campaign
May–June 1864

0   miles   15

Hal Jespersen

Petersburg

WARREN
June 18

Initial Petersburg
Assaults, June 15–18

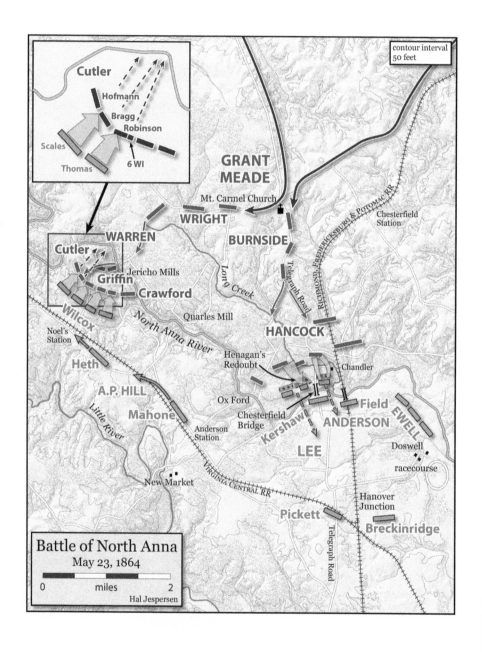

Battle of North Anna
May 23, 1864

0   miles   2

Hal Jespersen

Endnotes

1. Germanna Road is Virginia Route 3 today. The Orange Turnpike is Route 20 southwest of Route 3, then continues east as Route 3 from the intersection.

2. O. R. Vol. XXXVI, part 1, p. 615.

3. A stone marker marks the spot of Wadsworth's fatal wound. He died in Confederate hands two days later. See http://stonesentinels.com/the-wilderness/wilderness-battlefield-auto-tour/james-wadsworth/. Sixth Wisconsin battle accounts and events are from the Dawes Journal, Books 2 and 3, DAA, unless otherwise noted.

4. General Cutler reported only 1,269 men present for duty in the Fourth Division after the May 6 battle, 740 from the Iron Brigade. Most of the stragglers find their units on May 7. O. R. Vol. XXXVI, part 1, p. 459.

5. Cheek, Phillip and Pointon, Mair. History of the Sauk County riflemen, p. 94.

6. JCJ, Aug. 25, 1864, records the incident. Roster of Wisconsin Volunteers (RWV), p. 569 (The Internet Archive, http://www.archive.org).

7. The Iron Brigade trench line is now a one-way road, unfortunately named Burnside Drive, immediately north of VA Route 208, the old Fredericksburg Road. Analysis of Burnside's failure on May 10 is from Rhea, Gordon C., The Battles for Spotsylvania Courthouse and the Road to Yellow Tavern, p. 181.

8. Letters quoted herein are from the Rufus Dawes Collection, WHS, unless otherwise noted.

9. General Lee ordered two divisions of Ewell's corps on a reconnaissance-in-force to locate the Union's northern flank. Ewell withdrew at nightfall after a four-hour fight with Union Second and Fifth Corps troops. Casualties were heavy: nine hundred Confederates (with hundreds captured), and fifteen hundred Union. Grisly photos of dead Southern soldiers taken the next day provide lasting evidence of the war's tragedy.

10. Current US Hwy. 1 generally follows the route taken.

11. JCJ, May 23 and 24, 1864.

12. Derived from Harriet Dawes Wilson's The Accounting of Ephraim Dawes. Unpublished manuscript. Washington County Genealogy Library (WCGL), Marietta, Ohio. The site today is near the Georgia Route 61 overpass at Hardee Street, Dallas, GA, based on the Civil War Trust battle map. A bullet also grazed Major Dawes in the back of his head.

13. See: https://www.hmdb.org/marker.asp?marker=15167. The Civil War Trust has preserved much of the battlefield.

14. Letters from WHS.

15. Beach, Mary Dawes. Mother's Letters. DAA. Towsley provided a detailed and poignant account of Charley's last hours.

16. Wilson, Harriet Dawes. The Accounting of Ephraim Dawes. Unpublished manuscript. WCGL.

17. Dawes family records. WCGL.

18. Charley was fondly remembered for many years. In the 1902 publication History of Marietta and Washington County, 1700–1900 (http://www.archive.org), this was written: "[N]one was more generally known, and more universally beloved than Charles Beman Gates."

19. JCJ, June 2 and 3, 1864.

20. Conversations derived from Rufus Dawes letters to Mary. The surgeon endorsements note is preserved in the WHS. The three-page letter from Henry Dawes to Salmon Chase is preserved at the DAA. Rufus expresses embarrassment and disgust toward his father for writing Chase, but Henry's letter to Chase does articulate fatherly pride for his son's heroics. He also mentions Ephraim's service with General Sherman, refers to Beman Gates as "your [Chase's] friend," and is complimentary to Mary as "a very talented, well-educated and accomplished lady." Perhaps Rufus was too critical of his father in this instance, but his judgement was formed from years of experience, and none can argue his assessment.

21. Lucy's travel to Cincinnati with Uncle William to meet her wounded brother, Ephraim.

22. Dawes mentions Gibbon's comment in a letter to Mary.

23. The RWV notes that Private John Fuchs (of Buffalo, WI, Co. H) was killed in action this day.

24. The gallant and tough Joshua Chamberlin will somehow survive and return to command. Among many other accomplishments, the Medal of Honor recipient will write A Passing of the Armies: An Account of the Final Campaign.

25. EDC-NL. Letter of June 11, 1864.

26. Rufus Dawes letter to Father Henry, June 21, 1864. Rich & Peggy Dempsey Family Collection.

27. EDC-NL. There are five pages of recorded testimony. Col. Robinson will resign on July 9, 1864.

28. RWV. Pvt. Heinrich Schlueter, February '64 recruit, Co. F, killed in action this day.

29. Dawes Journal, Book 2. DAA.

30. ibid.

31. ibid.

32. ibid.

33. Bearss, Edwin C. The Petersburg Campaign, Vol.1, pp. 216 and 217. O. R. Vol. XL, pt. I, pp. 559–563 for mine sketches.

34. JCJ. Aug. 25, 1864.

35. Those absent officers receiving discharges are Captains Chas. Ford and Thomas Plummer, also Lieutenants Howard Huntington, Lloyd Harris, and John Beely. Officers present but waiting disposition of their discharge are Dawes and Lieutenants John Timmons, Wm. Goltermann, and H. B. Merchant. Dawes Journal, Book 2, DAA.

36. Derived from Rufus's letter to Mary this date. He expresses personal discouragement and contempt for the government administration.

Chapter Thirteen

An Honorable Life

Tuesday, August 9, 1864—Sixth Wisconsin Camp

Lt. Col. Rufus Dawes is brushing his horse, Bettie, as an orderly from Fourth Division headquarters approaches and hands him an envelope. Dawes salutes the soldier and pulls out the paper. It reads:

> Col, I have just received a communication from the War Department authorizing me to muster out yourself and 2nd Lt. William Goltermann of your Reg't.
>
> Very respectfully,
>
> R. Monteith, Capt. & A. C. M.
>
> 4th Div., 5th A. C.[1]

"Hurrah! Finally!" Dawes shouts so loudly that men nearby turn their heads. *But what about Timmons and Merchant*, he thinks. *Why just me and Goltermann?* Dawes hurries to find John Hall. "John, I can hardly believe it! After all this time, the war department agreed with my arguments—or at least decided not to fight it any longer. I wonder if my uncle or Mr. Gates had some influence. I'll be mustered out as a lieutenant colonel, but I don't care. I'm going home!"

Hall moves over to shake his friend's hand. "Rufus, I'm so glad for you—envious too. You deserve it more than anyone. I will miss you, though, that's for sure. But if I can find somebody else to challenge at chess, perhaps I can win a game occasionally!"

The next two days are spent signing over government property, accepting well-wishes from longtime comrades in the regiment and brigade, and visits with Generals Bragg and Cutler. Bragg comes to the Sixth's camp and meets with his old friend Rufus and with Captain Thomas Kerr of Company D, who will be taking command. Bragg comments, "Well, Rufus, I expect you'll have a happy wife at home. I'm not sure mine wants me back! Who knows when I will see her. Kerr, I know you'll do fine. God knows though, the old Sixth is just a shadow of what it once was."

Dawes responds, "Tom and I have just reviewed the roster. General, we've almost got fewer men left than we had in our companies back in '61! We crossed the Rapidan on May 4 with 370 officers and men. In the past three months, we've lost 227 killed, wounded, or missing.[2] And, we've got several in hospitals sick with the heat, bad water, or just plain worn out. I'm sorry to leave the regiment in such a state, but there's hardly a command in the whole army that is any better off."

Bragg shakes his head and replies, "Believe me, I know. I heard the number 'sixty thousand casualties' so far in the army! And there's still a lot of tough going ahead. I do know the men will miss you, as will I, but we all wish you, and your wife also, Godspeed." With that, salutes are exchanged, and Bragg is gone. As for General Cutler, Dawes accepts his good wishes and his explanation that attempts to thwart Dawes from leaving were "for the good of the service and the country." The two respect each other, despite their recent issues, and depart amicably.

The most difficult goodbyes are with the soldiers he has led and who will remain to see the conflict through. How many of these stalwart fellows will lose their lives or suffer wounds before it is all over? His good friend, tentmate, and mess companion, Dr. John Hall, will do his best to take care of them. The two will miss each other's company. Both are intelligent, articulate thinkers and have blended together to become as close as brothers. "I'll write to let you know how the Sixth is doing without you," Hall says. "You better do the same."

Friday, August 12, 1864, Marietta, Ohio

The day begins with more tragic war news. Such has become routine after three years of war. A major explosion is reported at the huge City Point, Virginia, army depot, right below General Grant's blufftop headquarters complex. Many men were killed when an ammunition barge exploded. Shells, body parts, boat pieces, and various debris rained down all around. Confederate sabotage is suspected. The disaster hits home as local boys from the 148th Ohio, Charley's unit, had been assigned to duty at the wharf. A friend of Charley's, a boy well-known to the Gates family and to the community, Joseph D. Clarke, age seventeen, is among the known dead. His father was local attorney Col. Melvin Clarke, killed at Antietam two years ago while commanding the Thirty-Sixth Ohio.[3] The news is even more reason for Mary to worry. Death is everywhere on the front line, and now it also strikes the rear. Would Charley have been there?

The weather today is torrid, well over 100 degrees. The messenger boy is sweating profusely as he knocks on the door with a dispatch. "Mary, it's from Rufus!" Betsey Gates calls to her daughter.

Mary runs to open the note, screams, "Thank God!," and hugs and twirls her mother in circles. "He's coming home!" she shouts, then runs out the door toward her mother-in-law's home. Betsey picks up the dispatch sent from Rufus and reads:

Washington D.C. August 12th, 1864

To: Mrs. Mary B. Dawes

Honorably discharged. R. R. D.[4]

Wednesday, August 17, 1864, Marietta, Ohio

William Jackson leans on the railing of the ferry as it begins to cross the Ohio River from Parkersburg, West Virginia, to Belpre, Ohio. He knows he is close to the end of the journey and the beginning of a new life. His thoughts are a mixture of exhilaration and dark uncertainty. *What will it be like living in the North? Will the people be friendly? What will I do to earn a living?*

Rufus Dawes looks at William and reads his thoughts. "Well, William," he says, "we are getting close to home, just a 14-mile train ride from Belpre to Marietta. What's the most exciting thing you've seen since we left the army?"

"We'al, sah, Ah have ta say it'd be Washington, dat's fo sure. Ah wuz hopin' ta see President Lincoln, but not much chance of dat. But all de big buildin's, all de hospitals! An all de officers! We coulda' used dat many privates, don't ya think?"

Dawes laughs. "You hit the nail on the head, William! Too many rear echelon officers, pushing papers and filling out forms. I think I had to see half of them and still didn't get it all straightened out. I'll have to go back to finish. I heard the president is meeting with Frederick Douglass this week. I think seeing Douglass would have been special, for both of us."

William looks at Dawes and recalls that hot day at Cedar Mountain almost two years past, the day his life changed. The colonel interrupts William's thoughts as he says, "Don't worry, William, everyone in Marietta is going to like you."

Rufus points out the Old Stone House as they pass by on the train. "We'll visit there tomorrow or the next," Dawes says. The train reaches Harmar, Bettie is unloaded from the rear car and saddled, and the two cross the Muskingam River Bridge to Marietta.

Rufus quickly dismounts and heads for the front door, while William shyly waits at the street with the horse. "Mary, I'm home!" Rufe shouts as he knocks and opens the door. Mary bounds down the stairs as Betsey and Bettie come in from the kitchen. "Rufe!" is all Mary can manage as she runs toward him, eyes brimming with tears, and embraces him as tight as she can. "I'm staying for good this time," he quietly says in her ear. "It's time now for us, time now for a family."

Betsey and Bettie hold back for a few moments, but then they, too, come forward and welcome Rufe with warm hugs. "Welcome home, Rufus! We are so happy for you both!" says Betsey. She *is* happy, of course. Her daughter is finally relieved of the constant worry and tension. But seeing Rufus in his uniform, safe now after such a long ordeal, is a painful reminder that poor Charley will never be with her again. Her tears reflect both joy and sadness.

William is introduced, and Betsey provides a snack as Bettie boldly bombards both Rufus and William with questions about the army and their trip. Rufus begs off quickly, though, as they all head up the street to his mother's home, where the warm and loving reunion is replayed with Sarah and Lucy. Ephraim hears the commotion and, rising from a nap, enters the room to greet his brother. For the first time, Rufus sees the evidence of the damage. Eph's lower face is covered with a bandage, a slit left open for taking water and soft food.

The brothers shake hands, and Rufe provides the first comment: "Well, you don't look *too* hopeless! I hope you're taking advantage of all the attention!"

Eph mumbles a reply, which Rufe interprets as "It hurts to laugh, so I won't."

Rufe has seen many gruesome wounds, but none belonged to his only brother. He knows Ephraim faces a very difficult future. It will be a fearsome surgical repair that, even if successful, will plague him for life.

There is dinner at the Gates home with Lucy Dawes as guest. Sarah stays home to welcome a seventeen-year-old nephew from Illinois, John P. Walton, who will be boarding while he attends Marietta College.[5] Beman Gates offers thanks for the safe return of a husband, son, and brother. They have all prayed for this day, and as it closes, the family does not linger, allowing Rufus and Mary to retire to Mary's room. The two have craved this moment for six months, and now that it is here, they feel a bit awkward. Mary's giggle about the absurdity of it dissolves their nervousness, and they realize how fortunate they both are, alone together at last. They are two people desperately in need of each other. The strain of separation has ended. The constant stress has disappeared. They hold each other close and love each other completely.

Saturday, August 27, 1864, Marietta, Ohio—the Corner

Rufus feels Mary stir next to him as the morning sunlight peeks through the window. He props up on his elbow as she opens her eyes and smiles at him. "Happy birthday, my dear wife," he says before leaning over with a kiss. "May this be the first of many more special birthdays we have together."

Mary kisses him back and replies, "Every day is special to me, so long as I have you here next to me, away from danger."

Before coming downstairs for breakfast, they talk quietly of Mary's parents. "Mother has been in such a depressed mood lately. I'm sure when we went through Charley's clothes … Well, it was very difficult for me too."

Rufus holds her hand and says, "It would be tough on anyone. Ma didn't remove Hen's things for a long time. That's why I didn't take much of Charley's for myself. I don't want to wear things that remind your folks of him; that would be awful. You did the right thing giving most of the clothes to the college for some of the students to use. Charley would approve, I think. Maybe someday we can bring a new son into the family who will help ease the loss."

Monday, August 29, 1864—the Old Stone House

The past week has seen Sarah Dawes quite ill with erysipelas. The skin infection is ugly and painful, and there's not much they can do but let it run its course. Lucy, Rufus, Julia, and Mary have spent many hours taking care of her. Ephraim is in Cincinnati to consult with Dr. Blackmon, who will determine if Eph is ready for facial repair surgery. His aide, Wesley, is with him.

Uncle William Cutler and Rufus sit together after supper. William comments, "Rufus, I'm glad to hear your mother is feeling better. If Ephraim is soon to have surgery, it would be best if she was healthy herself and better able to bear that stress. Now you say he's staying in Cincinnati until Dr. Blackman is available, assigned to a court-martial board? Well, perhaps that will be good for him. A sign of the army's respect for his judgment, certainly. But how are *you* doing? This civilian life is a drastic change from three years of active army service."

Rufus smiles in response. "I have to chuckle, thinking of Eph patiently listening to testimony from makeshift army lawyers! I did that for the longest time! Us Dawes boys can't seem to avoid it!" Rufe's mood changes in reply to his uncle's last question. "But, sir, as for me, I've never been happier. Yes, we have concerns—Eph and mother, the grief of Mr. and Mrs. Gates—but there's no regiment of soldiers to worry about, either. I do think of them, though. The Fifth Corps had a tough fight last week near Globe Tavern, trying to cut the Weldon Railroad. I know exactly where that is, but I haven't seen anything specific from the regiment. I sometimes feel that ..." Rufe pauses, and William hesitantly interjects, "You feel you should still be there?"

Rufus looks down and says, "Yes, I do sometimes. Mary understands, and I know I did the best I could for three years. But I think of those still there—boys I convinced to reenlist, soldiers still carrying the burden. Some of them were probably hurt or killed; some of the rest might think I deserted them. I've written to Dr. John Hall and to Captain Remington, but it's too soon to hear back. I'll try to find out more when I go back to Washington tomorrow. There are still ordinance and supply returns to straighten out. I won't get paid till the pencil pushers accept it."

William pats his nephew on the shoulder. "Rufus, there is no one who could question your decision to leave at your term's end. Tens of thousands have done the same. In fact, you stayed almost a month longer! And your service record stands as more than honorable. It's exceptional! Why, your actions at Gettysburg alone, likely saving the army that morning, will always be valued. No, you have *earned* your time away from danger."

Saturday, September 3, 1864, Washington, D.C.

Rufus Dawes is on his second full day in the nation's capital, making good progress in completing army paperwork. He meets an old friend and comrade while at the Treasury Department. "Colonel Dawes! You are a sight to see. I can't believe you've become a finance officer!"

Dawes turns and, with astonishment, moves quickly to shake the hand of a gaunt Colonel John Mansfield, Second Wisconsin. "John, it is you, isn't it? I thought you might be dead."

Mansfield responds, "I'm getting along fine, now that I'm out of Libby Prison! I got shot the first day in the Wilderness, and the Rebs picked me up. Being wounded at Libby is not a good thing, but I made it, and they let me out to be discharged. But I've been here in Washington for a week trying to get my pay. It looks like I'm going home without it. They say the records are incomplete. How could they not be!"

Dawes shakes his head. "So you were a prisoner of war in the enemy capital and now a prisoner of bureaucracy in our own!"

Mansfield grins in reply. "That's an accurate summary. You're discharged too? Have you heard from the Sixth after the fight last week?"

"Yes, and I'm heartsick over it," Dawes grimly replies. "Captain Hutchins and Lieutenant John Timmons were killed. Timmons was due to be discharged the same date as me! Our own war department doomed him! Cuyler Babcock is dead. He and I shared the same hot, dirty hole, dodging sharpshooters and mortar shells. I taught him some Shakespeare and Latin …" Dawes pauses to control himself. "There was no better young man. I had just promoted him. Hutchins had new bars too. Kerr was away sick, so General Bragg put Charlie Hyatt in command, and he had his leg taken off by a cannon ball. There are maybe eighty men left. Besides that, General Cutler was wounded in the face by shrapnel, so after the battle, General Warren dissolved the Fourth Division. We only had two small brigades anyway. Bragg and what's left of our brigade are now assigned to General Crawford. Hoffman's Second Brigade went to Griffin's First Division. I wrote my wife the other day that I'm sure I never could have lived through it. And there's no end in sight."

Mansfield sighs and, looking Dawes squarely in the eyes, says, "Rufus, it's a wonder you made it through without being shot somewhere. You were always in the thick of things. You need to go home and enjoy your life and raise a family. I think that's what God intends for you to do. We will both have stories to tell our children someday. It's been an honor to serve with you."

Rufus Dawes swallows hard, nods, and returns the compliment. The two veterans warmly shake hands again, more words unnecessary, and go their separate ways.[6]

Rufus Dawes is deep in thought as he walks away from his courageous friend. *Perhaps the guilt I feel is self-imposed. I do no justice to all my lost friends by brooding. I do owe it to them to live the rest of my life honorably and to keep the memory of their sacrifice alive.*

The day in the capital ends with spreading news of a terrific achievement. General William T. Sherman, once Colonel Mansfield's brigade commander at the first battle of Bull Run in 1861, telegraphs the Washington, D.C., War Office. The message reads, "Atlanta is ours, and fairly won."

Thursday, September 22, 1864, Cincinnati, Ohio—Officers' Hospital

Lucy gives her brother a long embrace. "Eph, I'll be here with Wesley to take care of you when it's over. I love you!" Ephraim returns the hug and turns with Rufus to enter the operating room. Dr. Blackman has invited a dozen medical colleagues to observe the procedure. Rufus and two assistants are present to hold the patient still. Dr. Blackman has advised that best results will be attained if chloroform is not administered over the open wound.

A focused Dr. Blackman states to the room, "First, I must cut from the corner of the mouth back to the angle of the cheek on each side, then just below where the under lip should begin, cutting again, running back toward the ear, thus separating a strip about one inch wide, but which will still be attached to the cheek near the ear. Then these two strips will be stretched forward until they meet, to be sewed together over a set of under teeth."

Ephraim closes his eyes as Rufus firmly holds one arm down while grimacing at the thought of the torture his brother is about to endure. Ephraim's convulsive reactions as the incisions are made feel to Rufus like the throes of a giant, but his brother makes no moan or sound. Ephraim gags on the blood and is told to turn his head for drainage. The work continues, then a pause. The sweating doctor says, "We must now secure the strip with these pins running through the upper part of the cheek to that below, and those secured by winding threads about the ends back and forth."

Rufus looks at the doctor in horror and is about to shout, "*No! Stop!*" But Ephraim weakly nods, as if to say, "We are committed now, get on with it."

Ephraim's agony continues with more cuts and pulls and sutures on the upper lip and jaw. At one point, Ephraim's chokes so violently that the false jaw and teeth are spasmodically ejected. Rufus is horrified, but Blackman keeps calm and decides not to replace them. "We will do that later," he says. "It will not be so extensive." The procedure is ninety minutes of hell. Ephraim's self-possession is remarkable, as he obeys every direction to turn his head this way or that, until the loss of blood and the pain exhaust him.

Saturday, September 24, 1864, Marietta, Ohio

Rufus Dawes walks into the Gates home and warmly embraces Mary. He has been on the train most of the day from Cincinnati, leaving Lucy to care for Ephraim. Betsey and Beman Gates join them in the parlor, all anxious to hear about Ephraim's condition.

"Thursday night was awful for him. None of us slept. But yesterday, he rested better," says Rufe. "He is not supposed to talk, and only sips water or juice through a straw. I don't know how he stood it! It was the bravest thing I ever saw. Doctor Blackman finally said it was finished, then looked closer, and decided he should do two more stiches! Poor Eph just trembled and held up one finger. I couldn't take it. I shouted, 'Don't touch him!' But then Eph held up two fingers, and the doctor put them in. I tell you, I would rather fight all my battles a second time than watch Eph go through that again!"

Major Ephraim C. Dawes after jaw surgery

Rufus and Mary walk to his mother's home, where Rufus provides a summary to Sarah and Aunt Julia, who is staying with her sister while she is still ill and worried so much about Ephraim. The family had received Rufe's telegraph message on Friday but had not realized until now the gruesome nature of the surgery. Complications, both short- and long-term, are always a concern, and he must endure another follow-up procedure. "I'm going to send William Jackson to Cincinnati on Monday to help Ephraim. He's trustworthy and a very handy young fellow. He wants to help all he can."[7]

Sunday, September 25, 1864, Marietta, Ohio

The family leaves Rev. Wickes's First Congregational Church after services, and since it is a pleasant fall day, Rufe and Mary cross Front Street to the park, watching the river traffic for a few minutes before walking arm-in-arm back to the Corner. Rufe had not slept well the night before, tossing and turning, moaning words Mary did not quite understand. He has had similar spells before. He usually is willing to talk about his dreams, so she decides to ask, "Rufe, who is 'Finton'?"

Rufe slowly stops and turns to her. "Did you hear me say his name last night?"

Mary can tell from the look on her husband's face that her question has opened a particularly painful recollection. "Yes, dear," she says. "You were having a nightmare. Seeing Eph go through his surgery just the other day would give anyone bad dreams. Is Finton one of the doctors?"

Rufe continues their stroll but is silent for a time. Finally, "Finton was a soldier. Company A. Just a young lad, really. Younger than Charley. He was killed this past June by a sharpshooter when we were near Bethesda Church. It was the same area and about the same time when Kate's stepson, Jackson, was killed. We were there just a few days, so our works were not fully protective. He and another man, Sergeant Fort, I think, had borrowed a Sharps rifle and were doing good work dueling with Rebs in a farmhouse who were trying to pick us off. Then a couple boys from the Seventh Wisconsin who were classmates of Finton's came to visit. They were having a good time, and he got careless. The Rebs were waiting for somebody to expose themselves. Somebody saw the puff and shouted, 'Look out!' Finton didn't react, and the bullet hit him in the head."

Mary is holding Rufe's hand and visualizes the horror. She is angry with herself for asking. Rufe walks in silence, then adds, "We thought he was killed. We could see his brains, and there was a lot of blood. He was one of the company favorites. The boys felt awful and dug a grave for him as soon as it got dark. But he didn't die! He lingered for hours. We couldn't understand it! Finally, they took him back to the division hospital. We then marched south toward Cold Harbor and later heard he somehow survived for several days. They must have moved him north at some point, because we heard he was buried in the cemetery that's been started near Lee's mansion at Arlington, right where we camped during our first winter in the army."[8]

Mary pulls him closer and says sadly, "Rufe, I'm so sorry. I shouldn't have asked—"

Rufe interrupts her: "It's all right, Mary. It happened, and there was nothing anyone could do. I've determined it's best for me not to keep these horrible things inside. In a war, awful things happen to good people. It could have been me or anyone. Maybe seeing Eph's bloody surgery brought Finton back to my mind. He's now in a cemetery being filled with young men just like him."

They walk in silence for a while before Rufe speaks again. "I do feel guilty at times, Mary. How and why was I spared? I'm human. I suppose it is normal to ask myself that question. There is no answer but to accept that God has a reason. I do feel I owe it to them ..." He pauses without finishing and turns to Mary. "I don't know what I would do without you."

Fall 1864–Spring 1865

The military situation around Petersburg has settled into trench warfare and stalemate. As this drags on, the Republican Party and President Lincoln worry about their chances for a second term. General Sherman's forces are on their march to the sea, but news of their whereabouts is slim. Then the Union cause is boosted on October 19 as General Phil Sheridan turns initial defeat into a smashing victory over Confederate general Early's command in the Shenandoah Valley.

Rufus and Mary continue to live in the Gates home. Rufus and Uncle William Cutler cement an already close relationship. Rufe accompanies William on several political speaking engagements in southeast Ohio. Both understand the critical necessity of Lincoln's reelection, realizing there are many ardent Copperheads in the region, some who have even threatened harm to William for his pro-Union and abolitionist views. The Democrats select former general George McClellan as their presidential candidate. McClellan favors peace talks with the Confederacy and is the man who Lincoln had previously relieved of command—twice.

There are also business ventures. Rufus works as a partner in sheep farming and as commissioned agent in the expanding oil industry.

Abundant oil reserves were found in southeast Ohio years ago. Rufus becomes an oil-leasing agent for William's land holdings in the area. Kerosene for lighting is now being refined by many companies, and oil is a hot commodity. There are meetings at the Old Stone House with oil entrepreneurs and trips to field sites, many in nearby Noble County. Rufus's efficiency and warm personality are perfect for this task. William Cutler is pleased to hear feedback from a New York capitalist buying oil lands through his nephew. "I never met a man who delighted me more than Col. Dawes," says he.

Ephraim suffers through a second painful operation in late October, returns to Marietta to recover, and is discharged from the army due to disability. He endures further procedures for dental implants that are installed by a specialist in the Ohio River town of Portsmouth. The surgeries and recovery take a toll on Ephraim, who is limited in what he can eat and, for a long time, is rendered mute.

Ephraim's recovery allows time for reflection regarding his relationship with Ella. It is a difficult period for them both. He begins to understand the family's misgivings about her, and she begins to understand the severe and long-lasting nature of his wound. The engagement is terminated by mutual agreement, and Ella is no longer in the picture. The ladies of the Dawes family breathe a sigh of relief and begin to discuss potential new matches.

Ephraim's servant, Wesley, works part-time at the nearby Burgess farm while he improves his reading skills under Julia's tutelage at the Old Stone House. William Jackson serves Ephraim tirelessly and loyally during the convalescent period in Cincinnati, just as he had done for Eph's brother. Rufus then finds young William a job in Marietta as a hotel waiter.[9]

Astounding news is heard from the Sixth Wisconsin through Dr. Hall! Captain John Kellogg and several others made a daring escape from prison in Charleston, South Carolina. They evaded pursuit by bloodhounds and journeyed through Southern territory for over 300 miles. Friendly Negroes assisted the escapees along the way, and the group finally emerged three weeks later into Union lines between Atlanta and Chattanooga. John is on a well-deserved leave to his home in Wisconsin, promoted now to major while in prison, but intends to come back to the unit. Dawes is elated. "Finally, great news!" he shouts at Mary while reading. "Good old John! What he must have gone through!"[10]

President Lincoln wins the November 8 election over the Democratic candidate McClellan. The news prompts an elated Julia Cutler to write:

Lincoln is handsomely re-elected—God be praised—now may slavery fall to rise no more—"Righteousness exalteth a nation, but sin is a reproach to any people" …

This success seems to breed more. The Confederate army under General Hood is shattered by Union forces under General George Thomas at Nashville, Tennessee. This essentially ends Southern hopes in the western theater. General Sherman's army reaches the sea at Savannah during Christmas, splitting the South in two. He brings war to the Georgia citizenry in a brutal manner and dooms the Confederacy in doing so.

Late on New Year's Eve, with six inches of snow on the ground, Julia Cutler records:

We have our New Years' feast to day. The turkey was very nicely cooked, also the vegetables, the canned strawberries were delicious.

Eighteen family members and friends are present at the Old Stone House for the festive occasion. Rufus and Mary enjoy the lively conversation, then depart to Marietta on the afternoon train. They are planning to build a home for themselves soon. It is time to become independent. And, although they do not know it, a child is on the way.[11]

New Year's Day, 1865—Julia Cutler Reflects on the Past Twelve Months

Last year was to our family a most eventful one, and it seems to me one of the saddest of my life, and yet I ought not to feel so, for God's chastisements have been tempered with his mercy too. January 11 … our sweet little Annie died of diphtheria—Jan. 18, Lt. Col. R. R. Dawes was married to Miss Mary B. Gates—Feb. 16, Kate L. Dawes was married to Rev. S. A. McLean … this made a great change and was a great loss to our family—May 5 my niece Louisa Cutler Fulton died—May 28 Major Ephraim C. Dawes was severely, at first supposed to be mortally wounded, at Dallas Ga.—April 18 little Eddie Walton died. In August Col. R. R. Dawes was honorably discharged from the service. In October Major E. C. Dawes was honorably discharged in consequence of his wounds.

The winter passes with business travels and meetings for Rufus and home planning for Mary. Occasional illnesses plague family members, including Rufus, who seems to have developed a bit of early rheumatism, probably brought on, Mary thinks, by his army service.

February dawns with wondrous news, as Julia Cutler records on Wednesday the 1st:

> Mr. T. B. Wilcox who had been getting Options on oil terri-tory in West Virginia is here tonight. The Gazette says that the Constitutional Amendment abolishing slavery has passed the House of Representatives in Congress. I thank God that he is thus inclining the hearts of our rulers to do away this great sin. It has already passed the Senate—and I trust that the State Legislatures will ratify the measure speedily.

By coincidence, a key component for General Grant's final victory plan also begins on this day. General Sherman's army leaves Savannah for points north. His targets are a secret—is it Augusta, Charleston, Columbia, Charlotte? The Deep South is in panic. Available Confederate forces to oppose him are scattered and will be outnumbered even if they converge. Charleston falls to Sherman on the 17th, and Wilmington to General Schofield on the 23rd.

By the end of the month, the successes prompt Grant to say, "Everything looks like dissolution in the South." By the "South," he means the Deep South, for at Petersburg, Lee and his stretched army are holding on. The Sixth Wisconsin is still there, augmented by draftees and volunteer recruits (as Rufus Dawes always advocated), held together by surviving veterans, and led now by four-times-wounded Thomas Kerr, who enlisted in Milwaukee as a private in 1861 and is now a lieutenant colonel. The Seventh Wisconsin is still there, too, but the other regiments and General Bragg are gone, transferred elsewhere or consolidated. The Ninety-First New York, a heavy-artillery-turned-infantry regiment, joins the Badgers, forming a three-regiment brigade of over three thousand men. Placed in command is the indefatigable John Kellogg, now a full colonel. They are still in Crawford's division of Warren's Fifth Corps.

In Marietta, Rufus and Mary decide to buy a lot on Fourth Street, diagonally south from the Gates home. Rufus contracts with a builder, and the foundation begins in early March.

Mary expects to give birth sometime in August. She and Rufus both know that any travel for her will be curtailed after that. On an evening soon after their "cottage" work has begun, Rufus poses an idea: "Mary, we have talked about a trip to Gettysburg and Washington before the baby comes. I think next month would be the best time. The weather should not be too cold or too hot. We could be back home before the carpenters start interior work, and I know you will want to be here for that."

Mary responds, "Well, I think that would be fine. I really do want to see where you fought at Gettysburg, and I know you would like to visit the cemetery there. And being in Washington will be exciting, especially now with the war nearing an end. So yes, let's plan that."

Rufus and Mary do not foresee how "exciting" Washington will be during their visit. The Confederacy finally unravels as April begins, and like a sinking ship, the end comes quickly. Richmond falls to Union forces on April 3. President Lincoln steams down the coast to tour the ravaged city several days later. A surrounded General Robert E. Lee surrenders his army to General Grant at Appomattox on Sunday the 9th following a frantic chase and several bitter battles. The war is over! Washington will never be a happier city!

Rufus and Mary join fellow Marietta citizens in celebrating the victory. To Rufus, it is vindication that all the pain and loss was not in vain. It is an exuberant young couple who board the train on the familiar route to Belpre, take the ferry across to Parkersburg, and ride the Baltimore and Ohio Railroad east though Harpers Ferry to Washington.

Good Friday, April 14, 1865, Washington, D.C.—National Hotel

They arrive midmorning at the bustling hotel on Pennsylvania Avenue. The recently finished Capitol Building stands magnificently 3,000 feet southeast down the broad roadway. The executive mansion is twice as far in the opposite direction but is obscured by budding parkway trees.

"Too bad you were not here last evening, Colonel," says the desk clerk. "The whole city was lit up. The Grand Illumination, they call it. Lanterns and candles in every window, celebrations and speeches all over town! But I'm sure this weekend will be terrific. General Grant is in town—staying at the Willard, I've heard, but only because that's closer to the president's house. The president and the general are supposed to be at Ford's Theater tonight. The play is a comedy: "Our American Cousin.' It starts at eight o'clock, if you're interested."

"Really?" says Mary. "Rufe, we should see if we can attend! I would love to see the president, and General Grant too!" When asked about tickets, the helpful clerk is pleased to arrange the purchase and add the cost to their bill. Done! Now for something to eat and then sightseeing on this sunny and pleasant day.

Rufe has seen Washington several times during the war, once describing it in a letter home as a city with "large buildings and magnificent distances." He once toured the Capitol Building from the support beams of
the newly finished dome down to the underground chamber once slated
for Washington's grave. The couple walk through the huge building and
over its grounds rendered colorful and fragrant with budding lilacs and
dogwood. It is a long walk toward the unfinished Washington Monument
and to the Smithsonian. By the time they take a street car back to the
hotel for supper, Mary is exhausted. As they sit at a table in the large
dining room, she says to her husband, "Rufe, I am so completely tired
out! If there is any possibility of seeing President Lincoln anywhere else, I
would just like to rest and not go to the theatre. I think I underestimated
how much this little person is taking my energy!"

"All right, Mary. That's fine. I'm sorry I led you on a hard march
today—I wasn't thinking. You know, I'm sure Mr. and Mrs. Lincoln
will be at Dr. Gurley's Presbyterian Church on Sunday. Dave Chambers
and I saw them there in the fall of '61. He has a reserved pew and rarely
misses a service. I'm sure he will be there Sunday for Easter. We could
see him then." The couple content themselves with the new plan, giving
up their hope of seeing Lincoln this evening.

The rest Mary desires is interrupted by loud disruption from the
adjoining room. Some fellows are obviously drinking heavily, and their
singing and swearing is loud enough to keep her awake. Rufe is about to
knock on their door in protest when the rowdies leave, and all becomes
quiet. Mary and Rufus sleep until morning.

"The president is dead! News of the assassination! Secretary Seward
attacked!" Rufus hears the newsboy shouting and the hustle in the hotel
lobby as he comes down the stairs Saturday morning. *What is that?*
Rufus is completely unaware of the 10:25 p.m. assassination. Fellow
patrons say the initial reports claimed the president survived, but the
direct head-shot was mortal. The great statesman dies in a small room
across the street from Ford's Theater at about 7:20 a.m. this morning.
Rufe buys a paper and hurries back upstairs to break the news to Mary,
thinking as he walks that fate kept them from being witnesses. Mary
shares the shock and grief felt by the nation. Later that day, she writes
her mother in Marietta, noting that she and Rufe "barely escaped seeing
the whole affair."

The city is shocked, and many are angry. Thousands congregate
at street corners, many threatening vengeances on those who seem to
rejoice in the murder, or even upon those who fail to exhibit emblems
of mourning from their homes. The military and police force are on the

alert for public disorder. On Easter Sunday, Dr. Gurley's church is so packed with mourners that hundreds cannot gain entrance. Near the middle of the church sits a vacant pew, draped in mourning black.

Rufe and Mary spend another two days in gloomy Washington before leaving for Baltimore. News of the manhunt reveals another shocking development: The actor John Wilkes Booth is the alleged assailant, and he resided in the National Hotel, room 228. This news shocks the couple. *Room 228! We were neighbors and didn't know it!*[12]

Wednesday, April 19, 1865, Gettysburg

They stand together along the Chambersburg Pike, then climb under the fence rails toward the railroad cut. Mary holds Rufe's hand as they walk through the field of death where he led the Sixth Wisconsin charge twenty-one months past. He recalls the sheer terror and violence. She recalls the painfully anxious days of uncertainty. "I now have a picture of it, Rufe. I mean, the land and the distances. I can't imagine what you and your regiment endured that day."

"It was the Sixth's finest moment, I think. Fitzhugh's Crossing comes close, I suppose," Rufe responds. "But we lost so many crossing this field. Yet not one man or boy shirked their duty." He pauses, then, "It had to be done. We had to take them. There was no one else to do it. But at every step here, I see the faces of the those who fell. It's like it happened just the other day."

They stand at the edge of the railroad cut now, and Rufe points down. "It was here," he says. "Their commander surrendered to me here. That ugly fighting for their flag happened right over there." Rufus turns to the east and says, "And then we were ordered to pull back to the next ridge," and he points down the cut to the wooded rise. "That's where we counted all our men, the ones who were left."

Mary squeezes his arm. "Like you, thank God," she says.

"Yes, like me." Somehow, he feels at peace. The explosions and screams are gone, the bodies and the blood too. And Mary is with him. But he tells her, "You were with me then, you know. And I'm glad you are with me today."

As they walk back to the pike, Rufe opens his heart and mind once more: "When we were at Soldier's Cemetery today, it all came back to me as if it happened yesterday. All those graves so neatly arranged, right where our men rested after we made it to Cemetery Hill. When we entered the gate today, I remembered leading the boys out, going the other way, toward Culp's Hill. Those headboards and stones are faces to me. George Stevens, Orrin Chapman, Tarbox, and Fletcher.

Anderson and Evans ... and Kelly. So many graves are marked 'Unknown.' The bodies were four days in the sun ... We could hardly tell who they were."[13]

Mary brings a handkerchief to her eyes. The thought of that grisly scene, spoken of so calmly by her husband, makes her shudder. *He has been hardened to it*, she thinks. *He saw so much death in those three awful years. He does have dreams, though. Still, he wanted to come back here, to see "the boys" again.*

Monday, June 19, 1865, Parkersburg, West Virginia

"Your beard is coming in pretty thick, bro," says Rufus to Ephraim. "You can hardly see anything."

Ephraim rubs his chin gingerly and responds, "It doesn't look too bad, I guess. Except these gore marks on my cheek. Just enough there to brag about. More than you can say!"

The two brothers are crossing on the Ohio River ferry to Parkersburg, and they are in a jovial mood. Rufus received the dispatch from John Hall a few days ago: "Reg't. in Parkersburg the 19th—can you meet?" Rufe is elated! A chance to see the boys and "Old Syntax"[AF] on their way home! Ephraim is an enthusiastic companion.

The Dawes brothers are waiting at the Parkersburg station as the train carrying the Sixth Wisconsin regiment arrives. Ephraim has never seen his brother so anxious, but he identifies with the feeling. These are brothers-in-arms, young men who have shared incredible hardships and dangers with Rufe, creating bonds that will last a lifetime.

Rufus can see them now in the cars as the train comes to a stop. Many young faces are looking out open windows. Rufus does not recognize many of them, the numerous draftees who were assigned since he left. The veterans are heavily outnumbered by them, but they are here! Coming down now is Lt. Col. Tom Kerr and Major Daily of the old Second Regiment. Greetings, hands shaken, shoulders grasped, a brief discussion to catch up on news. There is too little time.

Old Company K comes filing out, the men stretching and laughing and lining up for the roll before being temporarily dismissed. There will be no worries about stragglers missing the boat to Louisville; everybody wants to get home. The veterans see him now and hurry to greet their old commander. Here are Gallup, Van Wie, and Gordon, former enlisted men who have earned their officer bars. There is Crawford, St. Clair, Talty, Trumbull, Valleau, Winsor—all wounded at least once, all serving

---

[AF] Per Sergeant Mickey Sullivan, the soldier's nickname for Dr. Hall.

four long years. Here is Mickey Sullivan, a sergeant now, wounded three times, discharged twice, reenlisted twice, and feisty as ever. "Well, Colonel, sir, an Irishman would have two children by now!" says he. It is wonderful to know they have survived and are going home.

Then Dr. John Hall quickly approaches. There is a quick handshake and a big bear hug. "Colonel Dawes, Rufus, you look very respectable in your civilian wear! And this must be Ephraim?" Introductions are made, and Hall exclaims, "Major, I've heard about your surgery. My God, you are a brave soul! My congratulations! It appears it is healed very well. I would love to hear the details, if you don't mind. And, Rufe, I am happy to accept your invitation to stay with you for a day. Colonel Kerr says it's fine, says you outrank him anyway! Thank you! I'm looking forward to meeting your family."

John Hall impresses everyone with his sincerity and wit. He spends much of the train ride to Marietta quizzing Ephraim and inspecting the surgery. Ephraim is amused by the attention and quite accommodating. Hall finally meets Lucy and Mrs. Dawes and is pleased to have the reunion with Mary, who is now prominently showing her pregnancy. He feels he has known Mary for a long time. The three reminisce about Rufe's struggle to win Mary's heart, with Rufe crediting the good doctor for urging perseverance. On the way back to catch a boat at Parkersburg the next day, John and Rufus stop at the Old Stone House for a noon dinner. Julia is a gracious hostess, as always, and she is likewise impressed with the doctor. "Dr. Hall is tall and good-looking & appears to be intelligent and gentlemanly" is the way she phrases her evaluation that evening in her journal.

The two friends wish each other well as Hall's boat embarks for the trip to Louisville and his family in Green County, Wisconsin.

Beginning a Family
Monday, July 31, 1865, Marietta, Ohio

Beman and twelve-year-old Bettie Gates have left on an extended trip east to Massachusetts, with Betsey staying home with Mary, now in her eighth month. Mary writes her father:

My dear Father

I am going to have the most complete and convenient dining room closet that ever was. ... I entertain no doubt myself about being a pattern housekeeper. They finished tonight putting the

tin on the roof and the flooring is down all over the house and
the brick is laid in the basement kitchen. The rooms look large
and airy and pleasant. The mistake of not setting the house high
enough I will not allow to trouble me.

Sunday, August 27, 1865, Marietta, Ohio

This is a memorable day for Rufus and the Dawes family. First, it is
Mary's twenty-third birthday. Rufus and Betsey plan a nice after-church
family party at the Corner, with Rufe indicating, "Next year, I'll host it
at our new home!"

This is also a significant day at their First Congregational Church. The
Dawes family has signed a forty-three-member petition asking to be dismissed from the congregation. The purpose is to form a new Presbyterian
church. It is not a contentious departure; rather, the group is concerned
for the prosperity of Marietta College, which draws many students of the
Presbyterian order. Parents have become reluctant to send their sons to
Marietta because there is no Presbyterian church in town.

The petition is on the agenda this morning and is expected to be
adopted. The old church, while regretting the loss of this many active
members, is in fact treating the departure much like a new colony, with
moral and financial support to come. Land has been purchased at the
corner of Wooster and Fourth Street, and the new name will be the
Fourth Avenue Presbyterian Church.[14]

But someone has other ideas: Mary goes into labor. Rufus rushes to
services this morning with a different purpose than worship or the petition. He slips in to summon the doctor. The congregation cannot help
but notice, and the whispered word that "It's time" will be an embarrassment that cannot be helped. The first-born child is a boy, a wish come
true for both parents, and they name him Charles Gates Dawes, in honor
of Mary's brother, Charley.[15]

The proud father writes Beman and Bettie Gates the next day with
details of "the arrival of our long-expected stranger." Rufus is ecstatic,
as his wit and humor demonstrate:

Precisely at the first tap of the church bell at 10 o'clock Charles
Gates Dawes appeared on the stage. He weighed <u>ten and a half
pounds</u> and is not _fat_ at that. Mary endured her suffering most
heroically. He has dark blue eyes, light hair, and light complexion. He is said to resemble several people strikingly, and to be
exceedingly beautiful, but my judgement is that he differs little

in appearance from other babies, and he is homely enough to be President of the U.S.

Mary is coming on very well. ... [T]he excitement among friends was immense. The baby is also well, and very dignified considering his extreme youth, having said only enough to show us that he <u>can</u>.

You will be interested in the coincidence of her birthday, and of the child's weighing precisely what she did at birth.

Mary wishes Bettie ... to have patience, and baby "handsome" now will be "perfectly <u>beautiful</u>" by the time she comes home.

"Grandmother" desires me to say Charley sends love to "Aunt Bet," and she encloses a lock of hair which by use of a microscope you will find in this letter.

Very respectfully, Rufus R. Dawes

A short time after the birth, Mary writes her father about the new Charles, who they begin to nickname "Carta":

I want to bring him up to fill our poor lost Charley's place to you and Mother as much as possible, to show the same thoughtfulness and loving attentions to you that <u>he</u> did, and with a heart too full for words I come to you, asking your love to my boy. My prayer nightly is that he may be worthy of your love as the poor Charley whose name he bears, and in whose grave your and Mother's hearts seem so completely buried.

Mary has no reason to be concerned about her parent's affections for her Charley. The baby soon becomes the family focal point and a great source of joy, a new boy in a new home. Time is split with both grandparents. Sarah Dawes is a little farther away now, having moved from town to a home near the Old Stone House. Rufus and Ephraim are making money in business, and Mary becomes an efficient and cheerful homemaker, known for quality meals and for maintaining a clean, airy, and fragrant household.

Father Henry's settlement with Sarah frees her of the constant uncertainty of late alimony payments. The Dawes family has their own lives to live, so contact with Henry Dawes is minimal. Rufus politely responds when a letter is received, as he does here on February 6, 1866:

Dear Father—

I received some days since yours enclosing circulars from General Chamberlain. I shall give the matter proper attention. ...

I am glad to hear that your health remains good, and that prosperity smiles upon our relatives in Wisconsin.

My health continues very good, though I feel the effects of my hard service in the army with a predisposition to something like rheumatism. My wife is in excellent health and spirits, and our little boy, Charley, now near six months old, is an unusually bright, healthy, happily disposed child.

My brother has charge of the M&C RR office in Parkersburg. His health is good, and his beard now hides whatever disfiguration remained after his operation.

My principal occupation at present is exercising a general superintendence of coal traffic on the RR., viz. fixing rates, securing markets. ... The company allows me $1,500 per year for this service, which is quite liberal in view of the small amount of time required. ... I manage to keep certain other irons in the fire which I hope may prove moderately profitable.

My sister Kate's health is quite feeble this winter, so much so that she was compelled to give up keeping house. She is now visiting with us. ... I fear she will not live long.

I have been much interested in the establishment of a new church in Marietta. We have put up a building at a cost of $6,000, and have a membership of 75, and one of the ablest young clergymen in Ohio (New School Presbyterian).

Please give my respects to any gentlemen in Mauston who may be kind enough to enquire about me.

My friend Gov. Fairchild was kind enough to recommend me in strong terms for a Brvt. Brig. Gen'l. In a letter to the Sec. of War he says "... I know of no more gallant, brave and faithful officer from this state ..."

Your Son, R. R. Dawes[16]

Ephraim is doing well physically and professionally. All he needs is a caring life companion. She is not far away. On June 20, 1866, Ephraim and Frances (aka Francy or Fanny) Bosworth, the daughter of Sala and Joanna, are joined in matrimony.

In July 1866, Rufus receives a letter from the war department. This is the agency that threw multiple roadblocks in his path two years past, but now is the messenger announcing a coveted award. He is commissioned brevet brigadier general, effective from March 13, 1865, for "meritorious services during the war." The news is a source of pride to the family and the community. Rufus Dawes will be referred to as "General" from this time forward.[17]

Sister Kate continues to fail and dies in September at age thirty-six. She has an infant daughter by Rev. McLean named Kitty. Rev. McLean in Pennsylvania agrees with his wife's desire to have Kate's sister Lucy raise the child in Marietta. Kate's death brings sadness and grief to the whole family. Sarah has now lost her two oldest children before their time. Nothing is more painful than that. She needs and receives additional attention from her surviving children.

Julia has lost her faithful niece and companion. Lucy, Rufus, Jane, and Ephraim have lost an older sister who cared for them during the difficult childhood years in a broken family. Her letters and visits with the boys brightened their lives while they lived in Malta with Father. She was the tie that bound the siblings together, each one sympathizing, defending, and sacrificing for each other to survive what Rufus phrased as their father's "tyranny."[18]

The children, now responsible adults and on their own, do not abandon their father completely, despite his past tyranny. They will never return to him, but they feel bound by a higher calling to render polite respect at a distance. Henry Dawes is now sixty-two, living alone in his farmhouse south of Mauston. He begins to feel the effects of age and ponders his life situation. In March 1867, Rufus writes a carefully worded seven-page response to a surprise letter from Henry:

Dear Father

I received with great satisfaction your very pleasant letter. I am grieved to hear of your feeble health. ... By a long life of vigorous industry you have earned ... rest and quiet in your old age—and you should by all means shape your plans to that end.

It will please you to learn something of me and my family ... the last year or two.

Rufus tells Henry of the new home and of eighteen-month old Charley, "bright, happily disposed, handsome," and encloses a photograph of both. Not mentioned is Mary's second pregnancy. He describes his employment at the railroad (supervision of freight and coal interests from Marietta to Chillicothe and Portsmouth) and his annual income ($3,000 is expected this year). Henry is a businessman, so Rufus discusses Ohio and national monetary and fiscal issues. He mentions his political "radicalism," meaning he publicly supports "extension of suffrage to the colored men of Ohio." As to family, Rufus again refers to them as "my sister" and "my brother," rather than "your daughter" or "your son." He pointedly notes Ephraim's business acumen:

> My sister Kate's child, Kitty McLean, now about ten months old, seems quite sick. ... Lucy is bringing her up. My brother still has charge of the eastern terminus of the road at Parkersburg. ... He is doing very well and is one of the most shining, sharpest business men in this section.

Rufus mentions his old war horse, Katerina, and offers to pay for her upkeep rather than have Henry sell her. He perceptively closes with this:

> You must now have a fine, pleasant and convenient place with your many improvements. I would like very much to see the place. But my time is fully occupied now, and my duty is to "make hay while the sun shines." Close attention to business while I have youth and strength is the cornerstone of my fortune. Hoping to hear from you again.
>
> I am your son, R. R. Dawes[19]

Tuesday, July 30, 1867, Marietta, Ohio

Rufus Cutler Dawes is born. He has dark hair and complexion like his father. Both mother and child endure the birth in fine shape. Beman, Betsey, and Bettie Gates are traveling in the east and do not receive Rufus's telegram. Mary writes to inform them of a second grandson. An elated yet pensive grandmother, Betsey, responds:

Dear Mary

Our boys! While we rejoice with you we mourn afresh our own dead boy. How can we live without him? I will comfort myself with your boy. Our boy! I am glad that he is a boy and am glad he is black and now he must be R. R. Dawes Junior. I don't wonder that Carta was astonished and wanted him to get up. I suppose he will want him to ride his horse by this time.

I am sorry to lose the first weeks of the new baby, but he won't know it, and by the time we see him he will be his natural color and looking around and smart enough to learn and we shall all enjoy him very much.[20]

Monday, September 9, 1867, Marietta, Ohio

Henry's health continues to decline, and he writes Rufus again, asking for his personal assistance. Mary looks at her troubled husband and offers her wisdom: "Rufe, if you feel the need to go, I think you should. Despite the years of animosity, he *is* your father, he's afraid his end is near, and he's reaching for help. Perhaps a window is opening in his soul. But whatever you decide is fine with me. Mother and Bettie should be back next week to help with the boys."

Rufe smiles at his wife. She always says the right thing. After thinking more on it, he writes:

Dear Father

Yours of the 3rd was received today. I have hope from your improvement that the disease has expended itself.

Mr. Gates and his family are away. Mother and Lucy are also away. My wife is of course feeble with two babies to take care of. Mr. G is expected home Saturday. ... My plan is to start up to see you as soon as he arrives.

I sincerely hope that your fears are without foundation. You have a remarkably vigorous constitution and great vitality. I have confidence that you will rally.

Our sincere hope is that you may live many years to enjoy yourself in the fruits of your labors. ... We are now weighed down with obligations in our own families, and other established relations, which render impossible for us to change to be permanently with you, but you may depend on anything in our power.

Rufus retraces the long honeymoon train journey to Milwaukee (minus the snow, sleigh ride, and caboose adventure), thence on to Mauston. The trip three and a half years ago was much more enjoyable. He arrives at the hilltop farmhouse to find his visibly weak father sitting on the porch. Henry is alone except for the scheduled lady housekeeper. "The doctor says its dropsy," Henry says. "The swelling is very painful, and I don't know why it's happening. Our old doctor here doesn't know, either. I should think he knows how to send a bill, though."

Rufe stays up late that first night with his father, who cannot sleep well due to the discomfort. They discuss Rufe's army experiences and Henry's accumulated land purchases. There are chores Rufe takes on, wood chopping and horse tending, and reacquaintance with his wartime mare, Katerina. John Kellogg has moved to La Crosse, but there are a few Company K men around to visit, plus old Mr. Langworthy.

Rufus is there five days, and Henry is feeling somewhat better. Throughout the stay, Henry tries to keep Rufus there. "Rufus, it would bring me great pleasure to have you and your family move here. I can make it very agreeable for you. You can manage the lands and the tenant farmers. There will also be political opportunities."

"Father, you know I cannot do that," Rufe responds. "Mary will never wish to leave her family in Marietta. They still have trouble dealing with the loss of their son. Our boys are such a comfort to them. And Mother needs support too. I have already indicated all this to you." *And,* he thinks without saying it, *I have vowed never to live with you again.*

Henry sighs and nods slowly. Rufus is taken aback to hear his father slowly and sadly reply, "All right, I understand. I have made my bed long ago with you all. I did what I thought was my right as a husband and father and my obligation to establish prosperity. Your mother is a good woman. She deserves respect and such assistance as you can provide. I have no ill feeling toward her any longer."

As Rufe travels home, he is struck with the realization that Henry's words expose a lonely man who now desires attention from his children. Is there true remorse? Rufe is not sure. Henry remains a difficult man to understand.

Henry has a serious relapse a month later and fears he is dying. On October 31 a telegram arrives from Mauston:

To RR Dawes— I want to see you immediately— H Dawes

"Rufe, I'll go," says Ephraim. He and Francy are at the Dawes cottage, with Lucy there too. The five are discussing what to do. "It sounds serious in Mauston, but you were just there. I know he sent the message to you, but he will have to make do with me, like it or not."

Lucy joins in, "These attacks of his seem to come and go. I'll plan to go later, even bring Kitty along and stay the winter if I need to. You two men have business to take care of, and, Rufe, you and Mary have the boys now." Rufe is a practical man and sees the logic. But he marvels at their willingness to sacrifice for the man who has haunted them so many years.

Ephraim barely arrives in time, for Henry is failing quickly and passes away on a Monday, November 4, 1867. Eph telegraphs Rufe, who makes plans to travel to Mauston with sister Lucy as soon as they can. On November 6, Eph writes his wife, Francy:

We buried Father today. Quite a large attendance of the Dawes'—Ben, Jim & Luther of Uncle Edward's children, George and William Dawes, father's brothers. George is a plain, quiet, sensible man. William a man of evident ability, still more evident pomposity ... altogether one of the most peculiar men you ever saw. Such a house so full of things. ... [W]e have cleaned it up as much as possible awaiting Lucy's arrival.

I do not think he made a will. ... I am here at the hotel awaiting Rufe's arrival. I hope he will be here tonight. Father had a wonderful pile of everything. Half a dozen horses, 20 or 30 pigs, cattle, wagons, wheat, corn, oats, and all sorts of things that must be immediately sold. A good many are already inquiring about purchasing this thing and that. I have informed them all that we first bury a man before we sell his effects.

Poor old man. The more I see and hear ... it would have been utterly impossible for Lucy or any woman to have lived with him at all. Shall we remember only the good, "Let the evil be buried with his bones."

With all my love, yours as ever, Eph

Rufe and Lucy arrive at Henry's farmhouse and stay for ten days, clearing things out for sale. Rufus is administrator of the estate and, in his efficient manner, records the sales and manages the money. He writes Mary that people from all around "are constantly upon us in a perfect deluge to get things cheap—but we will work through gradually." He sends the money to Mary's father, Beman, at his First National Bank in Marietta for eventual distribution to the family. With consent from Lucy and Eph, Rufe signs a $380 contract for placing an eight-foot-tall stone monument at Henry's grave in Evergreen Cemetery, located a few miles west of the farm.[21]

On the 14th of November, he responds to Mary, who had sent a letter with a photograph:

> My dear Wife—
>
> We have a little quiet tonight for a marvel. Our customers have gone today to a horse race.

Rufe must stop writing. While at the blacksmith's to have a buggy repaired, he absentmindedly picked up a hot iron and burned his fingers. Lucy takes over:

> While Rufe sits with his hand in a dipper I will take up the pen. I am tired and homesick tonight. I guess Rufe is too. You may look for me home with Eph.
>
> Papa is looking at the picture. He thinks Charley was afraid the man would shoot him and so snuggles up to Mama for safety. Dear me! I wonder if you know what a paradise Ohio is. The house has been thronged with people from dawn till dark.

Then Rufe manages to add:

> Your letter was worth a great deal, and the picture worth millions.
>
> Rufe [22]

Mary Gates Dawes and
Charles (Carta) G. Dawes

The long, sad saga with Father Henry has ended. Aunt Julia and sister/wife/mother Sarah Dawes write to Jane in Persia on November 16, informing her of her father's passing:

Dear Jane—

I do not know if your brothers and sister have informed you of the death of your father. He died of dropsy on November 4th. … As his health failed he desired to have his children with him. … Ephraim was with him when he died.

Your father left no will. His estate … will consequently come to his family and is large enough to be a help and blessing to you all. Your mother prefers to waive her right of dower and takes instead an equal share with her children.

Jane's mother, Sarah, later described by a granddaughter as "the forgiving and uncomplaining wife," adds her thoughts to the letter:

Sister Julia has written all that we know of your father's death. That he turned to his own family in his hour of trial is a most comforting thought. God has ordered all things aright. That there is an equal division of property gives me more pleasure than I can mention.[23]

Rufus also sends his missionary sister Jane a letter some weeks later. He brings Jane up to date on the estate details, though it will take years of his able administration before all the property, which includes over 5,000 acres in four states, is completely sold. Rufus takes this opportunity with Jane to reflect on his family—past, present and future:

A most remarkable thing connected with the closing of this tragedy of family history is the perfect vindication of Ma's whole course. … I think Ma seems like another person already, now the great load is lifted from her. She is no longer poor, and the great dread of father is, of course, gone.

It has been eight years … since you left us. Poor Kate and Henry are in their graves, and now our father is gone, after a terrible retribution for a crime against his own. … We cannot give up hope of one more reunion this side of the grave for all who are left. Only we who have gone through the trials can know what emotions and remembrances would be excited ... and the joy and gratitude to the Providence that has so wisely and wonderfully worked out the result.[24]

General Rufus Dawes, Mary Beman Gates Dawes, and "all who are left" will always remember their eventful past, be thankful for what has been granted, and resolutely strive to live an honorable, enjoyable, and productive life.

Brevet Brigadier General Rufus R. and Mary Gates Dawes

Endnotes

1. Dawes Journal, Book 2. DAA.

2. *SWSW*, p. 294.

3. JCJ. Aug. 13, 1864. Father and son Clarke are buried in Marietta's historic Mound Cemetery. Clarke's beautiful home, built in 1855, is located on Fourth Street in Marietta, one and a half blocks from the Corner. It is now a museum named the Castle and is open to the public. http://www.mariettacastle.org.

4. *Dawes Journal, Book 2*. DAA.

5. JCJ.

6. Derived from Rufus's letters to Mary, Sep. 1 and 4, 1864. Dawes Collections, WHS. Also, Gen. Bragg's report in *O. R. Vol. XLII, pt. 1*, pp. 534–536. See *SWSW*, pp. 305–307 for further details. Hyatt died from gangrene a month after his leg amputation while in a Philadelphia hospital.

7. JCJ remarkably provides the specific surgery details based on Rufus's descriptions. Meticulous as he was, Rufus probably made notes immediately after the procedure, and perhaps Julia copied them for her journal.

8. *Sauk County riflemen*, p. 107, and *SWSW*, p. 283.

9. *SWSW*, p. 314.

10. John Azor Kellogg published the amazing story in a series of newspaper articles several years after the war. The Wisconsin History Commission published the complete account in 1908 as *Capture and Escape: A Narrative of Army and Prison Life*. It is now available online through http://www.archive.org. It is well worth reading for its adventuresome aspects, but also as insight into prison hardships and the prejudices openly displayed at the time. It is conjecture that Rufus heard the news through Dr. Hall.

11. JCJ provides the family information.

12. The amazing Ford's Theater and Booth's room experience is told in a letter from Mary to her mother and reported by a Marietta newspaper. Julia Cutler also notes the story in her journal after hearing of it from Rufus and Mary. Julia's account supposes that the rowdy fellows were Booth and his conspirators; historical facts, however, indicate that Booth, while in room 228 that day, did not meet there with his conspirators. No record is known of the Dawes room number, so the proximity of the two rooms—Booth's and Dawes's—is conjecture. The narrative closely follows the exact wording used in Mary's letter and Julia's account. The dates and itinerary after Friday, April 14, are speculation, though they did visit Gettysburg after leaving Washington.

13. The Soldiers Cemetery was famously dedicated by President Lincoln in November 1863. Union soldiers were exhumed from the battlefield or buried as they died from wounds. The effort was complete by March 1864, with 3,512 burials. Occasional remains continued to be found by local farmers and developers for decades. Section nine contains seventy-three Wisconsin soldiers, thirteen identified from the Sixth Regiment. Twenty graves are marked "Unknown" (http://civilwarwiki.net/wiki/Soldiers'_National_Cemetery_ (Gettysburg,_PA)#Union_Soldier_Burials). Rufus and Mary did not record any comments on their battlefield visit, therefore the narrative is created.

14. Dickinson. *A Century of Church Life: History of the First Congregational Church of Marietta, Ohio*. 1896. The Internet Archive (website). http://www. archive.org.

15. A bronze plaque is on the wall of the northwesterly parlor in the Betsey Mills Club, indicating, "This room, which was formerly part of his family home, was the birthplace of Charles G. Dawes." Assuming this to be accurate, the family apparently converted the first-floor room into a bedroom, probably for Mary's convenience.

16. DAA.

17. *ibid.*

18. From narrative written by Mary Francis Dawes Beach (daughter of Rufus and Mary). Dempsey Family Collection.

19. DAA.

20. *ibid.*, and M. Beach's *Mother's Letters*.

21. The farm was eventually sold and has remained in the same family ever since. The house exists today and is in the National Register of Historic Places. It is rented by the family to vacationers. Henry's monument leans slightly today, sitting alone and distant from the resting places of his family in Marietta.

22. DAA.

23. From narrative written by Mary F. D. Beach. Dempsey Family Collection.

24. DAA.

Afterword

Rufus and Mary began working on his Civil War memoirs ten years after he left the service, blending diaries and letters with his personal recollections. Handwritten journals formed the basis for Rufus's classic *Service with the Sixth Wisconsin Volunteers*, published in 1890. He intended the book to be a recollection of his military service, not his personal life. He intended it also as a tribute to the brave men he served with in the Sixth Wisconsin Volunteer Infantry and the Iron Brigade. *Service With the Sixth Wisconsin Volunteers* is a great achievement, especially considering the distractions imposed during its writing by his growing family, business obligations, and political activity.

The family preserved general Dawes's letters and journals, and most were eventually donated to either the Dawes Arboretum or the Wisconsin Historical Society. Mary requested that her surviving wartime letters be destroyed upon her death, and that request was honored. Only a few survived.

Rufus Dawes, greatly to his credit, chose to withhold many details of his military experiences while writing *Service*. His working journals contain numerous cross-outs and edits. It became obvious that he did so to avoid embarrassment to others or to minimize his own heroics.

To My Best Girl presents selected letters and journal entries exactly as they were written. The military actions, events, and narratives involving the characters, be they family, friends, or fellow soldiers, are derived from these written accounts. The conversations contained throughout the book, while fictional, are derived and paraphrased from the original sources. There are very few fictional situations or characters presented in *To My Best Girl*, and these few are reported in the chapter endnotes. The historical fiction format is an effort to bring the characters alive again in our minds.

Readers familiar with *Service* will notice many additional details regarding General Dawes's military service. And, of course, Rufus's memoir did not include the story of his life before and immediately after the Civil War. Conversely, many details contained in *Service* are purposefully omitted from *To My Best Girl*. This book is not intended as a rewrite of the wonderful Rufus Dawes 1890 memoir, but rather as an expansion of it.

I hope the reader has developed an appreciation for the extraordinary and honorable life this patriot led. His front line military service and his personal life are models of integrity, bravery, duty, positive productivity, compassion, and humor. Hopefully, you have become acquainted with Mary and with the family members, friends, and citizen soldiers who all served the righteous cause and lived their lives nobly.

Epilogue

Rufus and Mary Dawes will raise a lively and active family while living on Fourth Street, only a short walk from the Corner. Mary described their relationship this way: "love became perfect." They become parents to six children, four boys and two girls: Charles Gates (1865), Rufus Cutler (1867), Beman Gates (1870), Mary Frances (1872), Henry May (1877), Betsey Gates (1880). All will lead positive, successful, and productive lives.

Rufus worked for his Uncle's railroad, made money in oil, co-owned a local iron works with his brother and uncle, lost all he had in the economic Panic of 1873, but resolutely re-built his assets by operating a railroad tie and lumber company with offices at 161 Front Street. He was elected to the U.S. House of Representatives, serving 1881-83. In June 1882 Rufus revisited Gettysburg with fellow war-veteran colleagues and friends of the 47th Congress, including these former Confederate officers: Scales of North Carolina, Manning of Mississippi, Oates of Alabama, and Turner of Georgia. While in Washington he visited the graves of all twenty-four Sixth Wisconsin soldiers buried at Arlington. He served many years on governing boards at Marietta College, the Ohio Deaf and Blind Institute, and his church. Most importantly, Rufus was a wise and caring father and husband. Always mindful of his own difficult childhood, he once wrote home to Mary while at Congress:

> I believe in amusement for the young, all they can get, they have only one life, let its springtime be full of flowers. The only thing is to keep their pleasures innocent and pure.[AG]

[AG] Dempsey, Peggy. *The Dawes House*, p. 69

Rufus Dawes attended several Wisconsin Civil War reunions, always remembered by his men, always asked to address them. He could not get away to attend a New Year's 1885 Sixth Wisconsin reunion in frigid Mauston, Wisconsin, but his letter of regret was read to the 600 attendees and "received the closest attention." It was so touching that his former soldiers of Company K had it printed in the local paper. Rufus noted that in his "devoted company, 21 men were actually killed in battle, and 51 shot besides."[AH] He then related personal memories of each man killed. These surviving former soldiers knew that General Dawes remembered them, and they respected him even more.

At age fifty-one Rufus suffered complete "nervous exhaustion" and became physically incapacitated for months. Work on his memoir had recently been completed, work that Mary wrote "tired him so". Could those relived war memories have had an influence? We cannot know. He recovered but required physical assistance plus help from son Henry to manage his business. Relapses, injury in a fall, and steady decline eventually led to confinement in a tricycle-chair for his last few years. Once strong and virile, Rufus aged far too early. Yet, as Mary wrote, "he accepted the inevitable with his own brave cheerful spirit". Brevet Brigadier General Rufus R. Dawes died in his home on August 1, 1899 at age sixty-one. Mary missed him terribly. Mary Beman Gates Dawes, devoted wife, loving mother and grandmother, and witty companion, passed away on October 28, 1921 at the age of seventy-nine. Rufus and Mary are side by side in section four of Marietta's beautiful Oak Grove Cemetery.

Charles Gates Dawes, eldest child, will live a vibrant and multi-faceted business, military, and political life. He is most recognized as the recipient of the 1925 Nobel Peace Prize, and for being thirtieth vice president of the United States under Calvin Coolidge, 1925–29. A tune he composed titled "Melody in A Major" is put to lyrics in 1951 and becomes the hit song "It's All in the Game."

Two other siblings deserve mention for their contribution to history. **Beman Gates** and his wife, Bertie, founded the Dawes Arboretum near Newark, Ohio, a wonderful facility (visit dawesarb.org) that now houses the archives so essential for completion of this narrative. **Mary Frances** became the family historian. Her works, such as *Mary Beman Gates Dawes, Mother's Letters*, and *Grandmother's Letters*, are treasured sources of information about Rufus and Mary.

Three publications are recommended for those interested in more information about this remarkable couple and family. Peggy Dempsey's

[AH] Newspaper clip from EDC-NL.

The Dawes House: The Place Where You Are Always Welcome; Rev. William Roe's *A Memoir: Rufus R. Dawes; Charles Gates Dawes, A Life,* by Annette B. Dunlap.

Sarah Cutler Dawes will move from Warren to a house shared with faithful daughter, **Lucy Dawes**, very near the Fourth Street home of Rufus and Mary. Cute little **Kitty McLean**, the daughter of sister **Kate Dawes**, will be raised by Lucy but will die of pneumonia at age nine. Sarah will pass away on New Year's Eve 1896, outliving three of her six children. Lucy will live within walking distance of Rufus and Mary. The beloved sister and aunt will die on December 10, 1898, at age sixty-five.

Ephraim and Frances (Francy) Bosworth Dawes live for many years in Cincinnati. Ephraim managed a railroad and coal freight business, then a railroad company in Missouri. He went bankrupt in the panic of 1873, then started again as a contractor, builder, manager, and president of several railroads, then invested in southern Illinois coal fields. He amassed a superior collection of Civil War and Ohio Company records and histories. He became president of an Ohio veteran's organization, succeeding Rutherford B. Hayes and William T. Sherman. In short, he was extremely active in business, historical, and philanthropic activities despite being in constant pain from his horrible wound. Another financial depression in 1893 seemed to present a challenge his energy could not withstand, and he died in Cincinnati in April 1895 at age fifty-four. Francy will eventually move in with Mary, her cousin and sister-in-law. Francy became an expert wood carver; some of her work is displayed today at the Castle. The two widows will spend the rest of their days at the Dawes Fourth Street home. Francy, "Auntie Bosworth," will pass away in April 1925 at age eighty-four.

William Cutler suffered financial ruin in the 1873 economic panic and was forced to liquidate his properties, including the Old Stone House. He, wife **Lizzie Cutler**, and sister **Julia Cutler**, moved into Marietta. William and Julia collaborated in writing several histories and biographies of their ancestors Manasseh and Ephraim, utilizing the many papers that are preserved today in the Marietta College Special Collections Library. William dies at age seventy-nine, Julia at age ninety, and Lizzie at age seventy-nine. They are buried in Oak Grove Cemetery.

The Dawes, Gates, and Bosworth families are interred next to each other in section four of Oak Grove Cemetery. **Charley Gates** is there, too. His remains were relocated from Mound Cemetery after his father, **Beman Gates**, passed away in December 1894. "Grandmother" **Betsey Gates** followed Beman seven months later, three months after son-in-law Ephraim.

Betsey (Bettie) Gates marries William W. Mills who eventually becomes president of the 1st National Bank of Marietta. They will reacquire her girlhood home at the Corner where she established the Girls Monday Club focused on welfare of local women. Bettie died at age 67 in 1920 after a vibrant life of service to her church, the college and the community. Her husband expanded and dedicated the Corner as the Betsey Mills Club in 1927.

William Jackson worked at the Harmar train station and used his savings to open a successful grocery store. He sent his brother Moses to Spotsylvania, Virginia to rescue his severely abused mother and sister, taking care of them until their deaths. The Dawes family kept in close touch through the years until William died of tuberculosis in April 1886 at about age 40. Rufus Dawes composed a touching eulogy for his "devoted friend and brave and true man" which can be read at: historicalmarietta. blogspot.com/label African Americans, "William Jackson – Born a Slave".

General Edward S. Bragg returned to Fond du Lac after the war, becoming city postmaster, state senator and U.S. Congressman. He was a key delegate to several Democratic national conventions, served as the U.S. envoy to Mexico, and held consul general posts in Cuba and Hong Kong. In between he maintained his local law practice. Ed Bragg passed away in Fond du Lac in June 1912 at age 85. Wisconsin Historical Marker No. 339 near Fond du Lac provides a brief bio in his honor.

General Lysander Cutler was assigned to administer the draft in Jackson, Michigan while still recovering from his Battle of Globe Tavern head and face wound. His health deteriorated, and he died of a stroke in hometown Milwaukee one year after being discharged, in July 1866.

General John Gibbon, thrice wounded, saw the war through to Appomattox where he commanded the Twenty-Fourth Army Corps. General Grant appointed him as one of three commissioners to administer the surrender of Lee's army. He stayed in the army at the post-war rank of colonel, assigned to the Montana Territory. His column rescued George Custer's survivors after the Little Bighorn massacre. Other posts in the west followed until his retirement in 1891 at age 64. He was elected president of the Iron Brigade Association and Commander of the Loyal Legion. John Gibbon died in Baltimore in February 1896 and is buried at Arlington National Cemetery. Iron Brigade veterans financed his prominent granite monument. Gibbon River and Falls in Yellowstone National Park are named after him.

Dr. John C. Hall returned to his medical practice in Wisconsin where he also served one term as a State Senator and on the Board of United States Pension Examiners. Hall moved his family to Medical Lake, Washington in 1891 where he retired. He was president of the

Board of U.S. Pension Examiners at Spokane when he died at age 75 in November 1896.

Brevet Brigadier General John A. Kellogg returned to Wisconsin after the war, moving to La Crosse as a pension agent and then to Wausau, where he was elected as a State Senator. He died in Wausau in February 1883 at age 55, perhaps weakened by the severe trials of his war service. He wrote a memoir titled *Capture and Escape* which was published in 1908.

Rufus Dawes succeeded in contacting several former Confederate adversaries after *Service with the Sixth Wisconsin* was published. **Major John A. Blair** responded to Rufus' October 1893 letter from his law office in Tupelo, Mississippi. Reminiscing about the surrender of his Second Mississippi in the Gettysburg railroad cut, the major asked "what became of the sword I gave you?" Blair graciously reciprocated a bid for friendship with good humor, writing Dawes: "You say you have six children, and that I have two grandchildren, and upon this superior showing of forces you expect me to surrender to you again. I decline to do so ... but I will surrender to Mrs. Dawes if you and she will invade the hospitality of our home." Rufus' physical condition never allowed the two to meet again.

In July 1893 Rufus published a letter in southern newspapers seeking information about the wounded Second Mississippi sergeant he tried to assist amongst the battlefield wreckage of Pickett's charge. Mr. D. J. Hill, former private in the Second Mississippi, respectfully replied to "Gen. R. R. Dawes" from Blue Mountain, Mississippi. The man's name was **Christopher Columbus Davis**, wrote Hill, "a very brave man, even to recklessness". Davis survived the war to become a teacher, but sadly "put an end to his own life a year or two after the war." Mr. Hill noted that Davis was one of five orphaned brothers. One was a West Point graduate who remained loyal to the Union, joining a New York cavalry regiment, and "was killed at Brandy Station, Va."[AI] Hill explained that Sergeant Davis had "three other brothers in confederate service ... killed at different times and places ... It is presumed that grief at the loss of all his brothers and brooding over the result of the war may have unsettled his reasoning and suicide was the result."[AJ]

[AI] Col. Benjamin Franklin "Grimes" Davis, 1854 West Point classmate of Confederate Gen. J. E. B. Stuart and other Civil War nnotables, was killed June 9, 1863 while leading the First Brigade of Gen. John Buford's cavalry division. He is buried near Buford at the West Point cemetery. It is unknown whether Sergeant Davis was aware of his brother's death when he himself was wounded during Pickett's charge, fighting for the other side. (Wikipedia and FindAGrave)

[AJ] Blair and Hill letters from WHS.

Rufus undoubtedly absorbed the Davis story with sincere sadness. The wounded sergeant's fate had bothered him for thirty years. Perhaps he felt guilt for treating the sergeant's beloved flag as a birthday and victory trophy that July 4, 1863. There is no record of his thoughts, but in 1897 Rufus opposed a growing sentiment to return captured Confederate flags to those of a younger generation who "would make great glorification of them" as symbols of a cause whose "success would have ruined their country." Rufus respected Southern soldiers as "brave ... heroic and ... all around good fellows",[AK] but he also knew that the Mississippi flag was heroically captured at high cost, and that the cause for which he fought and which he helped to win was just and necessary.[AL]

D. J. Hill revealed that he had avoided capture in the Gettysburg railroad cut by covering himself with a bloody blanket next to two wounded comrades and feigning the moans of a suffering wounded man. "Your boys eyed me pretty close", he recalled, but left him alone. He was not bragging, just stating a fact. Now, as an aging veteran of a lost cause, he ended his letter to Rufus Dawes with:

> I am proud to say that there are no more peaceable, honest, law abiding citizens here than the old Confederate soldiers ... The federal soldier would hardly find better friends anywhere than among the veteran Johnnies who followed Lee and Jackson in 1861 to 1865.

President Abraham Lincoln had hopes that the war's sacrifices must ultimately serve to reunite the country, not to widen the divide. "Let them up easy" was his advice to a Union general when asked how to treat Southerners in conquered Richmond. Rufus Dawes understood that and sincerely did his part to befriend old adversaries. He was no doubt heartened that these Confederate veterans from Mississippi warmly reciprocated.

[AK] The Dawes House, p. 75

[AL] Confederate battle flags were returned to their home states by act of Congress in 1905. The Second Mississippi battle flag is now preserved in the Mississippi Department of Archives & History.

Glossary of Civil War Terms

Army **Military Map** **Symbol (XXXX)**	In order of size, largest to smallest, Civil War army units are as follows (still applicable today): army, corps, division, brigade, regiment, battalion, company, platoon, squad. See below for explanation of each.
Artillery Battery	Six or four cannons, each pulled by a two-wheeled ammunition limber with a six-horse team. Horse-drawn caissons carrying additional ammunition, plus several equipment wagons, complete the battery. Led by a captain and several lieutenants, with about 130 enlisted men and 125 horses. See cwartillery.com for an excellent summary.
Battalion **(II)**	Several infantry or cavalry companies, or artillery batteries, operating as a separate command.
Brigade **(X)**	Several regiments, usually three to six, commanded by a brigadier general or senior colonel.
Canister	Artillery ammunition used against troops; numerous lead or iron balls contained in a tin can, with a gunpowder charge attached. The can disintegrates upon firing, and the balls scatter with shotgun-like effect.
Cartridge	For infantry soldiers using a rifled or smoothbore musket, a sealed paper-wrapped "round" containing a lead bullet and gunpowder charge.
Colors	The US and state flags carried by a regiment.
Cartridge Box	Leather pouch with flap holding two tin waterproof containers, each holding twenty cartridges. Slung over the shoulder to ride on the hip.

Column of Divisions	A marching formation for an infantry regiment with two companies together in line forming a "division," each division behind the other, thus having five divisions for a typical ten-company regiment.
Company, Infantry (I)	One hundred soldiers at initial strength, led by a captain and two lieutenants. Disease, injury, and battle losses typically reduce the number significantly.
Contraband	Term for displaced or escaped slaves.
Corps (XXX)	Pronounced "core." Two to four divisions with supporting artillery batteries. Strength varied between 10,000 and 22,000.
Division (XX)	Two to five brigades, commanded by a general.
Earthworks/ Breastworks	Fortifications of earth and timber to provide cover from enemy fire; the longer the stay, the more elaborate they became.
Field Officer	One of the senior officers in the regimental command structure, typically three: major, lieutenant colonel, and colonel.
File	Infantry usually entered battle in two lines, or ranks, the rear rank close behind the rank in front. The two men front and rear were termed a "file."
Hardee Hat	Tall, black-felt Model 1858 army dress hat worn with pride by the Iron Brigade soldiers, initially with a black feather. Most Union troops were issued the smaller blue short-brimmed, flat-top cap, or kepi.
Haversack	Usually a leather or canvas bag slung over the shoulder for holding meal rations, most commonly hardtack crackers, salted pork, and coffee.
Knapsack	A backpack carrying basic soldier essentials such as spare socks, a shirt, sewing kit, etc., often with shelter half and blanket rolled on top.
Line of Battle	Infantrymen formed in two parallel ranks, one behind the other, bringing maximum firepower toward the front.

Military Crest	A position downhill from a hill's high point, offering a defending unit better fields of fire and avoiding exposure against the rear skyline.
Minié Ball	A conical lead bullet with three exterior grooves and a conical hollow in the base. It expanded under pressure inside the gun barrel. Rifled barrels made the bullet spin, improving accuracy and range. A skilled soldier could fire two or three aimed rounds per minute.
Musket	A muzzle-loading, single-shot, shoulder-fired weapon, either rifled or smoothbore, almost always fitted with a percussion cap nipple. The Sixth Wisconsin used .58 caliber, 56-inch long, 9-pound Springfield rifled muskets.
Noncommisioned Officer (NonCom)	Enlisted men with supervisory duties over enlisted men, under the command of commissioned officers. A full infantry company had eight corporals and five sergeants, the senior sergeant being the "first sergeant."
Order of Battle	An organizational summary of key units comprising a command, usually noting the names of major unit commanders.
Percussion Cap	Small copper caps with igniter compound that fit over a musket or revolver nipple. The trigger-released hammer strikes and ignites the cap, which detonates the gunpowder charge in the gun barrel.
Picket Line or Picket Duty	A small unit of soldiers placed between the main body and the enemy to provide early warning of an attack.
Rifle Pit	Term used for either trenches or individual holes dug for fighting positions.
Skirmishers	A thin line of soldiers, perhaps in groups of four, placed in front of an advancing main force for reconnaissance purposes and early warning.
Sutler	A person who follows the army and sells various provisions to the troops.

Bibliography

Books

Beach, Mary F. Dawes. *Grandmother's Letters.* Printed by Henry M. Dawes, 1926. Literary Licensing.

Beach, Mary F. Dawes and Otto, Mary Louise and Blazier, George J. *The Cutler Collection of Letters and Documents, 1748 –1925.* Marietta College, 1962–63.

Bearss, Edwin C. *The Petersburg Campaign, Vol. 1: The Eastern Front Battles, June–August 1864.* Savas Beatie Publishers, California, 2012.

Beaudot, William J. K. and Herdegen, Lance J. *An Irishman in the Iron Brigade.* Fordham University Press, 2003.

Cox, John D. *Culp's Hill: The Attack and Defense of the Union Flank July 2, 1863.* De Capo Press, 1993.

Dawes, Rufus R. *Service with the Sixth Wisconsin Volunteers.* 1890. Reprinted by the State Historical Society of Wisconsin, 1962.

Dempsey, Peggy. *The Dawes House: The Place Where You Are Always Welcome.* Peggy Dempsey, 2014.

Dunlap, Annette B. *Charles Gates Dawes—A Life.* Northwestern University Press, 2016.

Dunn, Craig L. *Iron Men, Iron Will—The Nineteenth Indiana Regiment of the Iron Brigade.* Guild Press of Indiana Inc., 1995.

Ferris, Mary Walton. *Dawes–Gates Ancestral Lines, Volumes I and II.* Privately printed, 1943. Indiana State Library, Indianapolis, IN.

Foote, Shelby. *The Civil War: A Narrative—Red River to Chattahoochee: Another Grand Design* and *Gettysburg to Vicksburg: Unvexed to the Sea.* Random House, New York, 2005.

Frassanito, William A. *Antietam—The Photographic Legacy of America's Bloodiest Day.* Charles Scribner's Sons, New York, 1978.

Frassanito, William A. *Gettysburg—A Journey in Time.* Charles Scribner's Sons, New York, 1975.

Gibbon, General John. *At Gettysburg and Elsewhere: Personal Recollections.* Originally published 1928. Big Byte Books, 2016.

Grant, Ulysses S. *Personal Memoirs.* Originally published in two volumes 1885, 1886. Penguin Books, New York, 1999.

Haskell, Franklin Aretas. *The Battle of Gettysburg.* Originally published 1908. Forgotten Books, 2012.

Herdegen, Lance J. and Beaudot, William J. K. *In the Bloody Railroad Cut at Gettysburg.* Morningside House Inc., 1990.

Herdegen, Lance J. *Those Damned Black Hats!—The Iron Brigade in the Gettysburg Campaign.* Savas Beatie, California, 2008.

Nolan, Alan T. *The Iron Brigade—A Military History.* Indiana University Press Edition, 1994.

Planz, Harry W. *Gettysburg—Culp's Hill and Cemetery Hill.* The University of North Carolina Press, 1993.

Rhea, Gordon C. *The Battles for Spotsylvania Courthouse and the Road to Yellow Tavern, May 7–12, 1864.* Louisiana State University Press, 1997.

Roe, Rev. William E. *A Memoir, Rufus R. Dawes.* Privately printed. Reprinted by Kessinger Publishing, 2009.

Venner, William T. *The 19th Indiana Infantry at Gettysburg.* Burd Street Press, 1998.

Archival Materials and Private Collections

Beach, Mary Frances Dawes. *Mary Beman Dawes*. Unpublished manuscript. Marietta College Special Collections Library.

Beach, Mary Frances Dawes. *Mother's Letters—Mary Beman Gates Dawes*. Dawes Arboretum History Center, Newark, Ohio.

Dawes Arboretum Archive. Rufus Dawes and family letters and journals. History Center Archives, Newark, Ohio. http://www.dawesarb.org.

Dempsey, Peggy and Rich. Dawes, Gates, and Cutler family letters, journals, and photos. Private collection.

Juneau County Historical Society. The Dawes Family Collection. Mauston, Wisconsin.

Marietta College Special Collections Library. Henry and Sarah Dawes marital separation documents and papers. Marietta, Ohio.

Newberry Library Special Collections. *Ephraim C. Dawes Papers, 1836–1905*. Chicago, Illinois.

Wilson, Hattie Dawes. *The Search for Sarah and Henry Dawes*. The *Tallow Light*, magazine of the Washington County Historical Society, Vol. 30, No. 1, summer 1999. Marietta College Special Collections Library.

Internet Resources

"A Brief History of North Hall—The First Building Constructed on the University of Wisconsin Campus." University of Wisconsin, Madison, Department of Political Science.

Andrews, Martin Register. "History of Marietta and Washington County, Ohio, and representative citizens." The Internet Archive (website). https://archive.org/details/historyofmariett01andr.

Baker, David. Various historical articles, news accounts, photos, and illustrations. Marietta, Ohio. http://earlymarietta.blogspot.com.

Burke, Henry Robert. "Judge Ephraim Cutler and Constitution, Window to the Past." 1998. http://henryburke1010.tripod.com/id52.html.

Cheek, Phillip and Pointon, Mair. "History of the Sauk County riflemen." Wisconsin Historical Society. http://content.wisconsinhistory. org/cdm/ref/collection/quiner/id/44929.

Civil War Trust (website). Civilwar.org.

Constitution, Ohio: The History of a Community in Washington County (blog). http://constitution-ohio.blogspot.com.

The Descendants of William Dawes Who Rode Association (website). http://www.wmdawes.org/

Dickinson, C. E. *A Century of Church Life: A History of the First Congregational Church of Marietta, Ohio.* E. R. Alderman and Sons, 1896. The Internet Archive (website). https://archive.org/details/centuryofchurchl00dick.

Jespersen, Hal. Professional cartographer and amateur civil War historian. www.cwmaps.com

Kellogg, John Azor. *Capture and Escape: A Narrative of Army and Prison Life.* Wisconsin History Commission, 1908. Wisconsin Historical Society. http://content.wisconsinhistory.org/cdm/ref/collection/quiner/id/28891.

Leger, Marie. "Marietta College's Lost Valedictorians: Their Similarities and Differences." December 9, 2011. http://library.marietta.edu/spc/showalteraward/Leger.

Library of Congress (website). "Civil War Glass Negatives and Related Prints." https://www.loc.gov/collections/civil-war-glass-negatives/.

Historical Marietta (blog). http://HistoricalMariettablogspot.com.

"History of the Antietam National Cemetery." Western Maryland's Historical Library (website). http://www.whilbr.org/antietamNational-Cemetery/index.aspx.

http://ironbrigadememory.blogspot.com/ by Lance Herdegen

http://www.ironbrigade.net/index.html by Terrence Lemke.

Marietta College 1835 to 1882 and Annual Catalogue. The Internet Archive (website).   https://archive.org/stream/catalogueofoffic00mari#page/n3/mode/2up.

Marietta College in the War of Secession, 1861–1865. Peter G. Thomson, Cincinnati, 1878. The Internet Archive (website). https://ia902604.us.archive.org/32/items/mariettacollegei00mari/mariettacollegei-00mari.pdf.

Onsager, Lawrence W. Transcription of a letter to the *Mauston Star* by R. R. Dawes, April 5, 1894, p.7. http://rootsweb.ancestry.com/-wijuneau/dawes1894.html.

Roster of Wisconsin Volunteers, War of the Rebellion, 1861–1865. The Internet Archive (website). https://archive.org/stream/rosterofwisconsi01wisc#page/494/mode/2up.

Rueben Huntley Letters, 1861–62. Unpublished. University of Wisconsin Digital Collections Library (website). http://digital.library.wisc.edu/1711.dl/WI.Huntley.

Rufus R. Dawes Diaries, Vol. 1 and 2. Wisconsin Historical Society (website). http://content.wisconsinhistory.org/cdm/search/collection/quiner/searchterm/dawes.

Showalter, Linda. Pioneer Prologue (blog). http://pioneerprologue.blogspot.com.

United States War Department. *The War of the Rebellion: a Compilation of the Official Records of the Union and Confederate Armies.* Government Printing Office, 1880. http://collections.library.cornell.edu/moa_new/waro.html.

CPSIA information can be obtained
at www.ICGtesting.com
Printed in the USA
LVHW040307140319
610627LV00001B/271